MW00636680

I Just Want You to

Remember...

A Story About the
Eternal Love of Twin Flames

Lala Agni

Lala Agni
I Just Want You to
REMEMBER...

His eyes have haunted her dreams since she was a child, yet she cannot find him. She calls for him through time and space, searching every crowd for the man whose name she has yet to learn. What forces are at play to aid two halves of the same Soul searching for their missing piece? They are known as Twin Flames. Two halves of One Soul. He is a massive movie star, and she an ordinary woman. The paths they travel through life could be no further apart, but what happens when fate intervenes? When they find each other, will they be able to overcome the barriers and find their way to each other at last? I Just Want You to REMEMBER...will touch reader's hearts and shake them to their core. This book will give readers an understanding of what is important to each of us and a faith in forces beyond our control.

This book is a work of fiction. Names, characters, businesses, places, events, locales, and incidents are either the products of the author's imagination or used in a fictitious manner. Any resemblance of the characters in this story to actual people, either alive or deceased or actual events, is purely coincidental.

No portion of this book may be reproduced in any form without written permission from the author. For permissions contact: alla_star@att.net
© Lala Agni

ISBN: 978-0-57883-812-0 (Print)
ISBN: 978-0-57884-121-2 (Digital)

Copyright © 2019. All rights reserved.
Copyright © 2020. All rights reserved.

About This Book

This is the story this world has never seen before.

Prepare to be shaken.

Prepare for a transformation.

Prepare for the revelation.

Prepare for the sacred truth of who you truly are!

This novel is a beautiful story of Eternal Love, carried in the hearts of one man and one woman through many lifetimes. Twin Flames, two halves of one Soul, lost in their current incarnation and destined to find each other again. This story is about what is important for each and every one of us. This story is about the reasons we chose to come from the realm of the Spirits to this planet, which many ancient texts call "The valley of tears." Our heroes will experience Pain and Joy, Betrayal and Nobility, Failure and Victory. But, above all, this novel is about the Power of Love.

Eternal and Immortal Love. Such Love will deeply touch your hearts and leave you in awe, and your World will never be the same.

You will never be the same.

This story will shake you to your very core. And I truly and deeply believe, it will shake the World as well...

- Helena Runi, journalist, psychologist, author, TV host, Member of the International Union of Writers.

Acknowledgment

My deepest and most sincere gratitude to Olena Dorunicheva, an honest critic, my inspiration, my editor, best friend and so much more; without you this book would not have been written.

My dearest Mother Lidiya and my two sons, Alexander Joseph and Thomas Nicholas.

Michal Madison for her help with creating a beautiful cover for this book.

All the wonderful people around the world, who stand beside me, believe in me, support me, and are there for me.

Thank you!

The Sky will be covered
With sparkling bright Stars
The leaves of the trees will fall

I always can feel you
Wherever you are
Because we are sharing
One Soul

I am always with you
You are always with me
In March, in July
In September

If you ever forget
I will help you believe
And awaken your heart
To Remember…
Lala Agni

Foreword from the Author

You are holding in your hands a story of Eternal Love. The existence of such Love is hard to believe. Infinite Love. Immortal Love. Love that never ends and lasts forever.

Have you ever thought about the fact that everything is created from and made of the Essence of Love? Living things and non-living things. Visible and invisible. All our feelings and emotions. Our happiness and sadness. Joy and laughter. All we can see with our eyes and what we are only able to see with our soul's eyes. All our hopes and dreams. Every particle of us, physical and non-physical. All of this is Love!

Do you realize *Love has no beginning and no end?* It does not appear or disappear. Its Divine energy exists forever. Love has always been and always will be! Forever. For Eternity. While universes and worlds rise and fall, are created and destroyed, to be created again, Love exists eternally. It was. It is. And it will be.

For many, many centuries, and even today, people have lived in fear of death. Not many of us truly realize that death simply does not exist. Death means "the crossing," but it never means *"the END."* Just remember this: *Nothing. Ever. Ends. Everything continues.* Death is our journey back home to the place each of us originally comes from, the realm of the Spirits. We return home to have a close look "from above" into the life we have just lived. We see what we did right and what we did wrong from that perspective. We look at the moments we were strong, and the moments we were weak, the times when we followed the voice of our Immortal Soul, and others when we followed the voice of our human Ego. Everything opens up to us. Everything becomes clear. When we go home, we take time to look at and understand our latest journey. We also take time to rest until the moment we decide to incarnate on Gaia Earth again. When we do, we will live, love, laugh and cry again, inspire and be inspired and do so much more, all over again.

Nothing. Ever. Ends!

Who do you think you truly are? Your physical body? Not really. Actually, your physical body is the tiniest part of who you are. You cannot even imagine how powerful, magnificent, unique, and incredible you are! *You are an Eternal and Immortal being of Light.* You were. You are. You will be. Forever.

When you love somebody, this Love forever becomes a part of your eternal and immortal essence. It will exist for as long as you exist. For eternity. Forever! Because pure, beautiful, true, and soul transforming Love is immortal.

This story is about such Love. I must tell this story to you because I am a living witness that physical death ends nothing. I am a living witness that Soul and Love are undying and infinite. We keep on forgetting about this truth in a million things we do every day. Unfortunately, we forget how beautiful, grand, and wise our own Soul is in our everyday life. We forget the Power of Love that is our very essence. We forget too many things. And I do not want you to keep on forgetting.

I just want you to REMEMBER.

Table of Contents

Chapter 1

Twin Flames

Who are they really?
Why do they come?

Twin Flames have an especially difficult task to integrate and balance their energies because very much is expected of them. They must yield to the Source, forget ego and be ready to merge so that their magnificent union can bring the change everybody has been waiting for: Creating shifts in the human collective consciousness.[1]

This story is about those who are called "Twin Flames."

Many sources say Twin Flames were created as one at the beginning of their existence. One Soul. One Essence, One Cosmic Energy Consciousness. The united creative energies of masculine and feminine. The yin and the yang. Unified into One. Inseparable. They existed as One. They functioned as One. They were One. It is as if they were the shore and the ocean, the clouds and the sky, the singer and the song, the poet and his poetry. They are the perfect harmony of all. But even such souls must leave the Spirits'

---

1   Zeyven Alexander Blackwell. *Twin Flame Revelation: Answering the Call to Save Humanity* (OutSkirts Press 2013,) Dedication.

realm to learn duality, develop, grow, become wiser, deeper, and stronger. And most of the time, Twin Flames incarnate with an additional goal; they come to help others.

For this purpose, they leave the realm of the Spirits just as all other souls do. They are often asked to do so by the higher levels of Guides and Keepers. If they agree, they know very well before incarnating the demands and requirements. They understand that their goals will be much more challenging and more complex than those given to other Souls. Twin Flames come not only to learn but also to serve the greater good of people and the planet. I will tell you more about it later.

Why are they called Twin Flames? Because their energy appears as Flares of Light, resembling Flames.

Twin Flame Consciousness separates into two and incarnates not as one human being but as TWO. One half of such a being takes a male's form with primarily male energy (yang), and the other half incarnates as a female with mainly female energy (yin). This way, in their physical incarnation, the ONE becomes TWO. But even while being in two physical bodies, separated from each other for many years, they continue to share the same energetic frequency. Here we can use the well-known expression "cut from the same cloth." No matter where they are, how far they are from each other, they are still one at their core. They feel each other, just like their own heartbeat. Some people also say about them: "Those two have one soul." And this is exactly what they are.

We all remember the ancient legends and myths about two separate halves of One. In different lands, at other times, people told these stories. Nowadays, they might sound like fairy tales, but it is not so. Twin Flames, or two halves of One, have always existed in all times.

But it happens rather seldom that they both incarnate in the exact same lifetime. More often, they separate, and only one of them incarnates on Earth. In such cases, the other stays in the Spirits' realm and acts as a Keeper or a Guardian, who supports, guides, inspires, and helps the other half. The one, incarnated in the physical body, naturally cannot see the one in the Spirits' realm with just their physical eyes, but they always feel the

2

other's presence. They can see the one in the Spirits' realm in dreams, or the moments between being asleep and awake, in visions, and at times when they find themselves "between the worlds."

The times we are living in now are exciting and very different. Our Gaia Earth is going through a vital process of Deep Transformation, which metaphysics call "The Quantum Transition." Some very ancient texts say this only happens once every 26,000 years! An old Chinese "curse" says: "I wish you to live in times of change!" It means times of transformation and change are never easy. It is one reason why The Higher Forces ask both Twin Flames to incarnate at the same time.

Before they meet on Earth, they live many years of their physical life far away from each other. They often live in different countries, with different cultures, and even on different continents. Each walks their own path and learns their own lessons. Then the moment comes when The Higher Forces help them find each other and, if possible, reunite them again. The purpose of such union is to restore the unity of all creations and destroy the duality of consciousness—the source of such terrible vices as *greed, selfishness, envy, lust, and cruelty*—all the "treasures" of Pandora.

Twin Flame relationships go far beyond the human definitions of the relationship between a man and a woman. If they both "wake up" and understand who they truly are, they love each other immensely, realizing and feeling as two parts of *ONE*. They understand each other with a half-sigh and a half-thought. But they are not united to just be together, love each other, and live happily ever after. Oh, no! That is not why they are here!

Their reason for incarnating in one life, at the same time, is both challenging and demanding. They are called upon to awaken humanity, improve and harmonize many people's lives by helping them *remember who they truly are*. They are here to help others understand that *the Divine is not outside but within every one of us!* Each one has a unique gift and a unique light they can shine, inspiring others to shine as well. Twin Flames come to help people to make this world a better, safer, kinder, brighter, more beautiful place. As you can easily imagine, this is far from easy.

If united, such couples are very bright and impossible to miss. In such unions, one complements the other perfectly. Together, Twin Flames usually achieve significant heights in whatever they choose to do. It could be science, art, healing, or any other area. Many of them work very hard towards improving the lives of women and children, improving ecology, raising awareness, and educating people on many, many important subjects. We can say that Twin Flames are *employees of Humanity*. That is the main reason why they are here. The Mission is not easy, as I have already said.

Unfortunately, nowadays, not many Twin Flames are in Union. Why not?

After finding their other half and realizing who they are to each other, many Twin Flames still choose to walk away from the union. Why is that, you ask, is it even possible? Would anyone reject their true One, the other half of their Soul? Who would do such a thing? Well, the main reason is *FEAR*—the fear of looking weird, strange, or even insane in the eyes of people. Fear of being judged, fear of being mocked, laughed at or ridiculed. As I have already said, they most often come from different cultures, religions, customs, languages, and upbringing. They usually deal with many obstacles, making their union, in some cases, almost impossible. Many refuse to overcome these challenges or are afraid to do so since it would change their current lifestyle.

The so-called "runner" usually does that. The runner is usually not fully "awake" and prefers to live his known safe ways and rejects his other half. Twin Flames do not unite in such cases, and this is very sad. We live on the planet of free will, and even Higher Forces must put up with it. A Twin Flame has the right to refuse the union; if that happens, each still *must continue working for humanity* away from the other. Unfortunately, separated, they are much less powerful. But there is always hope that the "runner" sooner or later will fully "awaken," and the union will happen after all.

Living and activated Twin Flame couples who are not united is quite tragic. Why? Because their Union creates an energy flow with constant access to vibrations of a very high frequency. This vibration helps them achieve significant results in their mission much faster. Twin Flames can be compared to lit candles, which in their turn can light up hundreds, thousands, or maybe even millions of other candles, i.e., souls. What does it mean? It means that the main goal of living Twins is to awaken, to light up as many souls as possible, *helping people REMEMBER*, understand, and fully realize that God—Absolute, Universe, High Consciousness—*manifests itself in every one of us! Each one carries Divine Power within!* Divine Light. Divine Wisdom. Divine Knowledge. Understanding this means becoming "awakened". It is *the most essential mission of Twin Flames.*

Handling the vibration of such frequency as Twin Flames, while being in the physical body, is like living inside an active volcano.

Being a Twin Flame means living in two dimensions simultaneously, in two bodies at once—two completely different lives, while being ONE at the core.

When they find each other, it triggers tremendous spiritual expansion in both. It starts the process of self-healing on an emotional, mental and physical level. Twin Flames are both compelled to become the best and highest manifestation of the One Soul they share, here and now, in this life, on this planet. That does not happen right away and is far from easy. Each Half must do *tremendous* inner work before they can unite. Twin Flames are the energetic flow of total unconditional love and infinite energy of cosmic Light and are part of a large Soul Group called "Light Workers."

Many people ask, "How can I find my Twin Flame?" The answer is simple: You can't. If he or she is physically incarnated with you at the same time, on the same planet, they will appear in your life when the time is right. Even if you don't want it or do not expect it, it will happen!

Just like it happened to me!

I found my Twin Flame. I found My Soul, My Heart, My Love. The one who is closer to me than my own breath, my own heartbeat, than the blood running in my veins. And at the same time, the one who was as far from me as the farthest galaxy.

How is it, to live a whole life, as a Half of One, to wait and search, to look for him every breathing moment, *FIND* him, just to see there was a world between the two of you? How is it possible to live with that? How to find the strength to breathe, to smile, to exist, to keep on going? How?

Now, allow me to tell you.

Chapter 2

The Keepers in the Mist House on a Lost Planet

How is it, to live a whole life, as a Half of One, to wait and search, to look for him every breathing moment, FIND him, just to see there was a world between the two of you? How is it possible to live with that? How to find the strength to breathe, to smile, to exist, to keep on going? How?
Now, allow me to tell you.

A woman with white hair laid a piece of paper with written text on the transparent-looking table floating in front of her as she leaned against the gracefully carved back of an ivory chair.

The table swayed as if on waves touched by a soft ocean breeze drifting into the hall through several open windows. It appeared to be the rather unsteady construction of an insanely romantic sculptor. However, a large blue vase with crimson peonies stood on it without even shaking.

The woman took a long deep breath, raised her head, and looked thoughtfully at her surprised companions.

"She has started writing a book."

"Already? How old is she?"

A man with a mane of wavy black hair, probably in his forties, with an athletic figure dressed in a light-blue knit pullover and navy-blue jeans, reclined lazily on a white sofa, his legs resting on a leather ottoman in the shape of a rhino. Open magazines with photographs of horses and old cars were scattered all over the floor. The yellowed, brittle pages of the magazines, hinted at their venerable age. Unrealistically handsome, with dark, almost Asian, almond eyes and perfectly chiseled facial features, this man seemed to have come off the covers of fashion publications of the mid-late 20th century.

He smiled and asked, "Thirty?"

"She soon will be forty," the woman with white hair answered. This woman could be thirty, fifty, even sixty-five; it was impossible to tell her age. She was beautiful, graceful, and elegant. She looked absentmindedly at the man, oblivious to his attractiveness or simply used to it after so many years.

"Isn't that kind of late?" he asked. For some reason, he looked worried.

"She hadn't thought about it before. And we could not do anything even though we tried."

"Have forty years passed by already? Time is passing by so quickly." A young, tall, graceful girl got up from her chair and approached the window, looking uneasily at the peaceful expanse of water, lazily swaying below.

Was this house standing on a cliff? Or was it floating in the air? It wasn't possible to say for sure. The girl narrowed her beautiful brown eyes. A whirlwind swirled over the ocean; a white cloud appeared from nowhere, looking like a fluffy dandelion head.

"I will not read her book. My soul can't handle that! I do not want to see her life again. It's hard for me. I still think we SHOULD HAVE INTERFERED back then and helped her."

The woman with white hair waved her hand in disagreement.

"Firebird! Do not start again! We agreed to this. We can only observe. We must not interfere!"

The girl with the strange name, Firebird, shuddered as if trying to drive away unpleasant memories. She ran a thin hand through her wavy dark hair.

"It's good that time flows by so fast out there," she said. "Otherwise, this torment would simply seem endless." Her voice sounded a little dull and stifled.

"Time flows by just the same everywhere. It always does, or it does not flow by at all! Time is only an illusion, in some way. Have you forgotten? That is why

8

suffering sometimes seems endless, on all the verges of the Universe," a soft, low voice came from the far corner of the bright living room. The room was hovering between the sky and the sea. It had comfortable, light furniture and paintings of shells and lost islands on the walls.

"Have you forgotten?" repeated the voice. The fourth participant of the conversation, a stately red-haired woman with golden freckles, looking like an ancient Scandinavian Queen, thoughtfully twirled her paintbrush in her hand. She looked at a blank canvas, then at the girl, as if about to paint Firebird's portrait.

Firebird's hand instantly froze in her hair. It seemed like time slowed down.

"Yes. You are right! I have forgotten," she answered. "But I want to REMEMBER."

9

Chapter 3

I Promise

This happened several weeks after I have found Him.

I wasn't doing anything mystical, just cooking dinner for my children on an ordinary day in January. My funny-looking little dachshund, Maxie, was running and jumping around me. Suddenly, everything disappeared before my eyes, going pitch dark for a moment. And then I saw...

I saw a place where the color of ocher and saffron prevailed. Instantly, I felt almost unbearable pain and distress. Oh, the pang of recognition— stifling heat from heaven and earth, scanty vegetation, though dry and barren, this desert-like landscape was exquisitely beautiful. All of this was heartbreakingly familiar.

I saw a man and a woman. I *KNEW* the woman was me, but from a very long time ago—hundreds of years ago. The man sat on the ground with his arms wrapped around her in a tender embrace. The woman was dying.

In the next moment, I was no longer an observer; I was *THERE*. I was this woman in his arms, with impossible chest pain tearing me apart. Words cannot begin to describe the excruciating agony. But the anguish in my Soul was much, much more profound. I *HAD TO LEAVE HIM*. I did not want to leave him! Horrifying hopelessness and devastating despair consumed me! How could I possibly leave him? Everything in me wanted to scream! Beg! Curse! I did not want to go. I loved him more than anything in existence! More than *ANYTHING*. I loved him! Oh, how much I loved him! I was woven out of this love! I was created out of this love! We were *ONE*. Parting with him was unthinkable! Unbearable! But my time on Earth was over. I knew it. And I couldn't do anything about it.

I was about forty years old. I looked almost the same as I do now, but my hair was plaited in a very long braid. The clothes I wore were almost weightless, bright, beautiful, and easily recognizable—an Indian saree.

The man, weeping bitterly, heart-achingly, was crying from pain, despair, and hopelessness. He knew I would be gone soon. He knew that no one, nothing could help me anymore. He held me tightly in his arms, tears streaming from his beautiful dark eyes.

"Lala, my Lala! Promise me! *PROMISE ME!!!! YOU WILL FIND ME IN ANOTHER LIFE!* You will find me again! Promise me, Lala! *PROMISE ME!*" he repeated over and over again.

I wanted to call his name, but I failed. I didn't have enough strength in me to speak. I desperately wanted to touch his face one last time, even if lightly, just with my fingertips. But I could not do that either. Hot, salty tears flowed down my cheeks.

Please! Oh, please! I prayed silently to someone; *let me touch him. Please, let me feel him just one last time.*

Instantly I felt the strength to raise my hand and caress his beautiful face. I was able to look deep into his impossible, incredible eyes. We stared into each other's eyes; for a moment, time ceased to exist—stars and planets stopped their eternal voyage. Eyes to eyes! Locked in existence. One Soul in two pairs of eyes—One Soul.

"*PROMISE ME YOU WILL FIND ME IN ANOTHER LIFE, LALA! PROMISE ME!*" he whispered.

"*I PROMISE you!*" I was able to say. "*I PROMISE you, I WILL!*"

Then the scene disappeared in pitch darkness. I found myself sitting on the floor of my kitchen in absolute disbelief. My little puppy was jumping around me, trying to lick my face, wet with the tears running endlessly from my eyes. Everything I had just seen disappeared, but one thing remained— that terrible, excruciating pain in my chest. If someone saw me at that moment, they would probably decide that I was simply insane or slightly out of my mind. I was sobbing and could not stop. I was hugging my puppy tightly, whispering several words over and over again. Like a spell. Like a prayer. Like a mantra.

"I found you!

I found you!

I found you!"

Now I understood why this strange chest pain had haunted me from my very early childhood. A pain that, at times, becomes completely unbearable. Dozens of cardiograms and examinations reveal absolutely nothing. Now it all made sense. This pain followed me into this life. Maybe it was necessary. Perhaps I had to have it to remember the promise I gave.

The Promise...

I gave it, and I kept it. I found him.

But what would it change? What could I do about it? Nothing. Absolutely nothing. It all seemed utterly hopeless. Hugging my puppy and shedding tears was probably my only option under those circumstances. What else could I do?

The man I gave that promise to, in this life, was one of the brightest and most famous celebrities in the whole wide world. He was a megastar—a movie star! He was known, loved, and idolized by millions of people. He had the same incredible dark eyes, same gorgeously shaped lips, slightly too full and too sensual for a man, and the same mane of wavy black hair.

Yes. He looked just the same. Only now, He was one of the highest-paid actors in Hollywood, the holder of many prestigious awards, one of the most respected and beloved stars in the world's film industry, highly admired and adored by both critics and ordinary people.

He was called the God of acting. A living legend, he held half of the world in the palm of his hand. Even little children knew his name. The phenomenon of his popularity and magnetism could not be explained by anyone. He was a star in every sense and meaning of this word. And he also had a wife and children, glory and power, fame and...

And yet, he was the very same man who cried, holding me in his arms and begging me to find him in THIS life!

How could that even be? Why? Why? Why? But this was the truth of it, and I could not change a thing. I could do absolutely nothing. In this life, he was as far from me as a distant Galaxy. For an ordinary woman like me, it was IMPOSSIBLE to reach out to him! Impossible!

But I did! I did reach out to Him. Somehow, I managed to do something that looked insanely impossible, at least logically! But Destiny is Destiny. Karma is Karma. What is written and meant to happen before we come to Earth will happen. And after all, I swore to him. I promised him. I gave him my word. I had to keep it. So, I did. I vowed to find him! And I did!

But it took me almost forty years of my present life to finally find Him. And it seems to me that I have lived at least a thousand lives over the past five years after I had already found him. It took me that long not only to reach out to him, the great and inaccessible Star, but also to make him believe me, to help Him REMEMBER. No, I cannot and should not say that I did it all by myself. If it were up to me only, I would have done absolutely NOTHING after learning who he was. But much Higher Forces intervened in my story, and I have done what I was meant to do.

How was I able to do that? How much of me did it take? What did I have to go through? How did I manage not to give up and not break? I will tell you all about it.

I will tell you about it, fully understanding and realizing that there will be quite a few skeptics among this book's readers, who will say, "There is no such thing as reincarnation! We only live once." Such an opinion sounds more than strange to me. Thousands of facts and dozens of years of deep research and exploration on this subject by world-famous scientists have made the denial of reincarnation, at the very least, rather odd. That would be denying the obvious. We can also deny oxygen because we cannot SEE it, but that would not be very clever.

There have always been, and always will be people, who do not want to admit this, no matter how much evidence you provide for them. Many times, in my life, I have come across such people. Well, then. That is normal. Everyone has the right to their own opinion and vision of the world.

Everyone has their own time to wake up, understand, learn, and see and accept the truth.

I will be honest with you; nothing puzzles me in the whole world more than the illogical idea that we only live ONCE. I always ask people who believe that a simple question: Answer me please, my beautiful Soul, where were you and who were you BEFORE you entered this life in your current physical body?

People, naturally, do not know how to answer. After all, it is only LOGICAL and OBVIOUS that the Soul *cannot* reach a high level of development in *just one life*. That would be the same as getting a University Degree in one week! Each life is another step, another year in the University of the Soul. It is another level, test, task, or many of them. As Souls, we are all at different levels of spirituality, wisdom, knowledge, enlightenment, love. *We all come to learn, to become deeper, wiser, stronger.* Each life on this planet is our classroom.

Think about it, everything in nature has the form of a spiral. Nothing ends. *It just continues.* That is how nature is. A day comes after night, and spring follows winter. After birth comes death and birth again in another form and life. *Nothing. Ever. Ends.* We are faced with déjà vu at almost every step we take. We meet people we have not ever seen before, but deep inside, there is a feeling that we have known them for thousands of years. Today we have the luxury to easily access any information we want and wish for without the risk of being burned at the stake by the "holy" Inquisition, as several hundred years ago. But still, many people do not know or deny the fact that trillions of galaxies, planets, and solar systems exist, similar to our own. The theory of not one but many Universes has been written about many times. Quantum Physics makes incredible new discoveries every single day!

I wonder how anyone can sincerely believe that there is only one planet like Gaia Earth and nothing else. Yet many people think we are the only ones in the vast Universe, and we should all pray and wait for a moment when Jesus (Buddha, Muhammad, Moses) will come and save us all. Why? Because it's familiar. It's comfortable. It's what we've been told for hundreds of years.

14

Many of us simply believe it without thinking to ask questions. After all, it is much easier to lay all the responsibility for our life and happiness on God's shoulders than to do something ourselves.

It is much easier to pray and to hope for the mercy of God than to take control of your own life, easier than taking responsibility for the thoughts in your head, words you say, things you do towards yourself and others. It is easier to pray and wait for God, or Gods, to bring you happiness than to work for it or fight for it. Unfortunately, only praying and waiting will not bring positive, joyful changes to your life. If someone puts you down, stand up for yourself, for your rights! Fight for your honor, your freedom, your dignity! Do not pray that an abuser becomes an Angel, or as I say, "the snake becomes a swan!" That will not change anything. If you hate your job, leave it! Change the place, the occupation, the city!

Do not kneel and pray for your boss to have mercy or coworkers to stop being nasty, or your job to suddenly inspire you! That will change nothing. Things will only change when you start DOING something, doing everything possible to make your life how YOU want it to be. Don't allow your family, or society, or religion to decide for you! You owe yourself joy, laughter, the fulfillment of your wishes! You have the right to be happy, to pursue your dreams, and to shine your light! So do something. Do not only pray! Act! Praying and waiting without doing anything only postpones your possible achievements and victories. It does not allow your talents to open and shine. It will only lead you to another monotonous, repetitive round of the same life in the next incarnation.

Positive Changes in our lives and on our planet will only occur when each of us takes responsibility for our lives and things that have happened, are happening now, or will happen to us. The change will arise when we consciously begin *to create our own reality.*

Reincarnation has been deeply studied and researched by famous scientists whose credentials and professionalism are undeniable. Hundreds of thousands of experiments have been conducted. Tens of thousands of pieces of evidence are documented. Hundreds of books have been written. Some of the most widely known are Raymond Moody's *Life after Life* and

Coming Back, my favorite, the most amazing of them all, three books by Michael Newton: *Journey of Souls, Destiny of Souls,* and *Wisdom of Souls.* I call those "The books of all books." This world would be a completely different place if everyone knew what was written in them. Other well-known books are three by Brian. L. Weiss: *Many Lives, Many Masters, Miracles Happen,* and *Same Soul, Many Bodies.* Tom Shroder's book, *Compelling Evidence from Children Who Remember Past Lives.* And *The Past Life Perspective* by Ann C. Barham. There are many more I could list, but you can do your own research.

Reincarnation is one of the fundamental laws of the Universe. To deny reincarnation, without at least considering its possibility, would be as strange as denying the law of gravity or the air we breathe every moment of our lives. We all live hundreds and thousands of lives. It would be wise to at least think about it and research it. We have all the information now at our fingertips. Denying our many lives is as strange as denying countless galaxies, solar systems, and planets. We have no right to live in ignorance anymore. We don't have time for that. We must finally know who we are, why we are here, and for what purpose.

Karmic Partners

KARMIC partners and Karmic Soulmates are also Eternal Lovers, much like Twin Flames.

When they meet each other, their feelings are similar to those felt by Twin Flames. They also feel an enormous magnetic pull to one another, unable to logically explain it. They recognize each other on the Soul Level. One soul will always recognize the other if they crossed paths in other lifetimes. This recognition happens at the level of inner awareness, in their very essence. Karmic relationships are never easy. But there's always the beautiful possibility they will be able to triumph over all the tests and lessons and finally be happy. Some of them stay together after paying karmic debts to one another. Others walk away, finding happiness with someone else. Each case is unique.

They may have had one life, dozens, or hundreds together. The more lifetimes they have known each other, the more powerful their sense of recognition. But they are not Twin Flames. The differences between karmic partners and TF are considerable, as are the goals they are given for their incarnations.

Karmic partners have many things in common, while Twin Flames MIRROR each other. Beyond their likes or dislikes, what they dream of and hope to achieve, they often even look alike, just as single embryo twins do. The most striking similarity they share is their eyes. As we know, the eyes are the windows of the soul. Since Twin Flames share the Same Soul, they have the same eyes. Very often, they even blink the same. Imagine the same face on two people. Male and Female. That is how they usually look. One Old Russian song has such words, "I do not need a mirror to see myself; I can just look at you." Looking at TF baby photos might surprise you. My own mother could not tell the difference between his baby photo and mine. Even the expression of our eyes is almost identical. That is the phenomenon of Twin Flames. That is the story I am living.

And now, let's go back to this story of Eternal Love.

Chapter 4

In the Mist House on the Lost Planet

"You know, there was a time when I wanted to die because I loved him too much. Or, to be exact, I wanted to die because he did not really love me. I was certain I had met my Twin Flame. We thought the same, laughed the same, argued, and loved the same films and books. We also had such similar eyes that everyone thought we were brother and sister."

Redheaded "Scandinavian Queen," Joanna put aside her paintbrush. The waves of the ocean kiss the shore on her canvas. The paints are translucent and light. Soft turquoise waves seem to be whispering old lost fairy tales to the wind and the clouds.

Helena, the woman with white hair, is holding a beautiful bouquet of wildflowers, about to put them into a crystal vase.

The girl with the fairy tale name, Firebird, looks at Joanna with her eyes wide open.

"Joanna! I would never believe you wanted to die because you loved a man too much!"

The handsome man, who looks like an Arabian sheik, playfully threatens the red-haired artist with his finger and laughs softly. "I do not believe it. I think he probably wanted to die because you loved him much less than your canvas, brushes, oceans, and flower-filled meadows."

Red-haired Joanna shakes her head seriously.

"I thought my life was over. Because without him, I could not breathe. And how can one survive on Earth without breathing? Impossible. Without breathing on Earth, you die."

"How did you manage to understand he was not your Twin Flame? If he wasn't your Twin, who was he? A Karmic Lover?" Firebird could barely breathe, eagerly wanting to know more about this story. The girl crossed her thin white fingers, impatiently waiting for the answer.

Joanna looked at Firebird's excited face. "Yes. Karmic. I finally realized it when I was almost dead from my 'love'. I only had two choices: to fall to the very bottom and stay there till the very end, or push off the bottom and swim back to the surface. I did the second. I put the broken pieces of myself together again and started over. I pushed off. I went up. I found a new career, hobby, and friends. I successfully wrote and published my own poetry and became famous. Only then did I fully realize, he simply did not love me. It's an excruciating realization, you know... But it must be faced. It must be done. He never truly and deeply loved me. And it means he was not my Twin, my Mirror, half of my very Soul. No. He arrived in my life as my Dark Karma. He came to claim old debts. He balanced our old mutual injustices and resentment of past lives, and he left. His heart, after all, was not even touched. He came as my executioner. Came to raise me high to heaven and then let me fall to the cold hard ground. He was no Twin. He was Karma."

"Bravo, Joanna!" said the beautiful man while dragging his fingers through his mane of dark wavy hair. "I truly admire your sharp mind and the power of your Spirit. Frankly, I'm glad you got over him and that excruciating love of yours. He didn't deserve you. You recovered from that pain and started a new life. It's always a beautiful experience—the endless possibilities for new friends, new dreams, and great achievements."

He came up to the artist and gallantly kissed her hand. He looked at the painting and saw mountaintops covered with snow instead of the ocean, which had been there just a moment ago. He pretended not to be surprised.

"Haan! Have YOU found YOUR Twin Flame? Have YOU met her?" Firebird asked suddenly. "I am certain you have your own fantastic story! Tell us! Who was she? Where is she now?"

Time froze. The clouds around the Mist House became an impenetrable curtain. The air was so thick you could cut it with a knife. A deafening silence fell on the room, not dead, not ringing, but a frosty, heavy silence. The handsome, masculine face of Haan became grim and sharp. Old pain flickered faintly in his beautiful dark eyes. The woman with white hair glanced at Joanna, then at Haan, shook her head.

"No. She still doesn't remember!" Helena whispered with her lips only.

The air swayed like a child's swing, and everyone managed to take a sigh of relief, and then Firebird said loudly to all three of them.

"Let's continue reading the story! We must know what she's writing."

Immediately, a white sheet of paper with written words flew through the window, into the room, and rested in Helena's hands. The clouds pretended to be soft chairs. The room became more comfortable, suddenly painted in the evening colors of philosophical thoughts, intellectual letters, and lengthy conversations about beautiful epochs, mysterious times, and places of a time long ago. Its inhabitants settled themselves comfortably and began to listen.

My story started a very long time ago. Knowing what I know now, I understand; it started long before I was even born.

I know that it may be almost impossible for you to believe what I am about to tell you. And still, this is the truth. I am a living witness of this fact: you can love the same man from one life to another. I am a living witness that death ends nothing. I am a living witness to the simple fact that nothing ever ends. *Nothing. Ever. Ends.*

I often say I wrote this book with the blood and the fire of my very Soul. I consider this book to be the mission of my whole life. Why? Because I am convinced our planet needs love stories such as mine. Gaia needs more true love stories. Only Love can and will save our World. Love is the only religion and the only truth. Without Love, we all are just bodies, like biological robots. Only Love makes us truly alive! Only Love makes us truly who we are at the very core. It turns the light on inside our hearts and makes us shine.

I want to believe this story will stay with people long after I am gone and maybe warm somebody's heart. Maybe it will help someone find a glimmer of lost hope. Maybe it will help somebody find the strength not to give up, to keep going towards what their Soul truly wants. Maybe it will help those who are apart come back together. And most of all, I want to help people understand, Love is Eternal. Love is Immortal. Love is forever.

This is not a myth; this is the truth.

My name is Lala.
I am a Twin Flame.
And this is my story.

Chapter 5

The Beginning

Before I tell you about my childhood, I want you to understand one essential truth. I am not sharing this story to judge those I will tell you about, nor am I writing this to cause you to pity me.

When I look back over my life, I see that the severe challenges brought me priceless experience and knowledge. That is especially true of the five years that passed since I had found my Twin Flame. I can confidently say: We choose the experiences we want to go through in our earthly incarnations. To be exact, our Soul or Essence chooses it. No, we don't do it alone. We plan it together with our Guides and Keepers. Some call them: "The Keepers of Destiny" or "The Keepers of Karma." In the end, the final choice for what we experience in our life is always our own. Yes, yes. The choice is ours only!

Why do we choose such demanding tasks for ourselves? You may ask. *Why don›t we choose something easy?* Because the expression, "What doesn't kill you makes you stronger," is a very true one. The more challenging the lesson, the stronger we become. The stronger we become, the higher our Soul Level and our Consciousness will rise. And when we do, we truly understand who we are and why we have come to Earth. Yes, it's our choice, only! For example, you may feel you cannot forgive your mother or father (somehow, the most advanced souls choose to experience a very harsh childhood). Or you think you cannot forgive the people who hurt you, who brought you a lifetime full of resentment, pain, and suffering. But what if I tell you that you

22

yourself have chosen this path, and because of it, you have become stronger? All your past experiences have made you who you are, *a faceted diamond, an unbreakable damask blade.*

There is an expression: "The Gods do not send us tests beyond our strength." The truth is, as I said, we ourselves choose the paths we take in each incarnation. The stronger our Soul, the harder the path we choose. Why? Because by going through pain, through multiple tests, we become wiser, deeper, and even stronger. I really wish it were different, but having once experienced hunger, you will never remain indifferent to the hungry one. Having experienced the hurt of rejection, you will not reject without reason. Having experienced pain, you will not want to inflict pain on others because you know from your own experience what it is like. We learn to appreciate the warmth of the sun after we've spent some time in a cold dark cave. We learn to appreciate the warmth and kindness of the human heart after we have experienced others' indifference or contempt. Do you remember this song?

> You live you learn
> You love you learn
> You cry you learn
> You lose you learn
> You bleed you learn
> You scream you learn [2]

This is what we constantly do. Some people come into our lives to inspire us, bring us joy, and teach us to laugh. Others come to teach us to rise after a fall.

I also want to tell you about my childhood and youth, so you can know and understand that even though I had no clue I was a Twin Flame back

---

2   Alanis Morissette, "You Learn," 1995, track #7 on *Jagged Little Pill*, Maverick, Rock, Pop.

then, I was still unbelievably strong from my very birth. I was a very tough cookie. None of the hardships, tests, pain, and suffering life constantly threw my way made me give up or break. That is how we are.

The Toughest Teachers

Do you know that while in the Dimension of the Spirits, no one ever wants to return to Gaia-Earth as a Tormentor! Nobody wants to incarnate as the one who must become a real TEST in someone's life. Nobody wants to live with the goal of hurting someone to toughen them up. And only the strongest do agree to assume this role. (Let me clarify this right away. I do not mean criminals, maniacs, and murderers. These creatures do not possess what we call "The Soul." They have rightly been called "non-humans" for centuries. But I will not dwell on this now. I am talking about other types of Souls and the different types of "hurt" they cause.)

The Strongest of Souls takes on the role of the tormentors of our earthly life. Do you know why? It is like a school. They give us the lessons of survival, of personal and spiritual growth. Often, it is our fiercest "enemies" in earthly life who turn out to be our most influential teachers. They teach us to fall and rise again. They teach us to bend without breaking, burn down, and rise from the cold ashes. They teach us how, after being hurt, tormented, with our soul worn out and crying, not to lose the ability to love and feel another person's pain.

It was a harsh and cruel school, but I chose these people and these events, or the Keepers and the Guides chose this task for me, and I agreed! I chose this school, and I have graduated from it. In my life, I have known a soul who took on the role of executioner in my fate, the tormentor, who became my toughest teacher, my brother Alexei. Another challenge, though much less severe, turned out to be my dearest mother.

You know, if there is a soul in this Universe that, upon before arrival to Earth, tells the Guardians of Fates that she can go through 77 lives in one, 77 most severe trials, 77 circles of hell, and 77 levels of purgatory and not give up or break, then that for sure would be my mom. And if one could say

24

that titanium or unbreakable Souls exist, it would definitely be her, again. My mother reminds me of the Great Pyramids that have stood for centuries, are still standing, and will be standing for millennia to come. It is impossible to describe in words the tests that her soul has chosen. But the word "to break" does not exist in her dictionary. Her life was a struggle. An endless, eternal struggle for the life of her closest and dearest people, and she did it silently, clenching her teeth and without ever complaining. Pyramids do not complain, right? They never collapse either. But sometimes, it is not easy for them to understand the suffering and tears of those who are smaller and weaker than they are.

Chapter 6

My Mother

My mother, Lidiya, was born in August 1936. She was only five years old when World War II began. Her father went to the battlefields, leaving his wife (my grandmother Tatiana), my mother, her little sister, and their little newborn baby brother. All men able to hold a weapon and protect the Land against intruders had gone to War. Like the other women, my grandma had to take on all the work of their now absent men. Grandma worked on a tractor in the fields for many hours a day. Someone had to take care of the youngest siblings; that responsibility fell on my five-year-old mother.

I won't write about the horrors of the war or the daily acts of unbelievable and heroic bravery at the battlefields and home fronts for those long, excruciating four years the war lasted; much has already been written about that. My grandfather, Alexander, returned home from the war before it ended, severely wounded in the brutal battle for Stalingrad. He considered it a miracle he was still alive. He told my mom stories about fighting for Stalingrad, which my mom later told me. Even imagining something like this is extremely difficult. There is a very ancient text about King Igor's fight with the enemies trying to seize Mother Russia. It was true even hundreds of years later: "Fight for your Motherland, even if you are already dead, rise and fight! They will burn you with fire. Rise and fight! They will pierce you with a sword. Rise and fight! They will kill you a hundred times. Rise and fight! Rise and fight!"

Life was not easy for anyone when my grandfather returned from war. But my mother told me my grandpa could do absolutely anything. He made an actual bicycle out of willow twigs. He could build anything and repair anything broken, so people constantly brought him things to fix or asked him for help. For his service, people shared what they had, mainly food. So, for his family, life was a bit less challenging than it was for the others.

Whatever hardships they had to go through, my mother says, love always ruled in their tiny little house. Her parents loved each other very deeply. Even now, mom recalls how the parents used to sing very ancient folk songs together in the evenings. The children were always aware of this strong bond, this deep true love between their parents. Having grown up in this loving atmosphere, she naturally believed she would find this same kind of beautiful love; she too would love someone deeply and be loved deeply in return.

But life had different plans. Horror awaited my mother with her first love, the father of my two brothers. At the very beginning, their relationship seemed wonderful, but unfortunately, with time, it burned out, turning my mother's life into absolute misery.

After graduating from High School at 18, my mom left the village she was born and grew up in and traveled several hundred kilometers to Odessa, Ukraine. She successfully passed the entrance exams and became a Polytechnic University student in Engineering. Soon she met her future husband, Vladimir, a fisherman. They dated for a very long time, without being intimate. Unlike today's world, it was common back then. They spent time walking along the beach, holding hands, sitting in front of her house on a wooden bench, and talking about everything under the sun until morning came. A year later, when Mom was twenty, they got married. After a very modest wedding, as they were very poor, they moved into his mother's house. Quickly, this imagined heaven deteriorated into a living hell, which lasted for ten long years. Vladimir could not cope with an old hereditary problem—alcoholism. He had managed to hide it from her while dating, but after she became his wife, he no longer tried. Soon he started drinking heavily every day. My poor young mother, exhausted from hard physical work, lived with terrifying fear for two little sons because of her drunk, aggressive, and dangerous husband. Her constant attempts to change, or at least somehow improve things, were completely futile.

Many women back then lived in the same conditions. Many live like this now. They lived every day in fear and torture. They cried silently, suffered silently, and many, unfortunately, passed this terrible habit of bearing it all onto their daughters. My mom endlessly loved her two sons. She dreamed of a better life for them, but she was absolutely terrified to go against her husband and her mother-in-law, who had never accepted and always deeply hated her. There were times when she had to grab her little boys and run, hiding with them in a huge cornfield, while her husband circled around in a drunken haze, knife in hand, threatening to find and kill them all. It would last for hours. It's hard even to imagine the horror those minutes and hours contained for all three of them! Having sobered up, he would ask for forgiveness and swear nothing like this would happen again. But he could never keep his promise. He really did love her very much, but not enough to overcome the powerful demon of alcohol. When he was sober, he was a good man, but he was rarely sober. When he was drunk, it seemed as if all the monsters of the underworld possessed him, cursing his family into endless suffering and torture. That continued, until one day, after living in pure hell for ten years, my mother decided she did not care anymore what people would say or think of her.

She had reached the edge. It was no longer possible to live every day terrified for her own life and the lives of her children. One day, she just took her sons' hands in her own, and the three of them simply walked out of that house without money or luggage or anything else. They didn't know where they would go or how they would survive. They simply knew they must run! A miracle was not going to happen. The monster would stay a monster. The laws of that country, like many others, have always been imperfect towards women and children. A law existed, but there was no way to make it actually work. It was impossible to convince an alcoholic to come to his senses. It was nearly impossible to make him pay child support and help his ex-wife and his own children start their lives from zero. With nowhere to call her own, she asked relatives and friends for a temporary place to stay with her kids. She worked three jobs 16 hours a day, every day. But she did not break!

A couple of years later, she managed to obtain a small apartment, granted for free by the factory she worked at back then. That was a common practice, and such flats were called "Khrushchev-era apartments" or "khrushchevka." It was a tiny two-room flat (a small living room, a tiny bedroom, and a miniature kitchen), situated on the fifth floor of a standard five-story building without an elevator. The name of the street they now lived on was called "Joyful" (the paradox of life)! Though tiny, having their own apartment felt like heaven. They no longer needed to live in other people's homes. Mom raised her children, my brothers, on her own, working from mornings till late at night. She also decided to go back to college and finish her master's degree. When she was 36 years old, she met my father. They were working together.

Even now, it's still a great mystery to me why my affectionate, freedom-loving, womanizing father wanted a relationship with my extremely serious and worn-out mother, a single woman with two children. But apparently, I will never find out what his reasons were. Could he simply have fallen in love with her? Knowing the little I know about my father, I doubt it big time, but then, who knows.

Mom did not pay any attention to his courtship for a very long time. Her plans did not include men or another marriage. She was busy studying, working, and raising two teenagers. She was convinced that one marriage would be more than enough with all the suffering it brought her and her sons. She no longer believed in men or the possibility of love. She certainly didn't think she could be happy again. But my father's extreme persistence seemed impossible to escape; he used promises, persuasion, and even blackmail. Finally, my mother agreed to marry him, perhaps again, fearing gossip and disapproval of her neighbors, coworkers, and those who talked behind her back. It was a time when an official marriage was a mandatory attribute. A couple could only live together and be considered "decent" and "right" if they were officially married. So, they got married.

Soon, it became apparent to my mother that my father loved every woman he met! In a word, he was a womanizer. A charming, charismatic womanizer! That was not something my mother had any intentions of putting up with. Only a few months passed after their wedding when it became clear as day to her that she could not live with him. But when she made up her mind to get a divorce, it turned out she was already pregnant with me. Did my father love my mother? I don't know. Maybe he did, in his own way. The answer to this question will forever remain a mystery to me. Did my mom love him? I think not, but I cannot tell for sure either. Mom still keeps silent every time I ask her. I only know that she decided not to keep on living with a liar and a heartthrob. I think she was absolutely right about that.

It wasn't even a question of whether or not to give birth to me. She had two teenagers, twelve hours of work every day, college, a tiny apartment, and no husband. To give birth to another child under such conditions would be simply pure madness. Besides, she was already 37 years old and Rh-negative. The pregnancy could turn out to be extremely risky, especially 40 years ago. But destiny interfered again. By the time my mother found out she was pregnant, it was already too late to change anything. Many years later, she told me how she begged the doctor to terminate the pregnancy with tears in her eyes. She explained everything about her desperate situation to him. But the doctor flatly refused. She was too far along in her pregnancy, and my heart was already beating.

Nobody was waiting for me; no one wanted me to come. I was not a desired, loved, or long-awaited child; I was a mistake, a misfortune. But I still came into this world, arriving almost two months before the due date. There were only two gifts my father gave me in my life: the conception itself and my name, Alla. He was a Muslim and decided to name me in honor of his God. That was all. He never existed in my life. I must admit that even now, I am still a bit jealous of those who have a person in their life to call this amazing word "Papa."

Somehow, my soul chose this particular man to play the role of my father. It was necessary for something. Now I know why I needed a father like him, to learn how to be unbreakable while being rejected, unwanted, and unloved. I guess this was the purpose of my childhood. I was being trained from a very early age not to break, no matter what tests I had to face.

Oh, there were too many of those tests. Had I prepared them for myself, or were these obstacles chosen by those who sent me to this planet? Did they choose my family and this fate for me? I'm not sure, but one thing I know for certain: Every soul comes here by their own choice. So, this means I was well aware of these challenges beforehand and agreed to go through them. But why? Why not choose an easier life? The answer is simple, the harder the lessons, the stronger we become.

Am I strong? Have I pushed more onto myself than I could handle? Maybe, when we are in the world of spirits, Earth life seems to us particularly fast, and all of these tests and sufferings do not seem as difficult? Maybe so. As soon as we come down here to the physical world, we begin to doubt our wise souls. We start to think that maybe we're not strong enough for the hardships we've chosen. But we're no longer capable of changing them. We must follow our chosen path, as that train already left the station and cannot be turned back. There's no going back. We have to go through what we must go through, what we've agreed on, what we've chosen. It's our obligation.

But how terrifying and distressing it was sometimes for me, as a little girl, unwanted and unloved. A strange, cold, unwelcoming world was my new reality. But I had to live, learn, grow up, and toughen up there to fulfill the destiny chosen for me.

For me, my mother, while an example of enormous strength and endurance, was also one of the toughest tests I had to go through. I call it "a test of rejection and loneliness." Though I spent my whole life next to my incredible mother, I always knew, always felt, she was neither spiritually nor emotionally close to me. Even more than that, my mom saw me as *weird, strange, a bit crazy*. If I spoke, I said something *strange*, not what *normal* kids my age would usually say. I guess everything about me somewhat scared or puzzled her. She did not like it and usually responded to me with these words: «It would be much better if instead of talking *nonsense*, you got busy and actually did something useful!"

Oh! That phrase! That mysterious phrase "better do something useful!" You can use it practically in any situation if you want to brush off anything or anyone like an annoying fly. Even now, I still profoundly detest those words. Of course, like any other little girl, I wanted to share everything with my mother (I had never had a father, my brothers were much older than me, so, naturally, there was nobody else to share anything with). But after several unsuccessful attempts to share something dear, secret, deeply personal with her, I shut up. Mom did not understand me. She didn't even try. She didn't have any time for that. She had too much on her hands. Besides working, studying, surviving a single mother's life with now three kids, she was fighting for the life of my two brothers, whom she loved immeasurably. And it was indeed an everyday battle, in the literal sense of this word.

She did not have time to deal with me. She did not have the time for my *weirdness*, mysterious wishes, strange questions, and hidden wounds. Still, I was just a little girl, and even though I had to grow up quickly, I still deeply and wholeheartedly longed for and needed her love, her approval, her affection. I wanted it so badly that I was ready to do anything under the Sun to deserve it. Yet, no matter how hard I tried, I never saw it.

Isn't what I want simple? I see other kids are receiving tons of love and attention without even trying. What am I doing wrong? I thought. Why is it always out of my reach? I just want a hug. I want mom to pat me on the head and say, "my daughter," "my dear girl," "my beautiful."

It is strange to admit, but I long for this even now.

Please, be sure to tell your children how much you love them! Spend time with them, speak kind words, share loving feelings. Praise and compliment them daily, even if it might seem they do not deserve it yet. Please give them your approval in advance. May it be your appreciation that your child has chosen you out of billions of other souls to be his parents. Love and appreciate him for being by your side, for loving you endlessly with all he has in him. As it might happen in the future, that you would turn out to be the only one truly and deeply loving and accepting of him. Life might turn its harsh side to your child, and many others will try to hurt him and bring him down. So praise him, love him, hug him, and let your child grow up feeling valued, cherished, adored, and appreciated. And then he will undoubtedly be happy: today and tomorrow as well. He will grow up believing in himself, shining his light for himself and for others.

As a child, I sincerely envied children who had affectionate mothers. My mother did not have time for that. Life for her was pure survival. A struggle. A fight. A test. There was hardly space in her life left for joy and peace, or even just laughter. But even now, when I am well aware of it all, I continue longing to be understood, accepted, and loved by my dear mother. I think, today, she probably accepts me. She probably loves me in her own way. Even though I wish, it was not love in "her own way," but just love—pure, simple love.

Even now, in her eyes, I am something incomprehensible and strange. My mother does not love me, does not understand, and does not accept me, and it will always be this way, I often thought. Those thoughts are painful and feel like many thin, sharp, cold blades driven into my heart. Unfortunately, all my attempts throughout the years to explain my feelings, or share something deeply personal with her, got smashed on the cliffs of indifferent detachment. I did learn to live with it; I did learn to accept it. But it never stops hurting.

Deep inside, for as long as I remember, I carried in me a strong, even sharp feeling of loneliness and inferiority. From early childhood, I understood that *something was not right* with me. I was *not like other normal children and people*. But I didn't have the slightest clue exactly what was *wrong* with me or how I could fix it.

Chapter 7

My Childhood. HIS Eyes...

I was a weird kid from the very beginning of my strange life. When I was born, my brothers were 13 and 15 years old. Our Mom continued to study and work at the same time. So, my brother Alexei had to babysit me. As a kid, I remember very little of my second brother Anatoly. He was rarely home, as he got married very young and moved to his wife Natasha's house.

The list of my *oddities* started from the moment I was born. I completely lacked the ability to cry. Odd? Yes, strange indeed, I agree. But this is exactly how it was. I simply did not know and did not understand how to do it. I *NEVER CRIED* until I was three years old, not even once. I also began to speak very early. At one year old, I was already chatting away. To be exact, first I began to sing, and then I started to speak. I could sing any tune by heart, having heard it only once or twice. I'd sing without even knowing the words, inventing them on the go. I was always singing everywhere possible. I still sing today, though not as often.

Singing has been my refuge, my way to escape reality, the fears, the sadness, the pain, for as long as I remember. My passions for books, music, and cinema became a similar refuge. And, for as long as I remember, I had only two wishes. No, to be exact, three: to find *HIM*, to become an actress, and to change the world so that it would be beautiful and sparkle like spring water in the midday sun. Of course, there would be a rainbow in this new world. And people would always be smiling; their hearts would have no fears whatsoever and only joy. Only Joy.

But does it even matter at all what we dream about? Or does it matter not? Some things are destined to happen, no matter what. While others will not happen, no matter how much we wish and hope and dream about them. Still, we dream! We must! This world moves forward because of the dreamers, those believing in miracles, moved by the pure power of the Heart.

In my early childhood visions, I saw myself sending kisses to a vast crowd while standing on the stage, scenes, and backgrounds constantly changing, replacing one another. I was absolutely convinced the time would come when those visions would become my life. That would be my future. Now, almost forty years later, I understand what it really was. I saw those visions with the EYES of my Twin. I saw HIS future, not my own! I saw what would happen to HIM, not me. But back then, there was no chance in existence I could possibly know that.

I was just a little girl who did not know how to cry and somehow absolutely felt no displeasure of being left completely alone. I have loved to be alone my whole life, perhaps because we are never truly alone. Besides us, there are realities invisible to our human eyes. The worlds and dimensions, and, of course, those I call "The Keepers." I always felt them. I always knew they were watching me, invisibly standing by my side. How could I know it? I just knew.

When I turned three, something happened that would affect my whole life. I remember that I was exactly three because that morning, my mother told me, "You are three years old already! You are not a kid anymore!" That night, for the very first time in this life, I saw his eyes in a dream. At that time, he was 12 years old. I remember that dream very vaguely. But I remember the FEELINGS, the sensations the dream brought me. I felt such a strange, out-of-this-world warmth inside me as if my very essence woke up and started to shine softly. This dream made me aware that I had to FIND someone. I was just a child, but that day, I started a pattern that lasted nearly my entire life, scanning the faces of all the young boys my eyes could only rest on—the boys playing with me in the playground, walking to and from school, playing sports in the yard. I was looking for SOMEONE. I clearly knew I was looking for someone! But whom? And why?

The day I turned *FIVE*, I had another dream. This time I saw his eyes very clearly and remembered them in the smallest details, right down to his every eyelash. I knew, I simply *KNEW*, I would *RECOGNIZE* his eyes from millions, billions of others. Even though I was still just a child, at that moment, I clearly understood one thing, I had to find *HIM*. I did not know why or how. I did not think about it! I just knew I *HAD* to find him. I had no doubt that I would succeed. Or maybe, He will find me, I thought. And when we find each other, all the rest will be like in a fairy-tale. Silly child! Silly, silly, silly child!

Another irresistible passion I had for as long as I remember was looking into the starry sky. I was drawn to it with an impossible and incredible pull. In the summertime, I used to go out to our tiny little balcony, or just outside of the building, and spend hours and hours looking up at the stars. Sometimes I was swept away by such a strong, inexplicable, and incredible longing for something that was far, very far away in that starry sky that I felt like crying. It was something, which I could not explain in any words. Somehow, I felt cut off from something loved, something dear and precious. Although, being completely honest with you, this feeling of isolation from something loved and dear has haunted me my entire life, not only in my childhood.

It seemed to me that because of some strange, wicked twist of fate, I ended up in a very, very far away place from my real home. Where was that *Home*? I did not know. All I knew, it was very far. And now I was in a place where everything seemed alien, strange, and incomprehensible. It is like if you lived your entire life in New York City, London, or Paris, and suddenly, overnight, found yourself in a small Chinese village. You do not understand the language, customs, habits, or why people act in a certain way. But you are there in the village, and you just have to get used to it all someway, get along with the locals, adapt your lifestyle, traditions, customs, likes or dislikes to your new environment. The time passes by. Slowly things start to seem normal. You almost completely forget your place of origin. You manage to fit in somehow. You get used to living there. But then...

A quiet summer night comes when you are looking at the stars, lying on the grass. Suddenly, you feel the pain hidden deep inside, and the tears sting your eyes and fall to the ground. And you let yourself cry because you passionately yearn for something you cannot even explain to yourself. Something is missing. Missing so badly, but what? How did you lose it, when? Can you somehow find it? You don't know the answers. You try to suppress that feeling, but it stays there, deep inside, it does not let you rest, and you do not know what to do with it. All you know, your true home is far, and you do not even know if you ever will be able to see it again.

Since an early age, I have had a habit of talking to the stars. I was sure then, and I still believe now, this is how I can speak with those who have known me for millennia, who hear me, who will help me or at least support me, guide me and give me strength when I need it. And the way my life was about to turn, I needed that strength! I needed it very much!

Yes, I was only five years old when I became aware of *his eyes*. And I was only five years old when my childhood was over.

When I turned five, I had to start kindergarten, but all the schools were already full. Alexey, my elder brother, was 18 years old. He was, what they later called, an "indigo child." He possessed strong psychic powers: telepathy, clairvoyance, incredible intuition. He had the gift of FORESIGHT, meaning he knew and saw what other "normal" people could not know or see. Maybe, many just did not WANT to know or see anything beyond the matrix, beyond things they were told to believe.

It rarely happens that these children are lucky enough to have family members who understand and support their incredible Gift. I know one extremely gifted woman who had a grandmother with the same abilities, the same power of foresight. Even though her parents, as *normal* people, tried to suppress the Gift, her grandma did not allow that to happen. But this is a very rare case.

Most of the kids with such gifts, especially back then, were completely alone. This was true for my brother. He was alone with this gift. Then it was seen as more of a curse than a gift. People who had it went through a lot of suffering. It was absolute torture! Just imagine! They SAW, they KNEW things, which were *THE TRUTH*, but they could not even tell or share it with anyone!

As a child, he tried several times to share what he knew with our mother, but nothing good came out of it. Our strict Mom doesn't comprehend such things even now, let alone back then. Could he share it with someone else? You may ask. What would happen, if he tried to share what he knew and saw with other people? Back then, he would definitely be put in a psychiatric hospital. Medical authorities would label him with a lot of diagnoses. People would frown upon him and screw their faces into smiles, but they would make a "cuckoo" sign behind his back. Oh! I myself know it way too well. I have lived it all! Even now, when you can't surprise anyone with the Foresight or Sixth sense, some people still look at you disapprovingly and put a condescending smile on their faces. Now, imagine what would happen back then…

Back then, it was simply forbidden! *NOT ALLOWED*. Kids and people with these abilities had to keep absolutely silent. My brother did not have any other way but to close up and pretend to be like everyone else among his friends and peers. He had to pretend he was only interested in girls, partying, and other nonsense like the rest of the guys his age, not what our Universe consists of and why we come into this life. My brother reminded me of Galileo—a great scientist who was almost burned at the stake by the church fathers for his "heretical" ideas.

Galileo, the Enlightened One, was trying to explain to religious fanatics that the Earth is by no means the center of the Universe, that it spins around the Sun, and not vice versa, and almost paid for that with his own life. He knew that he was right! But he couldn't prove it to the crowd of ignorant and close-minded people. There was not much he could do. He was one enlightened soul, facing a crowd of unawakened people. But still, he tried. Unfortunately, in their blindness, religious fanatics are still the same now, as they were hundreds of years ago.

My poor brother had to be alone with the knowledge that he had, forbidden to share with anybody. He read books avidly, and he often read them aloud to me, his little sister. Some books were so rare and expensive that he would spend his monthly salary just to buy one of them! And since I had the same "misfortune" to be born with the same gift or curse as he, I understood everything he was talking about perfectly! Who knows how my childhood would have been if...

But there is not a lot of sense in talking about "ifs."

It seems now I have already described so many events, so many memories. But I was still only five. It was so long ago, and yet I remember everything as if it were yesterday. My brother simply could not live with the burden of being different from everyone else. It was more than he could handle. So he tried to get away far from feeling different, lost, and isolated, far away from the knowledge he could not share with anyone, far away from the world in which he lived. He found an escape for himself, a horrific escape; he started doing drugs. He was broken.

I may be trying to find a good excuse to justify his actions right now. I love him. Therefore, I try to defend him. Grownup Alla is trying to justify a boy who turned out to be weak. Weaker than his little sister. Back then, little Alla began to live in such a hell that I am scared to remember it even now. The day had come, and my childhood ended. I remember that day in every detail. And sometimes, I wish I could forget. I wish...

It seemed like an ordinary late summer day. I was busy drawing a strange-looking picture—a bright green ground, a blue ocean, and a sky filled with many red, heart-shaped clouds. I heard the voice of my brother calling me from the other room and felt the pinch of sudden fear, cold, intense fear. But I got up, left my drawing and entered his room. He asked me why I had taken his cigarettes. I replied that I had not. And then, suddenly, abruptly, he grabbed me by my throat with one hand and lifted me above the ground! I looked into his eyes; the eyes of a NON-HUMAN were looking into mine. The memory of that moment makes me shiver with horror even now. I don't know how to explain it to you, but that was not a HUMAN! There was NOTHING human there and absolutely nothing like the eyes of the brother I knew.

Cold, suffocating fear consumed me with all its ruthless power. My brother clenched his hand over my throat. It was getting hard for me to breathe each passing moment. "Mom," I managed to half-whisper, half-hiss softly, as tears rolled from my eyes. But our mother wasn't there. No one was there; No one at all. Not a single soul would come to help me or save me. I knew that very well.

The beast that took over my brother laughed out loud. That laughter you hear in horror movies, but it wasn't a movie; this was my reality. "Nobody will help you," he told me, still laughing. Even the voice was not of my brother! He lowered me to the ground and told me to bring a knife from the kitchen. It was a serrated bread knife. "You took my cigarettes and hid them, and for that, I will cut off your hands," he said. The beast took my little hand, laid it on the table, and began to cut it! The pain was excruciating. I started to cry. But when he saw the blood, the "monster" vanished and my brother suddenly returned.

He looked with utter horror at the deep cut on my tiny hand and the knife in his. He threw the knife away and brought a bandage to cover my wound. Yet at the same time, he told me, "If you tell any of this to our mom, I will kill you!"

After that, he let me go back to the room where my mother and I lived. There was a curtain in that room, hanging over the balcony door. I hid behind it. I was so terrified that everything started to spin around me and became blurry. I felt the taste of my own blood in my mouth. I think I was close to fainting but tried my best not to. Since then, biting my lips when I feel pain became a life-long habit. I wanted to run far, far away. I wanted to hide so that no one could ever find me. My heart, the heart of a little innocent child, was scared to death. I felt something very terrible had happened to my brother. Somehow, I knew that life would never be the same again. I knew this terrifying horror was not over. With every particle of my trembling little body and soul, somehow, I knew that the worst was yet to come. I just sat there, shivering, behind that curtain, expecting the monster to return, take over what was my brother and do something terrible to me. It seemed that time had stopped. There was only fear. Cold, suffocating fear and nothing else. Nothing else at all!

And at that terrifying moment, I don't know why—I have no idea why—I remembered the eyes of the boy from my dream. I squinted my eyes almost painfully tight and tried to remember his eyes in every tiny detail I was only capable of evoking: beautiful dark eyes- lakes. It seemed I could drown in them. In the eyes of that boy, there was something that gave me strength. It gave me the strength to live. He will certainly find me, or I will find him, I told myself. "Find me, my beautiful boy! Please! Please find me! Save me! There is no one to save me. Nobody loves me. Nobody!"

Tears kept on rolling down my cheeks. The wound on my arm was throbbing. My throat was burning, making it painful to swallow. So, I kept holding onto "those eyes," like a drowning man clutching at a straw. Starting that terrible night and during my whole strange and uneasy life, those eyes kept me going! When my mom asked about the wound on my hand, I said it was an accident. The knife slipped while I was trying to cut a piece of bread. She believed me and asked no more questions.

My childhood was over.

My brother used to beat me up with three ordinary objects. In his hands, they became instruments of horrible torture—first, a long, black rubber vacuum cleaner cord. The only thing worse than the horrific pain it initially inflicted was the weals it left on my skin. They took so long time to heal; the agonizing misery lasted for several seemingly endless weeks. Next was a thick leather military belt, which also caused intense pain, but still not as brutal as the cord. The third one was a thick long rubber strip for practicing sports, also harrowing. But the excruciating suffering from the vacuum cord was by far the worst!

Do you know how I survived the moments when he was beating me? I counted the blows. One. Two. Three. Screaming and calling for help were useless. No one would come. I couldn't even tell anybody about this. Complaining and telling were forbidden! If I told someone, it would be worse. Much worse. At least, that was how he convinced me. And I believed him. Did my mom know? Yes, she did. But she would not, or simply could not, change anything though she did try. She made an arrangement for me to stay with our neighbor for part of the day. But my brother didn't like that.

When I would go to the neighbor's, an elderly woman whose door was just next to ours, my brother would bring me back home as soon as he saw I was gone and would beat me much harder for trying to escape. Unfortunately, several of my pitiful attempts to run away and hide at the neighbor's place for even a short time ended badly for me. So, it was better not to try to run or hide. Such was my life.

Do you know what terrified me the most? The MORNINGS. In the morning, our mother left for work. I would sit quietly as a mouse, watching her dress and get ready. I knew that my brother would not lay a finger on me while she was still at home. But the moment she walked out that door, it felt like all hell broke loose. Sometimes mom would let me go with her to work. It was absolute heaven for me. I would sit quietly somewhere in any little corner, like a silent, invisible blade of grass, and felt very happy. I could sit there for hours, thinking or dreaming or reading. I remember those hours as happy moments of my childhood because no one could beat me up, scare me, or humiliate me there. Those days were paradise for me. But they were very infrequent. So, there I would be again, seeing my mother getting ready to go to work in the morning. I'd long to ask her to take me with her but frozen in fear. What if she said "No"? Hearing "No" was like an emotional slap with the rubber cord, another confirmation of my hopelessness. Still, I would gather all the courage my little self possibly could and bravely ask, "Mom, can you take me with you?" But most of the time, my mom would say "No," announcing another death sentence for her little girl.

I am not a child anymore. I'm no longer in danger, yet I still wake up every morning terrified to death. Time has passed, but unfortunately, that childhood fear has never let me go.

Soon I started school. That was an opportunity for me to escape from my brother, even if just for a while. Unfortunately, at school, I became an excellent target for mockery. I was a classic example of a victim surrounded by a small, close-knit flock of young, healthy animals, ready to tear apart and torment this timid, sick creature that could not stand up for herself. When my classmates attacked me, I used to hide in a corner and just be silent. At school, I was a real outcast. And it lasted for many, many years.

Why did I choose this life and these hardships? Why did my soul decide that I could bear all this? Why wasn't I given the power to resist, to punish my offenders, when I was born?

I tried my best to blend in and be like everyone else. More precisely, I tried my hardest to become INVISIBLE, to merge with the wall. Unfortunately, I was not like everyone else, and children feel this otherness intuitively, on a subconscious level. And children never like others. They tend to be very cruel towards these others.

The ten years of school brought me so much suffering that I don't even want to talk about it. Yet, this pain also played a role in my destiny. It was given to me, so I could learn to fall countless times and find the strength to rise again and again, the courage to keep myself alive.

When the lessons were over, all my classmates, filled with joy and laughter, rushed home, shouting and talking happily. Oh, how I envied them all! I envied every one of them! Now they would go home, change clothes, do their homework. They would then play outside with their friends, visit each other, and have fun. Is it really possible to live like that? I'd ask myself. Live without being afraid, being scared every minute, every second? What a happy life it should be! Such reality was unfamiliar for me. I walked home very slowly, purposefully trying to postpone the inevitable. And terrifying horror grew with every step I took. I was going home. And there, at home, was my brother, my torturer.

With the money my mother had given me to buy my school lunch, I bought some treats for him. An ice cream, a sweet bun, several cookies, or candies. At least something. I carried it home in my shaking little hands, hoping with those treats to bribe my brother. Maybe if he likes it, he won't beat me up, won't torture me! I thought. I understood that he was emotionally hurting and in pain all the time. And, somehow, his pain got easier only when he was hurting me. I do not know how I managed to survive. Terrifying fear filled every single breath I took.

Singing saved me. Yes, singing entered my life to save me from my daily horrors.

At school, it quickly became apparent that I could sing. And not just sing, I was able to sing beautifully, even very complex songs. I was accepted into the school choir, where I soon began to sing all the solo parts. That gave me more well-wishers among my classmates. They hate you when you act invisible, but they hate you much more if you somehow dare to become visible. Usually, I would have refused to be in the choir and kept hiding in my little corner, but something in me was more powerful than my fears. Much later, I would know what it was. It was my enormous passion for Music and Art, a passion much stronger than even my anxieties of being bullied. I cared only about singing. It made me feel alive and breathing. I poured all my emotion, pain, fears, dreams of being loved and accepted into the sound of my voice. Nobody could explain why as soon as I started to sing, everyone around was deeply touched and even moved to tears.

"All so dear to the heart, we would turn into the song.
And the soft smile of a child, we would turn into the song.
And the sound of the sea, and the mother's eyes,
All that dear to the heart, we would sing sometimes."

I sang, and people would cry.

There was a simple explanation for that. It was not me singing those songs; it was my soul. My soul: hurt, lonely, and scared. Very scared. But apart from hurt, there also was a secret hope and memory of someone's eyes. I will definitely find THEM. And when I do, everything will be as wonderful as a fairy tale. I performed in the choir for several years. Our school choir won one contest after another: district, city, regional. People started to talk about me. Some important people began to show up to have a look at "the tiny, little girl with the incredible voice." They were going to send me with the choir to some extremely important competition in Moscow. But it all ended abruptly.

44

Not even for a moment did my mother stop trying to save my brother from drugs. She loved him and wanted to help him overcome his addiction. She firmly believed that one day she would find a way, and she did. Someone told her about a doctor, living many thousands of kilometers away, on the other side of the country. We quickly sold everything we could, packed up, and moved to that city, taking only the most necessary things with us. At that time, I was 12 years old. The new city and the new school treated me much worse than the previous one. But my singing saved me, once again. Only now, in addition to my shyness and intimidation, I had to deal with one more serious problem.

Suddenly, a very big ugly nose with a huge hump started to appear on my thin face. It grew more and more with every passing year. Whether it was genetics greeting me from some very distant ancestors of mine, along my father's line, or the working out of my Karma, or the consequences of some injury, I don't know. It doesn't matter where this creepy nose came from, but it was exactly like those painted on witches.

As if little Alla did not already have enough suffering, horror, humiliation, and bullying in her life, now she was given physical ugliness to hurt her even more.

Here is one of my ordinary days in school, just a typical day. I see myself sitting on the floor, trying to press myself into the wall and become one with it. I am surrounded by my classmates, mainly boys shouting, "Ugly! Ugly, nasty, disgusting creature! Get out of here! Terrible freak!!! OUT! Get out of here and die!" They kick me with their feet and spit on me. Yes, children can be ruthless, and they do many mean things without realizing it. But it did not make it easier on me back then. For some reason, instead of hating them, I feel pity towards those torturing me. I feel pity. It burns in my eyes. I want to cry, but not for myself, for them. Why? I do not know.

For a long, very long time, they called me mainly, "Hey you, Ugly!" Everything changed when I was nineteen years old. At that time, plastic surgery existed only in one city in the whole country. Moscow. My mom and I went there, and I had my nose corrected by a plastic surgeon. I will never forget his name. Igor Woolf. From an ugly duckling, almost overnight,

I turned into a beauty. Actually, it took one month. Still, for many, many years after that, every time I was told, "You are so beautiful!" I did not fully believe it. For a very long time, I continued to suspect mockery in every compliment about my appearance, so deep were my wounds.

Our move to another city and the doctor, found by my mother for Alexei, finally made my mom's hopes come true. As they said back then, my brother managed to "jump off" drugs, even though it did not happen overnight. It took a long time.

The most brutal year was the first one, and I'm scared even to look back at what horror it was for me. The thing is, in the most difficult moments of my brother's struggle with his demons, I was the only one constantly near him. He suffered from severe attacks of rage, attacks of unbearable pain, grief, and despair. There were attempts to take his own life. And I was always there beside him. Always. I became a sort of Guardian Angel for him.

Perhaps my brother's time slowly winning over drug addiction was even worse than my whole childhood. But still, I was there for him. I bandaged his wounds and prepared food. I catered to his unthinkable, sometimes absolutely absurd, requests. Scared and speechless, I was holding my breath with every movement I made. If he was in a fit of rage and pain, plates and cups, or any other object within his arm's reach, flew into my head. I was not allowed to leave the house or to have friends. I had to report on each step I was taking, every move I was making, shaking with every word I said. Even when he did not hit me, he knew how to, psychologically, keep me so terrified that sometimes I felt it would be better if he hit me instead.

Still, throughout the SCARIEST moments of my childhood and youth, in the most TERRIBLE and horrifying moments, those EYES from my dreams kept me alive.

But to be completely honest with you, there also were moments of such intense pain and utter darkness that I went up to the roof of our nine-story building and stood there on edge with only one desire, to make this final jump down. I wanted everything to be over. I wanted to end it all—the sheer hell at home, the humiliation and the bullying at school. Sometimes it seemed to me that there was no strength left in me. Nothing left at all!

In such moments, the only thing I wanted was not to live. But those *EYES* always held me, not allowing me to cut the thread, holding me on this planet, in this life. Starting from the age of five and throughout the following years, I saw his eyes constantly in my dreams. No, I didn't dream of them every day. But once every few months, that same dream would come to me again. So, I kept on living, one day at a time, one month at a time, one year at a time.

Chapter 8

In the Mist House on the Lost Planet

"One day at a time. One month at a time. One year at a time." red-haired Joanna dropped another page of the book and looked anxiously at Haan.

He sat behind the large desk with a monitor in front of him. It would have been invisible, but a glow surrounded the screen as photos of a little girl changed from one picture to another. The face of the girl was frightened. She had a big ugly nose, curly black hair, and huge, incredible, but very sad eyes.

Without turning, Haan asked quietly, trying his best to control his rage, "Was that necessary? Tell me! All of that, was it really necessary? Couldn't you help her? Couldn't you have given her a different family, different parents, or at least save her from the sufferings caused by her brother? I understand everything, of course! It was her Soul's own choice. But... Seriously! It's inhumane. Isn't it? As you remember, I was not here at that time. Otherwise, I would have interfered! But you were here! You and Helena, maybe even somebody else was watching over her life with you! As a last resort, this mission could have been moved to her next life. Right? Or you could just bring her back from that life! Why would you let her suffer? You could have taken her when she was standing on that roof! She wanted to leave. Why didn't you?"

"That would be absolutely unacceptable, Haan! Impermissible! We have no time left." The voice was cold and calm. The woman with white hair entered the room, melting a wall of bookshelves on her way, and came up to Haan. The wall

48

instantly reappeared behind her, only slightly disturbing the books: they trembled and swayed a bit but kept their balance. It seems only the volume of O. Wild had tilted, but nobody noticed that.

"You all know," she continued, "I was against this decision from the very beginning. But Lala knew she had to hurry. And she decided to take the hardships of seven lives into just this one. She knew that she could handle it."

Joanna laid down the papers she was reading aloud and said quietly, "We were not entitled to interrupt her life. But we did help, and we did support her as much as we could. Indirectly. We found a doctor for her brother. We helped her with the music, increased her abilities to tolerate pain, both physical and emotional. We prevented her from taking that last step when she was standing on that roof, although that was an intervention. You know, we are not allowed to interfere, but we did. We hoped no one would notice."

"But they did notice, didn't they?" Haan sounded interested. The strained expression did not leave his face, but his voice was no longer angry and strangled.

For the first time, a shadow of a smile appeared on the face of the white-haired woman, or did it just seem that way. "The Dark ones? No, they didn't. The fate of the girl was chosen perfectly. They did not even notice her back then; she was not deemed worthy of their attention. The Elders? Yes, of course, they noticed. But they, too, understood that we could not afford to lose her in her current incarnation. There is not much time left. All the pain, hardships, fears, and overcoming them, all this allows her Soul to make an extraordinary leap forward on the path of evolution and be able to fulfill her destiny and carry out the mission she was chosen for."

"And how did the Elders punish you for interfering in her life?" Haan asked, his voice seeming to warm up a little.

"I am supposed to stay here, in the Mist House."

"Forever?"

"No, just until she overcomes her third test and finishes writing the book."

The Snow Queen smiled for a moment, but then her face hardened again. "Let's not get distracted. She is going to need our help now more than ever. The Dark ones have noticed her. We must be extra cautious!"

"By the way! Has anybody seen my easel?" Joanna's voice suddenly sounded completely different—carefree and joyful.

Smiling, Firebird appeared in the doorway with a basket full of cloudberries.

"Your easel is still in the room with mountains, clouds, and waterfalls. Have I missed anything?"

Haan went up to her and took the basket. Looking out of the window, he saw thick trees, hills, huge granite rocks, and a turquoise glowing summer sky. He threw a couple of berries into his mouth, closed his eyes, hugged Firebird around her shoulders, and said, "Not much. Don't worry. It is only the beginning."

Chapter 9

My Little Pleasures

I had another passion that helped me survive my everyday battles, a beautiful colorful country—India. Since early childhood, I have been in love with it, and this love remains strong even now. I love that land with all my heart and soul! It all started when I was about seven years old. I begged my mother to take me to see an Indian movie for the very first time. It seemed as if I was in a trance for almost three hours while the movie played. Everything there was so FAMILIAR to me. From the moment I saw this film, I started to have this strange pain in my chest. Of course, I had no idea why. I found out only after I knew *Him*. Before that, I lived most of my life with this pressing chest pain. Countless cardiograms showed absolutely nothing. No doctor could explain it. But how could they know? They could not. After leaving the cinema, I told my mother, "Mom. Listen. That, in that movie. That is my *Home*, Mother! Do you understand? It is my *Home!*" But my mother, back then and even now, when I say something incomprehensible for her, cools me down with this one very familiar phrase, "Better get busy and do something useful."

Since then, I have taken every opportunity to watch every single Indian film in cinemas. Movie tickets were very cheap back then. So, when possible, I watched them multiple times. At home, I wrapped myself in curtains, tablecloths, pieces of fabric, anything I could get a hold of, imitating a saree. I read everything I could find about India in the school library; I searched and collected all the information available about this amazing country!

There was no way I could logically explain to myself or anybody else why I did it! Somehow, I could memorize the songs from the films without even knowing the language. It brought me great pleasure when people around me were really moved and amazed every time they heard me sing those songs.

There was also another country that attracted me with force impossible to explain. Egypt. Often in my dreams, I saw the Pyramids when they were still smooth and shiny in the sun. But that's another story.

India! I could not understand why I felt such a deep longing for this country. Now I know why it was so easy for me to memorize the lyrics of the songs, after hearing them just a couple of times in the films; why EVERYTHING about this place seemed so painfully familiar to me. Now, I know. But back then, I did not know. But I did know that seeing India's scenery, seeing the people, hearing the language, and listening to the music, made me feel alive. It made my life easier to live.

The years passed by, and I never stopped looking for him, for the boy with magical eyes so familiar to my own. I was so used to peering into the faces of the people around me. Whether it was on the streets, in school, in a movie theater, on a beach, I simply couldn't help doing that. It became a part of me. He became a part of me. Or has he always been? I did not ask myself such questions, or to be exact, I tried not to. I kept on searching and waiting for him! I was sure that I would find him! Oh, Powerful Forces of Light! Could I even imagine who "that boy" would turn out to be? No, I could not!

When I was 15 years old, besides seeing his eyes, there was something else I was allowed to remember. In the dreams, I started to feel HIS TOUCH. He gently, with just his fingertips, traced the outline of my face and my lips. The sensations of his touch were so strong, so real, and so intense that I used to wake up STILL FEELING them. Because of that, I did not allow any man to touch me until I was 21. I absolutely did not like any man touching me, even though sensuality was simply a part of my nature! I was looking for my man. I always knew that deep in my soul, it must be only *Him*. It can be only *Him*. It cannot be anyone else. Holy Guardians! How could I know where he was and who he was! And if I did know? I often, too often, ask myself this very question. *What if I knew from the start where and who he was? If I knew,*

52

would my life turn out to be different? What is the point in asking now? There is no point.

When I was 15, another event happened in my life that brought some light and joy into my dark world. Art again came to shine for me and help me. This is how it all happened.

I was standing at a bus stop and waiting for my bus to arrive, as usual, submerged in my own thoughts. Suddenly, I noticed that a young, gorgeous girl was looking at me very attentively. A few minutes later, she came up to me with a smile, and we started to talk. Her name was Karina. She asked me if I would like to become a member of the Gypsy theatrical troupe. It was a very famous company in the area, with professional musicians, splendid costumes, brilliant and beautiful performances, and sets. It sounded like a dream to me! She said I would have many amazing opportunities. I would be a part of their colorful performances and learn to sing and dance.

I told her I could only sing. But she assured me they would teach me how to dance as well. It all sounded so exciting! Frankly, it all sounded too good to be true. She told me that they often traveled around the country on tours and performed in different cities. Everything she said sounded like a fairy tale to me. But then, some words she said shocked me entirely. It shook me so deeply that I didn't know whether to cry or laugh; maybe cry and laugh at the same time.

"You see," she said, "you have a very interesting, I would say, very unusual face! This huge, hooked nose of yours! You are so..." she was silent for a moment, searching for words. "So, well umm, *un-pretty*. Please do not take it as an offense, as I guess this isn't something new for you to hear. Well, you're so *un-pretty* that it makes you very unusual and very interesting. We mainly have very beautiful girls, dancing and performing in the group! But I think you would be something like an exotic spice! Do you understand? I am convinced you would be a nice addition! So, will you join us?"

I understood perfectly well what she wanted to say. I was "*ugly*," but she softened it and said "un-pretty" at the last moment.

I told her that I would think about it. So, I thought to myself; *I am so ugly that I would be a perfect addition to a group of all pretty, beautiful girls. Next to my ugliness, they will look even more gorgeous. How very tempting! No, thank you. I'd rather keep myself from any more humiliation. I've had enough of that already in my life!*

But the pull of the stage and my passion for art and music was more powerful than my fear of humiliation. So, three days later, I decided to go there anyway. The stage beckoned me with uncontrollable strength! I was ready to agree to be a scarecrow among beauties if that would let me get on the stage and perform! I also passionately wanted to learn to dance in multi-flared gypsy skirts! So, I wasn't good-looking? Well, okay, I was well aware of that, and I couldn't change it! But I knew I could sing! And they couldn't take that away from me! So, I decided to go to the address the girl gave me, watch one rehearsal and see it all for myself.

I had been acquainted with gypsy music since I was a child. My mother loved and still loves it dearly. When I was a little girl, probably just five or six years old, the gypsy theater "Roman" was incredibly famous throughout the whole country. When they came on tour to our city, my mother and I went to every one of their concerts. One event I remember, as if it happened just yesterday.

After the concert, my mom and I were walking towards the bus stop on a summer evening. Suddenly, I saw the leader of this theater, Nikolai Slichenko, a phenomenal singer, dancer, and actor. He was walking on the other side of the street. I ran straight to him and said, "Uncle Kolya Slichenko! If I sing to you, will you let me join your theater?"

And I started to sing! I sang to him all the gypsy songs I could possibly remember, of course, shamelessly mispronouncing the words! I saw genuine surprise and admiration on his beautiful face. Even being so little, I understood that he was deeply impressed!

When I finished, he picked me up and said, "You are still very young, my beauty! But! When you grow up and finish school, come to see me in Moscow! Then, for sure, you can join my theater!"

And I promised him that I would definitely do exactly as he said! I was just six years old.

Now, at 15, I was going to the rehearsal of another gypsy theatrical group. It was not difficult to find the building where the rehearsal took place. I heard the bewitching sounds of violins and magical sounds of gypsy guitars from far away. Climbing up the spiral staircase to the second floor, I saw a young man, almost still a boy, maybe a couple of years older than me. He masterfully played the guitar and sang an old gypsy song in a completely magical voice. Seeing me, for some reason, he smiled at me sincerely and continued to sing. Later, I discovered he was the eldest son of the woman who founded and directed this troupe. She had an absolutely amazing name, Zarrina Amanovna. The boy's name was Zabar, just like the hero in "The Gypsy Heaven," a very famous movie at that time.

My appearance caused bewilderment and straight laughter among the troupe members: dancers, singers, and actors. Many of the adult members were mothers of girls my age. Of course, they all thought it was hilarious that such an ugly creature wanted to perform on stage!

But, to my surprise, the head of the troupe had a different opinion about me. She saw in me something that she then called "mannerism." I think now it would be called "charisma." Of course, almost no one took me seriously. But among those beautiful girls, there was one angelic soul, 14 years old, whose name was Albina. She had a kind and soft heart and obviously felt sorry for me. She promised to teach me all the dancing parts. And to my complete surprise! She kept her word. She did!

I was just obsessed with the idea of learning to dance well. I used to arrive two or three hours before the rehearsal when nobody was there. I was dancing and dancing and again dancing—practicing and polishing every movement. At first, nothing worked at all. I think a cow on ice would probably look better than my first several months of trying. But as the wise expression says: "Practice makes perfect!" That is a simple truth. My dancing started to look somewhat better, and then it became considerably better, then significantly better. Nobody knew that I spent hours and hours rehearsing the movements by myself. And then, one day, a few months later, I was assigned to substitute for a sick girl in rehearsal. That was my chance. Although no one expected anything from me, I suddenly, very naturally joined the dance sequence. Zarina Amanovna was sincerely surprised, and a tremendous sparkling smile appeared on her face. Unfortunately, nothing good was written on the faces of the others.

When the girl, who had been sick, returned, I was allowed to stay in this act. Although very few people liked it, the troupe leader decided to let me dance, so no objections were accepted. To be honest, I didn't have the perfect dance technique or the flexibility of more beautiful and talented dancers in our troupe. But somehow, for an unknown reason, the people in the audience would react most to my entrance on the stage. I could never understand it, neither could others.

Zabar once said to his mother, "You know, Mother, I do not know how to explain it, but when she dances in a group of girls, for some reason, my eyes are glued only to her. Something is incredibly fascinating about her; I would even say enchanting! Even though the rest of the dancers are more beautiful, and they dance better, for some reason, I end up looking only at her! Why is that?"

His mother smiled at him, "She has something others do not have. She has Magic! True Magic! It flows in her!" Still smiling, she added, "One day, you will understand what I mean!"

Once, I was so tired of the scorns and sarcastic remarks of the other girls and their mothers that I hid in the corner of a dark room and quietly cried. A dark corner always was my savior, my friend, my protector, my own little planet. There I could disappear and cry out all my aching pain. And exactly there, Zabar found me. With tears still rolling down my cheeks, I listened as he told me about his conversation with his mother. Did I believe him? Of course not. But I was endlessly grateful to him for his compassion, kindness, and support. I didn't experience it very often in my life, so my gratitude was endless.

The concerts were frequent. With time and my increasing skills in dancing, people received me more and more warmly. The audience liked me, which became apparent even to those who didn't want to admit it. Keeping that in mind, the head of the troupe did the unthinkable. She gave me a

SOLO! And not just any Solo! The solo dance of a BEAUTIFUL gypsy girl!!! Do you understand? She gave ME the role of a legendary BEAUTY!

At first, I flatly refused! That is just impossible! Me? Dancing the solo of a BEAUTY? Ridiculous and absurd! But then, at one of the rehearsals, when the whole group was present, she asks the girl who dances that solo to sit down and asks me to take her place in the middle of the room. Me! How can that be? How terrifying! How exciting! Are all those faces around me really full of mockery and sarcasm? Or so it seems to me, lonely little girl, who is used to being looked at by most people only in such a manner. Many years later, I found out that Zabar was in love with me. Even if I had known, I wouldn't have believed it back then. I was so used to being unloved!

The lump in my throat rose higher and higher. *Is it fear? Or tears? Or my suppressed pride?* I slowly get up from my seat. I take a shawl, wrap it around my shoulders, walk to the middle of the room and freeze in the starting position! Hands holding the shawl are crossed on my chest, eyes looking down. The music starts! The air is filled with several guitars, playing at the same time. The opening words sound:

"Her beauty could only be described if played on a violin by a true genius! And not just a genius, but the one who could play as if he knew the very soul of each string of the instrument."

As the violin solo sharply cuts the air, I take one step and throw my shawl high into the air!

I don't remember how I performed the dance! I simply can't remember! But when the last chord stopped, I came back to reality and finally looked up.

The faces, which just several minutes ago were filled with resentment and contemptuous grins, looked bewildered and simply shocked. There was dead silence in the room. Finally, the voice of Zareena Amanovna broke it.

"This dance will only be performed by HER! Only her! At all concerts! At all times! And please, no objections!"

Needless to say, it did not add to me any well-wishers. While they did not adore me before this solo dance, the appraisal by the troupe leader made everything much worse. Half of the group started to treat me like an empty space, openly ignoring me or talking about me nastily, as if I were not there. Now people started to think the director favored me. All kinds of ideas were offered, trying to explain why. But neither I nor anyone else knew for sure the answer to this question. She did love me and support me. Unfortunately, you can imagine how others "liked" that. But I was used to being abused, so if it bothered me and hurt me, it wasn't to the extent they intended. I made several attempts to refuse the solo, but I was cut off sharply.

"You must learn to believe in yourself and stand up for yourself!" the director told me. It was easier said than done. Plus, things were just about to get worse.

Envy and competition among ballerinas, actors, dancers, singers in theaters, and theatrical groups are known to anyone in touch with performing arts. I have heard the same problems exist in sports. Envy! I always saw envy as a beast, an ugly old creature made from dark gray smog, creeping into the hearts and souls of people and poisoning them.

Several months after my Solo, the director learned from her son that I could sing several songs in Hindi, songs from very popular Bollywood movies. As gypsies are tightly connected to Indians, she decided to include two of these songs in the repertoire of our concerts. No words can describe the audience's delight when they saw and heard a young, not very pretty girl sing in Hindi. Indian movies were a huge hit back then; people loved them tremendously! But naturally, nobody really could remember, let alone sing those songs. Somehow, I could. After the performances, I was often surrounded by a whole crowd. People DIDN'T BELIEVE that it wasn't a recording, but my own voice. They wanted to hear me sing without music or microphones.

So, I sang to them again, and they asked me to sing more and more. I saw neither scoffs nor disgust at my imperfect face with that huge, crooked nose. There was only joy, admiration, and happy smiles on their faces. Oh, the incredible power of Art! Art makes you beautiful, no matter how you look, especially if you do it with all your heart and all your soul.

A few months later, my brother came to one of the concerts, taking place in the biggest theater in the city. He saw me on stage, and that day became a true blessing, making my life much easier! He became much softer and allowed me to go, without objection, to rehearsals and concerts.

It didn't matter to me that while the girls were hanging out together, I was sitting alone with a book somewhere in the corner. The loneliness of being an *outcast* was no longer as much of a burden to me. I had been used to it since my childhood.

Every time I went on stage, I was thinking about *those eyes*. Sometimes I wondered if he was out there. What if he is here right now, in the audience and looking at me? So, I danced! I danced for someone who was farther from me than I could begin to imagine. He was very far away! Very! But I didn't know this, and I couldn't know! Oh, the strange destiny of mine.

Chapter 10

Changes

A year or two passed, and then something terrible happened in *HIS* life. I was about seventeen years old. That year, in my dreams, I saw his eyes filled with such unbearable pain and despair that I can hardly find words to describe it. When I woke up, my heart was pounding madly, and it was difficult for me to breathe. It felt like a multi-ton concrete slab was lying on my chest! I did not know where he was or who he was. I didn't know what exactly had happened. But I learned many, many years later.

That year, terrible grief burst into his life. He lost his mother to a cruel, ruthless disease. He idolized her and could not imagine his life without her. While I had no idea what, in the depth of my heart I knew something terrible had happened to him. Every minute and every hour, I prayed for only one thing: I want to share his pain. If not all of it, then at least some of it, so it could become more bearable for him.

I wished for it so desperately that I almost saw some kind of invisible light flowing from my heart to him, and it made him feel at least a little bit better. I fully believed that I could help him, and no one in the whole wide world could convince me otherwise! But in fact, no one could even try to do that because not a living soul knew about him.

Now I understand that Twin Flames *always feel each other*, even if they are in different galaxies. For them, time, distance, and space simply *do not exist*. But back then, I didn't know any of this. I just felt his pain and wanted him to feel a little better. Later, many years later, his mother, not from the surface of this Earth but the world of Spirits and Guardians, will play a significant role in this story. But I will tell you all about it a little bit later.

So, I kept on living my life. I kept looking for him. I did not doubt, not even for a moment that, I would find him.

You may ask if this strange quiet girl had any other dreams? You wouldn't believe it! Yes! I also wanted to be an actress. Oh, I cannot even describe in words how passionately I wanted that! There was nothing and nobody else in the world that I wanted to be! No other destiny even crossed my mind. The reason was clear to me since my very childhood. I have always seen how art affects people. Be it a dance, a song, a play, or a movie! People cry. People laugh. After seeing a good movie or hearing a piece of beautiful music, they became happier, brighter, and kinder.

I have always been convinced that the purpose of art is to invisibly and deeply touch our hearts and souls. The creative power of art is capable of changing us. Art makes us think, inspiring us to become a better version of ourselves. It makes us want to do something good for someone, hug someone, forgive someone, and love someone.

I wanted to be a part of this beautiful process with all my heart and soul. But remember, before the plastic surgery and the transformation of my "witch's nose," I used to be ugly. If I told anyone that I wanted to be an actress, they would laugh in my face! They always did.

Once I did make that mistake. I was fourteen years old and wrote about it in a school essay, "Who I want to be when I grow up." I wrote that I wanted to be an actress, which naturally caused an outburst of laughter and mockery.

"Hey! You, freak! Who will you play? An evil Spirit living in a swamp, Kikimora? Or maybe an old, evil and ugly Witch? That would be an absolutely perfect role for you! You won't even need the makeup! You can play it just the way you are!" They laughed, and I pretended that I did not care.

"But someone needs to play an old Witch as well. Right?" I answered, hiding my pain behind a mask of indifference.

Of course, after the plastic surgery, I was no longer called Kikimora or an old Witch. It was as if a shadow lifted off my face, and everybody started to notice my big, dark, expressive eyes (just like those of my Twin Flame) and beautifully outlined lips (just like his own as well). But this was still a while away.

As I told you before, I promised the head of the gypsy troupe "Uncle Nikolai Slichenko," who was known throughout the country, that I would come to see him in Moscow when I grew up. So, this was exactly what I did. When I was 17 years old, my mother and I bought two train tickets and went to Moscow. I was going to become a student of *GITIS* (State Institute of Theatrical Art).

For some reason, I didn't have any doubt about passing the entrance exams, even though my hooked nose was still with me! At the same time, I was planning to start working, as an extra, at the Theater of Nikolai Slichenko. I had no doubt they would accept me there, as well.

Why was an insecure, frightened, and ever-doubting girl, who lives in constant fear, so sure about all those things? You may ask me. It was my inner strength that kept me going, no matter what. This inner strength kept me alive. It did not let me go crazy or commit suicide in the most horrific moments. It never allowed me to give up. This strength, whose voice kept whispering deep inside, told me I could deal with everything, that I was strong enough to face all that I would face, including admission to the university, and later, maybe even fame and glory.

But, as we all know, our plans do not necessarily come to life. Perhaps, this is because there are some events we have no control over. Events may conflict with logic, morality, and sometimes even laws. Events that are often very unfair. Sometimes those events disrupt the life of one girl and her family. Sometimes they unfairly wreak havoc on an entire country.

The Higher Forces had other plans for my life, I guess. In August of that year (1991), a coup d'état took place in Moscow. That was the beginning of the end for this vast and powerful country where I was born and grew up.

The name of this country was the Union of Soviet Socialist Republics. The *USSR*. It was also the beginning of the end of my dream of becoming an actress. We could not stay in Moscow. It was unsafe, and we could no longer afford it: Farewell, equal opportunities for the rich and the poor. (There were, of course, differences in opportunities even during the times of Soviet

Union, as elsewhere, but your background was not important if you had talent and intelligence). All that was about to end—farewell, free education of any level for anybody and everybody. Farewell to the state assistance, free after-school programs, sports camps. Farewell to the country of my childhood. It is unbearably sad to say goodbye!

Unfortunately, Nikolai Slichenko was not in Moscow in August of that year, and to my great regret, I never had the chance to meet him and to say, "I am that little girl, remember?"

Another dream of mine had to remain a dream without coming true.

We returned home. A year later, due to life circumstances, we moved back to Odessa, where I was born. We left the city, where we lived for five years, and my gypsy troupe behind. I had to abandon my dream of becoming an actress as well. That was a big mistake. Starting that year and for all the years to come, I felt as if I was slowly fading away—slowly but surely. I had a Passion for that profession. I had the Fire. I had the Talent. I had the Dream. But... Yes, it's always that, *But...*

The "harsh 90s" were in full swing in the country. I was not the only one who had to say goodbye to my dreams. The established, quiet life of hundreds of millions of families started to collapse. The huge country was falling apart. It was not a good time to dream. All we could do is try to survive. There was no space to even dream of studying acting. Finding a job for my mother, due to her age and the country's whole situation, became impossible. There was not enough money even for basic needs. But what was worse, it wasn't even clear how to find ways to earn money for those basic needs. People were becoming "suitcase traders." What does it mean? People bought goods in one city, took a train, went to another city, and sold them for a bit more. Very often, it brought ridiculously little profit. Plus, it was physically exhausting and sometimes rather dangerous since the competition was huge. In wintertime, we had to stand in the open markets in freezing weather for many, many hours, trying to sell something. It was a true nightmare.

There were very few specialists in private trade among former citizens of a socialist society. Natural "businessmen" were rare. The rest just tried to survive. Factories, plants, all kinds of organizations were being closed down. Thousands of people found themselves with no job, no money, and not knowing what tomorrow would bring. It was true chaos! Of course, some "gifted" specimens quickly understood how one could get rich quickly by drinking the ruined country's blood. The rest of us survived the best we could. Or, having failed to adapt, we were dying of hunger and fear of the future. Poverty, hopelessness, banditry, lawlessness—these were the constant companions of Russia, Ukraine, and the rest of the Republics "freed" from the *USSR*.

My mother and I also decided to become "suitcase traders." Once we spent a whole month living in trains and train stations. It all felt like some kind of madness. But still, wherever I went, I continued to look for him. It was just an inseparable part of me. *One day, I will look up and meet his eyes*, I thought. And nobody could take away this faith from me. But I did not have to worry about anyone trying to do that. Nobody knew, and nobody cared.

Unfortunately, our "business," if we can even call it that, was over when we were robbed and nearly killed in one city. Luckily, we had just enough money to buy train tickets and get back home. We had to figure out something. We had to decide what to do next and how to survive. We took all of the more and less valuable things in our house to the flea markets one by one. Next, we started to sell valuable and rare books from our family library, which had taken many years to accumulate. Such were those times.

Every day we began and ended with the same question: *How can we earn some money and survive?* Sometimes my mother sewed beautiful aprons using our old German sewing machine. They had pockets in the form of hearts, strawberries, and flowers. She exchanged these aprons at the farmer›s market for groceries. Potatoes, onions, cabbage. That at least gave us food to eat.

And here, my baking skills really came in handy. There was a huge market in Odessa called "The Seventh Kilometer" (it still exists now). There you could buy pretty much anything under the sun. So, this is what I started to do. At night, I baked pies, pastries, and apple rolls. Back then, quick-acting yeast was still to be invented, or at least it wasn't sold in our country. It took many hours to prepare the yeast dough. I baked at night to have everything ready. In the morning, I packed my pastries in bags and went to the market.

The competition was immense—many other disadvantaged sellers, similar to me, and very few buyers. There were days when I came home empty-handed: with neither goods, nor money. The competitors, physically stronger than me or who worked by groups, could take away everything I had, including whatever money I made. I had those days as well, but it did not stop me. I had to take the risk. The money I managed to earn with my pies was little, but still, it was enough for us to hold on somehow.

I usually worked as a masseuse in the afternoons, having completed massage courses at 17. So pretty much every day, I was running around the city, visiting my clients, massaging backs and necks. I did pretty well because I probably possessed a healing gift in addition to my technical skills, so my patients felt great. I was a good masseuse but still didn't earn enough. Those times were poverty-ridden, wretched, and hungry, so there was hardly any work whatsoever that would be well-paid. And at night, I again baked my pastries.

One of my clients was an English teacher. She began to teach me in exchange for my services, and very soon, it turned out that I also had a natural talent for languages. Two years later, not only did I learn the language, but I also came up with my own system of teaching English to others. I began to give private lessons. Students would come to my place, or I would go to them. That greatly helped us to stay afloat in terms of money. I also continued baking cakes and pies on demand. And several times a month, I had a job singing at parties, banquets, and weddings.

Here I was, the youngest member of our family, taking on the responsibility for all of us. Like many others, my eldest brother had lost his job, and as he was the only one in the family working, things got extremely tough for them. How was I able to endure so much? I still don't know the answer. Perhaps I did not have the time to think of it at all. I did what I had to, that was all. Maybe I had chosen this destiny and this family to save my loved ones through these difficult years? Maybe so. Indeed, without me, they hardly would have been able to cope.

Do you want to know about my second brother? He began to paint. He finally started to do what he had a genuine, natural talent for. I am sure that he was not just a brilliant artist; he was a true genius. But when people are trying to survive, they don't really care about high art. What Alexey sometimes earned was barely enough for canvases and paints.

But most importantly, he was painting. It helped him with his inner demons. Several years later, his hard work and gift would bring him what he deserved: recognition, love of people, and even fame. He kept the beauty of our old city alive for generations to come. As for me, somebody had to feed the family, and I took on that role. After all, I had an example of my own mother-fighter in front of my eyes all my life. She was fighting silently without complaining. I followed her example and did the same.

Time was passing by. I was already twenty years old. Unfortunately, the young man I was looking for, with eyes so familiar to my own, was nowhere to be found. But when I was 19, I received an incredible gift. It was the gift, which finally put an end to my "ugliness." I got the letter from the Institute of Plastic Surgery. Back then, it was the only institution of this kind in the country! I found their address and read everything about them in the city library when I was 18. There were no smartphones back then, no internet, and no computers. It was tough to even call to a different city, let alone anything else. One had to go to the call center, which could have been located in another part of the city and be rather pricey. So, I only had one way. Within a year, I wrote and sent them several letters with my story and photos. I hoped they might be interested in my case and agree to help. That is exactly what happened. They wrote back to me and invited me to come to Moscow.

"This will not be easy!" the doctor said after looking at me. "It might take several hours, and the risks involved are pretty significant. Are you sure you want to do it?"

I was absolutely sure! I was more than sure! To cut a long story short, after the plastic surgery, overnight (to be exact, within one month), I turned from an ugly duckling into a swan. By the way, for that surgery, we did not pay even a penny. Maybe you can tell me, such things are unheard of, but facts are facts. The doctor read my letters, and his heart was deeply touched. He personally wrote to me and invited me to come. He personally performed the surgery out of the kindness of his heart. All my life, I will carry deep gratitude to him! I will never forget what he did for me!

A year later, I was 20. And I was beautiful. Very beautiful. But would you believe me if I told you that although being an eye-catching young woman, not only was I a virgin but never in my entire life had I even kissed a man! You can raise your eyebrows in surprise, or you can shrug your shoulders, but that was exactly so. I wasn't seeing anyone. I had never been on a date. It was as if I had built an invisible glass wall around me. I concentrated on work, making ends meet, and helping my family survive. Men, dating, flirting was not on my agenda.

You know, this is some strange curse for the women of my family. We usually spend our youth in loneliness, poverty, and hard labor. But to be honest, I couldn't even imagine being with someone other than the one I was waiting for and looking for. So unbroken was my faith in him and us. It had been with me since childhood, and it was unshakable.

Do you want to know how I spent most of my late evenings (especially in spring and summertime) almost my entire life? I guess I already told you about this earlier. I spent them outside, looking at the stars. I can spend hours like that. I especially love it when I can lie on the grass or a sandy beach and look at them. In such moments and hours, I always talked to HIM in my mind and heart. I also talked with those out there, beyond this Earth—those who watch me and hear me, give me strength, hope, support, faith, and courage.

"Where is He? Where?" I had asked this same question more than a million times. "Will I find him? When? How?"

But no answer came.

At that very moment, when a twenty-year-old me was lying on the grass, asking the stars questions about my beloved, the man I was searching for and longing for was already a movie star. And not only that! He was already married.

The strange fate of mine!

Chapter 11

The Sun and the Moon

At 21, my life turned upside down once again like an hourglass. An hourglass filled not with the grains of sand but with the minutes, hopes, tears, little joys, dreams, and sorrows of my life. Everything was, once again, turned upside down. It was as if, from time to time, someone big and ruthless would tip this hourglass over. And after that, everything that I'd gotten used to, that more or less had finally settled down, all that had started to get just a little better would go head over heels again.

This is how it happened this time. Because I had to work and help my family, I postponed my idea of studying at the university for a long time, but I did not abandon it altogether. And when I turned 21, I gathered my courage and applied to the faculty of foreign languages.

Why not at *GITIS*? You might ask. By that time, Moscow had become a city, absolutely beyond my reach, insanely expensive and elite. Those who lived through the "terrible 90s" remember very well how the country was falling apart. Actors, even the very famous, loved, and respected ones, were out of work. Theaters and Movie studios were being closed or barely surviving. Actors went to work in bars and restaurants or started driving taxis and loading boxes in stores. Tragically, many became broke and lost themselves in alcohol and other unhealthy substances. Some fled abroad. Others switched to any profession because acting could not help one survive this damned time in a country falling to pieces.

English language could provide a guaranteed income for the teacher because many citizens of my country traveled to other lands to buy goods they could sell afterward. Many simply escaped with the idea of never returning. Those with the lowest ethics became the most successful, making money from thin air, shaking up the public sector, or robbing their competitors. Now, the latter just traveled for fun. Everyone needed English. Immediately. The faculty of foreign languages was always mega-popular, even prestigious! The children of the elite usually went there. No more than 30 new students were accepted each year, though there were hundreds of applicants. I had a chance to be accepted, as I knew the language and even had a talent for teaching. Oh, my Guardians, how many more talents were hidden in my small stubborn head and thin little body? Still, everybody knew that bribery was absolutely essential to have that chance and actually be admitted. Naturally, I did not have the money for that. (Yes, bribery was common practice those dark times).

Fortunately, it turned out, there was a new faculty opening at the State University. A faculty of Philosophy with advanced English study, so if you wanted, you could get two majors! It was an absolute miracle!

The course promised to be truly complex because studying Philosophy includes almost everything you can think of—history, sociology, theology, cultural studies, religious studies, psychology, and much more.

I was well acquainted with philosophy, theology, and other mind-bending studies, thanks to my natural curiosity and the presence of rare books in my house since I was a child. So, I easily passed the entrance exams and became a student!

Wow! I was a student at the State University! I just could not believe it! Fortunately for me, I was among 20% of the students for whom the university education was still absolutely free.

Besides becoming a student and having an opportunity to get a master's degree, my thrill, joy, and happiness had one more reason. I was hoping to meet *HIM* among the students! Oh! Naïve little child!

Something else, quite amazing, happened, I want to tell you about. On the very first day the new students started our lectures, during one of the breaks, a tall, thin young man came up to me and said, "Hello, Witch!"

He said those words as if he had known me for at least the last 30 years.

I was surprised and even offended. Back then, I did not know the true meaning of the word *Witch*. I saw it as something terrible, wicked, and even evil.

"Why do you say I am a Witch?" I asked rather sharply, completely annoyed.

The guy smiled, "Because *you are* a Witch! Witch, meaning *the one who knows, the one who sees*. If you look at the whole word, you will see a *knowing mother*. They are also called *Seers* or *Sorceresses*."

Apparently, I looked rather funny, standing there all frozen and staring at him because he smiled again with a warm and open smile.

"I know how that is," he continued. "You probably always thought that something was wrong with you because you were not like the others. You must have felt very lonely and very often as if torn away from home, right?"

Astonished, I just kept silent, unable to find any words.

"It's all right, girl! Calm down! You're not the only one; I'm just the same! I'm Kostya! Nice to meet you! And you were, most likely, born in August? What is your name? Anna?"

"Alla," I answered quietly. "And you're right. I was born in August!"

It wasn't his extraordinary ability to know things about me that surprised me. I was more surprised, unspeakably delighted, thrilled by the fact that I had met someone just like me! As well as the fact that this young man didn't consider me some strange and weird creature. Not at all! He did not because he was exactly the same! Then he pointed to a guy with black hair, who somewhat resembled an ancient Chinese emperor.

"Look! Do you see him? He is also one of us!" Kostya told me.

The "Chinese Emperor" came up to us. He looked into my eyes, piercing me, to my very core, with his gaze. Then he looked at Kostya and told him, nodding his head in my direction, "The Sun and the Moon."

Kostya nodded his head in response while smiling happily.

70

This was the second time in my life I had heard these words, "The Sun and The Moon." The first time I heard this was when I was about six years old. Mom and I were at the local marketplace. There have always been many gypsies in our city. While my mother was buying something, I suddenly knew someone was looking at me. I could feel it. Two gypsy women, wearing beautiful scarves and multi-layered, multi-colored skirts, watched me very intensely. One of them was older, maybe about fifty, but now it's hard for me to remember. The other one was much younger, maybe in her twenties.

"Look at her, Radmila!" said the older woman to the younger one. "Look very carefully and remember her face! This child is The Sun and The Moon! And The Key! Not that often you see one of those. She took too much onto herself. Life will be tough for her! She needs to learn not to break. Hopefully, she will not! But truly, she will only fulfill her destiny in the second half of her life! Oh, she'll have a tough time!"

"*The Key*? That little girl? Oh my! Does she know who she is?" asked the young woman after a moment of silence.

"No! She is still too young! But she already feels a lot and remembers a lot! She does not know and will not know for a very, very long time *WHO* she really is. It will not be revealed to her until a certain time!"

They both were looking at me, as if I was something unreal and rare, freshly out of a fairy tale, like a blue unicorn or a fairy with wings. Then the oldest came up to me very closely, and, looking into my eyes, she put her hand on my head. She said only one word, "Firebird!"

Dozens of years later, I understood what she meant. Firebird in Slavic fairy tales is the same as Phoenix in the legends of other nations. Throughout my life, this mysterious bird has followed me almost everywhere. I found it in many unusual places and under the strangest circumstances. For me, the Firebird became a symbol of everything I do and a symbol of myself. I would even say, the symbol of my very Essence, my own Spirit, and my own Soul. But, after all, I was a *Twin FLAME*. No, I naturally did not know about it. But still, I was a *Flame*. So, *Firebird* was a suitable name for me. The gypsy women saw my very *Essence*. Was it surprising? Somewhat, but not extremely. Strange, inexplicable things have happened to me as long as I have lived.

She put her palm on my head as if blessing me and said, "Firebird!" With the touch of her palm on my head, for some reason, I closed my eyes. A wave of heat flowed through my entire body. I believe I was in a *trance* for several moments. When I opened my eyes, they were gone. It all happened so very fast that my mother noticed absolutely nothing. Or maybe it was the certain *magic* of a gypsy woman. This scene always stayed in my memory, every word, every feeling. And now I heard this phrase for the second time.

"Kostya!" I approached my new friend. "What does it mean? *The Sun and the Moon???*"

But both guys, exchanging glances, simply smiled. The "Chinese Emperor" was kind enough to tell me only the following.

"When the time comes, you'll find out!"

Despite all my attempts over the next couple of years to get additional information from them about what it meant, alas, they didn't add a word to what they had already told me. I discovered the meaning of that phrase myself many, many years later after I had found my Twin Flame.

Chapter 12

Dark Wedding

I became a student and submerged myself fully into the process of education. I was studying almost all my time and had no time to earn money. After all, computers, mobile phones, tablets, and laptops did not exist. Actually, stationary computers DID exist, but not at home. As for me, I didn't even have a phone line, let alone anything else. When classes ended, we would go to the library and sit there for many hours with tall piles of books. Money became a serious issue. There were days when I would have only an apple or a handful of nuts. Those times trained me to function with very little or no food for days and still continue to work.

A year passed. The first year of the university was over, and the second one began.

Once again, Fate intervened in my life. This how it all happened.

Natasha, my classmate, knew a man who urgently needed to find a place where he could leave his five-year-old boy while he was at work. Arthur, her neighbor, was a businessman. He was married to a woman, who was significantly younger than him, and they had a five-year-old son. While Arthur worked, his wife stayed home, taking care of the house and their child. Trouble came when she started having an affair with some young man. The woman took some valuables and documents with her and left her son with his grandmother, her mother. She left her husband a note, saying, "I have met the love of my life. I'm sorry. Please do not look for me!" Then she disappeared. As it turned out later, she moved in with this young man, less than 20 kilometers from Odessa.

The baby's grandmother could only take care of him on the weekends because she was still working. Arthur worked almost every single day for many hours. Because of that, he urgently had to find a nanny for his son. He started to ask everybody around if they knew somebody kind and trustworthy who loved children. That was how little Timka (Timur) found his way to my place. The first day I met him was Saturday, so I did not have classes. The boy spent all day at my place, with my mother and me. He turned out to be very smart, curious, and witty. But at the same time, he was spoiled like most kids his age: naughty, capricious, sometimes cried, then laughed. In a word, the boy was very unbalanced. To my surprise, I found out that he never called his mother "Mom." He addressed her only by her name. He also addressed his grandmother the same way, by her first name.

His health was not in the best shape either. The first day he arrived, he didn't feel too well. The kid was coughing and had a very stuffy nose. My mother was very familiar with medicinal herbs. She had been studying and using them for over 20 years. She knew exactly how to have him back on his feet in no time and immediately started working her magic. By the evening of that first day, he asked her, "Would you be my Babushka (Grandma)? " To which my mom immediately said, "Yes."

When the evening came, his father arrived to pick him up and take him home. But that became a challenge. Timka held my hand with all the strength he was capable of and said the words, which even now I cannot remember without tears burning my eyes.

"I just found my real MOM!!! I finally found her!!! And my Grandma, too! And you want to take me from them? I'm not going anywhere! I'm staying here! This is my HOME!" and he burst into tears, hugging me with both arms and clinging to me as if he was afraid that I would run away or disappear. I stood there frozen, unable to utter a word, looking into the eyes of his father.

Finally, I managed to say quietly, "Arthur, leave him with me until morning, so that he can calm down. You can pick him up tomorrow."

And the boy stayed. I put him to bed, told him a couple of fairy tales, and sang him every lullaby I knew (and I sure know a lot of them); still, he refused to close his eyes. He was afraid I would leave. Finally, he fell asleep after midnight, still holding my hand. My heart was breaking into pieces. *What kind of mother did this boy have? How could she leave him, just like that? How was that even possible? I had known this boy only for a day, and he had already gotten so deep into my heart. But she was the one to give him life! She was the one to watch him grow. She saw him take his first step. She heard him say his first word. How could she leave him?* It was beyond me.

He stayed in our tiny apartment the next day and the day that followed. And the next week, as well, which became two weeks, then three. He would agree to leave my place only if I walked with him and his father. If my mom joined us, that was even better. He was beaming with joy, having all of us there!

When I went to classes at the university, Timoshka stayed with my mother, and they truly enjoyed each other's company! Together they would go to the local market, cook dinner, bake cookies, and go for walks in the park. My mom even enrolled him in a chess school, and the kid turned out to be a pure genius! He was a quick learner and studied with pleasure. Mom also taught him to read and count in just a few weeks!

A month passed by. Two months. Timur became a part of our family, and his father, Arthur, fell in love with me. I understood that. It was the way he was looking at me, how he tried to take my hand and softly touch me any chance he had, how he nervously tried to find subjects we would both be interested in, how he thanked me for taking care of the boy, how he asked about my plans for the future, my dreams, my personal life.

He knew I loved roses. And almost every single day, he brought me bouquets of them! Every time a different color. I treated him with all the respect and sympathy he deserved. He was the father of Timur, first. Secondly, he was always kind to us, never hurting me or doing anything wrong. This man was 25 years older than me, a professional sportsman, tall, well-built, with bright blue eyes and a very masculine vibe. Many would consider him very handsome.

But I did not love him. I did not even think of him at all. I wanted to find the one who, I thought, was mine. The one I was looking for, whose eyes I have known since I was just a baby! I couldn't imagine anyone else next to me; I didn't want anyone else! But life, or Gods, or Destiny, decided differently.

The child practically lived in my house. This fact delighted my neighbors, who now had something to gossip about. This whole situation was strange and required some kind of decision. It was clear to everyone, including me. But I couldn't abandon my little boy, Timka! I couldn't reject him; that was completely out of the question. I did not know what to do. I simply did not know.

Soon afterward, one late spring day, Arthur appeared at our house wearing a beautiful suit. His son was wearing the same type of suit. Together they looked beautiful and sweet. Arthur held an enormous bouquet of a hundred roses, and Timoshka had a small box in his little hands. You should have seen how his face was shining.

"I picked it *MYSELF!*" he said, giving me the box.

"Open it! Open quickly!"

He was almost jumping, barely being able to hold his excitement. My heart froze. I felt a terrifying rush of chilling fear, which I tried to hide behind a smile. I opened an elegant little box.

Inside was a ring with a huge emerald surrounded by tiny diamonds.

"Will you marry us?" Timka asked. "I promise you to be the very, very best son ever! I will always, always listen to you and do as you say! And when I go to school, I will always get the best grades. And... And I will help you around the house, and...." He stopped for a moment, trying to find one more reason to convince me. It seemed like he was out of them, so he just uttered, "Say 'Yes'!!!"

His face was glowing, and he did not expect any other answer but "Yes" from me. His father stood next to him, silently looking into my eyes.

What was I to do? WHAT? Say No? And then, this child would once again be abandoned and rejected? I couldn't do that. I knew way too well what it felt like! I could not do this to this child. Could not!!! I knelt down

76

and brought him close to me. I hugged him very tightly but could not make myself say a word. He took this gesture as my positive answer. He kissed me loudly on both cheeks and ran to his father!

"Papa! She will marry us!"

The following two summer months flew by very fast, and I was in some kind of daze the whole time. Arthur reserved the most beautiful and expensive hall in the city for our wedding reception. He hired the best musicians, photographers, cameramen, so on.

My wedding dress was sewn by the very famous costume designer of the Odessa Opera House! The dress was truly royal. It was a replica of Angelica's dress from the movie "Angelica and the King" and was made from French lace and the finest golden brocade. It was a real masterpiece. I also had a headdress and a multi-tier veil to go with it.

As for me, during all these preparations for my OWN wedding, I felt as I was sinking deeper and deeper into a dark heavy cloud. I was getting thinner and paler. I was melting like a candle. But it wasn't only because I was about to marry a man I didn't love, thus going against my own ethics. No, that was not all. I was going against my own Soul. I was going against everything my Soul passionately longed for and deeply desired for so long; to find him, the man with those eyes, and stay beside him forever. And now I was going against it all. In my heart I felt, I was betraying not just myself; I was betraying HIM. I was betraying Us!

But this was not even the worst. As it turned out to be much later, my condition was also the result of black magic rituals done to me, a stupid naïve bride. Some people decided that I "didn't have any right" to marry that man. But I was clueless about that.

Arthur's ex-wife's relationship with her new man didn't go the way she wanted. She was having second thoughts about having abandoned her spouse. But the moment she considered coming back to Arthur, she learned that he was planning to marry me! Naturally, she saw me as an unwanted obstacle to her plans. She was not, as in that song, "the kind of girl, who gives up just like that, oh no"... She decided to get rid of me, to take me out of her way. When several attempts to talk to Arthur did not have the desired results, she decided to use an ancient method to make me disappear from the life of her ex and my soon-to-be husband. She contacted those who understood very well how to use black magic to get rid of a person. They were, unfortunately for me, real professionals of their dark trade. They were very knowledgeable, skilled, and extremely expensive. But she agreed to whatever they demanded. She paid them generously, and they did their work with skill and efficiency. Why would they feel sorry for me? They didn't know or care about me. After all, this was their job. Long ago, they freely gave their souls to the dark in exchange for wealth and dark powers. I doubt they were even able to feel any compassion whatsoever.

Of course, I wasn't aware of what was happening. I was just dying. Quietly. Every single day. With no emotions. With no desires. I lived in a colorless, dreary world of my own and saw neither joy nor happiness. I had no hopes for the future. Nothing brought me happiness, neither Arthur with his love nor my dear golden beloved boy Timoshka, who was the only reason I was doing any of this.

The price I had to pay for this marriage was very high. Too high. We got married in August. And the wedding itself passed, as in a fog for me, as if I wasn't even there. I just remember the moment when I looked at myself in the huge full-length mirror in this enormous royal dress of gold brocade. I was hearing the voices of the guests in the hallway, "Have you seen the bride? Have you seen her? She is so beautiful! So beautiful! Like a fairy! Like a Queen!"

And what about me? What did I feel at that moment, looking at myself in that mirror? I wanted to scream. I wanted to run and call for help. Just as I raised my hand to rip the golden wreath from my head...

"Maaam! Mamaaaaaa!" Timoshka bursts into the room. "Mama!!! You are so beautiful!!!! The most beautiful mama in the whole world!"

His face is shining with such joy, delight, and happiness that I can't help smiling back at him. He runs to me and hugs me tightly.

"Let us go, son," I told him, taking his hand. "People are waiting for us."

Like a scene from a black and white movie, the wedding quickly flashed by, and I found myself facing the marriage bed.

It was many years ago, and even now, it takes me so much strength to write about it. Even remembering that horror freezes me from the inside, making me tremble.

I remember as vividly as if it was yesterday, standing there, looking at the bed I am supposed to lie down on with my new husband. I start shaking like a leaf in a cold autumn wind, my teeth chattering. I simultaneously feel feverish and chilled as terror rushes up my spine! I stand, petrified, in horrific fear at the mere sight of that bed.

Fast-forward: I will tell you one of the reasons why it made me feel all that. Under the mattress of this same bed was a small amount of soil taken from the cemetery. Someone had taken soil from the grave of a woman with the same name as me. They took it at night while saying certain words and rituals. I would find out about it a year later.

Right now, I am that newlywed who must lie with her husband on this cursed bed. And I can't! I can't do that! But I have to! Right? I have to! I must! I am a lawfully wedded wife, and my husband has his legal right to have my body!

He comes up to me from behind and puts his hands on my shoulders. I want to scream and run somewhere very far away from this place and his touch. I want to escape this room. I want to hide somewhere, where nobody can ever find me or see me! I want to melt into the air. I want to disappear. I want to die, so this all horror is simply over.

At that moment, I remembered my childhood. *No one will come, and no one will save you*, a voice inside told me. And then a terrible thought came to my mind. *I need to drink some alcohol. I should get drunk, and maybe it won't be so scary! Maybe I will not feel anything!*

"Can you bring me some wine?" I ask my newly lawful husband. He is breathing heavily. His breath reeks of cognac. This smell. His touch. His voice. Everything makes me feel nauseous and disgusted, mixed with a paralyzing, ice-cold, terrifying fear. I have nowhere to run. I was the one who allowed this wedding to happen. I was the one who gave my word to this man. I was the one who promised him, love and family. I promised it to him and Timoshka. I knew this wasn't an ideal situation; I knew it wouldn't be paradise. I had hoped I could simply make the best of it. But I had no idea it would be a living, horrifying nightmare. This is too tough. Too unbearable. Too painful. Too scary! Heavenly Keepers! I want to scream! I want to cry! I feel like a sacrificial lamb about to be slaughtered. But I must carry on. I must!

No one will come, and no one will save you, a voice inside told me again.

No one will come, and no one will save you...

Arthur leaves and soon returns with wine. I gulp down a glass, asking for more; he pours me another glass. I drink it as well. The room starts to spin. The thing is, I do not drink! Alcohol, even in very small amounts, instantly gives me severe headaches. Until this night, I had had alcoholic drinks probably three times in my whole life, one-third of a glass of champagne or light wine at New Year celebrations. And now, in my insane attempt not to feel anything, I down two glasses! Everything is spinning, and the whole situation seems *a little bit less scary* to me.

My husband begins to rip off my golden brocade dress, nearly tearing it to pieces. And suddenly... sharply and clearly, *I see HIS EYES*, those very eyes I have been looking for all my damn life! My new husband slides his hands roughly across my skin. *I go NUMB.* I simply freeze. I turn into stone as if Medusa Gorgon had a look at me. I feel nothing. I only can see *HIS* eyes in front of me! His gorgeous, dark, dazzling eyes, like two deep lakes. Tears begin rolling down my cheeks, but I can't even feel them. I try my best to hold on and not to run, not to scream. Inside of me, there are only two words, *Forgive me.*

"Forgive me," I beg someone whom I have never even met but who seems to live in every particle of my Soul and my memory, in every particle of my very existence. "*Forgive me. Please. Please forgive me. Forgive me. Forgive me. Forgive me!*"

"What are you muttering?" My husband asks, abruptly turning me to himself. Seeing my face, he stops for a second. He was not a fool; he understood very well that I did not love him and did not want him.

But I was his wife, and we had just had a big, beautiful wedding. We had exchanged rings and probably promised each other to be together in wealth and poverty, in illness and health. Probably, I didn't remember anything, but I know that's what people usually say.

For a moment, he just looks at me.

"I see! You do not want this! You would be happy to find yourself anywhere else but here with me, even on the edge of the earth! I understand!" He reeked of alcohol. Looking into my eyes, he squeezes my face in his hands. I feel pain. But I was used to pain!

"You're so beautiful! So young! So innocent!" he continues, «And you are mine! *I PAID* for you! I have the right to have you! I want you and I will take you! Whether you want it or not! Do you hear me?"

He rudely lets me go, and I almost fall. He goes to the kitchen and returns with another glass of wine.

"*DRINK!*" He orders.

I drank all the wine. Unable to stand such a high dose of alcohol, I lost consciousness, and everything plunged into blissful darkness.

I came back from being unconscious because of such excruciating pain; I cannot describe it in words. It was as if a thousand swords were being heartlessly stabbed into my weak, exhausted body. The pain brought me to my senses, but only for a moment. The horrific shock immediately sent me back into the darkness.

When I woke up again, I was absolutely alone and unbearably thirsty. A lone night lamp lit the room. I tried to get up. It was nearly impossible to move, but I did. When I finally managed to stand up, blood flowed down my legs like a wounded animal. I collapsed onto the bed again. The sheet beneath me was wet—wet with my blood.

I closed my eyes and once again fell back into the darkness. Suddenly, I saw myself rising in some sort of blue tube. Then this *tube* became a corridor. I suddenly saw myself. Yes, it was me, walking towards me! But a very little me, maybe only one year old. I am dragging a plush dog, with funny button eyes, behind me by its ear! I hear my mother's laughter somewhere near, one of those rare moments when my mother laughed.

Then I saw myself at three years old. Then at five. My childhood, my youth. My dreams. Fears. Despair. Hopes. My...

"What are you doing here?" A familiar voice asked me.

I looked up.

"Grandma?" I looked in disbelief at the dear face of my grandmother, who left this planet when I was only 14. Only now, she appeared much younger than I remembered her.

"What are you doing here?" she repeated her question.

"You know what, Alyonushka," She had always called me Alyonushka, "You must go back, child! Go back! Now!"

And then, I finally fully realized where I was. At the same moment, as well, I realized what my Grandma meant with those words, "Go back now!" I was horrified by the very thought of going back! *Back? Back to that horror? Back to that pain?* No! I shook my head negatively.

"No!!! No, Babushka! I do not want to go back down there! No! Please do not make me! Babushka, how can you not understand? Please don't say that! Please do not make me go back! There is only pain out there, Grandmother! Only pain! Only hurt! It's bad down there! Terrible! There... There is so much evil, Grandma! *And HE...* He is so far away! *THEY* have separated us! They separated him from me! I do not want to go there! I don't want to go there! I don't want to be there *WITHOUT* Him! I won't go, Grandmother! I will not go!"

Grandma comes up to me very closely and softly touches my cheek with her hand. Looking kindly and affectionately into my eyes, she says, *"But HE is down THERE, Alyonushka! He is not here, and he needs you; he can't make it without you. You will find him, Alyonushka! You will definitely find him! Return, my child! Go back! Go back now!"*

I closed my eyes. And at that same moment, I felt my tortured, defiled body.

To my surprise, I saw that I was no longer lying on that damned bed. After a few minutes, I realized that I was in the hospital, in an empty hospital room. It was beginning to get light outside.

As I later found out, the following had happened. Having fulfilled his "marital duties," my husband decided to go to his friend's house to continue celebrating his marriage. The fact that it was the middle of the night did not seem to bother him. He left me bleeding. He just left. I'm not sure if it was Providence's or my Grandmother's efforts that saved my life that night; I cannot say for sure. But, somehow, a couple of hours later, he eventually decided to leave his friend's house and come back home. He found me cold and unconscious. After unsuccessfully trying to bring me back to life and seeing blood everywhere, he was terrified. I seemed to be dead, not responding to anything. He did not call an ambulance. He was afraid the doctors would report him to the police. So, he wrapped me in some kind of blanket, called a taxi, and took me to the hospital himself. I had multiple ruptures and severe blood loss.

They had to give me six stitches, which were removed two weeks later under general anesthesia since they were deep. It was a miracle I was alive, kind of…

When I woke up alone in the room, I was lying there staring at the ceiling over my head for a very long time. I was thirsty. But I did not have any strength to call anyone. I tried, but I could only whisper. I understood that I was alive. I did not see any point in it whatsoever at that moment. I did not want to be alive. I did not want to even exist. I wanted to be out there, with my Grandma. There, I felt no pain. There, I did not have to fight. There, I did not have to… But I was still alive. So, I also wanted to cry, and thank God, at least I had the strength to do so. I cried and cried and cried, tears flooding my face. I was crying out all my grief, asking the surrounding emptiness. *Asking HIM…*

"*WHERE ARE YOU? WHERE? Where can you be? WHY didn't I find you? Why didn't you find me? Why all this? Why? Why?*"

I was 22 years old, and the one I was looking for was very far away! But I couldn't know that then.

I wept, my wounded Soul falling into pieces. I cried, my body tortured and dishonored. I wept, staring at the ceiling in the empty hospital room, repeating, again and again, my stupid questions. The one I was crying about and I calling on was already one of the brightest stars in the World of Cinema. But I won't find out about it until years and years later.

Chapter 13

Meanwhile In the Mist House on the Lost Planet

...But I won't find out about it until years and years later.

Silence fell in the huge room cloaked with soft fog. All its borders were unsteady and transparent. The corners and walls looked like they'd been smudged with a photo editor. This type of silence occurs when very good and well-mannered people accidentally witness someone else's stupidity or meanness. Seeing something like that brings them into a deep shock. In such shock, they don't even know how to react. Should they, for example, get out of the room somehow to avoid further embarrassment and shame, or just try to pretend nothing had happened? Or maybe, they should interfere, not giving a damn about their reputation, and possibly find themselves in an even more awkward situation?

Haan's tall figure froze at the window, somewhat hunched. He leaned on his clenched fists against the glass; his head hung low. He looked as if he wanted to push the glass out with all his strength and fly away like a free, powerful eagle. A wall of heavy rain hung outside the window, drenching the entire sky. It was impossible to see anything through this downpour. The forest. The mountain. The sea. Nothing at all was visible. Only gray streams of water. Silent and indifferent.

"It was such a terrible, horrible story."

Joanna went up to him and put a hand on his shoulder, "But do you understand now?"

Haan looked up from the window and fixed his eyes on her. His beautiful dark eyes had turned red and were half-closed. He clenched his teeth so hard that his cheekbones looked sharper than ever. Every word he said was like the blade of a knife–sharp and quiet.

"Was it thanks to you that he returned just in time and took her to the hospital? Did you interfere?"

Joanna smiled with her eyes only and nodded. "To be exact, it was Helena. Even though she was already in her exile in the Mist House, she still was able to interfere and do something about the situation. This woman doesn't accept orders, and you can't forbid her to do anything. That is one of the reasons she has been living here for so long."

Haan looked at the woman with white hair and nodded as if thanking her or asking for forgiveness. Then he smiled at Joanna. Turning his face to the thin, gentle hand on his shoulder, he kissed it softly.

The woman with white hair laid a weightless page on the table, and it quickly disappeared, similar to those which were read before it, blazing into a million tiny sparks, which reminded one of the pure white grains of sand from some serene distant beach on a faraway island.

"It's not just a story, Haan. You know, it's the truth. Truth isn't only beautiful or only terrible. It does not need epithets. It is just the truth."

"Why can't I understand what you're talking about? Tell me, you were already living here back then, right? You were already here when all that horror happened to her?"

Firebird ran up to the table, where the last sparks of the previous pages were fading. "Have you already seen it all? I am not asking you why you did not help the young girl. That wedding. Some kind of dark, strange story... It seems so familiar as if I already saw it somewhere or heard about it. But I can't remember. I fully understand that Lala had the right to make her own choices and her own mistakes at that time. But she paid such an enormous price for those mistakes, Holy Heavens! Have you forgotten what a childhood she had? A dreadful, horrible childhood, goddamn it! It made her like that! She's still a terrified little girl, but in a body of a grownup woman, unsure, doubting everything, seeking everybody's approval and support, believing that she is unworthy of happiness and love. It gave her low self-esteem and a high dislike for herself! How could you allow all that? Why the hell didn't you help her when she was a little girl? Why didn't you help her before she agreed to marry that beast? Why did you allow all that? What is there, I don't know?"

Suddenly, the sound of rainfall burst into the room, rumbling thunder. One could hear the trees creaking, or was it clouds scratching the roof, or maybe some huge swing groaning and moaning on the other side of the window, which was still closed? Startled, Joanna looked up at Firebird.

"We must not interfere! As you saw, we already did, and it was very risky! If we had interfered more, the Dark ones would have noticed her! And if they noticed her back then, her protection would not stand even the slightest chance! We would lose her! We had to do everything possible and impossible NOT to lose her! She is our only HOPE!"

Joanna took a glass sphere on a wooden base from the shelf. It looked like one of those Christmas souvenirs people often brought to distant friends and relatives after traveling when they didn't know what present to get. But there was no snowman, no Santa Claus, no clock tower. Instead, a small log cabin was surrounded by dense forest and high mountains, with their peaks lost in a haze of clouds inside the crystal walls. It looked as if snatched from a different reality.

A tiny hurricane raged around the cabin. Leaves and branches were flying. The trees, huge compared with the house, were swaying wildly. Joanna waved her right hand over the ball as if stroking, calming it down. The sphere started to glow with warm light. The storm calmed. All the sounds of raging nature inside the round room also disappeared.

The woman with white hair sighed wearily, "Firebird! We must always try to outplay the Dark ones! Always try to be a step ahead of them! This is first. And secondly, we are not the Salvation Army. We are not the ones who save anyone! We are watching; we are the Keepers! We can give signs and omens, but we must not interfere!"

"That's strange. I was sure that our goal was to save her. Wasn't it? Did I miss something? Our goal is not to save?" Firebird looked like a ruffled chicken, hardly standing still. Her slender body was almost bouncing with impatience and resentment.

"You got it right. We must save, but not exactly her! Without her, we will not have any chance to save what we are trying to save here! Therefore, we can only watch. We will be her watchers and Keepers until she gains all her strength. But without suffering and struggle, strength doesn't come. As they say: 'What does not kill you makes you stronger!' and one cannot say it more accurately than that. Wait a little bit more, Firebird! Wait a little longer."

"Believe me, we all are here where we are right now because, sometimes, we did interfere a bit, preventing Lala from leaving, prolonging her life. And with prolonging her life, we also prolonged her torment and hope, and Her Love!"

Joanna smiled. She took Firebird by her hand and led her to the window.

"My dear girl, you will not be able to understand everything right now. There are many things you do not yet remember. For each one of us, the memory of karmic tasks opens up at a particular time, only after certain events. Yours hasn't happened yet. Take your time. Do not rush it. It's ok.

"Do you want to make some sunlight? Look. Place your left hand on your heart and stretch out your right one like this." She hugged Firebird, then quickly turned away and waved her head as if shaking off an unsolicited tear. Then she whispered the secret formula into her young friend's ear. The girl repeated soundlessly. Nothing changed.

"Add some love, Firebird. Whatever you do, do it with Love."

Firebird nodded nervously, pressed her lips together with a stubborn look on her face, took a deep breath, and as she exhaled, she smiled and whispered the right words. The sun appeared from nowhere, illuminating four people, the room of soft silhouettes blurred by the foggy corners and walls, and new pages of a manuscript swaying airily above the table. Some jasmine branches in a vase appeared on the table, enchanting everyone with their sweet, tart, intoxicating aroma.

Chapter 14

Farhan Ali

The year was 1997, and Farhan had recently turned thirty-two. He was gorgeous, talented, and mysterious. He was magnetic; something about him was bewitching. He was the dream of many millions of women from age three to ninety-three. He possessed everything anyone could possibly dream of. Yet, no one knew that deep down in his heart he still hadn't recovered from his terrible loss. Farhan Ali was born, exactly nine years before me, in the state of Virginia.

His mother was Indian and had a beautiful, very ancient name: Parvati. In Hinduism, Parvati is the beloved wife of God Shiva. She is also called "She, who gives Blissfulness" and" A Blessed Mother."

His father, tall, handsome blue-eyed Aman Ali, was an American man with a long list of Arabian ancestors.

Many years ago, when his father visited India on a business trip, he met his mother, Parvati, who was then a young girl, just seventeen years old. Their story of meeting and how they managed to get Parvati's parents' permission for this marriage could become a separate book. They were each from different lands, cultures, and even religions. Aman was a Muslim, and Parvati was brought up in the traditions of Hinduism. But Love eventually won. Parvati and Aman got married and moved to America. Soon they had a son and named him Farhan in honor of his grandfather, Aman's father.

A couple of years later, they had a beautiful baby girl, Fatima. Farhan looked very much like his mother, having inherited her olive skin tone and deep dark eyes. His extraordinary eyes made you want to plunge into them and never come up to the surface. These eyes were destined to conquer half the world. From his father, he took beautifully shaped lips, a bit too full and sensual for a man, making him even more tantalizing and seductive. His mane of thick, ebony black hair would be enough for several people, it seemed. His tall, slender figure was endowed with the grace of a panther. And, if all this was not enough, he was destined to be born under the most mysterious and mystical sign in the zodiac—Scorpio.

I read somewhere that Nature does not allow a Scorpio man to be born outwardly gorgeous. It is believed that Scorpios have so much natural Magic in them that to add physical beauty to it would be simply *too much*. Even without possessing physical attractiveness, the Scorpio man is capable of nailing you to the wall and making you obey his will with just one glance. "One look into their smoldering eyes, and you are a goner!" was written in one book. But when it came to Farhan Ali, he was an exception to the rule. Besides being a Scorpio, he was also fairytale handsome, like a prince from the "1001 Arabian nights".

Since childhood, he had had an inexhaustible passion for books and possessed a simply unthinkable intelligence, mixed with the naive charm of a five-year-old boy. It was impossible not to love him. Absolutely impossible! His teachers said it didn't matter what he did; he could get away with anything because no one wanted to punish him. And he was indeed a mischievous boy, a troublemaker, who got away with everything because he could melt a stone with just one of his smiles.

His childhood and youth were quite ordinary: school, college, university, friends, and sports.

He was very close to his father, Aman. They were best friends and understood each other, starting from the boy's early childhood and onward, throughout his life. As an elder brother, he adored and spoiled his little sister Fatima. But the most significant role in his fate was given to his mother, Parvati.

Farhan was not just attached to his mother; he idolized her. He worshiped her. She was the world for him. As for her, he was the most talented, most gifted, most brilliant boy of them all. He was the most amazing person in the whole wide world in her eyes. Parvati always dreamed he would become an actor, not just an actor, but the best and greatest of all. A true Star. A true Legend. Even for a second, she did not doubt that this is exactly what would happen. She believed unconditionally that her son would become a true star, and with his art, he would touch people's hearts deeply, helping them believe in the beauty of Love and life, in the wisdom of their own souls. He would help them be happier.

When Farhan was about 20 years old, they moved from Virginia to Los Angeles, California. His father opened his own company there. Fulfilling his father's dream, Farhan received a master's degree in International Law.

His mother worked in his father's office for part of the day and took care of the house and the children. In addition, she worked as a volunteer in various organizations that provided assistance to families with low income, especially those with children. She was a very bright woman, kind, generous, and hardworking. She worked many hours a day, but she would never deprive her own children of her love, care, and affection. She didn't try to control every step of her children, believing that the most important thing in a relationship with kids, was trust.

She brought her kids up to be free and independent. But at the same time, they could always count on her help, support and motherly hugs. Farhan would say many years later, "Everything that I have achieved in life, I managed to do only thanks to my mother, her faith in me, and her Love."

Yes, indeed. The mother's faith in her son and his future success had a significant impact on his career. She used to say to anyone who knew their family, "I do not need to worry about my children, especially Farhan. Whatever he does, he will always be the best of the best. Whatever he may choose to be, businessman, lawyer, diplomat, or actor, he will always be unsurpassed! If there is anything at all I am sure about, it is him."

For Parvati, her son Farhan was a megastar long before becoming one.

Since his very childhood, she cultivated this deep love and passion for the Cinema in her little Farhan. She went to see so many movies with him, and afterward, they discussed for hours what they had just seen. She also told him about the Cinema of her own native land. He could listen for hours to his mother talking about Indian Cinema. That mysterious, colorful world was filled with strong emotions, ancient stories, exotic melodies, songs, dance, and legendary actors like Madhubala, Nargis, Raj Kapoor, and many others. This love for his mother's homeland was passed on to him during his childhood.

"Look, son!" she would tell him. "Do you see? An actor can live hundreds of lives in just one of his own! But the most amazing thing about this art is that the actor can deeply touch people's souls! Their hearts! An actor can move them, touching something deep within their very essence! This could be enough for someone to change his whole life and the life of those around him! This is why true art exists. This is what true art is all about. It is created to deeply touch hearts and move people to live their best, love the deepest, and shine their brightest. This, my boy, is what I dream you will do when you grow up. Move people. Inspire and encourage them. Help them become stronger, brighter, happier. Help them understand important things. And if they have lost their way, help them find that way. If they have lost hope, help them find it again."

Parvati also taught her son Hindi, the language of her homeland. Because of that, it became possible for Farhan to watch not only the films made in Hollywood but later on, when VCR became available, many films from Bollywood as well.

So, from early childhood, he was well acquainted with both cultures. He absorbed the best of Hollywood and Bollywood, and later, he combined this in his work. By the time he turned 30, he was a star, both in the country where he was born and in his beloved Mother's homeland.

The work of Aman Ali, Farhan's Father, made it possible for the young man to contact many people from the film industry who knew his family. Parvati took advantage of this. Starting from when he was a teenager, she would introduce her son to those of her husband's clients who worked in the movie industry.

"This is my son, Farhan!" she usually said with her soft smile. "And mark my word, one day very soon, he will become a big Star! I have no doubt about it!"

Sport also played a significant role in the foundation and progress of Farhan's cinematic career. Football. Tennis. Hockey. Sport is the best school to learn how to fall and rise, to lose and win.

He started to take part in various theatrical plays and performances, first at school and then at university. His stunning looks, along with talent, grace, persuasiveness, and emotional expression, left no doubt that he had a bright future ahead of him. After university, he could easily have built a career in international law, but he never used his education for its intended purpose.

He had already participated in several successful television series, about a dozen theatrical productions, and three large-budget blockbusters at the age of twenty-five. His career was steadily moving onward and upward. You had to be deaf or blind to be able to resist his magnetism. Life continued on this course, gaining momentum.

At the same age, much to the dismay of the growing army of his female fans, Farhan got married. He met his wife, Cynthia, at a university party when she was only twenty years old. He was twenty-three. She was an American girl from a very wealthy and respectable family, belonging to old California's elite.

For a long time, her parents did not give their permission for this marriage. First of all, their daughter's sweetheart was a Muslim boy, and their family kept to the traditions of Catholicism. Secondly, Cynthia's parents didn't believe that becoming an actor's wife would be the best option for their only daughter. However, of course, they couldn't resist Farhan's charm. Two years later, the young couple got married.

So, here we have a young, handsome, beloved, successful man: a man who has a family, work, young wife, phenomenal career. Nobody thought anything could possibly go wrong. But disaster came without an invitation, unexpectedly.

When Farhan was on the set in another country, his father suddenly called him.

"Son! You must quickly come home! It's urgent! Mom is in hospital."

His heart froze in fear. The world stopped for a moment and lost its colors. He rushed home with the very first available flight, forgetting to eat, forgetting to sleep, and forgetting to breathe.

Over the following weeks, he did not move an inch away from his mother's side. He only ate when he was forced to. He did not sleep, only falling into the blissful darkness of oblivion, when his body simply refused to stay awake anymore.

Rapid, merciless cancer left no room for even the slightest hope. But he refused to fall into despair. He kept on hoping, no matter what. He trusted that God, in whom he believed with all his heart and soul, would never take away from him the dearest person in the whole world, his beloved mother. He believed in a miracle. Yet, Parvati grew weaker by the day. She would wake up for several minutes and almost immediately lose consciousness again.

In those short moments, when she was awake, she used to joke with doctors and nurses, say kind and gentle words to her son and dream about his future. She would tell him how he would receive all possible and impossible movie awards from all over the world. She talked about how they would then travel together to India, to her homeland, and she would proudly show him, her beloved boy, to her many, many relatives still living there. And he believed her. He believed her with all of his heart. But then Parvati slipped into a coma, and hope vanished.

He tried to stay strong. He refused to give up. He remembered that one day, back in his childhood, his mother told him about a very ancient prayer, which had immense power in it. It had to be repeated exactly 108 times, and after that, any miracle would happen. But it had to be read in the open air, under the open sky. So, he went outside, found a more or less deserted place in the parking lot near the hospital ward, and began to repeat this very prayer. With his eyes closed, he prayed and prayed, bending his fingers to not lose count. The moment one-hundred-and-seventh prayer was read, his mother left this world.

His father went outside, crying, almost not seeing the path in front of him. He found his son, repeating the last prayer. He went up to him and put his hand on his son's shoulder. Farhan did not respond. He just continued praying. His father was trying to find the courage to speak, but it took him several minutes.

Finally, clutching his son's shoulder, he said quietly, "Betta. (Son in Hindi) Betta! Mom is gone. She is no longer with us." His voice was trembling. He had to gather all his strength just to be able to keep on standing, to not break down. But Farhan did not seem to hear him or didn't want to hear. He refused to hear.

"Son…"

Farhan's voice began to tremble. Tears flowed down his cheeks. But he could not stop praying. He heard what his father had told him, but he did not believe it. He absolutely did not want to believe it! He did not want to! The last, one hundred and eighth prayer, was no longer needed.

During Parvati's funeral, it rained continuously and heavily. The gloomy sky was covered with dark grey clouds with no chance even for the slightest ray of the sun to get through. Mother Nature and the Earth were also crying. Farhan was walking behind the coffin, supported by two of his old friends. He could barely walk. He was not able to speak. Soon, all the rituals ended, all prayers were read, and all words were spoken. It was the time to say the last "goodbye."

But Farhan kept tightly holding his mother's hand, flatly refusing to let her go. He was mad with grief. His Mother had always been his life. His laughter. His joy. His inspiration. His faith. His whole world. And now, all of that would go away with her. No, he could not let her go. He did not want to let her go. It was above and beyond what he was capable of doing!

"I still fail to understand how I did not die with her back then," he would say many years later. "Since that day, life for me has been divided into two.

It became 'before' my mother's death and 'after.' I would never be the same after that day. This pain and this grief have never fully left my heart. But this pain and grief also forced me to become what I am now, to be where I am now. I swore to fulfill my mother's dream and become the brightest star in the Skies of the World Cinema, and I have fulfilled that dream of hers!"

Time moved on. Working fourteen hours a day became a kind of refuge for him, a safe harbor, where he could temporarily run from his pain that never healed. Two years later, his son was born, and two years after that, a daughter. His children, whom he adored and almost worshiped with all the depth of his heart, finally filled the void formed after the departure of his beloved Mother. His success as an actor was growing year after year. Besides being incredibly talented, Farhan was also courageous, preferring to go off the beaten track. He took up projects he considered exciting and challenging, even if others said they had no chance of commercial success. Prizes and awards were showered upon him as if from a cornucopia. He deserved them more than anyone.

And this is exactly that same man whose eyes I am searching for in the crowd. He is exactly the same man I am calling, lying in a cold hospital room. He is the One and Only. He is the one long-awaited! He is the one who is the missing part of my very essence, without which my Soul has no peace. His name is Farhan Ali.

But I don't know anything about it yet.

I still can't understand how it is even possible that I NEVER saw his face until 2014. I may have heard his name, but apparently, it did not ring a bell for me. Perhaps one of the reasons for that was a simple fact that I always loved old films. I would even say very old black and white ones. And most of the time, I prefer not Hollywood movies but classical Indian, Italian and French movies. From the early nineties (his blockbusters began to appear around that time), I hardly remember going to the actual movie theater. A cheap VCR finally appeared at my place, and I rented many tapes with my favorite old films and watched them repeatedly. My most beloved ones were, of course, still the Indian movies. I watched those old videos over and over again. They had this unique charm and nostalgia of a bygone era. Somehow all of his works just escaped my attention (or so it was destined to be). I never once saw his face. Otherwise, I would have *IMMEDIATELY* recognized those *EYES*! But it didn't happen until a most fateful night in 2014.

That night changed my life and my whole fate. But it's not time for that just yet. I'll tell you later...

Chapter 15

The Healing

I opened my eyes in the hospital room the morning after my wedding night, after my very first night with a man. I somehow managed to fall asleep. When I opened my eyes, the first thing I saw were the faces of my mother and my brother Alexei, both white with horror. As it turned out, having left me at the hospital to the care of doctors and medical staff, my newlywed husband went home to sleep. In the morning, he woke up as if nothing at all had happened, drove to my mother's home, and told her that I was in the hospital. "It's nothing serious. She will be fine very soon."

Seeing my mother and brother, I burst into tears again. I could not speak. I just looked at them and sobbed silently. My brother turned to my husband. He was so furious his face turned completely white, suddenly drained of all color. I was afraid he would hit him, and they would fight. Mom's face seemed bloodless and petrified. A moment later, a doctor entered the room and asked my mother to accompany him into the corridor for a "private conversation." My brother turned to Arthur and whispered to him, "If she had died, I would have torn you into little, tiny pieces with my bare hands! Bastard!"

I was in the hospital for three weeks. All this time, my mother tried to make me eat more. I was desperately thin. But she wasn't very successful, and my weight continued to melt away. I didn't know why: I did not feel any hunger. I had lost the sense of taste. I didn't feel anything. Somewhere along the way, I had completely lost any will or desire to live. But one more thing happened as well. This terrible experience had considerably sharpened my paranormal abilities. The news about the "clairvoyant girl who can *SEE*" flew around the hospital in a matter of hours. People constantly surrounded my bed, asking me question after question, which I answered indifferently in a dry, lifeless voice.

It all started one day when my nurse set up my usual *IV* line, the one hundred and fiftieth one. My hemoglobin was still too low; they couldn't make it go up. While she was doing all the usual procedures, she was thinking too loudly, if I may use those words, and I simply heard her thoughts. Not only did I hear them, but I also saw the people she was thinking about—all of those people, their present, and their future. I was in such a state I did not even question *HOW* and *WHY* I could see and hear everything. I did not care. That moment I was half dead, like a broken doll.

The wonderful nurse was busy thinking that she should not agree to her nineteen-year-old daughter marrying some guy named Anton. I don't know how and why I do it, but I always speak out before I even have a chance to think to stop myself. After all, I know very well *WHAT* people might think of me—crazy, weird, creepy, you name it. But at that moment, I did not give a damn. I was still alive, but I did not feel like I was at all.

"Oh, you shouldn't worry at all!" I told her. "He is a good guy. He loves her very much! So, what if she's 19, and he's 20! Let them get married! They will be very happy! They will have a son soon! What a joy for you! You'd better worry about your older daughter! The person she's seeing is so good-looking! He has money, but his soul is as black as hell! He'll ruin her whole life! Do not let her marry him!"

The nurse's face turned white as snow, and the dropper froze in her hands. That's how it started!

There were five beds in my room; only two of them were occupied by a young woman and myself. But after this incident, three more asked to be transferred to our room. At night, I would sing to them. My voice somehow was able to calm their pain. Each told me their whole life's story, then the lives of their children and relatives. I could clearly "see" all they were telling me about, as if I was watching it all on a huge screen, like a movie theater.

Not only could I see it all, I knew what those people thought, felt, hoped for, and feared. They called me the "Sorceress." Many people came wanting to talk to me. It seemed like a never-ending line.

When I was discharged, a huge crowd gathered. People gave me their addresses and phone numbers. They thanked me, hugged me, wished me all health and happiness. Oh, I wish I could have all the health and happiness they had hoped for me. But I was very far from that. From the hospital, I went straight to my mother's house.

Of course, returning to my husband's apartment was clearly out of the question. Timoshka stayed with me and my mom. He loved me very much, so much that he did not even like to have me out of his sight. He loved to hold my hand and shared everything with me. We built things with Lego, played chess, walked to the park or his chess school. He would fall asleep holding my hand as well while I sang to him and told him fairy tales. Arthur understood clearly that the boy was better off with me. But I still had the key to his apartment. We hadn't talked about divorce yet, although it was obvious that I would not live with him. Still, he did not want to give up. Oddly enough, he continued to hope that by some miracle, everything would work out, and I would come back to him.

Maybe he did love me in his own strange way; probably this is what it was, who knows? I did not know what love was. To me, this man was still a stranger—thick-skinned, insensitive, rude. But, most likely, he had always been like that. It's just that I was always thinking about my little Timoshka and did not even stop to think about taking a closer look at the person whose proposal of marriage I had agreed to accept.

I was used to being pressured, to violence. I didn't resist it. I thought I could withstand it all, as usual. I just tried to do the best for my little boy, but I failed. I had destroyed two destinies, or to be exact, three.

Arthur felt guilty and tried his best to make it right. One day a few months after the wedding, he knelt before me and said, holding my hands, "You have every right to blame me for everything that happened! I am very guilty! I beg you! Please, forgive me if you can! I love you so much! I cannot breathe without you! I'll do anything! Just name it! Tell me what you want. Everything will be as you want it to be! Do you want to go to Paris? Or to India? You have always dreamed about India! Tell me. What do you want? I'll do absolutely anything! I do not want to lose you. I can't lose you!"

But I didn't want anything. His touch, even the most innocent, terrified me to death. He sent me tons of roses, bought me the most expensive jewelry, which I later gave back to him. It seemed like he really tried to bring me back and did everything he could possibly do to make that happen. But I was numb. I was numb, not just towards him; I was numb, period. Frozen, I didn't feel anything at all. I had a very strange body temperature. It was below what is considered normal. I was constantly cold, and no matter how hard I tried, I could not get warm. Even when I got into a very hot bath or covered myself with five blankets, I was still icy cold and shivering. I moved around, did my homework, and went to the university. I talked to people when I had to. But it was as if I was a robot. I learned to wear a mask and almost succeeded in making people around me believe that everything was fine with me. But that was a lie—a big, fat lie!

The cold, numbness, and emptiness I felt were not only because of my first disastrous sexual experience and my husband's rudeness. Not only because the feeling of my own worthlessness, uselessness, and misfortune had returned to me, there was something else.

After leaving the hospital, I returned to the university. From the outside, everything seemed to be as it was before. But I knew, I clearly understood that something was very wrong with me.

I knew what was happening to me could not be explained only by the shock and stress of what I had experienced. No. I felt, with my gut, that there was something else. But what? What was it? I had no idea. I started to drink huge amounts of coffee to force myself to function normally because I did not have any strength for anything. I didn't feel like eating. I didn't feel like seeing anyone. It was a massive achievement for me just to drag myself out of bed. My mom would prepare all sorts of healing herbal brews for me. But nothing seemed to be working. Nothing helped me. I wanted to be completely alone. That was the only thing I craved, aloneness, complete and total isolation. That was the only wish I had. Nothing else! Nothing at all! Nothing!

After University classes, I went to a large park where I could find totally deserted pathways with no people. I wandered there for hours. I desired to be alone. Absolutely alone.

I also started to feel a terrible, overwhelming sense of guilt! Guilt before HIM. Guilt for having betrayed him. I had betrayed the one I was looking for all this time but never managed to find. I can't explain why it is and how it is, but with every cell of my body, every bit of my heart and soul, as long as I could remember, I always felt that I belonged to him and him alone. Him alone!

After all, I have always dreamed of only one thing. I would find him, or he would find me, and HE would be my first and my last. My one and only. The only man who would even touch me. I couldn't, and I didn't want to imagine my life with anyone else—only Him. But everything turned out to be totally different and not the way I dreamed. And for everything that had happened, I blamed only one being: Myself.

Having married Arthur, I went against myself. I gave my body to one who never should have had it, to one I had never loved, and because of that, I was paying the price. I felt dirty, dishonored, unclean. *How could I have allowed all this to happen to me? Was it something I had dreamed of all the years of my childhood and youth? Oh, no! Absolutely not! Maybe I had done something wrong? Maybe I deserved it? But why? Why did I deserve such a terrible punishment? Well, obviously, I might have deserved it somehow, since it all had happened to me!* So, I was telling myself.

Since that terrible night, and for many years to come, I could not get rid of that feeling of being *dirty, not pure, and unclean.* Every single day, every morning, and every evening, I would stand in the hot shower for a long time under the streams of hot water, scrubbing and scrubbing myself as hard as I could. Of course, I understood very well; the water would not help me. But I kept doing it. Apart from myself, I started to blame one other for everything, God. I was angry, very angry with God! I was in pain, and I was angry.

At that time, I was a deeply devoted Christian, a strong believer. I kept all the fasts and precisely followed all the rules and sermons. Unfortunately, I did not find any peace in religion. I had tried to force myself into it from a very young age, but it never worked. When I watched or participated in church rituals, I felt heaviness and pressure in my chest, sometimes even pain. I felt deep pain seeing people on their knees, their heads touching the floor, or kissing the hands of priests or praying over the casket or even a part of the body of a deceased saint. Almost every church has them. They call such parts "Moshi." Sometimes the church is named after the saint, whose body, after his death, was put into the church's foundation. The hardest for me was *Communion*.

As it was considered very important, I tried to force myself to drink the wine while the priest said, "This is the blood of our Savior." But everything in me refused to drink the blood and eat the body. No matter how hard I tried to convince myself, this was just wine and bread; I could not. I felt something was not right in that ritual. I was being given dark red wine and told: "Drink this. This is the blood of our Savior". How could I drink the blood of a Savior and eat his body? But I forced myself to do it. I thought that I must. And I always felt very unwell and couldn't even breathe freely for several days after Communion. Why did I force myself? Because I refused to listen to my own Soul. I simply convinced myself, I felt all that because I was a sinner, I was evil, and my Soul was dark. That led me to more fasting and being even tougher on myself.

I tried my very best to be a very good girl and do everything right. I did this for years and years of my life. And I sincerely believed that I almost succeeded at it. Unfortunately, probably because of it, I could not understand why *GOD* had forced me to go through all this. "Everything happens because of God's will," they told me. So, I believed that the horrific events must also be His will. But why? Why did I deserve that? I was sure that I did not deserve it at all. Did I want that much? Did I ask and pray for too much? I just wanted to be happy. I wanted to find *HIM*. I felt that I belonged to *HIM* and should not belong to anyone else. So, *WHY* did I get dragged through this whole nightmare? Why was I guilty? Because of my naivety? My softness? My stupidity? Or maybe something else? Questions without answers!

But the worst thing was, I started to believe that I had lost all chance of ever finding Him after what had happened. After that terrible night, I no longer saw his eyes in my dreams, which broke me completely. I blamed it on myself again. I told myself, *you will never find him because your body is not "pure" anymore, neither is your Soul. You do not deserve him. You do not deserve love or happiness. You deserve nothing! Nothing!*

A month passed by, another one, then three, then six. One day, returning home from classes, I got on the wrong bus. Its route passed through the old city cemetery. Let me tell you; I am terrified of cemeteries. I always was! I would never go there. I avoid talking about them, reading about them, or even seeing them in the movies. Even mentioning a cemetery gives me the creeps. I have a strange deep fear connected to them. But that day, seeing the high wall and many graves behind it, I suddenly asked the driver to stop.

I got off the bus near the cemetery wall, headed straight for the entrance gate, and went inside. It was completely empty. Absolutely no one was there. It was the middle of a cold, gloomy winter day in the middle of January. Although it was very cold, I did not feel it. A couple of months before that day, I stopped feeling cold from the outside. Why was it this way? I did not know, maybe, because everything inside me was cold, frozen, and lifeless.

Strangely, the cemetery did not cause my usual terror—quite the opposite. Suddenly, I felt unusually calm, as if I had come home. I stopped feeling the dull pain in my chest area, which had been with me for so long that I barely noticed it. It had become a part of me. The cemetery was very old and very, very big. I started wandering among the old graves, reading the names on the tombs, looking at the photos. I sat down on little benches near the graves, not noticing that it was getting really dark. I did not feel any fear. In fact, I didn't want to leave. I UNDERSTOOD something was very wrong with me. Something was not right, not right at all! But I had neither the strength nor the desire to fight this wrong and not right. My life was over. I was sure of it.

Him... No, I would never see or find him. So, why keep on living? What was the point? I did not see any point. I was just slowly, steadily fading away.

I began to walk to the cemetery every single day. Sometimes I would buy flowers and lay them on top of some old graves. I sat there for hours, talking to the dead people, calling them by their names on the tombs. They became my friends and family. The cemetery became my home. It was becoming more and more difficult for me to leave that place with every passing day. I wanted to stay there. But one day, something happened, which, as I understand it now, ultimately saved my life.

One morning, entering the cemetery gates, I saw an elderly woman selling flowers. She had just a few of them, and she asked for very little money. I decided to buy them all. But while I was handing her the money, she suddenly grabbed my hand. I can't remember her face now; even if I try really hard, I still can't. I do not know why.

She took my hand and said in a soft and very kind voice, "Sweet child, dear child, please listen to me! They want to ruin you! They haven't yet, because there is no darkness in you! Only light! You are bright as the Sun. But if you do not find someone who will heal you with prayers, ancient prayers to the Forces of Light, they will destroy you! Find someone, my sweet child! Someone to heal you! You know what, child? Go to the monastery, the one that was recently rebuilt. Ask for Natalia! She will help you! But don't come back here anymore, child! Do not come back! There is no place for you among the dead. They have cursed you using the SOIL! It was taken from the grave of a woman with the same name as yours! Taken at an exact dark hour, with words and rituals, only dark, lost souls have the knowledge of. The grave is here."

I was standing there, hearing her soft, kind voice, absolutely unable to move! I don't know how much time passed before I finally was able to talk and asked her, "And what did they do with that soil, grandmother?"

The woman was silent for a minute, all this time still holding my hand in hers. "They put that soil inside the bed," she said.

And suddenly, like a flash, it all became clear to me! I remembered that damn bed. I remembered how I was shaking at the mere thought of lying on

104

it. I remembered the cold, suffocating fear I felt even looking at it. "The soil in bed was taken from a grave of the woman with the same exact name as yours. That grave is here."

I remember the following events very vaguely, like it was happening in a dream or a thick fog. I got on a bus and went to my husband's apartment, where that night from hell had happened.

I knew that if I saw his car in the parking lot, then he would be at home, but if not... The car wasn't there, so he wouldn't be at home either. I took the elevator to the ninth floor. I still had the keys from that apartment with me for some reason. We were still considered married, or maybe I carried them in my bag as a reminder of my *bond*. I do not really remember, but I had the keys.

I opened the door and went inside, closing the door behind me. Slowly I walked up to that cursed bed. Again, I felt that unbearable horror. I was standing in front of it, terrified, shaking like a leaf as if it was going to attack me! Finally, I gathered all my courage, stepped closer, and lifted a huge, queen-size mattress. I had to bend it almost in half. In the center of the bed, I saw something like a bundle. I do not know how to explain it with words, but it blew mortal cold as if it was an old grave from the same cemetery I had just left. I took the bundle, wrapped in a woman's headscarf, in my hands. Unwrapping it, I saw the soil. I already knew what kind of soil it was. I did not know then that picking up the cursed items with your bare hands should be avoided in every possible way. One mustn't touch that sort of thing! But I did not know.

As soon as I had that damn scarf in my hands, I got a terrible spine-chilling vision: I was lying in a closed coffin, *and I WAS STILL ALIVE*. I was petrified and horrifically cold. I felt so sick that I had to sit down on the floor to catch my breath. I do not remember how long I was sitting there, breathing heavily, my heart pounding like a bird trapped in a cage. I felt a cold sweat appear on my forehead. I was freezing, and every cell of my being was trembling. At the same time, I felt an almost unbearable heat, as if I had a very high fever. At last, I gathered my strength and forced myself to rise from the floor.

I did not know what to do with that scarf and that soil. I put it into my bag and left the apartment. I decided to go straight to the monastery. I wanted to find Natalia, the woman I was told about at the cemetery. I often ask myself, *who was that old woman at the cemetery that day?* And the more I think of it, the more I suspect, perhaps she was not just a woman at all. Sometimes I think she was not even a human. Maybe she was one of the Highest, one of my Keepers or Guardians who came to save my life.

I arrived at the monastery and went straight to the church building. I saw a woman in a small shop where they sold candles, altar bread, and other church items. She was standing with her back to me, busy with something. But it seemed she felt my presence. She turned around and froze for a moment, looking into my eyes. Her eyes were silvery gray, deep, and penetrating.

"Good afternoon," I said and instantly fell silent. I didn't quite know what I was supposed to say.

'I'm looking for a woman," I continued, trying to sound calm. "Her name is Natalia. Perhaps you can help me to find her. You see. There was this woman at the cemetery. I, I met a woman at the cemetery. She was selling flowers. And, and she said that I was cursed. I found the soil under the mattress. In a few words, she told me to come here and ask for Natalia. She said Natalia would be able to do the healing for me so that the curse would be removed."

All the way to the church, and even when I was already inside, talking to the woman, I continued shaking as if I had feverish chills. My lips got dry and looked almost colorless.

The woman kept on looking at me cautiously.

"I suppose they cursed you because of your beauty," she finally said.

"I... I don't know."

"I don't know!" she gently teased me, kindly, without anger or a mockery in her voice.

"Have you ever seen yourself? It's hard to even take eyes off of you! Even though you look almost as pale as a ghost, a very lovely one! And your Soul is pure. I can see it in your eyes! I'll give you Natalia's phone number! She

106

doesn't take just anybody, but I am sure she will not refuse you. Call her and tell her I sent you. My name is Zina. Go and may Angels keep you, beautiful child! Did you understand everything?"

I nodded.

"Thank you! Thank you so very much!" My heart was filled with gratitude. I smiled at Zina and was almost about to leave but suddenly remembered the wrapped soil.

"Oh! One more thing," I turned to her again. "What should I do with this?

And I pulled that scarf out of my bag.

Zina looked at the bundle in my hand, and her face turned almost gray.

"Oh! Blessed Mother of God!" she exclaimed, pressing both hands to the face. Her gray eyes opened wide, filled with horror and compassion at the same time. She came up closer and looked at the bundle in my hand for several minutes. She was looking at it in such a way, as if I was holding a deadly poisonous snake. It seemed this wonderful woman could not believe that somehow, I was still alive.

"Who would hate you that much, to curse you like that?" she finally said. "This is made to make you find your death! I am pretty sure of it! Even looking at it is terrifying. It blows deadly cold, like an old, forgotten grave."

Then her face suddenly lit with disbelief and admiration.

"*AND YOU MANAGED TO SURVIVE THAT!* I cannot even imagine what kind of Force is protecting you, child! I can only say that it must be very powerful! Nobody would survive that!"

She again silently looked at me for a moment as if trying to see something. Then she said, "There is someone, I don't know who, but they guard you. They seem to be invisibly everywhere with you all the time. Not Spirits, and not Angels, more like people or, not actually, people. I cannot really understand who they are. I would call them *Keepers*, maybe. This curse was done professionally! Properly done! And they would not even think to have mercy on you, young, innocent child! Dark souls! Dark, merciless Souls! God sees everything!"

"Are you able to see what was done?" I asked.

107

"Yes. I understand some things and can see some other things, but I can't heal this. I only know that it was a woman who cursed you. To be exact, she did not do it herself. She hired somebody. It was done because of a man. You had stepped on her toes, had taken him. It is a rather common case. This happens a lot. But I have never seen a curse done like this! Usually, different methods are used—*Quarrel curse, Hate curse*—when two loving people suddenly start to hate one another and argue constantly, or feel nothing but cold indifference towards each other. All of those are done with one goal: to force people to break up, end their love, end their relationship. But in your case, the *Death Curse* was used. Poor thing! Well, you'd better call Natalia immediately! Do not wait! She will help you! And this," she pointed to the bundle, "leave it here! I know what to do with it."

The very next day, I was at Natalia's tiny apartment.

Natalia turned out to be a beautiful red-haired woman in her fifties, with piercing eyes, the color of the sky in June and soft sunny freckles, making her face surprisingly young and fresh. She told me to lie down on the snow-white fabric spread out on the floor.

She put two candles near my head, one on the left side and one on the right. Then two candles at the chest area, the same way, and two by my legs. So, I was pretty much surrounded by burning candles. She told me the same thing as the women at the cemetery and Zina at the monastery.

"There is a lot of light in you! You are like a waterfall in the rays of the sun. This inner light has helped you survive, but that's not the only reason. There is something else. You are one of those called, *The Key*. You will not be allowed to leave this Earth earlier than you are supposed to."

"*The Key*? What does it mean?"

"There are Souls who, once on Earth, can change the lives of many people for the better. Those souls are called *The Keys*."

"Me????? No! That cannot be!! You must be mistaken. I can't do anything at all! I…"

But she did not let me finish. She stopped me with a smile and replied, "You have a true Gift of Light in you, child! But what you do not have at all is *self-acceptance and love for yourself!* And that's bad! Very bad! But we will talk about that later. First, I need to snatch you from the clutches of death."

And so, she began "snatching" me from those clutches. She had a very old book in the Ancient Slavic language. I was struck by the fact that those texts were not addressed to the Christian God but to the old, very ancient Gods I knew not much about back then. Reading those unimaginably beautiful texts, she called on the Mother of the Gods, Lada. She called on the one who weaves the thread of human Fate, Dolya. The Father of Gods, Rod. In many Slavic languages, everything connected to family, ancestors, children, homeland has the same root of the word: ROD. Examples: RODina (homeland), RODiteli (parents), RODnya (Family) RODit (to give birth). So definitely, she was calling for a very Ancient Powerful Being, as his name was kept so lovingly in many languages for thousands and thousands of years. She also called on my Guardians and Keepers.

The feelings these texts created within me were incredible. At first, I got very scared. We were only two minutes into the first text-prayer when I clearly saw myself lying in an ice-cold coffin with the lid closed above my head. I was so terrified that I wanted to jump up, but Natalia held me tightly and didn't let me do that. She continued reading in her soft, calm voice. The closed lid on the coffin I saw myself in, gradually began to open slightly. And then, I saw a ray of light penetrating through the darkness. The coffin's lid was opening more and more, very slowly, inch by inch, and it was getting easier and easier for me to breathe. Life slowly began coming back into my body as if by a thin golden stream. And Natalia was reading and reading without breaks, I would even say, she was not reading, but more like singing an ancient, powerful, beautiful song.

"In the blue-blue sea, on the sacred island, lies the burning-white holy stone Alatyr. On that stone, Alatyr sits the Goddess Lada. Lada holds the white swan in her gentle hands. Lada plucks a small white feather from the wing of that swan. The wind Brother picks up the white feather and carries it away. So, be gone and vanish all the evil which was done to Alla, this pure child. May the evil leave her head, leave her eyes, leave her body, and leave her beautiful heart. If it came with the wind— then be gone with the wind, if it came with the water—then be gone with the water, if it came with the fire—then be gone with the fire, if it came with the earth—then be gone with the earth. From now on and forevermore. As it was, as it is, as it will be! The Guardians of Light, the Keepers of the Souls! I am asking you with my open heart: Guard, guide, and protect this child and save her from all evil. Guide her onto the righteous path. May all her deeds be in the Glory of Pure Light of her sacred Family in Heaven, from now on and forevermore. As it was, as it is, as it will be! From now on, until the end of time. Go sorrow, far away. Go, sorrow, do not come back. Go, sorrow, do not touch this girl. Go sorrow, forget her name, from now on, until the end of times."

It felt like the sun was pouring its warmth and light upon me with her every word, dissolving both my fears and the cold of the coffin, in which I was put by someone's desire, darkness, and greed.

I realized that Arthur's ex-wife had had a hard time with her young lover and wanted to return to him. But unfortunately, he did not want to see her. He didn't even want to let her meet with their son. She had decided that there was only one reason for such behavior in her ex-husband. That reason was me. She had desperately wanted to return home to wealth and stability, but I was in her way. So, she decided that all the obstacles to her coming back home would disappear if I died. She also wanted to be sure that I was gone. So, she paid for two rituals.

Natalia told me it was not only the soil in the bed, taken from the grave of a woman with the same name as mine. There was another reason why I was so drawn to that cemetery. In the same grave, they put a wax doll, which was prepared with specific dark ceremonies. It was given my name and represented me. That wax doll was pulling me to the cemetery, like to my own home. That is why I felt *calm* there. That is why I wanted to be there and had to force myself to leave. It felt like *home*. It is obvious to me now, if it wasn't for the Higher Forces, which interfered in my life back then, I would have found my *home* in that same cemetery, just as they wanted me to. But because of Fate and the help of the Guardians and the Keepers of the balance, I survived.

For a whole year, this amazing woman helped me get out of the darkness, where I was dwelling against my own free will.

She washed my face with water from seven wells, read ancient prayers for me, prepared mixtures with milk, honey and herbs, and poured melted beeswax into the water taken from under the bridge. We went to the forest on Kupala, the most powerful day of the year, the Summer Solstice. We had to come there very early and I wandered barefoot in the morning dew while she read some ancient runes. Slowly but surely, one step at a time, life was returning to me.

Although my marriage was still valid on paper, it had long ceased to exist. It shouldn't have existed from the very beginning, but what was the point in saying what should have been or could have been. I finally decided to ask my husband for a divorce.

For a long time, I didn't dare to do it. I was simply afraid of him. He became one of my nightmares, one of many in my life. When I saw him, my whole insides would curl up, shrinking, freezing. He was still trying to recover the relationship with me but seeing the expression of horror on my face every time he reached out just to touch me; he preferred to leave me be.

Finally, the day arrived when I decided to ask him for a divorce. Again, I blamed myself for everything, making myself the reason for all the troubles. It is not even a habit, but my lifestyle: taking the blame onto myself to make it easier for others. Still, he was in a rage. He tried to persuade me, then he threatened, then he begged me. He promised me to love me forever, to do and give me whatever I wanted, even the moon and the stars from the sky. Finally, he decided to use my weakest point.

"If you divorce me, you will never see my son again!"

Alas, I was so naive that I did not believe him. Well, I couldn't imagine how a father would want to deprive his son of all the love and attention the child was receiving in my house. But I was wrong again. When all the divorce papers were signed, my now ex-husband took little Timoshka with him to the children's theater.

I never saw the child again. Never. Arthur kept his word.

I did not expect that. I was devastated, my heart was yearning for my dear little boy. I cried a lot, talked to him in my mind, asked him to forgive me. I kept doing it for years to come.

For a very long time, I lived with the suffocating feeling of guilt towards this little boy. I had given him a home and a family and then taken it all away. Of course, he did not understand anything back then. And I have never had an opportunity to explain everything to him or ask for forgiveness. We have never met since the morning he went to the theater with his father.

I turned twenty-three that summer. Natalia's work with me was complete.

It had been almost two years since I last saw HIS eyes in my dreams, the eyes of my other half, of my cosmic beloved. And although the memories of those dreams had helped me move along, unfortunately, I wanted more than just the memory of a dream. A memory of a dream—how insanely little that is! I wanted those dreams to come back. They brought me strength! Strength, so I could patiently WAIT for the meeting with him! But dreams about him, as I said, had not been around for about two years. I felt miserable. It tortured me and made me feel lost and insanely alone in this life and this world. What if they would never come back? For the first time in my life, I decided to tell someone that I had been waiting and looking for someone since childhood. I told my story to Natalia.

Nobody knew anything about Twin Flames back then. While everybody knew the myth about the other half of the Soul, no one really understood it. Nobody expected it to be true in real life. It was simply considered a beautiful legend.

But to my amazement, when I got to the end of my long story, Natalia said, "I often felt that there was someone else's Soul next to you. But I could not understand who it was. It is the one who is always invisibly with you, near you, even though he is not physically with you. It is hard to explain in words. You are like two identical patterns overlaid, one on the top of another. You are alike. *You are always together*, and yet at the same time, you are not together.

"Now that you told me this, I finally understand the mystery. So, *it was HIM*, the one you are waiting for and for whom you are looking for. Probably your souls have never been parted before. And now you are separated, at least in the physical world. In the nonphysical, you are always together. I think that even now, you are there with him while he is here with you. No matter where you both are in this world, you are always with each other, always together. And I am sure, no matter where he is, no matter who he is, he is also waiting and looking for you, just as you are waiting and looking for him.

"I don't know how and when you will find each other, but I know for sure that *it will happen*. I just know it! Most likely, *YOU* will find him! I can't tell you how and when, but I know for sure that you will! It is written in your Book of Destiny! This is why you came to this Earth. This is why you had to go through everything that you've gone through. You will find him! I know you will!"

And that very night, I saw his *EYES* Again! And with them, Life and Hope returned to me. I will find him, or He will find me! This is meant to happen, meant to be! This is my destiny; it cannot be any other way. I believed again. I lived again. I hoped again.

Chapter 16

In the Mist House on the Lost Planet

... And with his eyes, Life and Hope returned to me. I believed again. I lived again. I hoped again.

Firebird finished reading the chapter and joyfully threw the page into the air. Surprisingly, it didn't turn into sparks, but into small white flowers.

"Those are daisies, right? Is that the name of those flowers? Daisies? I'm so glad that Lala returned to life and began to see the eyes of her beloved. Things are changing for the better. Something wonderful will happen, right?"

Joanna stepped away from the easel. Tilting her head to the side, she looked at her finished work. On the canvas was a daisy meadow, the edge of a blue forest, a dazzling blue sky, two bright suns, and three pale moons: a turquoise one, a golden one, and a cornflower blue moon.

"Yes, Firebird. These are daisies. I love them too. You see, you are already able to change reality. All it takes is Love! With Love, you can change any reality! We were all happy that this stage in Lala's life was over. Her life began to turn towards the light."

"Like a sun-flow-er?" Firebird was glowing. Joy was sparkling in her eyes, which looked like two shiny chestnuts, framed by long spiky eyelashes. Her shoulders straightened as if she had just thrown an unbearable burden off of them. Her legs were dancing, tiptoeing, bouncing up and down, spinning around. The soft hem of her white, slightly formless dress, wrapped around her knees like bindweed wraps around the tree. It was rising and falling again in a light cloud, accentuating her slim figure and thin waist.

"Oh, look at you, lovely girl! How pretty you are! Just like a sunflower yourself," Joanna jokingly smeared yellow paint on Firebird's nose. "You are a sunflower that follows the sun, Firebird!"

"Isn't it great that Lala met Natalia? Just on time! And she is just like you, Joanna, kind and fair, and even looks like you. She also has red hair and freckles. Could she be a relative of yours?" Firebird looked at the artist with curiosity.

Joanna turned away and began to put her paints into a box as if not hearing what Firebird said.

"I think I know how and why Joanna and Helena ended up here, in the Mist House," said Haan, looking closely at both of the women. «You didn't have permission to interfere, did you."

Helena maintained his glance and calmly answered, "No, we did not have permission. They believed the evil caused by Arthur's ex-wife to be balanced by the wrong decision made by Alla. Her decision to marry him influenced the character and entire life of both Arthur and Timur. Arthur would get married two more times, be rude, suspicious and jealous of both of his wives, and end up divorcing them. Now he despises all women in general. He is sure that women are just some vile, cunning, and ungrateful creatures. Now, when it comes to the boy, he…

"Do not!" Suddenly, Firebird cried.

She suddenly seemed to shrink, sinking her head into her shoulders and whispering, "Please don't say anything about the boy. I don't want to know!" She slowly walked toward the far wall. Scooped up a handful of cloud from the window, where the two bright suns and three pale moons were visible above the chamomile field, rubbed her fingers, twisting a foggy cigarette, inhaled deeply, and made a weird sound as if coughing or sobbing quietly.

"Girl, do not worry. He is alive! They will even meet one day!" said Joanna. But the downhearted Firebird had already left, not wanting to hear anything.

Helena shook her head reproachfully, "Watch out, Joanna. You are raising false hopes with that information. It is a psychological threat of the second level. I

115

just want to say that the boy will not believe his dad when he says she abandoned them. He will constantly try to run away from home, trying to find her. Then he will be silent for several years," she hesitated. "And everyone should be aware that we are responsible for all our actions. Pity is always subjective. Objectively, both sides committed evil."

Haan grunted, "Says, who? Didn't you interfere? Didn't you help? Or are you going to say that was objective? Isn't that a pity?"

"No. That was NOT showing pity! That was a necessity; this world has very little time left. We cannot lose it. We cannot wait for her another incarnation. And Lala knew this beforehand and agreed to this suffering with her eyes open, intentionally."

"I'll be careful, darling. That won't happen again," Joanna softly brushed the hand of the white-haired woman. "Calm down. We are still holding on. Firebird will return. She hasn't awakened yet; she still does not remember. It is tougher for her than for us."

Outside the window, the darkness of night had fallen. Only the stars and three shining moons were still visible. And this house itself, constantly changing, disappearing, and appearing in different places, probably, from the side also looked like a small warm moon. It was like a balloon floating above this earth, tied to it by an invisible thread.

Chapter 17

Soulmates

I often ask myself this question, *if I had known BACK THEN, where he was and who he was, would I have lived my life differently, or would everything have been just the same?* What is the point in asking? I would never know the answer to this question.

After I heard Natalia say, "You will definitely find him!" and again started seeing him in my dreams, which were more realistic to me than my real-unreal life, I was able to smile again. I was again able to look ahead with hope. I could live. I could breathe. And my eyes again started searching for his eyes among the faces of people I met. Of course, now you know that it was all in vain. But I didn't know that. I couldn't know it back then or was not allowed to know.

I wondered, *does he also see me in his dreams? Does he feel me? Does he know my soul is always there beside him? Does he know me without actually knowing me, as I know him? Is there any part of his ancient essence that remembers me?* I think yes. But men are created differently. Very few of them would pay much attention to such matters. Also, I guess his crazy rhythm of life probably, did not leave him much time to look too deep inside his very soul. Or maybe I am again making up excuses for those I love.

I was waiting for him. I was looking for him. I was searching for him.

The years went by and still, he was nowhere to be seen.

At 26, I graduated from the university and started postgraduate studies. I was fortunate; soon, I got a job as an interpreter at a travel agency. My hometown has always been famous among foreign tourists, and my studies and excellent English allowed me to become an interpreter for foreign tourist groups. They took tours around the city, admiring the most beautiful and interesting places. The guide would tell amazing stories about these places, and I translated them. Working like that was an absolute joy for me. I love museums, especially those with ancient artifacts. They are abundant in our city. In one of these groups, I met my second husband and father of my two sons.

I've explained the concept about Twin Flames—one Essence, one Soul, which incarnates in two physical bodies. And there are also karmic partners, whose souls have met in their physical form, not in one life but many. Both good events and not good at all might have happened between them. They could have loved or hated each other. They could have made each other happy or miserable. They meet in many lives, pay old debts, teach each other new lessons, and learn the old ones. But there is one more concept. Soulmates. If Twin Flames are like one apple cut in half, Soulmates are apples from the same tree, the same branch. My future husband and father of my two sons was and is my Soulmate. I also call him the "Angel of my life."

One morning my group of tourists was gathering beside a large sightseeing bus, preparing for the usual tour around the city. One person from the group was a little late, so we were waiting for him to arrive and join us.

"Ah! There he is!" someone said.

I turned around. Lit by the gentle morning sun rays, he was walking towards me calmly yet quickly. Tall, broad-shouldered, with a smile that could melt an iceberg, he seemed to be an organic part of this very soft, beautiful May morning, like a breeze or the smell of fresh green leaves. The moment I saw him, I felt absolute *PEACE*. It seemed that absolutely nothing terrible could ever happen to me while he was by my side.

Many years have passed since that moment. Yet I still feel that same absolute, almost unearthly peace, whenever this man is near me.

Probably you can't call anybody those emotive words "Angel on Earth," but that's exactly what comes to my mind when I think about Joseph. He

118

has incredible grayish-blue eyes, very pure and entirely angelic. It seems he cannot be angry or hateful, nor can he hurt anyone. Our second son Nicholas inherited the same eyes.

Joseph was like life-giving, healing water on my still hurting wounds. Wounds that had healed on the surface but were still painful and hidden deep inside. Those wounds were still bleeding. I felt surprisingly warm and calm next to this man, like stillness after a sandstorm or a terrible hurricane. Like after wandering through a dark winter forest, I suddenly walked out to a small log cabin. A door opened for me and, without being asked any questions, I was wrapped in a woolen blanket, moved close to the blazing heat of the fireplace, and given a huge cup of delicious hot chocolate. There was no more need for me to wander through the forests, through the winds and blizzards, no need to freeze outside or get soaking wet under the heavy, cold rains. Now I would be warm and safe. No one else would ever hurt me. No one would even dare.

He did not demand anything from me; I didn't ask for anything. He simply loved me with the purest love. From the first moment he saw me, love was pouring from his eyes, even though he did not utter a single word about it.

He was staying in Odessa for only two weeks. We walked around the city for long hours. Several times we went to his favorite ballet, "The Nutcracker." Such theaters and performances were rare in America. Even when the Ballet Troupes did come to the United States with a concert tour, they performed in auditoriums which were nothing like the Regal European Theaters. Usually, they had a simple stage, only essential lighting, very few scenery sets, and the price of the tickets is outrageous. We had a very, very vague idea about American life back then. Joseph had an expression of pure delight on his face when he watched "The Nutcracker" or a "Swan Lake" in the majestic, grand Odessa Opera House.

I was surprised that he had never seen anything like this since I spent my entire childhood in this very theater. This luxurious, fabulous, magical theater of Opera and Ballet was a trademark of my hometown. We also went to the Philharmonic House to listen to classical music. We took long walks around different parks and museums. I was very impressed by his intelligence, but most of all, my heart was touched by how he treated me. He did it with endless and incredible tenderness and delicacy. As if I was a fragile glass statue, he was trying to do everything possible not to break me. He even looked at me like if I was an angel, a celestial being that had fallen accidentally from a cloud. He still looks at me the same way.

Joseph told me about his family. He told me about the countries he had seen during his service as an American marine officer. Since he was an engineer, responsible for the construction and maintenance of various military faculties, he never participated in any military operations. His incredible sense of humor has caused me to laugh more next to him, than at any other time in my life. He sensed, there had been something in my life that had broken me. Maybe not completely, but to a large extent.

I don't even know what exactly he saw in me, but two days before his departure home, he simply pulled a ring out of his pocket and put it on my finger. I had no idea when he bought it or how he guessed my ring size, but this is how it was. No, he did not ask me to marry him. He just put a ring on my finger and said, "I know that you're the one I have been hoping to find. I know that you are the only one for me, and besides you, there is not and cannot be anyone else. You can think for as long as you need. Just know that I will be waiting for you."

I decided to tell him everything. I felt it would be wrong to hide something from the person who treated me like no one else ever had in my whole life. I told him everything about my childhood and youth. I told him everything about my terrible and ridiculous marriage. I told him everything. I thought my story would somehow frighten him and push him away from me. I told him about my *weird* abilities. He listened attentively, without interrupting. I said that I could see what others do not see, or do not want to see, or are simply afraid of, about my visions and dreams, my *weirdness* and *strangeness*. I expected him to change his mind, to decide not to marry such an odd woman. But I was wrong. It did not scare him away. He loved me and accepted me the way I was. He just loved me, as they say, unconditionally.

120

Then I decided that I would give myself another year, just one year more. If I did not find HIM, Joseph would become my husband, and I would go to his country.

My heart and my soul wanted to find HIM and be with him! But the years were passing, and it never happened! What could I do? How much longer did I need to seek and wait for HIM? Did I need to continue like this for the rest of my life? For every minute, every second, for years and years to come?

After all, I was just a woman. I was tired of loneliness, pain, hard physical work, the uncertainty of the future of my poor country and my own. But my soul longed for something else.

I wanted to have children and a family. I never had a father, that someone strong, warm and kind, who would hug me and hide me in his arms from the difficulties and worries of the world and life, at least for several moments. My soul longed to heal. I just wanted to feel warmth, love, and peace.

Joseph had an aura of the soft, gentle spring sun. When he hugged me, it seemed that neither trouble, nor grief, nor sadness would ever come even close to me. I felt so warm and peaceful in his arms. Intuitively, I also understood that he had come into my life for a reason. A cold and painful thought was creeping into my heart. *What if I NEVER find HIM—the one from my dreams?*

I did not want to allow this thought to grow deep roots in my heart, but I could not completely dismiss it. Doubts started to grow in me, like wildflowers in the fields after heavy rain. *Who is he? Who is this man, whose eyes I have seen since my very childhood? If my destiny is to find him and be with him, why haven't I found him yet? Why hasn't he found me? Does he even exist? No, I know, I KNOW, that he is out there somewhere, but WHERE? How much longer do I have to wait for him, look for him, hope... Soon I will be 27 years old, I still haven't found him! But what if I never find him? What if I am doomed to be alone for the rest of my life?*

Oh, no, I wasn't scared by the thought of being completely alone. I always loved to be alone. When I was alone, I could be sure nobody would hurt me. Aloneness became my refuge, my freedom. I could dream, read my favorite books, speak with the stars or try to solve the mysteries of life, destiny, and the universe. But the thought that I might never be a MOTHER was truly unbearable.

I have wanted to be a mother as long as I have existed! It has always been a big part of me. And it was clear as day that my destiny would probably not give me another man like Joseph! Another one like him simply *did not exist*. Angels do not come to walk the earth very often.

But at the same time, I wanted to be true to myself. I did not want to repeat the mistake of my first marriage. So, I took one year to think and wait. I wanted to be sure I was doing the right thing, both for Joseph and for me.

Meanwhile, where was my Twin? The one I was looking for, the one for whom I was waiting?

Well, during all these events, my Farhan Ali was at the apogee of his glory and fame. Was he aware of my existence? Perhaps, somewhere deep inside, he knew, at his very core, in the depths of his ancestral memory, or on the verge of dreaming or on the bottom of his soul, he knew. On the brink of all worlds, somewhere on the edge of lives, on the edge of conscious and unconscious, I hoped he knew. Twin Flames share one soul; therefore, they are always invisibly together. But his physical, earthly life had hardly given him a chance the think about it.

The year passed. That winter, I flew to Florida and got married. After marrying me, my husband became even more gentle, caring, and patient. He catered to my every whim as if he could not believe I was finally his wife, I was there with him, and I was his.

As for me, I became a perfect wife. Since I did not have a work permit at the time, I enthusiastically played the role of a devoted, conscientious housewife and enjoyed it very much. My handsome husband had been a bachelor until the age of 38, and somehow, before me, he hadn't encountered a woman capable of cooking real food, not just warming something in the microwave. Seeing his shocked face when he would return home from work to find the table set for dinner and the house filled with the aroma of freshly baked bread gave me lots of joy.

It was a pleasure to see him happy. He loved and respected me very much. And it was mutual. I looked at him in the same way as he looked at me: as if he was an Angel and a Savior. After all the horrors I had experienced, it was difficult for me to believe that such men like him even existed. He gifted me with friendship, care, and a feeling of family, warmth, and safety. I was trying to give him the same.

You ask me if I loved him. Yes, I loved him. I still do. It was not a usual type of Love. In my opinion, it was something much better. I even think, this is the main reason why we have been able to keep the same feelings for each other for so many years, till this very day. I was, and I am infinitely grateful to him. I sincerely admire him, deeply respect him, praise and appreciate him. And, as I said, all this has been preserved between us up to this day. I saw him as a treasure, one I received as a gift for my challenging life. Can it be called Love? Is it Love? Yes. Absolutely. Soulmates are the other type of Love, as I understand it now. Joseph is my Soulmate. He had been chosen or had chosen to come into my life to be my support and protection. He became the one who healed my wounds. And most importantly: he was sent into my life to become the father of my sons.

Yes, this is Love! Love comes in many forms. Soulmate Love is definitely Love! I was and remain infinitely grateful to him for every moment that he loved and took care of me.

Just a month after our marriage, I found out I was pregnant. The pregnancy was difficult, but together we coped, and before the birth of my eldest son Arman, my mother came to help me. She came and ended up staying with us permanently.

Arman, my little mysterious Scorpio, was born with olive-toned skin (why olive, you will understand later), dark hair, and those powerful, typical for a Scorpio, dark eyes—lakes. He was amazingly gorgeous from the moment he was born.

Not even two months had passed since his birth, and I was pregnant again. My second son Nicholas was born. A platinum blond boy with gray eyes, just like his father. Such children, who are only about one year apart, are called "Irish Twins" here in America.

123

You can't imagine how different they were. But my boys were inseparable. It still makes me smile, remembering the times when I put them both into the twin stroller and went for a walk.

One is swarthy, dark eyes, wavy black hair, a little macho heartthrob! Always serious, he has a piercing gaze from underneath. And next to him, his brother, a white-skinned, gray-eyed platinum blond. The contrast was so striking that it was impossible not to smile at them. People often asked me the same questions:

"Are they brothers?"
"Of course, they are!" I answered.
"Oh! Do they have different fathers?"
"No, they have the same father."
"Ah. You adopted the light-haired one?"
"No, I gave birth to both of them."

It was easy to understand the amazement on their faces. Little Nicholas looked nothing like me. His appearance was opposite of mine and his brother. I could never even imagine having a platinum blond little boy with grey-blue eyes. But on the other hand, we share very similar characters and gifts. To my happiness and my sorrow (because I know exactly how difficult it can be at times), Nicky is an *indigo child*. I even have many reasons to suspect he is a Twin Flame. But only time will show if I am right. I think it is our family tradition to have at least one difficult, talented child or a couple of them. In this story, Nicholas will play a huge role. One of the critical roles, truth to be told. But we will get there later.

So, I had two sons. As a wife and a mother, my life was ordinary and somewhat peaceful. When Arman was three years old and Nicky was two, I started working, since living on just one salary was very difficult.

It seemed impossible for me to find a job based on my education. I would need to study for about two more years if I wanted to teach either philosophy or foreign languages.

My university diploma, evaluated as a bachelor's degree, was not enough for teaching. If I wanted to finish my studies, it was necessary to take tens of thousands of dollars in student loans. I never had the guts to do that. Our financial situation was such that instead of studying, I needed to look for at least some kind of work.

But that turned out to be a huge problem. No one wanted to hire a person with no work experience in this country. But I got lucky again. I remembered my old hobby, face transformation with the help of makeup. When I was a child, I had seen several times how makeup artists worked at the Odessa film studio, and since then, I have always been fascinated by this art. It amazes me how a little bit of makeup can transform a person within minutes.

I was pretty much a self-taught makeup artist from age 16-17. It gave me a little a bit of additional income and a lot of pleasure applying makeup for brides, graduates, and birthday girls. I had a talent for it. So, I managed to find work as a makeup artist in a huge cosmetic department in the Shopping Center, not far away from where we lived. I started to work there, and financially it helped my family a lot.

So, I think, I was a good wife and a mother. I worked, took care of the house, my family and my boys. *But...*

I never stopped looking for *HIS EYES*. I continued seeing them in my dreams from time to time. Whether they were sad, happy, laughing, or thoughtful, I knew every expression of them way too well. I knew his every eyelash. He has very peculiar eyelashes. Long, thick and straight, not curled up, like most people's. If he blinked or closed his eyes, they were almost resting on his cheeks. I knew I would recognize those eyes from a million! I would recognize them the very moment I saw them. But still, a long time would pass before that happened.

My moving to another country, my marriage, the birth of my beautiful sons, a completely new life for me—none of these events affected the *invisible thread* that connected me with *him*. Not in any way.

My everyday routine, as before, consisted of scanning people's faces searching for *him*. What a strange destiny! Weird even. Ridiculous in moments. Sad. Yet, at the same time, there is such beauty in it. At least, I think so.

Yes, there is some sad beauty in it. There is also something eternal in it. Enduring. Unfading. Maybe... *True Love?*

You may ask if I hoped that my beautiful husband and my incredible children, my work, and my life would somehow distract me from thinking about *him* and searching for *him*. Yes, I did hope they would. But unfortunately, that never happened. *HE* was living with me, existing in me, breathing when I was breathing. *HE* was a part of me. What could I do? Nothing.

Years passed. The feeling of guilt towards my marvelous husband grew stronger and stronger deep inside my very essence. I started to believe that he would have been much happier without me. With each passing year, I was more aware that I would never stop looking for *him*, and I would never stop waiting for *him*. So, I started to think that my husband deserved a better wife than me. He deserves his own True, Great Love!

He deserved to be with a woman who would deeply, passionately love him. I tried to talk to him about it, but he only smiled in response. I knew that, in many ways, I was completely incomprehensible to him. I was certain he needed a woman of his own culture. A woman who would love what he loved. American football and steak, hard rock and hamburgers, chicken wings, and American TV shows. We never fought, never argued. Also, there was something else. He was and has remained a handsome, healthy man. And he had a beloved lawful wife, Me. But the problem was that after the birth of my sons, I could no longer bring myself to fulfill the same notorious *marital duty.*

At first, I used the sleepless nights with children as an excuse, then fatigue, then just about anything. But, no matter what, he simply continued to treat me with the most incredible tenderness and perfectly understood that I did not want this. Or I couldn't. Or both. I didn't want to and couldn't at the same time.

Anyone in a similar situation would require at least some sort of explanation from his wife. But not Joseph. He never criticized me, never said a rude word. He believed he must not put any pressure on me, that if

I ever wanted intimacy with him, I would come to him myself. But time passed, and it never happened. He was sleeping in the bedroom, and I stayed on the sofa in the living room. It was crushing my heart with an endless burden of guilt more and more with every passing day.

We lived like a brother and a sister. We laughed, joked, took children to the parks, celebrated family holidays. We lived together. But we did not sleep together. Five years passed.

Finally, I decided that I should let him go, so he could have the opportunity to be truly happy. I told myself that *I DID NOT HAVE THE RIGHT* to keep him by my side! I was sure, somewhere there was his true Love, a wonderful woman, who would become his real wife. Loving, easily understandable and understanding. Simple, passionate and humble, without all my *weirdness*. She would be for him something I could never be, even if I tried my best.

In 2008, I asked him for a divorce. Just like before, he agreed to it because it was what I wanted. He always did what I asked for or wanted. We had a very unusual divorce, compared to most people. It was quiet and peaceful, and oddly enough, our relationship did *NOT* change at all. Our children did not know that we had been divorced for ten years. Even before the divorce, we repeatedly had conversations that children would soon go to school, and Miami was not the best place for it.

We decided that the best thing would be to move to the north part of Florida, where schools were much better. We found a small town four hours away from Miami, where primary schools were among the best twenty in the country. Right after the divorce, I moved there with the kids. Joseph stayed in Miami. We told our children that a move was necessary so they could go to a good school, and dad had to stay, because his job was in Miami, which was true. Joseph was a construction engineer of Miami-Dade County. We also told them that dad would come to visit us regularly. And he did. Joseph began to come to us every two weeks.

After the divorce, I experienced all the consequences of my newly acquired status as a divorced woman and a single mother. I had to face unequal pay for labor, unemployment, lack of money, fear of tomorrow, and all the usual things of newly found *freedom*.

The schools were great, but there was practically no work. When finally, after months and months of searching, I was able to find employment; the pay was almost half of what I used to make in Miami. I wish I knew or could understand why I chose poverty, insecurity, and difficulties, again and again. I choose it over a stable and somewhat calm lifestyle, only because something felt *not right* in the depth of my soul.

More than once, I have tried to understand the reasons why my life, or my fate, or my guardian Angels, have always given me those two paths to choose from: the first one has tons of obstacles, traps, concrete walls and ditches, filled with muddy water; the second path is an easy and peaceful one. Over and over, I tend to choose ditches and walls, bumps and potholes, hard money, loneliness, and isolation from people. Somehow, I always choose the impossible and challenging quest for myself, one I am trying to solve with little chance of success, but still, I have kept doing it my whole life.

Now, back to my newfound life as a single mother. Unfortunately, in the beginning, I couldn't find any job whatsoever. It lasted for very long eight months. Then miraculously, I managed to get a cashier job at the supermarket. Of course, it was not my dream job. But I simply had no other choice. The work was tiresome, demanding, and very poorly paid. But still, it was a job. There was no time to complain, plus there was no sense in it. I just did what I had to do. I had no right to throw in the towel and give up. I had two children and my mother, who came to live with us after all her difficult years of struggle. I had to take good care of all of them. Perhaps it was another turn of my destiny, another one of the many tests. It was my duty at that moment: facing all those additional difficulties and obstacles and proudly overcoming them, feeling right, strong and pleased of myself. But to be honest, all I felt after my long working hours, was sheer exhaustion.

At the same time, I began seeing *him* in my dreams much more often than before. Sometimes he would come every night. I saw it as a good sign. *Can it be that he is somewhere near me? Or perhaps it meant that in some near and foreseeable future, I would find HIM? Or will he find me? Maybe I should do something for this to happen? But what?*

For some reason, I decided that if I wanted to find *him*, I had to do something to DESERVE *him*. I would have to struggle, beg, pray and work hard. Later, I tried to analyze why, while knowing that my other half was living somewhere, I did not wait for him as *his equal*. Why was I so sure *I HAD TO* deserve him first? Why didn't I rely on and trust in my fate? Why didn't I ever address him mentally and ask him to come to me and find me? Why did I consider myself inadequate and unworthy and constantly seek to improve myself? Make myself better. Worthy of affection. Worthy of love.

Well, the answer is simple. I suppose, in the body of a grown-up woman, I was still that little girl, lonely, laughed at by everyone, and hurt by the whole world. She knew and was sure that nothing good would just come to her without reason in this life. She must *deserve it*, fight for it, and work extremely hard for it. That girl was sure she must *earn happiness*. She must *deserve* love and affection. There is no other way. And if someone just gave her something, that little girl would try to find excuses not to take it. She was sure, she *had to* earn everything, even if it was hers from the very start. Was I trying to bribe my fate? Like bribing my brother in my childhood with a sweet bun, bought with breakfast money, so he would not torture me? Probably, yes.

I became a vegetarian and then a vegan. I didn't date any men, and I couldn't even think about them. My life consisted of two parts—work and home: home and work. I had not been anywhere since the first day I arrived in Florida in 2001. I patiently searched and waited for *him* while monotonous rows of days, weeks, months, and years passed me by. Still, I had no idea where he was and who he was until the tragic year of 2014.

Chapter 18

Fate

2014 was a year of terrible losses.

Actually, my troubles began even earlier. At the end of 2013, I almost lost my mother. But she survived. Hercules himself would envy her strength and thirst for life.

When she was in the hospital, I asked the doctor to write a letter to the United States Embassy, so that my brothers would be allowed to see her. She was in serious condition, and the doctors did not give me much hope. And then a miracle happened. My brothers were granted visas to the US, and not only them, but also my elder brother's wife, Natasha.

I had known Natasha since I was five. She was an incredible, marvelous person, without whom I could hardly imagine my life. More than six years had passed since I had seen her and my brothers. It was hard to believe I would see them all very soon! Only a month passed since we applied for their visas, and now they were coming! Natasha, my two brothers, and my uncle Anatoly (my mother's brother). Their arrival created a true miracle. Our mother began to recover by leaps and bounds to the doctors' surprise. A week later, she was at home surrounded by her family.

That New Year's Eve was one of the happiest events of my life. The whole family gathered at our big dinner table. Although we all regularly talked via Skype, we had not seen each other for six long years. The chiming clock on "NTV America" announced the New Year's arrival. 2014! The kids clinked their glasses of non-alcoholic champagne with us and screamed, "Happy

New Year!" We hugged. We laughed. We drank champagne and made bright plans for the future.

My eldest brother dreamed about driving a semi-truck through the whole of the United States! Natasha said that she would accompany him everywhere. They would see Niagara Falls, the Red Cliffs of Arizona and many other famous places. Alexei, my second brother, was planning to live in San Diego, where an old friend of his had been living for many years. He imagined opening his own art gallery. We all were absolutely sure he would succeed and that his paintings would be known worldwide. We told him that exhibition curators from all over the States would soon fight with each other for his masterpieces. He was a true genius, and we had no doubts about him.

And me, of course, I was dreaming of finding *him*, as always. Destiny would finally make this dream come true in the terrible year of 2014. But, sadly enough, I had no idea how it would be. Nobody, *NOT* a single one of us, could even imagine that this would be the last time we all gathered together like this, the very last time.

A month later, they all were going back home to Odessa. The night before their departure, l told Natasha my *terrible* secret. The story of *His eyes*.

We talked for a very long time, almost until dawn. In the morning, I took them to Orlando International Airport. Before entering the gates, she suddenly turned around and gave me one more strong hug.

"You are going to find him! It will happen very, very soon! I do not just feel it! *I know it for sure!*" she said. She smiled and walked away. She walked away into Eternity.

Did she really know that I would find him in just a few months? Did she tell me that because she was already standing on the edge of two worlds? Those, standing on the border between the worlds, know the truth, as many things open up for them. Did she know? Did she really feel that I would find *him* very soon, or did she say this to comfort me? I don't know. And I will never know. But her words were meant to come true very soon, and once again, turn my life upside down, bringing me the most challenging quest in my entire life, and perhaps of many lives. *Him!*

A few days after they returned home to Odessa, Natasha was gone from this Earth. She was gone and left a huge empty void in my heart. She was gone. Unexpectedly. Suddenly. She was a vast, tremendously vital part of my life, almost since I could remember. When we met, I was about five, and she was only 17. I remember meeting her as though it was yesterday. My eldest brother wanted to show her to me. He brought me to her house and knocked on the window. She came out. I remember her smiling face. She leaned over to me and said, "My name is Natasha! Can I be your friend?" And she became my friend for the next 30 years.

She was an incredible person. Full of warmth, compassion, love, and light, like sunshine! Everyone felt at ease with her. Everyone would come to her with all their pains, troubles, problems, or just for a cup of tea, a warm word and a hug. After seeing her, their pain was not as bad anymore. Problems and troubles seemed solvable. It was easier to breathe, easier to keep on going through all that life put our way.

It did not matter what she was going through in her life. She knew how to enjoy impossibly simple things:

A cup of her favorite tea.
A bouquet of wild lilacs.
A flower in bloom.
The first snow.
Her favorite film.
The rain.
An interesting book.

Almost anything would bring that warm smile to her face!

I used to visit her house every chance I had. Sometimes I would drop by, "just for a minute," and several hours later, I still was sitting with her, chatting away! I would give a lot to return to those teapot talks in her tiny kitchen where I could talk my heart out. Those were moments that one could not buy for all the riches of the world. Moments that would remain with me for all my life, warming me with memories, not allowing me to give up, not letting me break down.

She was gone! It was impossible even to believe. And that was only the very beginning of that terrible year.

Her passing knocked my brother Alexei down. It was a more terrible blow for him than even for her husband, my eldest brother. Like me, Natasha was a breath of fresh air in his life. Their lives were always closely intertwined. And then suddenly, she was gone.

A month after her death, Alexei fell very ill. He was diagnosed with cancer. Though he fought fiercely, he lost the battle. Or maybe his time on Earth was just over. He had accomplished everything he had come to do. Was it just his time to leave? Probably so. He was gone only a few months after Natasha.

He left this life as a beloved and respected artist. He was loved and admired. His works are now in private collections, in countries all over the world. He had managed to do a lot in his life and managed to leave a lot for the world. But, just like Natasha, his leaving created another hole in my Soul that nothing could fill. Have I forgiven him for my childhood? Yes, I did. A long time ago. When you genuinely love, you can forgive almost everything.

That year was far from being done with its mortal harvest.

A few months later, my uncle suddenly died of a heart attack, the one who came with my brothers to see my mother. A month after him, my mother's only sister, my aunt, died.

Everything! Everything just turned into a blurry black speck in some dark fog. At times, I could no longer understand if things were happening in reality or some muggy, pitch dark, hopeless, terrible, endless nightmare. A nightmare so long that I could no longer understand, what was real and what was not. I was living in a state of quiet horror, almost entirely losing hope of that nightmare ever ending.

In those dark moments, I still drew my strength from *him*. Just as I did in my childhood, just as I did and my youth. Just as always when it seemed all hope had vanished, memories of those eyes helped me keep going. The endless gray days passed by before me, turning into endless dark nights, and the nights again into the days like an infinite string of beads, a heavy rosary—black, gray, black, gray. There were no white ones.

There were moments when I felt as if I had fallen into the gap between the worlds. I did not understand who I was, where I was anymore, what was happening around me. Questions with no answers appeared and disappeared in my head like a fog: What am I doing on this Earth? Why do I breathe? Why do I exist?

One sleepless night I was attempting to read, but the words were all blurry. I closed the book I wrote this on the back:

"Many days, many years, many winters, many springs, and summers... I keep walking and walking this Earth. Every breath without you hurts me like fire. The air burns my lungs like burning wormwood. Why am I without you? Why did Force separate us? Why? Why are we apart? How can you separate the sky from the ocean? How can you separate the wind from the sky? How? Why would anyone or anything do that? What is the point of this all? How empty I feel without you! How lost and lonely I feel without you. Many winters, many years, many springs, I wander the Earth without you. Why am I without you? Why am I without you? Why?"

Then, one night in December, Destiny came to fulfill its purpose once again.

That night I felt *I had reached my limit.* No strength. No power remained in me. I thought I would not be able to handle anything else. Nothing else at all. I could not even imagine I was about to face the toughest test of my entire life. The test, I was born for and had come to this Earth to endure.

It was a warm Florida night in December of 2014. After wishing my boys good night, I went outside for a walk. I was trying to find some strength in the warm air and the stars shining above me, just as I had in my childhood. After walking for several hours in a small, deserted park, I lay down on the grass and looked up at the starry sky. Suddenly, a storm of pain and despair rose in me with the fury of a tornado! It was pressing my chest. Tears burned my eyes. A wave of rage washed over me! Like a massive tsunami, it covered me without any chance to escape or hide.

There was no more strength left in me. Only pain remained! *Only pain!* It burned out all I had in me! I needed to find some way out of the darkness. I had to! My Soul was sinking deeper and deeper with every passing moment. Looking up into the sky, I suddenly began to repeat the same words over and over again. Over and over again! Like a chant. No, I didn't pray! I did not ask! I *WAS SICK AND TIRED* of praying and asking, begging, pleading! I screamed! Or was it my Soul screaming? My heart screaming?! Because it was only a loud whisper, which left my lips:

"WHEREVER HE IS! WHOEVER HE IS! I WANT TO SEE HIS FACE! DO YOU HEAR ME??? I WANT TO SEE HIS FACE!!! WHEREVER HE IS! WHOEVER HE IS!
"I NEED TO KNOW HE EXISTS! I HAVE THE RIGHT TO KNOW! SHOW HIM TO ME! CAN YOU HEAR ME? SHOW HIM TO ME!!! SHOW ME!!!!"

I repeated those words, like a mantra, like a spell, like a prayer, again, again and again. Tears, freaking tears. Damn them! They just kept pouring from my eyes. I hated them! I hated to be weak! And I always saw tears as a weakness. This is why I hardly ever cried! But at that moment, I could not help it! I kept saying those words. I have no idea how long it lasted.

At some point, during my desperate speech to Heavens, my phone vibrated in my pocket, bringing me back to reality. I saw a familiar number on my phone display, stopped my flow of requests to the Heavens, and answered the call.

It was a good friend. He was a fantastic saxophonist, and his wife was a chef. At that time, they were renting a small restaurant in a hotel. They held banquets and organized various celebrations for different groups of people: anniversaries, birthday parties, weddings, etc. His wife cooked diverse dishes while their two children served food to guests, and he provided musical entertainment. During these events, I worked as a singer.

"Alla," said a familiar voice, "at the end of this week, we are going to have a banquet, a wedding anniversary, to be exact. I need you to please prepare a song called '*In Your Eyes!*' Remember, I told you about it a couple of weeks ago?"

"Of course," I replied. "I heard it! It's a wonderful song, perfect for a wedding anniversary! I will learn it within an hour. Do not worry! I will be ready to sing it by tomorrow."

We said our goodbyes. I got up from the grass and started walking home. While walking, I again looked up at the starry sky and repeated, "*Wherever HE is, whoever HE is, show me HIS FACE! I want to know! I must know! I have the right to know! Show me!*"

When I reached home, it was already quite late. I kissed my sleeping boys and went to my room, locking the door behind me. The house was sleeping. I sat in front of my monitor and quickly found the song's lyrics. I printed out the text. Now I just needed to listen to the music several times, and I would be ready to perform it.

I opened YouTube, typed the name of the song I needed in the search engine, and clicked on the first video that popped up. I began to listen to the music as I read the lyrics without even looking at the monitor. But at some point, I looked up at the screen...

Gods! Keepers! Heavens! Great Forces of Light!

It is difficult, if not *impossible*, to even describe in words what happened the very next moment.

THE WHOLE WORLD. STOPPED.
EVERYTHING. JUST. STOPPED.

Time. Space. Cosmos. Planets. They all stopped their perpetual movement. Nothing can convince me otherwise. I felt it. I knew it! The Universe itself froze for a brief moment. I do not remember either the sensation of my body or even the sense of my very existence.

HIS EYES were looking at me from the computer screen. His eyes, the very eyes I had been looking for every breathing moment of my strange, sad life! The eyes, imprinted into my very essence. The eyes, I knew from my very childhood!

Since childhood? Or had I known them for *ETERNITY*?
I was looking into his eyes!
It wasn't a dream!
It wasn't a vision!

I was looking into his eyes in this three-dimensional reality! Our familiar reality!

I did not know who he was at the moment, but I soon found out. Someone had created the music video using the fragments of his movies. In the description below the video, I read his name, *FARHAN ALI.*

I could hardly believe I'd never heard of him! How was that even possible?! The Higher Forces kept him hidden from me until this very moment. Soon I was reading everything I could find about Farhan Ali.

Every single word of his biography felt like a red-hot blade, cutting deep into my chest, paralyzing me, and preventing me from even breathing. "Phenomenon. Millions of fans. Dozens of prestigious awards. Dozens of films." The articles seemed endless! But, somehow, it was the word *"married"* that stabbed my heart the deepest.

He was a *Hollywood MEGASTAR*! It would be much easier for me to jump and touch the Moon than to reach out to someone like him! But for some reason, that didn't phase me. It was the fact that he was married that sent my world spinning. *MARRIED!* Seriously?!?! Suddenly, all I could see and feel was cold, pitch-black darkness.

A few minutes later, I was sobbing and laughing at the same time— laughing and sobbing! Thank Heavens, it was the dead of night, and no one was around to see this display of wild, relentless emotions!

Oh, I see! So, *THAT* is the one I've been looking and waiting for my whole damn life? That is the One, who I lived and breathed for!? *THAT* is the

ONE!? The one whose eyes helped me rise from hell, who gave me strength to live, to keep on going, to keep on fighting, to keep on believing! *A MOVIE STAR!?* Not just a movie star, a *MARRIED MEGASTAR*, Goddamn it!?

I did not know and could not know back then that his marriage existed only for the public. While Farhan and his breathtakingly beautiful wife Cynthia regularly appeared before the cameras and journalists as a loving couple, by the time I found him, they were married in name only. Their marriage existed for the sake of both their reputations and the family business. But I had no idea! Even if I had known, would it have changed anything for me? I do not thing so. He still was a *Megastar.*

Gods and Keepers of Karma! How can this be true?! How??? Are you kidding me?! It all felt like the absurd, cruel, horrible *joke* of some Gods, Guardians, Higher Forces, or whoever else is there!

Noo! It just CAN'T be true!!! IT CANNOT BE TRUE!!! It cannot be Him! Those cannot really be HIS eyes—the eyes forever imprinted in the very essence of my very soul! I wasn't looking for THAT man! It simply CANNOT be! It cannot be Farhan Ali! It cannot be this Mega Movie Star! It's Not HIM! Not HIM!!! Oh, please, Gods! Let it NOT be HIM!

My ridiculous, desperate attempts to persuade myself it was not him were of no use—completely pointless! I knew it WAS him. Every cell of my existence KNEW, He was the one I was looking for and waiting to find!

HIS EYES, which are so similar to my own, I would recognize *anywhere,* among billions of people, no matter how many millions of years passed. *No matter what dimension, beyond time and space, I would always recognize his eyes!* And I did. I did! So, now what? Now... Nothing! Absolutely Nothing!

Before dawn, I wandered out into the night air. The grass glistened as moonbeams danced in the dewdrops. I lay down and melted into the wet lawn as my world collapsed. All my stupid dreams and foolish hopes, everything that had given me strength to live, to keep holding on, to keep fighting—everything crumbled into a million pieces. He was a movie star. A. Movie. Star. He was as far from me as those stars sparkling in the sky, maybe even farther. My whole life seemed like a bad joke, a pathetic lousy joke.

Why do you torture me like this? What have I done? What is my crime? What is my fault? Am I guilty of something? Tell me! Answer me! What am I supposed to do now? What can I do? Nothing. There is NOTHING I can do! Nothing at all! So why all of this? Why? What for? This is the end! The end of everything! The End.

They say a person can live for many days without food, several days without water, a hundred or so seconds without air. But how long can one hold on without hope? And, what if that hope was the meaning of one's entire life? My hopes shattered. My dreams were destroyed. Done. Finished. Over.

What is the sense of living when there's nothing left to dream about? Try to find another dream, a different hope, a new meaning, so I could watch that one collapse as well? No, thank you! I was too broken, too exhausted, and too shattered. Inhaling and exhaling were all I could do, and even that seemed challenging at the moment.

What I did not know was, it was not the end.

That was just the beginning.

Or to be exact, a Continuation.

Because *NOTHING EVER ENDS.*

Everything only continues.

Everything!

Chapter 19

The Eyes of My Soul

I did not know that Karma and Destiny had completely different plans for me. I have a different *mission* if we can say so. Somehow, I had to *awaken* the Soul of my Twin Flame. To be exact, to *awaken his half* of our Soul. This quest was mine, given to me, a simple, ordinary woman, not possessing any power, wealth or extraordinary beauty. From society's perspective, I was just a middle-aged single mother who had no success, no special talents, no fame, not even a remotely decent job. Somehow, it had to be me. Me! No exception.

I would have to go through 777 levels of hell so that magnificent, bright, incredible, deep, and complicated man and megastar would not only know who I was but remember me. And not only remember me but believe me! I had to make him believe me with all his bottomless and complex Soul, to be exact, *his half of it!* Why? Because even though a very ordinary woman, I am, in some *UNTHINKABLE* and *INCOMPREHENSIBLE* way, the Twin Flame of this mega star man. A man who illuminates this world as brightly as the Sun in the sky. Only the Twin Flame can awaken the other part of the same Flame.

But I did not know any of this the night I finally found him. The only thing I understood was that the one I had been waiting for and looking for all my entire life, was way beyond my reach, and it always would be that way. That meant only one thing: everything had just collapsed. Both inside and outside of me! I had no hope. How could I have any hope? The pain of realizing it was unbearable. Possibly, you have experienced this at times in your life. Times when your Soul hurts so much that you start feeling this pain physically. I had a strange and terrible feeling as if I had a gaping hole in my chest. A void. A hollow. I found myself in a state too challenging to describe. It felt as if my heart had been cut out with a blunt knife and carried somewhere very far away. But somehow, I managed to survive. Somehow, I still could breathe, walk and talk. But that space, where I used to have my heart, now had a vast, gaping bleeding wound!

The worst problem is that it is absolutely impossible to get distracted from the pain, alleviate it, or forget about it, because there is no physical cause. My very Soul is crying and moaning and longing to connect with its other half! With Him! But He is way beyond the reach! And there is only one way out. One way out. I had to learn *to live with it*. But how? How?

I already said, I knew absolutely nothing about Twin Flames back then! At first, this information was simply hidden from me. I thought, probably the reason I was looking for him and waiting for him, was that I had loved him throughout many of my lives, or maybe even all of them. We incarnate hundreds, thousands of times. Many of us remember the pieces of one or several of those lives. Many do not remember anything. But He had always been a part of me, since my very childhood, and that meant I might have loved him many, many lifetimes. I thought this was the reason.

But what was the point of even thinking about it, after I found out *who he was*? It did not matter who and what we were to each other in the past. In this life, in this current physical incarnation, I was what I was, a simple woman; and he was what he was, *a movie star*. The Moon was much closer to me than him.

I was not going to do anything.

I couldn't even imagine WHAT one could do in such a case? Obviously, *nothing*.

I wasn't familiar with tears since I did not know how to cry until I was about three years old, which left all my mother's friends speechless, while the doctors were scratching their heads, "So what, she doesn't cry? It is good, isn't it? When she outgrows it, she'll learn how to do it, don't you worry." And I rarely cried, even in the bitterest moments of my life.

I did learn to cry. Doctors were right, even though, as an adult, it happened very rarely. I was used to keeping it all hidden deep inside. But after I finally saw him and knew who he was, it seemed someone had opened the floodgates in my eyes, as salty water flowed and flowed from them in an endless stream. I also started losing weight. Rapidly. I was melting like a Snow Maiden in the springtime, or like a bewitched wax figure on a hot summer day.

Amidst this cascade of emotions flooding my soul, I had to continue working and, of course, take care of my boys, be submerged into their lives, solve their problems, answer their questions, do the housework. I had to try to be a good mom, a good daughter, not a crazy one. Just normal one. Just ordinary one. Just average one. I would tell everyone that I had allergies to justify my endless tears. No one was surprised. In Florida, allergies are widespread.

I lived my everyday life like that mechanical doll I had seen in an old puppet show when I was a child. Her name was Tsarevna Nesmeyana, and she was a princess from an Old Russian fairy tale. She could not do anything but cry. She had streams of water, constantly flowing from both her eyes. I reminded myself of that doll. But unlike that rag doll, I had actual tears flowing in streams from my eyes. An old doll that somebody had forgotten in a dusty attic, who's winding doesn't end, so she's crying all the time and shaking her head. She does not want anything and is unhappy about everything. She is hiding her constant, never-ending pain and heaviness in the chest area, which worsens day after day.

I could neither take a deep breath in nor could I breathe out completely. I could not force myself to eat. I stopped sleeping. None of the tricks and recommendations to fall asleep I found online or in the books worked for me. And the worst thing was, I couldn't even tell a soul about it. It was absolutely unthinkable! An absurdity! Because in our traditional, three-dimensional reality, it looked like I was dying of love towards a movie star! *What nonsense!*

What impossible, indescribable nonsense! Me, an adult, a competent, vastly educated woman, one who had devoured thousands of books on psychology, philosophy, theology, archeology, anthropology. Me, in love with a film actor? Ludicrous!

I'm a hopeless bookworm, not a stupid teenage girl who suddenly has a crush on a celebrity! I am a grown-up, capable woman. I am a sister. I am a daughter. I am a mother.

Who could I tell about it? Gods! If somebody told me I would be pining for a movie star a month ago, I would have burst out laughing! Nobody would even think of telling me such pure idiocy! I never had crushes on celebrities, even when I was a teenager. I could never even understand such a thing. And now, look at me! Here I am! Ridiculous! What Madness!

Unfortunately, who he was and who I was in this three-dimensional world of ours, meant absolutely nothing to my Soul. My Soul did not give a damn about any of that! She was crying for him. She was screaming silently: *He is my Home, my Home!* My Soul yearned for Him. My Soul longed for Him, and she refused to listen to my reasoning. It constantly felt like my very Soul was trying to tear herself away from my body and fly to him. Fly to him. Fly to him.

What was I supposed to do with all of that? I did not know the answer to that question. Another extraordinary and inexplicable thing happened when I looked at his face. I didn't even know how, but knowledge about him, about his whole life, filled me up the same way that water fills a vessel. I knew everything about him, as if I had lived his life myself.

I wanted to have his photo, so I printed one of them from the Internet. It was this tiny picture, the size of half of my palm. I put it inside a book about ancient civilizations, one of those I kept in my car. As you already know, I am obsessed with books. I have them almost everywhere. After work, I drove to a deserted parking lot. I sat there in my car for about an hour just looking at his face, looking into his eyes. The very eyes I had been searching for and finally found. This was NOT how I imagined finding them. But what was the point of thinking of that? It was what it was. I could do nothing about that.

How would I explain what I felt looking at him? Imagine looking into the eyes of someone you logically and rationally know, he is a stranger, but in the depth of his eyes, *YOU SEE YOUR OWN SOUL*. You are *LOOKING INTO THE EYES OF YOUR VERY OWN SOUL*. It may sound strange, weird, bizarre, or ridiculous, but this is what it was. I felt it with every single particle of my very existence. I was able to do nothing about that.

Can you imagine this? Maybe some of you have experienced looking into the eyes of a stranger and knowing, intuitively *KNOWING*, this *stranger* is your *lost home*. He is your *HOME*. He is your peace, your strength, your wings you lost centuries ago! But He is far away! Very far away! And he does not have the slightest idea that you even exist in this world! Oh! What an unbearable pain to know that, to understand that, to realize that. And to know there was no hope. No hope at all.

I have always had that habit of talking to someone who hears me, but I don't see them with my eyes. I only can *FEEL* them. Somehow, I was born with it. For as long as I could remember, my invisible companions have been with me, the ones who know, the ones who observe, watch and maybe sometimes protect and guide me. I did not know what to call them, but I talked to them since I was a child.

"What should I do?" I was constantly asking them. *"What should I do? I cannot live without him! Can't! Do you hear me? I can't! I cannot even breathe without him! It hurts too much. It feels like I am trying to breathe in burning hot desert air in the middle of a sandstorm. How more severely painful can it be, when even just breathing hurts? Is this how my breathing without him is going to feel for the rest of my days?"* But *I MUST* be without him. And there is nothing I can do about it. Nothing!

I was weeping, sobbing and crying like a teenage girl. I hated myself for that and cursed myself uphill and down dale but I couldn't help it! Try to fight the hurricane or tsunami. I did try to fight it without much success. So, a week passed like this and after that another one.

Suddenly, a thought appeared in my mind, *A MOTHER! His Mother. I will talk to his mother!*

I knew, in some inexplicable way, that his mother, whom he loved deeply, had left this Earth years and years ago. No, I hadn't read about it; somehow, I just knew.

I decided that no matter what World, Dimension, or Level of Heavens she existed in, she would hear me! I knew and felt she was a Soul of a very high level and did not have to incarnate as often. I knew, she was not living among the people in her physical form. I felt, she was still in the realms of the Spirits! So, I decided to call for her and talk to her. She could try to answer me in a dream or deep meditation or a vision. I was sure she would find a way if she had something to tell me.

I would simply ask her to free me from this. Whatever it was! From this karma. From this love. From this quest. From this curse. I would ask her to save me from this punishment. It certainly felt like one. For some reason, I was sure that she could do it, that it was within her power. If anybody could do it, then that would be only her. So, I decided to wait for the night to come when everyone in the house was sleeping. But before that, I had to pick up my younger Nicholas from school and do a million other things.

A short side note along the way:

Since my boys were little, I would tell them myths and legends of different nations instead of fairy tales. I always saw those ancient myths as the most profound wisdom, passed on to us by our Ancestors.

I never perceived those legends as fiction or fantasy. I totally and fully believe that myths, epic ballads, legends, and tales were how the Sages of Ancient times conveyed to us the Secret Wisdom and the True Knowledge. They knew, the Dark would take over our planet for thousands of years. They will try to destroy anything that could prevent us from forgetting who we are and our true origin. So, the Sages of Ancient times created a way to convey the truth to us, by leaving it in the ancient legends. I had told my sons those stories since they were very little. One of those stories was the myth about *the halves.*

It says that once, a long time ago, powerful Beings lived on Gaia Earth who consisted of two halves, but were One Whole. Such Beings would not need rulers or authorities! They did not need anyone to tell them what they must or must not do for they already knew everything. They could tell good from evil, truth from falsehood, right from wrong. Such beings did not need Gods as they carried the sacred truth and knowledge within themselves.

Zeus did not like it at all. So, he divided this being into two and separated them!

Since then, they incarnate in two different bodies and each half is looking for the other. They cannot find any peace, no matter what they do or where they are, until they are together with the other half of themselves. Since that time, people have been looking for their *missing half* sometimes for many, many years, so they finally can feel *Home*.

My children were very familiar with this story.

So, I drove to the school and picked up my son, Nicky. We were quietly going home, as usual, when suddenly...

I see in the rearview mirror that my son was holding *HIS* photo and looking at him very closely. I could feel my insides freezing with fear. My children had never seen me with any other men or heard me even mention other men. They only saw and connected me with their father! And suddenly this! I am frantically trying to figure out what I should tell him. I had to think of something! Fast!

Then, I hear the calm voice of my child, "Mooom, is this someone from our family? I have never seen him before. *HE LOOKS LIKE YOU! HE HAS YOUR EYES.* Mooom! Who is this?"

"Uh, *my eyes?* Nooo, son! He is not from our family! This man. He is a Star, you know? A Celebrity!"

I am trying my best to *play an idiot,* as I call it.

"Well son, we women sometimes fall for all kinds of singers, movie stars, and other famous personalities. It's called, *having a crush.* All girls sometimes have a crush on someone, even grownup women sometimes do. It happens from time to time. It's kind of, how to say it, *a girlish thing.* Do

146

not pay attention. This means nothing. You see, most of the fans of all kinds of celebrities are women. We like bright, extraordinary, inspiring people. So, we are sometimes into celebrities and their work. Nothing surprising in that. It's just an ordinary thing."

Holy Heavens! What a fool I am being! As if I don't know that I can hardly outwit my *all-seeing* son. He sees right through me, just like any other person! But I had to try to save the situation somehow. I *COULD NOT* tell him the truth!

While I am brainstorming, searching to find excuses for this photo, my Nicky is silently continuing to look intently at the picture of Farhan.

"Mom!" he finally says, "You have never had any *crushes* on any of the Stars before! And I have never seen you have a photo like this one! *WHO IS THIS MAN*, moom? Why does he have *YOUR EYES*?"

"Son! Ok, listen to me! He, uh, well, he is just a famous man, a film actor! I like him, all right? I saw one of his movies, and I liked him. I printed out his photo because I think he is beautiful and incredibly talented. It doesn't mean anything at all! Just put it back inside the book and forget about it!"

Suddenly, he yells! "Mooom!!!!! *YOU FOUND HIM!!!! YOU FOUND HIM! YOU DID!!!*" His grayish-blue eyes open wide as saucers!

On hearing that, I almost fainted! I gripped the steering wheel so tightly, my knuckles practically turned white! My kid kept surprising me with his clairvoyance almost since he was in his cradle. There was *NO WAY* he could know I had been looking for someone.

"Found whom, darling?" I tried, desperately tried my best to keep my voice as calm as possible, but my heart was threatening to break through my ribs and jump out of my chest.

"Well ... How was it? You know! You told us that story about Zeus dividing them! He was afraid that *THOSE* could be too powerful together and would not need Gods, so he divided, separated them!"

"The legend of two halves? You are talking about *my other half*?"

"*YES!!!* Yes! *Your other half!!!* You found him!!!! Woooow! This is cool!"

I gathered all my willpower together and tried to speak kindly and calmly. "Son, that is just a myth, a beautiful Legend. And although such

I JUST WANT YOU TO REMEMBER...

things could happen, of course it would be *EXTREMELY* rare. This man is a Star. I'm not his other half. It is just not possible! By the way, he has a wife! He loves her. He has children. He is *VERY FAMOUS!* I can't be his half! It's insane even to think that! Ridiculous! Son, let's just leave this subject and forget all about it."

"But you *ARE* his half, Mooom! You have to tell him about it! You found him, and now *HE* must find you too! *He must know!* He is living out there, searching for you too, and does not even know where you are. He..." and suddenly, he falls silent, looking intently at the photo again.

"He is *VERY* unhappy, Moom! He has a lot of pain here," he says, pointing to his chest area. "*JUST LIKE YOU.* And he doesn't show it to anyone. He never does! You don't show it to anyone either. But I know, you have that ache right there! You must tell him! Tell him you're his half! And the pain will go away in both of you!"

"My sunshine, my amazing magical child! I can't tell him anything. Even if I wanted to, I just can't! He is *VERY* far away and *very famous!* I can't say *anything* at all to him. He is completely out of my reach! Me, his half? It is simply impossible! Forget it all, son! Please! And then, what about your papa?" I decided to mention his father to distract him from thoughts about the man in the photo.

"Papa is a different story! You love him too, very much, I know! But papa is not your half! This one is! You have to tell him!"

"My dear son! Let us, please, end this conversation about this movie star!! I can't say anything to *HIM*! And I will not! He is out of my reach! Do you understand?"

For a moment, my child fell silent. He was thinking.

"So, Mom! He is a famous guy, you say, right? A star, isn't he? Well, that means he has Facebook! Twitter! All those Stars do! Do you have a Facebook, Mom?"

"No, I don't. Never even thought about it."

"Then, create a Facebook page for yourself! I know how to do it! I will help you! And then, you will find his Facebook page and write to him, and he will read it, and he will understand everything!!! He will *KNOW*! You must

148

help him find you too! So two halves can find each other! *You have to write to him!*"

"Nicholas!" I was starting to lose my patience! "Listen to me! I will not do any of that Facebook/Twitter stuff! I am not interested in that kind of thing! And I will not look for him there or write to him. Give me a break! That is complete nonsense! He must receive millions of messages from his fans from all over the World! Do I look like a woman, crazy enough, to send letters to a movie star? What am I, a little girl? Total gibberish! I won't do anything of that kind! Forget it, son!"

I felt like a thief caught red-handed. I was getting angry with myself, which wasn't new for me. I was getting upset with my magical son, with my life, with the Gods and the Keepers, who had played such a cruel joke on me, and even with *HIM*, the Mr. Super Star himself, may the Almighty Gods extend his days and increase his talents for eternity. I felt sick and deadly tired of all of that.

"Mom! You must! Do you understand? *You MUST write to Him!*" I felt the weight of his grayish-blue eyes penetrating my soul. "And you know me, mom, I won't leave you alone until you do!"

I gave up. I didn't want to argue anymore. This whole situation was insane! Why in the world was Farhan so important for my child? Another mystery? Another riddle?

"Why on earth does it bother you so much, son? Why are you badgering me about this? What in the world has this movie star guy to do with you?"

"He must know you exist! And he must find out who and where you are! *It is very important!*"

"Why???"

He felt silent for a moment, looking straight ahead of himself. In such moments, his eyes turn deep silvery gray. He looks, as if he does not belong to this place or time. I know how it works. He *receives* the answers in his own way. He *sees* them. I also fell silent, waiting to hear what he would say. But there were no answers.

"I do not know why," he finally said. "I just know it is *important. It must be done.* What is his name, Mom?"

149

"Farhan. Farhan Ali."

"Farhan. He…" and suddenly, he stopped, his face shining with a bright sunny smile!

"Mooom!!!!" He screamed again! "This is Arman! Look! Our Arman! Wooow, Mooom! Look at him! He looks exactly like Arman!"

And then it dawned upon me! How did I not notice this earlier!? What a wild, *striking* resemblance with my eldest son!!! It is simply impossible! Same dark eyes—lakes, typical for Scorpio's penetrating gaze. Same smile. Same olive skin tone. No! No way! How the hell can it be? *HOW* can this even be??? Memories flooded my mind, "Is your husband Indian?"

"His father must be Arabic or Indian! Such a handsome little prince! Look at him! Those eyes!" Sweet Heavens! *WHY? HOW?* This is insane! Insane! But this was a fact. My child, my own son, looks like a man I have never even met in the real world, not in this life. And at this moment, it seems like I never will! And yet, my kid looks exactly like *him*! Maybe I can convince myself that I am nuts and have completely lost my marbles. I can go to a psychologist, and he might convince me that this whole story is my imagination. But how can the child I gave birth to, be my imagination? What would a psychologist say, if I brought Arman with me for the session? *Hello doctor! Thank you very much for helping me recover! I fully realize and admit now that I imagined the whole thing. I have imagined it since I was a child! Now I know for sure. It was just my fantasy! Thank you! By the way, doctor, this is my son! After that, the doctor faints, and now he also needs therapy!* The thought made me almost laugh!

As soon as we drove up to the house, Nicky bursts out of the car, yelling, "Brotheeeer! Hey, bro! Come over here! I'll show you something! You look like this guy. What's his name? Ali something. This guy is a movie star! He is mom's half, you know? Come, I will show you! You remember the story about the halves, which Zeus separated? Remember Mom told us? So! Mom has found her half! He is a movie star, and he looks exactly like you! Bro!!! Come here!"

What the hell is happening? What the hell is going on? I don't even know what to say. I just keep quiet and wait for Arman's reaction. *This whole thing looks surreal. Maybe I am imagining all this.*

"Mooom! What is he talking about?" Arman's voice pulls me out of my thoughts. The EYES of my Twin are looking into my eyes from the face of my son! HIS face, the face of Farhan in his child version! My kid! *Yes, I must be imagining everything. Everything, including myself, my whole life, my own child! None of this is real because HOW can this all be real?*

"So! We will create a Facebook page for mom! Then Mom will write to this dude! He will read it and be like, 'Wow! That is so cool!'" He keeps yelling at my second child from the kitchen.

I almost laughed out loud.

I imagined Farhan Ali getting my letter and being like, *"OH Allah Almighty! I have finally found my true Love! My one and only! I must run to her now, must find her and press her tightly to my heart!"*

Yes. Most definitely. That is precisely what will happen. That is exactly what he will do!

"Nicholas! I will not write anything to anybody! I have already told you!"

"You will, mom! You will. You know me, I won't leave you be!"

"Okay. Whatever. We shall see!"

There was no use arguing with Nick. I knew my kid too well. Maybe in a couple of days, he would just forget all about it. I hoped.

Chapter 20

Twin Flames

When we talk about Twin Flames, we can notice some common tendencies. These people are rarely young when they find each other. Almost always they have both already lived a large part of their lives without knowing each other consciously. They each have gone through their ups and downs, joy and happiness, grief and triumph, everything life throws our way. Very often they live very far from each other, sometimes huge distances. Frequently, they have different social statuses; one of the Twins may have a much higher position in society than the other.

Usually, the one with a higher social status is called "The Matrix Twin." In most cases, that would be the man. Before Destiny brings him together with his Other Half, he might not even think about his past lives, true Soul purpose, karma, and other esoteric subjects. He simply has no time for that. He is the so-called *RUNNER*. He is busy running. He runs away from the truth, from his old wounds, from himself, or after something like wealth, power, or fame. The other Twin Flame (in most cases, the woman) is usually called *Spiritual Twin* or *Awakened*. One of the *Spiritual Twin's* quests is to awaken the *Matrix Twin*. No one else would be capable of doing that. Why? Simply because the "Matrix" will not listen to anyone else but his other half.

The Spiritual Twin would often be aware of their ancient connection long before they get to know each other on Earth. Such examples are many, and I am one of them. As I have already said, the Spiritual Twin will have the duty of awakening the other twin to his divinity and spiritual power.

That means the Spiritual Twin will most likely be more psychic and in many cases, feels uncomfortable in society for the most part.

The Matrix Twin is not aware of who he truly is while living his everyday life in society. Before awakening, the Matrix Twin, in most cases, feels and acts like an average person. However, many of them may have a passion for books containing spiritual information without understanding why. The Matrix Twin possesses psychic abilities as well, but the real powers of their abilities are usually not used, waiting to be unlocked by the Spiritual Twin.

Another usual thing for Twin Flames is that their life circumstances are not conducive for togetherness. All possible and impossible obstacles exist between them. From the physical distance and social gaps to the different customs, languages, nations, religions, traditions, ethnicities, age gaps, and everything else you can even imagine.

Zeyven Alexander Blackwell writes this in his book *Twin Flame Revelation*.

> *Twin Flames have an especially difficult task to integrate and balance their energies because very much is expected of them. They must yield to the Source, forget ego and be ready to merge so that their magnificent union can bring the change everybody has been waiting for: Creating shifts in the collective human consciousness.*[3]
>
> *Twin Flames energies agree to split into the masculine and feminine aspects of God, incarnating as One Soul into two bodies and against all odds, attempt to reunite on Earth and begin the return journey home, to light a pathway home for humanity. A Divine Plan is to bring the Souls of Earth back home to THEIR POINT OF ORIGIN- GOD! But not God the Man with a white beard that sits among the clouds, GOD THE SOURCE. The unknowable essence that is present in every atom of every molecule upon the planes of existence!*[4]

---

3   Zeyven Alexander Blackwell, Twin Flame Revelation, dedication.
4   Zeyven Alexander Blackwell, Twin Flame Revelation, 8.

The Spiritual Twin is called *the chaser*, and the Matrix—or *unawakened* one—is often called *the runner*. You might ask me, is it really necessary to chase the runner? Is it really necessary to wake up the sleeping one? Wouldn't it be better to back off from a situation entirely and leave "the runner" alone? If he wants to pursue a mission to rise to his stardom and is not interested in searching for his Twin Soul or being with one, maybe it would be better to let him be? Maybe yes. But the *awakened* one cannot help it. The so-called «Celestial Plan» is now activated. Twin Flames have many tasks and many responsibilities to humankind. They can solve them only by uniting. Only together. When both know the past, they will create a beautiful present and change the future, not only their own but also that of the country, land, humanity.

The Dark Side prevents Souls from remembering who they truly are by keeping them focused on their desires for *wealth, power, sex, and conditional love*. Twin Flames must first remember who they are themselves, *then help others to remember*. So, does the Spiritual Twin actually have a choice to back off and *NOT* to at least *TRY* to awaken the Matrix one? The answer is simple "No." And in my story, you will see things happening to me that at the beginning of this quest, were not even possible to imagine. On finding out who he was, I decided to do absolutely *NOTHING*, convinced there was nothing I *COULD* do. But I had no choice. I would look at the sky and say, "*If I MUST* do something about it, let it rain!" and the sky would open, and the water would fall to the ground! I would say, "I want to see a white peacock!" And I would see one within several days! I would say, "May the waves of the ocean rise!" and they would! I would say, "I want a rainbow!" and close my eyes. On opening them, I would see a rainbow shining in front of me! No. I did not have a choice. I had to face a Shadow. What do I mean?

The Twin with very high social status is also called *The Shadow*. Why such a name? The thing is, the more material wealth and power a person possesses, the less power his very Soul, the true, eternal Essence of his, has over his actions. The more fame, worship, and influence such a Twin possesses, the harder it is to *awaken* him.

Do you remember what happened to the Atlanteans? Their thirst for power led them to renounce the original Truth! *Pride, arrogance, and greed*

154

made them lose connection with the Soul and made them the victims of the Dark Side. They started a war with their brothers and fathers, with their ancestors. It led to a terrible disaster. Myths and legends of many lands described it as the "War of Gods." This dreadful war caused the earth's axis to shift, the global flood, the death of many people, climate change, and the fall of the Great Empire of Antes or Atlantes, and many others. The fall of Atlantis threw civilization back many centuries. Those, who managed to stay alive, just needed to survive. Except for a small group, *The Keepers of the Scripts*, most people forgot who they were and where they came from for hundreds, even thousands of years.

So, the more power, wealth, and social status one of the Twins has, the more of a *Shadow* he becomes. In the third-dimensional world, many Twin Flames would be the opposite. One has it all in the material world. The other would have a simple life, but be very well aware that the world is not limited to material reality, there is something else. The Eternal, something that never ends. This truth, the Spiritual Twin must try to pass on to the Matrix Twin, the one endowed with wealth and glory. If the Matrix Twin believes it, he will become *awakened*.

Another tendency you can notice among Twin Flames is this: They both might already have families, or at least one may be married. But one thing should be clear here. *A TWIN WILL NEVER APPEAR IN THE LIFE OF HIS OTHER HALF, IF THE OTHER ONE IS HAPPY IN HIS EXISTING RELATIONSHIP!* If there is *LOVE AND UNDERSTANDING* between him and his wife or husband, the other twin won't be allowed to interfere. That would be against the Cosmic Law, in which *Love* is the *most sacred force*! But if the marriage of one of them, or both, is a loveless pretense and kept only for social status, Destiny will bring the Twin Flames together for sure. Then one of them, or both, will have to face a choice: Pretense or Sincerity. Love or Status. Matrix or Soul. Material or Eternal.

It happens way too often that for the sake of status, career, or wealth, or simply unwillingness to change anything, many choose to live a lie for years. They live a lie and constantly tell lies to people dear to them and even strangers. But mostly, they deceive themselves, cheat themselves, and lie to themselves.

And what about the Soul? After all, it does not need prestige or fame. It does not need social status and a fat bank account, an enormous house, multiple cars, or a collection of antique art. An immortal Soul needs someone who gives the feeling of peace and home. And if such a being is nowhere near, then the Matrix Twin starts to feel, so-called, *emotional burnout*. He might not understand why that is. He might ask himself, why do I feel like all the colors of life have left me? Why does my world appear black and white? I have everything my heart desires. I am surrounded by all I have been striving for all my life. I have it all, but why the hell do I feel no joy in living? Where is the spark of laughter, desire to create, the flicker of inspiration, the delight of imagination, bliss of dreaming and creating? What is wrong with me? But he may not know the answers.

At such a time in *HIS* life, Destiny helped us find each other, or to be exact, helped me find him. There's one more thing I want you to understand. *TWIN FLAMES ARE ALWAYS UNDER THE STRICT OBSERVATION OF THE HIGHER FORCES.* You can call them any name you wish to: Gods, Absolute, Source, Guardians. There are also those, I call *THE KEEPERS*.

The Keepers are those who activate the Spiritual Twin at the given moment. After that, they unfold events in such a way that even things that seemed absolutely impossible, become possible. Something that might seem completely unrealistic, becomes real. But at the beginning of the journey, it is the *awakened one* who has the most challenging mission to fulfill. This challenge was given to me. How do I walk this path, you might ask me? The most important thing is to make the very first step. After that, try not to give up, no matter what. No matter what people say, or how it looks from the outside. The Keepers will observe and help you create impossible, fantastic situations, so that you have a chance to achieve your goal. And the goal is to awaken the Soul of your Other Half, *help him remember*.

I DIDN'T KNOW any of this back then. I just thought that I was born with a preserved memory of a man I had loved not just in one, but also in many lives. Until a certain moment of this story, *I knew NOTHING about TWIN FLAMES.* Nothing.

Chapter 21

Maa

Fortunately, I didn't walk my path alone. As if by magic, there were people who appeared in my life and did not let me give up. I received help from *the other side as well*, from the realm of the Spirits. It was absolutely magical. The first Keeper, or the Guide from the Spirits' dimension who miraculously and unexpectedly appeared in my life, was *His Mother*.

As you remember, I wanted to talk to her. I wanted to ask her to help me somehow find the way to lift this quest off my Soul. Of course, I understood; I received it for a purpose. But whatever this purpose was, I was absolutely sure I could not accomplish it. I also understood that I could not do anything with it myself. I could not imagine how I would continue living my life as if nothing had happened when I constantly felt this aching of my heart. I hoped and somehow I believed, she would be able to help me.

It was after midnight. I had already put my sons to bed, finished loads of ordinary household chores, and finally, I was alone in my room. I typed in the search engine what I was looking for and made another startling discovery. A woman, looking at me from the monitor's screen, looked like me in my early 20s. But it was her eyes that especially struck me. It was impossible to believe, but they were so much like my own! I froze, staring into them. I think it lasted for a long time. I looked at her, feeling as if I had fallen somewhere in the void between the worlds and timelessness. I was, as if in a stream. I was in a flow where time doesn't exist, the past, the present, and the future exist *simultaneously*. The flow filled me with oceans of information and vivid feelings, sensations, emotions. This woman was so painfully familiar to me! *I knew her!*

I knew her with every cell of my body, every corner of my mind, every particle of my Soul. I felt that I had known her for a very long time. A very long time! I remembered her: her features, the familiar vibration, the sensation of *knowing*. The feeling of warmth and recognition in the heart, calming and soothing my agony and anxiety. I knew this woman as long as I had remembered the one who in this life was her son.

I tried to listen closely to my memory, to this ancient knowing hidden deep inside my very essence.

But then, someone knocked on my door interrupting me. My sleepy Nicky floated into the room.

"Mooom. I just had such a weird dream that..." when he noticed the face on the screen, he froze mid-sentence!

"Mooom. Who is that?" He thought for a second, "She looks like you! Why does she look like you, Mom?"

"It is, it is the mother of that man, that actor who looks like Arman."

"Really? The one who is your half? That is his mom?! You look like her! Can't you see? You look like her because you're his half!"

"Son," I said with a sigh, "why aren't you sleeping?"

"I am telling you I saw a weird dream! I was like on another planet or something, *and I had wings*! Like Huge wings! And *everyone there has wings*! It's like a normal thing there! Now, I can't fall asleep! Tell me a story. Tell me about Atlantis!"

"Fine. I will. Go, lie down. I will come over and tell you all about it."

"You have to write to him! Mom! *You must!*"

"Fine. Maybe I will," I said, sighing, knowing that arguing with this creature was useless! "Now, let's go to your room, and I will tell you stories till you fall asleep."

Finally, very late at night, when everyone was asleep, including my restless son, I printed a photo of his mother. I put it on my table, lit a candle and sat silently looking into her eyes for I don't even know how long.

It seemed like I could not find the courage to finally start speaking because I thought she might not like what I was going to say. But in the realm where she was, she already knew everything. Finally, I gathered my courage and said:

"Maa" (this is how they call a mother in India, and, as we know, she was born there).

"Maa," I said. "Please, forgive me for what I'm going to tell you now. And also, I am asking you to forgive me for my weakness and cowardice. I guess there is no need to tell you anything. You already know it all. You know that I've been looking for him my whole life. You know that I have found him. And you know, of course, who he is now, in this life. You understand very well that there is practically no chance for him to know that I exist. There's *NO CHANCE* for it, Maa!

"I do not know why and for what purpose this Love was given to me. I know. I have loved him in past lives. But I do not understand why my memories of him are still with me. After all, when we enter a new life, we must forget the past ones. Isn't that right, Maa? Although, of course, I realize that there are always some exclusions to every rule. But if our destiny is to *not be* together in this life, why did I remember him? Why did I wait for him? Why did I keep looking for him? Why did I keep hoping, dreaming, believing? And now I have found him, finally, after all these years, but what does it change? Nothing. Nothing at all!

"Maa, I can't love him! Please believe me; I cannot! This burden is unbearable for me! I am an ordinary woman, Maa. I dare to ask you: Lift this task off of my Soul, take this Fate away from me if you can. Lift it off of my heart. I can't do this. Please understand me; I can't.

"Yes, I understand everything. There is Karma. There is Destiny. Or whatever it is, I can't do it, Maa. I have no strength left in me. I don't see the path ahead of myself. I cannot even imagine there even can be a path in this situation. Allow me not to even look for it. Gift me the freedom from the duty to follow your son. Please…"

I went on and on like this for a long time, but I'll *NEVER* be able to explain what happened next.

I am not sure if it was a dream. Or a trance, a vision, I hardly would be able to give it a name, but maybe I do not have to. At one moment, I felt soft warmth on my right shoulder, as if someone was gently putting their hand there. I looked up, and I saw his mother standing next to me. The feeling of *RECOGNITION* was so strong that my eyes started to sting. I wanted to cry. Standing by my side was not *his* Mother, but *mine*! Somehow, I knew that this woman had also been my mother for more than one life, just as she had been his mother for more than one life. I knew that in those lives when he was my husband, she was also my mother-in-law. For many lives, my Fate intertwined closely with this woman. Unfortunately, my mother from this life, though I love her dearly and have always admired her strength, never fully either understood or accepted me because of my *strangeness*. With this woman, everything felt completely different. This Mother knew me in a way that even I did not know myself.

"My dear girl," she said, but not with her voice. The words appeared simultaneously in my heart and my mind. "My dear girl, I know how you feel and how tough it has been for you! I know how challenging it is now. I also know that it will get even tougher! Much tougher! With every step you take, it will only get harder! And each next move, and each next stage, will be much harder than the previous one. It is like existing in the middle of a fiery tornado! You burn, it becomes unbearable, and you run out, thinking, you cannot handle it anymore! But you will return inside the flame again, to burn again even brighter than before, because your Soul will not let you be! Yes, my dear girl! I CAN lift this off of you. It is within my power. But you must know, you must know this one truth! *ONLY YOU CAN DO IT.* Nobody else but you! Not a single Soul, but you. *ONLY YOU CAN.*"

"Only I can... WHAT, Maa? What can nobody else do, only me? Oh, Maa! Look at me! I am an ordinary woman! I *CAN'T DO ANYTHING*, Maa! *NOTHING!*"

"*ONLY YOU can do it, LAYLA, Only You!*"

"Layla?"

"Yes. Layla is your name. But Ram called you *Lala!*"

Ram... Ram... My heart ached from memories and feeling powerless, hopeless, and helpless. Gods, I wanted to cry! I wanted to just sit down on the floor, put my head on my knees, and cry, cry, cry.

"Ram," I said bitterly without even opening my mouth. "Ram now has a different wife, Maa. I was not able to hide my pain and bitterness. And He is a star. *A huge star!* He forgot his Lala, Maa! It is Lala who has not forgotten him! Why? Why, Maa?"

But I didn't get the answer.

"*No one can do it but you,*" she repeated softly.

"*DO WHAT? What* are you talking about, Maa? Tell me. Please explain it to me! Please!"

But she only shook her head. I knew she would not tell me what that mysterious "something" was that only I was capable of doing. Was it that important? Could I simply refuse it? Did I have the right to refuse, the choice to refuse? We both fell silent for a moment.

"You are not going to tell me what it is, are you, Maa?"

She just looked into my eyes while gently touching my cheek.

"And what should I do, Maa? How can I reach Him? After all, jumping to the moon is easier than..."

"*Write to him.*"

"What?"

"*Write to him, Lala!*"

"Write? But, what, Maa??? What can I write to a man like him? What words can I find? That is pure madness! Who he is and who I am! Where he is and where I am."

"*Write whatever is in your heart, Lala.* And do not be afraid of anything. From now on, I will always be with you. I will be by your side. My beautiful, brave girl! You will face a lot of hurts. A lot! You will try to quit it all, thousands and thousands of times. But you won't quit! Because you *KNOW* that deep down there, at the very core of his immortal essence, *he remembers you* and is waiting for you!"

A few days passed.

"Nobody can do it, but you. Only you can!" But WHAT exactly can't anybody do, except me? No matter how hard I tried to understand it, nothing came to my mind. However, my son's words sounded in my head and my heart over and over again, "You must write to him. You found him, and he must find you too! And when he does, it will no longer hurt right here" he had said, pointing to his chest area.

Maybe this is the reason? Perhaps I, somehow, can save him, heal him from that pain? Is that my task? Is that what nobody else can do, only me?

"He is very unhappy, Mom." Indeed, I saw that pain hidden in the depth of his impossible eyes, which are so similar to mine. So, could it be the answer? I did not see any other possible explanation. After all, there should be a reason why I was looking for him. A reason why this life didn't erase my memory of past lifetimes. A reason why I was looking for him as long as I lived and breathed. There MUST be a reason. Otherwise, none of this would make any sense! It was hardly possible that I had walked through my whole life with *him in every breath* to give up once I learned who he was! So, this must be a reason. Hidden pain existed deep inside his eyes, and in fact, not just his eyes, but the bottom of his very heart. I saw his tiredness, inner exhaustion he pushed deep down. I could see it. I could sense it. And there was something else, a sadness, which seemed not just old but almost ancient.

After losing his mother many years ago, it seems he never totally recovered from his terrible loss. Or was it much worse? When he lost his mother, he lost his Faith. Such a tragedy could have done that, causing him to no longer believe in Higher Forces. I have seen it happen before. I have gone through that myself. He believed only in hard work and protecting those he loved. He never said this or showed it to anyone, ever. But I knew it somehow. I felt it. Very religious in childhood, but now he lost his Faith. The loss of his mother was too unexpected, too painful, and too unfair. And probably, if he were honest with himself, he'd admit he wasn't a believer anymore. He tried to read and re-read thousands of books to find the answers to his endless questions, just as I had. But he did not find them there, or they weren't complete and did not satisfy him.

162

I knew what he felt. I knew how or why; I just knew! He had been angry with God for many years for taking his mother from him. Until the last second, he believed God would never do it. But it happened. And his Faith had burned out in agony and pain, not being able to accept such a loss. Being for many years closely watched by a huge crowd, he, like no other, could play a role. Play with his every smile, every gesture, and every look. It was his profession, constant self-discipline, plus genuine talent. Even when he was completely alone, he didn't stop acting. He had mastered this game to such perfection that he could lie even to himself. He could probably convince himself; he was perfectly all right. But he couldn't convince me. I saw everything. Not with my eyes, but with my Soul which we shared. *I heard him. I felt him. I knew him.*

I saw in him what is called *emotional burnout.* He had been burning so brightly and for so long that he had almost burned himself down. Still, he did not allow himself to stop or even take a break. He kept on going like a workhorse, day after day, year after year, while he had the strength. And even, at the moments when he had almost none left, he would find it. Such was his character.

But I could see it there, deep down. There was pain, exhaustion. Questions, *Why? What for?"* appeared in the back of his mind, from time to time. These questions were so strange and unexpected for him that he suppressed them, leaving them with no answer. I could also see that his magnificent wife, whom I infinitely admired—appreciating her beauty, grace, manners, and attitude towards her family—was as far from him as the farthest galaxy. They were both magnificent in every possible way, but they simply were different as sweet and yellow. That is not even a comparison of two colors. They were different substances. Different energies. Different vibrations. But as happens with many, they met early in life and got married while still being very young.

Such stories are similar to some extent. A young boy meets a young girl, they fall in Love, and their differences are not noticeable at the beginning. They love each other, and nothing else matters. For many years the power of their Love is enough. Opposites attract, I agree. But unfortunately, years pass by, the differences start to become more noticeable, and little by little begin to create an invisible wall between them. Usually, while they both motivate and inspire each other, moving together in life in the same direction, they still can make it work. But unfortunately, in most cases, sooner or later, one of them starts to pull away, grows, changes, and the other is left behind. Or they simply grow and change in *opposite directions*.

After that, they start to fall farther apart with each passing week, month, and year. Sympathy and understanding are the first to be gone on both sides. With time arrives annoyance, sometimes anger, frustration, perhaps even alienation. Later the lack of warmheartedness, genuine soul connection and the warmth of togetherness. At this stage, some people prefer to let each other go. Others stay together for the sake of tradition, business, or other reasons but try to find Love and affection with someone else. Sometimes they do not even fight or have conflicts. They start to live separate lives. Some even try to find the one true Love, because even the most inveterate skeptics know the concept of *soulmates*.

In the end, Love vanishes completely. It gets replaced by this beautiful and scary word, "obligations." Two people live together as business partners or as friends, sometimes close, sometimes not. Sometimes more like distant relatives. What they have in common is their past. In the best scenario, what they have left, is mutual respect. And, of course, "obligations." They also have children. Business. Property. Money. Status. In the public eye, they are a perfect couple. And behind closed doors: They are parents. They are partners. They are neighbors. But they are not the Lovers and not in Love like they used to be.

Their house becomes a place where they only come to sleep. And after waking up in the morning, they leave again. It's not the worst option, by the way. It is relatively peaceful. Calm. Many couples live like that. But after a while, a terrible creature called "anguish," or there is a softer word for it, "melancholy" settles in the house, which a long time ago used to be home. It now lives in that house and in the hearts of those inside that house. I call "melancholy" the Lady with Silvery Wings. She hugs you with her wings and

164

does not let you go. Over time, her wings turn dark gray and then purely black. I also saw her shadow in his eyes. It is no one's fault when people are different, neither his nor hers. It's nobody's fault.

A tiger who fell in love with a mermaid cannot blame her for not enjoying night strolls through the forests and the fields. And the mermaid cannot blame the tiger for not knowing how to live underwater or how magical the night mermaid dances are, in the shadow of the lonely weeping willows.

It happens rather often. Completely different people get together, thinking that their love will be enough to overcome their differences. And at first, everything is fine. If a conflict happens, it ends up with making up. They bury each wrong in forgiveness and kisses. But if this couple is not looking for an opportunity to strengthen the marriage, if they do not grow and do not change together, if they do not have true common goals and do not cherish their love, then sometime later, the Lady with Silvery Wings will drop by their house. Love is not only a holiday. Not only passion, longing, lovemaking. Not only ups and downs and everything together. It is also a FLAME, or you can call it a fireplace, where the firewood must be added from time to time, not allowing it to die. They must also protect this Flame from the rain and the wind. Or perhaps it is a flower, or a garden, that constantly needs to be cared for and nourished. Otherwise, neither the Flame nor the garden has any chance of surviving.

I have to say it here and now that neither then, several years ago, nor during all these years, while the events described in this story were taking place, had I such an absurd and even idiotic idea to take the place of his wife. No! Such a thought never even crossed my mind! As I mentioned before, I didn't even know that they were no longer married. Even if I had known, it would not have changed much for me. You can ask me what my goal was. I will be open and sincere with you, otherwise writing this story would make no sense whatsoever.

I DID NOT HAVE ANY PLANS AND OR GOALS AT ALL. None! Absolutely None! Take a moment to imagine this: His eyes followed me always, everywhere I went, as long as I could remember. I thought, and I believed, that it was my destiny. He would find me, and we would be happy. But it did not happen.

Then I got married, gave birth to my children, worked, survived, successfully and unsuccessfully, solved my problems, and from time to time; I tried my best to convince myself that fairy tales were over for me. I tried to convince myself; *HE* was just a dream, a dream not destined to come true. I tried to convince myself that most possibly, I might never find him.

But I never seemed to listen to my conscious mind and logical voice, neither then, nor now. I live, breathe and act with my heart, only my heart. I continued to wait and search for him. The idea of finding him was *living, burning, and vibrating with me as long as I could remember myself.* It was an essential part of me. It was a part of my very soul. Nevertheless, there were times when I was close to surrendering, to just giving up. I thought of accepting him being only a fairy tale, which had ended without even having started.

And then, suddenly, I find him! I find my Twin. I begin to read his soul, to understand him, to suffer because we will never be together. I accepted as a given that he was older and, I thought, happily married with children. It put barriers between us even more insurmountable than his fame, money, talent, and social status. Now I know it all. I accept it all. I accept the simple fact that I can do nothing under such circumstances. Still, I cannot tear him away from my very essence. I am trying hard. But I fail.

So, I turn to his mother in the dimension of the Spirits. I ask her to help me, to rescue me from the burden of this one-sided love, and in response, I hear: *"You must." "ONLY YOU CAN."*

And if there were such *magical keywords*, which would make me act, no matter what, those words would be: *"YOU MUST."* Or *"NOBODY ELSE CAN DO IT, BUT YOU."* That's all! The "Savior" program, somehow "installed "into my very core, would instantly *turn on!* Now I am thinking about how I can save him or help him or heal him because I believe it is much more important than helping and healing myself.

Everything I did, I did with just one thought in my mind. Maybe I am the one who can ease that pain of sorrow, hidden deep inside his eyes and his heart. Even if I cannot completely free him from it, I can share it with him. I will make it easier for him to carry.

If nobody can do it but me, as those were the words of his mother, then *I must do this.* Yes, that must be it. I must become some healing potion for his wounds. A potion that, perhaps, will bring back the faith to him, that his Maa hadn't gone forever but is alive, closer now, than even when she was beside him. Maybe I can somehow show him that besides the three-dimensional world, there are others. There are many others. Perhaps I can somehow return his faith in the Divine; however he imagines it to be.

Now I had at least some answers to my questions. Now I knew for sure that there is indeed Everlasting Love, which ends not with our physical death, but lasts for centuries and millennia. Now I knew for sure that the memories of past incarnations keep on living in us, that our lives continually intertwine with the same people for thousands of earthly years and by thousands of invisible threads of lives, laughs, loves, and memories, *forever connecting us.* And every one of us has specific tasks, which we must complete, as those tasks, tests, and quests are why we have chosen to come again into this world. Once again. *NOTHING. EVER. ENDS.*

Chapter 22

My Letters

I am sitting in front of my computer, looking at the screen. *So, this is Farhan's official Facebook page.* I have no idea what to write! Not the slightest clue! What should I do? Overcome with fear; I sense the absolute *absurdity* of what I am doing and planning to do. I have such a mix of contradicting feelings and emotions that neither God nor the Devil would be able to figure them out or understand anything about them. *What the hell am I doing? After all, hundreds of thousands of people will be able to read it. It's easy to say: "Write what is in your heart!"* Yeh, right. Just go ahead! Write whatever is in your heart and be judged by millions of people!

"Idiot!" I say to myself. "I am acting like a complete idiot! Close it all! Get up! Forget it all! Just forget it!"

But no! I feel as if someone's invisible hands softly lay on my shoulders. Then my heart heard his voice, which I had never heard, but seemed like I knew it with my every breath, whispers to me, "Write!"

"Dear Farhan, my name is," Gods, what nonsense! Erase!

"I would like to say a few words." Even greater nonsense! Erase again.

What a fool I am! What a hopeless fool, I think. And suddenly *I SEE HIM!* With my inner vision, the vision that can see through space and time, I see him standing on a terrace and looking at the ocean. My chest warmed up. My fingers sprinted across the keyboard.

And then, I wrote him my very first letter:

Have you ever asked yourself why people are afraid of loneliness? You are afraid of it also, even though you love it too. You love it, but you fear it more. You know, who has no fear of it? Me. I'm not afraid. Not at all. Can I say something? You are now standing on the terrace and looking at the water. You are looking at the Pacific Ocean. I am looking at the Atlantic. A vast distance separates us, and you think you are completely alone. You think no one sees you! And what if I say, I see you? Even though I am thousands of miles far away from you, I SEE you! What would you say to that? You are wearing a black shirt. Your gorgeous hair is waving freely in the wind. Do you want to hear something? You remind me of that very wind. The ocean breeze! You know why? Because you cannot be locked up, put into a cage, or somehow controlled or seized. You will break free! What? You are smiling? I know that you are smiling!
Soon the night will fall, but you will not sleep. Neither will I. You will keep on standing still at the same place where you are right now and keep looking up at the night sky. There is a legend, the legend of the Souls, which were born very far from our Earth. They come here to teach people to love. You hear me, my heavenly angel? People believe that such souls are rarely able to sleep well at night. They go outside and look up at the stars! It makes them feel a little better. It's like they can sense their distant home a tiny bit closer to them in such moments. You are standing out there now, while I usually like to lie down on the warm grass and look at the stars just like you do. Also, you want to believe that somewhere out there, among the stars, your Maa is looking down at you. You want to believe it, but you don't really believe it. Let me teach you one thing. If you close your eyes and try to turn off your head, you will feel her!
It feels like soft warmth embracing you. As if someone came up to you and gently covered your shoulders with a soft woolen blanket. Try it. Just

try. What? Are you surprised? You don't understand why I am telling you all this? And more importantly, why do you suddenly feel something? Right now! There, deep inside!

And you might wonder why the hell do I feel something? Some strange woman writes me some strange letter, what a big deal? But why do I suddenly feel this warmth deep inside? Who is she anyway? Ah, now you are curious about who I am. You are looking at my name. And it slightly surprises you. You are raising your left eyebrow and thinking that my name is definitely not real!

You want to know? It is my real name. The name of your God is also my name. Strange, isn't it?

What an interesting fan, never seen her before, you might think. And you will be wrong. I cannot be one of your fans, as I have no idea what your creative work is all about! I don't know anything about it yet. But I promise you; I will find out for sure. I will watch your movies and learn more about them. I do not have any doubts you are brilliant at what you do.

So, you see, I don't sound like an ordinary fan of yours. Then, who am I? Some little fool, in love with you, just as so many others? But little fool doesn't seem like the fitting description of someone capable of writing like this. Does it? So, Who am I? With time, you will know!

You have a strange habit of biting your lower lip. May I say something sensuous? I promise it will make you smile. Those are some eerily, impossibly beautiful lips you have. They could make even a nun slip into eternal-hell-threatening thoughts. Are you smiling again? Good! Who am I? Now you want to take a look at my photo? Wait! Do not look! I'm serious! What do you mean, why? They call me "Witch" for a reason! People say, if you look into my eyes even once, you will never be able to forget them! Just a warning.

I will finish this long letter, my Heavenly Angel, as it is already a deep night. I love the night, just like you do. Sleep well, my sweet prince! And wait for my next letter. Learn to wait.

I pressed the button. I sent the message. When I saw the whole text, I immediately wanted to delete every single word of it. I was terrified. I was shaking, like a leaf in the cold November wind. But I withstood the war with myself and left everything as it is.

Of course, I didn't know; he wasn't the one who was managing his official Facebook page. He had a personal account on Twitter, and usually, it was there where he would communicate with his multimillion army of fans. He rarely visited his Facebook unless there was something his assistant wanted him to see. I only found out about it a year later. Also, I didn't know that it would be one of his main assistants, his *right hand*, who would turn his attention to the *unusual fan* after reading this particular letter on his Facebook page.

This intelligent, beautiful, and powerful woman, Susan Malik, will play a big role in this story. I will tell you all about it later.

So, I had just written my first letter, and for me, it was already a huge victory—a victory of me, over myself.

You might ask me if I expected any reaction from him. I swear to you, I did not expect ANYTHING! I knew millions of people wrote to him, and most possibly, my letter would get lost among the comments of the others. And even if I wrote him more of those, those may never reach him either. Yet, I decided that *I had* to write to him. This way I finally could do something real, something I was able to do. Writing to him was also what Maa asked me to do. If those letters are supposed to find him, I was sure they would. If not, then, *Whatever*. So, I decided I would write more letters to him to make it easier for me to breathe. I was doing it for myself too. I was doing it to stop sobbing for weeks and wandering with a tattered and torn soul, with no strength and no desire to live. I'd been looking for him all my life, finally found him, saw who he was. That couldn't be the end of this story. It had to make some sense!

I decided I would be the breeze he needed to come back to life. I wanted him to begin to feel true joy in his heart again. It was another reason why I started to write to him. Of course, one letter was not enough. I started writing every other day.

Very soon, I realized I had nothing to fear. Everyone wrote short comments, and they all followed the same pattern: "Oooh! I love you! I love you so much!!! I love you! Love you!!!" Rarely, very rarely, would more meaningful comments appear! There were very few of them. I realized that the "millions" of fans couldn't care less about my long letters. They were so much absorbed in their love for Him; nobody would read mine.

No one except for him, I KNEW that if one day, at least ONE of my letters catches his eye, the invisible thread connecting our souls will become stronger. It will help me heal him. He will know me in THIS life, in this dimension, in this incarnation! Would he remember? I wasn't thinking about that. I wasn't thinking at all. I wanted to be his soft candlelight in the dark room, and the only way I could do it, was my letters. I was hoping he'd see at least one of them. And He did.

About two weeks had passed since I wrote him my first letter. And then, one night, I woke up feverish. My face was burning! My cheeks! My whole body was on fire, but most of all, my face. It felt as if I had entered a sweltering sauna. I sat up in my bed, pressing my palms up to my cheeks! And suddenly, I see the lines of my own letters, as if they were right in front of my eyes! I glance over the words I have written, and it takes me a moment to understand that I SEE WITH HIS EYES! Not with mine, but with his. I see what he sees! I feel what He feels!

His surprise. His bewilderment. His confusion. His curiosity! Even some childish joy, as if he was a child, discovering a huge toy fire truck under his bed on Christmas morning! I could clearly and articulately sense him thinking, what the hell? But with a sense of surprise and even admiration.

A whole range of emotions is boiling in him, like a tornado in the ocean. I feel every one of them. In the end, I hear his thought:

Who are you?

His index finger touches the small avatar, and a close-up of my face appears on the screen of his laptop. He's looking at me, taking his time, and examining all my features intently, peering into my eyes. I understand. He remembers. Something. Barely. Very faintly. But it was enough for the thin, invisible thread connecting us to twist, stretch, and become stronger. My

172

hero feels something he does not understand. My face, my eyes feel very familiar to him, but forgotten a long time ago. He is sensing something. But what it is exactly, he does not know and does not analyze it yet. I guess that Hollywood stars of his level rarely overthink their strange impressions, caused by someone else's avatar on their profile.

But this is only the beginning.

He closes my photo, and his eyes go back to the lines of my first letters. He frowns, he smiles, and he re-reads some sentences two, three times. *Interesting*, he thinks, *very interesting*. A smile plays on his beautiful lips, and I smile in response.

I got you, babe! I think of the words of the old Sonny and Cher song, smiling to myself. Now you will read everything and anything I write to you. You will not want to miss any single word from me, and you won›t even be able to understand why you do it. With every new letter, every word I write, you will feel me more and more, deeper and deeper. I don›t know if I'll be able to make you remember your Lala. But I will do my best to bring the joy back to your heart, so the world will start to sparkle for you with all its colors. I promise you, my ancient love. I promise you.

Curled up, smiling at my own thoughts, I finally fell asleep. In my dream, he held my face in his hands and, looking deep into my eyes, he asked me, *who are you? I want to know. I must know! Tell me, who are you?*

I answered him only, *"You have to remember it yourself. Try to REMEMBER."*

A couple of months passed like this. Every letter I wrote to him was still the result of a struggle with myself. Part of me screamed; I *must stop all this nonsense immediately. It is crazy. It will not end well. I should be living a real-life, interact with real people around me, not spending all my time acting absurdly, writing to a movie star.* Another part of me claimed that I was doing what I had to. It was my destiny and my obligation. These two parts of me fought each other for dear life, and neither one of them wanting to comply.

There was something else that prevented me from giving up and stopping. It was the Force, much more significant and grander than me. I could not logically explain it. I could only know and feel the presence of it. This Force led me, and it was impossible and pointless to fight it! I tried! Oh, my! I tried to stop so many times! But it was all useless! In the end, I told myself, *well, if nobody except me can do it, then, write, Lala, Write.* I told myself that I would and could stop any time I wanted to. I lied to myself. I was no longer the master of my own life and fate. I could no longer stop. Writing letters to him was already like breathing for me. For the first time in many years, I felt alive again. I learned to smile again, and the color of the sky, from gray, became turquoise blue.

One day he answered me.

Well, not directly, but he did.

About three months after writing my very first letter, for some reason, I wrote to him not one of my mysterious and lyrical letters but an entirely earthly one. It was about his hair. I did not like the style, just as I did not like his beard. I decided to tell him about it.

> *My Angel, tell me please, what have you done with your hair? What do you call this style? What color is it? Why the hell did you suddenly decide to change the luxurious black silk of your hair into THAT? You look like an aging leader of the Italian mafia! Forgive me, of course. Where is your boyish charm? Where is your charisma? Where is your spontaneity? I do not like this style! I can't see the real you; you disappear in it. It does not suit you when you wear your hair like that. And to be honest, I don't like your beard either. In my opinion, only a smoothly shaved face is irresistible.*

I followed with a detailed description of how, in my opinion, he should cut, comb and wear his gorgeous hair.

Well, I wrote it, sent it and forgot about it. But what I saw on Farhan's *FB* three days later sent me into a state of shock. It is one thing to feel and "see" things with an inner vision and another to see them in our usual three-dimensional world.

No, he did not write anything. He made a video a couple of minutes long. He was sitting in his car on the way to wherever he needed to go. He held the phone in front of him, first showing the right side, next his face, and then the left side. He was showing every detail of his new haircut and his new hairstyle. It was exactly the same as I had described to him in that letter. His face was also smoothly shaven! There was a sly boyish smile playing on his face; his eyes were sparkling with joy. They seemed to say, "Well, here's how you wanted it! Like it?" The words he was speaking on the video sounded philosophical and did not have much to do with his new-old look: "The mind with which you perceive the world belongs only to you, and the heart with which you love belongs to you only."

That was how that game started. The game, which seemed to say, "*Let the world think that I'm talking to them, but you know that I'm talking to you!*"

To say that I was happy is to say nothing! It was no longer "He does not even know that I exist on this Earth!"

Now he knew! He knew who I was and where I was! And not only that. He also made it absolutely clear, what I said, he paid close attention to and it was important to him.

I realized: Anything is Possible! Even things which seemed impossible are still possible! And this very thought led me to two conclusions. First, now I will be able not only to reach him and touch the deepest strings of his very Soul, I will make him believe me! I will make him *remember me*! And second, I could feel my wings starting to grow. I began to live and feel joy in life! I began to BELIEVE again, belief in my strength, in my unique light, in my happy destiny! But...

Wings are beautiful but very dangerous things. In this three-dimensional reality, life loves to snap and break them into little, tiny pieces! For someone who has asked what it feels like to soar up high into the sky, far away, above the clouds, it might turn out to be very painful to return to Earth and start walking again.

It's hard to take off. At first, it feels terrifying, but as soon as you are off the ground, it's beautiful, lovely, and magical! You become drunk from the feeling of flying. You break out of your reality, or it seems to you, you have escaped it. But the matrix, unfortunately, has a firm grip. It forces you, sometimes very rudely, to come back to it, asking yourself: *What is reality? Is "reality" only the things we can see and touch? But all of this will be GONE, so maybe reality is what we FEEL, sense, see in our dreams and visions. That reality stays forever! It does not disappear! So, what is reality?*

When I look back at the last several years, I think, *Heavens! I have come such a long way! Both of us have come such an insanely long and challenging way. This journey would be enough for a thousand lives!* And for me, every step on this path was the step towards him and about him. Unfortunately, I did not know any other way. He had been my alpha and omega, my breath, my thoughts, and my meaning of life. Him, and Him again! *What did I want to achieve? What was my destination? Where was I going?* I never even thought about it. Well, that›s not entirely true. I wanted him to recognize me with his very Soul. I wanted him to remember! *Remember!*

You might think I felt better after realizing he KNEW who I was, knowing that he saw my face, my eyes, knowing he was waiting for my every letter. But, no! Not at all. When it comes to Twin Flames, everything only escalates. I don't even think that such words as "things became a little easier" can be applied to Twins. Every next step, every next turn, every next breath, it only becomes tougher. Yes, now He knew me but this was no longer enough.

When the connection with him happened, it only got more intense! Every day it would get harder and harder to go on. Food seemed to be meaningless and sleep became my torture. Dreaming was the only way for us to spend time together in each other's arms, while we both were sleeping. Such were the given circumstances.

In our dreams, we began to see each other every day. There was one dream that kept coming back to me very often.

We are on the ocean shore, walking towards one another. Slowly. Very slowly. Step by step. Getting closer and closer... In dreams, *I PHYSICALLY* felt his touch. It became torture. He held my face in his palms, and I would jump up in bed, pressing my hands to my *burning* cheeks. When I woke up, I continued to feel his touch. It would get much more intense later. He would kiss me, and I would also jump up in my bed, my heart pounding wildly, physically feeling his lips on mine. I knew his taste. I knew his scent. I knew his every eyelash. Every trace of him. His heartbeat. His skin. His everything. I knew so much that sometimes it would even scare me. How can one Being know another in SUCH way? How? I just knew!

I could see what his eyes saw, not only mine. Feel what he felt. And there was no explanation for this. There were none. And a few months later, a telepathic connection appeared between us.

Later, I would learn this is entirely normal for Twin Flames, but I could not explain it back then. I began to hear his thoughts about me. At first, he did not speak with me directly. That would happen later. But when he was thinking of me, I heard it. *She is so deep!*

He thought: *This is simply amazing. How can so many things be combined in just one woman? She is gentle yet so passionate. She is wise, courageous, and at the same time, open like a child. She is brilliant and unique. Absolutely. Who would dare to write me so fearlessly, absolutely afraid of nothing! I wish I could do that. Why do her words affect me so much? I am touched, touched very deeply. Why? And those eyes! They make you look and look into them. I'm drowning in them. Why? I miss her when she doesn't write for a day, two, three. Why have I become so needy of her words, letters, feelings, and emotions? I've got to leave it all and forget it. I'm starting to think too much about this woman. Who is she? My faithful fan? No, it doesn't seem like it. She is different. She is not like anyone at all. Who is she? Where are these feelings coming from? Her eyes seem so familiar and even dear. But I could not have met her. I would remember her for sure! So, who is she? Where did she come from? She just appeared out of nowhere, captured me, made me think about her. Interesting. And it's strange. Very strange.*

I was smiling, listening to his thoughts, and told him silently, "*You know me. You just need to remember me. That is all. Remember…*"

I wrote him a lot of letters. I wrote about everything in the world and under the Sun.

He would always answer me according to the rules of the *game* he invented.

If in my letter I quoted Rumi, then a few days later, he would cite him. Or he would take one or two sentences from one of my letters, slightly change them, and use them as a thought or quote for a public speech. It delighted and amused me, as well as him.

If I asked him for something, he would always do that even though they were little things. It wasn't something hard for him to do, but still, it would please me and bring a smile to my face. Of course, it did not happen every day. But several times a month, at least. Sometimes more often. Usually, this would happen when I disappeared and did not write for several days. That was his way of letting me know he was missing me.

At first, I asked myself, *why is he listening to me? Why does he do as I ask him?* After all, he did not remember me. But all of us, as well as of course all the Twin Flames, have the *deep memory*. In that memory is kept everything we need to remember; we might not realize it consciously, but subconsciously we do. We might not understand why we feel a pull to this woman or want to run from that man, but "deep memory" knows why. Every significant experience we ever had in any of our incarnations, which shook us to the core, or meant a lot to us, or transformed us, is there. And most definitely, we remember those we loved deeply. *We always remember those we loved.*

Maa had told me, "Deep inside, Lala, he knows you, remembers you, and is waiting for you."

One day, I wrote to him that I had never seen the Pacific Ocean and asked him to come closer to the water. The next day he posted a video, where he was standing almost at the very brink of the water. He was standing there with a cheeky smile on his radiant and downright mischievous boyish face.

"There you go! Here is your ocean!" said his eyes.

If I wrote about some book, all of his subscribers (and me) received a quote from this same book a couple of days later. If I liked some shirt on him, he would often appear wearing it. But most importantly, what I hoped for and why I started all this correspondence, did happen. In some impossible and elusive way, his inner light seemed to be shining again! And the longer I was in his life, the more his light became noticeable.

His boyish charm returned, together with a spark in his unbelievable eyes. He bubbled like a brook in the woods in the joyful rays of the morning sun. But as soon as I disappeared, for two, three days, a week, his light would switch off. I could not bear seeing him like that. So, I always came back.

Was it my strength or my weakness? My wisdom or my stupidity? Was I a complete and hopeless fool, or was I a saint? I do not know.

Yes, I wanted to send it all to hell from time to time because as soon as I looked at this situation with my logical mind turned on, all of it seemed just absurd. Absolute nonsense. Entirely meaningless. But I was no longer able to leave. I just couldn't.

Seven or eight months of our first year passed by, just like one day. As the connection between us grew stronger, it became more and more unbearable for me to live like this. My Soul was a big white bird with huge wings, locked in a small, I would even say, very tiny cage. And this bird couldn't even move these beautiful, strong wings, let alone spread them in all their glory.

Twin Flames are very familiar with all these symptoms. The sudden rise of temperature, almost 105 F, without any logical reason whatsoever. Fever. Feeling hot, followed by chills. And severe pain in the chest, as if your Soul is trying to break out free and fly away. It is tearing, tearing away from this body, eager to leave and fly to him. Fly to him! But how? How? How can she fly out of the cage if her wings are squeezed by its bars so terribly that she can barely even breathe?

The more, the deeper he knew me, the more unbearable it was for me to be so far away from him. Even more unbearable was understanding that this separation would be for a long time. Perhaps even for a lifetime. This lifetime. But we all live in hope, don't we?

I wrote him a lot about almost everything. But when I wanted to write about my children, Maa told me, "Not yet."

His Maa, for the first several months, I only saw her in my dreams. But then came a moment when I began to see her without any need to fall asleep first.

For a long time, I did not dare start watching his films, public appearances, and interviews. When I finally decided to watch them, I damned everything in the world. At first, I could only last a couple of minutes. Looking at him was almost unbearable torture. But then, little by little, I was getting used to it. The more I watched and listened to him, the more I recognized myself in him.

179

I was shocked by how much we were alike! That was something no amount of logic or common sense would ever be able to explain. *I was looking at myself in the male form.* The manner of speaking. The way of building sentences. Frequently used words. Expressions. Turns of speech. It didn't seem possible, but it was just like that. And the most amazing thing was our gestures and facial expressions. We even blink in the same manner, smile the same, both have this fixed gaze from below the forehead and a way of squinting our eyes, raising the left eyebrow, you name it, what else.

I looked for information and read everything I could find about him! But while reading it, I would constantly realize that I *ALREADY* knew all that!

We had the same favorite cartoons in childhood, films, songs, books, actors, colors. Watching his interviews, I was looking into his eyes. In them, I saw my soul-bird, struggling in her tiny cage. At some moments, I would stop the video and look at him. What I did next probably looked like madness if somebody saw me.

Pure madness! But hypnotic and bitter-sweet. I would trace his face with my fingertips while looking into his eyes and let the tears fall. I seldomly allowed myself the luxury. In these moments, Maa would always be there. She laid her hand on my head and I felt support, deep love and understanding. Her touch was warm and calming and gave me the strength and the courage I needed so much.

"I can't live without him, Maa. Do you hear me? I can't even breathe without him! How? Tell me, Maa. How can I live without ever seeing his face? How can I live without ever seeing his eyes? You did not give me the freedom from this love. To be exact, I did not persist in such freedom, and now everything has become even worse. Much worse, Maa! This torture is becoming harder and harder. And what should I do now, Maa? What *CAN* I do?"

The pain in my chest from my soul tearing towards him became simply unbearable. The other reason for that pain was the simple truth that perhaps I would never even see him! The One who is closer to me than the blood running inside my veins, or my heartbeat, was as far from me as a distant Galaxy.

"My beautiful girl," she told me, "I cannot give you the answers to your questions. At least for now, I can't. I can only tell you one simple truth: When the time comes, you will know all the answers. You will know everything!"

"Will I see him, Maa? Tell me! Will I see him?"

"You will see him!"

"Maa, does he remember me?"

"I told you, Lala. Deep inside, he always remembers you! But he will remember you with his mind as well. But will he trust his mind? Will his mind and heart, the voice of his Soul, be able to stop fighting with each other and be at peace? It will depend on you as well, my girl! Do you have enough strength? Do you have enough courage? The time has come, Lala!"

"Time for what, Maa?"

"Time to tell him! You must tell him, Lala! *You must tell him at last, WHO YOU ARE!*"

Tell him who I am? That's exactly what I was afraid of the most! Even the idea of it terrified me! I had to tell him. I knew it. But I couldn't bring myself to do that. My courage would leave me as soon as I even gave it a thought. How can I tell him this?

I had written to him about so much. About writers and philosophers. About human nature. About ecology and history. About Vimanas and Vedas. About Gods, hidden knowledge, and the meaning of life. About love and poetry. I wrote to him about so many things.

I could create a whole book just with my letters. But I was still frozen by fear of writing Farhan about who I was, and why I have done all I have done! Why I just appeared out of nowhere. Why I have told him everything I have. I was also afraid to write to him that his mother was near me. I could see her, feel her, talk to her. Did I have the right? I wanted him to know, but would he even believe me? Most importantly, I had to tell him who I was! O, Gods! How can I say this? How?

How could I tell him that I am the one, he has loved for many lives, and I was the one who has loved him? How could I say to him that this was precisely the reason why I began writing to him? I knew I had to say that all

181

to him! I had to open him up to the truth finally. How much longer would I stay silent? I must do it, but how? How?

The day came when Maa said, looking straight into my eyes, *"The time is now! Write!"*

And I have written.

Chapter 23

Confession

In so many days, weeks and months, I am not sure if you managed to get used to my manner of addressing you as if I had known you for thousands of years. Or if you got used to me talking to you, not in the way someone would speak to a movie star, who you undoubtedly are but instead as if you were someone very close to me, someone I have known very deeply for a very long time. I even know that you admire me! I am some type of "Perfection" in your opinion. "A dream woman." Holy Heavens! Maybe I should buy myself a plastic or a paper crown and wear it on my head every day! Such a man admires me!

Oh, my gentle! Your fans would have torn me into tiny pieces if they only had the patience to read every letter I wrote to you during these months! What are you smiling about? Keep on smiling, Heavenly Angel. I adore your smile! When you smile, you look like a mischievous, naughty little boy! I know for sure, when I don't write to you, you miss me! How do I know? I'll tell you, even though you might think I'm crazy! But even if you do, it won't change the fact that I attract you like a flame attracts a moth.

What would you say if I tell you that I can hear your thoughts? What If I tell you, I feel you? I feel you with each cell of my body, every nerve like a bare wire. I fill you with every thought, every particle of my very existence. Will you be surprised? No. You won't be surprised. But you won't believe me. When I disappear, and you don't find the words written by me, you think of me; you miss me! You don't even know why this is happening? But it always does. Ask me, how do I know about that? I'll tell you how. Don't be in a hurry, my Angel. Oh, by the way, what are you thinking of my eyes? That you are drowning in them? Those are exactly your thoughts, aren't they? My eyes are just like yours. Have you noticed? Or rather, my eyes are like the eyes of your mom. I know, it hurts thinking of her not being there with you. I am sorry.

It hurts very deep inside, at the very core of your heart. You hide this pain from everyone, but I know it's there. I know. Also, you often wonder where the hell did I come from? Let me tell you something. You may not like it, and perhaps it will shock you or even make you angry. Because in saying this, I will touch upon something sacred for you—your mother. I will say it anyway. I will say it because I have to! I must, do you hear me?

Who am I? The answer is there, very deep, at the very core of you. It is deep in your heart! Not even in your heart, but in your very essence, your very Soul! In the part of you, which is immortal, eternal, and infinite. The answer is there. Will you be able to see it? Will you have the courage to accept it and to embrace it?

Your Maa is very dear to you. She is very dear to me as well. And you have to deal with the fact that I share her love with you because she loves me too. Yes, my heavenly angel. She loves me because she knows me! Just as you know me. Yes, you know me. You have known me deeply and truly for a very long time.

No. We have never met. To be exact, we have not met in THIS life. In this one, no. But we live thousands of lives! Do you know that? Thousands! That is precisely the reason why I just showed up in your life from nowhere.

I've been looking for your eyes for my whole life! Every day of THIS life! Ever since I was a little girl. But I found you only a few months ago!

Why did they let me find you only now? Why not earlier? Why not later? I do not know the answer to this question, perhaps, because the time has come for you to remember, for me to remember. Would you believe that my Beautiful Angel with sad eyes? What would you say to all this? That I am crazy?

But then why, why do you feel a flutter deep in your heart as you read my words? I will tell you why. Because there, deep inside, you KNOW me! You have known me for many centuries, for millennia. For many, many lives, we both lived.

And I've always been just like this. Maybe a little bit different, but I am sure, almost the same as now. Do you remember? No. You don't remember, not yet. Oh, how I wish you could remember! That is the only thing I want from you. Yes, my gentle. That is all I want. I just want you to remember... Remember me. I know you don't believe me now. But I know one day you will believe. Your Maa is standing right next to me. She has a yellow rose in her hands. Maa loves yellow roses. How do I know? Nobody knows this except you, right? But I do. There should be some explanation why I know such things."

I felt a soft, warm touch on my shoulder. I looked up and met the eyes of Maa.

"Lala, tell him! Tell him that you love him!"

"Maa, he hears these words a thousand times a day! He has for many and many years. He is used to them! They will not touch his heart!"

Maa just smiled and gently brushed my cheek with her hand, "Tell him, Lala!"

"Maa!"

"Tell him."

I took a deep breath and went back to my letter. Who am I to argue? At the end of that letter, I wrote these words.

And also, there is something else I have to tell you.
I love you

After that letter, he was silent for ten days. To say that my letter struck him is to say nothing. It was incredibly shocking for him. Shocking, yet at the same time, this letter gave him some answers. This letter awakened in him deeply hidden feelings and emotions; it also brought his deepest FEAR to the surface. The emotions, sensations, and feelings evoked by the Twin Flame have enormous, overwhelming intensity. Almost always, this is something never felt or experienced before. Something that cannot be logically explained. Such an experience may bring up the fear of the other Twin, sometimes even panic and terror, especially for the man.

As I've mentioned before, they call one Twin *awakened* or *the chaser*, and the other is called *the runner*. Here I need to explain something: The *runner* isn›t running away from his Twin because he doesn›t feel anything. On the contrary, he feels everything too deeply and too intensely! He experiences feelings he has never felt with anyone else before. Emotions, absolutely impossible to control. Something so powerful that nothing he previously experienced, can be compared with it.

For a man, king, and master of his own life and fate, controlling everyone and everything for many years, to receive such information is way too much. Too strange. Too unexpected. Too inexplicable. The easiest decision for him in such a situation was to get out of it all. Completely! He wanted to immediately cut it off and forget it all after reading my confession letter! I knew it! I knew since I could hear his thoughts! He wanted to quit this strange connection. He wanted to finish this strange communication. That was the easiest and the most convenient path to follow. After all, he was a Star! He was married, or the world considered him to be! So many eyes focused on him, on his every movement. Why the hell would he need this relationship? Was it even possible to call it that? And who with? With a woman thousands of miles away? A woman who was not of his circle, who was, yes for sure, fascinating, deep, extraordinary but at the same time weird, strange, maybe even crazy? Just break free of her at once! Cut it all off! Stop reading all her letters. Do not even try to understand these feelings! Do not even try to analyze them! Do not repeat in your head, over and over again, all the words she has written to you! Destroy them. Erase all of those words. Erase even the memory of them and her as well, from your mind! Forget it all and move on; just forget! He wanted to do that. He was ready to do that. I was prepared to accept that. But…

But his Soul, the same restless bird just like mine, would never let him do it!

He was silent. He was silent for a long time. When he finally spoke, he did not choose his own words. Instead, he quoted Shakespeare's *The Merchant of Venice*, the book I had adored since I was a child. (Of course. He was well aware of this fact from my previous letters).

He wrote:

> *"Beshrew your eyes,*
> *They have o'erlooked me and divided me;*
> *One half of me is yours, the other half is yours,*
> *Mine own, I would say; but if mine, then yours,*
> *And so all yours."*

His selfie accompanied the quote. In it, he looked completely different. His eyes had changed. They were so full of such intense emotional energy, that when I saw them, for a moment I forgot how to breathe. And these words! These words, *"One half of me is yours; the other half is yours, and so all yours."*

"What are you trying to tell me, my Love," I whispered under my breath, looking into his impossibly gorgeous eyes. "What? What do you want to say? Do you mean to say that you…" Oh! No! I will not think about it! I won't! I won't! I won't! Oh, Gods! And all the Guardians and Keepers of the Fates! What do I do with all this? How do I manage to handle all this? Most importantly, how can I breathe while being so far away from him?

A new day is dawning outside the window, and I was still sitting in front of the computer screen, staring into Farhan's eyes, unable to look away. I felt that if I stopped looking into them, I would stop existing. I would disappear as if I was never even created.

I fell asleep with his name on my lips. Like dozens of dreams before, he was holding my face in his palms. But this time, his eyes were burning me with a raging fire.

"Do you love me?" He asked.

"Is not it obvious?"

"Tell me!"

"Why?"

"Tell me!"

"I love you!"

"Say it again!"

"I love you!"

He took his hands away from my face, and his eyes fixed on the ocean waves.

"We are doomed to this hell, Lala," he finally said. "This hell will be our life, away from each other."

He turned around and looked into my eyes again. "I will hurt you! I will bring you pain! A lot of pain! Not because I want to, but because I will have no other choice! You will burn and burn and I, I will do nothing. You will cry but I won't be there to dry your tears. I will constantly take and take, giving you almost nothing in return. You still have a chance to leave! Leave now, Lala, while you still can! Leave now, because if you do not...."

Again, holding my face is in his palms, "If you do not leave now... Later, I will not let you go! I will never let you go. Do you hear me? I will torture you! I will torment you! I will make you suffer. But I won't let you go! I cannot! Because I need you! I need you like the air that I breathe! That is why I am giving you this last chance. Please find strength in yourself. Leave me now! Leave while you still *CAN*! While I still can let you go!"

I can feel the tears falling down my cheeks. I raise my right hand and trace Farhan's face with my fingertips, touching his insanely tempting lips. They are tightly pressed and firm, like marble. I look into the dark lakes of his eyes and shake my head no.

"No." I whisper in a barely audible voice. "No! I will not!"

From one of my letters:

I miss you. I miss you when my eyes are open. But I miss you even more, when I close them. When I am asleep, I miss you. When I am awake, I miss you. I miss you every minute, every second of every new day. I miss you.

Whether I am alone or surrounded by crowds of people, I miss you. When I walk along the ocean shore, whispering your name to the wind, hoping that it will carry my words to you. When I laugh and when I cry. When I am happy and when I am upset. I miss you.

I miss your voice and your laughter. I miss your hands and your impossible eyes. How long has it been since we saw each other last? A hundred years? Two hundred? Longer? I see you everywhere I look. I see you in the smile of a child, in the clouds that are racing across the sky, in a sweet couple of lovers holding hands, in fallen autumn leaves, and the cries of gulls gliding above the water. I feel the touch of your lips in the gentle caress of the sea breeze. I hear your laughter in birdsong early in the morning. Everything, absolutely everything, reminds me of you! There is nothing I can do about this eternal longing. The beautiful Lady with broad silver wings hugs me tighter and tighter with each passing moment. I can't escape from her embrace! I will be able to break free only when my eyes look into yours, when I touch your face, your lips, and your hair, with my fingertips. But will such a day come? Will it come?

A year passed, then a year and a half. The game he started, and I indulged, continued. At first, I enjoyed it; now, it no longer gave me much pleasure. I had a passionate wish for us to communicate not via Facebook but in the way simple people do: Phone. Skype. Messenger. Something as simple as that. I was getting tired of this game. He already knew a lot about me. He sensed me. I hoped that maybe he even remembered something.

Still, it wasn't enough for him to be able to believe me fully. I knew I had to do something so he would *BELIEVE*! So, he would remember me! The letters were not enough. But what else could I do? What else?

There is one more important detail I want you to know about Twin Flames, which is valid for some Karmic Soulmates couples as well. They constantly fight with themselves in the depth of their hearts and minds. Both always want to *break free from everything, forget it all and move on.* The reason for that is the lack of clarity. Neither of them can stand the uncertainty. But who can give any guarantees when it comes to Love? Especially Love like this, following them from one life to another. Twin Flames are very free-spirited beings. They cannot stand dependence and slavery, even in the name of Love. But the truth is, they are both dependent on each other and are both the slaves of this Eternal Love. They must embrace the *transformation* this Love brings to both of them. *There is no other way.*

You can try to run from yourself, but how long will you be running? Is it easy to face yourself? No. Not at all.

Imagine you live with a tornado raging inside you 24 hours a day, and you just can't get rid of it. There is an old song saying, "Lord! I can neither sigh nor breathe!" It is like that. Besides the "tornado," you, of course, are constantly trying to turn on your head and convince yourself that this is all "nonsense" and "just cannot be true!" Yet, Something or Someone much more Superior than you, call it God, the Supreme Source, Universe, or as you wish, will never let you give it all up!

Much later, I read in several books and articles the following phrase, *"Twin Flames always live each of their incarnations watched closely by the Higher Forces."* If you came to this three-dimensional world as one of the Twin Flames, you came not only to fulfill your karmic debts but also to do some essentially vital work. And many people's lives depend on how well you do that work, even if that sounds a bit *pompous.*

So even if you are having a hard time, The Force will never let you *send it all to hell.* Your Love, multiplied by fate, duty, karma, is an insurmountable life obstacle. That very obstacle you both want and don't want to overcome.

It is pure madness, a boiling volcano, relentless pain, and indescribable happiness all combined.

By the end of the first year, I fully realized that he was taking my words and ideas to heart, and not only that; he put them into real life. Every time I had an idea, a global problem was haunting me, whether deforestation or monstrous ocean pollution, millions of people living below the poverty line, or worst all, the suffering of small children; I wrote to him about it.

I always started these letters with the words, *"I am nobody, my Angel, no one will listen to me, but they might listen to you! They WILL listen to you. Tell them, my Love!"*

These words were followed by what, in my opinion, he could or needed to say to "them." "They" were the powerful, famous, and the rich of this world, and he was one of them. He had influence not only on the circle of the rich and powerful. He was followed by and heard by millions of people of all ages, religions, and social levels. They listened to his words. His ideas and deeds inspired many and many of them.

He was an excellent speaker, a genuinely gifted and phenomenal orator. Various schools and universities all over the world invited him to speak. He knew how to transfer his ideas to the heads and hearts of people of all ages, beliefs, and upbringings. He knew how to speak, what words to say, in order to be truly heard and understood. He was a true *inspiration*. He combined the vastest intellect with a witty sense of humor, the look of a prince from an Arabian or Indian Fairy Tale, the smile of a 6-year-old, piercing eyes, a deep sensual voice, charm and charisma enough for a dozen men, you name it, he had it. He was impossibly hypnotizing when he spoke; people listened. Such speeches could change the lives of many people for the better.

And now, imagine. Suddenly, in the most unexpected, incredible way, I was someone inspiring HIM. I have to admit; it felt darn good. I never thought much of myself. But if HE found my ideas good enough, maybe I was more than I used to think of myself. I could write five and sometimes ten sheets about something that had bothered me for a long time. I spilled my thoughts onto the keyboard and then sent those letters to him. Another realization came to me. As it was apparent, we could not be together under

191

the given circumstances, maybe I had to search and finally find him NOT for myself but some *higher purpose*. It must be so. Perhaps even some beautiful and noble purpose. One which we can fulfill together! Oh! That was an astounding realization!

That was the beginning of a new period in my life! Beautiful life! I began to breathe, rejoice, and feel his heartbeat as my own. Lady Sadness finally let go of my restless soul for the first time in many years. My soul was singing, speaking, sharing, dancing, living, and most of all, *LOVING*. Loving so profoundly, so honestly and so entirely that words cannot describe. Maybe only birds can sing it, or ocean waves echo it while kissing the shore.

I often said, "I am writing with the blood of my soul." My words penetrated deep into his heart and his brilliant mind. He never remained indifferent. When I wrote to him, *"Tell them, My Love! Tell them!"* He did! He spoke, and he acted! Others followed his example. A lot of others and, seeing that, my heart was singing!

In some small way, I knew I was a part of those good deeds, and the thought that at least someone in our crazy world would feel better because of the words I said to Him, warmed my soul. It also gave me enough strength to live and breathe, while still being so far away from him.

Chapter 24

Another Letter

You know, my gentle, what I've been thinking about for the last several years. It doesn't let me sleep! We live thousands of lives and incarnations. You do know, of course, that our Universe consists of myriads of galaxies, planets, and solar systems. We choose to incarnate and live on those where we can learn something to go to the next level. And the levels are endless. But for some reason, when we are here on Gaia Earth, in our three-dimensional world, do you know what prevents us from seeing the truth most of all? Our logical thinking! So-called *cold mind and logic*.

Strange, isn't it? After all, it would seem our minds are here to help us, right? But apparently, not always. Our cold, logical thinking, or our Cold Sober Mind, can become our most dangerous enemy! It is he who prevents us from remembering who we are and why we have come into this life. It's strange, don't you think, my Love? When our physical shell dies, our brain, the holder of our logical mind, remains here on Earth. But we, however, continue to understand everything and feel everything!

And most importantly, we *remember* everything! We know who we are, where we are, where we came from and where we are going! People, in their physical bodies, cannot see us. But we see and perceive everything! In the Spirits world, we remember every

193

minute, every second, not only of our recently finished life, but also of all the hundreds and thousands of lives that we had lived before. We also remember all those who were nearby. Those, who made us Love and hate, cry and laugh, create and dream, in ALL of those lives! We remember, understand, and realize *everything!*

That means, my Love, one significant thing! Our Deep Inner Memory is situated *NOT* in the gray matter in our heads! Not at all! Our Deep Inner Memory of everything we have ever experienced and been through, in all the levels of our existence, resides *EXACTLY* where our heart is pulsating. Where the Heart Chakra is—Anahata! It turns out to be, my powerful King, to comprehend the truth, you need to *TURN OFF YOUR HEAD!*

This idea is far from being new. I guess it is as old as the world. So, who are we? And who is God?

God is the ocean. And each one of us is a drop, a wave, *of this very ocean.* God is The Source, The Essence, and each one of us is *the same* Source and Essence in a smaller form. Why is it so hard for us to understand this? Each one of us is a miniature universe. Everything in this Universe is also in you, in me, in each of us! All of the questions and all of the answers are all in us! *You are the question! You are the answer!*

Carlos Castaneda, Nicholas and Helena Roerichs, Elena Blavatsky, Paolo Coelho, and many others like them, the so-called *awakened,* have spoken and written about this so many times! So, why don't we take a pause and just listen to them? Is it because we do not want to hear them? Or are we just being lazy? Or afraid? Somehow, it's much easier for many of us to live *WITHOUT THINKING* and asking questions and searching for the answers! It is much easier for us to live as slaves, following the laws and the rules, created by someone a long time ago and forced upon us since childhood. They force us to obey. Obey. Obey without *THINKING!* But it should be that way no more! It should not be this way, my Eternal Love!

LALA AGNI

Do you remember *The Alchemist* by Paolo Coelho?

> *"The Boy reached through to the Soul of the World and saw that it was a part of the Soul of God. And he SAW that the Soul of God was HIS OWN SOUL!"*[5]

The boy saw that THE SOUL OF GOD WAS HIS OWN SOUL! What else is there to add here, my King? So why is it so hard for us to see this simple truth? The answer is simple. Our Sober, Cold, Logical Mind!

I will remind you of another great thinker we both know. Ram Dass says, *"LOSE YOUR MIND TO GAIN YOUR SOUL!!!!"*[6] And *"Taming the mind is fraught with paradoxes. You have to give it all up to have it all. Turn off your mind. There is a place in you beyond the thought that already knows—trust in that!"*[7]

Do you know what the mind actually gives us? It grants us a billion fears and doubts. It gives us a million reasons and thoughts, like these: *You won't succeed! You cannot do it! Who are you to wish for that?! You cannot do this! You will fail! You will lose! People will talk behind your back! How dare you even think of that? Look at yourself!* These thoughts aren't the creation of your Soul; they are the creation of the *MIND!*

What do we have as a result? Instead of silencing our supposedly logical mind, we silence *OUR SOUL!*

And religions: What can be sadder than this? The most influential world religions at this moment in time, instead of guiding people to the truth, lead them away from it! Do you know why? God or Gods did not create religions. Gandhi said, *"God has no religion!"* The mind created religions! More precisely, people make them for a

---

5   Paulo Coelho, The Alchemist (Brazil: English translation published by HarperTorch, 1993), 154.
6   Ram Dass, "Ram Dass Quotes", www.ramdass.org
7   Ram Dass, Polishing the Mirror: How to Live from Your Spiritual Heart (2013)

single purpose: Power. Control of one group of people over another group of people.

Religions allowed some to rule, giving the rest no other choice but to obey. Religions made people believe that they had a very pitiful place in their life and on this planet, probably slightly more "magnificent" than an ant. According to what they teach us, we were born to struggle with only one hope, to be rewarded in "heaven" after death, of course, and only if we behave *according to the rules. Their rules!* Religious leaders proclaimed people slaves! But what can a slave do? Only *OBEY!* That is the *KEY* word—*Obey!* Obey, pray and repent. Repent, obey and pray. That is all that one's life is supposed to be, according to them.

Obey, pray and ask for forgiveness, and God will have mercy on you!

Pretty much, right from childhood, people are taught: Not only are you a pitiful powerless thing, living only one life. You are also constantly *GUILTY* of something. You were even conceived in sin. You are a terrible, evil, sinful, weak creature and must never forget it and continuously repent and ask for forgiveness while hoping you will be good enough not to go to *hell.*

None of this is the truth, my Love! That is the opposite of the truth. That is a terrible lie! People, believing in it, they break my heart!

Who could imagine such a God? Only a human mind, in a limited human body! Such things could never be created or told by The Divine Source!

Or it was much more complicated than that. It was an inhuman mind!

From many ancient texts, we could see that there were beings who came to this world, to Gaia Earth, declaring themselves gods. They killed and did terrible things to prove their power and force people to obey and worship them. Could this be possible? Of course.

The Beings of Light would come to Gaia as well. But the Dark Side was still too powerful. Religion twisted their teaching and words;

196

much of what they left, remains forever hidden from the eyes of people.

In Zeyven Alexander Blackwell's book we read

> *The Darkside's greatest triumph was in the engineering of religions around the beings of Pure Light, who arrived periodically to stir the SOULS INTO REMEMBRANCE!*[8]
>
> The remembrance of that simple fact, that *what they held within them was the Very God Essence…*[9]
>
> Oh! How much *I WANT THEM TO REMEMBER!*
>
> We, humans, are like ocean waves that are searching for and trying to explain this very ocean. Each one of us is a drop, and the ocean is God. Each particle of the wave consists of the same matter as the whole ocean. We, each of us, are this very ocean, and the ocean is each of us.
>
> Or there is a different way to say it. God is a body, and each of us is this body's cell. Is it difficult for a person to understand? Love in each of us is God. Compassion in each of us is God. We truly are created in the image of God! Gods! Absolute! Divine Source! *God manifests itself in each one of us!*
>
> Meister Eckhart said, "*The eye through which I see God is the same eye through which God sees me: my eye and God's eye are one eye, one seeing, one knowing, and one Love.*"
>
> We can be a source of joy for ourselves and others but we can also become a source of pain and grief. If you betray the one who loves you, it is not God who hurts your loved one! *You do!* We can be Gods for each other, or we can be demons for each other and ourselves!

---

8   Zeyven Alexander Blackwell, Twin Flame Revelation, 9.
9   Zeyven Alexander Blackwell, Twin Flame Revelation, 10.

It all depends on us. A drop has the same qualities as the whole ocean. We can create or destroy, inspire, or bring misery. It all depends on us!

Very few people question themselves: Where do we exist before we enter this physical world? And if, after just one life, for billions of years to come, we will be jumping from one cloud to another in a place called "Heaven," how will our Soul learn, grow, develop, advance? How? Each of our new lives is like the next class in school, the next level in the eternal game of life, the next stage of development.

If you did not pass something, did not understand, you have to come back and take this course one more time! Repeat it until you know it! Until you perceive it fully! Until you successfully pass all the Almighty Force of the Cosmic Balance exams, called *Karma.* How can people reject the obvious? How can people reject this fundamental law of our Earth and other planets, other Solar Systems, and other Galaxies?

You know, My Soul, what the truth is? The truth consists in the fact that our only boundaries are our fears and the doubts generated by the *MIND!* The society in which we live, the religion we grow up with, forced upon us by our parents, was also forced upon them by their parents.

But the ideals of the past, once-unbreakable laws, religions and traditions, all go through changes. Then a moment comes and the truth opens up right in front of our eyes! Now we have to make a choice. *To accept the truth or reject it.* Do we choose the path of chronic ignorance or a new one? That choice is up to us.

The removal of the law of Reincarnation from religions, which claim to be truth, light, and wisdom, has been a true crime against humanity! Against the Universal Truth! The idea of "one life, then hell or heaven" is not only completely lacking any sense whatsoever, but it is even dangerous! Such dogma leads a human to feelings of doom, hopelessness, unwillingness to live, and disbelief in any justice and happiness. Not only that. All the events that happen to us; all the people we meet, love, hate, learn from; all the things we try to learn, create and achieve: EVERYTHING loses any sense. All people in our life turn out to be random and all events accidental. *The tree without any roots!* You live once, it means you have no PAST, and your future is uncertain. Pray. Repent. Obey. Hope for Heaven. Is this ALL? According to "one life" religions, this is all. Any sense in it, and wisdom, any logic? No...

The truth is different. We are learning here on this Earth. We continue to come again and again *to learn*. We improve; we become calmer and wiser, stronger and deeper. We find our soulmates and other halves. We laugh, cry, inspire others and change the world for the better. That how it was; it is, it will be.

You know, the unwillingness of people to see what is right IN FRONT of their eyes surprises me. Despite the availability and accessibility of information nowadays, people still prefer to live in ignorance because it's easier! It breaks my heart.

Classical world history textbooks contain too much inaccurate information, and some outright nonsense. Forgive me for my harshness. Thanks to it we learn, after getting out of their caves, people began building monumental pyramids all over the world, on all continents, erecting huge megalithic structures, constructing cities and temples of unimaginable beauty, all by using technology we cannot even dream about understanding! I guess they did it with the help of a stick and a rock. Watch the movie series "Forbidden Archeology" or "The Technologies of the Ancients."

And what about the ancient spaceships? The manuscript "Vaimānika Shāstra" was created hundreds and maybe thousands of years ago. The Vimanas or "Chariots of Fire," described in detail, were, in fact, Ancient Spaceships. Again, their properties were far more superior to those we know now. In his work *"Vimana: Flying Machines of the Ancients,"* David Hatcher Childress puts together an incredible amount of extraordinary evidence that people used aircraft *thousands of years ago.* That means these ancient civilizations had advanced metal technology, electricity, and engineering knowledge. Plus, skills we, unfortunately, have no idea about, like *melting stone* technology or constructing temples out of stones, each weighing in around 800 tons (example: the city of Baalbek, and many others all over the world).

So who were they? Those people who possessed such information? Fallen angels? Gods? Possibly. But they were our ancestors as well! They had the KNOWLEDGE. Not any kind of religion or dogmas, but actual *Knowledge*! The Knowledge of the laws of the Universe!

There are many versions of what happened to the ancient Gods and then to the Atlanteans and their children. It could have been a war, a human-made disaster, a space invasion, some natural disasters, or all combined.

Ancient myths describe it as the "War of the Gods." What was ocean, became land, and what was land disappeared underwater! The axis of Gaia-Earth changed, and with it, the climate changed as well! Where there was a mild subtropical climate, terrible cold and glaciation began. Those, who managed to survive, regressed. The Golden Age ended. The Stone Age began.

Over the hundreds and hundreds of years, we have forgotten who we are, where we are from, and why we came to this planet. The Knowledge has been lost or destroyed on purpose! It remains only among the Guardians and in the ancient sacred texts. People started forgetting their true essence and power, and finally, they completely forgot. And then, those who wanted to rule, created religions for obedience and control. The true history was destroyed and rewritten again.

Will we ever find out the truth? I really hope we will. People are waking up. Forgotten or lost Knowledge is being finally revealed, people have started restoring their memory of past incarnations. The journey through past lives is gaining strength. Psychologists and parapsychologists have suddenly started discovering the secrets of the realization of wishes, time moves faster, time flies.

Cities covered with the sand of time, sunken fortresses and seemingly lost manuscripts, paintings, maps, all of a sudden appear out of nowhere and begin to reveal their secrets for those who seek them. People start to discover the simple truth: Multiple Universes and Galaxies, layers and levels of creation, multiple dimensions, all of those are within us! The smallest grain of sand and the Biggest Galaxy are created from the same building material— ENERGY! Remembering this, we will remember who we are.

I want to share one of my most favorite legends with you. It shows this all very beautifully in one story:

Once, a very long time ago, every human being was GOD. Everyone was at the level of creation. But the Dark Force interfered and humans started to abuse their Divine Powers. So, one day Brahma (the original Creative Energy, the Source) decided to take the Divinity back from Humans and hide it in a place where humans could never find it. But that was a problem. What place to choose? Brahma decided to ask all of the Gods, Spirits, and Beings of different levels to decide about a place to hide the Divinity.

Some said, "Let's hide it very deep at the heart of Mother Earth. People will never find it there!"

Brahma didn't think it was a great idea. "Humans will dig into the earth and find it," he said.

Some said, "Let's hide it in the deepest part of the ocean."

Again, Brahma refused and said, "Humans will learn to dive and will be able to find it.

"Mountains! Let's hide it on the top of the Mountains!" another offered.

"Humans will climb up the mountains and get the divinity," he answered.

After many, many hours of trying to find the solution to this enormous problem, the Gods gave up and said, "We don't know where to hide

Divinity! No matter what we come up with, eventually, humans will find a way to get a hold of it! There is no place left to hide."

Then Brahma fell silent! He thought for a long time and finally said, "I know what to do! We will hide it *in the center of their own essence!* Humans will search for it here and there. They will search for it everywhere and will not be able to find it! They simply will not even think to look for Divinity *inside their own true self!* Only when they are truly ready and awakened will they be able to understand where it had been all this time.

All Gods agreed that it was the perfect place for hiding the Divinity. And since then, humans have been searching for Divinity up and down! Digging Earth, diving oceans, climbing mountains, constantly searching for something they *have within themselves.*

And those are just a few of hundreds of letters I wrote to him.

The time kept passing.

Women lack logic. I guess this fact is well known to everyone. Even the women who can see and know more than others still lack logic. I was getting tired. The idea of giving it all up was a frequent guest in my head. More and more often, I thought about dropping it all. Over the years, this relationship in five-dimensional reality began to exhaust me beyond any level. After all, I was still a woman of flesh and blood even if I was a Twin Flame.

But the Seers didn't let me give up. They began to appear in my life as if by magic.

Chapter 25

The Seers

Fatima

During that period of my life, I experienced a feeling like when you go through something unimaginable, but you cannot share it with absolutely anyone. It is absolutely impossible and even unthinkable to tell such a story to anybody! Even though I have always been a hermit, all this started weighing on my shoulders as time passed. I was isolated from other people. I was becoming more and more reserved and remote. And maybe, through inspiring him with my letters and ideas, I was helping many people to become happier. Yes, I was getting his attention and understanding. But still, apart from that all, I was becoming terribly lonely.

As if responding to my heartache hidden from everyone around me, some amazing people started to appear in my life. That was a new twist in my extraordinary and unbelievable story.

One of the Seers was African. Her name was Fatima and we worked together.

She was originally from Senegal and belonged to an interesting group of Muslims. She told me that the form of Islam she and her family believed in, was closer to Buddhism than to original Islam and even acknowledged reincarnation. She was tall, slender, dark-skinned and incredibly beautiful. For about six months, we worked together but never had a chance to talk to each other.

Until one day, we happened to both work until late at night. After leaving work, we headed to our cars, and suddenly, she stopped and told me, "You know, I thought you were Indian! But I doubted because of your skin, as it is way too light, so I was not sure. Then someone told me that you were Russian. I was shocked!"

"You thought I was Indian? Why?"

She paused for a moment. "It might sound strange. But there is this very famous Hollywood actor. His mother was Indian, and his father has Arabic or Turkish background; I do not remember exactly. In my home country, Senegal, he is very popular! For some reason, he reminds me of you! I think of him every time I look at you. You see, your eyes and his. They are so similar, it's amazing! It's like... I don't even know how to explain it. But you probably know him! Farhan Ali!"

The parking lot got all blurry in my eyes. I turned so pale that it was noticeable even in the light of a streetlamp.

"Alla? What, what is wrong with you? You look like you have seen a ghost!" She reached out and touched my shoulder. "Alla..."

"No. Nothing! I am ok. I am fine." I was barely able to speak.

"Do you know him?" she asked me, looking deeply into my eyes.

"No! I mean, yes! Of course, I know him! Who doesn't?"

She took another good long look at my face, then opened her car, pointed to the seat next to the driver, and said, "Sit down! Tell me everything!"

I don't even know how and why, but I did tell her everything. When I finished my implausible and unbelievable story, she was silent for several moments. What she said to me next, I did not expect at all!

"I see." she said. "This is why *HE* came to my mind every time I saw *YOU*! You have one Soul and two bodies!"

"What?" I was completely shocked. The words of Nicholas came to mind that very instant, *"You are his Half, Mom!"*

"Yes!" Fatima continued. *"One Soul, but two bodies!* My grandmother used to tell me stories about such beings when I was little. She told those stories to my brothers, my sisters, and myself. Allah sends such beings to Earth *to light the way for others*. They are very blessed. Allah leads and guides these people. But their path is also a great trial. She also said that not everyone could handle such a test, only the strongest, the toughest. I always knew that you were *different*. Even your name is unusual."

"Listen," she asked, taking my hand into hers, "Does *HE* know? All of this?"

"Yes, he does. But I can hardly imagine he believes it. To be exact, he does not allow himself to believe. I am so tired of it! Sometimes I feel like the whole thing is just killing me. And Fatima, I'm not any different, believe me! I'm just an ordinary woman."

She just laughed at that.

"You're trying to be ordinary! Trying your best, but you are not very successful at your attempts. Me neither, trust me! But listen! There is one thing I know for sure. Allah Almighty will help you! You are on a mission, and *HE*, your beautiful Farhan, as well. I know that all the answers for both of you are yet to come. Now you are not alone anymore! Do you understand? You have me! *I believe you!* And I believe *in* you! I do! I know that what you told me is the truth. I have always been able to distinguish the truth from lies. You and Him— are One! That is what it's all about! Wow! Listen! I should bring you to our home. To Senegal. Will you come?"

"I would absolutely love to!"

She embraced me as if I were her little sister, although I was five years older than her. Suddenly, it became easier for me to breathe. And I knew I could continue living this strange, sad, but beautiful story of eternal love. I was no longer alone.

Unfortunately, in this book, I cannot describe in detail all the incredible, completely original and unique Seers that fate sent me. There were, for example, two Indian women. Madhu and Sumitra. Sumitra, herself, is a Twin Flame. Madhu is an absolutely unbelievable Seer and a healer who worked as a doctor for many years and possesses the Soul of a pure Angel. Even though they both knew perfectly well who he was, they always unshakably believed and still believe that he and I are "One Soul." They both saw this fiery *something* in my and his eyes. They both supported and still support me in every possible way on my journey.

There were others, *many others*. I want to tell you about only two more of them in greater detail. I want to do this, so you understand what incredible events can happen in your life and what astonishing people you can meet on your way, if you happen to be dealing with a Twin Flame, or you are one of them.

Chapter 26

Bastet

Bastet or Ubastet—Egyptian goddess with a head of a cat

This woman's name is Gina, but I call her Bastet.

At the time I was working in a large shopping center. She worked there as well, but in a completely different department, on the floor above. We never crossed paths until, one day, she was walking for some business through my department. She had already passed me, when she suddenly stopped, turned around and walked straight up to me. It might sound more than just strange, but I will simply tell you exactly how it happened, without adding anything, or leaving anything out. The age of this woman was impossible to say, she could have been 40, or she could have been 60. She was tall, thin, and seemed almost weightless. She had huge almond-shaped, emerald-green eyes and fiery red hair.

She stopped in front of me, looking intently into the depth of my eyes. It was as if she had known me for a million years, although, at least in this life, we had never met before. The conversation between us, which followed, I can't explain even now. But maybe, I just need to give up all the attempts to explain anything in this story. I swear to you, this was exactly what we said to each other! No matter how ridiculous it sounds now.

"Hello, Bastet!" I said. "Long time no see! What are you doing on Earth?" (Maybe I was trying to make a joke like that, I'm not sure. Those were just the first words I said to her.)

"I am here on Earth doing exactly the same thing as you are!" She answered me. "Our time has finally come. Kali Yuga must finally complete its cycle!"

(Note: *The Age of Kali Yuga* is characterized by debauchery, cruelty, deceit, envy, and degradation of the entire population of the Earth. People work from dawn to midnight literally for a piece of bread. They kill and betray each other for gold coins. Dishonesty is widespread and is considered to be the norm. Corrupted and greedy government pursues only its own interests, not taking into account the needs of the people. A rich person will be considered noble, truly noble, and the poor will become slaves. There will be wars, droughts, famines, natural disasters. Due to a lack of good nutrition, people will gradually lose their common sense, kindness, compassion, and the ability to think independently. That will reduce life expectancy; people will begin to die more and more from deadly diseases at relatively young ages.

Humanity will no longer be able to maintain the technological level. Environmental pollution will reach its climax, theft, and the decline of morals will intensify. In the future, peace and confidence will altogether leave humanity. Discord, confrontation, struggle, the killing of innocent, greed, lies, and all other imaginable and unimaginable sins will be the leading companions of those living in the period of Kali-Yuga. As a result, people will have to reap the fruits of their terrible deeds).

"The darkest time for this Earth should finally come to its end," she continued, looking straight into my eyes as if seeing through me. "It's time for people to wake up! It's time to *remember who they are!* Isn't it? Many are still not ready. Others do not want to. Some are simply being lazy and clinging to their usual lies. A calm, habitual lie is much easier to live with than the truth that burns their souls. Lies require no questions, but the truth makes you *THINK!* It makes you *ask questions and look for the answers.*"

Then I suddenly came to my senses and turned on the *normal person.*

"I am so sorry. I called you Bastet. I do not even know your name. It's just the moment I saw you, she appeared in front of my eyes."

"The Goddess with a cat's head! I know! It's more accurate to say *Ubastet.* She is also called *The Eye of Ra.*"

"So, are you Bastet herself?" I asked, and it seemed, at that moment, I had no doubts about that.

"I'm not sure about that," she answered thoughtfully. "I do not remember, just like many of us do not remember. After all, we were all forced to temporarily forget who we really are. But gradually, we begin to remember. Look at yourself! You do not even fully know what you are dealing with, or what powers you have, or who you really are!"

"You are absolutely right. I have no idea! And who am I?"

"You are a Warrior! Your armor is Love, Knowledge, and your burning fiery Soul! You burn like a torch, consisting of thousands of other torches! You can be seen from afar! You have a sword too! Although, the Sword has not been given to you yet! You will receive it later. HE will give it back to you!"

"He? Who are you talking about?"

"The one with the dark eyes. The one you were looking for!" She looked into my eyes as if she was reading my Soul. And then she said, "Come to my house, my dear Soul! You need some strength! Yours is running low. Still, you are only at the very beginning of your journey. Come tomorrow night. You and I live nearby. And don't you dare to think that you are alone! *You are not!* A great Power backs you up. Very great Power! There are still many things you will have to do. And right now, your energy is running low! Do come. We will do some rituals with the Spirits of the four elements— Fire, Earth, Water, and Air. They will heal you, soothe you and help you feel stronger. I will be waiting for you. And one more thing, it will be tough to make HIM believe. Very hard, my girl. But you can do it. I know. I believe you can do it!"

And she calmly walked away as if nothing had happened, leaving me in a state of complete shock and joy at the same time. I didn't even have to say anything. She read me like an open book. What a Gift!

As it turned out, we lived very close. When she opened the door, the first thing I saw was a statue of the Goddess Bastet, almost half the height of a human, standing by the massive fireplace. Also, I saw hundreds and hundreds of books everywhere my eyes looked.

Soon, I was sitting in a deep armchair, with a huge cup of herbal tea in my hands near the cozy and calming crackling sound of the fireplace. Bastet asked the date and place of my birth and his, both of our names, and then fell silent, compiling some kind of astrological map, which was completely incomprehensible to me.

Finally, she said, "I knew it! I knew this from the very beginning! From that very moment I rested my eyes on you! Rahu and Ketu! They are exactly in front of each other! They are mirroring! There you have your proof! *I KNEW IT!*"

"I…. What are you talking about, Bastet? Rahu and Ketu? What does it mean?"

"What?! Do you not know this story? Oh. You *MUST* know it! Now. Listen…."

Once upon a time, thousands and thousands of earth years ago, there lived a sage, to be exact a rishi, named Kashyapa. He had many sons. He called them Adityas and Daityas, after their mothers, his two wives. The name of one of them was Aditi, and the other's Diti. For a long time, Adityas and Daityas, two branches from one family tree, kept fighting to possess Amrita, the nectar of Gods that bestows immortality. To resolve this dispute, God Vishnu decided to resort to a trick.

He took the form of a stunning young woman. Mohini. She invited the brothers to share the nectar of immortality. Fascinated by her beauty, the half-brothers Adityas and Daityas agreed to this proposal. Mohini pushed aside Daityas, who fell into a trance from her beauty, and walked closer to Adityas! According to Vishnu's plan, only Adityas would drink the nectar, as he had always favored him.

210

When Adityas started savoring the Amrita nectar, one of the Daityas brothers suspected something was wrong and quickly joined the lucky group. He received his dose of Amrita as well. But The Sun and The Moon quickly exposed the cheat, waring Vishnu of the deception! Vishnu at once threw out his battle disc and cut off the cheater's head! But it was already too late! Daitya's brother had already tasted Amrita! Therefore, *his head* became the *Dragon's head* — RAHU, who in anger vowed to eclipse the Moon and the Sun at the first opportunity. His *body* became *the body or the tail of the Dragon—KETU!*

Since the rest of the Daityas brothers did not receive a single drop of Amrita, they later became known as Asuras, those who have not tasted the divine nectar of immortality. And the Adityas became known as the Suras, those who have tasted the divine nectar of immortality. Another name for Suras is the Devas, the deities of the light enlightened by Amrita.

RAHU AND KETU are two parts of the *ONE divided in half!* Rahu is the Dragon's *head*, and Ketu is the *body*, or, as they say, the tail! They are at an angle of 180 degrees from each other. Whenever the Sun or the Moon unites with Rahu or Ketu, *solar or lunar eclipses always occur.*

In astronomy, *Rahu* is the Ascending, or *Northern Moon Node*, the point where the moon's orbit crosses the ecliptic. As I already said, Ketu is the body or tail of a dragon. *Ketu* gives birth to comets and meteors and is also known as the Descending, or *Southern Moon Node.*

"So, my dear girl. You two are Mirroring. Your Rahu (Head) is in Scorpio, and your Ketu (Body) is in Taurus! He has his Rahu in Taurus and Ketu in Scorpio! *You are the head! And He is the body! You are the North Moon Node, and he is the South Moon Node!* You are all that is unearthly and eternal. He is all that is earthly and impermanent. You are the *ONE*, you understand? You are *TWIN FLAMES!* One Spirit, who came to this earthly incarnation as

211

two bodies! But you are stronger than him! Because you are the Sun and the Moon! What… What is it? What is wrong with you, my girl?"

Hearing these words, I almost dropped the cup on the floor.

"I… Nothing" I could hardly speak in surprise. "*The Sun and the Moon.* When I was little, two gypsies said the same words. What does it mean?"

"That means three things. First, you were born on the New Moon! Second, both the Moon and the Sun were in the Leo Constellation at the time of your birth. Third, this is how people, who are "halves," are also called. They are called "*The Sun and the Moon.*" Those like you come to Earth to pass some intense trials. Every next step for you will be more complicated than the previous one, and it will seem that this has no end, no finish line. Many people do not endure it and break down eventually. But for some reason, I believe in you. You are the Sun and the Moon! You are a Twin Flame! Now, look! Not only have you had the Sun and the Moon in Leo, but also Mercury and Mars. And your rising is in Aries. You are the energy of cosmic flame, Alla. In the world of Spirits, your name is *Firebird*, while his name is *Phoenix*! You two are one. You will burn his Soul with your flame, and he will remember his true Essence, his flame as well. I believe you can do it! I believe in you!"

I remembered the hand of a gypsy woman on my head when I was a child. The warmth I felt from it, and the single word she told me back then. "*Firebird!*" Over 30 years ago, she knew who I was.

They believed in me. Somehow all these incredible women knew who I was and believed in me.

I, on the contrary, had no such confidence. I needed time to process everything and come to terms with one Soul and two bodies. *Twin Flames?* I have never heard such an expression!

"Why such a name? *Twin FLAMES?*" I asked her after a short period of silence.

"Look at the fire in the fireplace," she answered. "You see, the fire is the Source or God, the origin of everything. Now. If I move the logs with a fireplace poker or throw in another log, what will happen?" With those words, she threw a small log. "What do you see?"

"I see sparks!"

"Exactly! Each spark of the original fire or flame is a small fire—*the identical essence of the original*, but just smaller. *Every Soul is the spark of The One Divine Creative Source*, but we have all forgotten this. As long as we realize it not, the Dark has power over us. Now imagine that this one spark divides in two. Same exact spark, but in two parts. Those are the Twin Flames!"

"I understand. So, what is the purpose of Twin Flames?"

"*To wake up and remember who they are and help others remember. Remember that each one of them is That Divine Spark!*"

Bastet went on, "There is one more reason why it is so hard for you to be without him. You two have never been apart before. All those hundreds, and maybe even many more lives here on Earth, you have *always been together*! So, the Higher Forces must have a serious reason for separating you two! By the way! You have two sons, right?"

"Yes."

"And one of them looks just like *HIM*, right?"

At these words, I dropped the cup on the floor! Luckily it was empty, and there was a rug on the floor. It did not break. Not one muscle moved on Bastet's face. Silent, with a soft smile, she got up from her chair, picked up the cup, and put it on the mantelpiece. She sat back in her chair, looking at my shocked face, smiling calmly.

"Why are you so surprised? It is almost always the case with Twin Flames. Either all of the children or one, most often the eldest, resembles the Twin. After all, this is not just your son. He is a 'link' between you two. All those lives when you were with your Ram, he was the son of both of you. Now, he is only yours. So, you shouldn't be surprised that your boy looks like him, or rather, he looks like both of you! But your second son is 'He who brings news and sees everything as it really is.' He is also from those who originally *had Wings!*"

She stopped abruptly and looked at me. Then she smiled, "Well, you know it already, right?!

I know? Sometimes it seems to me that I know absolutely nothing! But from his early childhood to this day, as I thought, a joke, I used to say to my Nicholas phrases like, 'Why are you so sad? Look! *Your wings* are also sad and dragging behind you!', or: 'Son! It's too late! Go to sleep! *Take your wings* to bed. Look how tired they are!' And the words of my child, especially when he was still very little, 'Mom! It always seems to me that *I have wings!* And I can fly!!! Mom! I saw a dream. *I was on the planet, where everyone had wings!'*

Bastet silently watched the emotions race on my face, then quietly continued, "You do know, I am sure, that there are myriads of galaxies in the Universe. There are myriads of planets and their inhabitants. There are ones that have two Suns or three moons, for example. On the others, people don't need bodies as dense as here on this planet, where we are now. There are those where wings are the usual thing. Others, where they are shapeshifters! There are many, *many of them.* But sometimes, we choose or are asked to incarnate somewhere very far away from our place of origin. The reasons can be different. Look at yourself. You have already lived hundreds of lives here, on Gaia, but still haven't got used to it!"

That was, unfortunately, a sad truth. I used to look at the stars for many hours since my distant childhood, feeling incredible and inexplicable melancholy and loneliness. I always vaguely suspected that somewhere out there, in the diamond-studded sky, was my home. Somewhere very far away from here, there was my real Home! When will I get there? Will I get there at all? I don't know.

"I still cannot understand how and why you two were separated in this life," she continued. "Probably, it is a *necessary evil,* as they say. You have always loved him. Always and only him alone. He has always loved you. It just cannot be otherwise, since you two have one Soul! There are a lot of questions for which there are no answers yet. The time will come, and you will find them. You are his ancient love. He is yours; you are his Soul, and He is yours! You have existed as long as he had existed. You are two parts of one—*Two Halves of the Whole.*

You terrify him, and at the same time, you fascinate and attract him! This is also very common for the Twins in their physical embodiment. He can neither understand nor explain his feelings. He has even tried to break free from this strange relationship. Cut it off. Forget it all and move on. And more than once! But he cannot succeed because *his half of the Soul is longing for yours*. What is divided wants to become whole again! It is not easy to silence the call of the Spirit. You have awakened him, but not entirely. There is a lot still ahead of you. You have no right to stop! You haven't come to this life and gone through so much to just give up! Only you can help him remember his true Essence! Only you. You alone!"

"Only you can do it," those were the words of his mother.

"Bastet! What does it mean to *awaken* him? I understand what it is, but…"

"This means to awaken his true Essence, his Soul! Glory, Power, fame, money have tremendous power over him. The measure of most of his actions now, is the profit it would bring and how it could be used in business. He began to listen to his mind and stopped listening to the voice of his heart! He no longer hears his true Essence, his Soul. In the life of those like him, it gets to the stage that they can find hardly any genuineness or sincerity. There's too little of all that is real, pure, timeless, eternal. But there is a lot of things, we can call 'the game.' He has lost his faith. Faith in something more than that game. Maybe he would like to find it, but he can't.

"He got lost and he lost himself in the bustle of hollow vanities, in the pursuit of things that have absolutely no value outside this world. But you can change that! Only you can! You have already changed a lot in him, but there is more to do. You scare him like a candle that can burn a moth. But you also attract him with your light, the one he had forgotten. His Soul has always remembered you. And it will be his Soul that will never let him rest until he can truly remember…

"Now, my dear girl-warrior, please close your eyes. I will give you some strength! You need it for him and for others too. Also, you need it to be able to hold the Sword".

"The Sword? What Sword?"

"Yours! Do not ask! You will know everything when the time comes!"

As for the Sword, I did not understand a thing back then. But what she was talking about happened exactly a year after our conversation, during a severe tropical storm.

That night, the eye of the hurricane was moving straight towards the small town, where I lived with my family. It was supposed to be the biggest, strongest, and scariest hurricane to hit this area for 25 years. Florida had been declared a state of Emergency. All who were able and could afford to leave, were leaving their homes. I stayed. The night of the hit, absolutely exhausted from all the anxious preparation, fears, and worries, I finally somehow managed to fall asleep, or rather, "fall into a dream," amid the darkness and wild howling wind outside the house. In this dream, I saw myself standing in a huge field. There were thousands and thousands of people around me. Filled with panic and horror, they were all running in different directions.

I heard a horrifying, blood-curdling roar! Above my head, there was something terrible and dreadful! It was hanging there, like an enormous sphere. It looked like a nightmarish ball of snakes and some infernal creatures! It was moving across the sky, and people were scattering away from it in absolute horror. But I was standing and waiting for it to reach the sky over my head. When the ball froze just above me, I realized fully that I absolutely had no idea HOW I could possibly stop IT or how I could possibly fight with IT?

I closed my eyes tightly and called for Him, "Ram! Come! Come to me now, Ram! I need you! I do not know what to do! Help me!"

And then I felt his presence near me. I stood with my back to him, and he was holding me, both arms wrapped around me. Suddenly, a huge SWORD appeared in his right hand, shining brightly like moonlight.

"This is yours! My Love! Take it," he said and put the Sword into my hand. For some reason, the handle's feeling was painfully familiar to me, but the weapon itself was very heavy. I could not lift it with one hand! I had to use both! I lifted it and screaming like a warrior, fighting on the battlefield for her people, land, freedom and love, with whatever power,

216

rage, passion, fire, and strength I was capable of, I thrust my shining Sword inside the very "heart" of the "sphere"! Right into the very center of it! A terrible howl broke out as the sphere began to fall apart, crumbling into several pieces.

I woke up because my mom was shaking me like crazy! My heart was racing and my hands trembled. Was it from chills or from a terrible dream? My pillow was wet with sweat and tears. I still felt his hands on my shoulders and the heaviness of my Sword in my hands, as if I was still holding it. My mother, in her usual orderly manner, tried to calm me down, "Stop it! Stop it now! What are you yelling about? I came running after I heard your screams! Calm down! We are completely out of danger; the huge storm is no longer a threat! They just said it on TV. *It split apart into several smaller ones and is no longer dangerous!* Why were you shouting so loudly?"

In response, I could only shake my head. I could still sense that wriggling sphere, my Sword, the howl across the field and that horrifying "something," falling apart to pieces after I thrust my Sword into it. Even now, I don't know what it was. The next several hours, the only thing that was pounding in my head was the question, *Who am I? What am I? Who am I? Who?*

Maybe someday I will know the answer to this question, or maybe not.

Chapter 27

The Mist House on the Lost Planet

"So, The Elders allowed you to help Lala again? Did you stop the hurricane and save people?"

"No, Firebird. This time, Alla-Lala did it all by herself," muttered Joanna, without lifting her head. She was looking at some manuscripts, spread on a large oak table with massive legs of a griffin, whose sharp feathers had been polished by centuries.

"Oh, really? Seriously? All by herself?" asked Haan quietly. He was standing half-turned to the women, leaning against the wall with floor-to-ceiling bookshelves. He held a clearly heavy book in a thick leather cover in his hands. You could see its title: The Gods of Orion. Great Tamerlane. Unknown facts.

"OK, she managed it with the help of her Twin. Technically, he gave her the sword." Joanna smiled, trying to conciliate.

"I guess you can leave the word "technically "out, huh?" Haan answered, narrowing his dark eyes. He closed the book, laid it on the wooden staircase attached to the shelves. Walking up to the table, he looked straight into the eyes of the red-haired woman. "Her Twin gave her a sword, with HIS help and the help of the SWORD, the Storm was stopped. Moreover, it was not a Storm, but another attempt of the Dark Forces to invade and gain full control!"

"Of course, you're right, my darling." Joanna didn't even try to hide her ironic notes. "Her Twin helped her a lot. Of course, his help was priceless. He handed her

218

a sword, which she did not know how to find. But, first of all, it was not Farhan Ali himself, who brought it, but his Soul, from another reality. Farhan Ali, at that moment, just to let you know, was drinking champagne in a nightclub and having a good time. And secondly, if HE is the main character in this story, why didn't he stop the Dark Forces himself?"

Firebird looked in surprise at both of them. The situation was not entirely clear, and she was waiting for someone to explain to her what exactly was going on.

Haan sharply raised his head, pursed his lips, and was about to throw a bolt of lightning at the arguer. But then he remembered, he was no longer Indra, so he just laughed and raised both hands into the air.

"All right!" he said, laughing. "I surrender! Lala has always been stronger than Ram. It's true."

"She is not only stronger than Ram, my dear," from the void, out of nowhere, in a haze of a light lavender cloud, came the woman with white hair. « In case you forgot, this planet's hope is on her shoulders, as well as her Twin, others like her, and those she awakens and inspires. She is growing, gaining experience, strength, and power, and learning to remember her mission as a warrior. If only she didn't have that Love."

«What do you mean "If only she did not have that Love?" Haan's eyes were sparkling, his beautiful face filled with both doubt and hope. "If she didn't have "that love", we would never have the chance to save the planet and defeat the Dark Forces. When Ram and Lala join together again, their powers can unite and grow stronger thanks to their love. What is left is just a little bit more of..."

"A lot more, Haan. There's still a lot more, unfortunately. More suffering. More struggle. More sorrow. More pain for her. He is her strength, but as well, he is her only weakness! The Dark can affect her and break her only through Him! We can only hope and wait," the white-haired woman sighed, "only hope and wait."

Chapter 28

Helena

Following Fatima and Bastet, other Seers appeared in my life. Each one of them was unique, and many were from different parts of the world. One day, a woman with the mystical and ancient name, Helena, appeared in my life. After her, several other Helenas appeared in my life, sorceresses, the wise, the seers. But this was the first one.

The very first Helena was, like the others, a woman of amazing soul and incredible fate. She was as extraordinary and as unusual as her life, which she spent almost entirely "on wheels" inside a moving train. For many and many years, she worked as the director of a restaurant car, and her whole life looked like a constantly fast-moving landscape, outside the window of a fast, rushing train. Cities, villages, forests and fields, summers and autumns, winters and springs, faces and places—that was her life.

It was this exact woman who had the most unshakable faith in him and me, the most unshakable faith in LOVE itself, as the Highest Power of all. She sincerely believed that my Twin and I would undoubtedly be together after all is said and done. Why? Because there is no way, it should or can be otherwise! Love conquers all!

It was her faith that kept me from giving up! As I've always been short of my own! She would persuade me and scold me. She cried with me and laughed with me! It was an amazing example of how a seemingly complete stranger can dramatically turn your life around and become so close to you as if they were your own family.

When she learned my story, still living on the other side of the planet, she made me do what would be the next turning point of this story about Twin Flames.

"You have to write a book!" she told me. "You absolutely must!"

"A book? Why?"

"Two reasons, my soul!" she replied. "First! He doesn't believe you yet. To be exact, he believes you, but not through and through! After reading your book, he will believe it! But you must appear in this book stripped to your bones, completely exposing your Soul. Do you understand? You have no right to leave anything unrevealed, hidden! Only then can he finally believe you! Only then can he really know not you—Alla, Lala, but you as half of his Eternal Soul. And the second: *Lala, people need this book!* You are aware that the last thousand years have been the worst and the darkest times for our Earth. Knowing your story, people will start to awaken. They will believe in Love again! And not just Love, but the one that has no beginning nor end. *True Love.*"

"Ages ago, people did believe in such Love, Love that can surpass time and life itself. But now, even the very thought of it, most of the time, causes either bewilderment or just a bitter grin. Not many people believe that such a feeling even exists! But it is precisely this faith that is the foundation of everything. Everything! Do you understand?

"The two of you are living witnesses! Witnesses that nothing ends with death! That life is infinite, and so is Love! That is why you should write that book! First, he will believe you, and then others will as well. Write! You must do it, my girl! You have no right not to! Do you understand? Write!"

His Maa also told me, "Write, Lala!"

I felt in my heart and knew in the depth of my Soul that they were right. I must do this, but I was terrified. It is easier to say than to do. Write it all, completely open up, naked in the heart and soul. Do not leave anything hidden. Tell everything. The force of True Light, where do I get the courage for such a thing? Write it all there: what I know, what I remember, what I want, what I feel. But I could not start. I was scared. I was scared to tell how I lived before him, how I dreamed, suffered, and how I had been looking for him. Yet I really wanted him to remember me too. Keepers of the Balance, I wanted that so much! I wanted him to be not just interested and curious or just entertained in those half-secret strange conversations with me, *but to remember*. Truly remember… Our lives. Our Love. Our Soul—the One Soul we shared.

So, I had to start writing.

Chapter 29

Double Rainbow

I wrote to him in one of my letters that I was thinking of writing a book. A book about my life. About my love. About how I was looking for him. How I found him and what happened afterward, how I managed to reach out to him, about my dreams, fears, doubts, struggles, everything. I decided to ask him what he thought about it, and if he agreed this was a good idea, he had to give me "a sign."

I wanted him to do it in our usual manner. I asked him to take a photo where he would hold his palms together, as the Indians do when greeting each other and saying "Namaste." The word means "God in me greets God in you," or sometimes it translates as "My God greets your God."

Since we had been communicating for an extended time, I was used to seeing him always do the things that I asked, no matter what they were. Well, almost always. But what I expected, unfortunately, this time did not follow. I was absolutely not ready for this.

He gave me no sign of approval of my idea. Not at all. Somehow, I felt that this idea didn't awaken in him either positive feelings or positive emotions. On the contrary, it awakened in him an emotion called "fear." I could sense it with every cell of my being. In my dreams, we still would meet every night. But even there, in the dimension beyond our physical bodies, he became silent and tense. He didn't like my idea. He didn't like it at all! It was clear that he wasn't happy or enthusiastic about it, so what now? What was I to do? Write it anyway?

But if he doesn't want it, why should I write it? What for?

Deeply stressed, I went to the ocean shore one day early in the morning, longing to find answers to my questions. For several nights I had not been able to fall asleep for more than a couple of hours. Even when I did, I would wake up with my heart racing insanely, as if it was trying to jump out of my chest. The morning of the second night, I went to the ocean shore in my attempt to find some peace and to find answers to my questions.

It was a very old habit of mine. Before arriving in Florida, I tried to find peace on the shore of The Black Sea. Now I was looking for the same peace on the shore of the Atlantic Ocean.

I don't understand why I totally can't imagine my life without "the Big Water." Even an hour's drive to the ocean is too far for me. Fortunately, the ocean is only 15 minutes away by car from where I live. Before or after work, I can always come and wander a couple of hours along the coast.

I do not know exactly when I realized that everything in Nature is alive! *Everything has a soul. Everything breathes and vibrates!* Perhaps that is why our ancient paganism, or to be exact "Vedism," was always closer to my heart than any religion. They saw and believed Nature as Divine. They glorified the *Sun as Father* and the *Earth as Mother.* We often see in ancient texts how our great ancestors talk to the Winds, Ocean, the spirits of the sacred forests, rivers, and lakes. They lived in peace and absolute harmony and union with Nature, the same way as Native American Indians. *In THIS,* I saw a pure truth. I was this way for as long as I could remember.

I was in the habit of talking to trees, stars, the wind and the sea. In the most challenging moments of my life, it was there where I went—the water, the sea, the ocean! All the elements were united there—Earth, Fire, Water, and Air. There, I felt much closer to those, whom I really missed: my brother Alexei, my beloved friend Natasha. There I talked with them, and with his mother.

I was wandering along the coastline for hours, asking those who were no longer near me, as well as the Higher Forces, to help me understand what I could not at that moment. Sometimes I asked them to give me a hint, a sign, to show me the way.

One day I asked his mother, "Maa! Tell me! *Who are we to each other?* Who am I for him, and who is he for me? Maybe all this is some kind of dream? Illusion? Some kind of obsession? What we are, who we are for each other?"

Suddenly, at that very moment, I felt something with my barefoot. I bent down and reached for it. I pulled out of the water a rather big, dazzling white shell, *consisting of two joined halves.* It was alive, whole, and beautiful. It was the answer—One, but two. Two, but one. Two halves of One.

Nevertheless, it did not stop the flow of my endless doubts, fears, and questions that remain unanswered! I do not believe in chance and coincidence, but neither am I crazy enough to feel a burden lifted with the mere sight of a beautiful seashell.

I continued to wander along the shore. I loved looking at the water. I loved the feeling of the sea breeze on my face. I would close my eyes and let it ruffle my hair, caressing my skin. At the touch of the Wind, I felt *him* because *he* reminded me of that very wind. I often wrote to him about it:

> *You remind me of the wind—the ocean breeze! Just like him, you can be gentle, passionate, and completely uncontrollable! Nothing can catch you or hold you against your will. One can only love you. You come flying whenever you want and fly away as soon as you wish. You are as impudent and wild, wistful and temperamental as he is! You can kiss or knock off the feet. You are dangerous, playful, sensual, and absolutely unpredictable. When I miss you, I go to the shore and let the Breeze kiss me. In his touch, I feel you!*

Every day without him was torture. Already routine torture, like an inevitable part of my usual life schedule. Still, it did not become easy or painless. It was Torture. I only felt a bit better near the ocean. Because I knew that he, just like me, also spent many hours looking at the water, his mansion in Malibu was naturally overlooking the ocean! He looked at the Pacific Ocean, and I was looking at the Atlantic. We both looked at the water, and we were both, at the same time, were thinking about each other.

Whenever I was on the shore, I asked the Wind to touch his face, softly, as if it was me. I asked the Wind to whisper words of love softly in his ear, as if it was me. I asked the Wind to hug him as tenderly, as if it was me embracing him.

That morning, as always, I went to the ocean in my usual attempt to find some answers. I did not get the sign from him. I was sure I would, but I didn't. I didn't know whether I needed to start writing the book. Yes, the seers and his Maa told me to write, but if he did not care... I needed answers.

It had been raining for over two days in a row. Clouds completely covered the sky. Even though it was already ten in the morning, it was dark and gloomy. It was late autumn. The sky, heavy with dark, menacing clouds, made the water look dank and unwelcoming. The waves looked unfriendly, even scary. That was the weather when I decided to take a walk on the shore.

Because of the rain, the beach was completely deserted. I did not carry an umbrella. I stubbornly walked along the coast, wrapped in a black poncho. After wandering for about two hours, I stopped at the water's edge, facing the ocean. I closed my eyes tight, and I said, "Listen. I don't know who I am, what I am, why I am here and what I am doing! But I need an answer! I want to know if *I MUST* write this book, if someone *NEEDS* it! Please, give me a sign because I'm feeling lost. I do not know whom to listen to, or what to do. I am asking you for a sign. Please, somehow, show me the way. Please show me the way. I do not know what path to follow anymore.

After a few minutes, I suddenly felt an intensely bright light on my face. I opened my eyes. What I saw is difficult to even describe in words! To do this, you definitely need to be an artist and be good friends with colors, shades, and halftones, or a musician able to listen to the melodies of clouds, wind, sun and rain, and then create a symphony of happiness from them.

There was a small gap in the sky, probably the size of a kitchen towel. Through this small, mica-like window in the heavenly chamber, the sun was shining brightly and triumphantly, directing its rays right at my face. My cheeks, ears, lips were burning. I was squinting my eyes from so much light, and a *magnificent RAINBOW in all its glory* appeared in front of me!

It was shining and sparkling in all the splendor of its fantastically brilliant colors!! It seemed that I was standing exactly in the middle of its semicircle! I was looking at all this indescribably beautiful wonder, yet, I was not able to make myself *believe* any of it! I squeezed my eyes, shut them tightly, very, very tightly. I stood like this for a couple of minutes, expecting to see nothing, when I opened them again!

It is impossible! It just can't be!!! I thought to myself, but when I opened my eyes again, what I saw made me just burst into tears. The Rainbow did not disappear. It became a *DOUBLE RAINBOW!*

Blessed is this Love! Whatever it is, blessed is this Love! I thought. Tears were pouring down my cheeks, mixing with the raindrops still falling from the sky. I felt sad that there was not a single soul on the beach, except for me, and no one else could see this miracle! Or so I thought. For a moment, I even believed I imagined the whole thing! Although, of course, I certainly knew that I did not make it all up. It just seemed *too impossible, too unbearable, and too fantastic!* Well, it can't be like that, right? Would it be possible that some Higher Forces sent me this incredible Double Rainbow as an *answer to my question?* No, right? Or is it actually possible? Can it be, or can it not be. It didn't matter. The bottom line was, I asked for a sign. *I got it.*

I was tired of asking myself questions, never getting a logical answer. Maybe I just needed to stop doing that, at least for a little while. The day after this event, when I came to work, my partner, who lived in a condo right on the ocean coast, told me, "You cannot even imagine what a rainbow I saw yesterday morning from my balcony! It was a Double One! Never seen anything like that in my whole life! It was something implausible!" And she showed me a photo on her phone.

There could be no more doubts. I had to write that book!

That very night, I started writing, and I kept writing for a whole nine months. Sometimes all night long without any sleep. I was not able to sleep. Neither was I able to eat. I lost close to 20 pounds and was scaring my poor Mom so much that she started to come to me several times a day with a plate of food in her hands and feed me like a baby! I did not dare to object! Mom threatened to do all the terrible things all moms threaten their kids with, if they do not eat; I just obeyed.

When I finished the book, it had over 400 pages.

It began with these words:

> *"You are holding in your hands a story of Eternal Love. The existence of such Love is very hard to believe. Infinite Love. Immortal Love. The Love, which lasts forever."*

Chapter One

This happened several weeks after I found you...

I was not doing anything mystical. I was just cooking dinner for my children. It was an ordinary day in January. My funny-looking little dachshund, Maxie, was running and jumping around me. Suddenly, everything disappeared before my eyes, going pitch dark for a moment. And then I saw...

I saw a place where the color of ocher and saffron prevailed. Instantly, I felt almost unbearable pain and distress. A pang of recognition, stifling heat from heaven and earth. Scanty vegetation. Though dry and barren, this desert-like landscape was exquisitely beautiful. All of this was heartbreakingly familiar.

I saw a man and a woman. *I KNEW* that the woman was me, and the man was no other but you, my eternal love! But it was a long time ago. It was hundreds of years ago. You were sitting on the ground and holding me in your arms. I was dying. I had excruciating pain in my chest. No words can describe this pain. But much more potent than this physical pain was the pain of my soul. *I HAD TO LEAVE YOU!* But I desperately did not want to!

I loved you so much! Oh! Gods only knew how much I loved you! *I was woven, I was created from this very love! We were One.* Having to part with you was unbearable to me. But my time had come. There was nothing I could do about it. I was about 40 years old. I looked almost the same as now, but my hair was plaited in a very long braid and the clothes I wore, were easily recognizable. I wore an Indian saree. You were crying, or rather, you were wailing because of pain, despair, and hopelessness. You knew that I would be gone. You knew that no one and nothing could help me no more. You were holding me tightly and repeating again and again:

"LALA! LALA, Promise! PROMISE ME!!!! YOU WILL FIND ME, IN THAT OTHER LIFE, YOU WILL FIND ME!!!! Promise me, Lala! PROMISE ME!!!!!!!"

I wanted to say your name, but no sound left my lips. I also desperately wanted to touch your face. One least a little, just with my fingertips. I could feel tears flowing down my face.

"Please," I pleaded in my mind to someone. *"Let me touch him."*

I had the strength to raise my hand and touch your wet cheek. I could look deep into your impossible, unbelievable eyes.

„PROMISE! YOU WILL FIND ME IN THAT OTHER LIFE!" You repeated to me again and again.

"I promise," I said. *"I PROMISE!"*

As you already know, the name of this book is: *I JUST WANT YOU TO REMEMBER...*

Chapter 30

Elephants and Angels

While writing the book, I kept on writing my letters to him. I included some of them in the book because they are also a part of the story. These are my thoughts. My breath. My life.

This is one of them:

> *I am your peace. I am the touch of cool water from a deep well, which stays fresh and cold even in the hottest summer. I am the water, which calms and heals your deep wounds. Share your pain with me. Share your fears with me. Share what you would never share with anyone else. Share it all with me. My darling! I will take your pain away. I can bear it! I'm strong enough for it, even if you don't think so. Let me help you with the burden you carry. Let me stand invisibly next to you, by your side. I will stand by you and protect you from anything that can hurt you. I will be your shield, your fire, your light! I will be your rest! Just let me...*

So, nine months later, a 400-page manuscript was finished.

I told him my whole life, starting with my childhood, searching for him and believing in us finding each other. Everything was in that book. The night I first saw and recognized him, everything following that night. Everything, right until the moment when I wrote the book's very last word.

LALA AGNI

In this book, I appeared before him, naked in my soul. I hid absolutely nothing. Only this way did I have the chance to awaken his soul. Only this way did I have the chance to make him remember, to make him believe. It ended with these words:

> *"Why did I survive all of this? Why did I write all this? Maybe because it was time for me to awaken and remember? Maybe, because it's time for you to awaken and remember? Or maybe, the time has come for all of us to awaken and remember. Awaken. And remember..."*

I wrote my last sentence. It was a very late summer night. Everything outside smelled of June, with its fragrances of leisure, high sky, and light aromas of blossoming flowers and fresh leaves.

My phone rang. It was one of my friends, the seer. "I'm not apologizing for waking you up because you were not sleeping anyway. Listen! I have to tell you something! In your very last life, before this one, you had a pet animal that was very dear to both of you. I can feel it! To be exact, I know it for sure! You must remember what kind of animal it was."

"Why? What for?"

"I don't know. But I am certain that this is very important. You must remember. Do you hear me? *TRY to remember!*"

Well, that's a nice thing! It's easy to say, *"try to remember!"* We are talking about events that happened, probably a couple of hundred years ago in a past life! Even if I do have that weird ability of my memory not remembering what happened a month ago, yet still have bright and clear memories of my past lives, it is still a rather complicated task. *What kind of animal did we have? What was it? A dog? A cat? Or maybe we had a peacock. How do I know?* It was already about three o'clock in the morning, the time people call the «witch's hour.» I finally lay down and, before falling asleep, told myself three times, without any hope of it helping, *"Remember! You MUST remember!"*

The next moment I am standing on a lovely little, incredibly picturesque lakeshore. Beautiful trees surround the lake and it seems perfectly round and smooth, like a mirror. The trees throw a pleasant shadow, lazily spreading on the soft grass. Their crowns reflect in the lake, forming a green picket fence in the water. The whole atmosphere seems filled to the top with magic and mystery. I am about 25 years old, wearing something like a salwar-kameez. It consists of tight-fitting pants and a dress. All my clothes are royal blue. I clearly love the same colors and the same man from one life to another. The weird creature I am. I have a long raven-black braid and my usually pale skin. And... I'm also wet from head to toes! I don't have a single dry spot on me!

"Raaaaam!!!! Stop that! Do you hear me?! Ram! *Stop that right now! Damn you! RAM!!!*" I am shouting, not in my native language, Russian or in English, but of course, I understood my every word.

I am trying my best to make my voice sound very angry. I try very hard, but I don't sound angry, not even close. In fact, I can hardly hold my laughter, but still, I'm trying to maintain a pouty face. Suddenly, I get a new spray of water, which drenches me once again. In front of me, I see an elephant!

Yes! *An elephant!* The man on the top of the elephant is my hubby Ram, happy as a sandboy, shining like a new silver coin in the Sun! He is sitting on the back of that majestic animal, apparently bathing him and me as well! He is naked down to the waist. His face expresses complete bliss, and he is smiling with the same smile that *he still has now. The same eyes. The same lips. The same hair.* He is tall and handsome. The elephant pumps more water into his trunk and showers me with it. Both the elephant and the rider seem to fully enjoy the process and look totally blissful, while only I pretend that I do not fully enjoy it.

"Ram!" I yell after receiving another splash of water.

Then, as elegantly as my wet look allows me, I turn my back on both of them. Then proudly, with my head held high, I walk ashore. I am pregnant. But my due date is still very far away. Maybe it is only three or four months. I walk up to the dry land and lie down on the warm grass. I feel such unbelievable joy; it's hard to describe in words. I have experienced nothing even similar to that feeling in this life. I felt as if I was *Nature herself. Mother Earth herself. Love itself.*

I closed my eyes and listened to the voice of my husband, who is now talking to the elephant, knowing very well that I could hear his every word. I could not help smiling.

"Do you think she really got mad at us, Appu? Or didn't she? You never know these women! It is impossible to live with them and it is impossible to live without them! You know what? Never get married, Appu! You hear me? If she really got mad at us, she won't feed me, and I would have to make the bread and cook the food all by myself. Appu! I'm not going to do that! She will not talk to me, and she will not kiss me! But she won't last for a long time like that, Appu! You know why? She loves to kiss me! She loves my lips, you know... Oh! Appu, she loves to kiss these lips of mine so much that her silence will only hold out a couple of hours! What do you say? Should we stay here for some more, or should we go see how she is doing out there?"

Guides and Keepers of the Balance! As I'm writing all this, I can't hold my tears just thinking how happy I was at that moment. Oh, I was so happy! I was breathing freely and deeply. The wind was full of Sun, sweet and aromatic. Everything around us smelled like warm raspberries, ripe mangoes, and fresh grass. The butterflies were fluttering not only in my stomach and chest. There was a myriad of them around, feeding on the meadow flowers. I felt like a bird, embracing the earth, the water, and the people with my wings. I loved them all. *And I loved HIM*; I loved my Ram so much. And he loved me too. He loved me just as fully and deeply as I loved him. *My heart was beating in his chest, and his was beating in mine.*

And what do we have now? It seems like a whole universe with millions of obstacles is between us.

I abruptly opened my eyes and woke up. My heart was pounding insanely with those two opposite feelings. I still felt the joyfulness and endless bliss I had in that life, and simultaneously, I felt the grief and deep sadness of this one.

"*How could you forget your Lala, Ram? How could you forget?*" I whispered in the darkness of the night. "*How could you forget?*"

And then I remembered. *An elephant!* Now I knew what kind of animal we had! Of course! An elephant! Oh, Gods!! I used to have an elephant as a pet! Appu! Why Appu? Who called him that? Me or Him? I did. Why?! Turning the light on, I look at the Ganesh statuette, the God with an elephant head on my table, the elephants on my blanket, the little elephant on my bracelet. I remembered seeing a coffee table with three elephants, holding a round glass desktop; I did not buy it because it was too expensive at the moment. Later, I could not find anything like it. That made me very sad. In my hallway there is an elephant on a small column and seven elephants stand in a line in the living room. Pajamas with elephants, blouses with elephants—So, I see now! That's why I always had two passions: Elephants and Angels. More precisely, elephants and any creatures with wings. My house is full of elephants and winged creatures. My mother has repeatedly told me, "I don't know what I will do with you if you bring home one more Angel or one more elephant!"

Now it was clear as day. *My Elephant, Appu!*

Suddenly, a clear and precise understanding dawned on me. After my untimely death, Appu had outlived me for only a short while. He died because he missed me. Ram was alone without Appu, without me. Ram, my beloved, if only fate had given me a chance to ask you to forgive me for having left you on Earth so early. You were so lost and so alone. But I could not stay. I could not...

I finished the book. Now what? How do I give it to him? At that time, Farhan was not even in the States. He was in India. While fulfilling his mother's cherished dream, he began acting in both Hollywood and Bollywood a few years before I appeared in his life. As well as acting, he collaborated with like-minded admirers, starting his own studios in both countries. In just several years, he already had an impressive track record of films, series, shows, and projects.

He had been living between the two countries for several years now. At that time, I needed to send this book to India, where he was shooting another film. He would stay there for several more months. I did not want to wait that long. My heart wanted him to have the book as soon as possible. I thought after he read it, he would understand everything and remember me.

There would be no more doubts left in him. Somehow, I also thought, after that, I would be set free. My "mission" would be fulfilled.

I copied the book onto a pen drive and decided to send it to his office in India. The address turned out to be so long that it did not fit into the lines allowed by the postal service. The poor post office worker, who had to fill out the electronic form for my package, could hardly fit it in and had to shorten and abbreviate it as much as possible.

I had finally sent the book to the man who used to be my Ram so long ago, and now was a movie star, who was so far from me, like the farthest galaxy in the physical sense, and yet closer than my own breath, in terms of spirit and soul. It feels so strange when someone is so far and at the same time is so close to you! Close, like blood running through your veins, *like the beat of your own heart.*

I could not even imagine the journey my book would take before it arrived at its destination, his hands. It would be a one-of-a-kind adventure.

Chapter 31

Adventures of My Book

I sent the package by *DHL*. All its movements were tracked and reported by email. A few days after its departure from the States, I received the following message, "The package was delivered. Addressee Refused."

Do you know what an ice shower feels like, or falling into an ice-hole? It was like an ice-cold knife was thrust straight into my heart, while my heart was flowing with warm blood. My hands and feet got colder and colder. Feeling weak and about to faint, I sat down immediately. It *is impossible! It can›t be true!* But there it was, written in a text from *DHL*,

"The addressee has refused."

I look at those words. I read them over and over again! I concluded that he had given his confidante the instruction not to accept any packages or parcels from me. While writing this book, I also continued writing my usual long letters to him. But I wrote rather rarely compared to before, maybe just a few letters a month. He knew, of course, that I was writing a book. He knew very well when and where I had sent it because I told him myself. Of course, I did! Apparently, now, it turns out that he did not want this book I had written: "with the blood of my soul." *He did not care. He did not give a damn. He refused to even look at it!*

What an idiot I am. Little, hopeless idiot! The addressee has refused. He told someone not to accept anything from me. Right? No. Not right. I am missing

236

something here. Who am I for him to warn anyone about me? Of course, he didn't say anything to anyone! He is running. He is a Runaway Twin. Right? NO! He is absolutely and completely normal. He does not need this book. He does not give a damn! I'm the crazy one here. I AM! And the biggest, pathetic loser in this Galaxy is also I am!

I was lying on the bed curled up, hugging a teddy bear and quietly shedding tears about my strange and absurd fate. Not that young anymore, irrational, stupid idiot, I was a woman who somehow believed some fairy tale of Eternal Love and hell knows what else. *Pathetic, pitiful idiot!*

Finally, after crying long enough, I got up and picked up the photo of his mom.

"See?" I said, "Everything was useless. He didn't even care to read it! It is over now, Maa. It is over."

But of course, it wasn't over yet. In fact, what comes to my story, there have been so many times when I cried, "Enough! It's over!" that I've lost count!

According to the postal service message, the package with my book arrived in India, but the recipient refused to accept it. The package was sent back to me and is currently in Ohio.

Well, *to hell with Him and with this package,* I think to myself. Damn both of them, together with my "eternal love" for him! Damn all of it! I am done! *Enough of all of this! Enough!*

But to my surprise, three days later, I received another message from the postal service, saying the package is again in India! What? Wait a minute! Three days ago, it was in Ohio, and now it is back in India? How is that even possible? Several minutes later, I received another email from them saying, "the packet is delayed."

Delayed? But by whom? Why? The message asks me to call them. So, I call.

They tell me, "Miss, the whole problem was when the package was delivered at its destination, the recipient had to pay the customs. He refused to pay it. If you pay it yourself, the package will be delivered to the recipient within a few hours."

I agree to that, and immediately go to the post office. But there, to my shock, I am told that the fee will be 982 dollars and five cents! If I pay that amount, then the package will be delivered. If not, then, with my consent, it will be destroyed. Of course, paying such an amount wasn't possible for me, and I give my consent for its destruction. I think everything has come to an end. But again, I'm wrong.

And now the fun part begins!

Four days later, my Nicholas comes up to me with his home cotton candy machine (Don't ask me why he bought it, for God's sake! I have no idea!). He tells me he's not happy with this purchase. It doesn't work the way he expected! "So, could you, Mom, please take it back? Please!"

I pack the machine in a box and stick the return label from Amazon on the top of it. I just need to go to the post office and leave it where they leave all packages of that kind. I finish all my chores and drive there.

And now, *pay attention, please.* Next to the post office, there is a supermarket, and I decided to drop by because that very moment I was craving some chocolate chip cookies. I swear for the life of me, I still can't understand why. *I don't eat them usually.* But at that moment, I wanted them with all the passion of my fiery soul!

Having bought the biscuits, I decide to eat them right away, while sitting in my car and thinking about my strange life and destiny. I finish the cookies with clear determination to stop it all. Forget it all. Let go and move on.

With this in mind, I drive to the post office, located in the same building as the coffee shop! And at that moment, it turns out that it's not possible to park nearby, as there are cars around the whole building (I have never seen it neither before, nor after that day). No place to park. Does everyone suddenly want coffee and donuts? I park my car in another parking lot, rather far away from the place, grab my son's parcel and start walking to the post office. When I get inside, I see that a female clerk is talking to someone on the phone!

She turns to me and points to the receiver, meaning she is sorry, but she cannot stop the conversation and asks me to wait a minute! I nod my head to indicate that I understand! I lift my box to let her know why I am here,

238

silently asking where I leave it? The woman nods to the far corner. I take the parcel there and leave it with the other boxes. I start walking towards the door.

"Three. Eight. Six," the clerk says to the receiver.

I keep on walking!

"Two. One. Seven," she goes on.

I reach for the door handle and begin to open it, thinking at the same time, *the number is just like mine.* I open the door. Before I step through the doorway, I hear:

"Seven. Five. Four. Five."

I slowly turn around and close the door! I walk up to the clerk and say, *"That is my number!"*

The woman looks at me as if Christ himself has appeared before her, accompanied by Buddha and Mohamed! After a minute of shocking silence, she asks in a trembling voice, *"Are you, Alla?"*

"Yes! I am Alla. That is my phone number you just said out loud!"

The woman kept on looking at me in disbelief. To prove that this is really me, I take my driver's license out of my wallet and show it to her.

After a couple more seconds of incredulous silence, she tells me, *"It's for you! It's India!"* She hands the phone to me, telling someone on the other end of the connection, *"She is right here!"*

HOW ON EARTH DID I GET TO THE POST OFFICE AT THAT EXACT TIME THAT EXACT MOMENT when they were calling from India about my package? I have no idea! But it happened exactly like that! I take the receiver from the clerk's icy hands and bring it to my ear. "Hello?"

"Hello!" The girl's voice has a soft Indian accent. "Is this ... (pause) Alla?"

"Yes, this is Alla."

The girl falls silent for a moment, totally taken aback, since she as well cannot understand how the hell I ended up there THIS VERY SECOND. Finally, she pulls herself together and tells me that they still have the package (To *hell with it!!* I think). And to my great surprise, it is not destroyed yet! So, do I want to pay a customs fee after all?

239

In a rather sharp tone, I tell the poor girl that I won't pay a thousand dollars for a flash drive, and they can throw it away and forget all about it! I don't understand why they haven't done it yet.

The girl, startled a bit, explains that the amount probably was announced to me in *Rupees* and not in dollars! In dollars, it would be about fifteen!

Now it was my turn to be confused! So, it turns out to be, I only have to pay $15, and the package will still be delivered? Yes, exactly like that. Finally, I say that I agree to pay the amount and would do it right away. The girl confirms that they will immediately take the package and hand it over to the addressee.

Then it dawns on me that the girl is speaking to me with a voice full of admiration, adoration, and even astonishment as if I was some pop diva. Well. Of course. The girl can see perfectly well to whom the package is addressed! What if He, the Great and Almighty King, knows me personally? Who knows?

After chatting with her for another five minutes, I finally hang up.

The postal lady is still white as a sheet. She silently listens to me as I inform her that I have to pay 15 dollars for that damn package to finally be delivered. She takes the money without speaking a word and looks at me with curiosity. When I thank her and turn around to leave, she regains her voice and asks me a mysterious question, "Do you mind if I ask you something?

"No, not at all."

"Tell me please, what is your religion? Which God do you believe in?"

At that time, I wore a pendant, looking like a small Ganapati (Ganesh), carved from a piece of malachite on a silver chain. It was obvious to me why she was asking such a question. She has just decided that my God, whoever he was, must be very powerful, since He brought me exactly where I needed to be, at exactly the right moment I was supposed to be there! I doubted it was a good idea to explain to the lady the rather complex system of Vedic teaching. It would consume too much time, and she would hardly be interested in that. Instead, I take off my Ganapati and show it to her on my palm.

"This one," I answer, smiling.

"And what kind of God is this?"

"This is Ganesh!"

"Who?"

That sweet woman has never heard about this deity. She gives me a pen, "Write it down, please!"

I do as she asks. But then, suddenly, I decided to give my Ganesh to her.

"Here! Take it!" I tell her. "Let him help you from now on! I'll buy another one for myself!"

A minute later, I get into the car, and everything that has just happened comes down on me.

Someone invisible seemed to be leading me by the hand, planning every step I took, every second, just so that I would be at the post office at that precise moment! Not a second earlier! Not a second later!

The Double Rainbow arises in my mind again. *"It is as if they are always in the presence of the Higher Forces,"* was written in one of the books about Twin Flames.

One thing was clear to me for sure. Some force guides me. And to doubt that fact would be rather foolish. Fighting this Force would also be also unwise and as useless as fighting the wind.

Why couldn't the postal service send me an email and explain everything? Why didn't they call me personally? Why instead, did they call the post office I had sent the package from? All these questions will remain unanswered.

The next day, I received a message that my package had been delivered and received by a woman named Shakti. (*Shakti* means a great, universal, divine energy).

On the same day, standing on the Atlantic shore, I once again asked for a sign. "Tell me, Spirits of Earth and Water, Guides and Keepers of Balance, will he read what I've written with all the love and fire of my soul? Please give me a sign. Please!" Again. These are the Ones who I came to in search of answers because no one else could give them to me. Several minutes after I said those words, a huge, beautiful dolphin jumped straight out of the ocean and flopped back into the water again.

"*Look! Look! Dolphins! Dolphins!*" The beach is full of people. They see what I see as well. The excited screams are heard from everywhere. The weather is wonderful. Many people are walking along the shore. I am holding back my tears. But these are the tears of happiness. The little girl in me, which still somehow believes in miracles and hopes for the better, just got a positive answer from brother Ocean, Wind, Sun, and Mother Gaia herself. *Yes, he will read it.*

I arrived home late at night and wrote to him.

> *Without you, I am a silent cry in the desert of silence, and amid a crowd of worshipers to their God, nobody but me feels such unbearable loneliness. Without you, I am ice even in the crater of an erupting volcano, and among the endless snows, I am nothing but a burning flame. Without you, my own breath burns my lungs. It is difficult for me to breathe when you are not with me.*
>
> *Teach me how to exist without you! Teach me how to smile sincerely when my heart wants to cry. Teach me how to find the strength to live and enjoy this life, knowing that our parting will be for a very long time, probably even till this life is over. Teach me how not to feel your breath on my face when you are thousands of miles away from me. Teach me how to find the strength to break free from Lady Sadness, holding me so tightly, embracing me with her silvery wings, just like before. Teach me how not to hear your thoughts and not feel your heartbeat in my chest! Teach me not to see what your eyes see and not feel your longing and pain. Teach me how NOT to be one with you. Teach me...*

Chapter 32

The Color Indigo

I do not know how much he anticipated the moment he could finally hold my book in his hands. Although, I'm lying here. I knew that, of course. After all, I know when he inhales and when he exhales. I also knew that he wanted that book very much because it could give him all in-depth answers to all of the questions he still had. Like who I was, where I was coming from, and how I ended up in his life. And most importantly, why the hell he, so powerful and famous, cannot get me out of his mind no matter what.

"My beautiful and powerful Sorcerer! It's all very simple. You are a Sorcerer who finally found his Sorceress. More precisely, she found you. You are a Wizard who, living among the mortals for so long, has forgotten you possess magical Gift and Power. You forgot your true Essence! And all of a sudden, appeared the one who has nothing special about her, with a small exception. She is you. Here you have all the answers you have been looking for.

"It is like two opposite worlds existing side by side inside you. One is your phenomenal intelligence, which makes you seek answers to all kinds of questions using knowledge, logic, and common sense. The other world in you is the infinite depth of your incredible Soul.

"But here comes the problem. You have lived for so many years in the tangible world of three-dimensional reality that you have begun to rely only on your cold, logical mind! This very inquisitive mind of yours is trying to find the answers to the question of who I am. And how is it even possible that I, a so-called simple woman, not rich, not famous, not a model, not a star, still managed to get so close to your Soul, touching the strings, nobody ever was able to touch before me?

"The truth is, my love, I never even tried to get inside your Soul. I simply was always there, you just forgot. I want you to remember.

"Do you hear me? I want you to remember."

My book was now in his hands. The second the lines and words I wrote with all my love, the fire of my very Soul, appeared on his screen before him, once again, I felt as if I had entered a heated bathhouse straight from an icy-cold street. In my part of the planet, it was daytime. Where he was, it was already the depths of night. His eyes, so deeply loved by me, so similar to mine, were eagerly reading the words I wrote. At that moment, I saw an extraordinary thing.

I have always been told that the color of my aura is predominantly something close to royal blue or an intense hue of sapphire blue. It is also called *indigo*. All my life, I have passionately loved this color.

When he began reading my book, I saw an indigo blue crystal where his heart chakra is. It looked like a royal blue sapphire. It was incredible, but the light in it was still very soft. As if someone had touched it with a magic wand and turned it on from inside. It was the same with me. I also have a bright blue crystal that was identical to his, sparkling and dancing in my chest. But mine was slightly bigger and much brighter, while his crystal was just beginning to glow. With every word he read, with every page he scrolled, his "crystal" was shining brighter and brighter, until suddenly, there was a luminous blue thread stretched between us, *connecting our hearts. Through time, through distance, through eternity!* It was magical. It was miraculous. It was amazing and something absolutely out of this world!! For the first time in many years, I was finally able to inhale deeply!

Oh! What a pleasure it was! All my life, one of my most passionate wishes was to be able to breathe deeply! But I never could; finally, now I was able to do that. It felt like heaven! An old song from my youth began to sound in my head:

"Our love,
The color of Indigo,
Just like this night,
The color of Indigo,
Just like the sky,
The color of Indigo, Indigo, Indigo, Indigo..."

I saw him just as if I was right beside him. While his eyes absorbed the words I had written, sometimes he smiled, other times he frowned. His eyes shone with joy, then filled with sorrow. I opened my entire life up to him in my book without hiding anything. I had to tell him about my childhood and youth and my first marriage. I told him everything that you now know as well. I did this, so he would know and understand what his eyes were for me, what the memory of him, the connection of our souls, and our eternal, never-ending love was and meant for me every breathing moment of this life. I wanted him to know that in the moments of pain, fear, and despair, His eyes and this love through space and time was my *lighthouse on the stormy ocean*, my *North Star*, shining from above, never letting me lose my way. My strength. My path. My hope. My compass—my heavenly and earthly compass.

He went on and on reading everything and could not put my book aside. He read all night. This was one of those rare moments in my life when I almost had no doubts. *After reading the whole book, he will believe me. Believe me with all his heart.* Naturally, it was impossible to finish such a volume in one night. That night my beautiful Wizard did not close his beautiful eyes because of me. But, oddly enough, this did not affect him in any way. On the contrary, he seemed to have discovered some never-before-known source of energy.

Outside his window, dawn had arrived, and with it a new day. I saw how my King had changed. He suddenly turned from a handsome adult man into a bright and sparkling boy. A smile was dancing on his lips (oh, those lips of his!). There was not a trace of fatigue in his eyes. He was bubbling like champagne in a tall crystal glass, glittering and sparkling in the morning rays of the sun! He looked as if his Soul was suddenly back with him after he had accidentally lost it somewhere. He looked as if he had been carried decades back, and now he had a whole life ahead of him, in which nothing was impossible.

There was also a big chapter in my book devoted to his Mother. For a long time, fear that he would not believe me, lived inside my heart. But he did. He believed me! He finished the next chapter, opened my photo, and looked at my face for a long time. Then he smiled, I sensed his thoughts— delighted, yet trying to understand the improbability of what was happening to him, or rather, to both of us.

"So, it turns out I knew you before! Or rather, was it not 'before,' but always?"

That day, I began to write a new story.

Chapter 33

The King of Wizards and the Witch

This story was about two different Worlds. The first one was the world of magicians, dragons, nymphs, dryads, spirits of rivers and lakes, fairies, elves, wizards, and witches. The other one was the world of mortal people.

An invisible wall existed between those two worlds. The King of Wizards was the most powerful in both of them, the Supreme Ruler among both people and magical creatures. He lived in an enchanted forest with his little son, also a Wizard. According to the laws of the crown, the King must live between the worlds, so he could easily move from one kingdom to another.

When he was still very young, he fell in love with a girl who was not like him. She was not a Sorceress or a Witch. She was a very bright, very beautiful, extraordinary being. But she was still an earthly woman, while he was a Wizard.

She only knew and understood one world, the earthly one. The world on the other side of the wall was unfamiliar to her, unknown, and incomprehensible. Still, they met and fell in love. Both of them were young and decided that their love would be enough for them to overcome everything.

They loved each other, got married, and had children. The wife had a beloved husband, a house, a wonderful cozy world filled with children, and lovely household chores. What else could one wish for to be happy? But there was a problem. While she knew and lived in one world, he lived in two! Two worlds. Two kingdoms. Many liegemen. Many issues to solve and enemies to fight and defeat.

Over time, the Wizard became more and more powerful. His world behind the invisible wall was becoming more and more incomprehensible to his mortal wife. She did not understand him. He did not understand her.

In the end, the same invisible wall formed between them as real as the one between the two worlds. The King had long been accustomed to this kind of life. During the day, he was on the side of the people, at night, on the Wizard's side.

There was the Forbidden Waterfall of the Forgotten Dreams in that enchanted forest. One day, while walking near this Waterfall, he saw a woman in the Mirror of the Water. She was a Witch, just like him. But she was on the other side of the Enchanted Forest. Upon seeing her, the Wizard's heart flipped upside down, beating as heatedly and quickly as in his youth.

This woman was his True Ancient Love. And not just love; she was the other half of his own Soul. It was clear to Him. He fell in love with her. But kings, wizards, and monarchs have their own rules to obey. He could not change anything in his life. He was responsible to his mortal wife and those under his rule. Yet he could not help loving the Witch, could not help seeing her. It would be like not breathing or not thinking, or simply not even existing.

So, they started talking to each other through this Forbidden Waterfall. They were unable to physically look into each other's eyes: neither in the kingdom of wizards nor in the realm of people. The Witch couldn't do it without his permission. He was terrified of meeting her in real life for fear that he might lose his self-control, and with it, the control over his life in both kingdoms. He knew and fully realized that once he looked into her eyes, into the eyes of His very Soul, he would no longer be able to live without her.

Only through the Mirror of the Waterfall could they see each other and talk to each other. This transparent but solid wall separated them. To see her, he just had to lie on the grass, close his eyes, and quietly repeat her name three times.

Of course, the name of the Witch was like my own, *Lallah*.

He called her, and she would come to him. That was how they would see each other.

So, this is the story I began to write. It consisted of many parts.

It was a beautiful fairy tale for both of us. The internet became our own Waterfall of Forbidden Forest. From now on, if I wanted to tell him something, I wrote another part. And it was a Witch who expressed to him all that I wanted to say to him.

I no longer wrote anything on his Facebook page, as I did initially. It was no longer necessary. I posted everything that I wanted to tell him on my own page. For almost two years, I kept my Facebook page solely to communicate with him.

I had no virtual friends. Even if someone offered me friendship, I did not accept it.

I didn't want anyone to know about our communication. From the beginning, I always thought of "protecting him" from unwanted publicity and the slight possibility of others saying anything negative about him. I was a witch madly in love, bewitched by my Wizard, but still smart enough to understand that simple fact, that my King lives in a different world and has his royal duties and responsibilities. But at least I still had the Waterfall—the computer.

Checking my *FB* had become his daily habit.

A few months after he received my book, another significant event occurred. We finally started talking to each other via Twitter, using, of course, fictitious names, but more on that later.

Time was flying by. This Witch intensely desired to hear the voice of her Wizard. I wanted a simple, *damn it*, ordinary telephone conversation. I was failing to understand why the hell this could not be done. And when I was unable to understand, I would become isolated and upset. I would rebel, disappearing "from the Waterfall" for a week or two.

The funny and maybe even weird thing was how we managed to quarrel and make up with each other telepathically and through *FB* and Twitter. If you think that the only thing I ever did was lovingly sing his praises and celebrate him as a deity, then you would be very wrong.

In the first year of our communication, I did sing his praises to be completely honest with you. But later on, I no longer treated Farhan as a famous star who had *the whole world eating from the palm of his hand*, as I used to tell him. To me, he was not a celebrity, but my significant other, someone very close and dear to me. He was my Ram, the one who used to make fun of me and tell me, his wife, at least a thousand times and a day, "Lala! You are as stubborn as 101 mules!" (Why specifically 101, I don't know).

Pieces of memories from past lives were falling upon me as though from a cornucopia!

Even my shadow of shyness towards him disappeared without a trace.

Would you really feel timid in front of your husband, with whom you have lived for twenty years? Or fifty? Most likely, you wouldn't, right?

I was connected to him through *multiple lives*, and no matter who he was *in this one*, a star or a truck driver, he was still the one who laughed at me, kissed me, made love to me and cried bitterly when I was no longer able to stay with him on Earth. *He was my Ram* and hundreds or thousands of other names he had in all those lives we lived. *I was his Lala.*

No shyness remained in me. I openly told him everything I admired in him and what I did not like very much or did not even like at all. I commented on things when he was right, in my opinion and when he was, as I thought, not that right. After the blind adoration he usually received, I guess, my directness was strangely pleasant, always seasoned with lots of humor; we both had this mildly sarcastic sense of humor. We quarreled and made peace, argued and reconciled, always physically far away from each other, whether we were living on the same continent or opposite sides of the planet. But soon, there came a day when he did something I could neither understand nor forgive him.

Chapter 34

Tropical Storm

As it happens nearly every year in late autumn, a severe tropical storm headed to Florida. Even Floridians who were tropical storm veterans, were quite terrified this time. The forecast was awful. We anxiously waited for the disaster to fall upon us with full force. Florida was declared the State of Emergency. Some were able to leave the state. Others decided to stay and prepare for the hit in the best way possible: large pieces of plywood on the windows, sandbags at the doors, documents, and necessary things prepared. Shelters were ready to take those in need. Of course, I told Farhan about everything. That year, we had suffered a lot. Exhausted from all kinds of preparations for the "strike" of nature, I managed to fall asleep for several hours. In my dream, I constantly saw him praying for me. *Keep her, her children, and her family safe. Please keep her safe for me. Keep her Safe!*

I do not know how I could describe the sensation of being hugged tightly by a person who is actually on another continent, but I felt exactly that. This hurricane had brought me back the knowledge of my Sword, which he gave me, and which I told you about earlier. Yes. I had all this. There was only one thing missing. Only one—*a simple phone call from him asking, "Are you alright?"*

The storm arrived with a frightening vengeance, partially destroying our house. Many things fell into disrepair. My mother, children, and I, though safe, had been terrified. Yet he was silent. *Silent...*

No worries. No offering of help. Not even a bit of empathy or simple, human compassion. No. I did not get any of that.

A few days later, when everything had more or less returned to normal, I decided that I'd had enough of these games! *ENOUGH!* If in real life he would not even call me at a time when my family and I were in serious danger, not even to find out if I was still alive, it only showed me how little I really meant to him. I am done! Time to end the games of the Witch and the King.

Absolute Stupidity—that is my name! He has a whole world on its knees before him. And I only have a computer screen and my love. He does not need me; I am not dear to him. That was clear to me now. Once again, I decided to stop it all and walk away.

If we can even call it that, this *relationship* had tormented me to my very limit in this dimension of reality. *APPARENTLY*, whatever I meant to Farhan that was not enough to dial my goddamn number. I decided that I had done absolutely everything within my power. Maybe, even more than that. My mission, if there was one, must be completed by now. I had had enough of this suffering and these games.

But I will still tell you about one of these games in particular. My favorite one. *Confession and reconciliation through one specific color.*

Long ago, he learned that I absolutely loved *the color indigo or royal blue*—the same color as the *crystal* we both have in our heart area.

One time, I wrote this to him.

> *If you want to show me how much you miss me and can't stop thinking about me, if I'm in your heart, if I'm in your Soul, if I am in every particle of your very existence and every thought of your mind, then wear this color, and I will know about it.*

So, every time he wanted to show me, he missed me, or we had a virtual fight with each other, he would immediately use all my favorite requests to make it up to me:

Photos and videos with him wearing royal blue clothes.

His hair a bit tousled, overgrown, not neatly combed, but falling freely on his forehead, *"because I like it when you look like a wild boy."*

A shortly trimmed beard, *"I like it because it outlines and shapes up your lips."*

Whole sentences and sometimes paragraphs from my book, my stories, and letters, which he used either in posts, in videos, or interviews.

All this immediately would be put into practice.

At first, I really enjoyed it! I loved it! MY words and expressions would bounce around the digital world as his own quotes—HIS quotes! I probably should have been a little upset. But no. I never felt that way!

On the contrary, it amused and pleased me. People around him would begin to use my particular expressions, courtesy of him, and later these expressions would scatter around the world like hot pies in a hungry family. That would only entertained me and made me laugh.

I was even proud of it. I cannot share my words, phrases, or expressions with you that Farhan would use. Otherwise, you will narrow down his identity in a heartbeat and I cannot allow that. I was his top and best-kept secret. I was the Witch behind the Forbidden Waterfall.

"I miss you. I yearn for you. I can't stop thinking about you." This is precisely what it meant in our game when he appeared on the screens wearing *"Royal Blue."* This was a game that we played with each other *in front of the whole world*, while the world *had no idea about it!*

Of course, this color looked incredible on him! If I sound like a woman in love, it's true; I was. For me, he was Incredible. Beautiful. Talented. Beloved. My Twin. My Half. My Soul.

There was something else, which kept me staying. Every time I tried to put an end to it and disappear from his life, he would start to fade away, as if someone turned off all the lights in a large, bright room. The longer I was gone, the faster his internal fire seemed to die down. As soon as I returned, the fire would light up again. When I was around, that particular light, or fire, sparkled in his eyes like magic and erased his age, turning him into almost a bright, vibrant teenager. When I was gone, the fire was gone. As soon as I returned, the fire ignited, and he would start sparkling again, shining and vibrating like a forest creek in the bright sun rays in the summer morning.

So, I kept writing, and Farhan answered me in a way everyone could read, yet no one would know, it was meant only for me. And I continued writing. I can't even recall the number of pages that I sent to him. Apart from the countless letters, fragments of the story "The King and the Witch," I also included pieces of two novels, *The Kiss of God* and *Forget-me-not*. There were fairy tales, poems, songs, short stories, ideas, thoughts, you name it.

These were thousands of pages! There was everything—life, tears, love, and inspiration.

But the hurricane had passed without a single call from him! Just a simple phone call would have sufficed. So, I decided that I meant so little to him that he did not even bother to call me at the moment of real danger. Did not even bother to find out if I was alive, if I was ok. Apparently, it was completely unimportant to him.

I disappeared for over a month. As always, he resorted to using all the *things* I loved about him as secret weapons—wild hair, quotes of my favorite authors or my own letters, wearing clothes in my favorite color, «indigo,» so on.

Before I write about what happened next, I want to say the following. I would be lying if I said I never longed for him to LOVE me! What kind of woman wouldn't dream about it? Is there a woman in the world who would not yearn for the one she loves to love her back? But allow me to repeat it, I never thought of destroying his family! And I believed he had a family. I was clueless that they stopped being a real family years before my appearance in his life.

I never intended to get between him and his wife. It never even crossed my mind. Never. In fact, I have always sincerely admired his wife, and when they argued with each other, believe it or not, it hurt me to the core to see it.

It was painful for me to see how these two people, who once loved each other a lot, seemed to be building an invisible wall between them, sometimes not even talking. Such periods of silence and rejection of each other had been in their family for many years. *It started long before my appearance.* There were times when they wouldn't even be seen in public together for many months. And if they did attend some event together, the tension between them was easy to read even by ordinary people, let alone those who can *see* beyond physical perception.

Since telepathy is a common thing for the Twin Flames, and a Twin can *see* with the eyes of the other Twin, sometimes I saw scenes of their fights as if I were standing in the room next to them. They argued, and both were right in their own way, both of them. They, just like all people, made mistakes. They both had issues with each other. They both hurt each other. Perhaps, even he was much guiltier than her in most cases.

They both felt worse after arguing, and I felt it. *While one Twin suffers, the other one is just as hurt.* If he felt terrible, I felt awful as well. If he was sparkling and full of joy, so was I.

When he was fighting with his wife, I wrote to him in our *secret* manner.

"What are you doing? What are you doing, Ram? Why are you arguing with her? Why argue? Do you feel better now? Or does she feel better? Do you think being your wife is like a pleasant walk in the park on a spring morning? It's not that easy! Believe me; she is also having a hard time. Please try to understand her! If you can't stand being with each other, why don't you just free each other and let each other go? But if you choose to stay together, please look into her eyes and FIND the young girl you once, long ago, fell madly in love with! Remember how she looked on your wedding day! Remember the moments, which brought joy to both of you, instead of criticizing one another. Remember what unites you two,

instead of what is pulling you apart. How can arguing and fighting help you two? It can't, Ram. It can't."

I am writing all of this not to appear to you as *Holy Mother Teresa*, not at all. I just share with you how it all was. As I said earlier, I write it so you can understand, Twins work like a mirror of each other. And if he is hurt, I feel bad as well. Yes, I have entered the life of a married man, as I thought. But by this time, I think, you can clearly see and understand that I, actually, was not given much of choice, if any choice at all. The earthly paths of the Twins are predetermined before they are even born.

When Twin Flames appear in each other's lives, *it's never a random event. They do not incarnate into the same lifetime randomly.* They don't find each other "just because." It never happens without a higher goal. When Twin Flames find each other, it's because they were destined to before they were born, just as destiny brought them together in the many lives *BEFORE* this one.

Did I want to be with him in this three-dimensional world? Of course, I did! For me, even breathing while living so far away from him was torture. But to want and to *DO* are two different things! I understood perfectly that my appearance in his life did not mean that we, as if by magic, would be together and live "happily ever after."

Of course, the Soul is always eager to unite with its Twin. But people have their own affections, tasks, hobbies, obligations, goals. Plus, do not forget, even though the Twin whose memory of the past wakes up first, longing to find the way for union, the other half might still be asleep and in no hurry. The other Twin might continue to rule his kingdom, with no intention whatsoever of changing anything. The *main reason* Twins appear in each other's lives is not for physical connection but their *Spiritual Awakening, Spiritual Growth,* and *Spiritual Transformation.*

So, what did I expect from him after that damn hurricane?! I wasn't looking for "happily ever after." Oh, no! I just wanted simple human empathy. I just wanted him to show he cared. Just simple human compassion. I did not think, it was too much to wish for. But it didn't happen. He didn't plan on showing me he cared. Or maybe he did not care that much, after all. I was just mere entertainment. Yes, we shared many things during these years of our story: creativity, inspiration, books, conversations, philosophy, humor, and flirtation. But I, probably, wanted the impossible. I wanted him not only to believe me, but I also wanted him to REMEMBER me. *Remember me on the level of his very Soul.* Remember me, the woman, who centuries ago used to be his beloved wife, his friend, his home, his inspiration. And most importantly, *the woman who was his Twin,* the other half of his very Soul, ready to help him find the answers to the questions he was always asking himself. *Who am I? Why did I come to this earth? Am I doing exactly what I came for? What are my tasks? Goals? Possibilities? Abilities? Why am I here?*

Or maybe I am lying? Am I lying to myself? I am not only a soul. I am a woman. Loving. Doubting. Suffering. I am not trusting even myself. Dreaming of the impossible miracle of him knocking on my door, holding me in his arms, and saying, "I'm back, Lala. *I remember you.* I love you. I want to be with you".

Is it true? Or not? Back then, *definitely not.* I would not even think of such insanity. Or would I? Maybe I would, but at the same time, I clearly understood the chance of such a scenario happening was very slim.

So, what did I want? I wanted him to know me, believe me, understand me, *and remember me!* I wanted to talk to him on the phone. I wanted to be able to see him sometimes. I wanted him to tell me about everything in the world, the things he would not tell anyone else. I wanted him to care. I wanted to know I was dear to him, cherished by him.

But most of all, *I wanted to look into his EYES.*

Oh! Those deep magical lakes that I have been searching for my whole life! I knew that if I looked into his eyes for at least a moment, my Soul would finally find Peace. We will look into each other's eyes, and two parts of our souls will become One. Our Soul will become Whole.

And then what? I do not know. He was a magnet, drawing me toward himself with inexhaustible power. Yes, I wanted to break this connection with him. Constantly. The reasons were obvious: *uncertainty and hopelessness.* I was playing a virtual game, one lasting for years. I was getting tired of it. I wanted more. I decided my game ended! I had lost. Game over.

After establishing a virtual, spiritual but nonphysical connection with him, I began to dream of a physical connection. I knew I shouldn't have, but I dreamed. I dreamed of kissing his beautiful lips, of holding him in my arms, being one with him, embracing him like the ocean embraces the sandy shore and the sky embraces the sea.

Oh, Ram. My Ram. Why couldn't I just forget you? Why didn't I forget you? It's impossible not to want you near me, Ram. Every particle of my existence remembers you!

Of course, I wanted him to *LOVE* me. I wished that with all my heart. But I was afraid to even think about it. I did not dare to allow such thoughts and constantly fought with myself!

But now, things were different. After the hurricane and his indifferent silence, *I felt very hurt.* To me, it became clear that I meant absolutely nothing. So, I disappeared from his horizon for over a month!

As usual, he did not like it. He tried all the old methods of winning me back. He wore my "indigo color" for several days in a row. Still, I was steady as a rock.

When I finally answered, I sent him another part of the story, "The King of Wizards and the Witch." In that part, I told him everything I thought about him. In that part, I told him everything I thought about him. Yes. I did write it twice. Are you laughing? So am I. I am a woman; I am a loving woman. To be exact, I am the words of the song "Woman in Love" by the brilliant Barbra Streisand.

I am a woman in love.
And I'd do anything
To get you into my world
And hold you within

It's a right I defend
Over and over again.
What do I do?[10]

So, a moment came when I could not remain silent anymore. And what followed? Keep on reading, and you will see.

---

10 Barbra Streisand, vocalist, "Woman in Love", 1980, by Barry Gibb and Robin Gibb, track 2 on Guilty (New York: Columbia Records).

Chapter 35

The King of Wizards and the Witch (cont.)

He was lying in the thick green grass of the Forbidden Forest, looking directly into the starry sky. The Stars were twinkling coldly above him in all their magnificent splendor. He closed his eyes, and his eyelashes laid soft winged shadows on his cheeks. Quietly, very quietly, he pronounced her name three times.

"Come to me," he said. Although he felt she was reluctant to answer his call, he knew she would come. He just knew. The King opened his eyes, got up from the grass, and walked to the Waterfall of the Forgotten Dreams. The Cascades of water were soundlessly tumbling from the cliff. The Moon and stars reflected in the mirror of water. A few moments later, she appeared. *His Witch. His Love. His Soul.*

Her raven-colored hair fell over her shoulders and almost touching the ground. Her thin cape fluttered in the wind. It shimmered with the starlight, just like the sky above them. Her eyes were glowing with anger. But they softened a little when she saw the color of the mantle he had over his shoulders. She called this color *The Color of Wizards, The Color of Our Love—Royal blue. Indigo. Sapphire.*

She knew every time he wore this color, it was to show her that his heart was crying and that his soul was longing for hers. But now, she had very little faith in it. Her faith had nearly vanished!

"My Lord and my King!" she said. "Why have you called upon me? And why tell me, are your shoulders wrapped in this blue cloak? What is this lie for? You want to show me that I am dear to you! But you don't have the courage to even look into my eyes! You can only talk to me through the mirror of this water but you don't have the courage to take a step towards me. When I was fighting the monster that threatened the world of people, you left me alone! You didn't care what might happen to me! And now you are calling me? The "color of our love" is draping your shoulders? Why? What for? *This all is a lie!* I mean nothing to you. Nothing, my lord! Nothing at all!

Her eyes glared with angry resentment, darkness gathering above her head.

"Do you hear yourself? Do you believe what you are saying, Lallah?" he asked quietly.

"I only voice how things really are, my lord! You do not love me! I do not know who I am, or what I am for you in this incarnation. Maybe I'm your favorite toy, your entertainment, the source of your inspiration, or perhaps just a beautiful fairy tale.

"Whoever I am to you, it's clear you do not love me! No, there is no love for me in your heart! And I deserve to be loved, not to be played with! Don't call for me anymore. Do you hear? Never! Never call for me ever again! And never again dare to wear THIS COLOR!

"Let the black color of the night hug your shoulders! Or the color of the day, the color of the morning dawn, or the color of the Sun! But never, you hear me, never again dare to wear this color! Royal Blue is forbidden for you from now on! Because it is the color of True Love! True, Deep, Eternal Love! He, who wears this color, is saying with it:

'*You are my life! You're my Soul! You are my happiness, my heart, my dream! Every day beneath the Sun, every night below the Moon, I think about you, breathing together with you! Your name has become my prayer, my spell! I see you in the stars and the green leaves of the trees; I feel you in the touch of the wind! In the raindrops! Because I love you! I love you! I love you!*'

"That's what that color means, my King! And if you ever again, even just once, dare to put on this color! It will mean just that! Do you hear me? Exactly those words! I will perceive it as you saying these very words to me, looking straight in my eyes! *I will take it as a CONFESSION!* Therefore, never! Do you hear me? Never again dare to wear this color! Do not torment my heart! Forget me! Do you hear? Forget!"

Two weeks passed after that letter. Farhan was silent. Good, right? I said what I wanted to say. But can I calm down and start living? No. I was dying because of uncertainty. It felt as if I had a tornado inside tearing me apart. I was falling to pieces. I was still waiting for his answer. Once again, it seemed that my soul wanted to leave my body and fly to him. Fly to him. Fly to him. I felt like a bird trapped in a cage so small, I could barely breathe in it, let alone spread my wings even a little. I could not sleep. I couldn't eat. I was simply trying to follow the path I'd chosen, to walk away and forget everything! But I was failing miserably. It wasn't working out for me. Not at all. More precisely, I couldn't do it! My soul was losing the battle because I loved him too much. I was melting like a Snow Maiden. I even wrote a story, *"A Woman Made Out of Wax."*

And then one night, I woke up sharply and suddenly, as if awakened by someone splashing me with ice-cold water. I grabbed my phone.

I saw a short video he made. With the help of some filter, *absolutely everything in it was Indigo.* He had first filmed everything surrounding him, then slowly turned the camera onto himself. Do I even need to tell you that *everything he was wearing was Indigo?* Or did you already guess? He smiled with his incredible smile, the smile of a guilty boy. Lowering his eyes, he nodded his head several times in such an easily recognizable gesture, meaning *"Yes"...*

It would have been a weird sight that moment if anybody at all saw me. It was about 4 a.m. I'm sitting on my bed, pressing the phone to my chest, laughing and crying at the same time, repeating, again and again, *"This cannot be! It cannot be! It is simply impossible!"*

Before me is a beautiful woman from the world of eternity and the realm of the Spirits with a smile on her lips and beautifully warm words, "*I told you, my dear girl! He will remember!*"

Chapter 36

In the Mist House, on the Lost Planet

"Everyone, get ready! Here comes the hardest test. The most painful one! Right here, we can lose everything we have been working for so hard and for so long. We might be thrown all the way back again and have to repeat everything from the very beginning, from her very birth. We will have to try again to raise a warrior. A Heroine. A Queen. A source of strength, love, inspiration, and happiness for many people." Helena, the white-haired woman, quickly got up and looked at the solemn faces of the inhabitants of the mist house.

They could see the endless snowy fields and the storm raging over them from the open windows. The snowy whirlwinds spread around for tens of meters, spinning on the ground as if gathering together their warriors. Warriors, made of snowflakes, ice, and frost, were rising upward, growing like gigantic icy genies, touching the sky with their heads. Three moons glowed through the clouds as they threw themselves at each other furiously, as if in a last, decisive battle.

Decisive it was. This was the final battle. The warriors of ice and wind exploded, hitting each other with icy knives, tearing away the thick white shrouds of their opponents, and falling to pieces just to rise again and keep on fighting their ice battle fiercely.

But not a single snowflake flew into the room with the four Keepers. Silence reigned in the house—cold, intense silence.

This time, Haan was reading the book. He read slowly, calmly, like a person already familiar with its content. Joanna was conjuring something over the large silver mirror. Looking into it, one would see: blue clouds floating in the sky, planes flashing as they flew by, a lost car, a crowd of people chanting the name of their idol, and a woman, Lala, with a royal blue scarf, slipping from her suddenly weak hands. A close-up image showed her eyes, as big as half the mirror, growing numb with unbearable pain. The mirror's image begins to fade; her eyes start to disappear.

Joanna starts whispering, "Breathe! Breathe! Breathe, Lala! Don't you dare give up! You are strong! Please, girl, please breathe! Don't you dare!" And she quickly does something with her hands, creating a protective dome of fire above the mirror and warming it up, trying to melt the frost, which has already begun to cover the screen.

Helena is sitting in an armchair, her head leaning back, eyes closed. At first, she appears to be unconscious. But taking a closer look, you can notice she's moving her lips as if talking quickly, asking questions, answering, speaking with someone she cannot see, someone present but invisible.

Haan's face looks almost tragic. He listens closely to her speech and suddenly comes to the mirror, holding his hands over it as if trying to warm it up.

"Do not disappear," he whispers. "Don't! Please don't! Lala, don't you dare! Breathe! Please girl. This is not the end. Not yet! Just stay with us! Stay! Stay! Breathe girl. Breathe! Hold on, Lala."

"Breathe, do you hear me?" Joanna says. But the mirror keeps filling with ice patterns.

"Can't any of you do something?!" screams frightened Firebird. "Help her! Please! Interfere! Do something! INTERFERE!! DAMN YOU!!!!"

Hann's face is almost white with tension, but he tries his best to stay calm. Looking into the cold female eyes in the mirror, he whispers, again and again, trying to make his voice sound soothing. "It's not over yet, my girl. It's not over. Please breathe... Do not do this... Do not... Breathe... It's not over... Not over..."

Sometime later, the room becomes empty. On the table lies the mirror, turned upside down; its glass frame looks smelted on one side. The huge clear windows are closed. The house looks still, quiet and serene. Only now, it seems, this quietness doesn't press you down and does not scare. Outside the windows, spring is emerging in the forest valley. Grubby remnants of snow lurk under the bushes. You can hear the impudent green blades of grass breaking through overripe foliage. You can smell the freshness of blue snowdrops that proudly spread their bells of thin china towards the warm rays of the sun.

Chapter 37

Tell Them, My Love

Many months had passed since he read my book.

I must add that the book was not only the story of my life and my search for him, the one with whom I share One Soul. It also contained a lot of my thoughts about many, many subjects. Religions and ancient wisdom hidden in myths. Fairy tales and ancient texts. My dreams of how I would like to change this world. What tormented me most and what inspired me most. I wrote about the destruction of Mother Earth by people, about the suffering of millions of young children. I wrote that in the pursuit of material wealth people have forgotten one simple thing: how to be people, how the things people owned *had begun to own them.*

I am not writing all this to show you: *Ah, here I am, such a good girl!* No. The truth is that I am a typical good girl—an ordinary and boring good girl.

I'm a girl, or to be exact, a woman who dreams and wants *to make a difference*, as strange as it sounds. I'm a woman, often feeling lonely, misunderstood by many, the one who had been hurt way too many times, living without love, but with a firm *faith* in it. I am a woman with a dream of changing this world and have been like this since childhood. Well, at least try to change the world *at least a little bit* by sharing with it *the love of my heart and the fire of my soul.* My biggest pain was always the suffering of women and little children.

While writing my book for him, the following thought occurred: *What if the fire and the passion of my heart can also light up HIS heart. Maybe he can feel*

267

exactly what I feel since we are each other's halves. It should not be that difficult! He might have deep concern about the same things as I do.

One day, when another moment of doubt threatened to overpower me, his mother asked me, "Lala! What do you really want?"

"I want what I'm not allowed to have, Maa. I want to be with him."

"I know that. But you are already with Him! That's the thing you don't understand just yet, my girl! *He is already yours.* He is already with you. Do you hear? He has always been yours, thousands of earthly and non-earthly years and lives; *He always will be yours! You will always be his! You have one Soul!* No one and nothing can change this, Lala! Such power simply does not exist!"

"I mean being with him in this earthly reality, Maa! And this is not possible!"

"Yes, Lala, this is not possible just yet. But besides that, what else do you want and wish for?"

"This might sound stupid, Maa, but I would like to do something that could change our world, make it a little better, brighter, kinder."

Once again, I thought it might be possible for me to impact this world with His help! So, whenever an important thought came to my mind, I once again wrote my letters to him, the letters starting with these words, "I am your Twin Flame, my love, yet I am just an ordinary woman in our three-dimensional world. I have neither fame, nor wealth, nor influence. They may not listen to me, *but they will listen to YOU, my Love! Tell them, Ram!*"

After those words, I wrote everything I thought he needed to tell the people and why he needed to say it to them. Millions of people were listening to him, not only ordinary people but the most influential and powerful people of this world!

He was, in my opinion, the greatest speech giver I had ever seen. The rich and powerful, inspired by his words, would improve many people's lives all over the world. My words and ideas would inspire him, and he, in his turn, would inspire others.

Once again, I felt immensely moved by this idea. I suddenly felt my heart singing with joy again. I felt the wings behind my back, and again,

I felt I could fly. I decided that this was precisely why we came to this world at the same time. We came to change it. He is a great actor, talented, famous, and rich. And I... I am just me, a woman who remembers our past lives together and loves him, a mother of two boys and the daughter of my strict Mother.

We were assigned strange roles in this incarnation. Was it I who chose such a fate for myself, or was it someone else? Or perhaps it was me and someone else?

Farhan had an immense influence on a massive number of people. I was well aware of it. Again, and again, I wrote to him, *"They will listen to you! Tell them, my love!"*

He had shown me clearly, more than once, more than ten, or even maybe hundreds of times, how important what I said was for him. My thoughts. My ideas. Especially after reading my book.

At first, I did not understand. *Why is Farhan listening to me? Who am I?* I asked myself. But I grew accustomed to the thought that in listening to me, he was, in fact, *listening to himself.* It was like the voice of his own Soul spoke to him through me. Deep inside, I understood; subconsciously, he knew and remembered me. Always.

As I already said, he was a phenomenal orator. He had an excellent education. He was fluent in several languages and often invited to speak to different people in other parts of the world. A brilliant speaker, with his own style, charisma, special masculine charm, vast intellect and sense of humor, he easily captivated any audience! He was listened to with genuine admiration. And every time, when he shared what I asked him to say in my letters, he looked directly into the camera and, with a subtle movement of his right hand, touched his lips now and then, barely, just with his fingertips (as if sending a kiss). This was another one of our *secret signs.* His eyes were saying, "You see, I am listening to you! This is for you!"

My writing, which started with my first letter to him, had transformed into something serious for me. I began writing like breathing! I just couldn't help it! I could not understand what was happening to me! It was as if I ended up in some space, where even the air itself was saturated not with oxygen but with inspiration! I already told you that I started the story "The King of Wizards and the Witch," apart from that, I began to write a series of stories, "Little Wizard," two novels, a series of stories "Wisdom of the Ancients," and a lot more.

I generously and wholeheartedly shared all my creations with him! I could not understand where it all came from; it just arrived. Entire scenes and chapters just appeared in my head, as if I saw them on the screen of a movie theater. It was unbelievable, but such things began to happen to me all the time. A dialog could appear in my head while I was standing at the crossroads, waiting for the light to turn green! I wrote on everything within my hand's reach! The blank pages of books, napkins, scraps of paper, leaflets, you name it.

The novel *Kiss of God* and the story "The King of Wizards and the Witch" appeared as whole scenes in my head. I only had to express what I'd seen in writing.

My days, weeks, and months passed like this. They passed one after another without stopping. Life was full of colors for me, and the sun was shining brightly. People were smiling at me. Birds were singing; it seemed like true happiness was everywhere.

Shine. Sparkle. Spread your wings, and fly with joy above the clouds, Lala! He loves you! He loves you! He loves you! I said to myself, raising my face to the sun's rays. Be patient just a little bit more, and you will be able to touch him. You will finally look into his eyes! You will feel the fullness of life and sense of your being, and with a smile, you will say to yourself: "You see! Everything was not in vain! It was not for nothing! It all was worth it! It was worth it every moment! Just you wait a little longer, just wait.

I started seeing the same dream every several days.

Chapter 38

The Dream

I am looking into the incredible eyes of a tall, luminous being. I am well aware that my physical body is sleeping right now, but my Essence, my Soul, is now outside the levels of Earth. This Being is much taller than I am. He is at least ten feet tall. He is millions of Earth years old, but he is still just a *baby* compared to others. He is one of my Guardians. His eyes are beautiful, somewhat frightening, and indescribable, shimmering with all the colors of a rainbow.

"Would you like to see other galaxies?" he asks me

"Sure, but…"

"Of course, we have only a few fragile moments. Not enough time at all, but I can show you from afar, briefly, how enormous this Universe is! And this is only one of them. It is infinite—*WITHOUT AN END IN SIGHT*. Do you understand? Of course, you don't. You don't understand, or rather, you do, but not entirely, because you're still in your physical embodiment!

"It's rather hard for you to imagine all of this. Your world also moves in a spiral, but many of you do not see it! You imagine everything to *be finite*, with an end. It's easier for you this way. What have you decided? Want me to show you something that will deeply amaze you? Something you could not even imagine in the wildest of dreams?"

I raise my dark eyes and silently look deeply into his rainbow-colored eyes.

He gets sad and then shakes his head. "*Him?* You want to see him, be with him, right?"

I smile guiltily and lower my eyes.

Then timidly raise them again. To my surprise, I see on his luminous face a mixture of human feelings and emotions. He is surprised, but I see admiration. He is a little angry but he cannot help smiling. The soft smile on his face makes him even more shining.

"It is just, you see," I try to make excuses, "you see, this is my only opportunity. You know how things are for us out there, on Earth. Well, how else can I be with him, and he with me? If not like this, there is no other way! At least for now, please try to understand."

The Luminous Being shakes its head. "I can't possibly understand you! With your thirst for hidden knowledge and information, you refuse such an opportunity! I invite you to see for yourself what is hidden from so many! Even from the enlightened ones! But all you wish for is for me to push the boundaries of earthly time and take you to one of your past lives?"

"Yes. I beg you, please. If this is allowed."

He shakes his head again. "Well," he finally says. "Fine. I will do it. Which one of those lives do you want to go back to? There were thousands!"

"The very last one, the one right before this one. It was very short, but I think it was the happiest."

"It's useless to try to persuade you otherwise. Right?"

I nod affirmatively.

For a fraction of an earthly second, he falls silent.

Then he speaks softly, "Well, what can I do with you? Go! Go to him, go to your Love." Then he smiles, shakes his head, and adds, "*You are so much a Woman!*"

And the very next moment, I am in a beautiful, sunlit field, blooming in every shade of green. I am in the strong embrace of his arms. I'm holding him so tightly I can hear his heart beating. It beats in unison with mine. I listen to him laughing, and the sound of his beautiful low voice fills me with joy.

"Lala."

I am overwhelmed by this sunny happiness, and at the same time tormented by such pain, it tightens my throat, so I can't breathe. Oh! If I only could—if only I had the power to stop time on Earth. If only I could stay in this life. Why was it so short? Why am I so rarely given happiness, and there is so little of it when I am? Why is that? Why do I always choose for myself some impossibly difficult tests? Why do I do that?

I want to stay with him! I want to melt into and merge with him, to be one with him. I want to dissolve in him. I do not want to exist without him. *Why am I without him, and he without me, why?* What for?

The Higher Forces know everything. But how little is what we know. So little. Are the lessons of Karma the lessons that I myself chose? Or were they chosen by the Elders? Questions, questions. And so few answers.

I draw back from him just a bit, wanting to see his eyes. As He holds my face in his palms, I feel like crying. I see it as a weakness. *I hate being weak.* I am a Warrior in my very Essence, and warriors do not cry! Or do they?

"I am weak, am I not?" I ask him an utterly stupid question.

"You? No. No." His fingers gently trace the outline of my face. His touch has been familiar to me for thousands and thousands of years. I cannot live without it. We are given a few moments. *Just a few…*

Chapter 39

The Fall from Heaven

"Tell me! Why then do we love?
Tell me! Why do we love each other?
Counting the days. Burning our hearts! Why?"
Leonid Derbenev

The Year of 2017 has arrived. Winter gradually moved into the spring, spring into the summer, summer into the autumn. Twitter had become the "Forbidden Forest Waterfall," for us, where the Witch communicated with her King. Months passed like this. We sent each other messages using false names. I wrote everything I held in my heart, as I always did. He used the same method of communication as he previously had on *FB*. He answered me with quotes from my favorite writers and poets, philosophers, ancient sophists, or my own words. Sometimes he sent me videos of songs, videos of his interviews, or pieces of the films, which he wanted me to see. That was his game. *HIS game.*

At the beginning of it all, I was enjoying that. Yes, I did. I found a million and one excuses for why Farhan could not just call me and talk to me. Over time I became more and more uncomfortable with this interplay. On the other hand, he seemed to be enjoying this game; the further it went, the more he enjoyed it.

It appeared that doing just about anything, was easier than dialing my number—paint his mansion in the color indigo, eat and drink, drive and work with the same color, wear my favorite shirts, or whatever I asked. Since dialing my number was impossible, it seemed obvious that seeing me wasn't even a thought in his mind!

Just make a call!!! Oh. No!

I didn't understand that at the time, but he calculated every move he made. If anyone suspected anything about our love, the color of twilight, he could easily say this conversation and the entire account *had nothing to do with him*. He could easily say he doesn't know who I am. Yes, I understand; Farhan was simply doing everything to protect himself and his reputation. (Here I go again, justifying everything, again and again, there's nothing I can do about it!) But this game was not open or honest towards me. *It had never been.* It was *his game*, not mine. *I was not playing.* He was. *But I did not know.*

Yes, his Soul remembered me and loved me. It could not be otherwise; it is IMPOSSIBLE not to love your Twin! But the Soul is *one thing*; the *thoughts and actions* of the one the Soul inhabits are *quite another*. I didn't know that either.

Unfortunately, forces unrelated to the Soul, often control our behavior, actions, and desires. For example, our notorious *Ego* has nothing to do with our *Soul*! *They are not connected.* As a result, if the Ego rules, the Soul is lulled to sleep.

You may ask, how is it even possible? Let me share an example. When a person is in extreme grief or terrified or under the influence of drugs or alcohol, they often do things *entirely out of character* for them and *not true to their essence, their Soul. Envy, greed, thirst for power and money, pride, arrogance, and ignorance—these result from Ego*, showing its control over the person, and *have nothing to do with the Soul or the true Self!* The saddest part is that people can spend years, decades, maybe even an entire lifetime living in *this state of Ego*. They live, walk, talk, laugh, etc., while their *Soul is sleeping*. To live without a Soul is terrifying.

The name *Buddha* means The *Awakened One*—the one who thinks, speaks, and acts *not as a Body*, but in *awake awareness as an eternal SOUL*, as the supreme, the truest I. When Twin Flames choose to incarnate in one lifetime, one awakens first and then helps the other awaken. I thought I was the awakened one and had done everything possible and impossible to help *him awaken*. I truly believed in the all-encompassing power of our eternal Love! I honestly thought he "woke up" and was now acting from his *Awakened Soul, not his Ego*. But I was wrong—Oh, how mistaken I was!

I had a very long path ahead of me until my Love could claim victory over his demons. Unfortunately for me, he had become used to living with these demons over the years. Dark forces do everything possible and impossible to *keep people from awakening*, especially people who have power and influence in our World. In such cases, they create unimaginable obstacles, nearly impossible to overcome!

Unfortunately, the Dark Forces control us on many visible and invisible levels, whether we realize it or not. They feed on the energy of our *fears and doubts, our longings and unfulfilled hopes*. They seek to keep us *away from the awareness* of our *true light* and *inner strength* because our *awakening is their death*. When we awaken, we stop feeding them; they lose power over us and die—to be exact, they simply *stop existing*.

Awakened beings remember, they have wings and they can fly. They understand clearly that they are *One with God, not separate!* They remember, the *Source of Truth and Light* is *INSIDE them* at their very *CORE*. It has always been there and always will be.

The awakened ones are rarely loved or appreciated by society or religion. But they aren't seeking outside approval. They follow their own path, *guided by their inner light*, not deviating, bowing to, or obeying anyone, impossible to control or manipulate. Seeing through lies, they cannot be bribed, overtaken by flattery or promises of power and will never again submit to the slavery of invisible Darkness! The Dark and their evil methods will never win over the awakened ones because their Soul, not their ego, is *the guiding force in their lives!*

LALA AGNI

No, I did not have the slightest clue back then that my beautiful Farhan was still far away from being "awakened." His Soul had been sleeping deeply for a long time. The Dark Force still held power over him, not allowing him true freedom, but he was not objecting too much.

We were very different, despite being One. For me, Love was God, the core of creation and the most sacred of all that has ever existed or ever will exist. But he had completely different values, ideas, and gods. Power, glory, fame, crowds worshiping him and money, big money, were more important and more valuable to him than anything else.

So, why did he continue our weird, unrealistic relationship? I will tell you why.

It was all a *GAME* for him; he *WAS PLAYING* with me—pretending to Love me! Game is the definitive word here. Did I know or suspect that? *Of course not!* Do not forget who was playing with me! An actor, and not just any actor, Farhan was one of the best actors walking the face of this Earth! Did I believe he was *sincere*? Oh, yes, I did! And you would have believed him too! I saw his sparkling eyes and his gentle smile in the videos and photos he sent me. He always remembered and used all of our secret signs. He addressed his words to me, respected my thoughts, ideas, and books. Plus, the secret color of our love, royal blue, was always present. *Yes, I believed him!* How could I *not believe him?*

Every time I tried to break away and leave this relationship, which obviously led nowhere, he did everything to keep it going. He held on, not letting me go. Whenever I attempted to escape, he did everything to convince me and make me believe *the impossible was very much possible. And I BELIEVED him. I did.* It was a ruthless game—a game where He designed rules that benefitted only him.

Had it *ALWAYS* been only a game to him? Had there ever been something, anything else? I was confused and didn't know. Every day *I found excuses for his every action.* I loved him too much, way too much! I was so focused and devoted to him that *I forgot myself; I lost myself in him. That was wrong,* but I did not understand it initially; I did not know how to be any other way.

"If you get what you want at once, it will quickly lose its value for you! Learn to wait!" he wrote to me. And I *BELIEVED* him! I believed with all my heart! Not in my wildest dreams did I imagine this was all a *game* for him. Soon I would learn that and find out *why* he played this game.

Oh, Love! You make us blind, dumb, and deaf! And here we're talking about the Love of a Twin Flame for her Other Half, so multiply it by a thousand!

As I later discovered, he needed many things from me: He needed my Light and my Love; without them, his Soul was falling deeper under the power of the Dark. He also needed my inspiration, passion, sincerity and laughter, the fire of my heart and Soul. His Shadow—the part of him controlled by the Dark Forces—needed my energy for food; there is nothing "tastier" than the pure, very high-frequency energy of the Twin Flame. My Love for him was as pure as you can even imagine. Nothing compares to this kind of Love!

Oh, stupid me. Even now, I often ask myself a question, *Am I just purely stupid, or am I a saint?* Maybe *both,* since I am a Twin Flame.

This Love had given me Wings—enormous wings, the color of a double rainbow. I left the Earth and was flying high above the clouds! But wings, you know, can be very dangerous! They lift you to such great heights that you would be shattered into millions of tiny pieces if you fall. I was unaware that my fall *was very close.* It was already starting to touch me with its ice-cold fingers, a touch as unavoidable as a touch of death. I did not know; the one who would cause me to fall was the *LAST* being in this entire Universe I would expect it from—the one I shared One Soul with, the one I believed in, the one I loved with every part of my essence!

I write all this because many of you think that meeting with your Twin, your other half, the one you share one Soul with, is like a dream come true! Many women and even men dream of finding their Twin Flame, thinking that everything will instantly be like a fairy tale as soon as they look into each other's eyes.

But the reality is *totally different!* When you find each other, the most challenging part begins. Sometimes even the most terrifying! *The battle between The Light and The Dark*. No, not a brief battle! If only it were ephemeral, I guess things would be much easier! No, this battle is, unfortunately, very real. Together, if the Twins unite, *they generate the highest frequency and purest vibrations*. That is the energy of *pure Love* and Joy, *a compelling energy force that can ignite many people's hearts*. In ancient books, I've read that the Twin Flames come to *increase the vibrational level of the planet*. They come to *help Souls to find their forgotten Mission*. You see, absolutely *everyone has a Mission and a Purpose! Every Soul!* But we were forced to forget all about that, and unfortunately, most people on Gaia still live their everyday life, rarely deciding to stop and think, *Why am I here?*

The path of the Twin Flames is *a long and thorny one*. But we chose to walk it and we do. The reason is rather simple, as I already said, *United Twins, with their energies merged, can play a massive role in the transformation of life on our planet, in the evolutionary transition of humanity to a new, higher level* of Consciousness. They can significantly accelerate the spiritual awakening of people by helping them activate their heart chakras. In simple words, people will again live, following their *hearts* without lies, deceptions, and pretense. But all this created a giant disadvantage to the *Dark Force* or the Dark Ones. Like the Light ones, the Dark ones are by no means a myth, a fairy tale, or fakery. They have always existed.

Strong emotions of low-frequency vibrations: *fear, envy, anger, desire for power, lust, doubt, irritation, greed, denial of the Soul's voice attract the Dark Ones*. When we experience such emotions and feelings, *we feed The Dark Forces*. It is their only food and the source of their existence. So, obviously, they really don't want to lose control over us. As I said before, the Dark Forces have extreme power over the people with *power, fame, wealth, and influence*. And my Farhan was and is one of them. Once awakened, *he could awaken millions among his audience*, and consequently, there would be a significant drop in the *food* for the Dark.

The Dark Ones are not only non-physical beings. Dark Ones can also be actual, tangible personalities in our well-known World of three-dimensional space. Many of them occupy prominent positions in world governments, managing our World and its events. They also do not want to see "awakened" among their flock. So, in every possible way, the vibrations of low frequencies are cultivated in us via media. *Lust. Envy. Greed. FEAR. Most of all, FEAR.* When we are afraid, terrified, and fearful, it is *effortless to control us and lead us whenever they wish us to go.* That is very sad and even tragic.

Therefore, the path of the Twins is never an easy one. *Never!* The Dark Force is interested in having everything remain *exactly as it is.* That is why they constantly interfere with Twin Flames both at conscious and subconscious levels.

Please, forgive me for this rather long digression from my story. This knowledge is essential to understand. I didn't know about it until much later after *Losing my wings and the brutal fall from Heaven.*

Back then, I didn't know any of this. I just loved and truly believed that I was loved back in the same way. *Silly goose.*

Shortly before he declared his *love* to me through the color royal blue, we chatted for several months via Twitter, as I mentioned before. But let me tell you how this happened the first time.

I found his account on Twitter by pure *chance*, if such a thing exists. And I found out also that he was in the habit of spending several hours each night, during his usual insomnia, reading what people wrote to him and even answering these messages himself. That was a well-known fact, but I hadn't a clue about it. When I found out, I created an account for myself. Since he knows me and my writing style, it was not difficult for me to let him know in just a few messages that it was indeed me. As soon as he understood, he created another account on Twitter with a name that, of course, I could not possibly confuse with anyone else, "*YourEternalLoveRam.*"

Our direct correspondence began at that point, if it can even call it "direct."

I wrote to him whatever comes to my mind. He didn't respond with many of his own words but sent quotes of the great ones or links to video clips he would like me to watch. Sometimes He sent me links to his performances before the public, links to fragments of his interviews, or parts of his films when he wanted to know my opinion about them. Sometimes he just sent songs. One of the songs he sent me was:

You are my drug,
Your Love is my drug,
I can never get enough of you.
I lost myself in your eyes.
What should I do now?
I know, I must run from you.
But leaving you is beyond my power.

There were, of course, quotes from my beloved Rumi and other great minds, and occasionally his own.

"I loved you before I knew your face."
"Before I even realized what happened, instead of blood, love for you began flowing down my veins."
"I have become one with you to such an extent that I don't know where my heart ends and yours begins, or maybe it's just one for the two of us?"

With every new such confession, my wings grew bigger and bigger; I flew higher and higher. My wings were growing stronger day by day. They became so huge that they began to touch the clouds. Even though I knew that maybe if I soared too close to the Sun, the wax would melt and I, like Icarus, would fall to the ground, I did not want to think about it. I wanted to fly and I was flying. I was gliding! The impossible no longer seemed impossible to me. *"Everything is possible! Nothing is impossible! Even what cannot be, still CAN BE! You just must keep on believing!"* I would say to everyone back then.

Silly goose. Oh, sorry. I have already said that before.

After his video in royal blue, indigo, all I could write to him on my Twitter page was, *"I don't believe you!"*

But, for some reason, it was important for him to *make me believe!* Many months followed when he only wore indigo color. Moreover, it seemed he enjoyed driving around in cars of this color, flying in helicopters and airplanes of this same color. His phone was the same color. His speeches, press conferences, interviews on *TV* channels and magazines were full of my words, ideas, expressions... *How could I NOT believe him?*

Oh! Of course, *I believed!* It really couldn't be just a *GAME*, right? After all, we had known each other for millennia before this life! We always shared One Soul and these deep, unbelievable feelings! Mysticism and all the visions and dreams are inexplicable from a rational perspective! So, how could it possibly be just a game for him? To me, *it was never a game!* For him, it was much more than that.

For him, all of this was so damn interesting! So, unlike anything he had ever seen or heard of—so mystical, romantic, and incomprehensible! So beautiful and magical! It inspires, moves the heart. After all, it entertains! He is playing *An Eternal Lover* in front of the whole world, but no one in the world has a clue! Exciting! And meanwhile, *he risks absolutely nothing!* He can still maintain the life he was used to—No changes are necessary. No real actions are needed. A perfect option? Absolutely! Indeed! Perfect for Him. But not for *the toy* the King is playing with, not for *the toy!* And the toy *was me!*

Unfortunately, I do not remember the name of the Brazilian writer who once wrote: *"What is more painful? To fall from Heaven or to fall from the second floor?"*

I fell from Heaven...

Chapter 40

The Abyss

It was October of 2017. I was living through yet another *dark night of the soul* and tired of not seeing Him, not hearing his voice. I was tired of that game and everything about it. For the million and first time, I wanted to «finish it all.» Even though the veil of my eternal love, I clearly understood everything was dragging on for *way too long*. With each passing day, it became more apparent that his plans did not include what I wanted so much: *eyes to eyes*.

I passionately wanted our eyes to meet at least once. Even if only for a moment! So, I could finally find in them my lost soul. And that was precisely what he did not want. Or maybe he wanted to look into my eyes but was afraid of it at the same time. Or He had other reasons. It changed absolutely nothing. Clearly, his plans included only one thing: simply leaving everything as it was. That was becoming very obvious.

Reality finally began to soak down into me and seep through my armor of *undying love and unwavering faith*. He was not going to change anything. Full stop. Did he remember me? If yes, fine. Did he believe me? If he did, great. If he did not, there was nothing else I was able to do. I have done more than enough. *The End!* This story of Eternal Love would not, unfortunately, have a happy ending. It's not up to me. It looks like I am just *a toy in the hands of the King*. I am just a toy in the hands of Destiny and Karma. I am sick and tired of being just a toy. This is it. *The End. El Fin. Konets! Finita!*

I shared with him my ideas for improving the world. As a celebrity speaking to his worldwide admirers, Farhan had given voice to my thoughts.

Children of the Earth, nature of the Earth, peace on Earth. Now he can continue *without me*. I accomplished my mission, if I even had one. And if he doesn't want to see me, and according to all we had up to this moment, this is exactly what it seemed, well then, there is no point in continuing any of this. No point at all.

I decided that I had already told him everything I had to say. I had done everything I had to do. Now I can leave his life. I can go and try to learn how to breathe, live, laugh, and rejoice, knowing that, in this lifetime, we will always be apart. After all, from a broader perspective, only this one lifetime physically separates us. I am sure I can manage. At least, I must try. Staying any longer didn't make any sense whatsoever to me. So, I wrote to him.

> *You know, my King. Probably the time has come to say goodbye. I'm tired, my gentle one! Your Lala is tired. I simply do not have any desire or strength to continue all this. I cannot do it any longer, and I don't want to. The rules of this game have always been yours and yours only. You know what I think? I think I have already said, or rather, written everything that I had to say and write to you. Now I want to finish this last chapter of this book, close it, and put it on the shelf. I will look at it, remember you and our story. I will keep it in the very depths of my heart. But I will never re-read it. It's too painful. At first, I didn't want anything from you. I just wanted you to remember me, to believe me. Later on, I began to dream of meeting you and looking into your eyes. But it will never happen, am I right? You will never do that! So please, just let me walk out of your life. Just let me go. Let me go with all your heart and soul. Because I'm letting you go. I love you. I thank you, and I bless you. Goodbye.*

Sharp, stabbing pain pierced my heart when his eyes read those lines. Let me go? Oh, no! In the world of a *smog*, he lived in, I was his *oxygen*. Who lets the oxygen go? How do you breathe afterward? My Great and Mighty Twin was not used to having anything taken away, especially something he *had zero intention of losing.*

But I was determined to do as I decided, to part and move on. The novel *Our Love, the Color of Indigo* was now complete.

A week had passed. As before, all the old tricks that I jokingly called "Come back, and I'll be anything you want" were in full swing: Sad videos, sad photos of his gorgeous, sad eyes. He enveloped the world in Indigo and sent the most beautiful songs to me. But I was firm as a rock. I kept my silence, not even considering coming back to talk to him, although I read and watched everything he sent me. I should not have, I know! But I couldn't help it! Each time I fell asleep, I saw us standing on the shore of some Cosmic Ocean, embracing tightly and unable to let each other go from the circle of our embrace. He was my soul. He was my love. How could I forget about him even for a moment? How could I leave him? I was aware that this would never end. *We are One for eternity.* But in this three-dimensional reality, I decided to put an end to it.

Again, I was wrong. Two weeks later, Farhan sent me a Private Direct Message *for the first time.* These particular words would lead me to my *Great Fall from Heaven.*

This time it was not a quote from one of the great minds, not a song or poem. These were the most ordinary human words, words from a man to a woman, addressed to me. He wrote:

"You know, I have one cherished dream! My dream is to meet you! Lala! You are my Magic. My fairy tale. You make my life so beautiful. If only I could see you."

I looked at his words, addressed to me and could not even move or breathe. It seemed that if I so much as blinked, everything would disappear and those words would be gone. But nothing disappeared. Reality slowly comes back to me and together with it, my wings, faith, and eternal Love. My sense of humor, spiced with natural sarcasm, returned as well.

"But this is completely impossible, my Love!" I sarcastically answered him. "There is no way you can meet me or see me! After all, I'm a

285

megastar! I live in a tall ivory tower, surrounded by a high stone fence!
You can't get close to me! And if I even get beyond the oak gates of my
tower, studded with iron spikes, immediately twenty bodyguards and a
crowd of a hundred thousand fans surrounds me! So, as you can see, this
is completely impossible! You can neither meet me nor see me!"

I may have been sarcastic, but my heart was singing! Not only my heart! My soul was soaring high in the clouds! I did not walk on Earth! Oh, no! Why? Why should I walk on Earth? I was flying in Nirvana! I slept on the rainbow and sailed among the raindrops over the fields of blooming forget-me-nots! O, love! What do you do with us? What do you do?

Just a few days after these words, one night, he tweeted that he would be in San Francisco the same month, October 2017. I still can't understand how all the following events took place.

I knew the following as a fact and repeated it to him like three thousand times: *"I am not one of your fans; I have never been and never will be! I would never go to the place where you are, just to be in a crowd of many thousands to look at you from afar! No! I would never do that!"*

But as they say, *"Never say never!"*

"You wanted to see me?" I wrote to him. "Well, so you will! San Francisco? October Twentieth? *I will be there!"*

I could not and still cannot understand how I always know the moment when he posts his messages. Be it a message to me personally or something he posts on his official page. I always know about it. Only a couple of minutes had passed since he wrote where he would be, when and why, and I already read it. When he posted that message, it was around four am where I live. After reading it, I searched for all the necessary information about this event. To my surprise, I saw that the ticket cost not five hundred dollars, as I expected, but only eighty!

Only eighty! Here I would like to add an emoji of a bitter, ironic smirk. Probably, I need to tell you a bit more about my life. I am always talking about souls, about creativity, about love, about my closer than a heartbeat but still very far away Eternal Love, my Ram.

At the time (to be honest, not only that period of my life but nearly always), my bank account was as low as the Ganges on a hot summer day before monsoon season.

The company where I work went broke and I got laid off. After a month of being unemployed, a month of fruitless attempts to find any type of job, I became a taxi driver. Yes. Me, the one who is saving the world with a mega movie star, billionaire, and philanthropist. The one talking about the long-lasting battle between Dark and Light, the mission and goals of Twin Flames and each Divine Soul, incarnated now on Earth. The one who managed to remember her past lives and her destiny. This same woman had to cabby daily to feed her family.

If you remember, I went through the harsh nineties in my homeland, a time of unemployment, hunger, and banditry. I was not used to sitting back and waiting for something in my life to change. I was always taking the reins into my own hands. Was I scared? Of course, I was. Big time! But I did not have any other choice. I had to support my two children, my mother, and at that moment, I also had unpaid bills for electricity and water. Since I live in a time and place of pure capitalism, no one would talk to me and ask me why I hadn't paid my bills. They would just come and cut the lines off. That was my reality and the reality of everyone else.

So, I became a taxi driver because no other options were available.

This job deserves a separate book. The stories would make you laugh and cry simultaneously. Maybe I will write it one day. Most of the time, I had to drive some rather inadequate personalities or not entirely sober. Sometimes they fell asleep while driving them to their destination and then I would wait for many hours until they woke up.

Once I drove to another state, nine hours there and nine hours back. I thought I would be able to make several hundred dollars. But to my shock, it turned out that the company I worked for only paid for the first 100 miles of one order and one trip. Gas was on me as well. So, for that 18-hour trip, I made about $90. The client scammed me. She knew the rules and ordered a trip only 80 miles away. But 20 miles from the destination, the girl told me a sad story of her life and begged me to take her home. It was late at night.

I felt terrible even thinking about asking her to get out of the car with two suitcases and figure out what to do next. She asked to change the address of the destination WHILE on the trip, and I did. The system updated the address and I kept driving. I took her home and drove back all night, being tired but proud of myself for making several hundred dollars, or so I thought. I was very wrong. After that, I wanted to quit! But there were no other jobs. This job paid very little, but still, it did pay.

Maybe some of you are curious, why didn't I ask *"the megastar, billionaire, and philanthropist"* for help? Well... You know me quite well already, so you understand, *I never would have even thought of that!* A woman who reaches up the clouds with her wings of love would not disgrace herself with requests like that to her Cosmic Eternal Love. Oh, no. Never! *I was sure my purpose was to awaken him. Love him. Heal him. Give. Inspire. Touch the strings of his heart. Never ask for something.*

When I found out where he would be, October 20th, San Francisco, California, my bank account had exactly enough for two tickets to this event. One hundred and sixty dollars. As if under a spell or I don't even know what, probably a love potion, I bought TWO tickets without stopping for a second to think about what money I'm going to buy plane tickets with, or where I will stay (hotels are not cheap there).

Oh, no! Why would I bother to even think much about such a "trifle"?! Love not only blinds us sometimes, but it also makes us rather unwise, to put it mildly. There is a very old Slavic expression: *"The one who is drunk is absolutely sure, the sea is knee-deep and easy to cross!"* For one in love, it seems to be the same. So, there I was with my two tickets. Immediately, I wrote a message to a girl I had known only for a couple of months. The message consisted of a few words, *"Lena, would you fly to California with me for a couple of days?"*

To my great surprise, the answer came immediately (she also had insomnia for some reason), *"I absolutely will! Just let me ask a couple of days off from work!"* (Little note: She was a tax accountant. It was peak season for her company. The chance of getting even one day off was close to the possibility of finding a snowball in hell. But she got it, no questions asked!).

My next problem was, where can I get the money for round-trip plane tickets? I studied several web pages and realized it would cost me about $350, and I'd just spent the last dollar in my bank account on event tickets. So no, I did not have the money. What would I do now? Suddenly, I remembered about sky miles.

I will not describe in detail the man who was born on the same day as my Twin, but I want to tell you a little bit. More than 15 years ago, I met him on an airplane. He was sitting next to me (another mystical story from my life that is almost impossible to believe). If it wasn't for this man, I cannot even imagine what my life would be like or the lives of my mother and my kids. I would never survive as a single mother on the income I had if it were not for this man's help. Almost since the day I met him on the airplane, he has become the Guardian Angel of my family! No less than that; I am not exaggerating even one bit. Everything I have at the moment in my life (the house in which I live, and a lot more) I have only *thanks to this man*. I name my son Nicholas after him, and he is the Godfather of both of my kids. To make this story even more incredible, this man is an actual *rocket scientist* who has devoted his whole life to Space and worked for 30 years at NASA.

Because of his work, he flew very often. I turned to him. He said he would check the number of sky miles and guess what? There were just exactly enough miles to purchase the tickets for this trip! *It must be a miracle; it must be fate.* I thought!

"But Alla!" he tells me, "

There's only one seat left on this plane! I don't know if your friend will have time to buy a ticket!"

I immediately call Lena. In the next 10 minutes, she somehow manages to buy that last ticket. To our complete surprise, when we got on the plane, our two seats were next to each other!

The day of the flight was just two weeks away. Generously Lena offered to pay for the two days and two nights stay at the hotel. "You can pay me back when you are able," she tells me.

I keep Farhan updated about all my plans via Twitter. When he learns that I am coming to his event, he feels both an overwhelming wave of joy and a blood-chilling fear. The storm of contradicting emotions, thoughts and feelings rises inside him like a tornado. It is a battle of heart and mind, a battle of mortal and immortal and you name it, what else. He wants to see me, and at the same time, he doesn't want to see me at all. He longs to hold me, and he wants to run away from me. I think he perfectly understands that as long as he doesn't look into my eyes, doesn't see me, doesn't feel me, he can keep this mystical situation under his rigid control!

But what happens if he does see me? If he does look into my eyes? Will everything remain the same as it was before, or...? What if our meeting provokes irreversible change? What if our meeting would make him want *something else in life*? Something different? Where would it bring him? Where would it lead him? Would he be able to control it all, as he always did? He didn't have the answers to any of these questions. What should he do now? Let me come and see him, just as I always wanted to, "eyes to eyes"? Or stop me and tell me not to come?

Until that moment, I had never felt such an enormous battle inside him. At first, I was afraid that he would stop me. I wrote to him, telling him I could feel the war raging inside of him. I said that if he told me *not to come*, I wouldn't! I would cancel the flight and the hotel and stay right where I was. I was waiting for him to stop me. But I waited in vain. *He did not.* The desire to see me got the better of all of his fears. I instantly felt the change in him. Eager anticipation replaced his haunting doubts. *She will be there! She will be near! I will finally see her!*

We were separated now by a distance of six hours of flight and a few more days. Neither of us could sleep and could barely eat. Such a fire of emotions was raging in both of us, impossible to transcribe in any human words! Sometimes the fear would leave him and suddenly surge inside of me. I was afraid, scared, terrified. I wanted to cancel it all and stay home.

What if he sees me and instead of delight, he is disappointed? After all, he had seen the most beautiful, most magnificent women in the world!! Women worshiped, praised, and adored for their magnificence, beauty, and talent. How could I possibly compete with any of them? That was simply unthinkable! Thousands of fans of all ages, skin tones and attractiveness levels were madly in love with him. *What the hell am I thinking? Have I got completely mad? Who the hell do I think I am? No! I must go nowhere and stay home!*

But not a single one of them, however luxurious and beautiful she might be, is the other half of his very soul, my heart was telling me. *Go towards your destiny, Lala! Go, and fear nothing! Love is on your side! How many years have you been walking towards this? To this very moment, when you finally see him, when you finally hear his voice, and finally, after all you have gone through, look into his eyes. Years of searching and waiting! Years of hoping and dreaming. This moment is coming at last. Now you want to step back, just run away? Back out of it? Oh, no! 'It's too late, baby now, it's too late' as the song says it. Go towards your destiny, Lala! Go, and fear nothing! Let your soul, Big White Bird, finally find her home and peace in his eyes. Let her...*

My heart, of course, was right. I have gone too far and I have fought too hard to stop right now. I must go. I must! But something deep inside, something else, was trying to warn me. I ignored it. *Love is on my side,* I thought. *Eternal and Immortal Love! My heart was pure.* What bad could happen to me? Oh, you cannot even imagine how wrong I was. *I was about to face my own death while being still alive.*

The day of our flight arrived. We left the house at about three in the morning to board the plane flying to San Francisco at 6 a.m. After six and a half hours of flight, we finally landed. Walking outside the airport, I clearly knew that he had not yet arrived there. I just felt it.

After I had received his direct message that he wanted to see me, to be exact, "*It was his dream,*" I hoped that he would write something else, but he didn't. He was completely silent. A sane woman would have *stopped right there* and *seen it as a clear sign of backing off*. But no woman in love is sane, not to mention one who is a Twin Flame. I am trying to find an excuse for myself, even though I understand they sound rather lame. *But I loved him, I believed him, I had my faith. I did.*

We left the airport and went to the hotel in our rented car. Driving on unfamiliar hilly roads reminded me of being on a roller coaster in one of our Florida Theme parks! The road went either sharply up or sharply down almost all the time. The legendary city of San Francisco appeared before us, not at all how we expected it to be. Since Farhan's event took place in one of the oldest cinemas in the city center, we reserved a hotel near that place.

In my opinion, the following words could describe the city. If you gather all the strangest people you can ever imagine from the whole wide world and put them all in one city that would be San Francisco. It was not at all like our quiet, beautiful and cozy town in Florida, where we lived. Residents of "Frisco" (as San Francisco is often called), please forgive me, but the phrase "The Ball of Satan" constantly came to my mind while being there. Or maybe we just were in the wrong area, pretty much downtown.

It was about two in the afternoon and it was outrageous for me to see the homeless literally on every single corner! They were just *everywhere!* In broad daylight, in front of everyone, they were either smoking weed or injecting drugs straight into their veins! The homeless people here didn't look like they ended up living the harsh life on the streets simply by some terrible misfortune or an accident. Absolutely not! Everything was completely different here. It was their own lifestyle; it was their own choice. A Street. A dirty sleeping bag. A supermarket cart filled with all kinds of junk. All sorts of drugs. It was their lifestyle, just like the rest of the inhabitants of this extraordinarily peculiar city. Everyone in this city seemed to have their own strange lifestyle. It was a weird place.

It seemed everywhere I looked, something shocking was happening. I saw women looked nothing like women. They were dirty, doing drugs in broad daylight, covered with piercings and tattoos, their hair greasy and matted. There were men dressed as women wearing absolutely wild makeup. Bright, tasteless jewelry practically covered them from head to toes.

Never in my entire life have I seen so many people in absolutely unimaginable outfits. There was a man covered with hanging animal tails. A woman who had a cloak made out of plastic bags cut into strips. A man who decorated himself with nuts and bolts. Punks with incredible Mohawks. People's expressions resembled someone lost, unable to comprehend where they were or why.

Even the city itself also looked scary. The houses were perched together, like flocks of birds, sharing sidewalls. The streets were narrow and somewhat difficult to drive through. By the time we arrived at the hotel, both of us were already so confused, tired and terrified that we wanted to immediately fly back home to our small, familiar and safe world. But we managed to pull ourselves together, although we continued looking at everything around us with wide-open, horrified eyes.

Our hotel, as I said, was almost downtown. The receptionist showed us our tiny room with two beds and a tiny window that looked into the wall of the next building. We were so scared by what we saw that we did not dare leave the room. Suddenly, to our pure delight, we heard somebody in the corridor, speaking Russian!

Something familiar and so warm in this crazy, weird place! It turned out to be a nice, sweet woman working at this hotel as one of the managers. In response to our stories about the horrors we had just seen, she only laughed and said that one could get used to pretty much anything with time. Having worked and lived in San Francisco for so long, she didn't notice how unusual the city was. She told us that we could walk around the city with no fear. The homeless, drug addicts and all those we saw as strange and scary were not dangerous or aggressive. But still, it was advisable to take walks during the day and be at the hotel after dark!

She told us Chinatown was nearby and we would surely enjoy it there. After we calmed down a bit, we decided to go out and take a walk. Chinatown turned out to be a charming place. It was like a small piece of China right in the middle of San Francisco. Red lanterns were hanging all around, tons of little Chinese shops with an unbelievable number of big and small, cute things, souvenirs, and whatever one could only imagine. All this, of course, was mixed with an incredible number of little Chinese restaurants. We enjoyed that place; we bought many souvenirs and took photos. Our Chinatown experience helped us breathe a lot more easily.

Suddenly, I stopped dead in my tracks!

293

"What is the matter with you?" Lena asked me.

"*He is here*," I answered her, as if in a trance. "*He is here!*"

At that very moment, I knew his foot had touched the ground; we were in the same city. My cheeks were burning like they always did when he thought of me. It felt as if I brought my face too close to a brightly burning fireplace. Simultaneously, my heart was beating so rapidly; I felt like I'd just run several kilometers without stopping or even warming up. But most of all, I could physically feel my own Soul! *The Big White Bird flapping her wings, finally be free.*

Since the night I saw his eyes and knew who he was, I felt this unbearable torment where my own Soul felt like a big white bird, struggling in her tiny cage. She wanted to break free, escape, and fly, fly, fly! To him, to him, to him! Towards the other half of herself. She wanted to become whole after such a long time apart. To unite and become one, as she was one from the very moment of her creation.

But you can't even imagine what this torment grows into *when you are physically very close to your Twin*. It becomes almost unlivable. You no longer feel human. You feel like Fire; you burn, burn and burn. That is all you sense. I was standing in the middle of Chinatown, clutching both hands firmly to my chest, as if I were afraid that my soul-bird would break loose and fly away. My eyes were closed—my face burning. My heart was beating in my chest, like a butterfly caught in closed palms. We were near each other. So close. Never before have we been so close!

The event Farhan was to take part in would happen the next day at eight o'clock in the evening. He knew my every move almost perfectly. I wrote him everything about where I was and what I was doing. Was he able to contact me? Of course, he was. But naturally, I *convinced* myself that he absolutely could not, as his day was planned minute by minute. He was busy with meetings, interviews, and all the usual things which come with the arrival of a star of such magnitude. That's what I told myself and *made myself believe.*

That night, of course, neither of us could sleep. He sent me a selfie against the night sky.

"If you can't sleep, neither can I," I wrote to him. "Why don't we not sleep somewhere together? I could tell you many interesting stories, my Soul, or sing you the lullaby of Umka, a little white bear cub from a lovely old, animated movie. Since my very childhood, I have loved this song; later, I sang it to my boys. They would fall asleep like magic, listening to it. Perhaps I could get you to sleep as well, my not-sleeping King.

"Then I would quietly sit and watch you sleeping. When we sleep, our Soul is flying freely, wherever she wants to be. During sleep, we are just what we really are. You probably look like a boy in your sleep, with your crazy naughty hair, your fan-like eyelashes, and your insanely beautiful lips with that cupid bow. I think I would definitely enjoy just sitting there and watching you sleep while your eyelashes throw wing-like shadows on your olive cheeks. Or we could silently look up at the stars, trying to understand where we came from into this world and why. Or we could have long, long talks about everything under the stars and beyond, the mystery of life, love, souls."

Little by little, the dawn started to break, and the morning came. That day, Lena and I decided to visit the only place that I remembered for its beauty and grandeur. The Golden Gate Bridge.

We decided to go there since we had plenty of time. Or so we thought. I felt like double espresso was flowing through my veins instead of blood. Despite the fact it was rather cool during our stay there, especially compared to Florida, I felt unbearably hot all the time. And it was me, someone, who freezes even in the tropical climate! My temperature elevated, but I knew from what I studied, read, and experienced myself, that it was normal for the Twin Flames.

I also did not feel any hunger or the need for food. I finally understood the meaning of the expression: *"For those, who are insanely in love, sunlight as food is enough!"*

That was about right! I felt I could pretty much live upon just air and sunlight just being next to him! I also had this strange feeling, as if while

295

walking, I wasn't stepping on the ground, but more likely, I was *hovering right above it.* My face was radiating in such a way that people passing by, were looking at me with amusement, and little children reacted vividly. When I walked by, they at first opened their beautiful eyes wide, as if they saw something right out of a fairy-tale. And just a moment later, their lovely faces would light up with such a bright smile that would quickly melt all the ice in Antarctica. They held out their little hands towards me, as if wanting me to pick them up and they would tell everything in their universal baby language. I could not just pass by any single one of them. I think we understood each other with no barriers at all.

I must have been shining with such light of joy that it was impossible not to be seen by anybody within a mile radius around me. That day, the word "Impossible" seemed to be the most ridiculous and stupid in the dictionary. I thought the Dark Ones must have created this word to control us and keep us from remembering our true nature. I was pretty sure *anything was possible,* anything at all. If the Sun can shine so brightly, why can't we too? So, I did.

My dear friend Lena was observing me and everything happening around me with an enduring expression of complete amazement. That same expression did not leave her beautiful face and bright blue eyes even for a moment. It was the first time in her life dealing with Twin Flames. Being a Seer by nature, she was able to see and understand a lot, but still, the events and how they were evolving amazed and surprised her deeply.

Farhan and I were so close to each other that it seemed if only I turned my head, if only I raised my eyes, I would look into his, drawn into those mesmerizing dark lakes. If only I closed my eyes for a moment, I would hear his low soft voice, calling my name: *"Lala."*

I knew the same things were happening to him as well. It was more or less understandable for me, but it all was way too complicated for him. He needed everything explained logically to be able to comprehend it. *But you will never find earthy logic when it comes to Twin Flames.* It simply does not exist. He felt me and sensed me just as I did with him. We were mirrors of each other, and everything he was going through, I was going through as well. At some point, he simply gave up. He abandoned his attempts to explain and decided just to let himself feel it, live it, and enjoy it.

Being so close for the first time in this life, the telepathy between us intensified; using a phone to communicate seemed almost absurd. Indeed, before we were made to forget, many thousands of years ago, *we could easily communicate with each other telepathically*, regardless of whether we were on the same planet, in the same galaxy, or on different ones. That is how highly developed beings communicate throughout all of the Cosmos.

I remember how I was amused by the question, "Why don't the representatives of extraterrestrial civilizations get in touch with us?"

The world powers spend billions of dollars building systems that can pick up signals from space. But it doesn't even occur to them that the extraterrestrial beings do not call us on the phone or knock on the doors. *They communicate TELEPATHICALLY*, and you only need to be able to *HEAR them*. Sadly, people who can't hear them, have a massive problem with the people who can hear them.

I will *NEVER* stop being deeply astounded by the fact that undeniable and irrefutable evidence of such advanced technologies exists on Earth that we, living today, *cannot even dream about or imagine*. And civilizations, hundreds and thousands of years before our time, *used those technologies!*

We observe the massive, gigantically sized temples of *Baalbek*. We look at the cities, carved into the rocks, like *Petra* and the enormous megaliths of *Puma Punku*, that appear as if cut out of softened butter. We know about thousands of pyramids all over the world. We don't believe in once seemingly unshakable truths, yet we believe what is written in our history textbooks, even though some of it is absolute nonsense. We believe that people built this miraculous city of St. Petersburg at the place of swamps in just several decades! What an absurdity! We look at the cathedral of Saint Isaac, a classical antique temple, covered with the symbols of the Sun, with huge columns soaring up into the sky, created, again by the technology not even known today and we believe that this is nothing, but just a simple church!

Today, with all the iPhones and smartphones, *we have the availability of information at our fingertips*. We are no longer tortured and burned at the stake for knowing something, as during the time of the *"Holy Inquisition."* Yet even now, many people continue to believe in such strange things that are hard even to imagine. How can this be? That is no longer a secret for anyone that there are billions of other galaxies, besides ours, quadrillions of other planets and solar systems. I have a question for you: What religion do you think they follow in the *Andromeda Galaxy?* How about *The Silver Coin Galaxy? Black Eye Galaxy? Whirlpool Galaxy* and many others? *What religion do they have?* Can you answer? The answer is simple. They do not have a religion. We are the only planet in the whole Universe, still ruled by religions, instead of the *True Spark of the Source living inside each one of us!* And I see this as a *tragedy.*

You know, I often hear the phrase, "It might offend the feelings of religious believers." But I am personally much more offended by the fact that from the Great Descendants of the Ancients, who once possessed the greatest knowledge and wisdom, we became a herd of obedient slaves, chained to religions and made to forget who we once were, who we really are! Why do we allow the Dark to deprive us of the right to know our True Great History? Why do we allow the Dark to deprive us of knowing *our true great Origin?* That not only offends me but also causes me unbearable pain!

I am infinitely insulted by the humiliation and belittling of human dignity by religions. Let alone how they treat women in some of them! And this is not surprising! In monotheistic religions, God is a man! The simple truth does not occur to anyone, that to create LIFE, it is necessary to combine feminine and masculine energies!

Religious leaders give people doctrines as the absolute and universal truth. *Yet where, in those religions, have you seen the concepts of Mother Nature and Mother Earth? How about space, Cosmos, Universe? What about that simple fact that you need to treat all living things and the planet you live on with love, respect, kindness, and compassion? Where is the knowledge about non-physical bodies? Ethereal, Astral, Mental, and the others? Those are inseparable parts of each and one of us! Are we not supposed to be aware of such things? Why is the Law of Reincarnation and Karma not presented? Where is the concept of the interconnection of all things? The power of Consciousness? The Higher Self? Where is all that and much more?*

It is not there. *And that insults and hurts me endlessly!* But I believe it! I truly and deeply believe, and I know that *everyone will wake up sooner or later!* And everyone will be aware of the Truth and Infinite Light we all possess for eternity. And when that happens, *no evil will exist on this long-suffering planet. Gaia-Midgard-Earth.*

But I have got distracted from my story here; I am very sorry. It still feels raw; *it still hurts!* Time has passed since these events, yet I'm still trying to delay the moment of my terrible *fall from Heaven.* I want to stay in the clouds just a little bit longer to philosophize, argue and dream. But time has come to tell you what happened next. It is time to go back to San Francisco.

The telepathy between Farhan and me, with our physical closeness, intensified a hundredfold. It seemed to me that *I felt and heard the beating of HIS heart in my own chest!*

"Where are you now?" his voice resonated in every cell of my body.

"I am looking at the Pacific Ocean!" I answered him. "I'm in a small town, not far from the city. It is called Sausalito! It looks like a fishing village; there's a small bay and houses on the hills. Amazingly beautiful and picturesque! I wish you could see it with me!"

"Do you love me?"

"Why are you asking me this same question over and over again, Ram? Isn't it obvious? I'm here, after all, very close to you! I will see you tonight! Of course, I love you! I have loved you for thousands of years and hundreds of lives! I've explained it to you a million times, but you still don't believe it, do you?"

"It's hard to believe, Lala."

"Then do not believe. FEEL! Just FEEL my Love, Ram! Why don't you just call me and talk to me?"

"What for? We are talking right now, aren't we? I feel a smile on his face. *I have not slept at all, Lala! Even though I tried very hard to fall asleep, at least for a little bit, but I could not! I could not get you out of my head; I could not stop thinking about you! You are so close! I was thinking: Right now, I could look into her eyes, hold her close, caress her face and hear her voice!"*

"So, what is stopping you? What is stopping you, Ram?"

"I don't know, Lala. That is so hard to believe, to explain. You are Fire; you are Flame. I always knew and saw it in you. You are like a volcano! Like a brightly burning candle, or not even a candle, but a torch! Fire attracts a moth, and it flies to the light, to the warmth! But what happens to the moth when it flies too close to the Flame? He will either die instantly or burn his wings and die soon because he can no longer fly."

"You are just the same Flame as I am, My Soul. Flame cannot burn another Flame. They only make each other shine brighter. We both share the same Fiery Soul and together we are only stronger, Ram! Why are you so madly afraid of me?"

"I wish I knew the answer to this question. But perhaps, I am afraid that my life will never be the same again. It will divide into two parts: "before you" and "after you." Or maybe there is something else. Maybe I am terrified to know something about myself and life that I didn't know before? Something that only you can open up to me. Am I ready to face it? Am I ready? I do not know, Lala. I wish I knew."

"I will still see you tonight, Ram! Although you will be on the stage, in your status as a movie star, and I will be in the hall, one of many thousands. But you will know I am there. You will feel me. And, when the event ends, there is one thing I want you to ask for, give me just a few minutes so that we can look into each other's eyes. I have been dreaming about looking into your eyes every breathing moment of my life, Ram. It's so important to me. I want to find my soul, which I lost when we were separated and came to this Earth as two people. I want to feel whole again, Ram. Just give me that, please. Am I asking you for too much, my Eternal Love?"

"Oh, Lala."

Lena and I walked along the Golden Gate Bridge and the surrounding area for a long time. We admired the greatness of the Pacific Ocean, the hills rolling down in their magnitude and huge, very old trees. Time flew by unnoticed. The evening was already approaching. Finally, we decided it was time for us to return to the hotel. But to our surprise, we could not find the place where we had parked our rental car. It was rather weird, to say the least. We thoroughly searched the parking lot for the tenth time and still failed to find our car. Finally, we decided to look for it in other parking lots. But it was not there either. It was like a scary fairy-tale for naughty little boys and girls. It seemed like a dark, evil wizard had cast a spell, causing us to wander in circles, unable to find our way out of the forest. In fact, the way out was right in front of us, but something blinded our eyes to be able to see it.

We were wandering between cars, pines, and hills, unable to find our car.

"Doesn't it seem to you that we are under the spell of some evil spirit? We are walking and walking in circles, but we cannot find the way out, as if someone or something bewitched us!"

"That is exactly what I was thinking," I reply. "Feels like that is exactly what is happening now. But why?"

I will find out the answer to this question in just a few hours.

In the meantime, we continued our search for another forty minutes!

Finally, I sat down on some steps and told Lena that I needed to stay there for at least a few minutes. I wanted to be alone for a short time, alone with my thoughts about the upcoming meeting with the one I had been looking for my whole life. I turned my face to the sun and closed my eyes. A few minutes later, Lena's voice brought me back to reality.

"Alla! Look! Here it is! It is where we parked! There is our car! We have been here so many times already! But each time, we simply passed it by! How the hell is this even possible? No! I swear! Someone was bewitching us! Let's go quickly, or we'll be late!"

But the traffic that day in the city was just insane. The cars stood bumper to bumper, without moving at all or moving extremely slowly. By the time we arrived at the hotel, it was already seven o'clock. And the start of the event was supposed to begin at eight o'clock. But we still had to get there!

We changed quickly and called a taxi, deciding we would get there faster that way. Wrong again. At 7:40, we were still in the car on our way to the venue. I wrote all my movements to him on Twitter.

Sorry, my Love! I am running late! We are still driving, and the traffic is crazy everywhere. I've probably lost my mind, my Love, but still, I will ask you something: could you please delay the beginning until I arrive?

Just a few minutes after sending this message, with my inner sight, I see him say to a woman, "Delay the beginning, please. People will not have time to get inside before eight!"

It made me smile.

Finally, we arrived at the theater, and what we saw simply brought us into a state of pure shock. Several thousand people had surrounded the theater, forming a tight circle. As I said before, Farhan was not just a Hollywood Star. Paying tribute to India, the land where his beloved mother was born, Farhan began working with Bollywood many years ago. He loved this land and these people with all his heart, and for many years he lived in two countries. He was a star with people who loved Hollywood movies and those who adored Bollywood movies.

He also took part in TV and movie projects in the Arab countries. He worked a lot in Turkey and the Emirates, Saudi Arabia and Kuwait.

He was an international phenomenon, and I have repeatedly observed huge crowds of people gathered wherever he appeared. But personally, as they say, I had never seen that with my own eyes. Now I had such an opportunity to personally witness the fame and the glory of the greatest of them all, Farhan Ali, my Ram.

As I already said, before the entrance to the theater, the crowd was enormous. There were people of various nations, languages and skin colors. Those who had tickets in their hands formed a huge line to get inside. And those who did not, were begging the lucky ones to sell them the coveted tickets at any price. (I still have that ticket!)

"Holy Mother of Gods! Holy Heavens and all of the Saints!" Lena yelled in my ear as the crowd buzzed so loudly it was impossible to hear ordinary speech! "What, in the name of Earth, is happening here? Has the world just ended? Will we even be able to get inside by midnight?"

That was an excellent question! In this congestion, it was hard for me even to imagine what time we would get inside to meet the Star of all Stars! So, I write to him.

My Soul! How stupid of me was it to tell you that I would never join a huge crowd so that I could look at you from afar! But look at me! Here I am, and that is exactly what I am doing! I'm still outside, Ram! I am standing in a huge line, and I do not know how much longer this will last and what time we will find a seat inside. No idea! But as soon as I am seated, I will write to you immediately! Can you make it possible that nothing starts until I enter the concert hall? Until I am there? Perhaps my love for you and our closeness right now has made me completely lose my mind to ask for such a thing, but can you please do that?

Exactly five minutes after I sent that message, the crowd murmured, "They put off the beginning until everyone is inside!"

Hearing this, Lena raised her eyebrow, just like Scarlett O'Hara, and shouted in my ear, "Does he always do whatever you ask of him?"

In response, I laughed like a child, accidentally forgotten at a candy factory! I was laughing, but my *Fate had her own laugh.* She decided to let me feel on top of the world before throwing me with all her cruelty and merciless force onto the ground. But more on that later.

We continued to move forward slowly. The magic called Farhan Ali, my Twin Flame seemed to possess people. I had the impression they were waiting to meet some Deity, not an actor, perhaps Zeus the Thunderer himself! The Supreme Sovereign of Olympus, who was about to appear before the eyes of mere mortals on a white cloud, surrounded by a host of beautiful gods and goddesses.

My friend was looking around, occasionally tossing phrases like, "Holy, Sacred Lands! Alla! This is insane! This is above and beyond my understanding! It's impossible! The magnetism of this man, his power over people, is out of this world! Look at this massive crowd! Alla, if they knew

303

who you were to him, who both of you are for each other, I am scared to even think about it! You probably would be torn into tiny pieces, with not even dust left! Just look at all this! Unbelievable! Simply unbelievable!"

And the crowd continued buzzing and slowly moved forward. There were Americans, Arabs, Indians, Filipinos, Europeans—people who had arrived from different cities and even other states. Everyone seemed a little crazy in anticipation of the moment when they would see their idol—their idol and my Ram.

People were quoting dialog from his films, singing songs, chanting his name. Finally, along with the last part of the crowd, I was inside the hall. Our seats were quite far away from the stage.

The program consisted of Farhan's interview with some big-shot journalists from several countries, after that, the demonstration of one of his films, after the film, they were to hold an open press conference. At this conference, people from the audience could ask him any questions and he would answer them. To communicate directly with their hero was a rare opportunity for his loyal fans. So, people were anticipating the event with a lot of excitement.

As soon as we finally got to our seats, I wrote,

I'm here, my Love!

Just a couple of minutes after this message, the lights went off! Silence reigned for only a second, and then the hall exploded with wild shouts and screams.

"Far-han! Far-han! Far-han!" the crowd screamed!

Lena was squeezing my hand tightly. I saw a mixture of delight, confusion, disbelief, and admiration on her face.

The screen lit up with a magic light. His face appeared on it. It was a compilation of highlights from many of his movies, in different languages, shot throughout the years, in many different cities and countries. His face, so dear and close to me, would appear on the screen expressing many emotions: unspeakable grief with tears silently falling from his hypnotic eyes, then

304

suddenly his face would become ruthless and cruel, then soft, playful and boyish, and then it changed and became so passionate and sensual, as if we were looking into the face of Sin himself, taking the form of a man.

The women in the audience gasped at once, as soon as on the screen appeared the moments where he touched gorgeous women in different love scenes from various films. And I do not doubt that each one of his partners was absolutely sure that *he looks ONLY at her this way! He touches ONLY her this* way! He was the God of impersonation. It seemed like this man could make even Satan believe anything! He dedicated all of himself entirely and unreservedly to each of his roles! He gave every cell, every drop of blood, every particle of his very existence to his roles. His acting was not only realistic and talented, but he was playing each one of them as *if it was the last role of his life! As if each breathing moment was the last one!* Oh, what a genius he is! I believe the world had never seen such a talent and never will!

He is Pure Magic! Pure, concentrated, undiluted Magic! The King of Wizards from my story!

The air in the hall was pretty cool, but I was so hot that I took off everything I possibly could without looking weird! I pressed a bottle of icy cold water to my cheeks; *my face was on fire.* I was seriously dreaming of plunging into an ice-hole somewhere in Siberia if that were only possible! Flame. I felt as if I suddenly transformed into nothing else but *Pure Flame.* Well, that is what I was! That is what I am.

The screen went dark. Intense silence reigned for a split of a second before the light was on again. A woman walked up to the stage and began talking about something, but no one wanted to listen to her. I felt sorry for a woman. It was her duty, after all. She just had to do her job and express gratitude to those who arranged the whole event. But the poor woman simply was not allowed to speak. The crowd wanted to see their God, and in the end, the woman couldn't help but simply surrender.

"Well then! My dear friends!" she finally said, drowning in the roar of the crowd, "since you would not allow me to finish my speech, you give me no other choice but to invite to this stage one of the most outstanding and amazing people I was lucky to meet and work with. Ladies and Gentlemen! *The One. The Only! Farhan Ali!*"

The side curtain was drawn open, and Farhan came onstage wearing classic black trousers, a snow-white shirt and a black waistcoat. (Should I mention it was one of my favorite outfits of his, and he, of course, was well aware of that?)

He walked onto the simple stage. There are no elaborate decorations or special effects—just a table and two chairs. One spotlight. One man. He walked out...

The audience simply RIPPED the silence apart! People roared, screamed, yelled with delight and adoration! It was just pure madness! How could just one man be a reason for all this? But he was. Never in my entire life, neither before nor after, have I been a witness to anything like that! And I don't think I will ever be.

The first second, I saw him, the roar of the spectators disappeared. *Everything disappeared! Completely. In an instant!* I felt as if I entered another dimension. As if on the screen of this cinema, I saw scenes from our past lives, one after another. Like a kaleidoscope. I already knew one of them: that life where I was his Lala, and he was my Ram!

"*Promise that you will find me! Lala! In another life, you will find me! Promise me!* "

"*I promise!*"

Suddenly, pieces of other lives began to appear in front of my eyes! Ones I had never seen before.

I saw myself and him in different situations, in other times, lands, places, and lives. Our appearance, surroundings and clothes changed, but only one thing always remained the same! *His Eyes and my Eyes! They always stayed the same!* Lives were flashing before me, like scenes from a movie! Not one movie, but many, very many; each movie, one of our lives. How many there were? *How many?*

I saw myself in some simple but rather spacious medieval stone house. Farhan was standing in front of me. He was tall, slender, and well-built; his beautiful face was pale with utter and unspeakable grief!

"They will come after me very soon, Peter!" I told him. "I can almost feel the cold of their ruthless, cruel hearts! You *MUST* swear to me now! Swear to me that you will renounce me! There is no way you can help me, Peter! There is no way! You must understand! You can't save me! You will only destroy yourself and our children! They will condemn me and burn me as a Witch at the stake! And you will be forced to look at that bonfire in which they will be killing me! But you must be strong and make them believe you are one of them! Make them believe you were my victim! I put a spell on you. I bewitched you! You did not know I was a witch! You must do it so that you can save yourself and our children! You hear me!? Don't you dare become weak! Peter! You must stay alive! You must stay with our children and try to get them out of this cursed land! Swear to me. You will do as I say! Peter! Swear to me!"

The next instant, there was a knock on the door.

"It's them! The servants of Satan himself! The Holy Inquisition! Open the door, Peter, and dare not argue or fight with them!! Remember what I told you! Renounce me! Save yourself and our children! We will see each other again more than once! *There will be other lives, my Love!* Remember, I told you *death is not the end! It is never the end!*"

I look deep into his beautiful eyes. My heart goes numb with unbearable pain, just like every time I need to leave him on Earth alone. I look at him, and with just my eyes, I tell him, *"I love you!"* He hears me!

The next moment I see myself in a cart similar to a cage. Keepers of the Destinies! Is this really my fate repeating itself over and over again? Cages for the body and the Soul, early deaths, separation from my loved one. In that dirty cage, they take me to the place of my execution.

"Burn the Witch! Burn the Witch! Burn her!" Their cries echo from here and there. I look at the crazy crowd around me. In the eyes of some, I see madness and joy! But the others, the rest, are driven by a blind, suffocating panic and fear of torture and a bonfire.

Oh! What a terrible time it was! Oh, what horror! For hundreds of years, people have been dying all over the Earth the most torturous and horrifying death imaginable, *being burned alive at the stake!* Men, women, even children. Hundreds. Thousands. *Tens of thousands!* Burning alive at the stake by Servants of Satan! Those using religion as the cover-up for their inhumane, merciless, ghastly deeds! And while doing that, they called it a religion of Light and Mercy, Truth and Forgiveness! In the name of this religion, they tortured and burned anyone possessing a spark of Light or Truth! Oh! What horrible dark times, which lasted hundreds of years!

They committed their terrible, bloody atrocities in the name of Jesus! In the name of the One, they *condemned to a horrible, unjust death for the Truth He had given!* The One who came to teach them about the *real Light and Wisdom!* But Darkness does not want the Light since the presence of Light destroys Darkness. It was not enough for them to only kill him. They also almost entirely destroyed the *real Truth about Him, about His life,* about *who He truly was, where He came from, who sent Him, and why.* His short and bright life was twisted and entwined with lies and half-truths. They did the same to a woman called *Golden Maria or Maria Magdalena. She was brilliant as a Star and pure as a dewdrop.* She was *His Divine and Sacred Love.* But her name was slandered; they proclaimed her to be something she had never been. How sad! How tragic! And later, to be sure the Truth would never come out, they erased from the face of Earth anyone who knew this very Truth! *Templars and Cathars,* and those supporting them, were blamed for "heresy," slandered, found guilty, and either brutally killed or burnt to death. They received *No Mercy!*

It was back then, when the monk, by the name of Arnaud Amairic, said his famous words to Crusaders, *"Kill them all and let God sort them out!"* And they were killing! Killing, torturing, and burning hundreds of thousands, including women and children! What mercy do you expect from Darkness? It worships the lie and hates the Truth. So, it destroys anyone who carries it inside and tries to share it with the World and with people.

And now it was my turn to die. I was not afraid of fire. Thanks to the Power of Light, I knew how to stop my own heart and leave before the fire began to devour my physical body, like the Venetian "witch," whose name was *Isadora.* Like many others, she and her ten-year-old daughter Anna were found guilty and burned at the stake, by the "great" Inquisitor and the fighter for "the faith" Giovanni Pietro Caraffa. Pope Paul *IV*. But this man was far from being the worst. Sadly known, *Tomas de Torquemada, another Grand Catholic Inquisitor,* was alone guilty of brutally torturing and executing over *2000 people!* He especially *loved* to torture women. Such times those were. They lasted *hundreds of years!*

The true meaning of the word "Witch" was twisted and distorted. Originally, it meant *"A Wise Mother."*

Unfortunately, not many of those, who were called witches and brutally killed, possessed the ability to "leave the body" before its physical death. But I knew how to do that. I knew. In my death of that life, I could enjoy one last thing! Those beasts, serving the Darkness and proclaiming lies as Truth, would hear neither my screams nor begging for mercy! As *mercy* was not a word known to them! Oh! How much I hated them!

My Peter is in the front row of the crowd who came to admire someone else's terrible death! He kept the word he gave me. If he as much as looked away, they would have killed him too! He looks at me, with no muscle moving on his beautiful, masculine face. His eyes were the last thing I saw in that life!

We'll meet each other soon! I love you! I tell him in my mind before my heart stops.

And then the next moment, *I see a warrior standing in front of me!* He is incredibly tall. People that tall do not inhabit our Earth anymore! It was many thousands of years ago! He has long blond hair that falls below his powerful, broad shoulders! But the eyes! *His eyes are still the same!*

"Do you want me to fight for those who, thousands of years later, will put us in oblivion, Darina? Can't you see? Can't you understand? Those we had saved! Those we had brought here on Vimanas to Gaia Earth when their own Earths were destroyed! They will repay us with dark ingratitude! Where is Earth Troara now? Where is Earth Deya? They don't exist anymore!!! We are the ones who saved them and brought them here, so they could build a new life, a new home! But I will tell you what happens next! The very people we gave our knowledge to and the wisdom of our Great Ancestors for hundreds and hundreds of years, those we taught to write and understand the runes.

309

Those we shared our knowledge about the laws of the Universe and Cosmos, and the ones we taught to build, create, and make things! Those we have taught to live by the law of consciousness, serving the Source and Light!! *They will betray us, Darina! They will betray us!*

"Do you think they will repay us with gratitude? No, my Soul! It won't happen! Do you hear me? It won't happen!!! They will repay us with the worst, *with OBLIVION*. All these nations, Arameans, Dravids, and others, will attribute all that *WE taught them to THEMSELVES*—destroying everything that points to us as the *origin* of their knowledge! They will erase any memory of us! They will destroy anyone possessing any knowledge of who we were and where we came from, as well! Do not look at me like that, my eternal Love! *I have SEEN it!* The priests have shown it to me! Thousands of years will erase even *MEMORY* of who were were—our names and the names of our peoples will be destroyed forever! And you want me to fight for them? Antlan will hold out this fight! We will stand!"

"No! No, it won't!" I shouted at him, deep despair resounding in my voice. I know that I can't convince him of anything. I know he will die, and I will die with him. But I don't want to give up. I can't.

"You know that I can see the future! My Soul, my Love!" I plead with him, "Please listen to me! Antlan will not stand! If the war starts, Antlan will fall! The axis of Gaia-Earth will change! What was the land, will become water! The everlasting winter will come to the lands where the Sun was shining before! People not taken away in Vimanas, or brought through the Star Gates, will die. Almost all of them!!! Only a few will survive! The time of darkness will come! What you are planning to do is Unrighteous! My *Soul! It is wrong!* You go against the *Holy TRUTH!* Against the Source, against the Light! You follow the Falsehood of the *Dark Oracles!* Those who serve the Dark poisoned your mind and your Soul! How can you not see it? *Their words are sweet and clever.* They make the voice of your true Essence fall into a deep sleep, similar to death! You can't even hear me! Me—your very Soul!

"*They only want Power! There is neither Justice nor Light in them.* Their strength lies in cunning, sweet talk, deception, and the ability to wait as long as it takes to poison minds and hearts. How many hundreds of years have they been poisoning the minds of the high priests?

"And look, what happened! *We are rising to war against OUR OWN KIND! Against our own fathers and brothers! How can this be righteous!?* How? Do not do this! Even if your words are true! Even if the world forgets us for thousands of years and our names disappear for centuries, I know the time comes, *and our Descendants WILL REMEMBER who they are!* Dawn comes after the night, my Love! *Do not go against your Soul! There is no truth in a lie and cannot be! There is no Light in Darkness and cannot be!* You will die! And Antlan will perish with you and our brothers and sisters! I know, they poisoned your father and he became dark. You can't help him or reason with him, but please do not join with him! Do not go against the Light! Against the Truth! Do not! *The Dark wants Power! Only Power! Nothing else!* Please! They are the fathers of the lie, and there is no truth or Light in them! In the name of our eternal Love, I beg you! Stop! Darkness is enveloping your mind and Soul! *Stop before it's too late!*"

On my knees, I am begging him, my beloved, knowing that I will fail.

He grimly but firmly looks at me and then kneels before me and takes my face, covered in tears, in his palms. In his eyes, I read sadness and iron determination. "*Darina! Remember just one thing! On this Earth or others, in the eternity and infinity of the Cosmos, I will find you again. And I will recognize you! I will always recognize you by your eyes! We have the same eyes, don't we? And whatever happens… Remember me! I will remember you as long as I exist!*"

Then I saw my death along with the fall of Antlan, or, as people called it centuries later, *Atlantis*. It was horrifying. The oceans were boiling! The Earth was moaning, and the land was breaking into pieces. Rebels fought against their own, destroying the once united nation with nuclear, climatic, tectonic weapons.

Oh, merciless Forces of Darkness! For hundreds of thousands of years ago, your tactics and methods have remained the same. *With the help of shameless lies, deception, and pretense, you turn brothers against brothers, fathers against sons, and watch them fight and kill each other! So many Lands have fallen because of your sweet-voiced lie!*

311

The Great Antlan has fallen as well, becoming the lost city on the bottom of the ocean. I died along with my warrior, my people, and my once beautiful and powerful land.

Before my eyes, our lives continued, changing one into another. I saw us in different times and different places on Earth. Pyramids with smooth, polished walls sparkling in the sun. The land of India with fairytale-like temples of incredible beauty. Whitestone columns soar into the sky, similar to those we see in Rome and Greece. One moment I was wearing simple peasant clothes, laughing, picking ripe apples and putting them in a basket. The next, I was in luxurious ancient Indian garments, embroidered with golden and silver threads, walking along a marble hall under a canopy of columns laced with carvings of unspeakable beauty.

Lives were changing faster and faster, and it was becoming hard for me to remember any specific details. There was one thing I understood for sure. *There were hundreds and hundreds of them.* Maybe thousands. And another thing was clear to me. In each one of them, I loved him. Even if we were enemies, and I had to hate him, I still loved him. He and I didn't have cloudless happiness in most of our lives. Not at all! As I see it now, the last life before this one was, probably, the happiest.

Abruptly I am thrown back to the *present moment.* I opened my eyes and saw myself in the theater, where the one I loved thousands of lives was standing on the stage with a crowd roaring, screaming, loving, adoring and worshiping him.

Younger women whistled, shouted, waved their hands and jumped from their seats at the sight of him. Ladies slightly older were crying. Some young girls were sobbing hysterically, screaming his name and stretching their arms towards him. Older women were crying quietly, wiping away their tears, some with a handkerchief and some with just a palm.

Lena continued squeezing my hand and repeating over and over, "This is simply impossible! Impossible! Unbelievable! Just unbelievable!"

And me... It was as if I were there and at the same time, I was not there at all. I watched the things around me in some kind of fog as if from the side.

From the very moment my eyes saw him, *I felt ALIVE*. For the first time in my long life, I felt truly, deeply, *immensely ALIVE*. I remembered the words of my mother; she said them to me quite often, "You have absolutely *no LIFE in you!* Some people are sparkling! Vibrating! They are full of life! But for you, such things are nonexistent!"

Only now was I finally able to understand the meaning of her words. Probably my dear mother was right.

I really was like *NOT alive* until that moment. At that very moment, *I felt EVERY living cell* of my physical body! *EACH cell was vibrating, breathing, and LIVING.* For the first time in my whole life, I was truly, in every sense of the word, *ALIVE!* And I knew for sure; I had lived for thousands of years and thousands of lives!

A famous American journalist appeared on the scene. He briefly introduced himself to the crowd, shook hands with Farhan and sat on one of two chairs. Farhan took his seat in front of him. The crowd fell silent, preparing to listen to every word of their idol. In the front rows of the hall, just before the stage, people were waiting for their chance to ask Farhan a direct question and get his answer to it. To have this opportunity, some of them had come here almost 24 hours before the actual event. People had waited all night and all day to be the first to get inside and be able to ask him one question. And even if they didn't have the opportunity to ask him anything, at least they would be able to see Him from the closest distance possible.

The journalist asked his first question, and Farhan took his microphone. He began to respond in a rather odd way, to my great surprise, not like his usual speaking manner. He seemed uncomfortable, shy, somewhat lost and as if he suddenly found himself entirely out of place. His voice sounded surprisingly unconfident and broke several times. It seemed that even pronouncing words was not that easy for Farhan Ali, *the greatest orator in the world.* He was sitting half-turned from the audience, and it seemed that he was trying his best not to look into the faces of the people. The journalist kept asking questions, Farhan kept answering, but I felt as if there was someone else in the place of the famous actor who rules the heart of half of the planet!

I have seen dozens of interviews with Farhan and his performances in diverse audiences, from students at prestigious universities to the wealthiest and most influential people in this world. He was ALWAYS *absolutely confident* and at ease, no matter who was in front of him: millionaires or ordinary people.

A brilliant speaker and intellectual man, he easily and with grace could answer any question, speak on any subject, and sparkle with wit and warm-heartedness on any issue. Be it Italian cuisine or cybernetics, cinema, or world politics. He had been doing this for twenty years. So, what was happening now? Because of some mysterious and inexplicable reason, he seemed to be a completely different person. It was as if this handsome and powerful man suddenly turned into a 15-year-old teenager, dragged onto the stage in front of a huge crowd, and forced to answer some strange questions! And nobody had taken the time to explain to him why he had to do that and what he needed to do!

He was staring at the floor. His voice was breaking now and then. He would suddenly lose the thread of conversation or answer out of line or say something irrelevant. When the audience's first moments of madness and euphoria passed, the people naturally noticed. Here and there, people began to whisper

"What is the matter with him?"

"Why is he so shy?"

"Why is he so embarrassed? He doesn't even raise his eyes, like a girl on a first date!"

My friend heard and understood everything perfectly well. She squeezed my hand, and with an angelic-devilish smile on her face, she spoke in my ear.

"What have you done with your poor boy? Huh? Look at him! He can't even raise his eyes. Your greatest in the world movie star—your Twin—is afraid to look into the audience. Your great speaker can't even string a sentence together! It's all because of you! Can you calm him down? Go ahead! How do you communicate here? I don't know, telepathically? Go ahead! Talk to him! Save your boy! See, he is in trouble!"

314

I was not able to even speak, but her advice made sense! I began to try to calm him in my mind. *My soul! Do you hear me? Are you acting like this because of me?*

A hot wave hit me, and I heard him. *Damn! What is wrong with me? What the hell is happening? I am acting like a stupid teenager! God knows what! Why is this place so damn hot?!*

This place has nothing to do with it, my King! It's hot because we're close. Twin FLAME, understand? Flame! We are parts of one Flame! We are both BURNING. That's why it feels so hot. Take it easy. I won't eat you up alive! I promise! And do not be afraid to look into the audience. You will not see me because I am very far from the stage! Calm down! Take a few deep breaths! It is ok, my soul! It's all right! You are my ruler of the world, not some little boy, are you, my love? Come on! Pull yourself together, Ram!

Farhan took a deep breath several times. His voice became smoother and calmer, and he slowly turned and looked at the hall, where thousands of people were watching his every move.

"That's better! That's much better," said Lena. She was clearly enjoying all this. "It is just awesome! This is just really cool! I'm witnessing eternal love here! Unearthly love! Oh! Lucky me! What did you tell him?"

"I told him to calm down and that I am very far away from the stage! He will not see me!"

"Wait a minute! *Is he AFRAID of you?*"

"I, I do not know, Lena! I have no idea."

In about an hour, the interview ended, and they told the people that now they could ask him their questions. People rushed closer to the stage. People in the back attempted to get to the front and break through the crowd who came early. Television cameras and a projector showed the people asking questions on the big screen. The first person asked his question and Farhan answered. As the second person came up to the microphone, suddenly, I felt something cold piercing me like the blade of a sharp, merciless sword. This cold was not of a physical origin.

The feeling was so sudden; I had no time to be prepared for it. It was as if I found myself in some blood-freezing, horrifying, terrible place

315

within one fraction of a second. And in that place, there was no sunlight, no warmth, no sounds of nature, no human voices, nothing. Emptiness, cold, and fear, was seeping through not just my bones but also squeezing my very Soul, my very Essence! There were no EMOTIONS in this place. More precisely, there were no LIGHT emotions. Love, Hope, Faith did not exist in that place! Have you seen the Tarot card, "Three of swords"? It shows three blades piercing through the middle of a heart. That was what I felt in my heart at that very moment. And the blades felt icy cold in my hot, bleeding heart, which just several moments ago was full of joy, hope, and love. Now it was paralyzed with *pain and cold*. It happened so quickly and hurt so badly that I almost screamed. But even if I had, I doubt anyone would have heard me.

I took Lena's warm shawl and wrapped myself in it, trying to warm up even a little bit. At this moment, the second person received his answer and the third was approaching the microphone... When Farhan suddenly rose and said, *"I apologize to all of you! But unfortunately, some unexpected circumstances have occurred, and I must urgently leave you!"*

The hall hummed indignantly! What does it mean, he has to leave? He's leaving several thousand people who have flown from other cities and even states for this event and waited for this moment for many hours? How can this even be?

The indignation of the crowd was quite understandable! Was it even possible? Was this really happening?

It's like you bought a ticket for a two-hour performance. You sit in the theater and enjoy the play of your favorite actors! But suddenly, 40 minutes later, the main character interrupts the performance and says that he urgently needs to leave. How should people react to this, especially if there are several thousand of them? But Farhan reassured them all with the following phrase, *"I beg you! Please do not worry! I will be absent for only a bit! And while I am solving my problems, you can watch one of my movies. By the end of the film, I will be back and continue to answer your questions. And I promise you not only to answer absolutely every single one of them, but I also promise to hug every one of you who wants a hug from me!"*

316

The crowd buzzed approvingly. Farhan bowed again and quickly left the stage, disappearing behind the curtains. *Everything inside of me just froze.* I am not even sure I was even breathing. With all the complete and cruel clarity, *I suddenly realized exactly what had just happened.* But what I understood, my Soul refused to understand. My Soul—the bird with white wings, was again locked in her cage with no way out!

"When he returns, I will go and hug him! If you do not mind, of course!" Lena chirped in my ear like a happy bird in the spring forest. But, when she saw my eyes, she stopped abruptly. The smile disappeared from her beautiful face.

"Alla! What's wrong? What happened? Alla! Are you alright? What is the matter?" She squeezed my hand again. "Your hands are icy cold! Alla! *What's wrong with you?!*"

"*He will not come back, Lena!*" I finally was able to find my voice. "You will not be able to hug him. He is gone. *He will not return!*"

"What do you mean? What do you mean he will not return??? Why?! What are you talking about? Of course, he will! Are you trying to tell me that he has just lied to all this wild crowd and simply took off and left?"

"Yes."

"WHY?"

I just closed my eyes and shook my head. *No.* But for Lena, it wasn't easy to believe such a thing. As a devoted friend, she squeezed my hand once again and said with a smile, "He will return! You will see! And I will go and hug him! Even if you do mind!"

The screen lit up again. Farhan›s dear face and his oh so loved and so-familiar-for-many-thousands-of-years eyes appeared on it. Again... But I could hardly see what was happening on the screen. My mind knew and understood very clearly, WHAT *had just happened and* WHY *that happened.* My Soul was crying *NO!!!* No! No! But that was pointless. In heartbreaking protest, my soul-bird was again smashing her wings against the thick, unbreakable rods of her cage. *But she could not break out! She could not escape! She could not be free! There was no more hope!*

The movie ended, and the crowd waited for the return of their Idol. An hour passed and the darkest night reigned outside; Farhan had not returned. But the audience refused to leave, still hoping for a miracle. Only I knew that there would be no miracle. I had a crazy idea to tell all these people that they would not see him, *and the reason for that was standing right in front of their eyes.* What would they do? Nothing, I guess. They simply would not have believed me.

Finally, one of the organizers decided it was wrong to keep people waiting any longer and told them *Farhan Ali would not return.* The crowd began to murmur angrily. People were distraught.

"But he said he would come back! He even said he would hug everyone!" They told each other, but another twenty minutes later, they finally accepted the simple fact: His Majesty is gone. People started to leave.

"The stars have their own quirks and their own crazy lives," they said.

"Well! We did see him, right? We did! So, it's still rather cool, don't you think?"

"He might have something extremely important to do and simply could not come back! You never know what is happening in his life."

"The most important is that we saw him! I have recorded everything on the phone! Now I'll post it on YouTube!"

"He is just a dream, right?! Ahhhhhhh! What a man! He is unbelievable, isn't he?"

People were headed home or to their hotels. They were quite happy and content, no matter what.

Lena and I went outside to wait for a taxi. Silently, Lena looked into my eyes as if trying to tell me something or ask me something but could not find the courage to speak. We silently drove to the hotel and went up to our room.

Something happened to me that I had never experienced before. *Complete NUMBNESS!* It was as if I were under general anesthesia, but somehow, I could still move and talk. But my feelings simply weren't there anymore. It was like someone *had TURNED them OFF.* Who did it, why, or how? I did not know, and I didn't care. I simply felt nothing!

Nothing at all! Dead! Some power cut off all my feelings and emotions in me.

Now I know why. The numbness arrived so I would be able to bear it all. After all, this was only the first blow of that night. I would have to withstand several of them. I silently sat on my bed without taking off my clothes.

Lena was like a tigress raging around in our tiny hotel room.

"*COWARD! He is just a damn coward!*" She suddenly snapped and threw the pillow against the wall. "He just left! He simply ran, like a terrified rabbit, when he realized that you might be among the ones, asking him those stupid questions! Yes? I'm right?"

"Yes, you are right. But it's not only because of that." I answered. I heard my own voice somewhat remotely. It was surprisingly cold and deadly calm, completely unlike my usual tone. "He also escaped because he was afraid that I could *damage his reputation.*"

"WHAT? Damage his what? How? How could you damage his reputation? What are you even talking about? In what manner could you possibly do that, Alla?" She sat next to me, looking deeply into my eyes.

"It's very simple." My voice sounded hollow and ruthless, like an ice floe breaking against another ice floe. "He thought that I could play some trick. Do something inappropriate. Embarrassing. Maybe even insane! Maybe, right there, amidst all that wild crowd, cameras, and journalists, I would start asking something about him and myself! Maybe I'd start screaming hysterically that he is my eternal love, and I am his, and we are Twin Flames! Maybe I'd start to sob or laugh! Maybe I'd start yelling into that damn microphone the things that only he and I know... Or I'll throw myself to his feet, like some of his female fans do. Who knows what else, right? Who The Hell Knows?"

My voice broke. A lump grew in my throat. But my face remained stone-like and completely unemotional, which seriously scared my dearest Lena. She took my face in her palms, lifted it to her eye level and forced me to look at her. Tears glistened in her eyes.

"Alla! Cry, please, would you? Or, you know what? *Let's cry together!* I will hug you and cry with you, ok?! Just don't frighten me like this! You

319

are not like yourself, Alla! It's terrifying! I feel like I am talking to the dead woman! *You are not alive!* Come on! Cry! It will make you feel better, at least a little, Alla!"

Perhaps, it was her anxious eyes and tears cascading down her face because of MY pain that broke the ice in me. This ice had been saving me from a thousand blades, piercing every particle of my barely beating heart.

Immediately pain consumed me, swallowing me whole! All of me. All I ever was or have ever been. Anguish dissolved me, leaving nothing but itself. I finally spoke, barely able to pronounce the words. I felt my chest as if it had just been forced open with an *iron crowbar!*

"He thought that I was capable of such a thing," I said. Each word was like a nail pounding into my hands. "He thought that I could disgrace him! Compromise him! Harm him! Just imagine what a nightmare it would have been! Those thousands of people in the audience would have seen it. And thanks to telephones and television journalists, in an hour or two, spreading it all over the whole damn world! And the great and infallible, his majesty the King, Farhan Ali, would have to answer uncomfortable questions! Like, who is this crazy woman and what the hell is she talking about?

Oh no! Could Mr. Movie Star allow this?! No, of course not! He would never allow that! He hastily retreated, preventing the slightest possibility."

I started laughing! I continued talking, laughing, not feeling the tears pouring from my eyes! *Damn, be these tears! Damn, be this goddamn movie star whose words I believed, whose eyes I was searching for all my cursed life! Damn, be my life. Damn, be the day I found him! Damn, be the day I wrote him my first word!*

"He," I continued, laughing and crying, ignoring the face of my faithful friend distorted in pain. "He! That damn idiot! He thought that I was CAPABLE *of doing such nonsense!*

"He! *The one who should know and feel me with his very soul and heart!*

"He! *The one who has known me for thousands of lives!*

"He! *The one who read my book, and hundreds of my letters!*

"He! *The one who knows my whole life! My very soul!*

"He DARED to think that I was *capable* of such *nonsense!* He dared to believe that I am capable of making myself an idiot in front of the whole damn world and at the same time bringing disgrace to Him! His damn majesty! The King of the world! The Lord of the mountains, seas, and ruler of the women's hearts!

"*He Who Is One With Me!*

"*He Who…*"

I covered my face with my hands. I could not continue. What was the point? I had to face another issue. I was having a hard time breathing, the challenge increasing with each passing moment, inhaling felt like breathing burning air during a desert sandstorm. It hurt so much that I clenched my fists and bit my lips, trying not to scream. Where my heart was, instead of a shining blue crystal, there was a massive, terrifying black hole. Lena rushed to me and hugged me as tightly as she could. She was crying with me.

"Alla, what if… I mean. Maybe…" her voice sounding hopeful, "Maybe he understood everything? He realized that he had made a mistake that he was wrong about you! That you are not like that! That you are completely different! And maybe tomorrow, He will call you! And you will see each other! And explain everything to each other! And, looking into each other's eyes, you both will know the truth! *If he only saw you once! He would understand everything!* Perhaps…"

"No, Lena. *There is No perhaps!* That is not going to happen! He will not see me! Not now. Not tomorrow. *Not ever!* Don't you get it yet?" Behind the veil of tears, I could barely see anything. I was like a half-dead Niobe, a symbol of grief, a monument to my stupidity and eternal love. There I was, a warrior of Light, a Twin Flame, The Sun and the Moon, standing in the middle of some cheap room in some cheap hotel in San Francisco. A warrior of Light? The Sun and the Moon? Oh, no! I am nothing! Nothing!

"Who am I, after all, if you think about it?" I said, almost whispering. "Who am I? Why should the Great Farhan Ali deign to give me five minutes of his precious time?"

"He is right." I continued, seeing the things around me as if in a cloud of thick gray smog. "He is absolutely right! Who in the world am I? Who, the

321

hell do I think I am? Who? A model? A Miss Galaxy? A Star, like himself? No. I am nobody. Nobody! I am a jobless, powerless, ordinary single mother! Who is he, and who am I? He is absolutely right. He is right."

"Alla ..."

"Forget... Please. I beg you, beautiful soul! Let's just forget it all! Let's sleep."

I lay down, pulling a blanket over myself, making it clear to my beloved friend that I no longer wanted to speak.

She also got in bed and quickly fell asleep. My chest pain transformed from severe to dull. Tears still were flowing from my eyes, soaking into the washed-out cheap hotel pillowcase. I looked at the glare of a streetlamp on the wall.

"LALA! PROMISE ME! YOU WILL FIND ME IN ANOTHER LIFE! PROMISE ME!"

"I PROMISE You! I PROMISE You! I WILL!"

Searching for Answers

I wonder, why haven't people yet found a way to run away from themselves? Why?

Some kind of inner impulse made me pick up the phone. I wanted to see what was happening in his life on this ill-fated day. The day, which began with me smiling at the sun, with me waiting to finally, after all these years, meet him, and ended with vicious, bitter disappointment and pain, from which I had no escape.

Fans had flooded Twitter with videos. I began watching one and just froze! The crowd started gathering near the theater the evening of the previous day. People were ready to wait all night and all day for the chance to see him closely, ask him their questions and get the answer. The most devoted and the luckiest of them all hoped for a selfie with him. What could be a bigger reward for a fan?

322

There was already a huge crowd in the morning, not to mention the evening, just before the event. Farhan arrived at the venue about 30 minutes before the show's beginning.

It's very interesting *HOW* he arrived!

The great Farhan Ali didn't arrive at the events through the building's main entrance. That would be unreasonable and perhaps even dangerous. It is clear why: wherever he appeared, there was always a huge crowd, and not everybody in it was sensible or could control their emotions. But this time was completely different! This time, he decided to change his usual pattern for some reason. Instead of arriving quietly, unnoticed to the back door, he, who hates limousines, drove one of those directly to the main entrance! The one with a wild crowd awaiting the beginning of the show.

I watched as his limousine stopped in front of the main entrance in a state of complete shock. People were completely stunned by such a turn-up. He opened the door, got out of the car without any escort or bodyguards, *and went straight into the crowd.* For a moment, people simply froze with surprise and disbelief, but the next thing, a real doomsday, began. The crowd rushed to him, surrounded him, and it seemed it didn't bother him at all. His eyes were peering intently at the hundreds of faces surrounding him as if he was looking for someone.

"I will be wearing a long black cardigan and a beautiful chiffon scarf, the color of our love—royal blue!" I wrote to him the day before. *"You will easily recognize me!"*

And that is *precisely* what he was doing—searching for me in the crowd, but I was not there! I was not there and could not be, because *PRECISELY* at that moment Lena and I were unsuccessfully trying to find our car that had suddenly "vanished" from the parking lot!

"Doesn't it seem to you as if we are under the spell of some forest spirit? We are walking and walking in circles, but we cannot find the way out, as if something bewitched us! It feels like some Force is confusing us on purpose, so we can't somehow find our car and can't get out of here!" Lena asked me then, giving voice to my own thoughts. *Now I could see WHY!*

He *wanted* to see me after all! *But not face to face.* He wanted to see me in the *CROWD!* This way, if anything happened (like if I ran to him, throwing my arms around him, did something outrageous, or worse, something "crazy"), he could easily explain to the media that I was simply some poor crazy fan of his. Not a big deal! If someone asked him whether or not he knew me, he would simply say "No." There have been hundreds of women of all kinds who threw themselves on his neck and under his feet, who fainted and shouted God knows what at the sight of him. So, if I did anything like that, it would not surprise anyone! He would be completely safe! *He thought I WAS CAPABLE of such nonsense!* How sad...

Yes. It was clear and obvious now. Meeting me personally, face to face, was never Farhan's plan. Is that so? Yes, it is! But it would have been wonderful and extremely kind, if his majesty's greatness had been so thoughtful and generous *to inform me about it!* But who am I, after all, for his excellence to notify me about anything? Right? Yes, he wanted to see me! But not the way I thought, dreamed, hoped, or wanted. *It was his game again,* and *the rules of this game were his and his only!* Who am I to change them? A Twin Flame? The other half? Oh, please! Fairy tales! None of this real! None of this even exists! Do I exist? I was not so sure of that anymore.

He slowly moved through the crowd! People seemed to lose their minds from this unexpected generosity and the close proximity of their hero. His dark eyes continued to look intently into the faces of the people around him. People were shouting, whistling, women were crying and stretching their hands towards him. But his eyes were looking for me! I was certain of it! He was sure that I would be there! But I was not and could not be. I *simply wasn't ALLOWED* to be there that very moment! Who did not allow that? I found that out many months later. One woman who, like me, was a twin flame, would tell me, *"The Dark Ones would never let you near him! And they will keep convincing him in all possible ways so that he never comes near you!* Because your physical contact would mean a *Connection,* and a *Connection would mean the end of their power over him!"*

Naturally, every pair of Twins is unique, and for each couple, things might develop and progress differently. Sometimes Twins collide physically but then part just as quickly to go through their individual transformations in separation. Later they can reconnect, ready to be together and bring the Light of their Love into the world.

But our case was not like that. *Our physical contact would have connected us and changed everything in our lives and the lives of many other people! It would also mean the Dark Ones would lose control, not only over him and me but with his fame and influence, over millions of other souls.* The Dark could not let it happen! And as in fairy tales, the forest creature is tricking a lone traveler among the trees, not allowing him to find the way out, the same way they were tricking and confusing me, *not letting me come near him. Not letting our eyes meet and two parts of our Soul unite and become one again.*

He was looking for me in the crowd, but I was not there. And *OUTSIDE* of the crowd, he didn't have the courage to see me!

I put my phone aside and stared at the ceiling. What a weird day and what a crazy strange night! The emotions, feelings, and pain experienced that day would probably be enough for several years, or maybe even several lives. *What should I get from it? What lesson should I learn? What was it all for? What was it all about? Why? What is the point of all this? What is the sense?*

Alas, I was too tired, too exhausted, and drained to even think about it. My energy was on the ground. It seemed that I barely had the strength to inhale and exhale, and my heart hardly had enough strength to keep on beating.

Again, I closed my eyes, feeling the hot salty water streaming from my eyes, making its way down my cheeks and disappearing in the cheap hotel pillow.

Who have I been for you in this life, Farhan? What have I been? I asked him with my very Soul. *How can you be so cruel, so heartless? How can you cause me such terrible pain, having known me for thousands of years? Or maybe there is a reason? Maybe I've wronged you somehow? Maybe I am paying this debt to you for other lives? Could I have been as insanely cruel to you as you are to me now? Could it be possible? Maybe! In hundreds of earthly lives, anything could have happened! After all, there is always a reason for all things! Everything always has roots in the past.*

But then why don't I remember anything? How come all that I remember is that I've always loved you? It has always been only you in all my lifetimes. At least I do not remember anyone else. If we are one whole and share one Soul, how can you hurt me so much? Can't you feel that my heart is barely beating? Why are you doing this? Why? How can you justify yourself? Or am I to be blamed for it all? Maybe. But people must not hurt each other like this, burn, tear apart and destroy each other this way! They must not! Must not! Why do they? Why do we? Why do you? Why?

I stared into the darkness of the night, not seeing anything. I closed my eyes once more and got a burning sensation as if covered in hot sand.

Who have I been for you in this life, Farhan? Who was I for you? Who am I? I was asking him again and again, trying to find the answer.

The answer rang in my head as only four words.

You are a dream!

A dream? I answered. Meaning, *I am not real? I do not actually exist?* That is why you are hurting me so? *Because you can't hurt a dream?*

The silence was my answer.

Why are you hurting me so? Why are you burning me in this hellfire? A thousand blades have been piercing me! What for? Why? Why?

Silence...

I stared at the gleams and sparkles of a streetlamp projected on the ceiling, asking myself the same questions, to which there were no answers.

Chapter 41

Susan

That night was far from ending for me. It was around three in the morning when my phone's screen lit up. It was a text message. The number was restricted.

Alla, this is Susan M. You know who I am. Before I say anything else, I am sure you clearly understand, this message must stay strictly and completely confidential. If you are not sleeping, and for some reason, I'm sure that you are not, I need to talk to you. In half an hour, a car will be waiting for you at the hotel entrance. Let me know if you can meet me. It is important! I have some things I need to tell you. I am sure that my information is very important to you. I will tell you the rest when we meet.

I reread the message several times.

What in the world is going on? Susan M.? Susan Malik? His legendary omnipotent, omnipresent, almighty assistant? The "iron lady" of industry, his right hand? What in the world does she want from me? And what in the name of Earth can she tell me? And why the heck does she need me at three in the morning? But she wants to tell me something? All right. Whatever it is, I will listen.

I quietly got out of bed. I looked at Lena. She was asleep. I didn't even have to get dressed, as I was still wearing my outdoor clothes. I looked in the mirror. In the moonlight, I saw a pale face and eyes which looked as if no life remained in them at all. I was a candle with no fire. Cold and dead candle. What am I doing in this crazy, strange city? Or more precisely, what am I doing in this crazy, strange life? Whatever the almighty Susan wants to tell me, can she tell me anything that I don't know yet? I doubt that.

Oh! How wrong I was!

I quietly walked out of the room, trying to make as little noise as possible, silently closing the door behind me.

I took the elevator down. Just in front of the hotel entrance, I saw a black car. I don't remember the model. Actually, at that moment, I did not give a damn about it. I was so exhausted, shattered, and crushed that reality no longer existed. It was as if I was watching myself from the side, *a blown-out candle.*

I went outside. The back car door opened, and I saw a woman I recognized immediately. I often saw her photographs near Farhan since she accompanied him almost everywhere. I walked up to the car. The woman gestured to get inside, moving further back and freeing up space for me. I sat next to her and closed the door. The driver started the car. We started moving slowly along the night streets of San Francisco. I turned to Susan and looked into her eyes.

"Let's start our conversation after we arrive," she said.

I just silently nodded.

I noticed that Susan could hardly take her eyes off of me. It felt as if she was trying to examine my face thoroughly. Apart from the surprise in her eyes, there was also bewilderment and even shock. However, she remained silent. Fifteen minutes later, the car stopped in front of a giant skyscraper.

"It's here," said Susan. "Patrick will be waiting for you. When we finish, he will take you back."

I must admit I was so naive and stupid that I thought she was taking me *to him* for a moment. Deep inside, my hopes suddenly resurrected again, my heart started beating violently, and I involuntarily gasped and put my hand to my chest. Susan turned and looked at me. It was not for nothing that she was the powerful right hand of the triple powerful Farhan Ali. She understood everything.

"No," she said. "I am not taking you to him."

To my surprise, I heard notes of sincere compassion in her voice.

I looked into her dark, beautiful, intelligent eyes, penetrating me to the very core. I felt like I wanted to either fall through the ground or turn around and run away, like an upset little girl. But my pride did not allow me to do that. To my surprise, I still had some left. This same pride did not let me lie to her and say that it was not what I was thinking. No, my pride did not let me neither run nor lie.

In reply, I just smiled bitterly and slightly shook my head. We walked to the elevators. Silently went into one of them, and Susan clicked on the letter "P."

A penthouse, I thought indifferently. *Well, of course. Where else should the rich and powerful stay?*

While the elevator slowly crawled upwards, Susan kept her eyes fixed on me. Finally, she said, "Even if there were a crumb of doubt left in me about all this Twin Flame thing, it would have melted now like the snow in the sun. I am standing in front of you, and still, I can't believe what my eyes see. If there were such a mirror in which a man would see his female reflection, then *Farhan, looking at his own reflection, would see you!*

Her words struck me. I looked her straight in the eyes, trying to understand what she had in mind and what she wanted to talk about.

"Oh!" She said with a laugh. "How well I know that look from under the brows! Merciful God! *How alike you two are!* Impossible! Just impossible!"

The elevator stopped. We went out and silently walked to the door; Susan opened it and invited me in. The room was truly unbelievable in size, luxurious furniture and a beautiful interior. Silk curtains and cushions on sofas. Vases with fresh flowers. Drinks and fruit trays. All this seemed to imprint in my memory without causing any emotion.

I do not know why luxury and wealth have caused me neither special admiration nor much enthusiasm. Somehow, I have always looked at people and considered only their human values. *Kindness, compassion, empathy* have always *touched me deeply.* Millions in their bank accounts or the size of their house, a car for half a million dollars, or the cost of their villa and yacht have never mattered to me and meant *absolutely nothing.* If I found a person unpleasant, he remained such, even if he ate, drank and slept on gold. But if I enjoyed being around that person, I didn't care if he was a homeless man or an Arabic sheik.

Susan pointed to one of the beautiful soft sofas.

"I'll be back in a minute," she said.

I sat on the sofa, still feeling as if everything happening to me was some kind of weird dream, or if all of it was happening to someone else and I was just watching. Of course, I suspected that most possibly, what she was going to tell me was unlikely to be something sweet and pleasant. But I tried not to let myself out of the I-don't-give-a-damn-anymore mindset.

Susan returned, holding a small black folder in her hands. She sat opposite me and handed it over. I looked at her with a silent question in my eyes.

"Open it," she said.

I opened it and froze. I saw my face! It was a photo of me at my previous job a few months before they laid me off. I was standing in front of one of my clients. Makeup brush in hand, I was enthusiastically explaining something to a woman in front of me, sitting on the tall chair for a makeup application.

In a daze, I turned the pages, looking at my photos taken in different situations of my ordinary life: walking to my car after work, walking along the beach, immersed in my thoughts, not noticing anything around. I am refueling the car, going to the cinema with my children, loading groceries into the trunk. Of course, I immediately understand; obviously, someone had been watching me and took these photos. In addition to photographs, there were detailed reports on me: year of birth, place of birth, my schools, where and when I worked. Where and when I studied. All the addresses where I had ever lived, also personal reports of those who had collected all this information. Apparently, it was more than one person.

Personal evaluation read one of the reports.

330

I pretended to be one of the buyers, who spoke poor English. I asked her to help me. We talked for about fifteen minutes. During our conversation, I was undeniably fascinated by her. In my opinion, she is beautiful, very intellectual, I would even say brilliant, with a good sense of humor. She speaks English fluently. I could not help but notice her eyes. They are amazing. She is very natural and authentic, without pretense. She's sincere in conversation, not afraid to express her opinion on any subject.

I was very grateful for the beautiful words that this man had written about me, but I did not want to read any more of it. It all was strange. So strange! I turned the page.

It seems she loves her sons very much. She is extremely protective, as if afraid to lose them. She usually takes them with her everywhere she goes. All three look rather happy. She often holds their hands, even though both of them are almost adults. They joke and laugh a lot. I could see that the kids are also very attached to their mother. She loves children in general. If she comes across a child in her daily life, she will always stop and say a few words. Children seem to love her too. She also loves dogs. She loves to be alone. She can sit for an hour in the car all by herself, thinking or reading a book. She likes to take walks along the ocean. In these moments, she does not notice anything around her, as she seems immersed in her own thoughts. Apart from her sons, sometimes she spends time in the company of a tall, beautiful woman who looks like a close friend. In a month of observations, I saw her with a man only once. According to a previous report, this man is the father of her children. Though they divorced in 2008, it seems they have maintained a great relationship. I would even say that he still loves her. They went to the beach, and he took pictures of them all. All three looked quite happy. Apart from this man, there were no others.

331

Attached to the report were quite a few photos.

"So," I said, "I guess, what I have written in my four-hundred-page book and hundreds of my letters over two years was not enough for him. He also needed to compile a dossier on me. Why? What for?"

Why did Farhan need all these reports? After all, he never intended to see me, and now it was as clear as day.

"This is only a small part of the reports about you, Alla," she replied. "There are reports from two more investigators who have followed you at different times. Also, besides this one, there are reports about everyone with whom you have ever had close contact."

"*What for?*" I repeated my question.

Susan only waved her hand. "In my opinion, the answer is obvious, Alla. He wanted to know everything he could about you! He wanted to know if you *were REAL* and how much truth is in what you have written to him. Also, up to what degree is it true."

I just smiled bitterly, "So he doubted if I was real?"

"Alla! Even I doubted whether you were real or not! Same as a few more people who follow your every written word! It was not only Farhan! He is a public person, a star. A megastar! There are thousands, tens of thousands of people, who try to approach him by hook or by crook in every imaginable and possible way. I think you understand!"

"Yes. I understand," I answered with a bitter grin. "How many people do follow my every word, Susan?"

"I cannot tell you this; there are not many of them, but they exist and it is part of their job. Alla," she began and stopped abruptly. She seemed unable to decide how to start her story about why she called me here. I waited patiently.

"Alla," she began again, "I hope you understand that this conversation should remain purely between you and me! And one more thing, Farhan does not have the slightest idea about me meeting with you. Nor is he in any way aware of what I'm going to say."

She was silent again for a moment.

I nodded, although what she said was already obvious.

"Alla," she stopped again and inhaled deeply. It looked like saying, whatever she was going to tell me, was true torture for her. I felt something terrible washing over me. My heart trembled with fear, and every cell in my body tensed up. Just like when I was little and knew, in a moment, I would be hurt, humiliated and physically abused, and there was nowhere to run and no one to come and save me. For a fraction of a moment, I wanted to scream to Susan that I want to know NOTHING else, and run, run, run away from this damn room—run very far away. Hide from all this. Hide! But I ordered myself to stay where I was.

"Alla, I do not want Farhan to," Susan paused, unable to finish her sentence. Finding her courage, she started again, "*I do not want Farhan to continue to USE you!*"

This word struck me. As if someone silently came behind me and thrust a sword into my back, I involuntarily shuddered and looked into Susan's eyes. Part of me hoped I might have heard her wrong.

"Yes, Alla, this is exactly what he is doing. *He is using you.* And we all do the same, together with him. I believe this must stop; it's not right! It is terrible and wrong! Even though there is a large share of my own guilt in it. Since I started it, consider it late repentance; I regret it now. Very much!"

I kept silently looking at her, my eyes wide open with shock and hurt.

It seemed like she could no longer watch the bewilderment, pure shock, and raw pain in my eyes. So she got up from the couch and went to the huge panoramic window, where the night city lights were reflecting.

"I will start from the very beginning, Lala." She faced me again, "We all call you that. Lala. So does he."

She took a deep breath.

"His page on Facebook was always maintained by my team and me. My job was to read his fans' comments, to keep an eye on what they say. There are people in charge of his Twitter and those who manage his accounts on other social platforms, forums, fan clubs, etc.

"As you know, Farhan has a huge empire and he is known not only in the States. He is idolized in Africa and Asian countries and especially in India, where he is involved in many projects.

333

"I don't think you are fully aware of how we do things in our business. It is all pretty complicated! But recently, the film and television industries have started to undergo a real *crisis of IDEAS!* There are practically no worthwhile scripts, interesting, original texts, novels, dialogs! It seems that everything in the world has already been written, played, and filmed! We have many professional and unprofessional writers, screenwriters and so on, but it doesn't help much. *People have had a surfeit.* People have already seen it all and heard it all, and it is getting harder and harder to surprise them."

She stopped for a moment, as if gathering her courage again, and finally continued. "Farhan is a brilliant businessman! It's not easy; I would even say, close to impossible, to reach the very top as he did, without having any patrons in the world of cinema! That world is rather dirty, cruel and even ruthless! It's harder, much harder to stay there, on the very top, yet he has.

"Farhan is bright; one might even say, phenomenally brilliant and as well insightful. He has made himself thanks to his excellent talent, dedication, being a crazy workaholic and perfectionist. He created himself by always intuitively knowing what he needs to do to please the audience. He knows how to behave and not behave, what to do and what not to do. He knows what he can say and how to say it and what he should never discuss. He knows what to show and what to conceal. When to smile and when to blink. When to be playful and when to be serious. He knows when to be sweet or stern. He is an *actor through and through.* A brilliant genius. One of the best actors in the world, if not the best.

"In part, he is exactly that King—Wizard you described in your story, 'The King of Wizards and the Witch,' but only in part. With years passing by, there was no longer one Farhan Ali. There were two of him! Then three, and sometimes even more. One of them is the skillfully and thoroughly created *IMAGE* that he shows to the world. The second is the one that 'got carried away with playing God,' which are your words! I couldn't have said it better! It was you who once wrote to him, 'You got carried away with playing God, my Love! You have played it for so long that you lost your personal code of honor. You think that *ALL* is allowed to you, and everything should be exactly as you want it, when you want it and how you want it to be!'"

334

"And the third Farhan is the one he was before becoming this *God*, this *Idol*. The real him, the true him. Perhaps, *ONLY YOU* truly and deeply know and understand this third one! I believe you are the only one who does. But when it comes to Farhan himself, he avoids his third and true identity as much as possible."

She fell silent for a moment, then continued, "Ah Lala! I was also playing God, like Farhan. But I have changed. You managed to touch my soul very deeply with your incredible story! Lala! There is so much I want to tell you that I'm afraid I don't have enough time. But one of the reasons I am telling you all this is that *I DO NOT WANT him to continue using you and what your talent creates!* It must stop! You are so gifted! You do not even know how gifted you are! But I know as well for sure that even after what happened today, he unshakably believes that he can get you back whenever he wants to. He will do everything to achieve it. But I do not want it to happen!"

"How is he using me, Susan? What exactly do you mean?"

She moved away from the window and sat in the chair in front of me. What she was going to tell me was not easy for her. I waited patiently.

"Farhan has hundreds of millions of fans around the world," she continued. "Among them, sometimes we come across truly talented, gifted people. Since they do not have direct access to their idol, they write their ideas, texts, and dialogs directly to Farhan's social network accounts! Some of them use the multiple emails of his studios. Some send their work through regular mail to his offices, or even to his home address. We carefully look through them and if we find something interesting, we use it in our business! Our enterprise is not only movies for the big screen! There are also numerous series, soap operas, short films, commercials and many more. All ideas that are at least remotely interesting, we use in business! It is an enormous gluttonous, greedy machine! Do you understand?"

"You mean... Do I understand it correctly? You make money, using his talented fans' texts, thoughts and ideas? Is that right?"

"Yes. We do that too. If you think about it, why not? They write, for example, an interesting script or telenovela, or offer an idea and give it to him for free. As a gift! This way, they hope if he likes something they had created, he will invite them to work either with him, or on his team. No one forces them to do that. They do it fully by their own free will. So why not use it in our business?"

"Wait a minute. You are saying that the ideas of Farhan's fans feed your business. But what about those authors, creators of those texts and ideas, Susan? Do they get anything in return for having their work used?"

"No," she answered, averting her eyes after a moment of silence. "Most often, they just give it as a *gift*, hoping to be invited to work with Farhan, or just wanting to meet him face to face."

I shuddered and shut my eyes from yet another blow of piercing pain, tearing me to pieces. I remembered my own words I wrote to him after sending my book, *This is my gift to you! You can do with this book whatever you want!*

Everything inside me froze. It seems that even my heart slowed down and began to beat quieter. I was the one who gave him everything I had. Me. Me. Me...*It was me.* I put my heart and soul, my words, thoughts, feelings, ideas, everything I was or have ever been on a golden plate with the silver lining. I brought this plate to him and said, *Take it, my Love! All this is yours! All that is mine is yours! All that I am is yours!* So, who do I blame now? Only myself! My head was spinning, as well as the room around me. I closed my eyes again, trying to breathe. Breathing was turning into a big issue for me with every passing minute. Simply breathing...

"Your ideas were the best we've seen for several years," Susan continued. "Or perhaps, even the best we've ever seen in the many years of our work. *You are unique!* What you create does not resemble anything else. *It captures all attention, sincerely touches and moves something deep inside.* It's impossible not to succumb to the influence of your writings. Yours were the best among all we've ever seen."

The true meaning of what she was saying, or was trying to say, was slowly penetrating my mind, infiltrating deeper and deeper. The blades of the swords were now piercing me from every angle, every time I inhaled or exhaled. There was a type of torture during the time of the Inquisition;

they would pierce your body with a sharp cold knife many times. In the beginning, you would scream with pain, but after they had done it hundreds of times, there would come a moment when you would not be able even to cry. I was coming close to that as the meaning of Susan's words finally seemed to sink in.

"So," I said, almost whispering but trying to keep my voice steady, "everything I wrote during all these years... He was using it in his business? He needed me only for his damn business, right? Is that what you are trying to tell me?"

She was silent.

I clenched my teeth, struggling to maintain even a drop of control over the emotions written all over my face, but I was failing. The pain swept over me stronger than ever. *Pain. Shame. Resentment. Hurt.* Bitter as raw wormwood. *Disappointment. More pain. More pain. More...*

I wrapped my arms around my body with all the strength I had left, trying not to crumble into a million pieces.

"So," I continued, "*everything he did*, all the indigo shirts he wore with eyes full of Love! All these phrases he addressed as if to the whole world, but in fact, to me. The songs, videos, words, quotes—*ALL of that* he was doing in order to just keep me on the hook, right? So that I would continue to write? So that I continued to create enough material for his goddamn business? *Is that right?* He made me believe that he cared for me so that he simply *could continue to USE ME?*

Use Me!

Use...

Me..."

I whispered the last words almost soundlessly. My voice broke down. The world around me was slowly falling into pieces like shattered glass. *Shattered glass!* I felt like I was dying—falling into an endless, dark, freezing tunnel, snow swirling all around me. I didn't feel pain here. Finally, No Pain! Eternal emptiness—void of all emotion. There's no air here either. The cold, open space squeezed my head and chest, not letting me breathe. Why would I? The dead do not need to breathe. *After brutal betrayal, one could no longer continue living either. They are dead.* I kept falling deeper and deeper into the tunnel.

Endlessly

　　　Falling.

　Falling.

　　Falling.

　　　Falling.

White sparks began flashing in my head like fireflies. Silence. Bitter cold. The fall. Sparks. No breath. No life. It didn't bother me at all. Who cares? At least it is calm down here. No pain. No sound. No emotions. Nothing. And suddenly, I felt someone was with me in that tunnel. I sensed their presence. Someone I did not know. But I felt no fear. I heard them whisper inside my head, "Breathe! Breathe! Breathe, Lala! You are strong. Breathe! Do you hear me? Don't you dare die! Don't you dare!"

Who is here? Whose voices are surrounding me? Who are these people? Are they even people? Am I losing my mind? Suddenly, the chilling cold disappeared, the voices vanished together with my thoughts. I felt someone›s hand drew a circle of fire around me, trying to warm me up, trying to protect me. Suddenly, the icy hole pulling me into its cold bottomless mouth changed its shape, becoming a sparkling drop, exploding and splashing icy water onto my face. Abruptly I drew in my breath. Somehow the air smelled of wood smoke. Sobbing, coughing, I opened my eyes and found myself lying on the floor. Susan›s face was white with fear. Her eyes looked huge. Her voice trembled with relief on seeing me open my eyes.

I closed my eyes again, shutting them with all my might. Can I just disappear? Right now, can I? May I dissolve in the air? May I? No? Why? I don't want to live like this. I don't want to continue. I choose not to be. I don't want to exist. I want to be gone—gone like snow in spring. I do not wish to continue this fight. Everything is meaningless. Everything is useless. Everything!

"Lala! Heavens! Lala! Thank God! Are you all right, girl? Can I help you somehow? Tell me what to do? Just tell me!" Through a veil of water, or was it my tears, I looked at her beautiful half-blurred face, alarmed and leaning over me. I brought myself up into a sitting position. I covered my face with my hands, trying to pull myself together and stop shaking like a leaf in a storm. But that was not something under my control at the moment. Finally, I just gave up and let myself weep.

I didn't even notice that while doing that, I was repeating the exact words over and over again, "*No, this cannot be! No! This cannot be! This cannot be, this cannot be, this cannot be...*"

So, *here is the truth!* The simple fact, as cold and horrifically cruel as it can possibly be. He never loved me. He never cared. He never remembered. He never... Nothing... *He just used me.* Used me! This is it. That is all. Here is all your power of love, you little stupid fool! Little. Worthless. Fool. None of this was real. None of this!

I don't know how long I wept. I lost all sense of time—lost in my tears. I slowly came out of the fog because Susan kept calling my name, hugging me, stroking my hair and wiping away the tears from my face. Powerful Susan Malik, a legendary woman well known by everyone in the industry, was wiping my tears, saying my name over and over again.

"Lala, Lala."

Tasting blood from my bitten lip, I looked up and suddenly asked her, "Where is he now, Susan?"

But she didn't have to answer me. Before she could even open her mouth, I "saw" where He was at that very moment. I saw a huge room in a luxury hotel—a small company of well-dressed and not very sober people. A serious bartender, mixing cocktails at a small counter. An incredibly gorgeous woman with straight blond hair and extremely long legs was leaning over the armrest of the chair, where my King—who was never mine—was sitting in a relaxed pose. My devil. My demon. My tyrant. My Twin. The great businessman and unrivaled actor, the "ideal" man and the Lord of millions of hearts, Farhan Ali.

The breathtaking blonde gently brushed the luxurious locks of his hair away from his forehead with her fingertips. His hair disheveled, his gaze detached, the touch of a smile was wandering on his legendary lips.

With long elegant fingers, his strong dark hand gently stroked her knee. She was wearing a short silver dress that looked more like a shirt—perfect knees of perfect legs of a perfect woman and his long, elegant fingers on them.

I suddenly burst out laughing!

"Lala!" Susan's face was frightened again, "Lala!"

"What a beautiful woman!" I said with a suddenly icy, calm voice. The numbness that first swept me in the hotel room came to my aid now once more. It has come again to save me! Well! Just in time! I was still crying, and I hated myself for it. *Such a weakling! Take a blow, Witch! Take another blow from your King of Wizards! And don't you dare fall apart! Breathe and stop crying already! STOP!*

But I was powerless against those damn tears. At least I stopped feeling anything at all. I looked into Susan's eyes. She did not understand what I had just said.

"A gorgeous woman!" I repeated. "Tall, slender blonde. Delicate facial features. Gray eyes, or blue? Silver dress. It looks like she loves him—little fool—and her legs, good Lord! She is so perfect."

"Lala, how do you...."

"How do I know?" I interrupted her, smiling bitterly, "I have the misfortune to be the damn Twin Flame of this striking and oh-so-gorgeous ruler of the world! This angel and demon can put on any disguise, any mask! Pretend to be anyone and anything under the sun! Who can make anyone believe in whatever his majesty wants them to believe! Sometimes *I just SEE with his eyes! Even if I DO NOT WANT to! I see it anyway!*

"Tell me, Susan," I continued, looking up into her eyes. "Tell me, how many of them? How many women, like this blonde, does he have?"

Susan lowered her eyes in silence.

"Many! Right?" I answered my own question, laughing bitterly. "There have been many."

I dropped my hands and stared into the space in front of me.

"Lala! Lala, I know how you feel now. Believe me. I know."

I just shook my head. *No.*

"Lala! Listen to me! Please listen! Yes, he played with you like a cat with a mouse, used you, made millions on your ideas and creations while you were working for mere pennies. He's been with many women while you were *living and breathing only him!* I am not trying to justify him! But what I am trying to say is, it's not that simple, Lala! Actually, it's way too complicated! I was hoping you could try to understand one thing. At least try, no matter how strange it may sound, knowing his actions."

She touched my cheek and said something I didn't expect to hear, leaving me once again, in pure shock! No. Those were the last words in the world I expected to hear at this moment!

"Lala, I KNOW THAT FARHAN LOVES YOU! He LOVES you, Lala!!!"

What she just said was so ridiculous under these circumstances that a second later, when the meaning of what she said finally penetrated my mind, I burst out laughing. But this time, my laughter was full of pain, tears, and sarcasm.

"Oh yeah! Right! Of course, *HE LOVES ME! He is just dying of love for me!* Right now, at this very moment, when I only want to stop breathing, he is so full of love for me that he finds himself in the passionate embrace of some beautiful statuesque woman! *Yes! Sure!"* I continued to laugh, wiping my inexhaustible tears with the back of my hand, although it was pretty useless.

"Of course! I believe you! *I totally believe you!* You're absolutely right! Of course, *he LOVES me!* He loves me very much! So much so that he would not even turn his head *if I died.* His love is especially strong tonight when I am here because of him, but he is oh-so-very-busy and can't see me!"

Susan sat next to me, taking my hand.

"Why are you trying to console me, Susan? Why are you even talking to me? Who am I? Why did you suddenly take my side? You are a powerful assistant of triple powerful Mr. Movie Staaa! And I am just some little nobody! Why do you waste your time telling me all this? I am not worth it."

She reached out and wiped my tears. "Can you hear me out, Lala? Perhaps then, you will be able to understand why. Just try to listen to me. Will you?"

I nodded silently. The words about his love for me sounded like the most ridiculous joke one could ever imagine.

And the great and powerful Susan Malik, who turned out to have a beautiful and compassionate heart behind the "iron lady" mask, began her story.

Chapter 42

The King and the Witch – Susan's Version

"I have known Farhan for more than twenty years. I know his family closely. I know his wife and her family. In fact, I am his remote relative as well, something like a distant cousin from his mother's side. He has three main assistants, but he trusts me the most. Sometimes I have to be with him twenty-four hours a day. Of course, you can imagine how you can get to know a person by being with him for so many years, days and hours.

"I went through a phase of falling crazily in love with him and dreaming that one day he would love me back. But it lasted only about a year at the beginning of our collaboration. That love burned out pretty quickly! Because I met a man for me.

"The more I knew Farhan, the more I realized that I was wrong about many of the qualities of my employer. I saw that there was more than one Farhan! He has many faces! He is a real magician and instantly feels and knows what this or that person, or a group of people, expects from him and how they want to see him. I have already told you about it! He accurately reads the slightest shades of a mood of both an individual and the whole crowd.

"When it comes to women, he doesn't even have to snap his fingers to have any of them fall at his feet. You know that very well. *He FEELS each of*

343

them, whether it is a secretary, a businesswoman, a sophisticated diva, or a young and innocent virgin. After spending a few minutes with a woman, he knows everything about her! He knows how to look at her, what to tell her, how to touch her. He knows what makes her happy, what makes her sad. Women lose their minds not so only because of the way he looks, his sensuality and natural magnetism, but more because of his ability to deeply *KNOW and feel* each one of them! He reads their hearts and souls like an open book!

"He chooses the ones he wants and does so whenever he feels like it. Rejection for him is almost impossible. You won't believe this, but he would like for one of them to reject him. If he meets a woman he cannot not conquer in 15 seconds, his eyes light up! It means *a challenge!* It means the game *tug of war* has started. He long ago lost interest in women who fall in love with him within three minutes. He has had more than plenty of those in his life. The ones who give him a challenge, those do turn him on. Because he needs to win them over, conquer, charm, subdue and bewitch them! But he seldom meets that kind.

"He is attracted to the strong, intelligent, self-sufficient and unique women. The ones who can match him! *Be equal to him!* If he meets such a woman, he gets a spark! He falls for her, but, unfortunately, his spark quickly fades away.

"Usually, such an affair lasts from several weeks to several months. Farhan understands, of course, that he hurts a woman when he tells her it's over. But he believes that both of them are adults, and both of them are aware of what they do. Moreover, each one of them is well-informed that he is married, so from the very beginning, they have to accept his terms and conditions and play according to his rules."

I covered my face with my hands, unable to believe what I just heard.

"But this is terrible, Susan! *That is not the man I know with my very Soul!* I do not know this one! He is a complete stranger to me! And how can he do all that while he is married? What about his wife, Cynthia? Does she know? How can she stay in all this hell?"

344

"I can't tell you everything that I know, Lala, but his marriage, for quite a bit of time already, has just been a mere performance. The continuation of a successful business project."

"Holy Heavens! Is that so? So, it's all a lie! His marriage is a lie. His image is a lie. Everything he made me believe is a lie! And I thought he was practically a saint. I called him 'My Heavenly Angel,' and the world thinks exactly the same! An ideal husband who has never, in his whole life, been with any other woman but his wife. A perfect father. A perfect brother. A perfect son. He is perfect all over, to the moon and back! I saw people in other countries that erect altars, devoted to him, and pray to him as God! How can one lie like that? How can one lie with every word, every look, every smile and blink of his eyelashes? And who are all these women? After all, not a single actress with whom he worked had ever…"

"*Actresses are his TABOO, Lala!*" She interrupted me. "He never starts a love affair with his coworkers. Never! He treats all actresses he works with, with the deepest respect and admiration. He had only one affair with an actress, a Spanish actress and model, Beatrice Sanchez. It was a deep romance and the longest one he ever had. It lasted for several years. In public, they both, of course, denied everything. But he really was into her. She wanted him to leave his family and marry her officially. Of course, it wasn't something he ever planned to do. In the end, they broke up. She continued to love him, and he too could not forget her for a long time. Although after her, he had other affairs. I knew he continued thinking about her until one day," she stopped for a moment. "*Until one day you appeared.*"

We looked into each other's eyes, and she repeated, "Good Lord, when I look into your eyes, I am hot and cold at the same time! *In your eyes, I see Him!* It is incredible! What an unbelievable, unthinkable test you both have chosen for yourselves in this life!"

"Tell me, Susan. You said his marriage was part of a business project. What do you mean? She found out about his affairs, but chose to stay with him because of his empire?"

"Yes and no. I mean, not exactly like that. His wife has been with him in show business long enough. She knows how things are done there. We are talking about private clubs, closed parties with a sea of expensive alcohol, soft and sometimes heavy drugs. The most beautiful women are inevitable components of such gatherings. She is not so naive as to not understand the obvious. It is a part of his life! Many years ago, when he was young, talented, and was only at the beginning of his career, he married her. He was passionately in love with her, the beautiful, bright, intelligent girl. She is the only daughter and her family belongs to the old Californian elite. Naturally, her parents were initially against their daughter's choice. But he won both her love and their respect, trust and approval. For years, it was probably a perfect family, a perfect marriage. They have endured a lot. Lengthy shootings that lasted days, nights, weeks, and even months in locations all over the world. Ups and downs. Success and failures. Triumphs and disappointments. But their love could not stand the test of world fame and all that came with it.

"The burden of such enormous fame is a heavy one, Lala. Very heavy! And part of such a burden is becoming a member of the so-called 'circle.' Those closed clubs and parties, with a sea of alcohol, drugs, and beautiful women, are a part of it. At such gatherings, besides "having fun, "and sometimes even instead of having fun, they also make big decisions, sign deals, contracts, so on. To be rich, famous, and powerful in the world of show business, means taking part in things like that! Sometimes things are even scarier than those. But I don't want to mention them. I have already scared you enough. If you don't participate, don't show up there, you will be out!

"In most cases, that would mean the end of your career, especially for those who once were outsiders. Farhan was one of them. So, once he was 'let in,' *he had to play by their rules.* The rules of that "big game." He pretty much had no choice. You play by their rules, or you are out!

"The wives of such stars know this and simply turn a blind eye to it. Being the wife of a famous person means *prestige and a high position in society!* They do not intend to lose their status, just because their husbands are not perfect. The main thing is that he remains a star for the rest of the world! At first, it hurts, yes, of course! But then, they get used to it and accept it as part of their lives. They stay in these marriages for fame, status in society, and the multimillion-dollar income of their husbands.

"But, when it comes to Cynthia, Farhan's wife, she does not care much about his earnings, as she is from a wealthy family. But prestige, the family name, reputation and status are essential for her. Rumors of their divorce have circulated for a long time. But her parents demanded it is kept a secret, in strictest confidence. They want to protect their good reputation, the family name, King Farhan Ali and their daughter's business, and protect their grandchildren from exposure in the media and the press. She agrees that she must help keep the family's reputation by all means! They have not been living together for a long time, each has their own life and interests but they regularly appear in public as a beautiful, loving family. It is not our business to debate, and people close to Farhan don't discuss these issues at all; *it's a corporate taboo.* She plays her role as his wife in public, and he appears as her devoted husband. But, as I already said, she has her own life and he has his own. And naturally, for one like him, multiple women are nothing unusual."

I didn't want to hear anymore! *I didn't want to know anything else!* I wanted to leave and just forget it all like a terrible nightmare.

"Susan, why are you telling me all this? Why do I need to know all this? What does any of this have to do with me? Why the hell do I need to know about his lovers, women, wife, parties, affairs? What for? I do not need any of this, Susan! I don't! Please, can I go?"

"Oh no, Lala! Not now! I have just started. Now stay and listen! The more you know, the easier it will be for you to understand that everything is not that simple! Neither for him nor you! Believe me, if I hadn't known everything about you, from the very first words you wrote him and up to this very day. If I *hadn't BELIEVED you, I would have never interfered!*"

She went silent again for a moment and then continued.

"I was the one who suggested hiring private investigators to find out everything about you."

"You? Why?"

"Because I saw what was happening to Farhan from the moment he read your first letter. I knew perfectly well that he did not believe you. But I also knew he WANTED to believe you. I offered to find out as much as we could. I said, 'Let's see what is true of what she tells us, how much of it is true.'

"In addition, we were already using your materials in full flow. It was a perfectly justified decision. I also wanted different people to talk to you PERSONALLY and have their own opinions about you. I was not at all surprised when they were charmed by you."

For the first time on this scary and strange night, I smiled slightly.

Susan continued, "As I said, I have known Farhan for a long time. At first, he was not at all what he is now. The demons of narcissism and darkness gained power over him gradually, throughout the years. You know, there are many fairy tales about how a hero successfully passes very difficult and dangerous tests but fails the trial of *unlimited power* and freedom. He fails when people start to see him as a Deity and praise him. He fails when *everything becomes accessible and allowed*. With time, the hero loses his true self, becoming someone else. You remember, of course, the words of *John Dalberg-Acton*:

Power tends to corrupt, and absolute power corrupts absolutely. Great men are almost always bad men, even when they exercise influence and not authority, still more when you superadd the tendency or the certainty of corruption by authority.

"Do you remember, in your book, you wrote that his mother came to you in a dream and said, '*No one else can do it. You are the only one who can!*' You said you did not understand what exactly it was that no one else could do but you. Reading your book, I understood it very well. I knew exactly what she meant. No one else but you can get *the true Him* out of *what he has become*, influenced for years by *fame, power, money, permissiveness, and, how you say it, 'playing God.'* Only you can *move him, help him, inspire him to look for the true Him deep inside, find him and bring him back!* I truly and deeply believe it, Lala! As much as his mother believes! Honestly, I believe she guides you, as well as the Force, which is far *beyond human comprehension.*

"The first breakdown in him occurred after the sudden death of his Mother. He loved her very much and wanted to fulfill her dream—to become a star. For this, he was ready to do almost anything. He undertook any project, any role, without reading the scripts or discussing the fees. He wanted to prove to her, to himself, to the whole world that he could succeed! He could do it! Even the story of his marriage is primarily an opportunity to prove to Cynthia and her parents he can accomplish anything!

"He and his wife are very different. It seems they even see leaves on the trees and the clouds in the sky in different ways. At first, their love was enough for both of them to feel happy. But time passed, years passed, Farhan was soaring higher and higher. The more he became *God* in the negative sense of this word, the more he was losing himself. Power and money change people, it›s true, and there›s no getting around it! Playing by the dirty rules of "the circle" to stay where he was, did not help either. I am not trying to find excuses for him, but what choice did he have? He got to the top by his own sweat and blood, by working 16 hours a day, every day for years! And when faced with the choice: Lose it all, or accept the rules of *the big game,* he chose the latter.

"In addition to being a brilliant actor, he is intellectual and a great communicator! He likes to conquer. He enjoys playing, acting, being loved, adored and worshiped. It is no wonder. As far as I know, all great actors are like whimsical, selfish children. But no one knows his deepest secret! He never shows anyone how much *fame, power, and money really mean for him!*

"His biggest fear is to fall from the top and lose his megastar status! That would be the worst thing imaginable for him! Big money and great power hold him tightly *in the grip of their claws.* Although he possesses a lot, he wants more. A lot more! He is excellent at wearing masks and knowing how to hide what he needs to hide and only showing people what they want to see.

"Can he brilliantly manipulate people to achieve his goals? Yes, he can! Can he do the same with women madly in love with him? Yes, he can."

I shivered. The last words made my skin creep.

"Susan. I get it. I've heard more than enough. Really! I deeply appreciate everything you have told me. But I don't want to know anything else. I am exhausted, Susan. Please, can I..."

"No, Lala! You can't. You must stay until I tell you everything, I've got to tell you."

She took a deep breath and continued, "I understand. None of this is easy for you to hear, to say the least. I realize *you did not know any of this and did not see it!* Perhaps you even wonder how it is possible that you, the one with whom he shares *ONE Soul*, saw and felt *nothing of it!* Here's how I have come to understand it.

"Over the past year, I have studied the phenomenon of Twin Flames like a maniac! I have spoken personally with a few of the most powerful Seers, as you call them. That's another reason why I consider it necessary to tell you all of this. You probably think, 'How can this demon, which hurts me, uses me, and manipulates me and others, be a part of me? I am nothing like that!' But you are not a part of this demon. You are a part of the Farhan, over whom the demons of fame, power, and money have no control. *You are his Soul, Lala! You are HIS SOUL.*"

"Susan," my voice sounded somewhat calm, probably because I was exhausted beyond compare, on both a physical and nonphysical level. "Don't only blame him, please! What happened is not only his fault. Did he ask me for anything? No. I did everything by my own choice and of my own free will. So, how can I blame him for simply using what *I MYSELF* gave him with love and an open heart? He was not the one who found me. *I found him.* He was not the one who asked me to give. I did it myself. So how can I blame him? I can't; that would be stupid and unfair.

"After all, Susan, He never promised me anything." My exhaustion had reached the point where even blinking seemed too hard to do. "No, he promised me nothing," I repeated. "He did not ask me for anything. I gave

350

everything to him myself. I was giving and giving and giving. It was always just me. So, I have nobody to blame but myself!"

"Lala! I have no words! My dear girl, *even NOW*, even after all I have said, after all, you know and all he has done to you, *you're ready to defend him?* Are you justifying him and putting all the blame onto yourself? What kind of Soul, what kind of heart do you have, dear? Are you even a human?"

I closed my eyes again and quietly said,

"*I love him…*"

But I instantly opened them up again, *stunned by my own words! I was unable to believe what my mouth has just said! How could I? How? Oh, no! I'm definitely crazy! Insane! No doubts, completely insane! No matter how much he hurts me, I am flying even higher and loving him even more! No! I am not normal! My mom is right! I absolutely need to see a psychologist, or a hypnotherapist, a psychiatrist, or hell knows who else! HOW could I SAY this, after ALL he has done to me??? How could I?*

Susan looked at me with a faint and somehow gentle smile on her lips. "I know that! I know…" she replied.

"Susan, *I must be just crazy… Or seriously stupid. Or both!*"

"No! You are neither crazy nor stupid. You are Farhan's Twin Flame, *HIS LIGHT*, his mediator. Your love is the only hope he has to not lose this light forever! *Mediator between him and God*, him and the *Source of Light itself!* Without you, he has no chance to stop being the many-faceted dark wizard he has become and return to his authentic self, who he really is! Do you know why he is so afraid of you? I will tell you why!"

"In one of your letters, yes, I have read them all, forgive me, and I have done it more than once. In one of your letters, you wrote a story about a beautiful young woman and a wise old man. This woman came to a wise man and, with tears in her eyes, she asked him, 'Tell me, teacher? Why do people hurt me so much? Why do they pay me back with dark ingratitude for all the good I do to them? Why am I suffering so much? Why is the world so unkind to me?' And the teacher answered her, 'Because your Soul is pure, and for the people, *it serves as a mirror!* And in this mirror of your Soul, *they see themselves, just as they are.* They see their true self! How many would like it? Only those *whose Soul is as pure as yours*. But those who are not, *will hate you for showing them the truth*. That's why you receive evil from them! *Look for people who are like you!* Those as pure in Soul as you are. With them, you are at peace and smiling at the Sun instead of shedding tears.'

"This is precisely the reason why you cause such fear in him! You are the mirror in which Farhan can see the simple and complicated truth. He might be standing on the top of the world, but his Soul is in shadow.

"I doubt you even realize that people, who are lucky to get to know you, begin to find in you a source of strength and inspiration. People are *moved by you*, your passion, openness, your fire! You become the very oxygen that makes it easier to breathe, live, hope and believe. I find it in you. Those on the team who know about you, do as well. And most of all, Farhan himself."

She fell silent again for a few seconds. Then she got up, poured herself a glass of water. She brought another one for me, sat next to me, and continued. "By the time you appeared, he had almost fully turned into that enchanted Prince Narcissus, who sincerely believed that he had seen it all and done it all. That there was nothing left in the whole wide world that could surprise him! I could see in him the signs of burn-out more often. He was like a man who had sated himself with every possible luxury in feelings, emotions and material things. He had seen and experienced it all. *What is next? What is all of this for?* These are not the kind of questions he wanted to ponder. So, he pushed himself to the limit in work, so there was no time left for him to be alone, face himself and think. He did everything to fall entirely exhausted in the evening, sleep for several hours, and then again do what he did yesterday, the day before and five or ten years ago.

"Permissiveness and being one of the *circle*, the *elite* with their *rules*, destroyed his family. His profession, which he used to love so passionately and enjoyed so much, no longer brought him the drive it used to. And his multiple lovers, no matter how beautiful and bright, became part of an almost ordinary routine. Each of his women was stunning and unique in her own way. It would be hard to imagine otherwise. He had seen plenty of beauty in his life. He was looking for something else. In addition to brightness and beauty, she had to 'catch him' with something else. Something extraordinary and unique. Something which he had not seen before. But even when this happened, it didn't usually last that long. Over time, it started to look like his affairs with women were no longer for pleasure or entertainment. It seemed to me as if *he was looking for something, or rather, someone!* Although he did not even know, or consciously realize, what exactly or who exactly he was looking for! Once he enters a new relationship, he hopes that finally, he has found her. The one he was looking for! But time passes, a week, a month or two, and she turns out not to be *The One*. She doesn't have that mysterious something he's constantly searching for yet failing to find. He tears up all the threads and walks away. He keeps on looking and searching.

"Now I understand that his subconscious was searching for you! After all, *the Twin is always looking for his other half, whether he is aware of it or not! He was not aware.* And this brought him into the arms of many lovers, where he found no peace, no joyfulness and no harmony for his heart because none of them *were you!* No matter how bright and beautiful each one of them was, how much she loved him or wanted to make him happy. None of them *were you and could not be you.* And he was always searching *for you* and no one else. As simple as that."

"Oh, Susan!" I interrupted her with a heavy sigh, "He already found me two years ago! And today we were very close! And what?"

"Lala. Don't you know about the Running Twin? The one running from his truth, his Soul, himself?

"Yes, I know about it."

"Well, this is what we have here! I repeat I am not trying to find excuses to justify his actions. Unfortunately, a "runner" is exactly what we are dealing with. For two years, I have been closely observing what has been and still is happening to him since you appeared in his life. I have also studied The Twin Flames phenomenon very carefully in every way I found possible. I have spoken with several knowledgeable people. I have already told you: if I hadn't known everything about this unbelievable story, from the very first words you wrote to him and up to this very day, *If I hadn't BELIEVED you* and what you two are for each other, I would have never interfered!"

353

"Believe me, Susan, I truly, deeply, with all my heart, appreciate what you are doing now. I could not even imagine that I would be having a conversation with the great and incredible Susan Malik!"

"Great Susan Malik?!? You obviously don't even know yourself at all, Lala! You do not understand or realize that you have managed to do something that no one has ever done before you. Many tried, no one succeeded. Only you did.

"One very expensive clairvoyant in New York told me that Farhan's Soul was nothing else but Excalibur itself. The legendary sword of King Arthur. Metaphorically speaking, Arthur had no idea it was destined for him, only him, to get the sword out of the stone. At the same time, you have no idea that *you are the only one who can get his soul-sword from the stone and make it shine in the Sun again!* The words of his mother 'Only you can!' Do you understand them now?"

I just shook my head. *No.* I didn›t understand. I only understood that he was with another woman at that very moment. I also understood that I might never even see him again.

"Maybe you're right," I said. "Maybe there is some truth in your words, but unfortunately, it doesn't make it all easier for me."

"I know, my girl, I know that! But let me tell you the things one after another, as we always go wandering off-topic." She stopped to have a drink of water and continued. "I could see the emotional burnout in him over the last few years. It seemed that everything he did, he was doing in autopilot mode. Nothing gave him pleasure anymore. There were times when it was simply painful to look at him. He was turning into a shadow of himself. Many people began to notice that. There was glory. Money. Women. Films. But something was missing. Spark in his eyes. Joy. Laughter. Happiness. I wanted to help him, but I didn't know how.

"Then one day, I am looking through his fans' comments on his *FB* page, and I stumble upon your letter. I begin to read it, and it completely captivates me! I'm just amazed because the style and the form of this writing are nothing like anything I have ever seen before. I reread it so many times that I can even retell it.

354

Have you ever asked yourself why people are so afraid of Loneliness? You are afraid of it also, even though you love it too. You love it, but you fear it more. You know, who has no fear of it? Me. I'm not afraid. Not at all. Can I say something? You are now standing on the terrace and looking at the water. You are looking at the Pacific Ocean, and I am looking at the Atlantic. A vast distance separates us, and you think you are completely alone. You think no one else sees you! And what if I say, I see you? Even though I am thousands of miles away from you, I SEE you! What would you say to that? You are wearing a black shirt; your gorgeous hair is waving freely in the wind. Do you want to hear something? You remind me of that very wind—the ocean breeze!

I could not help smiling. "I am delighted and very flattered that what I wrote, touched you so much!"

"*Touched* is not a strong enough word, Lala! It seemed to seep through my very veins into my very core! But my surprise was still ahead. I would meet Farhan later that evening at his residence, and what do you think I saw when I got there? I found him *on the terrace, in a black shirt looking at the ocean, with hair disheveled by the wind!*"

I smiled again, imagining the whole picture. The image warmed my heart.

"That time," Susan continued, "I attributed it to a mere coincidence. Before we started talking about business, I said I wanted to show him something. I showed him your letter! First, he began reading it rather indifferently but as he kept reading, his face changed and he furrowed his eyebrows. 'Who is she?' he asked me. 'What an interesting style. *Bewitching!* I will reread it later again. Does she always write like that?'

"'I don't know her,' I answered. 'I've never seen her before. But her style indeed is very unusual.'

"And we went on to discuss our urgent matters. When I was about to leave, Farhan said, 'Susan, about the girl that wrote that message! It's an interesting fan. Let me know if you see anything else from her.'

"So, of course, I let him know. Starting from your first letter, I watched everything you wrote on his page and passed it on to him. But very soon I realized that *he was watching you himself.* However, he did not show it. At first, we did not have any mercenary interest in your writing. But it appeared after a couple of months. We could not allow such texts and ideas to remain only in texts. You were an open treasure chest.

She fell silent again, as if thinking, or maybe, feeling regrets. "We were using almost everything you sent to him! Did we feel any guilt? Not really. Even if we did from time to time, we continued. We have done this many times over the years. It's part of our business. We were having some serious problems with several rather big projects when you appeared. Your gift and your talent came right on time! Within a year, you helped us resolved all those problems. Especially when you started writing pieces of your novel *The Kiss of God*, the story "King of Wizards and the Witch", the novel *Forget-me-not*! There were finished scenes and complete dialogs! Later we got a hold of your book *I Just Want You to Remember*, in addition to your letters, sketches and stories! We had found a goldmine! You gave us all plenty of work! We understood that such material would be enough for years to come!"

Suddenly she stopped again. Again, she shocked me with what she said, *"Forgive me, Lala. Forgive me, my girl. Forgive us all if that is even possible.* We knew we understood that what you wrote and created was personal, meant only for him.

"But on the other hand, it was the material for creating music videos, commercials, television series, films and so on. You gave him all these excellent concepts, heroes, complete scenes, fresh ideas in your beautifully unique style. It was your way of seeing things, feeling them, understanding them, putting them into words. As I already said. It was a *goldmine*. I would even say *a diamond mine*."

She fell silent again for a moment and continued, "A year or so later, you began to disappear from time to time. Farhan and the whole team who knew about you, obviously did not like it at all. It was not something he, or we, could allow to happen. Farhan did everything, so you would believe in his love, believe that everything is possible. 'By hook or by crook,' he sustained this faith in you, skillfully using what he had learned about you."

She looked at me. I remained silent. Well, what could I say? Another cold blade of the sword stabbed my heart. There were so many today. I almost got used to this sharp, sudden pain. Susan read it in my eyes.

"But there was something the great Farhan Ali was unable to foresee and predict," she continued. "I think the will of the Higher Powers did not allow him to know how deeply you would impact him, how unexpectedly and imperceptibly he would begin to change.

"At first, it was simple curiosity, then interest. Of course, not that deep initially but it was becoming deeper and deeper as time passed and as he got to know you better. He started to enjoy playing that game with you, which he invented. He liked it a lot."

Another thin, sharp sword stabbed my heart!

"Then he began to admire you sincerely and did not even hide it from me. Yes, he did use you. I'm not looking for excuses for him. Yet, at the same time, each day, you meant more and more to him. Setting the snares for you, Farhan himself fell into his own trap. He hadn't noticed the moment when you began to mean too much for him. The moment when he no longer could be without you."

She got up, walked to the window and looked at the still sleeping city. I patiently waited for her to continue.

"We often fly to different countries," she went on. "These are usually long-haul flights. He got into the habit of rereading your letters and stories during these long hours. He told me, 'How can one woman combine so many different things? It is as if she is all the women in the world *merged into one!* There is so much gentleness in her, and at the same time burning passion, bottomless depth, wisdom. She is not afraid to say what she thinks. She couldn't care less about my fame! Wait! How dare she!' And he began to laugh like a boy, not seeing what I saw. And what I saw, I had not seen in him for many and many years. *The spark in his eyes was back.* The light! And with this light, I could see the very joy of life! The more time passed, the more striking was the change in him. I can tell you for sure; there was one Farhan Ali *before* you. And then there is another one *after* you.

357

"You know, we are making so many films, series, and short love stories. But the most amazing story of love, I was able to watch *with my own eyes*. And I feel blessed because I did! I still do! Love has great power! After knowing you, I do not doubt it anymore. It is like the 'water of life' from those old fairy tales. *It touches something dead and makes it resurrect and raise its face to the rays of the Sun again!* Yes, yes! I, like many people on our team, use your words," she said with a laugh.

"Farhan seemed to begin to glow from the inside. He became softer. He started to notice things he never seemed to notice before. He began to hum and quietly sing under his breath. That certainly had never happened before. In 20 years, I had never seen that! He started to use your words and phrases. He was thinking of you more and more often. I have been with him for so long I can read him without him saying a word. When he submerged himself in thought about you, his face changed, features softened, the shadow of a smile played on his lips. Of course, he believed that the whole thing was only some pleasant entertainment, with a bonus in the form of your texts, letters, novels and ideas.

"But when you disappeared, *the light in him was gone instantly*, like *a candle in a stormy wind*. Yes, your words again! When I mentioned it, he would tell me how important and valuable you were for 'the empire' and all of us. That we should not lose the "diamond mine." He needed to get a haircut like this and get dressed like that, so that you would come back. But I understood that there was something else there. Much more than just 'the empire.'

"With each passing day, week, month, it was more and more evident that he could not be without you. He was changing. He was transforming right in front of our eyes. People around him began to notice it and comment on it. He even read the books you liked, digging into all the topics you mentioned in your letters. But the most dramatic change happened to him after he had received your book.

"He quickly devoured those 400 pages. I could see that the commotion he got as a reaction to your book was intense and very strong. But to my surprise, shortly afterward, his mood changed dramatically for the worse. I could clearly see why. You entered the space *no one had ever entered before.* No one dared. No one was even allowed to! You touched such depths in him, places he didn't even know existed. He didn't like it, not at all. He changed for the worse again, becoming impatient and aggressive.

"It was as if he finally understood and admitted to himself that you meant much more to him than he wanted to believe or even accept. He realized that he needed you! Just you! You as a woman! You as you, not simply someone he could use for his empire! It meant that he was not in control. You were. You could leave anytime you wished, meet somebody else and continue to live your life the way you did before him. But for him, *life without you would never be the same again.* You were in control of this situation, not him. Obviously, the almighty King was not pleased with this realization. The phase of the so-called 'Running Twin' had begun. It was as if he was trying to prove to himself that he could easily manage without you. The King cannot be weak; he must not be weak! And he took it as a weakness.

"I read your book also. It shook me to my very core. I began to study the phenomenon of Twin Flames. The more I knew, the more the things 'clicked' and made sense. And the more amazed I was to be a witness of such an extraordinary, true story! Later I decided to meet and talk to several, as you call them, Seers. And I have something to show you."

She left the room and returned with several pages of printed text. She handed one of them to me. I obediently took it and began to read.

Dear Susan,

My apologies for not immediately responding to you. I wanted to take my time and look into the connection between these two people as deeply as possible. It took me a few days. Of course, I remember the complete confidentiality of our communication. It is a part of my work, so you do not have to worry about it. I appreciate your trust and I am not going to break it. I must admit that what I will tell you may sound rather strange but it's exactly what I see. It is up to you to believe me or not.

This woman, Alla, and Farhan share one Soul. They are one Soul divided into two bodies, two halves of One. I am very grateful to you for this experience, as I have not encountered such a phenomenon in my work. Although, of course, I have heard about it. Such a phenomenon is extremely rare, and their paths are never easy. What can I say? These two did not accidentally meet. From the viewpoint of our ordinary, everyday lives, their reasons for meeting one another are too complicated to put in words. They were chosen for each other by the Higher Forces for a specific purpose, a mission. Otherwise, they would not have incarnated at the same time. It's too risky. A lot depends on them. I can't say exactly what they must accomplish; their Keepers guard this information.

At this point, the man does not seem to know what to think about any of this. He certainly loves her, but he doesn't seem to realize it, or understand who she is for him. Theirs is not even Love as we know it or understand it. His love for her is more like a reflection of her love for him, an ancient mirror. She is his guiding star in the night sky. She has always been the one for him—the only one for many lives. There is no other and cannot be another. Whether knowingly or unknowingly, she supports him along the way, as she is the spiritually stronger out of two of them.

There is something else. Two people sharing one Soul are always together, even if they are worlds apart. *Distance means nothing for them.* They are always close to each other. It's hard to find the words for them. But imagine that they live in each other! She lives within him. He lives within her. They don't communicate as other people do; it's a telepathic connection. Even if they do not see each other for months or even years, *they are always together—inseparable.* No matter how much he wants to run away from her and the feelings she evokes, he will fail. If she tries to run, it will be the same result. They are connected forever. I have no idea what will happen next. At the moment, I see that he intends to leave everything as it is. The Force, and the One Soul they share, is much stronger than his human will, mind and logic. Only time will show how long he can resist it.

When I finished reading, she handed me another page.

Dear Susan,

I am delighted that you have turned to me with this. I have been familiar with Twin Flames for about five years now. Once, about three years ago, in deep meditation, I saw the faces of world-famous people who are Twins! One of them was Farhan Ali. So, you can say I am not a bit surprised. This woman, without a doubt, is his Twin. It is obvious and easy to see. But at this point, it will be pretty difficult for him to believe such a thing. His heart chakra is almost entirely blocked and has been out of balance for quite a long time. And let me speak quite frankly here. Perhaps this will sound strange since millions love Farhan Ali, but a person with a closed heart chakra *has no love or acceptance for himself.* Deep down, he believes he is not worthy of such love. He believes that 'everybody loves for something,' so he struggles to understand and accept the fact that she loves him simply for himself! She loves him just because she loves him. Such a simple truth is hard for him to grasp. Actually, Lala has the same issue, absence of self-love and self-acceptance due to her harsh childhood, loneliness, a series of losses and life tests. They *mirror each other*, which is natural for Twin Flames. If she learns the art of self-love and self-acceptance, she will help him as well, as they are connected, like two halves of one shell.

Now, what and how he feels about her. You see, her appearance in his life requires changes, and he is not ready to change anything. Sorry, but I see how strongly he is attached to the material side of life. He is like a genie in the tale of Aladdin, who is a slave of his Lamp. *The genie has unlimited power, but the price of this power is to be a slave of what gives him this power.*

The intensity of the feelings, brought by a Twin Flame, completely knocks one off balance. For Twins, *"usual," "normal," "ordinary"* things are hardly possible between them. A man who controls everything and everyone, will run away from this hurricane of emotions. It will be like that until his Soul fully awakens and *the light in him becomes stronger than his ego and the need for control.*

Although you should not forget, Twins are always being watched by Higher Forces and this story is very far from its culmination.

I hope I was able to help you.

Sincerely yours...

Susan handed me the third sheet.

Dearest Susan,

Yes, I have received the photos and the dates of his and her birth. Thank you.

In my 22 years of practice, this is only the third case of Twin Flames I've seen. They are as rare as white peacocks. Between the two of them, she is much stronger in Spirit. She leads him with her love, like a lighthouse on a stormy sea. They have always been together and always will be on the Soul level. But in the framework of our three-dimensional reality, unfortunately, too many things separate them. He is logical, reasoning that there are many obstacles between them. Unfortunately, his Soul is asleep now and he does not hear its voice! Regrettably, as I see it, they have not physically met each other yet. The Dark will try to prevent that. Because as soon as they look into each other's eyes, *the CONNECTION will happen.* It will produce the vibration of incredible Force. If it happens, the Dark will lose its power over him and her. Because of that, their union is not yet possible. The Dark will simply not allow that.

In addition, he must wake up and make a conscious choice. He will need time for it. But if she, tired of fighting, abandons him, his Soul will lose its only chance to awaken and thus come back to her Power and *true Light*. She is very strong, and hopefully, this will not happen.

Yours sincerely....

The fourth page.

Dear Susan,

One more thing I would like to add to what I had said earlier. These two, as I mentioned, are chosen by the Higher Powers. They have shared many lifetimes together; they are much more than just a man and a woman for each other. He is very unhappy without her. She is the sacred light of his Soul. The one who makes him feel alive. The one who makes him feel the inspiration! Still, he has no intention to risk or change his life because of her. She, and this whole story of Twin Flames, seem like a fairy tale to him. He doesn't trust his feeling or believe her completely. Of course, they did not meet by accident, but were chosen for each other long before they were born. You asked me about the future. Unfortunately, there is a block. Their future is closed for me. When the answers are not apparent, we have to take it as it is.

Sincerely yours...

I finished reading and handed Susan the last page. Outside the window, the night was giving way to a new day. For a while, we were both silent.

"This is just a small part of the material I have gathered, Lala," she finally said. "But, I think you see the idea. Your path is a very tough one, girl. The chance of victorious love and your physical union with him, under the given circumstances, is negligible. But still, it's there! Lala, I believe in the two of you! I do, even if both of you do not! This story cannot end here! I do not believe that the Force of Light, as you call it, or God, as I call it, chose

363

both of you to walk this path so long and so far, so that it would end like this. No, Lala! I do not believe that! And I consider myself incredibly lucky and blessed because Fate has allowed me to be a part of this story of Eternal Love. Not fictitious. Not a mere myth. But a true one. A real true love story! I am endlessly grateful for that!"

Surprised, I looked into her shining eyes.

She continued, "Yes, Lala. About an hour ago, you told me that you consider it an honor to speak with the *Great Susan Malik*. And I will tell you this; I consider it an honor and a blessing to have met you and talked with you, to see your incredible eyes and Him in them—His Soul in them. Because before I met you, I have only seen you in his eyes. Now I have seen you both, two, but One. I am grateful for that! Very grateful!"

"Oh, Susan," I answered with a laugh, "Please! I am just an ordinary woman."

"Ok, *ordinary woman*, I will not embarrass you anymore. But I'm glad I could tell you all I wanted to tell you. Now, do you understand why everything is so complicated? Why is this all so not easy? Neither for you nor him."

"*A slave of the Lamp*," I said. "How did one of those people call it? He is a slave of the Lamp, like a genie. And this Lamp is his crazy life! *A Slave of Glory, Money, and Worship*. If he looks into my eyes, he will risk breaking free of this Lamp! What can I do here, Susan? There is nothing I can do! It's hopeless."

"Lala, both of you have chosen this path. Both of you have come to fulfill it. So this is not the end, my girl, only the continuation! You always say, '*Nothing ever ends, only continues!*'

"Lala, for all of us, who knew about you one way or another, life has changed a lot. You made us see things in an entirely different way, a way we never even thought possible. You have the power *to touch people deep inside*. No one who knew about you, or read what you have written, could stay untouched and unaffected. I will not tell you exactly how many people know about you, but those who do, have taken your words to their hearts. And I am one of them. I will give away one more little secret. *We are all on your side*, even though we are employees of Farhan. And I suspect he might be well aware of that. You have become a part of our lives and a part of who we are now. Again, we will never be the same because of you, your passion, strength, wisdom and endless love. None of us will ever be the same, including the one you share one Soul with, Your Twin, the great and almighty Farhan Ali.

"That's why I decided to tell you everything. I think *you need to cut off all contact with him completely.* Not only because he must stop using your talent and what you are creating, but also while being torn away from you, he can understand *who and what you are for him.* I have consulted the Seers. And they agree on it. As long as you 'feed' him with the energy of your love, he will not be able to fully realize why the two of you belong to each other. His Soul cannot fully awaken, while you are with him. *Be gone. Completely gone.* Let him face his Soul and, through the Mirror of it, see why the two of you belong together, who and what you two are for each other."

Silence reigned in the room again.

"I still can't believe that you have taken my side in this!" I finally said.

"Oh! Lala! Just please, don't tell Farhan!" she laughed. "And do not write about it in your books. And if you do write, change everything so that he never guesses that it was me. Otherwise, I will lose my job! But seriously, I want to ask you something, my Heavenly Angel. Yes, yes, I know!" she laughed again. "Those are your words! You called him this many times, when in fact, *the Heavenly Angel is you,* not him! So, tell me, Heavenly Angel. After all that you know now and what I have told you, how do you feel? I hope you do not hate him, do you?"

I sighed heavily.

"No, Susan, I don't think I can hate him, no matter what. But I feel wounded, hurt, mistreated, fallen, maybe much more than that. Of course, you have made it all a little easier for me since you have told me everything. You literally *saved me.* At some point in this crazy night, it felt like my heart would stop! But now, at least, I can breathe. I am very grateful to you, Susan! Endlessly grateful! Of course, continuing communication with him is totally out of the question. I have no intention to keep on playing his games. I am done with it! I will try to find my own path without him and walk it, hopefully with dignity. And he must find his own. I guess I have already told him everything that I needed to. It's time for me to go."

We both went to the window.

"Where is he staying?"

"At the hotel, a mile away from here."

"Good. I should be going already, Susan! Thank you for everything! From the bottom of my heart! Thank you!"

"Can I hug you?" She suddenly asked.

And we shared a strong, tight hug as if we were good friends forever. But then, we live thousands of lives. Who knows how many times this incredible woman and I have crossed paths; maybe it was her Soul recognizing mine.

"Hold on, darling! Hold on!" she said and led me to the exit, giving both of my hands a tight squeeze. "You are in my heart, Lala. In his too. I know it. No matter how hard it is to believe now. May your Angels guard and guide you!"

The doors of an elevator opened and closed. The hotel lobby was completely empty. The driver was still waiting for me near the entrance. I got inside the car and apologized to Patrick for keeping him waiting so long.

"Don't mention it, ma'am!" he answered me seriously. "This is my job!"

As the car glided smoothly through the predawn city, my mind again threw me back to the very first night I first found him. My whole life—all the years before finding him—I was hoping, waiting, dreaming. All these years after finding him—the same thing—hoping, waiting, dreaming. All my stupid attempts to appeal to his memory, all my letters, tales, stories, novels, advice on how to change the world, making it a little brighter, a little kinder, a little better, at least for somebody. My friendly jokes, irony, tenderness, words of love! *Love! LOVE!* It all was nothing. Nothing at all! Although wait, not entirely nothing. Those were the golden eggs of one dumb and blind golden goose. *Stupid and blind.*

What a strange joke of Gods. What an ill twist of Fate. All my life. *My whole life.* Fatherlessness, poverty, violence, trauma, pain, lack of love and acceptance, the indifference of loved ones, and my Fate. There was only one hope that lived inside me, in every cell, every breath, every heartbeat — *a boy and his familiar eyes.* So close and dear, so loved. *This boy cannot fail me.* He will find me, and everything will change. Or I will find him! And then, there will be a new, beautiful life! He will protect me. He will save me. He will heal me, understand me. He will love me. *Love me...*

I found that boy. And where am I now? What has changed? Nothing! Absolutely Nothing! Nothing has changed at all. I guess I'm just not worthy of either love or happiness. But I was happy, wasn't I? I was. For a little while, I was. So, I'm lying to myself. He made my heart skip a beat when he turned the world into the color of indigo. My boy has done that for me. *My boy who has never been mine.*

It was I who created and wrote him tales and stories during sleepless nights. It was I, criticizing or admiring him, entertaining him, loving him. It was I who cried with joy, looking at him, standing at the Ocean, or dressed in royal blue. I was the one who begged for signs from nature and guidance from the Seers and his mother. I was the one dancing at the ocean shore, singing in the rain, extending my hands trying to touch the rainbow. It was I who...

I'm fucking crazy! Blind, stupid, and crazy! I do not curse, but it seems the most appropriate word for me now.

There is only one positive moment in this whole story. *It is a true and authentic one.* Like Susan said about it. Maybe this story could prevent someone from being as endlessly stupid as me. He is an actor.

He is an actor through and through. The best one in the world! What chance did I have not to believe him? None. Besides, *I wanted to believe!*

So, I believed. *I believed him with all I had in me.* And now I am dealing with the consequences. Golden goose. Stupid. Blind. In love.

It turns out that I was working for the movie empire of Farhan Ali. Instead of a salary, He paid me with sweet selfies and videos of him wearing royal blue. I wanted to cry but instead, I laughed bitterly. What else was left for me to do? The situation was like some of those old tragicomedies. You can cry, you can laugh or do both at the same time, anything goes. I could say, of course, I gave my all to him. I threw myself to his feet. I was walking on sharpened blades, like a mermaid from the story of Andersen. Poor little Mermaid.

But once again, I found him, wrote him, and was dying of love and happiness when he responded to me. I walked on clouds and lived in Heaven while he was reading my book, my stories, tales, letters. He read what I wrote! *HIM! The MEGA star, almighty King,* the god of cinema, the legend, the phenomenon, the owner of a million hearts. *HE read what I, some little simple woman, wrote.* And He not only read it, *but he RESPONDED to it!!* Oh! I should be happy! I should be jumping and dancing with joy, damn it! I should buy myself a paper crown and wear it at all times. *I had grabbed the attention of SUCH a man!* Hurray to me! Bravo to me! Bravo! Viva la Diva! Damn it!

But I am crying. Crying. Why? Because I'm not just a "little simple woman", a "little nobody," who was lucky enough to be noticed by some big movie star guy. I'm not just a single mother with not even a normal job and reliable source of income. I am his Twin Flame. But I am not just his Twin Flame. I am also a woman. A woman, he hurt very badly! Was he just playing? Yes, he was just playing. Did he fall in Love? Oh, no. Susan's words of him loving me, *I believed not a bit.* Probably he was just fascinated. Not in Love but fascinated with his new toy. An exclusive one. Exotic. And most important, *profitable.* Very profitable, as it turned out to be. Why the hell do I live like a tramp when my ideas are so expensive? Just golden they are, damn it. Golden enough to make the heart throb, Farhan Ali, present me with several of his mesmerizing smiles and the words, *"I dream of seeing you."* How hard is it for an actor to play Love? It must be the easiest role of all. The most familiar one. And me? *Golden goose. Stupid. Blind. In Love.*

My sobbing turned into laughter again. I read it somewhere that one particular characteristic of a self-sufficient woman is talking to herself. Funny. I thought I was full of insecurities. And here I am, laughing and crying at the same time, like a very independent, self-sufficient woman. What a brilliant discovery!

A couple of blocks from the hotel, I asked the driver to stop the car. I said I wanted to take a walk.

"Ma'am! I cannot do it! The area here is very unsafe! Even during the daytime, it's not at all advisable to walk around here, not to mention the night!"

"It's almost morning, Patrick! Stop the car, please! I am a self-sufficient, strong, independent woman!" I said, trying to hide sarcasm, pouring out of my every word. "I will certainly be able to stand up for myself. Please, stop the car, Patrick!"

I saw the shock in his eyes and smiled as I hoped charmingly. "I just want to get some fresh air."

Patrick obediently stopped the car. I got out and walked down the dimly lit streets. Some of the homeless were asleep in their sleeping bags. The street was quite lively. Representatives of all the strangest types of human beings talked with one another, smoking weed, injecting some kind of muck, vital to them, down their veins, discussing something. They were living their normal every day and every night life. Strangely, their appearance no longer scared me. It seemed I was no longer fearful of anything. The thing I was afraid of the most, had already happened. I walked past them and apparently, the look I had on my face, somehow made them silently let me walk ahead, until one of them blocked my path.

"Heeeeeeeey! Yaaa Baaaaaabyyyy!" He said, drawing out vowels! "Why yaaa so saaad? Hell, there is no face on yaaa! Who huurt yaa? You tell Johnny who huurt yaa! I'll tear his head off! Come here yaa baaby! Come! Have yaa a seat! Tell me what happened ta yaa?"

The way Johnny looked was utterly unimaginable. His hair and beard were so dirty and tangled that they had turned into a solid gray mass. He was wearing dirty jeans and, for some reason, several T-shirts, one on top of the other. His eyes, though, were an amazingly bright blue color, and on his addled, dirty face, they seemed to live their own life.

He put his arm around me and led me to his dirty sleeping bag.

Farhan again appeared in my vision. He was putting on his jacket and talking with that same beautiful blonde. "I can't say when exactly, Mel. You know my crazy schedule!" He came closer to her, put a hand on her neck, and gently kissed her cheek. *"See you later, my fairy."*

This image hit me like a whip across the chest. It knocked the rest of the air out of my lungs and girded me with pain. So sudden, sharp and unbearable that I screamed and pressed both hands to my chest. Johnny couldn't understand what had just happened, but he thought things must be horrible.

"Heeeey! Baaabe! Baaaby!!! Hey guys! This gaaal raiiit heere in really bad shape! Doonn yaa worry gaal, yaal be all raaaait! Come over heeer! Come!"

The next moment, I remember, I was sitting on Jonny's sleeping bag. Dirty gray faces around me, with shapeless hair, unkempt beards, and weird shining eyes. They were looking at me with genuine sympathy. Johnny came up with a brilliant idea that maybe I needed a "dose" to feel better.

"Mackeeey!" He turned to one of the guys who looked from thirty to seventy years old. Mackey was smoking something.

"Mackey, yaaa dameet moron! Yaaa give the gaal a smoke, will yaa? Yaa see the gaal ees really baad!"

Mackey handed the cigarette, or whatever it was, to Johnny, who, in his turn, passed it down to me.

"Heeere! Take it baaaaby! There is still enough foo yaa! Heeere, yaa go! Easy, gaal, have a smoke and tell us eeverything yaa have! What happened to yaa? I saaay ya gaal, we kick his ass, thaat moron who huurt yaa! Just tell us whaats his name! We will find eem, don' ya worry! Don' mind we are like... simple guys! We know how to kick aaasses of 'em morons (he used much worse words), who huuut good gaals like yaa! Come on! Smoke and tell us all!"

I almost burst out laughing just thinking how those guys, standing and sitting around me, would go and try to kick the ass of a Movie Staaa Farhan Ali! That would be worth a look! Such a pity they would not be able to even come close to him! But still, I have no doubt that they would go and tell him everything they thought of him!

"Yeah, gaal! We go to thaaat jeckass of yaaars, and tell eeem, "Hey, yaa snake! Ya come outaheere and tell us, why yaa huut thaa good gaaal?! Come on! Have a smoke naaw, dooon' yaa worry! Yaa no need to pay. It's on us!"

I held in my fingers a cigarette with marijuana, or the devil knew what was in it.

I looked at it. *Why not? Maybe it will be my cure for stupidity? Maybe it will ease my pain? It is not a big deal to smoke weed once in a lifetime, right? It does not matter, after all, where it will take me! I am no longer here anyway. I do not exist anymore. I am nobody! I am nothing!* I could still see with my inner sight the recent scene in all of its cold cruelty and splendor. His fingers caressing the perfect skin of the perfect blond woman and his low beautiful voice saying to her, "See you soon, my fairy!" *Fairy! Probably the hundred and first of his! Oh, Guardians of Fates! How painful! How unbearably painful. Hurts! Hurts like a bitch!! I want to forget. Forget everything! Forget!* So, I brought the cigarette to my lips.

And suddenly, I hear, loud and clear, my son Nicky's voice. (I can't explain it! I just can't!)

"Mooom?"

I jumped to my feet, looking around. But how could Nicky be in California? He was not here; he couldn't be! But I heard his voice, I did! Nothing could convince me otherwise! Now I understand that it was his voice, the voice of my child that saved me.

I gave back the cigarette to Johnny and said, "Thank you, guys! Thank you so very much! I will go now; I am fine, I swear! And you're right! He's a snake, my boyfriend, I mean, ex-boyfriend, I guess. He is much younger than me. You know, I thought it was special. I thought he was different… Then I got pregnant and told him about it. And guess what? He just vanished! He was just, gone, you know. Did not explain anything. Did not call. Did not leave a note. Just 'Poof,' gone! I thought something had happened to him! Found out from his friends where he was, and I flew here to see him. I thought, he loved me, you know. But he told me, 'That is your problem, baby! I don't need no kids, no family, and no shit like this!' So, to hell with him! I can handle it myself! I will not smoke weed, guys! Thank you! I don't want to harm the baby! I need to go back to my hotel! Thank you! You are the best! Just the best! Thank you, all! Gotta go!"

The guys had completely dumbfounded looks!

"I ssuppose, heees rich, thaat snake of yaars! Theyaa aall jerks! So, he just used yaa and kicked yaa out! Tell us whaaat his name will ya?! Wee find eem!"

"No, guys! I can't tell you his name. He is indeed a rich snake! Do not worry about me. I will be alright! I have to go now, guys, thank you!"

But they did not let me go alone! Three of them, including Johnny and Mackey, volunteered to be my escort!

"We're just keepeen watcheen. So, nothing bad happens to yaa!" Johnny explained to me. I was escorted to the hotel's door by those I was terrified of only yesterday and fled from like a plague! How strange and unpredictable the world and life can be! We run to those who hurt us. We run away from those who can heal our wounds. How strange it is.

I went up to my room where Lena was still sleeping quietly and peacefully. I stroked her hand. *Kind and wonderful girl. Thank you. Thank you for being here with me!* I lay on the bed over the bedspread, didn›t bother to undress, and finally closed my eyes. What an insane and endlessly long night! As soon I closed my eyes, I fell into a dream. I found myself on the same shore where he and I had always met.

He was standing with his back to me, looking at the water.

Two feelings were fighting in me. Pain and resentment made me want to turn and run away from him, but my Soul was flying to him as it has always been. After all that had happened in the past several hours, it remained unchanged. He looked completely lost and impossibly, unimaginably lonely. I went up to him and stood next to him. He looked at me and again stared back at the water.

Finally, he spoke, "Do you hate me?"

"No," I answered after a moment of silence.

"Have I lost your Love?"

My silence was his answer.

"I have."

"No." I finally answered with a heavy sigh. "Whatever you and your physical body do, will never affect my Love for you, Ram. This life on Earth is all temporary. There, the Dark Ones control you. You are in your Shadow, Ram. But without them, we cannot grow. *Overcoming their influence, we become stronger, deeper, and wiser. Without them, our development would have stopped.* Your Soul, in its essence, is eternal and pure, my Love! The Soul receives a body to grow. To become stronger. I love your Soul, Ram! I love you forever. Nothing will change it! And you love me too. But the "love" you have for me on Earth *is NOT love. It is greed.* You want me to live for you only. Create for you, write for you. Breathe for you and worship you. Be dust at your feet. You want me to continue giving you all I have and more. You want me to be happy with just giving and serving you with my every breath. *That shall be no more, Ram!* As long as you are in your shadow, you can only dream of me. That is all you are going to have. Dreams! When you are your Soul, and not your greedy Ego, I do love you, Ram! I do."

"Then say it to me."

"I love you."

"You know what I think, Lala? I would have died a long time ago without your Love. My Soul would have plunged into the full darkness."

"I doubt I would ever let that happen. You know me. I am as stubborn as 101 mules, as you have been telling me for many lives! Or maybe, I am just as stubborn as you!

"Tell me, Ram. What would you do if I were next to you now, there, in the physical world?"

"I would bury my face in your neck and breathe you. I would hold you in the ring of my arms and would not let you go."

"What else?"

"I would kiss you."

"How?"

"Softly, gently, very tenderly, and very slowly. I would savor your lips, Lala! I love them!"

"No! I love yours! I am crazy about them! Addicted to them and losing my mind over them! I think you have the most beautiful cupid bow in the Multiverse!"

"Same as yours!"

We look at each other and start laughing. The pain melts inside me like last year's snow. I come closer to him. I raise my eyes to look straight into his. He takes my face in his palms and looks straight into mine.

"I'm tired, Lala. All that fight, out there on Earth. I'm tired."

"I know, my Love. Me too! So tired! I am beyond Exhausted!"

"Lala, it's hard to fight them. They know how to control us!"

"The Dark Ones? *Of course, they do.* They use different approaches for each of us, though. With you, they use *wealth, glory, power, women!* With me, they use *sadness, hopelessness and helplessness, sending tons of fears and doubts.* So much that I can hardly breathe. Sometimes I feel that breathing is the only thing I have enough strength to keep on doing, Ram."

"And yet, you are much stronger than me. You constantly give me your Love, your power, your Light!"

"What else did you expect me to do, my Love? Is there any other way I can make you stronger? How else can I give your Soul the strength to wake up and shine her true, powerful Light?"

"Just love me, no matter what. Just love me."

Lena's voice brought me back to reality. "Alla!!!!! Wake up! Coffee!" She said, placing a fragrant paper cup in my hand.

"You know what? The hell with him! With your idiot Flame! The hell with him! Let those who didn't get us cry and sob!!! We are beautiful! We are... Ok, get up! Get dressed! I will take you to an Italian restaurant! According to TripAdvisor, San Francisco has the best Italian restaurants! Do you like the carpaccio? Have you ever had it? Actually, it does not matter! Come on! Hurry! It's my treat! To hell with your Twin. Whatever! *HELL WITH HIM!!! He doesn't deserve you! A coward!* We'll find you a guy, much better than him! The best one! Get dressed! Let's go!"

Chapter 43

Going Home

Book of Answers

Our last day in San Francisco, I remember it as a blur. I don't know if you have ever been in such a state. You look at everything around you, and it feels as if it is happening to somebody else, and you are just watching in a cinema seat! It was such an overload for me—events, emotions, people, thoughts. I was so exhausted I became somewhat disconnected. I lived through the day in a salutary blurry haze. My brain reacted lethargically to the faces and objects around me. We indeed went to an Italian restaurant, but I do not remember the taste of the food. My Soul existed separately from my body. It seemed to soar above me and above this strange city, which had brought a big, brutal ending to my life-long love story. At least, I thought so.

And those timeless questions dominated all other feelings, repeating themselves in my head over and over again: *What am I doing here? Who am I? What is the purpose of my wandering around this earth? Was I living in a dream that was my reality? Or is my reality just a dream? What is real, out of all the things that surround us? Maybe the material world, which our eyes can see, is just an illusion, a matrix! Perhaps the truth is entirely different. What we see through the eyes of our immortal Soul, what we feel with it, THAT is real! All material is going to be gone. Only what is eternal will stay.*

Feelings. Emotions. Compassion. Love. Those stay with us! As part of our very Essence, that will travel with us from life to life, guiding us and leading us! Why is that so hard to see, to feel, to understand? Why is it so painful to wake up in the real world for me when I DO understand all that?

The day passed by quickly. The night passed just as fast, with lightning speed. I vaguely remember how we checked in and got on the plane to fly back to our hometown. The plane quickly gained altitude. The pilot's voice informed us what time we would arrive at our destination and some more irrelevant, for me at that moment, information. I was sitting, silently staring into space. I guess it looked like I was staring intently at the back of a chair just in front of me.

Lena's voice finally penetrated the fog in my mind. She seemed to have been trying to tell me something for several minutes. "Do you plan just to continue sitting silently and staring into space, Alla? Have you even heard anything I just said?"

I looked at her, totally embarrassed. She was not to blame for anything; she did not deserve such treatment. She was the only person who was near me. She was the only person helping me go through losing my wings and falling crushed onto the ground.

"Forgive me, please. I'm not the best company right now. I don't even know how to explain it. It is like I am here, but I am not here at the same time. As if lost among the worlds. I have lost my way. I have lost the thread. I don't know who I am, what I am, why am I…"

"Yes, I understand. I mean, I do but of course, not totally. Not like you. I so much wish I could change anything, but… Okay! Look. I will let you be and leave you alone with your thoughts and feelings and the Forces that lead you and guide you. If that is what you want, of course. It's only a pity that I haven't thought of bringing a book with me. You don't happen to have any with you, do you? We still have several hours of flight. It would be nice to read something."

"A book?" And it dawned on me. I had a small book, one that easily fits into my purse. But I had completely forgotten about it! When I was leaving home the night of our flight to San Francisco, it was around midnight. The house was sleeping, and I quietly came out of my room without turning on the light. Suddenly, I stopped. The flight was to last six hours, so I decided it would be a good idea to take something to read with me. I went back to the bookshelf, and in the dark, I simply grabbed the first one my hand could touch, without even looking at the title. I put the book into my bag and completely forgot about its existence. Only now I remembered and took it out of my purse.

It turned out to be one of the books of my favorite author, Paolo Coelho and called *Brida*.

I had no idea what it was about. I had seen it on a shelf in a bookstore recently and bought it. I brought it home but somehow had never had a chance to read it. It was with me the whole time we were in San Francisco, even in the theater when I was looking at him. It was with me when I spoke with Susan. It had been with me every moment of these two insane days and nights as a *silent witness to all the events*. I pulled it out of my bag and handed it to Lena.

She took it and began to read with interest. She also adored Coelho.

The fatigue and events of the last two days finally took their toll on me. Closing my eyes, I fell into the blessed embrace of Morpheus. But what I saw in my dream was creepy and cold. I was wandering through a thick, cold night fog. I was frightened and chilled to my very bones. I was wearing something white that looked like a burial garment. In the distance, a female voice mournfully sang a strange, terrifying, and at the same time, somehow beautiful song with the following words:

You are wearing a white dress, just like a sweet and innocent bride, but he will not come for you. Death will be holding you tight; your Soul is now doomed and lost. Lost. Lost. The snow will be cold and deep. Deep. Deep. His Soul is not waking up; he will be forever asleep. Forever asleep. Forever asleep...

I am walking through this terrible icy fog and calling his name. I feel how I am becoming weaker and weaker with every step. I am calling him by his

377

name, the name he had in that life where we were so happy, where I left so early and promised to find him. *"Ram! Ram! Ram! "*

But he does not hear me. He does not hear me.

"Alla! Are you okay?!"

I suddenly woke up, apparently pale as death, and with an expression of horror frozen in my eyes. "I am fine," I replied, panting. "I am okay; it is nothing! Just a nightmare. A crappy nightmare!"

To escape from what I just saw and calm my breath, I nodded at the book in her hands. "How is the book? Interesting? Do you like it?"

"Ah! Yes! Very interesting! I can't believe it. *It is about you two!* Did you intentionally take it with you? Did you want to show it to him?"

For a moment, I froze, unable to understand what she was talking about. Finally, the meaning of her words penetrated my mind. *"A book about the two of us? What are you talking about?"*

"I am talking about this book you gave me! It is about Soulmates! When he wrote it, the concept of 'Twin Flames' did not exist yet. He calls them 'Soulmates—Halves of One.' This book is about you. Even the woman described here is almost exactly like you! Not on the outside, of course, but inside! He even writes about the fall of *Château de Montségur* in France! How those two hundred and twenty Cathars, men and women, were burned at the stake on 16 March 1244 by the Catholic Church Inquisition!!! All of them at the same time! Such horror is almost impossible even to imagine! You have told me so much about it, and he writes of it here! But mainly this book is about this young woman, Brida. She is learning the secrets of magic, ancient sacred knowledge. Looking for the answers, she follows her own path and meets her other half! I swear at moments, it feels as if Coelho wrote it using you as his inspiration!"

She stopped for a moment studying my face, then asked, "Wait a minute. *You didn't KNOW? Haven't you read this book???*"

I just shook my head. *No.* She silently handed it to me. I opened it randomly, and the first lines I saw were these:

"'I want to learn about magic,' said the girl. The Magus looked at her. Faded jeans, T-shirt, the challenging look adopted by all shy people precisely when it's least needed. 'I must be twice her age,' he thought. And despite this, he knew that he had met his Soulmate."[11]

I felt goosebumps on my neck! I frantically turned the pages. What my eyes saw shook me deeply, to my very core. How could it even be possible? It was as if I was reading *about myself and him*, about Farhan. If apart from being a Twin Flame, I, as everyone else, also had soul mates, soul-guides, and soul-teachers, then I truly believed for quite a long time that *Paolo Coelho was definitely one of mine.*

When I saw words about Tarot cards, I remembered my deep longing for those ancient symbols to open their profound secrets to me. But for so many years, it hadn't happened, as if they were hiding from me. I read about them in many books. I often held them in my hands, but I still did not ask them any questions. It seemed as if I wanted them to find their way to me and reveal their deep mysteries. My eyes continued to run across the text. The words were insanely familiar, and at the same time, I was reading them for the first time in my life.

The next page I read made my heart tremble.

"We form part of what the alchemists call the Anima Mundi, the Soul of the World," said Wicca. The truth is that if Anima Mundi were merely to keep dividing, it would keep growing, but it would also become gradually weaker. That is why, as well as dividing into two, we also find ourselves. And that process of finding ourselves is called Love. Because when a soul divides, it always divides into a male part and a female part."[12]

---

11   Paulo Coelho, Brida, (Hammersmith, HarperCollins, 2009), 9.
12   Paulo Coelho, Brida, 37-38

Divides into a male part and a female part, he clearly writes about *Twin Flames!*
But he calls them "Soulmates."

> *"But how will I know who my Soulmate is?" Brida felt that this was one*
> *of the most important questions she had ever asked in her life.*
> *"By taking risks," she said to Brida. "By risking failure, disappointment,*
> *disillusion, but never ceasing in your search for Love. As long as you keep*
> *looking, you will triumph in the end."*[13]
> *"The essence of Creation is one and one alone," she said. "And that*
> *essence is called Love. Love is the force that brings us back together, in*
> *order to condense the experience dispersed in many lives and many parts*
> *of the world.*
> *"We are responsible for the whole Earth because we do not know where*
> *they might be. Those Soulmates we were from the beginning of time.*
> *If they are well, then we, too, will be happy. If they are not well, we*
> *will suffer, however unconsciously, a portion of their pain. Above all,*
> *though, we are responsible for re-encountering, at least once in every*
> *incarnation, the Soulmate who is sure to cross our path. Even if it is only*
> *for a matter of moments, because those moments bring with them a Love*
> *so intense that it justifies the rest of our days."*[14]

Familiar words and familiar situations, describing other people and
someone else's life, but it was about me. Paolo Coelho knew and wrote about
something that had always been a part of me, if not the *whole of me*. This
knowledge has lived in me for as long as I remembered. First, it appeared
in my lucid dreams. Then it was born out of feelings. Out of conversations
with beings, I called the Light Ones. The Guardians. The Keepers. Later,
when the Internet appeared and so many resources got accessible, I found
confirmation of what I had known for so long there as well. Twin Flames,

---

13   Paulo Coelho, Brida, 38-39
14   Paulo Coelho, Brida, 39-40

many years ago called Soulmates, were mentioned by many philosophers, researchers, writers, who were also Seers. I was not alone in what I knew. There were so many of us. But still, many were afraid to talk about it openly. I kept turning the pages.

> "We can also allow our Soulmate to pass us by, without accepting him or her, or even noticing. Then we will need another incarnation in order to find that Soulmate. And because of our selfishness, we will be condemned to the worst torture humankind ever invented for itself: loneliness."[15]

Of course, Lena was right. When he wrote this book, the name "Twin Flames" didn't exist yet. The "two halves" were simply called "Soulmates." But now we know this isn't exactly right. "Soulmates" are something different. In one of my favorite books by Michael Newton, *Journey of Souls*, he writes about "Soul groups. "It would be similar to having a family in the realm of the Spirits, similar to the one we have here on Earth. Soul groups would consist of different numbers of Souls. Some were small and others big families. These groups have known each other for a very long time. They often incarnate together, taking different roles in each life for mutual development. They can be members of our family, siblings, cousins, parents, best friends, teachers, husbands, wives, and much more. That is why Soulmates can be many, each with their particular role in our current incarnation. Soulmates are not One Spirit, incarnated in two bodies. Soulmates are like apples from the same tree! While the Twin Flames is one apple, divided into two halves. But in this book, as we already know, Paolo Coelho calls two halves, Soulmates or Soul Mates.

You know, I cannot even tell you how many hundreds of times, while reading the books of this author, I caught myself thinking that I was reading about my own feelings, my own fears, doubts, searches for the truth, dreams. How many times, reading his books, I told myself that I should learn to

---

15   Paulo Coelho, Brida, 40

talk to people like he does. Help them see the eternal truth gently and unobtrusively, just by making them THINK, *look deep inside, see the Light, see the answers.* As he writes in *The Alchemist,*

> *The Boy reached through to the Soul of the World and saw that it was a part of the Soul of God. And he SAW that the Soul of God was HIS OWN SOUL!"*[16]

These are the most powerful words ever written.

I felt almost physical pain while reading negative opinions about his work from unknown "writers" who know better "how to write such books" and, of course, from religious fanatics of all kinds. Oh, I just can't stand fanaticism! Maybe this is one of my life lessons in this incarnation: learning to have compassion for them. To recognize that everyone has their own path to the truth, to the Light. Their own path to awakening. How far am I from being fully awakened? It looks like I am still a very significant distance from it.

My eyes went back to the words.

> *"'But how will I know who my Soulmate is?' Brida felt that this was one of the most important questions she had ever asked in her life.*
> *"'By taking risks,' she said to Brida. 'By risking failure, disappointment, disillusion…'"*[17]

Well, one could hardly blame me for not doing that. I took risks all the time. When I flew to San Francisco, I knew that such a scenario was possible. I just didn't want to think of it! I did not want to believe it.

---

16   Paulo Coelho, The Alchemist, 154
17   Paulo Coelho, Brida, 38-39

It would be completely senseless to think that the book ended up in my bag "*coincidentally.*" No, it didn't accidentally accompany me every minute of these last two days, which seemed to be an eternity! I kept randomly turning the pages as if someone invisible was speaking to me through them.

> "*The whole of man's life on the face of Earth can be summed up by that search for his Soulmate. He may pretend to be running after wisdom, money, or power, but none of that matters. Whatever he achieves will be incomplete if he fails to find a Soulmate.*"[18]

Those are my words; those are my thoughts, feelings, beliefs and my whole life! Paolo Coelho. He was not my Twin, unfortunately. But I was sure we were coming from the same place, somewhere in the endless levels of Eternity! Some Force, watching from above, gave me this book to be by my side when I was falling from my Heaven. Why? To give me answers? Yes. I believed in all he had written! No matter how high we soar, no matter what heights we reach, we will never find true happiness until we find the *one.* And after we do, this sacred eternal Love will open all the secrets of the Universe to us. *Love is the only bridge, the only force, capable of uniting us with the higher aspects of ourselves, with Absolute. With God.* But then, why had I ended up so broken?

I continued turning pages.

> "*Don't bother trying to explain your emotions. Live everything as intensely as you can and keep whatever you felt as a gift from God. If you think that you won't be able to stand a world in which living is more important than understanding, then give up magic now. The best way*

---

18   Paolo Coelho, Brida, 62

to destroy the bridge between the visible and the invisible is by trying to explain your emotions."[19]

This Great Love is beyond time and space.

Is this the answer? Just take this all as a gift? Did I need this pain for something? For what? For me to experience what I was afraid of and stop being afraid? I turned several pages.

> *"She feared pain, loss and separation. These things were inevitable on the path to love, and the only way of avoiding them was by deciding not to take the path at all. In order NOT to suffer, you had to renounce Love."*[20]

I was already on this path. I have been walking this path for a very, very long time. Could I now walk away from it? Is it even possible to leave this path? Do I have any choice at all? At least any?

I turned several more pages.

> *"It's true that I feel unworthy. I always think the spiritual search was made for people better than me."*[21]

As they say, hitting the nail on the head! Why is it me–the Twin Flame, the other half of this Lord of the Blue Screen, this great sovereign of hundreds of millions of hearts? This man can both lie and inspire, save and destroy, create and shatter into pieces? Could there be some kind of mistake? How can I, an ordinary woman, be the only one capable of turning him to Light? Bring him back to his own essence! How can it be me? How?

---

19 Paulo Coelho, Brida, 87
20 Paulo Coelho, Brida, 97
21 Paulo Coelho, Brida, 102

I turn over several pages.

> *"Why are you wasting your time with me?"*
> *"Because you are my Soulmate! You are a Half of me!"*[22]

Maybe this is the whole point? Is that what this is all about? The only explanation? *"Because you are a half of me!"* So, what am I to do now? Keep on going? No way! Right now, I didn't want that! That wasn't the way I imagined *the reunion of the two halves of one Soul* would be! Not at all! So, what should I do now? I turn several pages more:

> *"At some point in our lives, we all meet our Soulmate and recognize him or her,"* he went on. *"If I were not a Magus and couldn't see the point of light above your left shoulder, it would take a little longer for me to accept you, but you would fight for me, and one day I would see the special light in your eyes."*[23]

So, does it mean I have to *fight for him*? So, he can see the *Light in my eyes*? King of Wizards. Magus… Unawakened one. Fight more? *More?* No! I had enough of this fight. *I have lost, haven't I?*

"*We are responsible for the Universe because we are the Universe. Love is the key to understanding all the secrets! Only Love.*"

Yes, I understood that. I have always understood that! But what were my chances of making him understand that? And most importantly, does he even *need* this knowledge and this Love? Does he even *want* it? Why did he do that? Why he dragged me through all this hell, which almost killed me. I survived and was still alive, but I was not sure of that! I turned several pages and froze.

---

22   Paulo Coelho, Brida, 112
23   Paulo Coelho, Brida, 114

"His heart was afraid. As he looked up at the clouds or down at the precipice, he realized that this woman was the most important thing in his life; that she was the explanation, the sole reason for the existence of those rocks, that sky, that winter. If she were not there with him, it wouldn't matter if all the angels of Heaven came flying down to comfort him-Paradise would make no sense."[24]

I smiled bitterly. I would *love* that to be at least *partially* true. But I did not believe it anymore; I did not believe those words for just one reason. You do not hurt the one who is *"the explanation, the sole reason for the existence of those rocks, that sky, that winter."* No, you don't... But he could! And he did! I turned several more pages.

"He looked up at the sky, still full of low clouds. God was the God of the Brave. And He would understand him because the brave are those who make decisions despite their fear, who are tormented by the Devil every step of the way and gripped by anxiety about their every action, wondering if they are right or wrong. And yet, nevertheless, they act. They do so because they also believe in miracles."[25]

Oh, another "hitting the nail on the head!" So, maybe instead of feeling down and broken, I need to feel proud of myself? How more accurate those words could ever be. *"And yet, nevertheless, they act. They do so because they also believe in miracles."* Yes. True. I was this weird creature who kept believing in miracles despite anything and I mean *anything* in life, even when miracles did not happen. Or maybe, they did happen but not how I wanted them to be. Maybe this whole situation will open me to some new depth of what I can handle. Of how much I can forgive. Maybe those changes in him, Susan mentioned, were indeed the *miracles* I have created with my Love

---

24 Paulo Coelho, Brida, 162
25 Paulo Coelho, Brida, 260

for him. Even if I failed, maybe I still won. Maybe because of my bleeding heart, I simply cannot see how much I gained. Right now, I only see my loss. I turned the page.

"Love was the only bridge between the visible and the invisible known to everyone. It was the only effective language for translating the lessons that the Universe taught to human beings every day".[26]

How few of us really believed that? How many understood? People, blinded by greed, envy, and thirst for power, or simply their attempt to survive, how often in the everyday fight for a piece of the sky, did we think of that? I did think of that and believed that. And had my heart shattered to a million pieces. Yes. I understand. But I do not anymore. Yes, I see. But I do not anymore.

I put the book aside, deciding to read it at home carefully. But then I changed my mind and took it into my hands. I closed my eyes. If this book had all the answers for me, it has one more. I had lost my way, and I simply needed to know what I should do next? What? With that question, I opened the book. These were the words I saw.

"Now listen to me," said Wicca sternly. "Every day from today, at an hour of your choosing, sit down alone at a table and spread the tarot deck as I did, completely at random. Don't try to understand anything. Simply study the cards. They will teach you all you need to know for the moment."

"The pictures seem so simple," she thought. A woman forcing open the mouth of a lion, a cart pulled by two mysterious animals, a man sitting before a table covered with sundry objects. She had been taught that the deck was a book, a book in which the Divine Wisdom had noted down the main changes that take place during our journey through life.

---

26 Paulo Coelho, Brida, 261

But its author, knowing that humanity learned more easily from vice than from virtue, had arranged for this sacred book to be transmitted across the generations in the form of a game. The deck was an invention of the gods".[27]

So, here is my answer. As clear as it even can be! I think the time has come for me to fully open the door, leading me to the path of knowing and understanding the seventy-eight card symbols created by Gods and given to us as the symbols *to understand ourselves and the world around us better.* But what if they do not want to reveal their secrets to me? This magical book tells me they will. So be it. I will try, and I will not put it off anymore! The time has come.

My dearest Paolo Coelho! From my small world to the wide one of yours, I pass over my deepest and most sincere gratitude and send you my Love and my Light! Your books have helped me so much! Brida became a silent witness of another turning point in my life. It gave me the answers I so much needed and warmed up my heart. I no longer feel so lost. Thank you. Please, keep on shining brightly, helping us see the Light in our Dark Nights of the Soul. We have so many of those during our lifetime. May your path be long, happy, joyful, and blessed by the True Force of Light!

---

27   Paulo Coelho, Brida, 43

Chapter 44

Home. The Curse

The plane gently landed. I was going home, carrying a broken heart in my chest, which at first I had to hide from my all-seeing son Nicholas. I would try to reassemble it again using my kids, everyday worries, and little joys of life. Also, I would have to learn to live without my great idea of rebuilding the world and this "Twin Flame's Mission" story.

Alas, my attempt to hide something from Nicholas turned out to be as impossible as awakening my famous Twin. He easily *read* me as if I was an open book the moment he looked at me.

"Mooom! Where have you been? You said you were going to Miami for job training. But I do not believe you! You were not in Miami! Something happened, right? I can see it, Moom! Just tell me the truth! I think this has something to do with *HIM, right? Am I right?*"

I really wanted to lie, but he easily sees a lie, especially when it comes to me. So, what's the point of lying?

"I flew to San Francisco, son. Farhan wrote to me that he wanted to see me. I thought we could meet for at least a few minutes, you know. Maybe look into each other's eyes, have a word, or two. But..." I fell silent.

"But? But what? *He got scared and ran, didn't he!*"

I was dumbfounded. Did he guess the reason for Farhan's behavior or read my thoughts?

"Nicky! How? How did you...."

"Mooom! Everything is written on your face! So, this is exactly, what happened, right?"

"Yes. Yes, you are absolutely right." I was ashamed to even raise my head. I felt like a little stupid county girl, questioned by her strict farmer-daddy after returning from her first party with alcohol and classmates. "I can't even imagine how you guessed, but you are absolutely right! So, I flew there for nothing."

I sighed heavily. I raised my head and looked into his eyes. Well, this is life. Sometimes our children are much wiser than us, while we behave like little children. "I follow my Soul! I believe in this! I see no obstacles! *Love is leading me! Love is on my side! I am a Twin Flame!*" There is an old song with these words, "It wasn't that hard for him to deceive me. I often do deceive myself." I think those in Love right now and those who loved at least once in their lifetime, understand me pretty well. And if you are a Twin Flame, finding after years of waiting and searching your other half, you would not only understand but shake your head agreeing, *with a heavy sigh and a sad smile on your face.*

When you, with every particle of your very existence, are deeply in Love, you do not listen to others. You do not heed anyone's warnings or reasoning. Sometimes you even curse all those who dare talk against your Love or do not wish, as you think, to understand you! You love, and you believe, he loves you too! And now, you are no longer even a human! Oh, no! *You are a great Magician!* You are a *Sorcerer! A Magus!* The Elements, the Spirits, and the worlds are all within your power. Yes, you are all that! But also, you are something else!

You are a slave! Yes, just a slave. You do not even *belong to yourself* anymore. But you can't see it or *refuse to see it.* You love, and you believe that you are loved! You are happy. You are in the heavens, walking above the clouds and everyone else…

And the next moment, *you are thrown from your Heaven and broken and shattered to a million pieces!* You are defeated. *Humiliated. Ashamed. Crushed. Destroyed.* And no one can help you or heal you. You are alone in your grief. *Alone.* Your non-awakened Twin has run. He flew away like a bird. He has the right, his reasons and his own well-established life. Both of you, in most cases, are of mature age. But he behaves like a "normal and reasonable" person, unlike you. Whether his actions are noble or vile, whether hurting you and going against his own Soul is the right or wrong thing to do – we are not to discuss here. Usually, *he gives you hope, and then he takes it away.* But at least, from a "normal" point of view, he has some kind of logic. While everything you do, from the same point of view, you act like a senseless, foolish child.

And what to do, after you have lost your wings and fallen from Heaven? There are many options. You might give up and admit defeat, silently and secretly drop tears from time to time and wait for your next incarnation. Or you can try to awaken your Twin, no matter what, with a very slim to none chance of that ever happening. You can go to the mountains or the forest. You can go to a monastery, meditate or pray for his joy and happiness and for all of humanity. You can begin writing poems and novels, creating beautiful paintings, becoming a healer, a teacher, *someone who inspires others and helps their hearts feel less pain and more joy.* You can build a family with a kind and wonderful man, have kids and give them all that Love you had for *HIM*... No matter what you decide to do, *you will have to do something!* Because otherwise, your Love will burn you from within. *You have to use that Fire to shine and warm the hearts of others.*

Still, many could not handle the pain of betrayal by the one they loved so deeply. They were not strong enough to forgive themselves or handle being judged, misunderstood, and ridiculed by others, so they simply slipped away. They cut the strings holding them to this physical life, making a massive mistake in both the human world and the world of Spirits. I have been on that edge way too many times, and now I would cry to them: *"Wait! Stop! Stop my girl! Do not leave! Not yet! I will help you! Let me help you! I've already walked this road and can help ease your pain by telling you everything about it. I will tell you about your happiness, dreams, and hopes; if you listen, I will tell you! Do not be afraid! You are not alone! There are many of us! We went through all this, and it made us stronger, my girl! It made us shine brighter and stand taller, like a Lighthouse in the dark stormy sea! Stay with us! Sister of Light!*

391

Stay with us! Together, we will make this world Brighter! Please believe me. We will!"

But this is what I know *now*. Back then, I think, I was still on the side of the street with those who wanted to be gone from this world—those who felt *lost, hurt, betrayed.*

How could I explain my condition to my wonderful boy, my son? I only remember I felt humiliated. I was speaking slowly. I was carefully choosing my words, saying that, unfortunately, even good moms like myself, and I wanted to hope I was not that bad, sometimes make such stupid mistakes. I was even trying to smile. I was trying to show him that it was not that big of a deal after all. There was nothing to worry about.

"I should have been more rational, son!" I said, with, as I thought, a sunny smile. "I should not have gone anywhere! But I leaped in there, like a silly teenage girl! It's all my fault. I should have been more sensible. I should have thought more with my head, not only with my heart! If he truly wanted to see me, dreamed about it, as he did say, *he would have called me on the phone, like normal people do,* right? But I was not thinking. So now I am dealing with the consequences. And Nicky, let's be completely honest here. If you look closely at all this communication via Twitter and Facebook." I sighed heavily, *"It's complete nonsense, son!* But at least I will no longer cloud my head with all these delusions! Now, I can put a full stop to it, telling myself that I have done everything that I possibly could! Right? So, it's all just fine. No need to think about it no more!"

But my child was absolutely furious, his silvery-gray eyes throwing lightning! He could not believe such a thing! He demanded that I tell him everything as it was, from the beginning to the very end! And knowing my child, I knew he would not let me be until I told him the truth. So, I shared almost everything with him, softening the sharp edges as much as possible but did not mention my meeting with Susan.

After this conversation, I hugged and kissed him and went to cook dinner, attempting to escape from my sad thoughts and the pain in my chest, *as if it were possible.*

Hours later, I would find out what Nicky did after our talk. It was already very late, and everyone was asleep. But I couldn't seem to fall asleep as I used to a long time ago, anytime and anywhere, oh, those blissful times! My mind was spinning. I replayed every event of the entire trip, moment by moment, again and again, like a broken record.

You probably have been in this state, after having failed, when you begin to think, *What if…*

What would have happened if we hadn't lost our car and hadn't been late for Farhan's entrance to the event, when he was looking for me in the crowd? What would have happened if Lena and I hadn't gone out to see the Golden Gate Bridge but had come to the theater earlier and joined the others, waiting for him in front of the entrance? But why would I do such a thing?

"I am not a fan of yours," I told him many times. "I am your…" *I am your what? Twin Flame? Other half? Love of all your past lives? What difference all this makes now? None.*

What would have happened if I demanded him to confirm his "great desire" to see me! Just demanded him to call me and say it with his own words before I set foot on the plane! No, even better, make him promise that he would not run away at the very last moment, like a scared rabbit into a burrow. Or, not even that! It would have been much better if I simply had said this, "So, do you really want to see me? Awesome! Wonderful! Get on a plane and fly to MY city." Invite me to a café. Yes, everyone knows you, you are afraid that people will pay too much attention. Then put on some disguise, goddammit! Reserve the whole damn restaurant for one evening. Surely you can afford it! And let's drink some champagne to us, for being one Soul. No? You don't believe it? Ok! Then to the fact that we have met! To the fact that we have found each other in this crazy world! No? Not good enough? Then let's drink to me for working for you! You and your goddammit empire!

Ha! Daydreaming again! *What if…* is the road to *nowhere.* Live here and now, Lala! *Here and now.* And do not delve into the past. The past does not admit any *what ifs.* The things Susan told me, No; I did not believe that he loved me, not in the slightest! It seemed like a strange mockery after all that had happened. But I can dream, can't I?

393

I took another gulp of oxygen before disconnecting the patient from the artificial respiration apparatus due to the complete futility of continuing to torment him. Last breath! Enough. That is it. I picked up the phone, intending to cut off the only channel that directly connected me with him. However, when I opened the app, I read the following:

Farhan! This is Nicholas! I just wanted to tell you! You are a bloody coward! COWARD! And you are not worthy of my Mom!

I froze in bewilderment, looking at these lines. Tears started to choke me. My son, my dear Nicky, was standing up for me against the king of cinema. My Man. My dear little man. As reckless and impulsive as his mother. Of course, if I had known my son would write this, I would never have allowed it. As for him, this is still an adult stranger. His mother is an adult woman who, to be honest, never received any promises or anything of the kind from this very king of cinema.

On the other hand, this whole story partially started with Nicholas and his words, "*Mom! He has your eyes! He is your half, Mom! You have to write to him!*"

But what Nicholas had written was a couple of hours ago. And I knew *for sure* that Farhan had already read the words Nicky wrote. There was no point in being either glad or mad. Was my son right? Or was it all my own fault? I was where I was... No point in overthinking it. Whatever happened, had already happened. Why didn't I just move on?

I began to scroll through the latest photos of him in the media. You ask why? There is a good answer "*just because.*" People use this answer when there is nothing else to say. They used it when they do something illogical, irrational, or simply senseless. Well, I have done so many stupid things in the past couple of years and the past couple of days, that it would be enough for a couple of lifetimes. I was a fool of a woman, so one more stupid thing, one less. Who cares? I was again looking at his photos. On several of them, my demon was in the company of dazzling, breathtakingly beautiful women, looking relaxed, pacified and quite happy with his life. He was standing next to a gorgeous blond woman in one of those photos. Seeing her sent a sharp pain through my body. I instantly recognized her! It was *that very woman* who was with him that night in San Francisco. She was gorgeous! Stunning. *Perfect.*

"*See you soon, my fairy!*" I closed my eyes and tried to convince myself I do not give a damn! It no longer hurts me anymore and I do not care. But unfortunately, it was not working. "Fairy." Indeed, she was. Of course, I was nothing like her! Who am I? A middle-aged single mother, exhausted by life's constant stress and everyday survival. Trying her best to make ends meet, pay the bills and have enough groceries to last until the end of the month. That is who I am. Put me near that perfection of a woman, probably around 25, and have a good laugh! I am ridiculous, goddammit! *Pitiful, stupid, pathetic idiot!*

I clenched my teeth, not wanting to cry. After all, this should not even bother me anymore. I closed my eyes and tasted my own blood in my mouth—a stupid habit of biting my lip in the moments like this. When scared, when hurt, I always do that. Why did I do it then? Because of pain or because of hatred? Suddenly, a merry-go-round of images started flickering in front of my narrowed eyes. I think I reached out for the curtain. Or for the bedspread on the couch. I remember holding onto some fabric, attempting to slow down the fall. My head is spinning, spinning and spinning. There are so many images in front of my eyes that I feel nauseous.

I tell someone, "No! No, please. Please do not!"

And some hissing, nasty voices answer me, "Look! Look, you little fool! You have to see thissss!"

"I do not want to see this! I do not want to see this!" I think I'm screaming but only a moan comes out of my mouth.

"Look! Look! There were lotssss of them! They were all beautiful! NOTHING like you! And you know what? He loved them! He really did love them, not like you! *Little fool! Fool! Fool!*"

"No! Please…"

"Oh! We can show you more! *MUCH more! Look! LOOK!* See for yourself!"

Images were changing one another as if on a movie screen. My Soul and never-mine Farhan Ali and his breathtaking women. Many! Many of them. Intertwined arms and bodies, his lips finding theirs, their arms around his neck, their fingers in his gorgeous hair, them moaning and melting with him, screaming and whispering his name. I do not want to see any of this! *But I see it! I see it all!*

The thin glass of orange juice I was holding shattered into pieces in my hand, leaving a few deep cuts. But I felt nothing.

"And you! *You don't even know the taste of his lipsss! Little fool!*" giggled the chorus of nasty voices of some vile creatures.

I knew who they were. I understood very well exactly what was happening. The dark side had faithful servants on the so-called lowest astral level of the Planet, as long as it exists. Never in my entire life had they been able to approach me! And now they did. They did because I didn't have an ounce of strength left in me to fight them. I broke down! I broke! As if dirty water flooded me, covered me, and I was drowning in it. It was sick and terrifyingly dark! I still don't know how it happened but honestly, I was gone! *Lala, the one which consisted of Love and Light, was gone.* I was no more! A beast, I had nothing in common with, took my place. But still, it was me. Dark swallowed me like a hungry, vicious monster! I became the darkness, consisting only of hatred and one burning, overpowering, evil desire!

REVENGE!

REVENGE!

REVENGE!

This desire hit me, breaking through the armor of all my goodness, my Light, and my Eternal Love. Just like a spear. *Right through the heart.* I still remember the feeling. The spear was sharp! It was cold, yet the cold was burning me. It took away the ability to breathe! To think! To feel! Only one thought pulsating in my every cell, like a forgotten neon sign in an abandoned dead city. Those lights flashed on and off, on and off. *Revenge!* Take Revenge on him! Revenge for my pain! Revenge for my humiliation! For all the lying and pretense! For using me! For making me believe in what was never there!

Take Revenge! Take Revenge! *Take Revenge! HE HAD NO RIGHT!* This monster had no right to use me, to lie to me, to give me hope!

Now, *make him pay!* This almighty God and movie star is pretty sure that such a sad little thing as me is capable of doing NOTHING *to him! Oh, how wrong he is!* Almighty King has no idea who he is dealing with! I learned the darkest and the most powerful rituals long ago. I had to know my enemy well to be able to fight it. The Dark Masters themselves taught me. Seeing my powers, they accepted me into their very small circle, as they hoped that one day soon, I would become one of them. I knew such words which even the craziest ones, practicing dark magic, *had no guts to use!* Well, I do! So! My dear sweet love boy! *I saw YOUR power! Well, now you will see MINE!* An eye for an eye! Blood for blood! Pain for pain! I will make you pay me for my every tear, for every moment, when *I believed you* and you *used me!*

The hissing giggle grew louder! It should have alerted me, brought me back to myself! But that did not happen! I knew how I could take REVENGE on him! So, I am a witch, am I? Well, I⋅ll be the kind of Witch they tell those spooky stories about on Halloween night, the one flying on a broomstick and cooking potions from the hearts of innocent boys!

I lit the candle. I yanked Farhan's photo out of the frame. I whispered several dark words over the fire and saw it turning almost red. I brought the picture close to the fire. Was I aware of what I was doing? Of course, I was! I have long been familiar with magic. But the woman performing the ritual of dark magic wasn't really me. Dark took me over and fully possessed me *for the first time in my life!* I slowly drew the photo to the candle and set fire to one of its corners! My heart was pounding as if it wanted to break out of my chest and fly away! *It did not want to be a part of me.* Because what I did *was not a part of me!* It was dark, while, in my essence, *I had never been dark.* But at that moment I became it! I only wanted one thing. I wanted him to *hurt, hurt, hurt!* As much as I did! Oh no! More! Much more! *A thousand times more!*

"*I knew the pain, tearing me into pieces. I knew the pain, burning and destroying my very Soul, who loved you so endlessly,*" I whispered, burning his photo with the flame of a candle. "*So now, I am cursing you with pain to torture*

397

you both days and nights! Days and nights! And may this pain not allow you to breathe, sleep, smile, live and exist!! As tears burned my eyes, so let the never-ending agony burn your Soul with hellfire, not letting you be in peace for one breathing moment! Go, Pain! Go! Bring sorrow over him. Go, Pain! Go! Take sadness with you. Go, Pain! Go! Destroy his joy-happiness. No rest for him when the sun is shining. No rest for him at night in the moonlight! Smoke into his head, darkness into his eyes! Grief into his heart! Grief into his heart! Sorrow! My dear sister, obey me and enter his dreams and his thoughts so that he can't eat, sleep, live in the days and dream in the nights unless in your embrace you keep him tight! Both days and nights. Days and nights! Like blood beating in his veins, let his heart groan, howl, cry from longing! Suffer you will, toil! I am cursing you to not have peace from now on; hurt, sorrow, agony is all you ever will know. All you will ever know...."

I continued to say my terrible dark words. And I kept on hearing the quiet evil giggles, but that did not stop me. I realized perfectly well that the Dark Side was having their Great Celebration! They had finally got me in their claws! How many years they had tried! How many times and never got anything! No matter what they threw my way, I did not break—until now. And finally, I am here, where they wanted me to be for years! Broken! Torn. Destroyed. Lost. Shattered. Pitch Darkness replaced the pure white Light in me. But I didn't care. I kept repeating my terrible words, trying to burn his photo with the candle flame. But it was far from easy. *The picture wouldn't burn!* The fire went out over and over again! I tried to burn it again and again from different sides but it would burn for just a few seconds and the fire continued to go out. I got angry and decided to burn it right from the middle! I held his face directly above the flame, but it did not want to catch fire. Finally, the paper *under his eyes began to blacken*, but at that moment, *the fire went out again.*

I saw the burned black holes under his beautiful eyes! *His eyes? Or mine? Our eyes. Ours. The eyes of the same Soul!* I froze and suddenly came to my senses. Abruptly I stopped the ritual. Terrified, as if sharply awakened from a nightmare, I stared at the photo of him in my hands. What have I done? Merciful forces of Light! *What have I just done?* I pressed his burnt photo to my heart; then I threw the blackened candle away from me! I was shaking and shivering like a leaf left on the tree through the winter storm. I felt excruciating pain *in every particle of my body*. Breathing was torture. I felt a burned and bleeding open wound in place of my heart. I was freezing as if I were lying alive in a coffin carved from a block of ice!

The tears were burning my eyes and falling onto his photo in my hands. *"Forgive me! Please forgive me!"* I was whispering, looking at him. Was I asking for *his forgiveness or my own?* Part of me understood that I had not finished the ritual, and I had not used so-called "keywords." Without those, he would not get hit as much as he could have been. But still, I could have done enough to harm him, as I knew how terrifying and damaging the anger of a White Witch turning dark can be. I needed to reverse it! I had to reverse it! But how would I reverse an unfinished spell? I was so cold and felt so wrong on all the levels that I was close to fainting.

I put down his photo, almost falling as I got up. Barely able to move, I got myself under the sizzling hot streams of water in the shower. But standing there for 10 minutes, I still couldn't get any warmer. I was shivering and horrified! I felt as if someone, something, was violently attempting to tear my soul from my body, and she was resisting with all her might. I closed my eyes and hugged myself with both hands. I got out of the shower and wrapped myself first in a huge towel, then in two blankets. I had a fever. My hands were shaking. Everything around me was blurry. I found some over-the-counter flu medication in the cabinet. I took four pills instead of two. I guess they contained some sedating ingredient, as only a few minutes later, I fell asleep and saw...

There, under a huge tree, spreading its willow-like branches, its crown rising high into the sky, his mother was waiting for me. Dressed in something white that shimmered like a cloud, her silhouette was shining but her face was sad. I slowly approached her, afraid to even speak. She turned to me and spoke first.

"Do not blame yourself! Do not get tortured by your own guilt! Such things can happen even to the strongest ones! The pain breaks us down but your Light is stronger! You did not harm him! Because your Love for him is much more powerful, more ancient than any rituals and words of the Dark! Your Love has shielded him from even your own anger, Lala! You did not harm him. *You shielded him with yourself!*"

Perhaps I did want to ask her how I had done that, but I woke up sharply, still wrapped in towels and blankets, only now I was burning, as if on fire. The full realization of what I had done drenched me like a splash of icy water. How could I have done that? How is it even possible? No matter how angry I was with him, *I still LOVED him!* And yet, I did and said all that? How? But my heart remembered the words of his mother. This memory warmed my Soul, still shivering in horror. She said I had not harmed him since I shielded him with myself. *Shielded him with myself?* What does that mean? I would know soon enough.

Two days later, I decided to treat my children to a cake. When recalling their favorite taste from childhood, many immigrants from the former USSR will undoubtedly remember the taste of homemade cakes, frosted with icing, made with boiled sweetened condensed milk. Cans of those were hard to find back then. When you were lucky to get a can or two, you felt on top of the world! Our mothers, and later we, boiled them for hours in a pot of water (without opening the cans, of course). As a result, we had a magnificent caramel dense mass, which we used as icing between each layer.

I decided to recreate this simple treat from my childhood and share its taste with my sons. I bought two cans of sweetened condensed milk, and like many years ago, I plunged them into a large saucepan and set it to boil for two or three hours. Just as I turned the burner on, I heard a knock on the door. A postal clerk had brought a package with seedlings for my mother's garden. I signed the delivery receipt and took the plants to the garden. Then, I went to my room and peacefully started to translate a rather big text I had received the day before. The house was quiet. The children had gone to school. My mother was paying a visit to a friend of hers. The text I was translating was quite complex and voluminous. I completely submerged myself in work for at least two hours. Suddenly the awful smell of an empty frying pan left on a burning hot stove filled the house.

Oh, Holy Heavens! The condensed milk! I entirely forgot about it!!! I jumped up and ran to the kitchen! The hot pan is on the stove. I had answered the door and failed to turn down the heat. The water has thoroughly boiled away, leaving only the cans of condensed milk on the bottom of the pan. I don›t even know how long it has been without water with the heat turned up high! I grab a kitchen towel, wrap it around the pan's handle and quickly transfer it to the sink. And…

The instant the hot pan touches the cold sink, both cans EXPLODE from the sudden temperature drop! The boiling hot sticky mass splashes all over my face! Luckily for me, I manage to close my eyes before it hit me! It saved me from becoming blind. At that moment, I still didn't understand how lucky I was. At first, I don't even feel the pain. I'm in absolute shock! The damn viscous, hellishly hot mass completely covers my eyes and my face. I blindly grope for the faucet of cold water, trying to wash it all off as quickly as possible! A few minutes later, intense, horrific pain begins spreading all over my face. It's getting stronger and stronger. Every second, every minute, becomes more and more agonizing!

For the next few hours, I am struggling to soothe the unbearable burning, even a little bit. I use everything I can get in my hands. I find it impossible to suppress or conceal the anguish, so I yell and cry. I am scared to even look in the mirror at my burned face.

My kids come home from classes along with my mother! The poor things look at me in shock! My beloved angels, my sons, were suffering more than I did because there was no way they could help me. Nicky held his hands over my face as Reiki healers do. Arman read aloud all the information he could find on the Internet about treating severe burns. At that time, I didn't even have a job, which meant I had no health insurance. You can't get to the hospital without insurance! I mean, you actually can, but the bill you will receive after would be many thousands of dollars, which of course, I did not have. Such was my reality.

Quickly having reviewed all her reserves of the healing herbs, consisting of many cotton bags of dried roots, flowers and leaves, my mother makes me an ointment of herbs and a mix of oils! She puts a thick layer of it on my face! An hour later, the pain no longer slashes me with red-hot arrows and does not pluck my eyes with fire anymore. At least now, I can tolerate it. The most severe burns are under my eyes. *UNDER MY EYES!* Exactly *AT THE SAME SPOTS,* where the candle's fire burned dark holes *under HIS eyes on His photo!*

"*Shielded with yourself.*" That is exactly what happened! Being a Light One in my very essence, loving him with all my heart while performing the rite of black magic, I *unconsciously turned the power of witchcraft against myself.* A Twin always protects her Twin! No matter what! It's like a warrior's shield! And I became such a shield for him, closing him from my own spell and my own anger. I shield him with myself from myself. Now it all became clear.

The following week passed like a bad dream.

I hurt! I was in physical, emotional and spiritual anguish. I didn't know what to do or how to find any strength to go on! I had to talk with someone, someone who could give me some answers. I knew who could do this, Bastet—The Eye of Ra.

Chapter 45

Bastet

The Answers

Bastet opened the door and froze. A scarf covered my face; only my eyes were visible.

"What happened to your face, Lala? Come in! Come in quickly! Get in that chair, baby girl! Let me bring you some tea, and you'll tell me everything!"

Just like the very first time I came to her house, I was sitting again in the same armchair, by the massive fireplace with the statue of the cat goddess Bastet, looking down upon me, as some little mortal woman, lost in her current path and incarnation. I probably was too little and insignificant to a great Goddess, or maybe indeed, she felt compassion for me and remembered her own lives when she was just a woman.

Bastet, my hostess, entered the room, carrying a huge cup of tea in her hand, spreading the marvelous aroma of many herbs around the room. I guess, even if she gave me some ordinary tap water, it would also have an amazing aroma and a healing effect. That was the kind of woman she was.

I took my time telling her about everything that happened in San Francisco, my conversation with Susan Malik (without naming her, of course). I told her about how I burned my face after attempting to burn his photo, and many other things. She listened to me very carefully, not missing a single word, only shaking her head from time to time. Finally, she said.

"My dear girl, what I will tell you now may sound rather harsh, maybe even cruel. But that will be exactly what you must hear. I can understand your pain but what happened to your face was thanks to your own utter stupidity! *You know that you and he are ONE!* How could you let this all happen?"

"If he and I *are one*, as you say, then why was I blind and clueless of what he was doing all this time? Why didn't I see his multiple lovers? Why didn't I see that he was using me, playing with me, like a cat with a stupid mouse, using my feelings, hopes, dreams to his own advantage! Why didn't I see any of this, if we are one, as you say Bastet? What I saw and what I felt, *was completely different* from what the *reality was and is!* If we are one, *I should have known!* But I didn't know anything! I did not know anything at all, Bastet. *Nothing!*"

"I will explain, Lala!" She said after a moment of silence. "You see and feel *his SOUL*, and *the Soul can neither lie nor pretend!* The Soul is pure! But his Soul *DOES NOT CONTROL HIM!* His Soul only occasionally raises her head and opens her eyes! And as soon as it happens, he is immediately attacked by the Dark! He does not listen to his Soul, Lala! He is listening to the mind! Do you know what that means?

"The human brain is pretty much just a receiver! It is entirely empty initially! All thoughts appear from *OUTSIDE*. The Dark Ones broadcast at *low frequencies and low vibrations*, the *Light Ones at high!* While you are at low-frequency vibrations, the Light Ones *cannot reach you*. They simply cannot get through to you! No matter what they try to tell you, *you will not hear them!*

"*All doubts, fears, pain, anger, resentment, jealousy—all these come from the Dark Ones!* Why? So, that you lose your pure vital energy, which serves as *their food!* The more you lose it, the worse it gets on the physical side for you! Insomnia begins, panic attacks, depression! The Dark ones do everything for a person to stay precisely on *LOW-frequency* vibrations as long as possible! When you were trying to burn his photo, you were under the influence of the Dark Forces. That's why it happened! You have punished yourself! As for Farhan, at the moment, he is *eighty percent controlled by the Dark Ones* and only *twenty percent by his Soul*, which *you hear and feel!* That did not happen to him in a day; he gradually moved towards this state for many years.

"You were sent to him precisely *to be his Light* and not to descend to low-frequency vibrations! The Dark controls most of what his physical body does! All this was hidden from you, yes! I knew about it when you first came to me! But I didn't tell you anything, because if I had told you, *you wouldn't have done ANYTHING.* Meaning *he would not have the slightest chance of waking up!*"

"You are right! If I had known all this from the very beginning, *I would have done absolutely nothing!*"

"Exactly! There is no untruth in what you knew and felt inside of your very essence. You are connected with his Soul since you share one! And his Soul *loves you! Loves you deeply, truly, and for eternity!* But I repeat; his Soul does not control him! He does not listen to her voice and even if he does, he does not follow it! He follows the mind and his mind follows the low vibrations. If you look at what he is most striving for, it is easy to see! The Dark Ones prioritize *business, power, money, fame, sex, and material pleasures!*"

"Bastet! He is the god of lies, do you understand? A God of *deceit and pretense!* He can lie with every wave of his legendary eyelashes, with every smile, with every breath! Gods! And I used to call him my Heavenly Angel! How stupid I am. Stupid and naive!"

"Lala, he is an actor! Not just any actor, but one of the best in the world, possibly even the best! What surprises you so? They were right when they told you that he has *many faces.* But the one who loves you is *the real Him.* Only no one gives any power or freedom to the *real Him,* and even when it happens, it happens rarely and very scarcely.

"Do you think he understands it? No! *He has no clue!* When a person UNDERSTANDS that the Light is fighting with the Dark inside him, we can say *the Dark is already half defeated!* But when a person does not suspect the Dark has control over him, it is very difficult for the Light to win, because there is NO CONSCIOUSNESS. Farhan does not comprehend what is happening to him! He believes that he controls his life and actions, when in fact *the Shadow controls him.* That is one of many reasons why you were sent to him!

Your purity and Light are there to help the Light in him win over the Dark! Do you understand?

"Bastet … I don't think I understand anything anymore … What should I do with all this?"

"Lala! Twins are guided to each other only when they can reach the level of Connection! Of Alliance! If there were not *any chance*, you two would never have found each other! So, there's a chance!"

"I'm not that sure. Actually, I don't think there is any chance whatsoever! And tell me, why I can't sleep with other men while he can do it with tons of women. Why can't I even let someone else touch me?"

"Because you are more awakened than he is! You understand that sex without love is a low vibration; you know it and feel it. You do not want sex! You want *to make love! Create Love.* That's a completely different thing! For you, making love is not just a desire to satisfy your flesh. You feel the need for a spiritual connection with the one your Soul needs! For you, it's only him. But if you think that you two are separated only because of him, you are very wrong! *The guilt is also yours!*"

I could not believe what I've just heard. *"Mine? I am guilty? Guilty of what?"* I was startled, really shocked by her words!

"Yes, Lala! *You are guilty!* You are guilty of NOT LOVING YOURSELF and NOT ACCEPTING YOURSELF! Tell me, do you love yourself? Do you forgive yourself? Do you accept yourself the way you are? Do you have that *unconditional love towards you?* Tell me!"

I was so shocked by her words that I could only shake my head! For as long as I remembered, I liked nothing about me! Of course, my childhood and youth's circumstances, my whole life, in general, did not help me much in "loving and accepting myself the way I am." The words of my dear mother got to the surface of my memory. "And why would anyone love you? What have you achieved in life? Some people accomplish so many things! And what have you done?"

It was my old, unhealed wound. My strong mom never seemed to see anything good in me. And no matter how painful it might have been, I got used to the thought that I was worse than anyone around me and did not

406

deserve the right to any admiration or happiness. I held the deeply rooted belief that one MUST *deserve love, happiness, and respect.* I felt I had nothing, or close to nothing, worthy of any of those.

My father never needed me and was never present in my life. In the eyes of my dearest mother, I was woven from all kinds of not, particularly positive qualities. At least that's what she told me throughout my life. Maybe she felt or thought differently. I cannot know for sure. Where would this self-love and self-confidence come from?

For many years I have had a dream to accomplish something glorious, so my mom would change her mind and be proud of me. If only I could get an Oscar or something like that. But such a chance is rather slim, to say the least. The way things were going on in my life, I guess an Oscar was hardly possible for me, even in my distant future.

Somehow it was apparent to me; the people who achieve something great in life do not care much about anyone else's opinion. Do you have to be self-confident and at peace with yourself and the world to be successful and auspicious? Usually yes. Well-balanced and confident people achieve a lot because *they know who they are, what they want, and typically do what they are passionate about and enjoy.* In harmony with themselves and the world, they don't seek *external praise.* Unfortunately, I was not one of them. All my life, it seemed the world told me that everyone was better than me, and I was unlovable. Everything in my life told me this, over and over again. I heard it so often; I believed it was true.

Do you want some advice from a Twin Flame? Whoever you are, wherever you are, please never get tired of *loving your children.* Remind them you love them as often as possible. Please do not get tired of praising them and telling them how much *you believe in them.* Please support them in developing their talents and all their good undertakings. This way, your children will become strong and confident adults who will follow their dreams, achieve their goals and be happy.

Bastet silently watched me as I stared at the wall wiping away my tears.

"No, Bastet!" I answered. "I have no love for myself. I don't have anything to be loved for!"

She paused for a moment. Finally, she said, "Lala, do you remember that the Twins *mirror each other?* Where do you think his narcissism comes from? *He is just like you!* He does not have this inner love for himself! That woman was absolutely right; the Anahata, heart chakra, is blocked!"

"Farhan does everything to *receive love from the OUTSIDE!* He needs love from all those crowds, worshiping him and praising him! Why? Because *he does not have it inside him!* All those women, his lovers—he needs them for that same reason! There is *no inner love in either of you, Lala!* You cannot be together at this stage! If the Higher Ones interfered and united the two of you at this stage, you would not be able to *put up with yourself reflected in him,* and he would not be able to *put up with himself, reflected in you* for more than a few days! You would kill each other! The lack of unconditional self-love and self-acceptance in both of you has resulted in *this huge imbalance in both of you!*

"*You are only in the Spirit, and he is only in the Body.* But neither of you has any *inner love!* So, how can you be united? You see him as a demon only because you *DO NOT ACCEPT YOURSELF!* Everything that he has, *you have it as well!* If *you* were in *HIS* male body, and he embodied your female form, *you would behave exactly the same as he does now!*"

I stared again into her incredible green eyes. The soft glow shining through them seemed to carry powerful and bright energy that could soothe, taking away my pain and confusion, straightening up my thoughts and opening up new, previously unknown ways to see past events. But too many revelations landed upon me that day.

"Bastet, is this really true? *Would I really behave the same if I was a man and lived his life?*"

"Absolutely. Yes! You must be the *LIGHT* for him, Lala! The Light!" she continued. "You were given to him so that you could guide him *back into the Light!* But without learning *to love and accept yourself, you cannot do this! You must learn to value, accept and love yourself!* And only after that will you be able to learn to rise *ABOVE* his actions in his physical form! *We all are Spirits, playing our given roles.* We receive a costume—our body; a scenario—our life circumstances; and the stage—this planet. In each performance, *we have goals, purposes, and missions.* The requirements of Twin Flames are intense. You must learn to rise above his actions in physical form and *see him as a Spirit* who has lost connection with himself. You are the one to help him return to that connection. But first, *you must learn self-love!* Only after that will you be able to learn to accept him in ANY *form,* calmly! Just as you calmly accept his roles in his movies, knowing those are just his roles. You will learn to accept the roles he plays away from the movie set. *You will learn to love you in him and love him in you!* Love, not because of something, just love. *Love with no conditions. Just love yourself and him for everything and nothing. Love you for just being you. Love him for just being him! That is your goal. Do you understand? That is where you must be.*

"Are you there yet? No, Lala! Not at all! At first, you idealized him! He was your Heavenly Angel with white wings. You saw in him only his beautiful qualities, which, of course, exist in great quantity. But you did not see his hidden dark side, which is also there! I am not telling you he is a Heavenly Angel, as you used to call him. He is far from being one, just like the rest of us. But he is your Twin! *Your Twin* with all the light, dark, and half-tones in him! And this Twin resides in the body of a person with deep inner traumas no worse and no better than the rest of us.

"I repeat, my beautiful girl! *You must be his Light! His true Light. The sacred fire of his Soul.* The spark of the Source, the GOD in him! But look what has happened to you instead? *You have lowered yourself to hatred, jealousy, resentment and anger! So, how can you get him into the Light and resurrect that Light in him if you have lost it?*"

I closed my eyes and took a deep breath. Why should it all be so complicated? Why?

"You are blaming him," she continued. "You are angry with him and jealous of him; you criticize and hate him! *These are all low-frequency vibrations!* You have forgotten, *your Love is eternal and UNCONDITIONAL!* You can lift him out of the darkness in which he lives. But YOU FIRST MUST LIFT YOURSELF, Lala! *How can you do what you both came for if you both lose the Light?*"

I only shook my head. "So, what should I do, Bastet? What am I supposed to do with all this?"

"You must raise yourself from the low to the high levels, Lala. You need to change the vibrations in you and around you and start to listen to the Light, not to the Dark! To do that, you need to generate a state of *Unconditional Love within you. Love towards YOURSELF first of all!* After that, and only after, will you be able to show Love towards him, the entire world, and every Soul in it. No matter what their stage of development. *Love is the essence of the SOUL.* Do you understand? *When you are in that state, you don't have irritation, anger, envy, resentment, grief, hopelessness, sadness, condemnation.* None of that will exist in you! Such Love directly connects with the Divine Energy and all the Souls on Earth and beyond! It is hard work! *But this is exactly what you must do!"*

Silence hung in the room. Finally, Bastet spoke again. "You think you love him! But can you assure me that your love for him is UNCONDITIONAL? No, Lala! You can't! You love only his Light! The earthly one, the dark one, you are still not able to accept. Especially his dark side, a Narcissist!"

"Narcissist? But how? Bastet, I always knew from Greek Mythology that Narcissus was madly in love with himself! But didn't you just say that there is *NO self-love and no self-acceptance in either of us?* If he doesn't love himself, how can he be a Narcissist?"

"This is who he is. He is always trying to convince the whole world that *he is perfect!* He is constantly playing roles and wearing masks. Why? What's the reason for that? He is doing everything to receive love from the *outside.* Because *inside him,* self-love is nonexistent. People who love themselves do not need or crave *love from the whole world.* They do not strive for recognition, worship, and admiration from others. They do not seek it. People who love and accept themselves *are at peace with their Souls,* with their higher Self, and with the world. *They do not need to prove anything to anyone!*

"But if a person lacks self-confidence and self-love, he will try to receive approval, admiration, recognition of his superiority and uniqueness *from others.* And no matter how much of it he gets, it will *never be enough!* It's like a coffee mug without a bottom. Even if the whole of humanity worships him as God, disappointment, and restlessness *are always there, hidden deep inside from everyone else* under the multiple masks he wears. Do you remember the story when Christmas toys were returned to the store because they were '*not making the person happy*'? If there is no joy in the Soul, no love in the heart, *nothing can make such a person truly happy.* The body disconnected from the Soul is dead. That is why Narcissists are often called 'Soul-less' or 'Lost Souls.' They have lost connection with their true Essence. They do not know who they truly are. Lost in the dark, they have little hope of ever seeing the light at the end of the tunnel.

"Your Twin seeks the approval of others, honor, money, envy, and the ability to have the best of the best in everything, but ... Only while the *world recognizes him.* Only if the *world admits* that yes, indeed, what he has is *the best and he is the best.* And what his feelings toward you? This is simple. The Dark Ones constantly whisper to him, "Don't take any action! Don't do anything! *Stay away from her!* If anyone finds out, imagine what will happen. Scandals. Gossip. Ridicule. Newspaper headlines. People would look at you like you're a joke! Do you want that? This whole story sounds more than just weird! It is delusional. Insane! Leave everything as it is! Don't you dare to change anything! You are not insane. Are you? Like the words in the song, 'Conceal, do not feel, do not let them know! You must reject all ideas, thoughts, feelings about her and this entire story! That is what you must do!'"

"They seek to convince him you are weird, crazy. You want something from him. You're dangerous for him. You are this; you are that! *They will not let him be!*

"*His Soul remembers you and loves you!* But his body and mind want to live as they always have—the old familiar way. He tells himself, why change? Meet her? Look into her eyes? *AND?* Then what? Will I be able to leave her in the way I leave others? And if I stay, what will happen next? Also, what about the people who idolize me? Would I look like an idiot in their eyes? Will I be happy? Am I ready to annul my whole life before her and start a new one with her?

"*Because AFTER he sees you, nothing will be the same for him; nothing will be the old familiar way!* He knows it. He feels it. He realizes it way too well.

"No, Lala. *He is not ready for you.* And you cannot blame him for that. But as you can see, *you are not ready for him either.*"

It was quiet for a moment, except for the ticking of the clock in the hall.

"This whole thing is absolutely hopeless," I finally said. "We have no future. Farhan is a star and I am just an ordinary woman. I can't do anything! And is it really necessary? Why, Bastet?"

"Ordinary women?" she said, smiling mysteriously. "You? *An ordinary woman?* Allow me to show you something, my child."

She went to one of the bookshelves and took out a book. "Are you familiar with this book?" She asked, handing me a small manuscript.

I looked at the name *Twin Flames Revelation: Answering the Call to Save Humanity. Part One,* written by Zeyven Alexander Blackwell. I turned the book and read what he wrote on the back.

> *Twin Flames are presently re-uniting to complete their mission at the critical juncture in Earth's ascension. Humanity has long been trapped by the forces of darkness and today stands poised to emerge from the dark and rise to a higher dimension. However, unseen forces are working hard to stop this, and it will take the combined efforts of advanced Souls and Twin Flames to bring the balance of power back into humanity's favor. This book details the journey of one such Soul, his Twin Flame, his Soul Mates, and their journey prior to and after answering the call to help liberate humanity...*[28]

While reading the words, I felt my face *burning*, the same as when I was near Farhan. I put my hands to my cheeks.

"Face *burning*?" Bastet asked, smiling. "Yes. I believe the author of this book is a Twin Flame.

---

28 Zeyven Alexander Blackwell, Twin Flame Revelation, back cover

"Not only that! He is one of the 'Keys,' as they are called; you and Farhan are also. As far as I see, you have not read this book yet. In my opinion, this is the only book revealing the truth of who Twin Flames are and why they are here! I am absolutely convinced of it and I am sure you will be as well.

"I am giving this book to you but I want to tell you a bit about what he writes and read a few sections to you. There are some essential things you must know about who you are and why you are here.

"Zevyen says that Twin Flame couple do not always incarnate together. The consciousness on some planets is so low vibrational and dense that the Higher Forces only allow one Twin to incarnate. It's safer that way. So, one Twin remains in the Spirit realm and acts as a guide to their physically incarnated half, helping, so he doesn't lose his way. The risk is much higher when both incarnate at the same time. So why is such a risk taken?

"He tells about a call that went out from the *Grand Collective Council* requesting ALL who were willing to help the souls of Gaia Earth transition to a higher dimension. Yes, our planet has been in desperate need. But this isn't an easy task. Even entering the Earth Matrix is far more complicated than you can imagine. Not even an *ascended being* can simply come waltzing into the physical realm of Earth, in all his or her magnificent brilliance, and solve humanity's dilemma. Every soul, even ascended masters, avatars, and world teachers must become completely human, incarnating with no awareness of who they are as eternal beings or knowledge of their vast capabilities.

They must live as humans... WAKE UP and REMEMBER THEIR POINT OF ORIGIN, THEIR POWER, AND THEIR MISSION, within the allotted time or risk relegation back to a lower dimension for yet more eons."[29]

She continued to tell me about this complicated process and the significant preparation a Twin Flame must make before entering the Earth plane! "Like other sixth-dimensional beings, Twin Flames have to descend in

---

29 Zeyven Alexander Blackwell, Twin Flame Revelation, 156

vibration so they can make the shift to the dense form and limitations of third-dimensional life on Earth. It says here, each level down takes up to one thousand earthly years! So, you can imagine!

The higher the dimensional being, the greater the work that had to be done to FORGET THEIR GREAT KNOWLEDGE AND CONNECTION TO SOURCE![30]

"He writes about The Darkside and the necessary precautions the Twin Flames must take. They must enter Earth in a way that doesn't attract the attention of the Darkside! For this, so much of the Soul Essence must be withheld. Though each of these Souls is remarkable in their own right, they must appear incredibly ORDINARY when they are born as babies, or their mission could be at risk.

"THE WORK and activation of the TF protocol happen towards the end of the cosmic cycle (Kali Yuga), as Humanity seemed highly likely to be slow to awaken, even after significant prompting. As I mentioned, when the Twin Flames incarnate simultaneously, there is the risk they might both lose their way. But he says that if at least one of the Twins awakens by the end of Kali Yuga, then their joined energies 'will prove a POTENT FORCE, upon [their] physical and spiritual reunion!'[31]

"You see? Even if ONE is awake! And this one is you! So, you still have a significant amount of work ahead! You have no right to be weak. Pay close attention to the words in this book, maybe even read it a couple of times, so you understand *who you are, what you are, and why you are here!* You have not risked and done so much, for thousands of years, to stop right now when the time is crucial. That is what the Dark wants!! Do you understand?

---

30 Zeyven Alexander Blackwell, Twin Flame Revelation, 156, emphasis mine
31 Zeyven Alexander Blackwell, Twin Flame Revelation, 161, emphasis mine

"There's something I want you to read. I want to see your eyes when you do." She found what she was looking for, and with a soft smile, gave me the book. I took it and read the highlighted words aloud. While reading, it seemed the whole world just disappeared!

There truly is some danger to our souls in journeying to Earth. We could get lost for a very long time![32]
'UNDERSTAND THIS, Etherielle, and BURN IT INTO YOUR MEMORY... NEVER FORGET THAT I WILL FIND YOU NO MATTER WHAT HAPPENS! BY THE LIGHT OF SOURCE, I WILL FIND YOU! IF YOU, BY CHANCE OR MISFORTUNE, FALL AND ARE AT RISK OF NOT ASCENDING WHEN TIME COMES, I WILL FIND AND LIFT YOU UP IN THE... I AM DIVINE WILL FORCE, AND I WILL NOT REST, UNTIL THIS HUMANITY IS LIBERATED AND YOU ARE BY MY SIDE, MERGING BACK INTO ONENESS.' As Jonanon declared this sacred vow, his aura flashed SAPPHIRE BLUE.[33]

"Sapphire blue!" I whispered. "Royal blue—Indigo! Our color!" I looked at Bastet with tears in my eyes and went back to the book.

Etherielle smiled in comfort at his strength and power, and she rested in his embrace. Her confidence restored, she felt safe and able, once again, to take on a legion of dark forces. TOGETHER THEY WOULD BE UNSTOPPABLE, awe-inspiring, dynamic force![34]

"Holy Heavens!" I said, "*I will find you! No matter what! I WILL FIND YOU AND LIFT YOU UP! I WILL NOT REST UNTIL THIS HUMANITY IS LIBERATED.*"

"Yes, Lala! Exactly! This mission is not about only you and Farhan; *it is about humanity and this planet!* Ordinary women? You wish! Because if you were an ordinary woman, you would have an excuse to give it all up and walk

---

32 Zeyven Alexander Blackwell, Twin Flame Revelation, 163
33 Zeyven Alexander Blackwell, Twin Flame Revelation, 163
34 Zeyven Alexander Blackwell, Twin Flame Revelation, 164

away! But you do not have that luxury! You are *a Warrior of Light* on a Cosmic rescue mission. You came here to fight the Dark and to win! So, continue to walk this path you chose for yourself!

Let me share a little bit more. Zevyen writes that before incarnating to Earth, Twin Flames, along with other Beings of Light, enter *The Sacred Temple of Forgetfulness*. They are washed in unique light and sound frequencies *that dissolve their fifth-dimensional bodies* while still preserving THEIR ESSENCE. Then, they all are guided down to the fourth dimension before descending to Earth. No matter how hard they try to hold onto their truth, only tiny memory fragments survive. So, you only remembered his eyes, but this was enough for you to be able to find him.

"Please read the highlighted words on page 171."

> *Meanwhile, back on Earth, the first of the advanced souls had begun to arrive. Their arrivals would be staggered over the coming centuries and their placement strategic. All would face great hardship...*
> *Thus, the final battle for the souls of humanity had begun. All would play their role, but would they be successful? And what of Twin Flames? Of all the soul groups to incarnate, they held the greatest capacity to change the course of human soul evolution, yet, it required their strategic meeting and melding on the physical plane against remarkable odds. Timing would be everything. THEY WOULD BE AMONGST THE MOST HUNTED BY THE DARKSIDE, WHO WOULD THROW EVERYTHING AT THEM TO KEEP THEM APART...* [35]

"This is what you are experiencing! This is what you are living! Please, turn the page and read his *Final Message to the Reader*."

---

35   Zeyven Alexander Blackwell, Twin Flame Revelation, 171.

We stand at the crossroads in human and planetary evolution. The time for ascension is at hand, though there still remain forces that are working against this. STAY THE COURSE, LIVE IN YOUR WISE AND LOVING HEART, AND WE WILL MAKE THE TRANSITION TO THE HIGHER DIMENSION SUCCESSFULLY. EARTH AND GALAXY ARE COUNTING ON YOU![36]

"Do you understand now?"

"I, I think I do, Bastet," I said, closing the book and taking a deep breath. "I think I do. The book is indeed phenomenal! I wish I had read it before. Maybe if I had, I would not have done all these stupid things. Why only now has it found me?"

"Things find you *when you are ready for them to find you*, Lala. You were ready for this book today, and it found you today! You have only seen a very small part of it, but I am sure you will find many more answers there. You have said to me enough times, 'I am just an ordinary woman. He is a megastar!' The fact is those are just *the costumes and the roles you chose for this incarnation and this life.*

"Nobody is ordinary, my girl, and you know that better than anyone else! Everyone is unique, with their own distinctive gifts, qualities, and missions. This book clearly says how much is required from Advanced Souls, especially from Twin Flames. Do you remember what he wrote? *'If one Twin Flame soul loses his way, the other would always act as a homing beacon to call, pull and guide the other half home.' His home is you. His Light is you. You do what you do, not for him or you. You do it for all of us. You, as Light, along with the Light of other Twins and advanced Souls, are here to fight against the Dark.*"

She took a deep breath, then got up and walked over to me. She took my hands in hers and squeezed them as if she wanted to pass me her strength and faith.

---

36   Zeyven Alexander Blackwell, Twin Flame Revelation, 173.

"You are a warrior of Light, Lala, and you are his Twin! As I already said many times, you have no right to give up! That should be clear to you now. And you have no right to judge him for his earthly path either! *Rise above it all and Love his Soul!* Even with what you recently went through, nothing has changed for the Soul you two share! Yes, he loved you and used you! You must rise above it! *Focus on yourself! Work on yourself! Wake up completely, and then you will be able to help him! Because you are never really apart!* Do you understand?"

I nodded.

"He is your Enchanted King, Lala!" she continued, looking intently into my eyes. "You do remember the tale of the Snow Queen?! Once a beautiful and sweet boy, Kai gets a fragment of a cursed mirror into his heart, and it turns into a piece of ice. He becomes cruel and cold. He believes only in a logical mind and Power. Everything kind and beautiful seems fake and ugly to him. The Snow Queen takes him to her ice Kingdom. Meanwhile, Gerda, the girl who loved him, walked half the world to find Kai and melt his icy heart, defeat the Snow Queen and take him back home! Gerda's unique Power to save Kai is *in her heart!* Her love for him is her most extraordinary Power. Nothing can stand against it! *Farhan is Kai, and you are his Gerda!* You have no right to stop. You can't stop and quit everything because it's difficult or because it hurts. You must carry on. You must overcome everything that gets in your way to melt the heart of your Kai-Farhan and do what you *both came here to do.*

"You have accepted and loved his Light, so now accept and love his Shadow. It depends on you how soon he wakes up. Heal yourself first. Start meditating, find a good psychologist, regression specialist, parapsychologist, energy healer. You need to heal all your childhood traumas and wounds, remove all the blocks, learn and practice self-love and self-acceptance. It is long and fraught work, I know! But without doing it, you won't succeed in your mission. Without it, whatever you do, you will slide back into dislike and rejection of yourself, and *he will mirror you at that.* Learning to love and accept yourself will help you to accept him in all his complexity. And as a

418

result, *awake his soul. Making yourself stronger, you are making him stronger! It's all up to you!*"

"I don't know if I can. I really do not know!"

"I know, you can! Lala! You are strong. Remember! Twin Flames are here to help people get to the next level of consciousness. Such a level, where the Dark Ones are no longer able to influence them, use them as slaves and 'food.' Our development is their hunger! There are still very few Twins on Earth, but there will be more and more of them every year. You, Farhan, and the other Twins living and fighting- are *the pioneers.* You have the hardest time. Those coming after you will have it much easier. But I believe in you and Farhan! *I believe that you can rise together as the beacon of light in the power of your true eternal Love!* Many others believe as well! And you should believe, Lala!"

After leaving Bastet, I again went to the ocean shore. There was just too much of what I needed to think of alone. I thought she would tell me to send it all to hell and forget him. But it turns out I had to continue to fight.

But what is there to fight for? For the love of a man who does not love me or is too afraid to love me? Or the great mission to unite the Twin Souls, defeat the Dark Ones, help the Light Ones, and lead people to a higher state of consciousness? Help people remember that within each heart lay a Spark of God, the One True Source. Is that my goal?

Who is right? Susan? Bastet? Zeyven Alexander Blackwell and his amazing book? Who am I? An ordinary woman or a Warrior of Light? Or maybe both? I sat on the sand and stared at the water. I'm probably just a woman. And at the same time, a witch. A Twin Flame. Half of the soul. I'm also the mother of my sons. My mom's daughter. A lonely soul. And this soul is wandering all by herself along the ocean, looking for the meaning of life, knowing, it seemed, already everything and knowing absolutely nothing.

I always felt that there were some Guardians above me. The Guards. The Keepers. The spiritual beings who know all about me, who look after me and if not help, then at least they won't let me leave this life before I accomplish everything I need to do. They find a way to tell me about my great and small goals in life. About my mission. About why I chose this path. Why each time, breaking through a concrete wall, I find another one behind it. Endless amounts of difficulties and problems. What for? But my Guardians are often silent. Probably they can't tell me the answers yet or are not allowed to. They only whisper to me, *"Hold on, Alla! Breathe! Breathe!"*

Time will pass before the new chapter starts. Maybe...

Chapter 46

In the Mist House on the Lost Planet

Joanna lifted a glass souvenir ball standing on a shelf in a cloudy room. Inside the globe, the golden season of autumn has arrived. She gently shook it, creating a swirl of yellow and red leaves. They were dancing in the air and falling over a wooden log cabin that stood in a dense forest at the foot of majestic mountains. Outside the room's huge open windows, leaves fell, reflecting in the ball like a mirror. Two autumn suns and three moons were spilling their warm, calm Light from the purple and blue sky. Firebird sat at the window, completely immersed in her own thoughts.

"Tell me, are all the Twins like that?" she finally asked.

Haan, working on some kind of mosaic or puzzle made of fragments of transparent colored glass on the table, grunted, "Like what?"

"Like that! Do they all hurt, betray, lie, manipulate and deceive? Are they all narcissistic, selfish, power-hungry, unhappy, lonely?" She turned sharply to Joanna, "Did you have something like that with your Twin?"

Joanna cautiously put the glass ball with the log cabin in the forest back on the shelf and looked at Firebird with love and compassion.

"Not all Twins are like that, Firebird," she answered. "Not all of them are weak. Not all of them are strong. It's different for everyone. But more often, while they hurt and betray each other, they learn to love. Learn to remember. Learn to be strong and independent. Learn to forgive. The latter is more complicated. It's

421

easy to be a slave to your own feelings. Believe it or not, crying, suffering, loving selflessly, and altruistically is easy. It is much more difficult to walk away from the sleeping Twin, leaving him alone with his insecurities, narcissism, selfishness and desire to manipulate you and everyone who loves him. It's hard to leave when you love, but you can't change his character or his attitude towards you, or the way he chooses to live his life."

Joanna's voice trembled a little, but she pretended to cough and went to the table. She picked up a crystal pitcher and poured herself a blueish drink with silver bubbles. She drank it eagerly but continued to speak calmly and compassionately.

"You will not believe it, dear, but not all Twins can awaken their other halves. Sometimes you need to come to Earth with him more than once. Again, and again. And every time, you will love him again. There is a big chance that, while in his shadow, he will either immediately reject you, or say that he loves you, play with you, use you, and reject you later. Who knows which one is better? But you will come to him again and again. Life after life!"

Firebird looked at Joanna in surprise. "But we all know that Twin Flames come to Earth at the same time to change the world for the better? They must unite their forces, their Light, and start to create. Create what will touch people's hearts, encourage, inspire and motivate! Books, paintings, films, scientific discoveries, divine energy, peace instead of war, and so much more! How can any of them betray or run away, or hurt the other? They have a mission! A tough, beautiful, and noble mission!"

"You see, Firebird, the problem is, in the beginning, we don't remember our missions, we don't know our tasks, and we don't or can't remember our halves. That brings a lot of mutual pain, mistakes and deception. But with each next life, the Twins get closer to each other, becoming more and more aware of who they are. They become more and more talented, powerful, and loving. And the one who is awake finally catches up with the Runner …" saying that Haan walked up to Firebird and softly kissed her on top of her head. He pulled out a cigarette but changed his mind and threw it out of the window. While falling, the cigarette burst into golden sparks, which turned to small yellow maple leaves, and, beyond the lower border of the window, completely disappeared.

LALA AGNI

The girl looked up at Haan as if trying to remember something. Something in him… Something suddenly seemed so painfully familiar. But then she smiled and asked, "Will Lala and Ram be together? Will their love win? They have met thousands of times in thousands of lives. Probably it's time already for them to unite and complete the mission they were called for, right? And by the way, what is their mission?"

The woman with white hair appeared in the room unexpectedly. "They must save their world, Firebird," she said calmly, coming to the window and looking out at the falling leaves. "Time is running out; you are right. Now the planet is about to make another quantum transition. If high vibrations become predominant, there will be a New Earth! Love is going to be the one and only Law there! But if low vibrations will prevail," she paused. "Let's hope it will not happen! There is still time! Lala and Ram are now stronger than ever. If they unite, others will unite as well. In such a case, both the Earth and humanity will enter the Golden Era, known in very ancient sacred scripts as a wonderful and happy land, full of harmony, love, and joyful people."

"And if not? What if they do not unite because HE will never get the courage to see her? What then?" Firebird looked around the room, into the face of each one of them.

Haan and Joanna turned away to the window, pretending to admire the falling leaves. The sight was truly enchanting. The suns were setting; the moons were shining brighter. The sky turned turquoise, cornflower blue, and golden. The wind waved streams of yellow and red leaves, reminiscent of a dancing gypsy wearing her ruffled skirt. Absolute silence filled the room.

"And if they can't learn self-love, become free, and finally meet, then… Then another planet will become deserted. And somewhere far away, we will have to start all over again." The woman with white hair came up to the narrow wall cabinet and opened it. She thoughtfully took a glass ball into her hands, the same globe that just a moment earlier Joanna had held in her hands. She also shook it a little. Admired the golden autumn swirls and looked at the rows of other glass balls, much like the one she cradled in her hands. They stood beside one another on the shelves in the cabinet. Each was different, City landscapes. Village streets. Deserts. Snow-covered forests. Palm trees and seas. Mountains

423

and forests. Everywhere you could see movement—snow or rain, wind, waves, tree crowns, flowing rivers ... One thing you couldn't see were people. Those were the lost planets, where people failed to choose Love.

'Well, they both continue to their search for the truth." she said, closing the cabinet but still holding the ball with the log cabin in the autumn forest in her hands. "Let's hope for the best. Let's not lose our faith in our Lala. She's smart and powerful. She loves Him, and He loves her too. It's time for our King to step out of his Shadow!"

With those last words, she put the glass globe on the table.

Chapter 47

The End of the Game

I turned to face the ocean water. For some reason, the lines from my favorite book, *The Maid of the Pharaohs*, appeared in my memory.

On the other side, my beloved is standing.
The water in the river is rumbling between us.
The Crocodile rests on a sandbank.
My beloved is waving to me.
But I don't have a boat to get to him.
The Crocodile rests on a sandbank.
My beloved is calling my name.
But I have no wings to fly to him.
The Crocodile rests on a sandbank.
'You, the beast of the river
I will give you my right foot.
Just let me go to my beloved!
You, the beast of the river
I will give you my right hand.
Just let me go to my beloved!'
'I don't want your right foot
I don't want your right hand.
I want to swallow you whole!
Then you can wait for him.

Wait for your beloved one.
In the place where no longer
You have to part with him![37]

How I loved this book and these lines: *"Then you can wait for him, wait for your beloved one, in the place where no longer you have to part with him!"*

But I could not do this. I had to live apart from *my beloved*. Perhaps for a very long time. Perhaps even as long as this life lasts. Yes, that was the reason why all my unshed tears were burning my eyes, why my heart was beating with pain and my Soul was looking at me with her huge sad eyes from the cage she was locked in. What could I tell her? How could I calm and soothe her? Unfortunately, I had no words of comfort for her.

I sat on the sand and stared at the water for a long time, watching day disappear into the night. The words of Susan, Bastet, and others shuffled through my memory like a deck of enchanted magical cards. Over and over again.

"He is an enchanted King—your Farhan, Lala! And only you can free him from this spell!"

"He is a slave to a lamp! Like the fairy tale about Aladdin. The lamp is his crazy life."

"Remember Gerda from Andersen's fairy tale *The Snow Queen?* She went through many trials, walked across the whole world to save Kai from the kingdom of Ice. *You are his Gerda!"*

But I didn't feel strong enough for that. Where could I find the strength to keep moving on? I did not understand what to do next. I was completely lost. However, one thing was absolutely clear for me. I knew I had to leave this game, the game he invented, which we played following his rules. *I was always a loser in this game*, and he was the winner. I was done playing it!

---

37 Elizabeth Herring, The Maid and the Pharaoh, (Pravda, 1988), 124. The translation from Russian is my own.

After wandering until dark along the coast, I finally returned home. At first, I wanted to say goodbye to him by writing another chapter of my story, *The King and the Witch*. I even knew what I was going to write. I would call this chapter *"The Grail of Power."* The Dark Lord would offer my King a golden chalice that belonged to another dark magician, the Lord of Broken Dreams. This chalice, or rather, the golden grail, gave the one possessing it immense power over both worlds—the world of people and the realm of wizards. But in return, my King would have to give the Dark Wizard his memory of me. I mean, of the Witch. The King agrees to this, giving up eternal Love to gain complete and absolute power.

I spent several long night hours writing and editing the text, but then I was severely disappointed. The whole chapter mysteriously disappeared when I tried to copy it to the FB page. Gone, like it never existed! Apparently, the Higher Forces did not like this "ending" of our story. Still, I did not want to leave silently without saying a word. So, I wrote a different text and posted it on my Facebook page.

LIFE WITHOUT THE SOUL...
Do you know what I call Sadness? I call her a Lady with silvery gray wings who hugs me and holds me in her embrace sometimes very tightly, not letting me go.
I end up wrapped within her wings when I see people neglecting their Souls as if they did not even have one. Many religious people think that taking care of the Soul means visiting churches and temples or performing religious rituals. When, in fact, taking care of the Soul simply means *LISTENING TO WHAT SHE TELLS YOU AND FOLLOWING HER VOICE, choosing her voice over anything else.* But how many people do that? Not many.
The terrifying truth is that people of this three-dimensional reality value anything else *over* the voice of their Soul! Position, money, reputation, prestige, what people would say of them, etc. The only thing they do not know how to do is how to open their hearts and

listen to the voice of their Soul, which resides inside their very hearts!

Look, what happened to LOVE? What happened to the most powerful Force in the Multiverse! It has turned into anything but what it truly is! Try telling people that Love in our hearts is THE ONLY way to transformation and Enlightenment. They will laugh at you and call you crazy! Love is the only Force that is capable of moving people! But people instead are motivated by other things! People are motivated by fear, greed, ego, envy, jealousy. Mostly GREED! That goes on and on from one life to another, turning into a never-ending cycle. Love is the Force! But the dark side makes love appear as a *weakness*.

Love is the only truth—the only religion. Act out of Love. Think out of Love. And the world would transform into a magical place. But Love has nothing to do with being humiliated, lied to, or being used or being treated wrongly!

People give too much time and effort to taking care of the temporary things. When they have a house, they want a bigger one. When they have a million, they want ten million. They are never satisfied. GREED takes over their hearts, becoming the ruler. But a moment will come when, no matter how much they have, they lose the feeling of TRUE JOY. Why? Because for years and years, they were taking care of pleasing their body, completely neglecting the voice of their Soul. But do you want to know what life is without the Soul? *That is a life of death.* When you live your life, listening to your Soul, following your Soul, respecting and valuing her guidance, *you live a life of JOY.* You really do LIVE!

When you neglect your Soul, you are not truly living at all. You are a biological robot, a machine. The Soul is what makes you ALIVE. Without it, you are not living. You walk, talk, smile, make money, visit parties, and have lovers, but YOU ARE NOT LIVING! *That is a LIFE OF DEATH!*

You think, it is important to become successful, to achieve something from society's point of view?

But I will tell you the truth if you are ready to hear it. Your Soul, your true Eternal Essence, does not care how rich or poor you are! Your Soul does not care how much money you have in your bank account, 23 dollars or 500 million. Your Soul does not care what religion your body follows. Religion usually comes with the place of your incarnation. You can be a Buddhist in one life and a Christian in another; you might be in another Solar system and another Galaxy in the third one, where religions don't exist. *The Soul does not care about your religion.* She doesn't care about your position in society either! She doesn't care if you are the head of a major corporation, a movie star, a Miss Milky Way Galaxy, or a single mother of 7! *SHE ONLY CARES IF YOU HEAR HER, IF YOU LISTEN TO HER, IF YOU FOLLOW HER VOICE.* So, ask yourself, do you follow the voice of the Soul, *or do you follow the voice of your fears, greed, ego, and anything else?*

And now I will tell you one little secret! Your Soul knows and sees everything you do. When one day, your physical life is over, do you know who will judge you? Do you really want to know? You will be surprised; *IT WILL BE THAT VERY SOUL OF YOURS!* It will finally have the right to talk to you because it could not, while you were still in your physical body! While in the body, the Soul was a *prisoner of your mind, ego, greed, envy,* and anything else.

Without the body, now she will have the freedom to talk, and you will have to hear what she wants to tell you! There is no escape from the judgment of your own Soul! But there is something you can do right now, if you choose to, of course. Stop running away from the voice of your Soul. *Stop pretending you do not hear what she tells you.* Finally, look into her eyes, embrace her and make peace with her! She is there, right where your heart is beating! Hear her voice. Listen to her voice and never listen to anyone else but *HER.* Whatever questions you have, find a quiet place, close your eyes, breathe several times deeply and *LISTEN TO HER VOICE INSIDE YOUR HEART!* Listen! *You will hear!*

It may take several attempts, but you will hear! She will answer every question of yours! And every single answer will be accurate and true. It is that easy! Yes, it would require courage for some of you because many have forgotten how to listen to her. But be patient, and it will come! Whenever you are in a situation where you do not know what to do, ask yourself this simple question, *what would my Soul say? What would my Soul do?* Then do whatever she tells you to do! There is no other truth, only this one because your *Soul is the Spark of Original Source*, which is God! There is no other truth but this one! *Your Soul is nothing but Love, itself!* Fears, doubts, anxiety, greed, jealousy, hate *never comes from the Soul! Never!* They come from the Dark Side. Do you want to obey the dark side? I do not think so. So do not! Obey your Soul, and you will always be *on the right path!* Your Soul would never tell you to pass the hungry, or sad, or hurt somebody, or use somebody! *The Soul is not capable of that!* When you help another person, *you help yourself.*

When you save somebody, *you save yourself!* When you make someone smile, you will smile. When you help someone heal, *you heal yourself!* And stop being fearful of death. Death does not exist; it is only an illusion! *You are a Spark of God—Source. Eternal and immortal Energy!* That Energy cannot be destroyed, disappear or cease to exist. It only changes form! It transforms, but it remains forever! *You are forever!* All your Love is forever! You cannot lose anybody because they all will exist forever, just as you will! May the Force of True Light lead you solely on the path of Love, kindness, and compassion. Underneath it all, *we are all ONE.* And for Love, nothing is impossible. When you live, think, talk, and act out of Love towards yourself and everyone else, *nothing is impossible!* Love is the most powerful Force in all Multiverse, and no obstacles exist for this Force! *Love is your Soul, and your Soul is Love.* No other truth exists.

After that, I went to our "waterfall of the forbidden forest" on Twitter and wrote, *"I hope you will have good memories of me."* These were my last words.

The night was over, and the morning had come. I deleted my Twitter account, our only direct connection with each other. Of course, the Omnipowerful Farhan Ali knew all the possible information about me, and if his majesty wished, *he could have found me in a blink of an eye* or at least *called me.* But finally, I understood, *this was never his intention. So, be it.*

Chapter 48

Alina

Now I guess it was time for me to start fighting with my own demons. Change me. Seek and cultivate *a love for myself*, confidence, *and self-sufficiency*. Suddenly, I realized that I did not have any idea what I should do or even where to start? What am I supposed to do? Meditations? But I have tried them for years and multiple times. Unfortunately, they have never worked well for me. Or perhaps I was doing something wrong. What else? Psychology? I was always into it and read anything and everything I could find on the subject. But those times I had the opportunity to talk to classical psychologists, I got annoyed with their conservatism and absolute absence of professional curiosity and desire to look "out of the box." However, *parapsychologists* would be a completely different story. I knew from personal experience that almost all people with "The Gift," or the "Seers," as I call them, always choose to enter the field of either *philosophy or psychology*, very often *both*. I knew as well that many psychics, and clairvoyants, practice as psychologists. This way, they can help people, having an official diploma from a traditional institution. It makes their hard work somewhat easier. That was exactly the kind I needed to find. But how? Where? Where would I find a parapsychologist who would be able to see me the way Bastet could. One who would not think I had completely lost my mind if I told her my story? The problem seemed impossible to resolve.

Trying past life regressions would also be a wonderful thing. From what I had read over many years, I knew that nothing could be compared with the effectiveness of this method. It was a quick and effective way, with one small exception. I had to find a good regressionist who was also a *SEER*. Where would I find such?

It turned out when I asked myself that question, I already knew her! As the saying goes, the Universe always gives us what we need and when we need it.

I had known Alina for about a year. We met at one of the forums dedicated to the decrypting of ancient legends and tales. It was one of Alina's strong points. She was very knowledgeable in this topic, not only from the familiar three-dimensional sources but also from her own immersions through meditations and regressions into the depths of our great ancestors' lives, into the days when epics and tales were real events of that time. On one well-known radio station, Alina, being a radio blogger, used to share amazing information and discoveries with her listeners about the real life of our forefathers. About the ancient Gods, about the deep knowledge hidden in the ancient myths. After just several minutes' talk, we started to communicate, and a few days later, we found out there were oceans of things and passions we shared and had in common. As they say, "they found each other." We could talk for hours, sharing books we read, films, videos, articles, personal discoveries, and so much more with each other.

She lived in another state. For about a year, we had communicated via the Internet. All that time I had no idea that she was a professional psychologist, parapsychologist, and regressionist. We always discussed our discoveries, but never our professions.

Two weeks after my long talk with Bastet, I talked with Alina about who Koshchey was in the Slavic tales and Kashyap in the Indian epic and how those two were connected. Suddenly I asked her if she, by any chance, knew someone who could help me find an experienced regressionist. Alina was shocked by my question. She was sure, I knew who she was by profession.

One thing led to another, and once I told her that I needed her help as a specialist, she immediately invited me to come to her place for several days. At that time, she had successfully practiced past life regression for the last eighteen years.

For the first time in my life, probably, I decided I would not try to find a million and one excuses not to do that because it was only about me, myself, and I, not my children, my family, and my duties. The familiar feeling of guilt squeezed my heart when I decided I would not put it off and just go, but I imagined it was the heavy black rock and threw it into the Ocean.

Atlanta, Georgia, was not that far from me, and I could easily get there by car. My burns had more or less healed. At least they had healed enough to be covered with a thick layer of foundation and concealer.

So, armed with a supply of coffee, protein bars and my favorite music, I hit the road. I was driving up to a large bright house seven hours later, which was surrounded by trees and flowers in bloom. A couple of minutes later, I was sitting in the elegant living room of my friend, now also my psychologist and regression specialist.

I must admit that I felt very uneasy, to say the least. Of course, beyond any doubt, I clearly knew that Alina was, as I called such people, "one of us," meaning one of the Seers. But at the same time, I have never in my whole life had an appointment with this kind of therapist! Never! What if she tells me that all this story was just my damn imagination? We are talking about a professional psychologist with 20 years of practice under her belt! *What if she tells me... Ah, maybe it is even for the better if she tells me I am nuts. She will use some hypnotherapy to erase this whole thing from my memory! Actually, that would be just perfect. Maybe then, I will move on, become "normal," and... And what?*

My slender, beautiful hostess graciously entered the room with a small tray in her hands, interrupting my thoughts. The tray had two cups of tea and a small basket with little cookies.

"Do you like baking?" I asked her.

"Oh! Absolutely! And believe me, everybody loves it! I love taking my time to bake fresh pastries! It gives me a feeling of joy, and the aroma of baked goods in the oven is beyond compare!"

"I absolutely agree! You won't believe it, but I love baking as well! It's my little addiction, besides books, candles, and the Ocean."

434

We both laughed. Alina put the tray on the table, handed me one of the cups, and took the other. The room immediately filled with the smell of summer alpine meadows.

"What a wonderful aroma! What kind of tea is this?" I asked.

"Oh, take a sip! These are the herbs from the *Altai region*, the real ones, collected at the foot of Belukha Mountain. My friends often send me these teas—this one, in particular, has some incredible powers. It clears your mental field and opens your eyes to the hidden!

"And my dear Alla!" she continued with a soft smile. "Please, relax! We've known each other for a long time! *Much longer than just this incarnation!*"

"Yes, I understand! Believe me; I completely understand that! But the thing is, you see," My usual eloquence completely abandoned me that day. "I am something that you might not yet be familiar with, have heard of, or know. This thing is not quite usual. Many people have never heard of it, and many of those who have, do not believe in it. It may sound like absolutely ridiculous nonsense! If I had not lived through all this and experienced it all myself, I probably would have been thinking just the same!"

I fell silent for a moment. Alina was patiently waiting for me to continue. But I somehow was terrified even to say it out loud. Finally, I gathered as much courage as I could and said, "The thing is, have you... *Have you ever heard about «Twin Flames?»*

"Of course!" She answered with a soft laugh, her eyes sparkling. "And I have worked with them as well! But you are right; they are very rare. And this is one of the reasons why I knew you were one of them the moment I saw you."

"But, how?" I looked at her in complete astonishment.

"Oh! That is very easy, my dear girl! The energy of you guys is impossible to miss. Twin Flame energy is like a huge bonfire in the forest, with such spurts of flames flying up to the sky, it's impossible *not to see.* I have seen this phenomenon only twice in my life before you. So, relax, my dear, *I know exactly who you are!*"

Tears of joy or relief sparkled in my eyes as Alina gently took the cup from my hands, lifted me from her comfortable white leather sofa and hugged me tightly!

"Crying is not just allowed," she said without even a hint of a joke, "but is highly encouraged! Don't bother holding those tears inside, my Love! Let the pain go away together with them! We need that to help joy come in its place! And so, you can fully understand my gifts and powers and have full trust in me, I need to show you something. Please, wait here; I'll be right back."

She left me for just a few minutes and returned with a laptop in her hands. She opened it up and spent a couple of minutes searching for something. Finally, she found it and turned the screen towards me. I froze. My own eyes were looking at me from Farhan's face. Oh, how well I knew this face in every detail. I knew it for what? Hundreds of years? Thousands? But with his face came the memories of the things I *wish I could forget*. Those memories caused the sensation of a cold blade in my heart and made me shiver, even though I was almost sure I was already used to it.

"How! How did you know that?" I asked her. *"Is his name written on my forehead?"*

"Pretty much," Alina laughed. "Let me tell you a little story. Many years ago, I took classes with a young woman, Sofia. She was *a huge fan of his*. We spent time together at least a couple of times a week, and we often watched his movies. I was always fascinated by him. Not because of the way he looked or his obvious talent. There was something else in him. *Something very ancient*, hidden deep inside, *living, breathing and vibrating in him*, but it seemed he was *unaware of it*. His eyes had the vibe of something *ancient* that words cannot describe. I tried to explain to myself what it was but could not. Years later, I met my first Twin Flame client. Surprisingly, this client was a man. He was living his normal life, was married, had a career and two grown-up sons, when one day, while in Canada on a business trip, *he met a woman*. They spent less than an hour talking together, and his world turned completely upside down. *I mean completely!* He spent over a year visiting traditional therapists but unfortunately found no answers, until the Guides brought him to me. He said those words, *Twin Flames* in one of our hypno-regression sessions. That is when I first heard of it. I started to dig into anything and everything I could find about them. One day, listening to him talking, I caught myself thinking there was something familiar *in his eyes.* But at that moment, I could not recall where I had seen it before. A couple of weeks later, Sofia and I went to see the new movie with Farhan Ali. And then, it dawned on me! Holy Gods of the North! *This man was also a Twin Flame!* I had no doubt about it! So, I started to pay more attention to his life. I was mostly curious when *SHE* would appear, his other half. Who is she going to be, where will she come from? Several years passed by and she still had not shown up. I had another case with Twin Flames and after several years of research, I was able to see the unique kind of energy only you guys have. It reminds me *of 'Flames'* indeed. When you and I started to communicate, I went onto your Facebook page. I was curious and wanted to see your photo. *As soon as I saw your face and your eyes, Farhan Ali's face appeared instantly in my mind! Same eyes,* with that same something ancient in them, *same vibe, same energy, same feel!*

"To make a long story short, Alla, I knew you would come here, into this very house, *over a year ago!* I was waiting for you, my girl! I hope you understand now; you have come to the right place and the right person. *I know very well what and who you are.* It is not an easy path. For all the Twins, the road is different yet somewhat similar. You all have come to fight the dark, to *make a change.* That was never easy on our planet, especially in the last thousand years. You came to me to find the answers to your questions. And we will try to find them. But you must be ready to work. *Work, Alla! It is intense inner work!* You will have both victories and failures, ups and downs, and the desire to drop it all and send it all to hell. But remember, when you work on yourself, *you are also helping him.* Away from your physical elements, *you are one.* Two flows of energies intertwined and united together into one *for eternity.* Therefore, whatever you know, he will know as well. By healing yourself, your wounds, your traumas, and your insecurities, *you will help him as well.* It hurts a lot now, I know. I can read it in your eyes. But the more you can see and deeply understand why things are the way they were and are, the easier it will become for you to keep on following your path. Do you understand me?"

I silently nodded. I was ready for my next step. I was ready.

Chapter 49

Regression
Returning to the Past

As I mentioned, Alina was a regressionist. Who is it? A regressionist is a guide to our past lives. Many years ago, psychologists and psychiatrists using hypnotherapy in their practice noticed that some people during the sessions of deep hypnosis, while immersed in their early childhood, would sometimes "skip" further back. They would remember the death that preceded their current birth. And then another life, which they had lived before this one. And then another one before that one, and many others.

Over the decades, the technique of deep immersion "into the past" has improved significantly. Many conductor regressionists use the methods developed by their predecessors to awaken the patient's memories of past lives or reincarnations. *Why is this method so effective?* The answer is rather simple.

It is a great way to access the information, *encrypted and hidden in our subconscious.* In most cases, Past Life Regression can uncover the reasons and causes preventing us from living life *fully today.* The simple fact is, *we are all the result of our past lives,* experiences, emotions, mistakes, choices, and the paths we have or have not taken.

Nothing in our lives is coincidental. Absolutely *nothing!* What you love or dislike, what you strive for, what you dream about, what you fear. The roots of all this are in the past. Everything, not only on our Earth but also throughout the Universe, has a *cause-and-effect* link. Everything *has its root and its reason.* It simply cannot be otherwise.

After talking with many of their patients, some well-known regressionists began recording what they heard. Many excellent books have been written, contributing to the confirmation of the law of reincarnation and helping many more people understand. With every passing year, more and more people have learned that we live more than once, in hundreds and thousands of lives.

My favorite book of all is *Journey of Souls*, written by Professor Michael Newton. The book describes twenty cases of people of different faiths and world views entering a superconscious state during regression sessions. The book helps us find the answers to many questions: *Who meets us in the world of Spirits after our physical death? What happens to the soul before the next incarnation? How does the soul choose the conditions and the goals of the next life? What is our purpose on Earth?*

Destiny of Souls is another brilliant work of this author. It is hard to underestimate the contribution of this amazing professional to the world and the people. He studied this subject for over 40 years, and his credentials are *unquestionable.* He was also the founder of the Michael Newton Institute for Life Between Lives Hypnotherapy, which trains professional regressionists. I consider his books, his research, and his work simply *priceless gift to Humanity.*

Of course, you can argue and doubt. You can do your own research or continue your search for the truth based on what has already been put into your head by somebody else. The choice is always yours.

I choose trustworthy, passionate researchers. Time is changing very fast. The history, which was called alternative, is about to become mainstream because people are starting to think more often about inconsistencies between the latest discoveries and old "official" versions.

Many things written in conventional history books also start to look like a joke in the light of recent findings. And not only that. More and more people, far from physics, are becoming familiar with *waves, frequencies, fractals, energies, and vibrations.* People are becoming aware of the incredible discoveries of many: *Ernst Chladni (Chladni figures), Dr. Masaru Emoto,* and his amazing work about Water Consciousness. Schumann's resonances of our planet and how they have been dramatically changing in the last several years, influencing our lives on all and every level. People are starting to think of and get familiar with many other things they had not even thought of before. As Nikola Tesla said, *"If you wish to understand the Universe think of energy, frequency, and vibration."* More and more people are becoming aware of it!

Some children recall their past lives, calling relatives, living in nearby or distant places, by name. Many are still alive and confirm these stories of their recently deceased and reincarnated loved ones. Some Seers have long known both their destiny and their past lives. And now, everyone wanting to find the answers to important questions, can do that with the help of a regressionist. They help us find the beginning of a thread in a tangled ball of our past, which we cannot remember on our own.

Both Bastet and Alina told me that I had to do the intense *inner work* and learn *self-love and self-acceptance so that he could do the same.* Only then could he truly love me, and I, in turn, could see myself, not only him, *but both of us in the mirror of our Soul.* Only this way could we have a chance for a future together. How this is all connected? Our loved ones look into us as in a mirror. If you love him and him only, *forgetting yourself completely,* then he will see in that mirror of you only *his own reflection.* In this case, he will leave as soon as he gets tired of your *all-absorbing* Love. But if He sees *both of you* in that mirror, two powerful, self-sufficient, and happy people, then Love has a future. A beautiful future! For that to happen, you have to heal the old wounds, spread your wings and learn to fly above the clouds fearlessly. Learn to fly!

In this life, the origins of my insecurities, wounds and absence of self-love come from my family. The most significant burden for my Soul was the failure of all the attempts to forgive my parents. Like an unbreakable slab, this load was lying on my heart, forcing me to the ground and not allowing me to breathe deeply.

I could forgive neither my father, whom I had never known nor my mother, for what I had to go through in my childhood.

After almost 40 years of this life, I was exhausted and fed up with my bouts of fears, doubts, and panic attacks. They had haunted me for as long as I remembered.

Morning has always been the hardest time of day for me. I was terrified of the mornings. In the morning, my mother used to go to work and I was left alone with my brother, the one whose Soul had chosen to be my torturer.

Yes, at that stage of my life, of course, I knew that Souls, while being in the dimension from where we come to live our next life, never feel the desire nor joy to go into their physical embodiment as a torturer. But very often, our enemies become our most vital teachers. They make us grow stronger and able to overcome obstacles. They teach us how to rise above our fears, pain, and doubts. I can understand it now. But when I was a little girl, I did not know any of this, and my Soul lived in fear, doubt, and loneliness. I had to try to heal it.

"I will tell you a little story," Alina told me before starting my first regression session. It is called: 'Where would we hide the Divine Power?" Listen…

Once upon a time, many thousands of years ago, all people living on Gaia-Earth had the Divine Power. Each one of them was God since their Souls had achieved the level of Creation. Many myths and legends tell of this Golden Era lasting thousands of years. But The Dark Side found its way to our blessed planet. They found a way to penetrate the minds and Souls of People-Gods. The result of this influence was terrible. People-Gods started to use the Divine Power the wrong way, harming and hurting themselves and the others, being possessed by greed, envy, thirst for power. That lasted for a long time! Finally, Brahma—the God—Source of all the Creative Energy and thus everything that exists, decided to stop that!

Brahma decided to take the Divine power from People-Gods, who had started to use it the wrong way, and hide it in such a place where they would not be able to ever find it!

442

But unfortunately, even Brahma could not think of such a place. Finely Brahma decided to call other Gods and ask for their advice.

"Let's hide the Divine Power in the depth of Mother Earth." Some said.

"No," answered Brahma. "People are smart, and they will find a way to get it from there."

"Then let's hide it on the bottom of the Ocean!" Said the others.

"Not the best choice either," answered Brahma. "People will get it from there as well."

"How about the top of the mountain! The highest and the most dangerous one! If people even try to get there, the risk of dying before reaching it would be too high! They won't be able to do that!"

"No," answered Brahma. "You do not know people well enough! They will get it from the top of the highest mountain!"

After all the propositions, the problem remained unresolved. They all kept thinking for many days and nights but could not think of anything else. Until one moment, Brahma rose and proclaimed.

"I got it! I know exactly where we would hide it! That is a place where they will never even *THINK* to look! I will hide the Divine Power in the very center of their Essence! *They will always have it with them and in them, but they will never guess to look for it there!* They will search for God near and far for hundreds of years but will always fail to find what is within them, each one of them!

And the Gods understood how brilliant the idea of Brahma was. And since then, God and Divine power are hidden in everyone's Soul Essence, incarnating on Earth life after life, but very few of them know that each one is *Divine by their very Essence*. Every single one of them, at their very core, is God.

"And now that you have heard this story," said Alina, "we will try to help you find that Divine power inside of you! You always had it but forgot about it! And I want to help you remember. Are you ready?"

"Yes. I am. I know this story very well; it is one of my favorites! I read it several years ago, and I even shared it with him in one of my letters."

"Good. I am glad you did! So now, please, relax and close your eyes. I need you to breathe in deeply seven times and breathe out seven times! With each breath you take, you will breathe in bright sunlight, which will fill you like a vessel, healing you, renewing you, and restoring your strength. One. Two. Three. Deeper and deeper. Four. Five. Even deeper than before. Six. Deeper and deeper. *SEVEN.*

I felt that I was falling, falling, falling, through an endless Cosmos. The very next moment, I saw myself suspended in a transparent blue space, surrounded by many very tall shining figures. I call them the *Fathers*. They were looking at me with almost earthly, human emotions, most of all Hope. They hoped that I would find the strength to handle anything I would encounter on the journey they are sending me on. There was also deep and sincere empathy because they knew my path would not be easy. I saw endless, eternal wisdom and kindness in them.

Sadly, seeing myself from the current "here and now" viewpoint, I feel great anger and resentment towards them. I want to cry. I want to scream at them! I want to blame them for everything I have endured. I want to blame them for everything that happened to me and what will happen in the future. But most of all, I feel hurt and bitter because they separated me from Him and sent us into this incarnation, distant and apart in every single way possible with close to zero chances of being together.

In my physical body, tears suffocate me as I begin to cry.

As if from far away, I hear the voice of Alina. "Send them Forgiveness! Send them Light and Love!"

"No!" I almost scream! "No! I will not! I do not want to! First, they called for me! And then they sent me here to experience pain, to live this torture!! They have separated us! *I have never been without him before,* but they believe it was *necessary.* They consider that what I have to do on Earth can only be done by me and no one else. But I do not want to do it! I do not want to live like this! I do not want to!"

I shiver and tremble. I can't seem to stop crying.

"Not a single Soul is sent down on Earth *against her will!* You have agreed to this! You came to Earth of your own free will! *It was your choice! Only yours!* Both of you answered the call and agreed to this task. *You both agreed because you wanted to help people remember their Divine origin!* You wished that with all your heart! And you must see and remember it yourself. Now I will count to THREE, and you will go *farther back! Go Back! Look what happened before! One. Two. Three!*"

I see myself in a giant ball, looking like trillions of little shining multicolored suns create it. I look like a baby. Maybe about a year old. I also shine like those little suns with a kind of golden light. Suddenly, next to me, I see another baby who looks just like me, only he is a boy. In my heart chakra area, I have something like an *indigo-colored crystal. The boy has one as well.* But his crystal is a little bit smaller than mine. For some reason, I understand that I am stronger than him. Not much, but stronger like a twin who was born first. We turned to each other and I feel this incredible, *absolute Love.* There's a complete absence of all earthly fears or doubts or anything like that. *Only Love and Peace. Love and Peace.*

The indescribable feeling of Peace and Love is tough to express in human words. The next moment I see two hands reaching out for him, picking him up and taking him out of our sphere. I understand that they took him into the physical world first. It's strange but I do not feel any anger or fear in his absence. I know *it is only temporary.* I clearly understand that *it's impossible to separate us because we are one.* I am just peacefully waiting for my turn. I also begin to see the pictures of my future life on Earth.

I see a terrified little girl. She is hiding behind a red curtain; knowing what is ahead of her will be extremely scary and painful, and no one will be there to rescue her. But looking at all this from my sphere, I understand that I can get through this. I am strong enough. So, I am just watching, calmly watching.

I see myself at my elementary school, sitting on the floor, surrounded by boys and several girls the same age as me: *"Ugly freak! Get out of here! You do not deserve to be among normal people! Freak!"* they say, kicking me with their feet. I hunch and crouch as much as possible, but it doesn't help much. Blows hit me non-stop. But for some reason, instead of hating them, I feel a burning pity! Not for myself. For them! In the "golden sphere," I consciously choose to go through that as well! Images change into one another—my childhood and youth, my tests, my hopes, my little joys, my future earthly life.

I get to the point where I see my future mother and father.

I clearly understand. No one wants or needs me there, to say the least. Me coming to both of them is terrible news, especially for my future mother, who already has a couple of tough teenagers on her hands. I am neither needed nor wanted. And yet, *I CONSCIOUSLY choose to go through it*. I choose to experience the *REJECTION* from my very first seconds of life in the physical world. I chose to go through that. I also decided to endure the experience of being beaten, tortured and humiliated, not only for my "ugliness" but also because I'm "different."

I am the one who chooses and agrees to go through all I must go through in my physical life. I understand that it has to be this way, for me to become stronger. I must learn to fall and rise, to bend without breaking. I need to go through this harsh school to achieve something significant in this incarnation. I am the one who agreed to take such a path. Who am I to blame? *It has been MY decision all along! My own!*

After that, I again find myself in a circle of tall luminous figures. Now I understand why they are looking at me with hope and infinite, eternal *kindness and compassion*. They love me and count on me. They believe in me and are blessing me. And now I can do what I must. I finally can send them Light and Love. Forgive them. And forgive myself because I chose and agreed to such a path.

I see the moment of my birth and my mother. I suddenly understand how little Love and joy she had seen in her life. I saw how few bright days she had and how much her own heart suffered. I understand what a difficult path her Soul chose for her earthly life.

Feelings of deep compassion take me over. I hug my mom, filling her with my energy of pure sunlight. I see my father and allow myself to cry. *"You have never been in my life! Papa!"* I find the strength to forgive him as well. After all, I chose him as my father. I needed that for some reason.

Then I ask the Higher Ones, who blessed me on my earthly path, to allow me to spend several moments with Him. That same moment I found myself in his embrace with my head is on his shoulder. I wrapped my arms around him, melting into him and with him. We are one, intertwined in a tight embrace. Just a fraction of a second passes, and I want it to last forever. I do not want to come back! *Coming back means leaving Him! Oh, how much I do not want that!*

But Alina's voice calmly tells me, "Leave him and come back."

A hurricane of protest rises inside me! But she repeats her words with a calm, soothing, but firm voice.

"Come back, Alla. *He is already yours. You two are one.* But to be together with him here on Earth, you still have a lot to do. If you insist, you will only postpone the moment both of you are waiting for—the moment of your togetherness. So, now you have to say goodbye to him. I will count till five. And when I say 'five,' you will come back into the here and now without arguing! One... Three... Five."

And I came back.

"Now, please try to stay still for a couple of moments," she said, gently touching my hand. "I will bring you a cup of tea. You need it now."

She left the room and came back in a couple of minutes.

"Drink!" she said. I just obeyed, drinking sweet, flavorful herbal tea.

"*Twin Flames come to Earth with a mission.* I am sure you have already heard it a million times," she said while I was drinking my tea. "They are called on by the Higher Forces. They agree to come into the three-dimensional world as male and female and walk part of their lives separately. This way, they are living and learning, rising and falling, falling and rising again, getting enough strength and experience. While going through all that, they reach such a level of consciousness one day, when they can finally unite and do what they have come to do. But their separation is only physical. At the spirit level, they *continue being one.* There are always many obstacles between them. No other ways are even possible. That is part of this path."

Alina fell silent for several moments and then continued. "You and he are so-called 'Key Twins.' It means that one of you, or both, has a huge impact on millions of people. So far, it is him, your Farhan. Once awakened, *he will awaken many people and guide them with the true light of his Soul!* That means you are capable of the same thing. You can touch the hearts of many thousands of people with your inner light! Probably even millions. You can help many people feel stronger, wiser, help them see who they truly are, help them *believe in themselves, in their true inner powers, believe they are capable of changing their own lives and the lives of many others!* You can do it all!"

Her words shocked me.

"Me? Are you talking about me?"

"Yes. Yes, you! I am talking about you! *You are his mirror!* Whatever he can do, you are capable of doing *just the same.* He became famous to the whole world thanks to his hard work, passion, dedication, and his great talent, which means you can do it too! You can rise in this three-dimensional world to the same level as him! Do you understand? If he could, you can do it as well! You are two halves of one!"

"Me? *On the same level with Him? HIM???*" I laughed out loud, without even trying to hide my sarcasm. "Well," I said, still laughing, "that would only be possible if he suddenly loses all his stardom, and everyone leaves him all alone. If no one needs him anymore, he loses his talent and money, friends and lovers. Only if all his fans in 150 countries forget him, and he comes to live in a tiny house a mile away from me. Maybe then *I can be on the same level with him!* But even then, I think I would have to try really hard.

"Heavens! Alina! *He is a genius!* This man is so talented, clever and brilliant! Give me a break. He is a Mega Star! Probably even stray dogs know his name! Mothers give his name to their newborn boys! Not in a million years, never in my whole damn life could I come even close to...."

She stopped me with a subtle motion of her hand.

"Well, then let mothers give your name to the newborn girls, all right? And, please, Alla! Let's leave behind already this intense dislike of yourself and constant self-abasement. Leave it, ok? Starting today, it is a new you and a new life! Do we have a deal?"

I nodded silently. "I will try. I will give it my best, damn it!"

Alina smiled and nodded back to me.

"Oh, by the way, Alla, *give me your left hand, please.*"

I silently gave her my hand and she immediately turned it palm up. She just glanced at it briefly, as if confirming her idea, and again lit up with her incredible smile!

"I knew it! I am such a genius! *I knew it!*"

She looked at my questioning face with her shiny eyes!

"*You've got a mole in the middle of your left palm!* Do you know what that means?"

I shook my head. *No.*

"There is an ancient legend. Some Souls, before their incarnation, promise to find each other in their earthly life. To make it easier for each other, *they are born with the mole right in the middle of their palms.* The woman will always have it on her *left* hand because a Woman lives by her heart. She always follows her Soul and her inner Truth.

"The Man, her Twin, *will have the same mole, but in center of his right palm!* Because a man follows *logic.* He tries to explain everything from the point of view of his cold and rational mind. Does your Farhan have *the same mole as yours?*"

I had not the slightest clue if he did or he didn't. So, I only shrugged.

"Don't move!" she said, rising from her chair. "Stay here; I'll go and bring my laptop! After all, he is a Star, your Farhan, which means, for sure, we can find almost any information about him online. Wait here; I'll be quick."

And she went out, leaving me there, still hovering somewhere between the two worlds. A part of me was still in his embrace, and this part did not want to come back and connect with the part of me that was here. I closed my eyes and allowed both parts of me to connect with him. I laid my head on his shoulder while his head rested on mine. There we were standing, somewhere between worlds, in a cosmic radiant and infinite eternity, outside of space and time.

But again, I was brought back to reality by the bell-like voice of Alina entering the room.

"I told you! I was right! I didn't doubt it for even a second! Here! Look!"

She turned the laptop screen towards me. It was a YouTube video where some famous esoteric astrologer was reading the lines of his palm. They used a photo of Farhan where he was welcoming a joyful and lively crowd with a wave of his hand. Then they enlarged the image of his palm several times to make the lines clearly visible to the viewers. He explained something while I was looking at his palm in pure shock. I was not able to tear my eyes off of it. *I was looking at a mole in the center of his palm. His right palm. In the same place as mine.*

If standing face-to-face with each other, I held my left palm in front of me, and he put his right palm against mine; our moles would *touch in our connected hands.*

"Well, now I am going to tell you what you should do, my dear. It is one of those tasks that you must fulfill! *You must write a book and tell this incredible story of your Love,* including everything you have lived through to this day. I know it for sure! You have to write, my dear; your book will deeply touch many hearts around the world. People will find answers in your story, recognizing themselves in you and him. Those who hear your story will be inspired, and their hearts will start shining brighter. People will remember who they really are, and other Twins will find support and courage there. *You must write!*

"This is the second time I have heard about the book. I have already written one, Alina! But it was for him only. I thought, when he read it, he…" I just shook my head.

"And now, you must write it *for the people.* Write not with your mind, do it with the power of your burning heart and Soul. All people have gifts and unique Spark of the Source in them; yours is *touching people's hearts.* You are real. You are open. You are sincere. People will know it. They will feel it! You must write, Alla! Write!

"And another thing. *Tarot cards!* Those 78 symbols are the whole world! The whole Universe! They are connected with Astrology, Numerology, Mythology, Symbology, and so much more! Allow the depth and the wisdom of those cards to open their secrets and the mysteries to you. They will if you fully open your heart to them! And when it happens, with that knowledge, you will be able to help many people! Do not ask me how. You will understand it yourself when the time comes.

"*Learn to smile and be happy without him, Alla!* Find peace within yourself. Find the light within yourself. *Start to shine on your own!* And when you do, help others to heal, believe and shine. That is what you must do, my girl! *It is what you must do!*"

Chapter 50

Letting Go

We did tremendous work, and finally, I could see some changes in me, in my attitude toward myself. I finally realized that I could love myself *just for being me and not for something in particular.* I could find peace and joy in myself, forgive myself, get to know the new me!

Four weeks had passed since my return home from Alina, when I slowly began to feel *I was whole even without him,* even with him being far away from me. Yes, I was a "half," but as a half, *I still could be whole.* After all, as the seers told me multiple times, separation is possible only in physical; in Soul, we are always together, we are one. Distance, obstacles, misunderstanding, or absence of Love—they didn't mean anything in the World of Spirits! *We still have One Soul—We are still One.* This thought gave me strength and confidence.

Four weeks had passed since my last "goodbye." I did not check his social media, did not search for news about him. I did not know what was happening in his life. But when I finally decided to have a look, I almost snapped again, returning into the old game we used to play, to be exact, he used to play with me, and me following his rules.

It seemed that only a shadow remained of Farhan. His bottomless eyes were lifeless, filled with pain. His severe thinness showed creases on his beautiful face. Bitter folds of sadness or discontent appeared around his lips. And in almost all the videos and photos, he was wearing blue.

"*Come back!*" It meant only one thing: "*Come back!*" But this time, I knew the truth of it: *coming back would mean going back and play his game.* No, I didn't want that. Even if it was necessary for him to sparkle again and smile, I did not want to play that game! I had the right *not to want to.*

A few days later, he gave a speech to a rather large audience that consisted of wealthy and influential people. Just before that day, he told me in my dream: "You used to say, 'Tell them! My Love! They will listen to you!' So, my Beloved! I am going to do so! I am going to tell them! You will see it with your own eyes!"

His speech lasted only half an hour, but I spent several hours in front of the monitor. I watched the video over and over again, constantly pausing it as tears choked me—tears of pain, joy, and gratitude combined. I felt as if someone was tearing my heart to pieces. He turned and directly faced the camera as if looking into MY eyes. Into my Soul! He addressed his words to the hundreds of people in the audience and the millions watching the recorded broadcast, but he spoke directly to me, *using MY words. And I knew it.*

"I want to share something essential with you," he began, "something I only recently realized. Do you know what truly keeps us from breaking while the world around us is falling apart? What gives us the strength and desire to live, create, shine our true light and inspire others? What keeps us from giving up, what breathes new life into our being, what gives us hope? What sheds light on our darkest moments? Do you know what it is? Its essence was present at the world's beginning, *the spark creating everything in this Universe.* It is a word, a feeling familiar to everyone, big and small; an emotion felt and experienced by each of us. We read about it in books and hear it in songs and poems. We all crave and search for it. We fight for it, we live for it, and even die for it. It is something that gives us wings and lets us fly! *What is it? LOVE!*"

He looked directly at the camera when he said, "*Love!*"

This is for you, his eyes told me.

I knew it. I felt it in my soul.

"Money," he continued, "money gives power to those who possess it—a lot of money gives a lot of power! Tonight, I am standing in front of the wealthiest and most influential people in the world. I am one of you. So, what should we do with all the money and power we have? The choice is up to each of us! What will you do? You can spend this money on encouraging wars and intolerance between people based on religion, cultural differences, or anything else that divides us. There will always be plenty of people who are dissatisfied with governments, laws, or systems. If they aren't already disappointed, you can teach them how to be unhappy, hand them weapons, and send them to "fight for justice." Unfortunately, *this path leads nowhere.*

"You could build a marble palace and surround it with extremely high marble walls, isolating yourself from the world. You could buy an island and prepare an underground bunker, just for yourself, in anticipation of the apocalypse. You can collect priceless pieces of art worth millions. You can have a park full of cars, private jets, a soccer team or two. The possibilities are endless.

"*Or... You can choose a different path and change someone's life!* You can build schools, hospitals, and kindergartens with your money. You can tear down the tall marble wall separating you from the world and instead *let the people come to you.* Let simple people become a part of your life and your heart. You can make them feel equal to you, no matter where they come from or who they are. You can hug them. You can make them feel happy and powerful! *When you do something to change their lives, yours will change as well!* Maybe all of us with power and wealth should consider becoming a little kinder, don't you think?"

As I listened to Farhan, I again felt my heart wanting to break free out of my chest and fly away. *Fly away to Him. Fly to Him.* His words profoundly touched me to my very core. I was so proud of him. And I loved him again. Again? Or always? Always! Oh, this silly heart of mine.

"Look, what are we doing to our planet?" Farhan continued. "What are we doing to our Mother who provides a home for all of us, who feeds us, gives us water, and warms us with her body? *We are poisoning her seas, rivers,* and oceans. *We cut down her forests!* We spend millions of dollars improving weapons and creating new ones so we can destroy each other on a larger scale. Look at us! Is it even possible to call us 'Human,' 'Wise Men'? *Hardly so.* We do not act like wise men at all. Mostly we behave as irrational, spoiled, ungrateful children, killing our own Mother Earth. But what are we without her? Without her care? Without her heat? Without Her Love. *What are we, Without, HER LOVE?"* As he said the last two words, he again looked straight into the camera and *into my very Soul!*

The screen behind him lit up, showing a beautiful rainforest, green trees soaring into the turquoise-blue sky, wild animals and birds living in peace and harmony. Suddenly, the serenity disappeared! What was once full of life was replaced by horrific destruction, death, and despair. A song started playing, words and music by one of this planet's most gifted sons. We lost him and many others before him. It seems we fail the best of our sons and daughters only to cry over them when they're gone.

What about sunrise?
What about rain?
What about all the things
That you said we were to gain?
What about killing fields?
Is there a time?
What about all the things
That you said was yours and mine?
Did you ever stop to notice
All the blood we've shed before?
Did you ever stop to notice
This crying Earth, these weeping shores?
What have we done to the world?
Look what we've done
What about all the peace
That you pledge your only son?
What about flowering fields?

Is there a time?
What about all the dreams
That you said was yours and mine?
Did you ever stop to notice
All the children dead from war?
Did you ever stop to notice
This crying Earth, these weeping shores?[38]

I closed my eyes. I could never watch this video and listen to this song without my heart feeling ripped apart. The Great Son of Mother Earth and Humanity wanted to show us, help us see, think, get terrified with our deeds and change something. He called it "Earth Song." Michael Jackson, a legend, an artist, a man with a child's heart—a heart hurt, broken, and betrayed too many times—created a song with a profound message. His message touches all of us, even those who do not know English. It was not the first song he wrote like this. Others were: "We Are the World," "Man in the Mirror," "Heal the World." But "Earth Song," in my opinion, is the most powerful of them all. It left every particle of my very Soul *trembling and crying.*

Oh, what we have done to the world, to the children, to the planet, to ourselves! The song ended, leaving the audience in complete silence. Dead silence! Finally, Farhan's voice sounded deep and quiet, as if repeating the same questions I had in my mind and heart, the same question, expressed in this song:

"*What have we done to the world? Look what we've done!*"

I closed the video. I forgave him for everything. *Because of THIS,* I forgave him for everything and anything! I again opened the only channel that connected us directly. Twitter. Yes, I had deleted my account but I thought

---

38 "Earth Song." Track #20 on HiStory: Past, Present, and Future, Book I, Epic Records, 1995. Michael Jackson.

that I could restore it. I tried. But I failed. Of course, I could easily create a new one. But I suddenly stopped.

I could see I was about to make the same mistake again—the one I had made not once but many, many times before. All it took was a word, look, smile, the blink of his eyelashes, or a profoundly beautiful speech, and I was running to him!

Running!

Running!

Running!

Running and forgetting everything—forgetting the past pain, his unwillingness to see me in real life, playing cat and mouse with me, using me and my Love for him to his advantage. Just look at me! I would fall at his feet and would be ready to trade my whole damn life for one smile of his. No! *That is wrong!* Yes, I loved him. I have loved him for thousands of lives. I have loved him endlessly, wholeheartedly, selflessly, with the Love of a Twin Flame! *But I could no longer let him play with my fate, my heart, my life …*

Take your pride, Lala! Hold it in front of you like a shield! I said to myself. *Does it hurt? Sure! Sure it hurts! It's ok! You can handle it! You survived San Francisco. You sure can get through this! For his Soul to shine, you must first shine yourself!*

Easier said than done. *But I MUST do it! Must!*

Two months passed since that day. Yes, I changed and managed to forgive myself for some things—extremely challenging for someone who had seen only her faults for several decades. My pain of being away from Him was still there, living and dwelling in my every cell, torturing me every breathing moment, not giving me any peace. Or was it my Love for him? *I must learn to love and value myself over him.* He was still my Life, my Sun, and my Moon! And I had to learn *to put myself there instead of him.* I had to become my Life, my Sun, and my Moon! *Forgetting yourself is the same as betraying yourself!* No matter what excuse you give! I must learn to put ME first! Well. That was a hard thing!

We can be confident and strong, educated, intelligent; we can understand everything. But there are some things, beautiful in their very essence, which can deprive us of our will, strength, pride, and common sense.

Love is a wonderfully beautiful feeling. Love is miraculous! It inspires, gives wings, and helps to achieve the impossible. But unfortunately, sometimes it also destroys us.

I tried my best to convince myself that even without him, I could still be radiant, happy, full of life (you can continue this list to infinity), but nothing worked for me. I have not outgrown him, had not become stronger or more conscious. I still felt "not whole" without him. I still had that nagging pain in my chest. My Soul "bird in her tiny cage" still wanted to break free and fly to him. Fly to him. *Fly to him.* I guess I didn't get past the threshold of my low-frequency vibration. In the end, I decided that I had to come up with the "Formula of Non-Love." That was the name that I made up for it. I decided that I had to find a way to disconnect myself from my Twin! For myself, and others like me! But alas, no matter how hard I tried to find the method for it, *all my attempts were in vain. I never found it!*

But there MUST be some method! There must be something! Something I could do!!! There had to be some way to break this connection! To cut it off! To block it out! Therapy! Deep Hypnosis! Anything! There HAD to be a way! I didn't want to go on anymore. I did not feel like I could or wanted to. I had no strength left in me to keep up with it!!! All I felt was powerlessness, hopelessness, and helplessness!

"*Mission?*" I said to myself sarcastically, "The heck with that Mission! Warriors of Light? The heck with it as well! What am I supposed to do? Do I need to help people remember their Divine nature? Raise the Vibrations of Love on this planet? What does all this have to do *with me?* What kind of warrior can I possibly be? I am just a simple, ordinary woman! As ordinary as can be! What has any of this to do with me?"

But then suddenly, as if something or someone interrupts me, I stop my inner monologue.

With my inner sight, I see my sword and the endless, countless moments where I am on the battlefields, different times, places, faces, beings, realities, and maybe even different worlds and dimensions. But I am never alone. *He is always there with me*, fighting by my side. *I am everywhere and every moment with him! Even in the moments when he is not right there next to me, he is still with me!* So, why on Earth am I alone now? I am alone, aren't I? *Absolutely alone!*

"You are not alone, Lala. Do not be afraid. We are here. There are many of us, Twin Souls, Light Workers. *We all are Warriors of Light and Love!* We all feel each other and give strength to each other at times and moments of despair. You gave your strength to many of us multiple times, whether you were aware of it or not and we are giving it to you now. *You are never alone.* We are here with you. The only thing you must remember is that you love him! And he loves you! And this is forever! Do you understand? *Forever. Everlasting, Sacred Love.*"

Who is this? Who is talking to me? My Angels? The stars in the sky above? The souls of other Twins? My Keepers? Or is it my insomnia? My severe, endless as the sky, insomnia. How wonderful it would be if I could finally disconnect for at least some time from THIS reality and fall asleep.

I guess I'm talking to myself. Hello, madness! And who said, this is madness? Maybe this is my way out to the higher frequency vibrations and a deep philosophical and metaphysical view of earthy events.

There's a place where our souls are free. The chains of fear, doubts, ego, social and "moral" norms, and cages don't exist. There, we are unaffected either by the Dark Forces, controlling him through his "dark ego," or me, through my lack of self-acceptance and my belief that I am not worthy of Love and happiness. There, far away from this dimension, in the space I call *"in-between-the-worlds,"* we are two luminous eternal beings, sparkling and shining with the color of "Indigo." The light shines from our crystals, in our heart chakras and surrounds us as one being. There, we are looking at each other and say only three simple words.

"I love you," he tells me.

"I love you," I tell him.

No other words are needed—no other words.

But from that place "in-between-the-worlds," I always have to return here to this reality. And here, in this earthly reality, I stubbornly and persistently want to find a way to forget it all! *I'm tired. Deathly tired. Why would I need this Cosmic, give me a break, Eternal Love with all of these emotions and feelings of insane intensity in my ordinary life? Why? What for? To breathe? To live? Because of this Love, I cannot breathe and can hardly find any strength to live. So, what for? And what about him? Why does he need me? To have my tales and my letters? My ideas, thoughts, my concepts, and my knowledge? To entertain himself with watching all my useless attempts to awaken him? To make him see, understand, remember?*

I feel as if in a cloud of fog. Am I actually falling asleep? The angry, black prickly insomnia melts away, and I fall into a room with blurry bluish walls and windows that open wide into a luxurious garden, full of roses and the scent of phlox. There's also something tender, soft, and smelling like honey.

I am hanging in the air and swaying slightly in the waves of the fresh spring wind. Where is this wind coming from? The air behind the open windows is calm, and not a leaf is moving on the trees. Oh well, it is not important. I calm down. Gently, lazily, my thoughts flow out in a slow stream. They cross the room, seeping under the wall, which turned out to be a closed door.

There, behind the wall, people are talking. I do not see them. Only a stream of my sleepy thoughts is with them. I catch bits of their conversation.

"Don't talk nonsense! *He loves her. He is just stubborn!*"

"He obviously *cannot see...*"

"He would have died a long time ago. *She guards him!*"

"Yes. His earthly life could have ended already, if it was not her love, protecting him!"

"Gerda. She is his Gerda."

"She keeps the fire of his Soul alive!"

"She has nothing because he...."

"We cannot interfere!"

"Haan, what are you doing?"

460

"Lala, you must breathe! And you must write! *Breathe and write, do you hear me?*"

I see a face of a man over mine. Beautiful man. Farhan? No. This is not him. But he looks like him. Who is he?

"Do you hear me, Lala? *Breathe. And. Write.*"

A sudden bright flash and I opened my eyes. I had dozed off in a chair, with the window wide open. The wind is warm. The room smells of roses.

Who was talking? Whose voices were those? Who is this man? Why does he look so much like Him? He said, he said, "He would have died a long time ago. *She guards him!*"

Is that so? Am I guarding him without even realizing it?

Suddenly, hundreds of pictures came flooding my inner vision.

A fire starts in the room where he is working with other people. Smoke, voices, panic! He is well, with no injuries. In the next image, he slips on the roof while filming a scene, gets away with a sprained ankle. He falls off the top of a train another time, injures his shoulder, painful, but nothing serious. It could be worse. Much worse. Next. A big private jet with him aboard. Suddenly all the systems collapse. Shock, panic, horror! Then a miracle happens. They manage to land the plane. Everyone is shaken, but well and unhurt. The plane landed on its belly. Another accident, part of a ceiling in a very old building, falls right when he decides to step aside. And more, and more and more. How did I suddenly remember all this?

Do I work as his Guardian Angel? No. I just love him. *So, I live as his Guardian Angel. I am his Twin Flame, so I AM his Guardian Angel.*

"Do you hear me, Lala? *Breathe. And. Write.*"

Well. I think I can do that.

461

Chapter 51

Tarot. Fifteenth Arcana

"And so to magic my soul, I've given,
If, haply, by spirits' mouth and might,
Some mysteries may not be brought to Light;
That to teach, no longer may be my lot,
With bitter-sweet, what I need to be taught;
That I may know what the world contains
In its innermost heart and finer veins,
See all its energies and seeds
And deal no more in words but in deeds."
Johann Volfang Goethe, *Faust*

I know almost everything about the Guardian Angels at this point. I know how they choose us, shield us, save us and avert troubles. They lend their shoulder to us, their wings as well, so we can live. Their wings do not have feathers. *Those are rays—rays of pure Light and true Love—*the force of the Energy of Life. When we love someone, *we also protect and guard them.* But not only that. Together with Love and protection, we give them our vitality and fortune. If they love us back, they do the same for us. But if they love us not, we lose our own life energy and fortune. With every passing month and year, our Light shines less and less. In such cases, we must close the door and leave them behind. Otherwise, we risk losing our Light almost completely. That must never be allowed. Though I studied many things, read many books, and worked through many subjects searching for the answers, I still know so little!

Several more months pass. I calmed down a bit, composed myself, and saw that I could be a Guardian Angel for my loved ones. I realized that I have very many rays in my wings. I have plenty of them, and I want to share them with people. I want to help them in their moments of sadness and despair, shining my soft, warming Light for them, healing them, and comforting their hearts. Also, I finally started to write this very book you are now holding in your hands.

And I finally opened my heart fully to the wisdom of the symbols of Tarot!

Tarot opened the door into a whole new world, for me—a world full of mystery and secrets, questions and answers, kings and queens, knights and pages, hermit and high priestess, emperor and chariot, and a lot of those things I had not known deeply before.

For many nights I studied the meaning of each of the seventy-eight cards. They hold the key to understanding the deep essence of everything in existence. Through them, one can see the past, present, and future. Our fears and dreams, our conscious and subconscious. The will of the Light and the intrigues of the Dark. Light and shadow. Happiness and pain. Our truest essence. Our deepest core. They reveal what we want to see, and what we do not want to see, what we show to others, and what we hide even from ourselves. Their depth is incredible!

I plunge into this world, reading books, filling my diary with comments and discoveries. In the middle of the nights, I spend hours studying the smallest details of the drawings created by the genius of different artists throughout time: The Ryder White Tarot, the decks of Ciro Marchetti, Marseille Tarot, Arcanum Tarot.

I keep digging into all the information that I can possibly find, but I can't help the feeling that there is something important I am still missing! The different masters' interpretations sometimes coincide and sometimes differ and even contradict each other. I know I must understand the secret essence

463

of the cards in addition to interpretations. Let that essence become a part of my own. But how?

For many hours I've been trying to comprehend the meaning of the card "Hierophant" but failed. I do not like his adherence to dogmas and his strict looks. He is often interpreted as "marriage," but my subconscious could not agree with it! The Hierophant's prototype is the Pope! How can that be about marriage?

The "Justice" card didn't want to reveal its secrets to me either. After all, everyone has his own concept of justice! What is just for the wolf is evil for the sheep he will eat.

But most of all, I am intrigued about the Fifteenth Arcana—"The Devil." The thing is that this card is usually interpreted quite one-sidedly. But to me, it was clear; this particular Arcana was not that simple at all. Most decks show him as some horned monster or a beast. That also seemed entirely wrong to me. The ugly, terrifying beast, which makes your blood freeze in veins, would make you only run away in fear! But this card was not about that at all. Why does he have such power over people? He seduces, tempts, turns lives upside down, lies, gives, and immediately takes away. You can play with him, but it is impossible to win. He is strong and intelligent. Perhaps those he managed to deceive didn't see him only as a monster. They saw him as something else. What and who did they see in him? Why do they follow him? Why didn't they run away? What kind of tests does he bring? Why does he bring tests at all? What is the lesson there? I did not understand this Arcana. I was stuck and could not move any further; I felt mediocre and powerless. I did not know what made me so annoyed. None of the meanings of this card I had read gave me the answers. Something was still missing. So HOW can I interpret it? How can I comprehend it?

One night, after spending another long evening studying the Fifteenth Arcana, I fell asleep at around three in the morning, still holding the card in my hand.

The next thing, I find myself in a magnificent huge library, in an old castle. Three walls are covered with tapestries and decorated with works of famous artists. A huge fireplace occupies the center of the fourth wall, built of sooty stone, with ancient weapons all over it. Friendly fire is burning and crackling. The reddish, uneven light of the fire and yellow glow of wax candles in heavy candelabras illuminate the room.

I'm sleeping and this is all a dream. I think to myself, looking around. *Yes, definitely a dream!*

I see ceramic and stone figurines on the black marble mantelpiece— small figures of gods and deities of different lands and times. And everywhere you rest your eyes, there are books, books, and more books. Their gilded bindings made of soft old leather speak of antiquity and the secrets and knowledge they keep. They are tempting, calling for me, whispering my name. I walk past them, gently touching their bindings with my fingertips. An irresistible scent of mystery fills the air. I carefully pick up one book, sit down in an armchair, and am about to open it.

But suddenly, hearing a rustle, I raise my eyes.

I see a man, with huge silvery-gray wings, standing in front of me! He is naked down to the waistline and looks like the statue of David by Michelangelo. His skin is a honey hue, and I can see fireplace flame and candle reflections in it. His raven-colored hair falls in waves below his shoulders. The almost perfect features of his face make him look very masculine and courageous. Somehow, I understand that he can be harsh at times and maybe even cruel, but his beautifully defined lips soften his face. He smiles as I meet his gaze! Oh, Gods!! *These eyes!* You have to possess some incredible willpower to not lose yourself and all the remnants of your will and reason, just by looking into those bottomless oceans—these dark blue powerful eyes. So royal. So unbelievable. They mesmerize. *They call. They beckon.* Here is the real danger. *His eyes!*

"I hope I have not scared you," he says in a velvety, smooth, low voice.

I take a deep breath, trying to pull myself together, come back to my senses and calm down my frantically beating heart.

Fifteenth Arcana! The Devil! I think to myself. *But how can he be so beautiful? Why is he so insanely beautiful?*

"Did you think I would be an ugly monster, with horns and streams of human blood all over me?" I hear his sarcastic voice.

He can read my mind and hears my thoughts! I realized. *And not only my thoughts, but also my feelings and emotions! Well, what else did I expect? After all, he is the Devil!*

"You know, it is absolute nonsense," he continued, "when people portray me like that. But I do not mind! After all, it is not me they paint as a beast, *but their own fears.* To look deep inside yourself takes much courage! Not everyone has it. But when I come into their lives, I make them do it! I make them leave their comfort zone. I make them choose! *They have the right to choose!*"

"I sincerely thank you for coming!" I said, tilting my head slightly. "I would like to talk with Hierophant as well. I do not understand him either."

"Hierophant? Oh, boy! But you can't stand him. Why would he come?" He answered me with a laugh.

"You are right! He is not my favorite! All his dogmas and rules! I must understand him anyway. But mostly I want to understand you! Tell me! Tell me what you are, who you are, why you have come?"

"I will, Fire Soul! I'll tell you what I can! But not everything. A lot of things you will have to understand and feel yourself!"

And he sank onto the fluffy carpet, folding his luxurious wings.

"Do you remember what happened to Adam and Eve and how it was all turned upside down? I guess this is a habit of people. *They like to turn everything upside down to blame somebody else for their own deeds.* The truth is, I wanted people to have *KNOWLEDGE.* They have the right to knowledge. They contain the same essence, same Source, as the Creator. With knowledge of Good and Evil, they could discern one from another! I wanted them to live like Gods, which *they are in their very nature.* They have a right to make their own choices! I am against slavery—*Any slavery*—even if imposed with good intentions! *A man must be free and choose his own path!* But in order to *KNOW,* it is necessary to stop being an *obedient sheep.* It is necessary to leave the Garden of Eden. For each man and a woman, this would be a different place. *To KNOW, you need to take the thorny path!* I wanted them *to KNOW.* I still do!"

"Yes! I remember that!" I answered him. "And I completely agree with you! But sometimes your methods...! Especially when it comes to Love!"

It seemed like, against my own will, my eyes became fixated on his lips. I could not help it. I felt millions of butterflies fluttering their wings inside me!

I wonder what the taste of those lips is, I thought to myself, but suddenly realized what exactly was going on! *What a Devil!*

"Hey! *Stop that!*" I almost yelled, trying to sound angry and annoyed.

"Stop what?" he asked, gently touching my cheek with his fingertips and taking my breath away. All I wanted at that moment was to close my eyes, so his touch would last forever. By the force of my will, I made myself open my eyes and look straight into his bottomless oceans!

"*Stop it!*" I tried to make my voice as firm and disinterested as possible, but unfortunately, it didn't sound like that, and we both knew it. Well. I knew who I was dealing with—nothing to be surprised at.

"But if I stop," he said quietly, in almost a whisper, "how will you understand who I am and why I come into the lives of people? Especially in Love! After all, I am directly connected with Love—with *Karmic Love, to be exact!*"

"Explain it to me with words! No need to demonstrate!" I said, trying to make my voice not sound disappointed. But he knew and understood everything. After all, *he was the Devil.*

"*Are you afraid?*" he whispered, bringing his face close to mine, up to the point I felt the heat coming from him, and the butterflies fluttered their wings inside of me again.

"Yes! I am!" I answered. You can't hide anything from him anyway. What is the point in lying?

"Fine!" he answered. "Let me know if you change your mind!"

And he crossed his arms over his chest.

"I have many shades!" he continued. "A lot of shadows! Therefore, defining me is not easy! Even if you ask about Love, I can have many variations.

"Suppose I come to a man or woman who is married. This marriage can be, for example, many years old. Everything has settled down into a mundane, everyday gray routine. Love, passion, and unity of souls no longer exist. Nothing! Life together is a duty, an obligation, a habit, a tradition, society's rules, and the things they jointly own: everything *but Love*. On the outside, such marriages appear to be fine, even perfect. The more miserable the people are, the more *"perfect"* they try to look for others. But behind closed doors, nothing but emptiness remains. People who once loved each other now barely talk, or even worse, they quietly hate each other. They feel trapped, in a cage, with no apparent way out. Finally, they just give up and go with the flow, forgetting who they are, what they really want, and why they came to this planet and into this physical embodiment. Their soul development stops. The flowing water in the mountain river turns into a stagnant swamp. *That is unacceptable!*

"At this moment, I bring Love into their life. This Love can be of all kinds and colors. It depends on the spiritual level of the person! For some reason, people constantly make a mistake, believing that I bring only deceitful Love, Love, which is untrue or false. But that is not always true.

"I also bring *Karmic Love*, and it is eternal, and indeed, *true*. However, it can have many shades and hues! And then people have a choice. They can reject this new, false or true Love. By rejecting it, they might see the person they have been living out of habit for many years in a new light. They might discover her or him all over again. They might *fall in Love after many years* of both forgetting the meaning of this word.

"In this case, who can ever say that *I did something evil?* Just the opposite! I brought the opportunity for their emotions and feelings to go through the fire of temptations, betrayals, and disappointments and be reborn with beautiful Love, like a phoenix from the ashes. *Love, which before seemed lost.*"

He again gently touched my cheek, "I admire you, Fiery Soul!" he said. "You are something else! You had the courage and even dared to call for me!"

"Did I call for you?" I was surprised.

"Yes! You have been calling me for a long time. Trying to understand me from the books' descriptions, you often used to think, *I wish you could tell me who you are YOURSELF!* So, I responded to your call, unable to resist your courage and charm and thirst for knowledge and the truth. But you know how they portray me! What if I showed up to you just like that? As a beast?"

I shrugged. "I do not know why, but I have never seen you that way! You are the Shadow that leads to the Light. Without knowing the Shadow, it is impossible to go out to the Light. But in the Love, you bring, there is a lot of pain and suffering."

"That's right, my Brave one! But would you really understand what you understand now, and would you know what you know now if you hadn't experienced such Love?"

"No," I answered after a moment of silence.

"You see? People say: 'No pain, no gain.' They are right about that! Finding the truth is never easy. *Finding yourself* is even harder. But this is what must be done."

"What's your name?"

"Don't you know? Lucifer. It means the Light Bringer. Before the church turned me into a monster, people compared me to the Morning Star and the planet Venus. In the symbology of Tarot, I am the Shadow and the Light that you find in yourself and every human. Yes, the Love I bring is never easy. Far away from being easy. But through the Shadow, through trials, through fears and doubts, I force people to stand *face to face with themselves!*"

"Tell me more! I could listen to you forever!"

"Careful!"

"Oh yes. You are putting me off my guard."

"I'm a master at that! Good. Keep on listening. In Love, I make people 'lose their minds'! And you know very well that to find your true essence, you need to lose your mind first. It is necessary to disconnect the 'ratio' and trust only your inner truth!

"I make people feel desires so strong that they overshadow the voice of reason. It is a fatal passion. But! Here lies a very thin line.

"A man must be very strong in order not to *LOSE HIMSELF*. I will help a person understand whether this Love is Ancient and True, *REAL ONE!* Or a trap, a fraud, a lie! An emotional addiction. Tyranny."

"Through such Love, I make people look deeply into the eyes of *their own souls*. Really deeply. Because often that's what most people are afraid of the most – *themselves*! Most people keep on running from themselves for their entire life.

"Sometimes, with such Love I make a man, or a woman fully submit to the will of the other. This relationship is toxic! It can *BURN*. Sometimes both people are obsessed with each other. Other times only one is obsessed with the other and can neither live, nor exist, nor breathe without the other! To keep the other nearby, they will use anything possible—blackmail, betrayal, jealousy, manipulation, threats! Anything! That is 'obsession!'"

"I can bring unhappiness and suffering—a *SHADOW*. But if you think that I come to the weak ones! Oh, no! *NEVER* to the weak! You know very well what it feels like to deal with me!

"Yeah! I know! I sure do! I have experienced your strength myself! You have burned me until no more than a handful of ashes was left!"

"It's true! But what happened after that?"

"I survived. I was born again! I have risen like a phoenix!"

"Exactly!"

"But this was an unbearable test! Excruciating. I would not wish this on my worst enemy!"

"It's true! But this is *the experience*. That is the shadow through which we go towards the Light—our own *inner Light*! I will make a person walk away from society's rules, religion, culture, and system! But, as I said before, I do not come to the weak! And most often, *I do not come of my own free will!*"

"What do you mean?"

"It means, my Fiery Soul, *I am Karma! I am Fate!* As I said, I'm not always and not necessarily vicious! They often interpret me like that! But you do know; this is not how things really are. The truth is, most of the time, *I just have to be the karmic inevitable 'evil.'*

"In most cases, I appear in the lives of those who need to repay their old debts to Mother Karma! She is the one who knows no mercy! I am just a slave of hers. And who creates Karma? *People! People do it themselves!* Such Love may be deep and passionate in this life, but it can also have rather gloomy and even tragic roots in the past ones. Perhaps there had been *hatred, violence, unfulfilled promises, fateful vows, or the use of dark spells.* All of those things create heavy Karma. Those two meet again in yet another incarnation, and such Love brings a lot of torture, suffering, and pain. It also creates a chance for one or both of them to *make things right* and learn and understand the lessons they failed to learn in past incarnations."

"Wait a minute!" I said, fully realizing what he had just said. "So, you have nothing to do with that! You, as you said, are a *servant of Karma.* So, it turns out to be, PEOPLE *themselves* create the preconditions for your appearance in their life! *But why do they always try to blame you and only you for everything?*"

"Because it's easier! It's easier to dump your guilt onto someone else than to admit your *responsibility!* They blame me for everything in the world! But I'm used to it! As I said, I have many shadows. I make people look inside! Deep into themselves! I make those two experiences such a depth of passion and sensual pleasures that it becomes both their blessing and their curse. It's hard to resist—almost impossible. People became slaves of it.

"Do you want me to show you how it feels? So, you can understand?"

"No!!! I almost screamed. "No! No need to show me! Just tell me about using words!"

"As you wish," he said with a smile, which showed clearly, he was well aware of his power! *Devil!*

I heard a lot about you! A cunning tempter! A merciless seducer with no heart! You are a real demon! How many women have you destroyed? Pushkin's lines from "Don Juan" came to my mind.

What an excellent illustration of understanding such a fateful love. Donna Anna, pure and right. She is fighting and fighting very hard. How can she love the one who killed her husband, her enemy! Unthinkable! But she fails. Her life and life of Don Juan became the payment for this forbidden Love.

"What about relationships, where both Love and hatred are present at the same time? Is that you too?" I asked, forcing myself to look into his incredible, depraved eyes.

"Yes, Fiery Soul. That's me too. In such relationships, everything is present at once. Insane attraction, impossible to resist. The desire to run from the one who is the reason for such uncontrollable magnetism and emotions. It's wanting to possess and at the same time wanting never to see her/him again. '*I can't stand being with you! And I can't stand being without you!'*"

"So... What should people do? What should they do if you appear and bring such Love?"

He thought for a moment. "Everything will depend on *people themselves*, on their Karma, and the stage of their Soul development at the moment. People *MUST learn to hear the voice of their Souls*! If that voice says *STOP!* Then they must stop! The most terrible sin is when people *betray themselves*. But if people reject Love in the name of money, power, greed, etc., *I will not leave them in peace even for a minute!*

"I am a *TEACHER*, Fiery Soul. That is who I am. My lessons can be cruel and painful! But this is how a steel blade is forged! People should act, not following the body, which is given to them temporarily, but *following the Soul, which is eternal!*"

For several moments we both fell silent.

"I have to go now!" he finally said. "Now close your eyes, and when you open them, I will be gone."

I did not want to admit that I would like to stay with him longer. There was so much in him—this whole mixture of shade and half shadows, good and bad, right and wrong, true and false. I wanted to embrace it all, to comprehend it! But I understood that my time was up, and he wouldn't tell me anything else. I simply obeyed and closed my eyes. But what I felt the next second made me forget how to breathe!

I felt a touch, light as a feather, the touch of his lips to mine. But even if I really tried, I doubt very much that I would be able to find the words to describe the feeling. One thing I know, if he were to repeat this same touch even once, ever again, I'm afraid I would follow him wherever he was going. *Such was his power.*

"This is for you to understand better what it feels like to fight me," he whispered, and his breath touched my skin, burning it.

"Goodbye, Fiery Soul! Goodbye."

I opened my eyes and saw my room with the candle was still burning on the nightstand. The clock display showed 1.11 a.m. I touched my lips with my fingertips as if in an attempt to hold his light kiss on them a bit longer.

Yes. You are right! You are very hard to resist. I thought to myself. At the same time, I could not help smiling.

Now I knew what to do and how to see and feel the secrets of all of the Arcana. They will come to me and tell me everything themselves.

The next one was "Hierophant."

That night gave me a second wind. Starting from my meeting with The Fifteenth Arcana, the Tarot cards revealed their secrets to me, answering my most difficult questions. Very soon, I felt confident enough to share my knowledge with people. I combined the wisdom of the Tarot with all the knowledge I accumulated from all the books I read and things I knew from other seers. I was trying to help people find the ways and find the answers with all my passion. Help them see the Light at the end of the tunnel to give them hope and warmth amidst the cold waters of life, which are almost always unpredictable. I called myself *a candle.* A candle is not as bright as the Sun, but it has enough Light to show the door or the pathway to those lost in the dark. Whatever that dark represents— betrayal of those we trust and love, our sadness, fear, doubts, or something else. I truly believed that people knew the way out and the truth inside themselves, all they needed, was a little warmth and a little light to believe it. And I was just that.

Alina was right. I had lit my own fire in my heart, and with this fire, I was able to light the fire in the hearts of the others. Those who had simply forgotten they'd always *had it within!* They, too, were created from the Spark, the sacred Source of all existing! They were divine, and they were creators! They have just forgotten. *My passion was to help them REMEMBER.*

It made me feel strong. I finally FOUND MYSELF. I found my own path— this path was not all about Him—it was my own! I was no longer asking myself those questions: *Who am I? Why am I here? What am I doing on this Earth? Why do I walk, why do I live, why do I breathe?*

473

I finally knew the answer. *I am a Candle*. My Light and warmth are strong enough to light someone's path and warm someone's heart. It became my goal, passion, inspiration, and life.

Also, I continued doing the hard inner work. I kept facing my fears, healing my many wounds, and learning to *love, value, and accept myself*. All my hard efforts were finally yielding some results. I found my way and my calling. I was helping people see their Light, believe in their strength, and change their lives. What can be a more honorable path than this?

"Learn to shine with your inner light, and you will teach others to do the same." "Love yourself, and you will teach others to do so." How true were those words!

I finally learned it.

It gave me back the wings that He once gave me but then took back.

I learned to fly again.

> To fly without him.
> > To shine without him.
> > > To inspire without him.
> > > > To laugh, enjoy life, rain, and the sunlight without him.

Was it a tough school? Oh yes. It was! Was it worth it? I believe so.

And what about Him? I forbade myself to follow his life. I forbade myself to look at his face, read his interviews and watch his films. I forbade myself to cry and ache for him. But I still did not have enough strength always to follow this set of rules. I did allow myself to deviate from it sometimes. But only sometimes.

His Soul still spoke with mine—his half was talking with my half. In dreams, we still would meet on the shore of some cosmic ocean and stand there for a long time, embracing each other as One. We would look into each other's eyes for a long time, finding in them our strength to continue our earthly journey. But now I knew.

My eternal Love was a sacred fire in me, which had finally brought me to my true destination—finding my true self, I finally found my way, my calling. And I also knew, even If the Light of our Love could not connect us in this incarnation on the face of this Earth, still this very Light could help me to unite others.

Love is a cosmic eternal flame. The base of all creation in the Universe. May it shine its Light in me and illuminate the pathway of those I meet on the many crossroads of life.

Who am I? The answer is simple.

I am Lala.

I am a Twin Flame.

Chapter 52

The Will of the Gods

Two years later

Susan Malik looked out the window of a picturesque two-story house at the magnificent view opening before her eyes. Late autumn in the state of Virginia was worth being painted by the most talented artists. All the colors one could imagine intertwined in a magical dance of trees, branches, leaves, shadows, late flowers and neatly trimmed shrubs, surrounding the house. They looked like some mysterious giants, standing and protecting it from the evil forces and Lady Sadness who sometimes visited the mistress of the house. The sun still warmed the earth, but the freshness of winter, ready to take over, could already be felt in the crisp cool air.

"What do you see? " she asked a woman bending over a small mahogany table. The table was decorated with a multicolored mosaic, created of different pieces of wood. Altogether, it looked like a multi-ray star. Right now, it held a spread of Tarot cards. The faces and the figures, painted by the unsurpassed master Ciro Marchetti, were revealing their secrets to the woman, looking at them.

"Nothing you would like to hear from me, Susan." The woman replied.

She was about forty-five years old. She was dressed somewhat exotically: a long green woolen skirt, a cherry-colored sweater with bright orange roses and a turquoise shawl, draping her shoulders. Her dark penetrating eyes seemed to see something beyond this room, beyond this reality. Thick,

476

fiery red hair, which you can only see among free-spirited and bright Irish women, fell around her shoulders.

"Susan, we have known each other for many years. You know that I always tell the truth. The chances of these two meeting each other face to face in the foreseeable future are close to zero! Your Farhan is just one stubborn mule, let me tell you! We need no less than a miracle for him to take a step towards her! You know, I've seen so many stories in my lifetime that I could write a saga-novel! But these two!"

She felt silence for a moment as if trying to find the words.

"Susan! Let me try to put it in words. I would say a Holy Temple exists in his heart, and your Lala is this Temple's only Goddess! But she is imprisoned there. The door to that Temple is closed.

"He told himself this story must be over. Lala was his fairy tale who became a reality by some miracle of God. But he made himself close that book. Now he is trying his best to continue his life as if she had never been there. He is not used to blaming himself. He believes he has done the right thing. He closed his heart to her and retained his empire and his title of the King. He thought this way would be better for both of them. He also convinced himself that she deserves better than him. She will be able to find another man and be happy. This stubborn mule is dead walking without her. Let me tell you! Yet he will do absolutely nothing!

"He also believes he has lost her forever. And since he has lost her, there is simply no point in doing anything! It's too late now. What's done is done. What did you say about him being a romantic hero? Someone who loves beautiful gestures? This one? I doubt it a big time! All I see is a hardheaded stubborn mule! How long has it been since she disappeared from his life?"

"A little over two years."

"Hmm... Long enough. Did Farhan try to contact her?"

"Yes and no. He tried to make Lala come back using his old game. He wore her favorite color and used her phrases in his speeches, just as he had always done when he wanted to win her back. But this time, it did not work. Then he invented a new method. He was sure this would melt her heart and cause her to come running back him."

"Really? What was it?"

"A movie!"

"A movie? No way! Are you serious?"

"Absolutely! Have you not seen his last movie? The film is completely devoted to her! I bet he only agreed to this role because he pretty much was playing himself."

"Wait a minute. Is that the one which is called 'Perhaps you're my Salvation'?"

"Yes, exactly!"

"Ah, I see! Yes, I saw it. Although the film itself is, frankly saying, rather weak, Farhan is amazingly organic and natural in it! So, he somewhat moved their story to the screen! In that movie, he is a playboy! Rich, spoiled, cynical, who has seen everything in this life. He thinks nothing can surprise him anymore. Until one day, by a will of providence, he meets a girl who couldn't care less about his money, lifestyle, and so on. She is nothing he had ever met or seen before, and she completely knocks him out of his usual rut! He is also wearing, what do you call it? Indigo? Her favorite color, right?"

"Yes, I call it *'The Color of Their Love'.*"

"Yes, it is the prominent color throughout the whole movie! It's everywhere, especially in the clothes he wears! The film was beautiful and expensive! Although it wasn't too successful. Too personal, I guess. In my opinion, the storyline wasn't written very well. The ending was way too predictable. So, he dedicated it to her? Of course, he did. Why am I asking? He for sure hoped that she would come back and play by his rules once again. But obviously, she did not. Men! How often they underestimate us, women? *She is stronger than he thought she was and prouder than he could imagine.* She gave her heart to him once on a silver platter but *she will not do it again.* Actually, she is *just like him,* just without his shadow. The mirror of each other! *The Twin Flames.* What else is there to add?"

"Exactly."

"But his plan just didn't work out. She never returned. And I can tell you, she will not, even if he dedicates to her not one, but 20 movies, 150 interviews, and 500 public speeches! She loves him, Susan! We both know that! But she learned, the hard way, *how to control her feelings.* He took a big part in the process of her learning! She keeps herself in an iron grip, either because of her pride or because she is trying to change herself and achieve something in this life. Or maybe she simply no longer sees the point. *And she is right!* If you look at this, what is the point? Plus, I do not think she is fully over the pain he caused her. Cards show it too. She doesn't trust him at all. Deep inside, she is still terrified he will cause her more pain *if she ever lets herself trust him again.* She has chosen to walk her own path. I believe she is absolutely right!"

"And Him… It turns out he has deep feelings for her, which surprises him. He might even laugh in your face if you dare to say it out loud to him. I don't doubt his love for her, Susan! But he believes there is no future. Not in this life. He did not come to her when she was waiting. Then she left. He did not stop her. *His majesty* is not used to running after anyone. He is too used to women falling at his feet. She was a giver in their story—giving, giving, and giving whatever she had, while he allowed her to worship him and love him. She simply got sick and tired of doing it. She turned her back on him and shut her heart. I have no clue what we can do about it. He will not go to her. She will not come to him!"

Silence filled the room for a couple of moments. Then Susan spoke.

"You know, Bella, he ran from her as if a thousand demons were chasing him! And since the divorce with Cynthia finally became public about a year ago, he's been living as if today was the last day of his life and tomorrow would never come! As if he found a 'self-destruct' button. I've tried to reason with him, but you know, he never listens to anyone! This legendary stubbornness of Scorpios! He practically stopped eating. He drinks dozens of cups of black coffee a day, works till he drops dead, smokes like a damn maniac. Bella! My heart is breaking, and my soul is bleeding! I can't watch him burning himself to ashes in front of my eyes! People think he is suffering because of his divorce from Cynthia, but *they divorced years ago.* They just would not talk of it publicly. For three or four years, they pretended to be a perfect family and couple to maintain their image, reputation and family empire. But since the divorce became public, her family has pretty much taken full control over his studios, and what they are doing isn't any good. Those kinds of movies and projects are forgotten before they are even released. The most terrible, he does not even give a damn. He has read three dozen scripts in the past several months and chose not a single one of them. Nothing makes sense to him, and I know the reason! Her! Lala! But try to mention her name to him! *Stubborn mule, you are absolutely right!*"

"Yes, everyone is sure he is lost because of Cynthia. Many believe their break-up is temporary, and they will get back together! They played the 'perfect couple' for dozens of years. People do not like to be disappointed. Some even put bets on them. Some say the divorce is fake and simply a *PR* move to increase their popularity. The tabloids are shouting about it constantly! The yellow press has finally found something to talk about!"

She took a deep breath and shook her head.

"Susan!" she continued, "did you try to talk some sense into him?"

"About what? About Lala? Bella, darling! Lala is a subject, a territory, off-limits for everyone, including himself! But, yes, I did. I spoke to him. Once! We have known each other for over twenty years. It is useless for him to try to hide something from me. Especially when it's something I already know and see for myself! It was two months ago. We were flying to the Emirates. The flight was long, around 15 hours. I swear to you, Bella, it was scary to look at him. The further we go, the worse it becomes! He reminds me of a man sitting by the river, dying of thirst but refusing to drink! *Forbidding himself to drink!* As if punishing himself for something. He's *haunted, exhausted, shattered.* And I know he constantly thinks of her. *Constantly!* I know it! I see it in his eyes! She is *there with him, in him,* but he doesn't let himself face it!"

She fell silent for a moment, took a deep breath then continued.

"When she disappeared, he did not even pay much attention. He was a million percent sure of her undying, unshakable love to him. He was sure she would come back. He was certain she would again join his game and play by his rules, because she loved him so much, and she would forgive him anything. He did not doubt her love for a second! But she did not come back.

"A month passed by, two, three, four. But she was gone. He began to panic. He tried to entice her to return, doing everything that had worked so brilliantly before. You know, Bella, my dear, sometimes even brilliant and deep men behave like primitive and arrogant alpha males."

Both women looked at each other and laughed.

"You see, Bella, he had tried everything except just one little thing—*talking to her*—just talking to her like normal people do! Like you and I are talking right now! *Games?* Absolutely! *Talking? NO!* But, she didn't respond to the games. He waited. Then, finally, six months later, he gathered up the courage to dial her number for the first time. But this courage wasn't enough *to talk to her!*"

The red-haired lady raised her eyebrows in surprise. Curiosity sparkled in her eyes.

"You mean Farhan Ali! A man, who has them women eating from the palm of his hand, *did not have the courage to say a word to this one?*"

"Exactly!"

Susan smiled bitterly. She brought red wine from the bar, poured some into two large old goblets with very long stems. They looked as if someone took them from the props of films about great ancient Kings.

Both women raised their glasses, looked at each other, and took a sip without clicking them.

"I will tell you more! It was more than once! He has called her many times but hung up every time she answered." continued Susan. *"And yes, this is the legendary heartthrob, Farhan Ali!"*

Taking another sip of wine, she came up to the window. She wished she could admire the mesmerizing beauty of nature but her heart was too heavy.

"You know, Bella," she turned to her friend again, "when it comes to Lala, he suddenly becomes himself. The real Him, the one I used to know about twenty years ago! Not the image he has skillfully created for the public. But the real him! I think this is another thing that scares him to death. With Lala, *he cannot play!* He is so used to a life of playing all kinds of roles. He thinks, if he is his true self, it means eliminating who he has become, who he is today—the great, the famous, beloved, and worshiped by millions.

"At least, this is how it was before. But now, it seems like everything in him has turned upside down. In my opinion, he no longer wants to continue living by simply *playing his many roles*. Because it seems to me, he suddenly has realized that he is *mortally tired of all the masks and all the games*."

The storyteller raised her glass, looked at the light through the wine, admiring the violet-red tints. She took another sip.

"The wine is perfect! Yes, Bella, we did talk. After having flown in complete silence for several hours, I finally decided to rip off the band-aid with one brutal question.

"Farhan," I turned to him. There was no point in beating about the bush. I decided that if he did not want to talk, I would try another time. "Farhan! How long do you think you will last if you continue living in self-destruct mode? You have been doing this for over a year now! You barely touch food. You smoke three packs of cigarettes a day. You survive on just coffee and the devil knows what else. Have you seen yourself in the mirror? Your clothes are hanging off you! What are you doing to yourself? Please tell me! I'm scared! It hurts me to see you like this! For the sake of all Gods, Farhan! We both know why this is happening! Why are you so goddamn stubborn? *You love her!* You can do to me whatever the hell you want, *I know that!* And she, she loves you too! Why don't you simply talk to her! Farhan! How much longer are you going to slowly fade away like this?"

He closed his eyes and smiled as if he had no strength left for taking even another breath.

"Until I fade away completely, Susan!" he answers me. "Nothing can be changed... I lost her and my chances and hopes that something could be any different. It's too late now. She will not forgive me and she is absolutely right! How have I been living, Susan? I've always seen myself as a King! I've believed that everything was within my power. Everything would be as I say and as I want!

482

And I really believed it was so! I thought that more fame, more money, more success, more love and worship would bring me more happiness!

"Yes, I've been working for years, like a maniac. I am a self-made man. I have built my empire with my sweat and my blood! For me, the measure of everything has always been my success and my benefit! But most of all, *the love of my fans!* I could never have enough of it! I always wanted *more, and more, and more of it! More fans, more rewards, more worship, more love!* But the higher I was rising, the louder this «something strange "inside me tried to talk to me. This "something strange "I had no name for. But it would never leave me be! I did not know what it was. A feeling, an emotion, a sensation, or all of that together? I did not know. But it made me want something else! Something I did not possess yet. *But what was that exactly?* I did not know, or to be exact, *I did not want to know.* Now I understand what it was. It must have been my very Soul! *My very Soul, Susan!* She was crying, she was trying to reach out to me, but I did not want to listen!"

"And then she came into my life! Lala! She just appeared from nowhere! Like a fresh sea breeze in the middle of a damn desert! Not like anyone I have ever met, or ever seen in my entire life! There is so much in her! I was asking myself this question over and over again! *How can one woman combine it all?* She is romantic, loving, kind, gentle as a rose petal, and at the same time tough as nails, bright, deep, unbelievably gifted, open, and brutally honest. She couldn›t care less about the fact that I was the Great Farhan Ali— the King of Kings! She did not give a damn about it! Of course, she grabbed my attention! I remember the exact day and moment when you first showed me her letter! She was extraordinary and it was easy to see. I was flattered by her attention. I understood, of course, she was not just a fan. I saw that she was different. I enjoyed her Love, and later on, I used her talent to my advantage! *I used her!"*
He fell silent for a moment and closed his eyes!

"Bella! It was such grief on his face. I cannot even begin to describe it to you. When he opened his eyes and looked at me, I saw pain—anguish and deep sorrow! I opened my mouth to say something, but he did not let me, making a gesture with his hand.

"I made her believe that I loved her!" he continued. "You know everything about it. You were there! And she did believe me! It was not difficult for me to convince her. After all, I am an actor, right? A lover! *A romantic hero, aren't I?* This role was not hard for me to play. I was playing with her, just the same way I was playing with countless women before her. Was it really me, Susan? Was it really me who lived like this for all these years? I can't even tell you when she became the oxygen I needed to breathe. If you look at it from a rational, logical point of view, this connection is weird. More than weird, probably even stupid! But if so, then why did I feel her so deeply, *almost from day one?* Why were her eyes with me *wherever I went?* Her words made me feel, think, search for the answers. Why? Because she was so far? Like a dream of the unknown? Mysterious, strange, and incomprehensible? Maybe so.

"Yes, I have used her unique talent, her stories, her fairy tales and told myself: *Hey! Why not? After all, she is the one who is giving them all to me as a gift. So why couldn't I use them?* In my turn, I was giving them to my viewers. Didn›t she say we had a mission? To make this world kinder, brighter, better? That›s what I was doing! I was doing this with the help of my work while using the material created by her talent. I gave people beautiful cinema stories of Love and devotion—Love that lasted through years and even lifetimes. Maybe that was the way it was supposed to be? Her stories of Eternal Love became the property of the audience. So what? I loved being the hero of her tales. Her One and Only, Her Eternal Love, *Her King of Wizards.* I enjoyed this game. I thought that she enjoyed it too. But I was wrong. I was playing; *she was not!*

"But what the hell was she expecting? What was I supposed to do? Fly to her little town, meet her and, and then what? What next? Even thinking of that was more than ridiculous! To me one thing was obvious: we are playing our sweet game, and both are enjoying it. Nothing else can be or should be, or would be, right?

He got silent again, and I was just patiently waiting.

"But then…"

Silence again.

"The longer I was in this game, the more I felt I no longer knew what all of this was. Me! A King of Kings got confused because of some little woman out there, one I had not even seen! Yet, it seemed *she lived in my every cell*! How could that be? I did not know. And later, it turned out that she was not playing! I was. She was not! She was *living all that*, Susan! With all her heart and all her Soul which she says, we have one! She is very extraordinary, Susan. *Pure magic.* Absolutely unlike anyone! There is no one like her in this whole goddamn bloody world, I swear! *No one!* But I have played with her heart! I played with her feelings while she was loving me, living me and breathing me! I have lied to her, used her, pretended that I loved her!"

He sighed so deeply that I felt the lump in my throat.

"Farhan," I said, but again he stopped me with the gesture of his hand.

"I did not know," he said very quietly, "I did not know. *I was never pretending to love her*, Susan!"

He closed his eyes as if he wanted to disappear, so hard it was for him to say those words out loud. He told them without opening his eyes.

"I was never pretending to love her," he repeated. "*I LOVED her!* I loved her from the very second I read the first line of her first letter! When I first saw her eyes, I loved her. It seems that I had always loved her, even before I knew her! Or maybe I am going crazy! But how could I not know about it? How blind was I *to not see it*? It was so clear! How? But I did not know."

He fell silent again.

"And now I know but it's too late. Susan, I have lost her—lost her forever. Maybe it's for the better! Maybe she will meet the one worthy of her, who will give her what she deserves. She deserves everything under the Sun, Susan. One like her deserves it all!"

"Farhan..." I finally said. "Don't you think it's rather stupid just to give up? You love each other, and this is obvious to me! Don't you think that before you let yourself turn into a shadow, you should try at least to talk to her? *Just talk to her, Farhan!*"

"I talk to her all the time, In my thoughts and my heart. I did not know how to do it before, but she taught me. Or maybe I used to know how long ago, and I just forgot. I've read a lot about Twin Flames. Even though logically, I still can't fully accept it, somewhere deep inside me, I know that's what we are. I can feel her! *Always.* If I didn't, I would have gone insane already. I need her to be able to breathe, Susan. And if I am still breathing, it's because *she is always with me.*"

"Don't you see? You're not only causing yourself to suffer. You're making her suffer as well! Farhan! Tell me, please, for God's sake! Why are you such a stubborn mule? Through time, space, circumstances, you are connected through all things! *You two are one!*"

"I know that now. I do. I also know that her Soul loves me! I know it and feel it. But the Soul is one thing, while the body is another. I do not want to lose my dream of her, Susan! That is the only thing I have left. If I try to make this dream a reality, I could lose it. I'm afraid to disappoint and to be disappointed. Do you understand? Leave me with my fairy-tale, Susan, and let me be. Please."

He waved his hand and turned away.

"I realized that any further attempts, trying to convince him otherwise, would be useless. He is stubborn, like a hundred mules. You think he is afraid she would disappoint him? Nonsense! He worships her! He is afraid SHE will be disappointed in HIM, and this way, he will lose her Love. To him, losing her Love is losing his only light and his only will to live. He will not risk it! Never…"

Silence hung for a few moments in the cozy living room. The silence magnified the sound of logs crackling in the fireplace.

Finally, Bella said, "Susan, listen to me, my Love! They are Twin Flames! *They need physical contact!* Once those two look into the eyes of each other, they will no longer need words. The connection occurs precisely through their *EYES, the mirror of their One Soul.* They are *One Soul!* That is why he is so afraid of seeing her. He both wants this connection and is terrified of it.

"So you see, everything is rather simple! What we need to do is to make them meet each other! Face to face, do you understand? Push them nose to nose so that they are together for at least a few seconds! And then! *That would be their point of no return!* They would not have a way back and not be able to separate after that! They are both so powerful and together they are powerful twice over. They belong together, Susan! Two halves are meant to become whole! *All we need to do is to make this happen.*"

"Bella! Do you think I haven't thought about it? Of course, I have! But how? He will not go where she is. He is afraid of it. She will not go where he is! She already did it once in San Francisco. You know perfectly well what happened there! Poor girl! Remembering that night and her eyes full of pain and denial still make me *shiver to my bones! She will never risk it again!* So, how will their meeting even be possible?"

"Hmm… Great Susan Malik! It looks like your usually sharp mind is taking a break now," Bella giggled. *"They need to be brought together in such a way that both of them are clueless about it!* Here is the solution to your problem! How do they say it? 'If the mountain does not come to Mohammed and Mohammed does not come to the mountain, you need to make a small earthquake and they will certainly collide!' Something like that! You know what? Let's go to the kitchen. I have one brilliant idea!"

487

They entered a spacious, rustic-style kitchen. Susan sat down on a cozy corner sofa and watched Bella pour freshly boiled water into two cups. Then she took a rustic wooden box out of the cabinet and put it on the table. Opening the lid, she took out two gray pellets that seemed to be small bundles of dry grass rolled up into a ball. She solemnly placed these balls into the cups and watched them start to unwind in hot water, releasing a flower that looked like a small chrysanthemum. It slowly opened its petals, rose to the very edge of the cup. Susan gladly inhaled the delicate aroma of sweet jasmine, autumn flowers, and tart green tea leaves.

"I don't remember where I read this story," began the hostess of a tea ceremony. Handing one of the cups to Susan, she took a seat in front of her. "There was a similar situation in this one beautiful love story. He and she were madly in love with each other for many years! But both would rather be on different planets than within a hundred miles radius! She was sure he had betrayed her, while he was convinced that she hated him with passion! Something like this!

"I don't remember the details. But the two of them ended up in a log cabin somewhere in the mountains by the will of fate. There wasn't a soul for miles and miles around that place, plus it was wintertime! They didn't have any other options but to face each other and finally talk after many years of avoiding each other in every way possible! They yelled at each other and blamed each other but ended up making love, just the way it is supposed to be! There were some other circumstances as well; I don't remember exactly. Maybe she didn't even have a car and one of his friends or a taxi driver took her there. Anyway, as I said, I do not remember the details and this is not important! My point is that we need to plan everything so that they end up together in the same house with no way to run! Then everything will go as it should! Hopefully!"

"Sounds like a movie!"

"Susan! *Life is crazier than any movie* you have ever heard about or seen. Give me a break! You know it better than anyone else."

"I do. Well. All right, let us imagine for a moment we manage to somehow organize Lala and Farhan's meeting with each other, like the love story you had just described. Why are you so sure it will go fine from there? Who knows how he will react? How will she?"

"Oh please, Susan! *They are Twin Flames!* You know what it means! They react to each other as soda reacts to vinegar but on a much grander scale! The force of attraction between them is so great that they are often scattered across different continents and for a good reason! When they look into each other's eyes for three seconds, on the fourth, well, you understand. They are not just a man and a woman. They are Flames! Fire, my girl! They burn! Each of his chakras will unite with each of hers. Each of his heartbeats with hers. *Each of his breath with hers!* It is not some earthly sex we are talking about here.

"These two do not have sex! *They make Love, and I mean Love with a capital L!* Their connection will occur at all levels! *Soul, body, energy, emotions—everything merges!* And with this connection, they connect to the Source! Their strength multiplies a thousand times! Their united vibration can affect the vibration of the whole planet. Did you know that? I am not joking! That is why the Dark Forces are trying to prevent it by any means possible! But we will try to outplay them!

"Listen, Susan!" She continued, looking into her friend's face, where she saw mistrust and a million doubts. "Listen! On the level above the physical, their union is eternal and sacredly powerful! They have always been, always are, and always will be *together*! Their meeting will set in motion the realization of their mission. Twin Flames always have a mission and I think it's time for them to start fulfilling theirs! If the Supreme Forces do not approve it, if at least one of them is not ready, they will not let us do it, you hear me? We will fail and both of them will go on with their miserable lives away from each other. But if they are both ready and I feel they are, we will succeed! Of course, we cannot ignore the fact that the Dark Ones may try to outplay us, to pull out some of their dirty tricks, but at least it's worth a try! Do you understand me?

"Yes, I understand! Of course, I do, but. Ok! Let's say you're absolutely right! How are we going to bring them together? Like in your story? *In a snowy log cabin somewhere in the mountains?*"

"Exactly!"

"Bella," Susan looked at her friend in pure shock! *"I thought you were joking!"*

"Absolutely not! When was the last time you saw me joking? I am always extremely serious! On the other hand, I just don't see any other way for those two to finally meet each other, if we do not make it happen. You said yourself; he does not look his best! So, we'd better take this matter into our own hands. Wait here a minute; I'll bring my laptop! I have a particular plan in mind and I will explain it to you in just a moment!"

Bella disappeared into her little bedroom and returned with a laptop. She sat near Susan and her fingers ran across the keyboard at lightning speed.

"Here! Just what we need! Look!"

She turned the laptop to Susan so that she could see the screen. The photo looked just like a place from a fairy tale. A majestic forest with sharp crowns of tall fir trees, soaring into the sky, sparkling in the rays of the sun, a mountain river running down from the hill and in the middle of it, almost as if painted by a skillful romantic artist, stood a house. It was picturesquely beautiful but at the same time a warm and cozy log cabin, which somehow harmoniously merged with the snowy forest and Blue Mountains around it.

The text under the photo said the following:

The Smoky Mountains in North Carolina. One of the most beautiful places on Earth. This luxury log cabin is located high in the mountains, right in the middle of a magical, majestic forest, almost in the heart of the National Park. You will feel like you are a million miles away from all the noise, crowds, cars and city life roads. The house is equipped with everything for you to have the time of your life. No matter what season you come, we promise: what you see will remain in your heart forever. A mountain river flows near the house. The house has a spacious living room with a massive fireplace for romantic evenings. There are fireplaces in each of the three bedrooms, as well. There is an incredible library and a kitchen that will amaze even the most demanding enthusiasts who love to cook something special. A wonderful terrace for pleasant evenings with your significant other or with your family is here for you to enjoy and so much more. We guarantee you the most unforgettable experience you will treasure in your memories for years to come!

"Sounds perfect!" Bella stopped reading and turned to Susan! The text goes on but the idea is clear. It is exactly what we need! How do they say it? 'Just what the doctor prescribed!'

"I see," the voice of Susan still sounded somewhat skeptical and full of doubts. "You want both of them to end up there, in this paradise-like forest in that fairy tale house. Now answer me, please; *how the hell can we pull it off?*"

"Oh boy! That's easy! First of all, we book this place, let's say, for a week! Secondly, you mention to Farhan that you were planning to celebrate New Year's Eve in the mountains with several close friends and already found the house and even paid for the reservation, but at the last moment, everything changed.

"You can think of any reason—someone gave birth, someone is getting married, getting engaged, has just gotten pregnant, your grand grandmother is turning 100—and you must be there! *Think of something!* The point is that you must convince him your plan of spending the week in the mountains has gone to pieces! But you already paid for the house and it would be a pity if it stayed empty on these dates! You tell Farhan something like this: 'Listen here, my dear boy, why don't you go instead of me! Just think of it! Majestic Mountains. Fresh, crisp air. No people for miles and miles around. Absolute peace and solitude. You can spend all the time you want to heal your body and spirit. Reflect on life and your eternal Love, find peace within yourself. Read books, and so on. Just imagine, nobody in a 10 miles radius! No one will pester you, ask for an autograph, or try to seduce you! Heaven on Earth for one week! What can be better? What do you think about it, my dear boy?'

491

"You simply need to persuade him. Let's imagine he agrees.

"But BEFORE he arrives at this house, the day before, or even several hours before, we have Lala arrive! I can already see this picture: You invite Lala to visit North Carolina! We can think of what to tell her, for example, to meet you and several of your very close friends. Maybe tell her they are Twin Flames, just like herself and dream of meeting her! Think of something! On the given day, she flies to North Carolina! One of your people meets her at the airport and drives her to the place. While on her way, you call and tell her something like this: *'Forgive me, my dear girl, but unexpected circumstances just suddenly occurred, and we won't be arriving until late evening.'* Your driver takes her there, lights the fires in the fireplaces, makes sure she has everything she needs, hands her the key to the cabin and leaves. Now, she is there alone, supposedly waiting for *you to arrive.* She suspects nothing. A couple of hours later, Farhan arrives at the cabin as well! He suspects nothing either! He thinks the house is empty! He opens the door with the key you gave him! Lala hears someone coming and thinks it is you! She runs to the door to greet you and instead, she sees Farhan! Farhan sees her! Bang! *Eyes meet eyes!* Just exactly what we need!"

"*Wow! Just Wow!!!*" Susan clapped her hands in total amusement and admiration with her friend. "Bravo! *Bravo maestro!* What a glorious plan! Bella! I had no clue you were such a romantic! You just opened yourself to me from an unexpected perspective! I am in absolute shock, in the most positive meaning of the word. Have you ever thought about writing movie scripts?"

"Not yet. Maybe I will start doing it later when I retire."

"Ok, genius! Let's just imagine we can try to put this plan into reality. Persuading Farhan to spend a week in the mountains away from the world, in his current mood, it doesn't seem it would be difficult at all. But Lala! What should we tell Lala?"

"Hmm... We'd have to think about it. What is your Lala up to these days? What does she do? I bet you keep watching her from a distance, do you?"

"I certainly do, Bella! I follow her because I love this woman, and I love Farhan. My heart bleeds for *both of them!* I sincerely want these two to stop torturing each other finally and at least talk! It is so rare to see such Love in our world! You know that I've met her and saw her eyes! Oh, Bella! *Her eyes!* That is just something unbelievable! *Their eyes—hers and his— are like a mirror!* When I told her the whole truth about him, do you know what she said?

"She said that she still loved him.

"Bella! Heavens! How did you…Well, why should I be surprised? You are one of those—a Seer!"

"I like to be called a 'Witch' much more! It sounds scarier for 'little' bad boys! So, what does she do now?"

"A little more than a year ago, she finally decided to take a chance and work closely on the gift she's had since her childhood. She is just like you, a 'Seer' or 'Witch,' if you like that word better. Actually, I think she would like 'Witch' better, as well. One of her most beautiful stories is called "The King of Wizards and the Witch." She has started her own blog and a YouTube channel, giving advice to people, inspiring them, motivating, teaching women self-love. She helps them see their uniqueness and "true inner light," as she calls it. She has quite a few subscribers, which is not surprising. She is original, sincere, and intelligent. She has a real gift of touching 'that something' deep inside people's hearts. She likes to inspire people to think, ask questions and find the answers. I am convinced that all Twin Flames possess this same gift. She puts all her soul and passion into everything she does. People feel it and are drawn to her like a flame in a cold forest. You can watch her videos and read the comments people leave her. Her subscribers and clients adore her. She writes and makes many videos about Twin Flames, relationships, Love, finding strength and courage when it seems completely gone, how not to give up, and how to find your inner light and wisdom within. People are attracted to her because of her warmth and light. It does not surprise me at all. She is just like Farhan—*the same magnetism, same charisma, same passion, the same impossible eyes!*"

"Hmm... I see. Does she use anything in her videos? I mean, any tools? Or does she just talk? Does she rely on any specific esoteric system? Does she use anything besides her gift of clairvoyance and ability to connect to people's hearts?"

"Well, sometimes she just talks, but she often refers to astrology, numerology, knowledge about energies, chakras. She uses Tarot as well, just like you do! She handles these cards with the greatest of respect. Considers them a great ancient system of Symbols! She also tries to explain it to people. In some of her videos, she talks about how you can learn to understand their language. Although I have tried to learn how they work and what they mean, nothing seems to stay in my head. It requires time, passion and dedication. I do not seem to possess any of this. Bella! Why are you shining like your grandmother's freshly polished copper pan?"

Bella was not just shining. She looked like she was ready to clap her hands and to jump onto a bed, like a six-year-old!

"Susan! Susan! Susan!!" Bella hugged her friend. Her eyes sparkled.

"Susan! Tarot!!! *Your Lala is using Tarot!* Gods! And who am I? I am a *TAROLOGIST*, Susan! But not just any tarologist! *I AM A TEACHER!* I have published two books, and I'm working on a third one. You know that! Plus, you are well aware that I'm considered one of the leading experts in this field! That, by the way, is one of the reasons why we met! Here is the solution! Lady Fate is on our side, I swear! Listen to me! You call your Lala! If she loves Tarot, she must have heard of me. And if she hasn't, you will enlighten her! Tell her that I am your best friend, I am dying to meet her, and so are a few of my best students. Tell her that I saw her videos and work and I want to accept her as my student. I was very impressed with her, and I want to share with her all the knowledge I've accumulated throughout the years! Tell her that we are planning a little, "white witches" gathering, in the good sense of the word.

"I give you my word. One like her would never say 'No' to such a proposition! It shouldn't be too difficult! You call her and tell her that we will spend several days in a log cabin in the mountains, surrounded by virgin forest! We will be discussing the most profound topics, reading books, sharing our skills, knowledge, secrets, reading cards in different life situations and so on! We are going to celebrate New Year's Eve in front of a burning fireplace, in our pajamas with glasses of sweet red wine in our hands!

"*I guarantee you; Lala will say 'Yes!'*

"For her, *meeting people like herself is like a seven-tier cake for a sweet tooth!* I don't even have to look at cards to know that she will accept this proposal. I just know! When she arrives, let the driver meet her and take her to the empty house! There he will give her the key. You call her, apologize a thousand times and say that you are late, your flight has been delayed, or something of the kind! You and everyone else will arrive in a few hours. She can make herself comfortable in that cabin and have some rest. A couple of hours later, Farhan, who does not suspect anything will arrive, do you understand me? As I have already said before, Lala hears the door open, thinks that it's us, runs out and just like in that song, 'Where have you been for so long, my love?' *Eyes to Eyes!* My Gods, I am ready to dance! I *can FEEL it;* I know it will work! I know it will. I believe so! I will beg all the Spirit Guides and Keepers to help us, Susan! *We will unite them,* darling! We will!!! True Love is on our side!"

There was a smile on Susan's lips. She looked like a child who had figured out how to eat all the candies without ever being caught.

"Bella! I have a business proposition for you," she finally said. "I want to offer you a job as a screenwriter! You're a genius. That is a ready-made script!"

"We'll write the script later, Susan! This story of Farhan and Lala is a ready-made script, don't you think? I tell you that this is a true love story that is actually happening! A story of Twin Flames—The story of *Eternal Love!* But I think Lala should write it herself! Our responsibility is to play our part to ensure this story has a happy ending! Because if these two do not get together, there is no end at all. It's hanging in the air. *That is wrong* and we must change it and *make it right!* We will do just that!

"And we will start right now. Make yourself another cup of tea, and I will call and book this house from December 27 to January 2! It is November now, so there is a chance it will be available for use on those dates!

"Bella! Wait a minute! Maybe we should talk to both of them first? Maybe he will not agree, or she can't make it?"

"No, Susan! *Let's trust that the Forces of True Love are on our side!* I am sure they are! I am calling!"

Chapter 53

Two Weeks Later

"Susan? Susan Malik? Is this really your voice I hear again?"

I was sincerely happy to hear the voice of this amazing, strong woman, although I felt the cold touch of fear in my heart. *What if she is calling because something has happened to him?* Although if it had, I would have felt it, I would have known.

"Susan! How are you doing, darling? It seems a thousand years have passed since the night we spoke! It feels like I have lived a hundred lives since then! I hope nothing bad has happened?! Is he...Is he all right?"

"He... Well... Lala, I can't say that he is *totally* all right, although, thank God, he is alive and more or less well, at least physically. Aren't you following him on social media?"

"No, Susan. I have forbidden myself to do it. I stopped following his life altogether. I talk only with his soul. Since our conversation in San Francisco, a lot of water has flowed under the bridge. I have learned a lot I didn't know before. I see a lot of things differently now. I have grown emotionally, mentally, and spiritually. I have become strong and independent. At least I want to believe so. I do not need him to live, breathe, smile, walk my path and shine brightly. I can do it on my own, Susan. I even wrote a song, more like an anthem for women, '*I Can Stand on My Own!*'

"I learned that *a woman must never make a man the center and sole meaning of her life. A woman must shine her own unique light. Always.* And if a man wants to be with her, she must be an equal partner. If one is on the throne, and the other one serves and sacrifices, this only leads to heartbreak and resentment. Farhan was the center of my very existence, every breath I took, the sun in the sky, the wind and the ocean. *That was wrong. I had to learn to stand in my own power, gift, and light.* It was tough, but *I had to learn to do that!"*

"Oh, Lala. Indeed. I see you are a different woman now. Even your voice has changed. But if you do not follow him, you would not know. He dedicated his wax figure in one of the museums of Madame Tussauds *to you!"*

"What?" I almost dropped the phone.

"Yes. Yes, dear! Exactly as I say! The one in London. The great Farhan Ali decided to immortalize your Love. His wax twin is standing there wearing an outfit of you know what color, with a red rose in his hand! Search the internet. There are a lot of photos."

I had to sit down.

"He wears indigo? And a red rose? But the rose is..."

"Your favorite flower, and a symbol of you, as he thinks. And yes, of course, indigo! What else did you expect? The color of your Love! 'The color of Wizards' as you called it in the story of the King and the Witch."

"But, Susan, wouldn't it be easier to just talk to me?"

"Talk to you? Oh no! Absolutely not! He would rather buy the moon and paint it royal blue than take a step towards you. Actually, I'm calling you for a different reason! I really like your work on your blog and your YouTube channel! I am so proud of you!"

"Do you? Oh, Susan, I am speechless! I feel so honored you are familiar with my work."

"I am more than just familiar, darling. *I adore you!* And actually, this is the reason I am calling! Have you by any chance heard of Isabella Sullivan?"

"Of course, I have! I love her! She is an esoteric, one of the best tarologists of our time and the author of two books: *The Language of the Symbols* and *The Soul Lives Here.* I have both of them. She's simply amazing! Why are you asking?"

On hearing those words, Susan was ready to dance. She tried desperately to contain her excitement and keep her voice calm.

"I am asking because she is my old and beloved friend. I have known her for a long time, and she was one of those I consulted about you and Farhan as well. She has seen your work. She knows your story very well and wants to meet you! Dreams about it! *She asked me to make it happen!*"

The words of Susan left me in a combination of shock, delight and disbelief. It sounded like a dream or something like a Christmas miracle. At first, I didn't even know what to say.

"Isabella Sullivan wants to meet *ME*?" I finally said.

"Exactly! And not just meet you. She wants to teach you and share with you all of the knowledge and experience she has gathered from her many years of work and research, if you agree of course. We plan to spend several days in the mountains of North Carolina. Imagine a log cabin in the woods! There will be only a few people—you, me, Bella and her two best students who are also friends of ours. By the way, one of them, like you, is a Twin Flame! We plan to discuss mystical topics, learn Tarot cards, watch old Christmas movies, drink hot chocolate and eat gingerbread cookies! New Year's Eve we are planning to spend sitting by the crackling fire wearing soft fluffy pajamas with a glass of red wine! We will arrive there on December twenty-seventh and stay until January second! What do you think about it? Will you join us?"

"Pajamas?" I asked with a laugh. It just sounded too good to be true. "Why pajamas, Susan?"

"Because *we love pajamas!* Don't you? In your stories and letters to Farhan, you mentioned many times that pajamas were your favorite type of clothes!"

"Oh, Susan! You know too much about me. It is absolutely true! I am very passionate about pajamas, and if it were possible, I probably would seldom take them off!"

"Yes, my girl! I know everything about you! So, what do you say? Will you join us?"

"Susan, I don't even know what to say. To see you, to meet Isabella Sullivan, to spend several days in a house in the mountains. I've never been in the mountains in my entire life! It all sounds like a fairy tale!"

499

"Well then, I guess its 'Yes'?"

"Yes! Yes!" I said twice with a happy laugh!

"All right, my girl! I am delighted you agreed! It will be unforgettable, I promise you! I will forward the flight tickets to your email address. Is that all right?"

"Susan! I do not want you to pay for my tickets and accommodation!"

"Lala! My dear sweet girl! Please do not hurt my tender feelings with your words! Do you remember whose assistant I am? And I guess you are aware that my income is way above average. Believe me; I can afford a lot of things. Besides, the cabin belongs to my friend and it will not cost me a penny! So, the plane tickets are just a trifle for me! You will simply give me and everyone who will be there pure and great delight by joining us! Yes, by the way! You do know how to bake gingerbread cookies, don't you?"

"Of course, I do! I love baking them, Susan!"

The joy of the upcoming trip and an opportunity to meet such unbelievably amazing people just swept over me with a sunny warm wave. I was thrilled and was ready to share this happiness with the whole wide world.

"I will come with great pleasure, and I promise to treat you all not only with the best gingerbread cookies in your life but with many other unforgettably delicious things! You have my word! Be ready to gain a couple of pounds! Oh, Susan!! Thank you! Thank you! Thank you!"

"No. Thank you for agreeing to join us! I have to run now, my dear girl!! See you in December! I will send you all the information in your email! Pleasure talking with you!"

"Pleasure is all mine! Bye for now."

"Bye."

The phone went quiet. I was still smiling. What a completely unexpected and indescribably wonderful proposition. Almost a week in the mountains, a small cabin, logs burning quietly in the fireplace!

Oh, what magic it would be if I happened to find myself there just with him—just the two of us—and no one else. We would be sitting near the fireplace, flames dancing, logs crackling. A blizzard is swirling outside the window and I am safe in the circle of his arms. I see flames reflecting as I look into his dark eyes. My eyes wander to his lips, too beautiful and sensual for a man. I reach for them and…

Ok, that's enough! Stop that! Just stop this very moment! I said to myself.

Or what? Do you want to go back to pain? You really want to take more knocks and then spend nights sobbing and rocking yourself to sleep? No, right? Good girl! That is not happening! Go and, as mom says, "do something useful."

I knew my mother would be very happy if I asked her to celebrate New Year's Eve with the boys alone. Those three have their own little "mafia" with secrets I am not allowed to know. At least they think I do not know about the secret stash with candies and cookies they have in Grandma's room or fun TV programs they watch till very late when I am not home. Once I came home a couple of hours earlier than I was supposed to. I found all three of them in my mom's little bedroom eating candies—all three of them. "Do not tell Mom," my Mother said. I pretended not to see or hear. But even now, remembering that makes me laugh. It's true. I don't allow SUCH an amount of sweets all at once, but…I pretended I didn't know. They do have fun, the three of them. My mom seems to be trying to give my boys what she hadn't been able to give me in my childhood—love, laughter, their own little secrets. They will be happy to have New Year's Eve, just the three of them, while I will sure enjoy my little break in the mountains.

Later that same day, Susan called her best friend.

"Bella, you were absolutely right! She knows you and admires you! Yes. Of course, she agreed! She is coming! Farhan? I am sure he will not change his mind at the last moment! He clung to this idea, like a drowning man to a straw! For him, mountains and complete aloneness, in his present, state are exactly what he wants and what he needs, even desires. Yes, he will take a private jet, of course! Lala will be there around 3 p.m., and Farhan at about 7 p.m.! *No, he doesn't suspect anything!* Nothing! Nothing at all! Neither does she! She absolutely bought my story and was extremely happy! I hope she will still be happy when, instead of you, *she sees him. Her Angel and Demon,* as she calls him. Bella! Let's pray to all Gods that our idea works out. I swear I'll buy that champagne Don Perignon for a thousand bucks a bottle, and you and I will drink the whole thing! Let's hope those two will not run away from each other or kill each other! What? You don't think they will? Are you sure? Well, *we will know soon enough.*"

Chapter 54

27th of December

The Greatest Forces of the Light! It is so beautiful! Like a lost land from old legends and fairy tales! So unbelievably beautiful!! I looked out the window while my plane was flying lower, soon to land in Asheville, North Carolina. My mood gradually shifted from a state of joyful expectation to absolute delight.

I grew up on the Black Sea shore, and for many years I have lived on the coast of the Atlantic Ocean. But I had never seen the mountains! And now, in front of my eyes, I saw a chain of smoky peaks which, as I knew, went along two states. North Carolina and Tennessee. The sight of a snow-covered ridge with stone needle-peaks, soaring up to low-hanging clouds, seemed to sew sky and earth together. It aroused a kind of solemn thrill and tears of joy deep in my Soul.

These magnificent mountains have been standing for thousands of years and will be standing for thousands of years more as silent witnesses. Wise and eternal! People will be born, will live, love, die, and be born again. And they will keep on standing, silently and calmly, witnessing everything great and not that great, of everything that passed a long time ago, is happening now and will happen in the nearest and furthest away future. They always will be here, as Guards. Observers. *Keepers of time.*

The plane landed smoothly.

Since I had only a small carry-on suitcase with me, I did not have to wait for luggage, so I went straight to the exit.

Just as I expected, I saw a tall, respectable-looking man holding a sign with my name on it in his hands. Apparently, he already knew what I looked like, as he smiled at me even before I read his sign. He came up to me and took my suitcase. He was tall, rather attractive, with radiant gray eyes and thick hair touched with a bit of "salt and pepper."

"Welcome, ma'am!" He said. "My name is Stephen. Let me help you. You seem to be dressed very lightly for our weather at this time of the year!" he said, looking at me in surprise. I had a pair of jeans, a blue sweater, and a black poncho over my shoulders.

"It's pretty chilly out there, ma'am."

"Don't worry, Stephen, this time I do not plan to ski. And I hope I will not freeze to my bones near the fireplace inside the house because this is what I mostly plan to do. We usually do not have fireplaces in Florida. Pity, because what can be more romantic than a fireplace. Don't you think?"

"Yes, ma'am! I absolutely agree! The house has three of them. I am sure you will find them delightful. The car is in the parking lot. It will only take a few minutes to get there. The cottage is a bit remote; I have to say. It is in the mountains, but in about forty minutes, if the traffic is good, we will be there!"

"Thank you, Stephen. Can I ask you something?"

"Of course, ma'am, anything!"

"I am begging you, Stephen, *please do not call me 'ma'am'!* My name is Alla, or some people call me Lala. Choose whatever you like or your own version but please, don't call me ma'am." I said, barely holding back a laugh.

I hated to be addressed that way; the word ma'am brought into my head the image of a very old lady, between 85 and 95, who wears glasses and holds a dog on an elegant long leash and looks at everyone with an expression of deep displeasure and disapproval on her face.

"No problema ma… Sorry, Lala!" he said, warming me with the rays of his charming smile.

"That's better, thank you!"

My phone rang in my bag. The number was hidden, which could mean it was most likely my dearest Susan. I answered the call.

504

"Lala! This is Susan! Have you already landed?"

"Yes! Yes, just a moment ago! Stephen met me! We are heading to the car."

"Ah! Ok. Very good! Lala! I am having a little problem here. So, the gang and I won't be joining you until tomorrow morning! Stephen will give you the keys and light the fires in the fireplaces! You just relax and enjoy yourself! The cabin has everything you might need. If you need anything else, just give Stephen a call. He lives about 25 minutes away from you. He will get you anything you might need. Please, feel at ease there. Make yourself at home. You can even bake the gingerbread men cookies. You will find everything you need for that in the house too. Just make yourself comfortable, relax, and enjoy a quiet evening at the fireplace with a book and a cup of tea. You can also watch some romantic movies. I know there is a whole collection of them there. In a word, rest, relax, enjoy, and the girls and I will see you tomorrow! Ok?"

"Ah… Yes, of course, Susan! Thank you! So, you are arriving in the morning?"

"Yes, my dear! Tomorrow. By the time we get to the cabin, it will be around noon! Make sure those cookies are ready. We will be hungry! Do not feel lonely! If you need anything, call Stephen immediately. He will take care of everything!"

"Please, do not worry about me! I love solitude! Especially in the mountains, with a fire burning in the fireplace! What could be better?"

"And I will bake the gingerbread cookies, don't you worry! Tons of them if you want! I can bake our Russian pirozhki as well! You know, such sweet little pies, with filling in them. If I can find the yeast, of course."

"Good, dear! Bake anything you want! We will eat everything! I hug you tightly and see you tomorrow!"

"See you tomorrow, Susan."

I put the phone back into my purse. While I was talking to Susan, we made it to the car.

Our Range Rover flew like a quiet silver bird along the almost empty road. The snow was everywhere, but Queen Autumn was not yet giving full power to Lady Winter. Here and there, I could still see the trees, covered with multi-colored leaves of multiple shades. Red, yellow-red, yellow-green, red-brown, and all of them together. The evergreen fir-trees, resembling ladies with their lush crinolines, were lining up along the road. Their sloping snow-covered branches were like soft shoulders, wrapped in snow-white lace. They were swaying in greeting, promising miracles and Christmas gifts. Christmas was only a couple of days past and the Spirit of something magical was still present in the air.

"A ball. I am going to the winter ball. The requirement for the ball is *plush pajamas*," I whispered to myself and laughed happily. I can't stand all these receptions and all kinds of formal events. There's always the fear I might be dressed incorrectly, inappropriately for that specific crowd. Or I might blurt out something against the etiquette. Or while walking on the red carpet, I might decide to take off my shoes if they are too tight. So, pajamas and the informal company of wonderful people sounds like a perfect celebration to me.

We made another turn and *I saw a fairy tale place*. The house was standing on the hill and right in front of it, a small mountain stream was running down happily over pebbles, while sparkling in the rays of the still bright winter sun. Snowcaps were visible here and there on each side of it.

The house was what Americans call a "log cabin." It was large and unrealistically beautiful. I got out of the car and looked around. I could barely believe in the reality of what I saw around me. I felt like a little girl from a fairy tale, every step filled with magic, mystery and expectation of something one cannot even say in words, yet what the heart truly and deeply desires. I felt as if I could meet a hero from an old legend or a fairy tale behind every corner. Father Frost, or Santa or some other winter wizard, waiting for me to enter that house. I will knock on the door and hear a voice.

"Who is knocking on my door? Who wants to enter my home?"
"It is me, Father Frost! Lala!"

"Is your heart loving and kind? Because if not, you'd better run! Anyone who enters this home with an evil heart, will turn into a piece of ice!"

"Let me in, Father Frost! I have a kind and loving heart!"

"Come in, then!"

I will come in and make some tea for Father Frost. I will light the fire in the fireplace made of ice. Then I will wait for the Twelve Months—Twelve Brothers to come out of the forest too. Each possesses his own magical power, but he can only rule his month while holding the magic staff. When his time is up, he gives the magical staff to the next Month— His brother. Brother December will hit the ground with his staff and a sleigh with three horses will appear! *Troika!* And Brother April will fall in love with me, a poor stepdaughter, sent to the winter forest by her evil stepmother to bring her snowdrops. Those flowers only appear in spring. To make this possible, Brother December will give his staff to Brother April for just a short moment so that spring comes in December and I can get my snowdrops. Then, April will pass the staff back to December and I will be happy with him for eternity. No, actually, this will not happen. Brother April is not my half. The name of my half is Kai, and he has the piece of cursed mirror in his heart, which turned it into ice. That Ice I could not melt, *even though I tried very hard...*

I shook my head! Such beauty is around me; I should be feeling like one of the happiest beings in the world, but no, instead, I am trying to find something to weep and suffer about, going through my painful memories, thinking of what could have been, should have been or would have been, if only...

Stop that! Just stop! I said to myself, took a deep breath of unbelievably crisp mountain air, and smiled again, looking at the enchanting beauty around me.

Stephen pulled my suitcase out of the trunk and smiled broadly, seeing the expression of complete bewilderment on my face. I studied the house and the forest around me and probably looked like a child forgotten at a candy factory.

"Lala! Let's go inside! You are going to freeze! You will have enough time to look at everything. I promise."

Inside, the house was spacious and enchantingly beautiful. It's impossible to compare the charm of a wooden house with anything else. I think a marble palace, or a medieval stone castle would not have impressed me in the same way. Ancient whispers of long-forgotten coziness, security, something very familiar and warm filled me. Something I had known for thousands of years. I guess my inner memory pulled out my ancestors' wooden houses from its archives—warm, friendly homes where families lived in love and harmony. The warm, honey-tinted wooden walls and floor and the expensive simplicity of such dwellings, bring feelings of refinement and beauty. *Warming. Soothing. Healing.* The house feels alive. *He embraces you gently and invites you to rest your weary body and Soul.* It feels like Home—a long-forgotten home you spent years searching for and finally found.

I just could not shake off the feeling of being enchanted. Anyway, why should I?

As Stephen said, there were three fireplaces in the house. In two, Stephen had expertly lit the fire.

"Keep adding these logs into the fire, so it doesn't go out!" he told me, pointing to the logs, forming symmetrically arranged piles in iron baskets beside each fireplace. "If you need anything, anything at all, please call me right away!"

"I will be sure to call! Don't worry, Stephen! Thank you for everything!"

And Stephen left.

I was alone in my enchanted forest, in my magical, enchanted log house, with burning fireplaces and snowflakes, quietly falling outside. Soon night would replace the day.

A few hours passed unnoticed.

Outside the window, it was already completely dark. It is incredible how mesmerizing a fire can be on a quiet December night. *I could keep looking at it, listening to the sound of the crackling logs forever,* I thought.

I glanced at the clock ticking loudly on the wall. It was almost seven in the evening. I took a log from the iron bucket and placed it carefully into the fireplace—the fire wrapped around it. Suddenly in one breath, I felt as if *I was* that log! I felt as If I had been lit on the fire. My temperature jumped up so sharply and unexpectedly that I felt, as if I was floating above the floor. The room started to spin and became blurry. My heart was beating so rapidly it seemed it would break my rib cage and fly away. I was looking around me, bewildered, trying to find a reason for such a sudden and drastic change.

I felt a strange sensation, as if my heart had stopped for a moment. I pressed both of my hands to my chest, and that very instant, *I felt Him! I felt him with every particle of my very existence.* My heart raced again, reminding me of the bird in the cage! I felt *HIS* closeness almost physically. Or maybe, the word "almost" cannot be used here. But I will still use it. I could almost feel his breath touching my face—the scent of his cologne mixed with the scent of his skin. I seemed to have known his scent for thousands of years. I saw his eyelashes, each one of them. His cheeks with light stubble, as if he had not shaved for several days. I felt frosty cold air touching his face as if it had touched mine!

But my face was *burning! Hot lava flowed through my veins instead of blood!* I knew when and where I had this feeling the last time. *San Francisco!* Then we were very close. *But why am I feeling all this right now? Why now? There is no way he's somewhere near!*

At this very minute, he is probably somewhere very far away! Maybe in Europe, maybe in Dubai, maybe somewhere else. But definitely not anywhere near! No, there must be something wrong with me. I am just an insane, crazy woman. Or maybe it's the mountain air and this magical place. Yes, this must be the reason.

I got up and went outside into the cold night, as I was—in my light T-shirt and jeans—without putting on any coat or even a sweater. But the frosty mountain air did not cool me down. My face, together with the rest of me, was burning like fire, no matter how long I stayed outside. The sky above me was crystal clear, sparkling with billions of shining stars.

I'm sure it's because of the sharp change of temperature and climate, from summer to winter, I thought. It was the only reasonable explanation that I could find for myself at that moment.

I went back inside. Suddenly, *visions of past lives consumed me like a snowstorm.* I pressed my forehead against the log wall, trying to shake the feeling of being inside a frantically swirling tornado. Scenes from different lives flashed—one after another, again and again, creating a mosaic-like pattern— in front of my tightly closed eyes.

I pressed both palms to my cheeks. My face was practically on fire and the burning increased with every passing minute.

I took a large ceramic cup, went to the refrigerator and pushed the ice lever. Silently, in a strange trance, I watched the cubes of ice fill the cup almost to the brim. Are those the same ice cubes the Ice Queen gave to Kai? The ice cubes were part of a puzzle. The Ice Queen ordered Kai to put them into the word "Eternity," but it was extremely hard. The longer he spent trying to do that, the more his heart was turning into ice. Gerda would have to hurry if she wanted to save him. *"You are his Gerda, Lala!"* I remembered the words of Bastet.

I poured water into the cup. I drank this Snow Queen's cocktail. Still, the fire within me raged.

What's wrong with me? What is happening? Alas, I got no answer. No explanation. There was no logic in what was happening. No clues. I am burning. I am the fire. I am flame! Wait a minute. Yes. It makes sense. I am a Flame. So why should I be surprised? But still, I must try to do something with this burning, or I will simply become ash!

From ash, you will rise, like a Phoenix! I reasoned with myself. But I had another idea! Shower! Ice-cold shower!

In the bathroom, I quickly undressed and turned on the cold water. Me and cold water? I am someone who hates the cold in any way, not to mention cold water! But there I was, standing under the icy cold shower, without even a wince or shiver. No, *something definitely was not right with me.* Very soon, I realized that icy water was pretty much useless. It wasn't able to cool me down, as I was burning *from the inside.*

510

I do not know how long I was standing there under the streams of cold water. Once I realized it was absolutely useless, I closed the tap and got out of the shower. Near one of two washbasins, I found many fresh, clean towels together with two soft, warm bathrobes. I thanked in my heart the one who so kindly provided all these things and wrapped myself in one of them. I caught a reflection of my face in the mirror. It struck me. My eyes were shining with some ancient mystical fire! My usually pale cheeks were glowing like garden peaches in July.

"Hmm. *What a gorgeous Witch I am,*" I said aloud and gave a wink to myself. I was feeling weird. It was very strange. But that moment, I wanted to burst out laughing with a bell-like laugh, find myself a broomstick or a cloud or just a pair of wings and fly over the snow-covered earth, dusting all the humans with some magical stardust, making all their dreams come true!

My black curly hair was falling over my shoulders in complete disarray, as if on purpose. My face was glowing without any make-up, my eyes were sparkling flames. My lips were full, sensual, and alluring.

I smiled at my reflection and finally seemed to get used to this internal fire.

It all is happening because of the mountain air, because of this enchanting, magical place! I thought to myself. An unknown and almost unfamiliar sensation of complete happiness and unity with the world, with everything, moved in strong waves inside me. I finally could comprehend the meaning of the expression "*when the soul sings the songs.*" But why my Soul was singing, I could not understand. Yet, I could feel every part of my physical and non-physical being trembling, as if in anticipation of something. But what?

Suddenly, I heard the sound of a closing front door. *Stephen must be back!* I thought. Running out of the bathroom in my cozy robe, I suddenly realized! Damn it! There was nothing besides me under this robe!

So what? I told myself. It is a very thick bathrobe! *It is so long that it almost touches the floor,* covering me from my neck to my toes, quite modest and chaste!

After pulling the belt tighter, I entered the living room.

"Stephen! Are you…" the words froze on my lips.

It was not Stephen! I saw the figure of a tall dark-haired man in a long black coat. My heart sank for a moment. No. *It just stopped beating.* It just stopped, and then, a moment later, it started fluttering like a thousand butterflies caught in a thin net. The man turned to face me, surprised by the sound of my voice and froze in pure, undiluted shock. *The Universe stopped.* All the planets, stars, and galaxies—all of them—stopped their movement for a moment.

"For what has been created as one shall be united as one!"

What was that? My thoughts? Or did someone say these words? Or...

I probably would have collapsed but the kitchen wall supported me. I managed to grab onto it with my hand. I was looking into His eyes. *HIS eyes!*

The eyes I had lost all hope of ever seeing. His luxurious silk hair, caressed now by the snowy wind, fell freely over his forehead. Melted snowflakes transformed into shining water droplets, reflecting the flame of the fireplace. He probably had not shaved for several days, stubble framed his lips, overly beautiful for a man and so painfully familiar to me. And yet, I was seeing them for the first time in this life. His eyes seemed even darker and more powerful. What a long path! What an endlessly long, exhausting path we were walking to arrive here. *Here!*

He looked at me, not believing his eyes. When the first seconds of numb shock passed, he slowly, step by step, walked towards me, not taking his eyes off mine for even a second! I could neither move nor breathe nor believe that this was happening for real.

He came up very close to me. *HIS EYES! Oh, Gods, His Eyes!* How many years, months, days, hours, and minutes have I spent praying to all the Forces to be allowed to look into *these eyes?!* In his eyes, I could see billions of stars, worlds that were born and died, just to be born again! I could see the Milky Way and *Eternity itself*—the shortness of one life and the infinity of Soul and Love. I saw floods of feelings and emotions—Love. Pain. Fear. Surprise. Joy—the entire spectrum danced in his eyes. But apart from all that, in his eyes, *my Soul finally returned Home!*

As if still not believing I was there, that I was real and not an illusion, he slowly raised his hand. He gently touched my face with his fingertips:

512

my hair, cheeks, lips… So very gently, as if he was afraid, I would melt away. I felt as if the one, touching me, was not a man of flesh and blood. Oh, No! *He was the ancient pagan God, woven from energies and the eternal flame of all creations.* I closed my eyes for a moment but then opened them again. Waves of light, energies, flames of all colors were rolling over me one after another, and to continue standing straight seemed to be an impossible task. I no longer knew where I was. *On Earth? In Cosmos? In Heaven? Who was I? A woman? A human? Or was I something else?* I no longer knew.

"*Lala*," he whispered, taking my face in his hands—like in my dreams near a cosmic ocean, in the silence of other worlds. He did it with such incredible, indescribable tenderness that tears came to my eyes and flowed down my cheeks. I closed my eyes as he timidly kissed my tears, barely touching. Then, just as endlessly tenderly, he began to kiss my eyes, my cheeks but for some reason, he avoided my lips as if not wanting to frighten me.

His lips, the tips of his fingers, every cell of him was radiating *cosmic, eternal fire,* which instantly spread throughout my own entire body. The pleasure of his touch was so intense I felt as if I was dying in sweet intoxication.

"*Lala*," he repeated, caressing my face… His voice, soft and powerful, so bewitching, hypnotizing, enchanting, *felt almost physical.* Like melted bitter chocolate, spiced with Caribbean rum and Indian spices, it was running through my veins instead of blood.

"*Lala*."

I finally gained the ability to move and did what I had dreamed of for countless days and nights, what I did so often in my endless dreams in thousands of those days and nights. I let my fingers run through his jet-black hair and covered his lips with mine. I didn't want to wait any longer! Not a minute. Not a second. Not a single sigh. *Not any longer! I've been waiting for so long! Too long!*

And then…

How can I find the words to describe this?

It was me, and at the same time, it was not me. Me—the woman I was now, and the woman I have always been in every single one of those thousands of lives. Those lives when I loved him. But that moment. What was it like? I will try to explain. Imagine that you have been walking through the desert, not for forty but a thousand years! You have lost all hope of reaching an oasis. You have even completely forgotten the meaning of the words, "hope" and "oasis." You have not only forgotten the taste of fresh, cold spring water but you have even forgotten the meaning of the word "water." Then after walking and walking through this desert for a thousand years, you stumble and fall from a cliff. You scream in horror, thinking you're about to hit the bottom of a rocky gorge and die a torturous death. But instead, you find yourself in a cool mountain river! How? At first, you do not even believe this is all happening, but later, you drink the water. *You drink, and you drink,* and you are both *happy and terrified.* You fear the river and the water will turn out to be a mirage, a phantom, *an illusion.* Or if it is real, someone or something will take it away from you, or you suddenly will wake up, and the water will turn out to be *just a dream.* It's hard and almost *impossible* for you to believe *the water is there and real, and you can drink it.*

He was this water for me and I was this river for him. That is what we were, just minutes after we touched each other. It was insane, passionate, strange, beautiful, eternal, and indescribable.

Our bodies had become two powerful magnets; the force of the pull between us was so indescribably strong, so intense that nothing in the Universe could separate us. It seemed to me that if the taste of his mouth was taken away from me, I would not live. I would die. Because now, knowing this taste, *I would never survive without it.*

His taste was my Surya, my Ambrosia, my Drink of immortality! When his lips were not on mine, I wanted to scream! And he understood that. The desire to dissolve in him completely, melt and disappear with him and in him was so strong. It burned through my entire body. Each cell of it!

Oh! Where was my natural shyness? It Vanished! It was as if his body had been molded, created just for me! Only for me—and mine for him, for him alone! His hands shamelessly glided over my skin, and I was like a

514

flower, starving for the sun. My body curved under his touch and followed him in complete obedience to his will. I longed for it without an ounce of shame. And he, in turn, obeyed me. He seemed to have known my body for thousands of years.

Intuitively, instinctively, he knew what I wanted and gave it to me. He gave and gave. Again and again, dissolving in my pleasure and my moans. He followed me, and I followed him. He was my slave and my master. I was his slave and his mistress. He was my God, and I was his Goddess. If only it would never end! If only it lasted and lasted! Forever!

In this sacred dance of our bodies, two parts of our souls swirled in a cosmic dance, penetrating each other and returning to their original nature—whole, *one creation*. It was a sacred, a holy spectacle! We were crazy and shameless. But what shame can there be when the Sea makes love with the Shore, and the Sky makes love with the Earth?

At one point, he stopped and whispered, "Lala! Open your eyes!"

I could hardly lift my eyelids.

"*Look at me!*" he said.

I silently obeyed, drowning in his eyes, darkened with passion and contained desire.

"I want you to look at me! *Look into my eyes, Lala!*"

The next moment, our bodies united! I screamed his name! I threw my head back, involuntarily closing my eyes but he, by an incredible effort of the will, made himself stop for a moment and repeated, "*Open your eyes, Lala!*"

A breath later, I no longer existed. Scattered into myriads of cosmic particles, I became stardust, looking into his eyes!

I burst into pieces, instantly becoming whole again, only to explode and burst out again—Again, and Again, and Again!

What was it? Two parts of the same planet or star that at cosmic speed rush towards each other with only one purpose—*to become whole! To become One!* It is a fiery tornado, in the eye of which there are two—him and me. For a moment, all laws of physics disappear entirely, and only whirlwinds of energies remain. One moment, they shine with all the colors of the rainbow, and the next, they shimmer with only one color. Orange! Red! Violet!

515

Indigo!
    Indigo!
        Indigo!

Stars and cosmic whirls still circled me, intertwining again and again in a magical pattern, until, finally, everything fell into blissful darkness, flickering here and there with far away shooting stars.

I just fell asleep. I fell into a deep sleep like a wanderer who, finally, after a long and exhausting journey, *returned to his homeland.* He came home to a place where he was waited for, loved, and cherished. Where hearts and souls were open to him, he was safe, nothing to fear, nothing to run from or after. He was finally home. *My Soul was finally home after all the struggle and tests and hurt and fights and sleepless nights and walking barefoot through the winter forest. I was finally home.*

Chapter 55

No More Darkness

His side of the story

I slowly opened my eyes, surprised to find him looking at me, his face shining with joy, peace, and a touch of disbelief that I was there—there, near him, with him.

One look at him sent blissful warmth and joy into every particle of me—physical and not—entirely replacing the fear and panic I usually felt first thing upon waking in the morning since my early childhood. Now everything was different. Now, my body reminded me of a cloud, floating in the sky with gentle spring sun rays bursting around me—a very unusual sensation.

His face—impossibly beautiful—was so close and as dear as I had always remembered it, yet different, somehow new. It was as if it was him and at the same time, not him at all. I raised my hand and traced his cheek, chin, his lips. It was still hard to believe he was near me—not a dream, not a trance, not a vision. He's here with me. He is mine!

"Have I slept long?" I finally asked him.

"No. Just a few hours." he laughed happily.

"Oh, Gods! Farhan! I don't even know how or when I fell asleep!"

He gently ran his fingers over my palm, over my hand, touched my neck and stroked my hair.

"After you told me for the one thousand and fifty-first time *that you loved me.*"

"Oh! Really? Are you sure you did not dream of it? Mistaa Heartthrob and a Movie Staaa?" I answered mockingly, raising my left brow just like he always did.

"Of course, I could be slightly mistaken, especially since after the *one thousand and twenty-fifth confession, I lost count!*" He took my hand in his and pressed it to his lips, sending warm waves into my every cell.

"You seem to glow from inside, Farhan," I told him. "It is you and at the same time, it's not exactly you. Do you know how you look? It's as if you were standing in a dark room, sunlight barely peeking through the windows covered by heavy black curtains. But someone walks in, pulling the curtains back, allowing brilliant sunlight to burst into the room. All the shadows, dark corners and monsters created by half-darkness completely vanish. Sunlight transforms and animates everything, infusing life into places where it seemed to have disappeared forever. This is how you look! Why is it so, Farhan?"

"Lala, oh my Lala! The way you speak is incredible! How do you do that? The way you put words together makes my heart tremble like a million butterflies. It feels as if Rumi himself were speaking through you."

"Maybe it's Love that makes us poets? Tell me, my King," I asked, touching his cheek with my lips. "Tell me, what suddenly changed you so much? Why do I know you and do not know you at all? Has this Light always been hidden in you, or has it appeared just now? You appear to be woven of a billion solar sparkles! What has caused such magic, my beloved King?"

"What has caused such magic? You! *Your eyes.* I looked into your eyes for a mere second and saw my own lost Soul there. You were absolutely right," he continued. "You told me so many times that in your eyes I would find me—the real me I lost a long time ago—*the true me.* That is exactly what happened. I don't know, Lala, if I will ever be able to get used to how I feel when I am looking into your eyes. I cannot explain it with any words. When I look at you, *my Soul kisses your Soul, and your Soul embraces mine.* It is unimaginably beautiful, extremely powerful *and a little bit terrifying.* I can't hide anything from you. It makes me drunk without alcohol; it delights and frightens me at the same time. Now I finally understand why I was so terrified of your eyes! Deep inside, I have always known this is exactly what would happen! I am an actor, I have played thousands of roles. It has been a way of my life. It has been my *whole life*, Lala. Good or bad or both, but it has been my life. When you were given to me, when you came, I thought there was no place for you in that life of mine. How could I have been so blind? How?"

"Farhan…"
"No, let me finish, my Love."
"Say it again."
"Say what?"
"My Love!"
He brought his face closer to mine.
"*My Love*," he said, kissing my eyes.
"*My Love*," he said, kissing my lips.

Then he pulled back slightly and laughed softly. "Let me finish, my crazy and beautiful Witch! I have so much to tell you! So be patient and listen!"

He fell silent for a short moment as if gathering his thoughts together and then spoke again. Even his voice seemed to sound different than before. It was the calm, deep voice of a man who finally found the answers to all of his questions.

"While you were sleeping," he began his story, "I replayed—over and over again in my head—what happened to me since the moment you entered my life. I want to tell you *my version of our story*.

"I doubt that my storytelling skills can come close to yours, so try to be patient and forgiving."

He ruffled my hair as if I was a child, pulled me towards him. I rested my head on his chest while he hugged me tightly with both arms. As in my youth, when I would fall into heaps of autumn leaves and inhale their smell with hunger, pleasure and pure delight, now I closed my eyes, greedily breathing the scent of his skin. *Oh, how I had missed him!*

"I used to think that you appeared in my life by chance," he continued, "as if from nowhere. But later, I realized one thing. Sometimes we are calling for someone, or, as you say, our Soul is calling for that someone, although we might be unaware of it. Perhaps that's exactly what happened to me. My Soul, the one we share, called and called for you. But back then, I didn't understand it. I could not understand it, even if I tried.

He ran his fingers through my hair again and continued.

"By the time you came into my life, I thought that I had already seen everything and experienced everything that I could experience. By that time, I had lived a big part of my life already. I had done a lot, seen a lot, and achieved a lot. There were ups and downs, losses and smiles of Fortune, fame, money, women, a marriage, a divorce, powerful people wanting to be friends with me, Love and the worship of millions, so on. I was betrayed, hurt, manipulated and used by other people and I had done the same. I had seen everything, experienced everything, done everything, or so I thought. For decades, I was living in a harsh world and the rules of that world were simple: the stronger one eats the weaker one. You destroy or get destroyed. Oh, Lala...

"Years and years of my life, stone by stone, I had been building my empire, my world. I knew this world was not perfect, but it was just the way I wanted it to be, or almost. In my eyes, the world I had created was my greatest achievement. I was proud of it. I considered it to be as unshakable as was possible. Even the unhappiness of my marriage became a part of this world over time.

"My wife played her role and I played mine. We had acted like a 'perfect couple' for so long that it became natural for us. It seemed almost 'normal,' as if this was the way it was supposed to be. Many people live like that, wearing masks and pretending when others are looking, but barely talking when nobody is watching. It can be even worse; behind closed doors, they hate each other. Yes, something inside would ache and whine from time to time, but I convinced myself not to pay attention to it. I trained myself to silence the voice of my inner core—the true part of me—the part which is the original Spark of God and in every one of us, as you said it many times in

520

your letters. I trained myself very hard not to hear it. I suppressed it. I tried to make myself deaf to this voice. With time, I became a master of the trade. Thinking I had won, when in fact, *I was losing.*

"As the years passed by, I forgot how to listen to and hear my Soul. Even the very idea of listening to my Soul seemed ridiculous. I lived in that room you just described with the windows closed, draped with heavy curtains, not allowing fresh air or sunlight to enter. But I wasn't aware of it. Or I didn't want to know. In the eyes of the people, I was the King and in my own eyes, I was the King as well.

"Yes, I was playing God, as you once wrote to me. I have played it for so long that I started to believe it was true. Anything I wanted, I would get one way or another. It became an ordinary thing for me, the norm of my life. My life was exactly how I wanted it, and I wouldn't allow it to be otherwise. I didn't want anything to change. I only wanted more of what I already had. Yes, again, you were right. *Greed possesses us when we disconnect from our Souls.*

"And then you appeared. Now I can understand; I have been waiting and looking for you every moment of my life. But that thought didn't even have crossed my mind back then. Still, you came. You burst into my life like a fresh ocean breeze bursts into a room through open windows and doors. There was no escape from you. But was there a place for you in my life? In that empire I had created?

"Of course not. Still, you came. Destiny created a way! What was meant to happen had to happen!

"Did I believe you? Of course not. But you struck a nerve in me from the very beginning. You touched something alive and forgotten in me, something intensely deep and profoundly personal. I did not let anyone enter these depths, not even myself. But you went there anyway. I did feel something almost instantly, from your very first words! But I could not understand what it was, even though I tried very hard. In the end, I wrote it off as a mere curiosity. After all, I was always attracted to unsolved riddles, and you seemed to be one of the most complicated of them! For a very long time, I didn't think you were a real woman of flesh and blood. You were an interesting virtual fantasy. Something that does not exist and indeed cannot exist. As they say, '*too good to be true.*'

"While, my empire and my world, on the other hand, were real and tangible. At least I thought so. It's strange how immersion in Shadow changes your perception! It's as if someone takes spring out of your heart, replacing it with winter. Do you know the fairy tale about a loving girl from a poor family and a boy with an icy heart? He wanted to live in the palace and be a King. *Forever!* For some reason, I remembered it just now. *When you do not live from the heart, you see everything in a distorted mirror.* The important becomes unimportant and the temporary seems so necessary and genuine. Truth becomes a lie and lies appear as truth.

"But the more you were present in my life, the deeper you were entering my Soul. Or have you always been there?"

"You are speaking just like me, Farhan!" I was surprised by his sincerity, eagerly catching his every word. I mean, until now, I only knew my side of the story. I did not know what he had gone through while living the story of our eternal Love away from each other.

"Am I not the other half of you?" he answered, kissing my hands and hair. "I should speak like you, shouldn't I?"

I breathed in his scent. Again. What a blessing to lie in his arms, breathe him and hear his low caressing voice, to feel his fingers gliding over my skin, causing warm waves to wash over my body. It was strange; while this life had deprived me of these feelings until tonight, I have known these sensations for hundreds and thousands of years. *I have always remembered them!*

"When I read your book," he continued, "I was astounded. It affected me too strongly and too deeply, in many unexpected, unexplainable ways. While reading it, there were moments when I felt like the hero of a beautiful ancient legend—*Farhad and Shirin. Leila and Majnu. Aivengo and Rowena. Lancelot and Guinevere.* It flattered me. But, believing it seemed impossible; my logical mind wouldn't allow me to believe in this *fairytale* you wrote. No, I simply couldn't.

"After I finished reading it, I felt fear suddenly rush through me. I didn't know why it was there. Fear is weakness, I thought. And there is nothing I hate more than to be weak or to lose. Yet the fear remained, arousing my anger, frustration and even aggression towards you. An unimaginable storm of inexplicable emotions raged inside me. The only way to cope with it was to close my heart—close it to you and everything about you!

"You can't even imagine how 'dark' I was when you appeared in my life. But I was clueless. I didn't understand what it meant 'to be dark' until much later. But I was just that. "Dark." I was sure I had complete control over everything. Everything and everyone obeyed my will. Everything happened exactly the way I wanted it. Almost always. A demon of greed possessed me in every way possible. I was blind, and I was deaf. My Soul, crying bloody tears, tried to make me hear her voice. But I kept shutting her out.

"You came, and at first, you saw me exactly as I wanted the whole world to see me—an angel with huge white wings. You weren't seeing the other side of me—the me I was becoming by pulling away from the Light and submitting to the Shadow. No. You did not see that, or maybe you weren't allowed to see. You called me 'My Heavenly Angel,' and it flattered me. From the very beginning, I knew you were different. *Very different!* But I couldn't even begin to imagine who you were or why you came into my life.

Of course, I was well aware; I was far from being a "Heavenly Angel." On the one hand, I was flattered by how you saw me; on the other hand, I was angry and annoyed that I was nothing like that. You became a mirror for me, showing me my past self. Your words, love, passion and fire, turned a light on in me that I had spent years carefully extinguishing. You want to know why? I guess it deprived me of my control over everything I had, and everything I thought I wanted. Control has been my God and my Master for many years. Then came a moment of clear realization: You were the only woman, or to be exact, the only being on this planet who could help me regain the real me I had lost, the only woman to inspire me to listen to my Soul. But it made another thing very clear: It had a price! And the price was no more, no less than *rejecting all control!* I did not want that! I hated even the thought of it! The Shadow still had too much power over me. My Shadow was too strong. I blindly obeyed it. For many years I knew no other ways. So, I chose to shut myself off from you! But I didn't want you to know. You had something I could use. And I had every intention to do that.

Despite your vast intellect, talent and depth, you were still just a woman! I have always known my way around women. I told myself you were no different than any other. I convinced myself of that. In psychology, they call it "devalue." I was a narcissist and a manipulator. I was asleep, living for years in the Shadow. What else would such a beast do? Now I am terrified when I look back and see what I have done and who I had become!

I convinced myself you were weak, while I, on the contrary, was invincible. *I was one of the most powerful men in the world, while you were some little woman who loved me so much.* Because you were so loyal to me, I could easily manipulate you and make you do whatever the hell I wanted or needed. I thought I had complete power over you. As a businessman, I saw how I could use what you had written and sent me. It seemed you were clueless about how incredibly talented you are! I used that to my advantage and had no remorse back then. I told myself that you gave me everything on a silver platter, so why shouldn't I put it to good use. Now that I see what I did, I feel disgusted! Absolutely disgusted!"

"*Farhan. Don't.*"

"No, my Love. Do not say anything. I guess I had to go through it all. But what a long and exhausting journey it has been, Lala! Where did you get the strength to bear all this? How did you manage to endure so much and not break? I can't even imagine! And you loved me! Me! While I did not deserve even a hair from your head!"

"Farhan. You do not have to…"

"Yes. I have to, Lala! I must! I must tell you everything."

"I didn't see what or who you really were," he continued. "I was entertained, amused and flattered by your Love—the Love of such an extraordinary woman! I didn't believe a bit about us being two halves of One—Twin Flames! It seemed ridiculous. I was deaf to what my Soul was trying to tell me. But, you had something that I needed. Your talent! A talent you seemed unaware of! You continued sending me brilliantly creative messages. I needed those. You were giving them to me by your own free will, asking nothing in return. I just had to show you a few signs from time to time. Show you that I was thinking of you, make you think I believed you, and I loved you. For me, it was a game—an exciting game!"

He paused for a moment as if thinking, remembering.

"But I didn't know I would fall into the same hole I had dug for you. I fell into each trap I had prepared for you! The most amazing thing is, *I did not see your strength.* Your unbelievable inner power! It wasn't there because you had money or position or anything of the kind! No! You had inner power simply because you followed the Light, the Eternal. You followed Love!"

He gently lifted my chin and looked into my eyes. Such tenderness and sadness filled his eye; my heart skipped a beat.

"Will I ever earn your forgiveness, Lala? Will I ever be able to heal the wounds I created in my ignorance and blindness, the pain I caused you?"

"Farhan…"

"Please, don't answer me now. Let me finish. You shared everything so openly with me; the way you saw life and people, Love and feelings, wisdom and other important things. You were pure, gentle, so open, and so sincere. You made me think a lot. You made me cry and laugh. You pushed my boundaries about so many things: life, the world, myself.

"The fire of your heart filled everything you said and did with depth and passion! I started to realize you knew many things that *I knew nothing about.* It was like a revelation to me. I've read twenty-two thousand books and I rightfully considered myself vastly knowledgeable in many subjects. And here is this little woman who knows more than me and somehow is wiser than me, stronger than me, deeper than me. It turned out that this little woman—who I thought was weak and under my control because she loved me so much—*was not weak at all.* I didn't have as much control as I thought after all. I didn't like that! I felt annoyance mixed with anger and something even similar to hate."

"Holy Heavens!"

"Yes, I know. I think my Darkness began to hate your Light. *My Demons began to hate your Angels.*

"The instant I realized this, instead of an enjoyable game and mere entertainment, you turned into a *threat!* This little woman, madly in love with me, with no power, money, or fame, became a threat for me, the Great and invincible Farhan Ali! You were a threat to the "me" I had become, a threat to my familiar world. I began to ask myself questions that I had long ago refused to ask: *Is there really any sense in what I'm doing? What am I trying to create? What am I trying to achieve? What is real and what is false? Where is real me, and where is the pretense? Who am I? What am I? Why am I? Is this all I want, or is there something else? If there is, then what is it? Where is it? How can I find that?*

"When you disappeared from time to time, I hated the feeling that everything became empty and gray without you. As if the colors of the world around me suddenly disappeared, everything became black and white— even soundless, like in a silent movie. But I always found a way to get you back into 'our old game,' as you called it. I understood perfectly that sooner or later, you would get sick and tired of all this. But I also knew how strong your Love for me was, so I thought, if it happened, it would not be anytime soon. And even if that moment came, still I'd probably find a way to make you come back. I had almost no doubt about it. As you know, I can be a presumptuous mule who believes that everything in this world belongs to me and happens—only if I want it, as I want and how I want it! But again, I was wrong.

"It all ended after you came to San Francisco."

At the mere mention of that city, my body immediately froze and turned into a block of ice. He felt it instantly.

"Lala," he said softly. "Look at me."

I silently raised my dry, prickly eyes and tried to pull away as if I could sense waves of danger and pain coming from him.

Gently, as if I was woven from the wings of butterflies, he touched my face.

"Still hurts?" he asked.

I lowered my eyes. I didn't want to tell him how I survived that night nor about my meeting with Susan. I did not want to say anything at all.

If only I could completely erase the memory of that pain and agony. That cold numbness and falling from heaven to the relentlessly cruel, cold hard ground. I wish I could forget.

'My Love," he said gently, laying me next to him and kissing my face, barely touching it with his lips. "My Beautiful, my Gentle!

Please, Forgive me.
Forgive me.
Forgive me. Please!

Oh, how could you stand all that? How could you manage to keep loving me? Loving such a monster?"

"Probably, somewhere in the depths of my heart, I have always known that very deep in that monster, my Angel lives."

"Maybe it was this faith of yours and your Love that created this Angel?"

"No," I answered, kissing him back. "My faith and Love just woke him up! Tell me, did you feel me, then in San Francisco?"

"Oh, Lala! That was a real madness! I thought I was just being crazy and had lost my mind! Not only did I feel you, but I also heard you—in my head, telepathically! Pure insanity! Especially in the hall! I acted like a damn idiot! I could not put two words together! But then, suddenly, your words appeared in my mind, as if from nowhere. You said something like, 'Ram! Take it easy, my Love! I won't eat you up alive! I promise! And do not be afraid to look into the audience. You won't see me. I am very far from the stage! Calm down! Take a few deep breaths! You are my ruler of the world, not some little boy, are you? Come on, Ram! Pull yourself together! Breathe!'"

I smiled and looked into his eyes, nodding my head.

"What?" he said, laughing. "Oh, no! Did you say all that to me that night?"

"Almost word for word, Farhan! So, you did hear me! I just can't believe it! I constantly tried to convince myself that I imagined everything since none of this existed in real life! Countless times I told myself that I was simply crazy! That it was just my imagination! Oh, Farhan."

Tears rolled out of my eyes.

He dried them off my cheeks with great tenderness and embraced me tightly again.

"How magical it is all, Lala!" He said with a deep sigh. *"Love is the purest magic!* I have been an idiot, running from everything as if all the devils of hell were chasing me, running away from the most beautiful thing in the Universe! I did run! I ran, causing you tremendous pain, and I knew about it! But I thought that I was doing the right thing! I thought it was what I wanted, to keep everything in my life just that way it had been before you. But while running, for the first time, I realized that indeed I could have lost you! This thought and realization I remember even now. It felt as if my heart froze and even stopped beating. Suffocating, freezing, *numbing terror.* I desperately tried not to pay attention to it. I tried not to think of you, not to feel you. I went to some stupid party I didn't care about and got drunk."

And got yourself a gorgeous woman! Mel... I thought. *But what was the point in talking about that now?*

"Next day, I left the city. I had to keep going with my crazy life and doing my usual things. But it felt as if I had a *huge gaping burning hole in my chest, at the place of my heart.* The pain was physical! Everything in me screamed, 'You *lost her!*' But I told myself, *She loves me too much to leave! I can always get her back.* I was wrong.

"You vanished. I did not believe it was forever. You had been gone many times before when you got tired of playing the game by my rules, and I always found a way to get you back. But days followed days, and weeks became months. Nothing that worked before to get you back worked anymore. And I wanted you back! Badly! But to make you part of my real life, simply dial your number or meet with you. No. I had no such intentions. I wasn't ready to do that or did not want to. I was happy with our old game, and I had no desire to change anything in my life. Life of a powerful King, Mega—damn it—Star!

"However, time passed by, and you were still gone. Even my speech to a multi-million audience that I had written using your expressions, words and ideas, even that song of Michael Jackson you love so much, changed nothing.

528

You were gone. You had left my life as if you had never been there. It was not what I expected. Not what I wanted. After all, I was sure you saw and heard my speech! How was it possible that after that you would not come back! You had to! I had never done anything like that for anybody as long as I lived! But you did not. And it became clear that you had no intentions of doing so. Even then, I did not want to believe I would not get what I wanted! I always did! I always do! It took me months to fully realize: That was it. You were done with me.

"In some inconceivable way, we had switched places! Now YOU had power over me! I was following your every word and every step! I watched your videos and read every article, story, or post you have created. I was angry, jealous and pissed! Before, everything that you created, was for *me*! Now, you were creating all that for other people. I read the comments and saw people loving and adoring you! I hated that! *You must be mine! Mine only!* And all that you create must also be for me! It was clear; you had found the strength to rise from the pain I caused you and move on. To live and create without me, while me without you—that was a completely different story! Without you, I could find no peace, no colors—everything around me suddenly turned into an old black and white movie. The most beautiful and unique women seemed flat and uninteresting. What I used to find thrilling and exciting, whatever I used to find so much pleasure in, suddenly stopped being all that. *Everything reminded me of you*—colors, smells, roses, ocean, sky. I saw you in everything. I hated it, and I started to hate you! Severely!"

"Oh, Gods! Farhan, that's terrible!"

"Yes, exactly! Now I understand it clearly, that there have always been two of me! The light one in me loved you. The dark one in me hated you. And I gave my will to the dark one!

"Finally, one day, almost a year after you left, the emptiness and colorlessness of my life became unbearable enough for me to dial your number finally, but when I heard your voice, I became a damn coward— No! *I did not dare speak to you!* You were a thousand times right in calling me a coward; that's exactly what I've always been when it came to you and everything about you.

"A few months later, I realized, your Love has never been a weakness which I could use against you. *Your Love was your Strength! Your Power! Your fire and your only truth.* It did not make you weak! Just the opposite! *It made you strong! Invincible.*

"I also realized as well: I really had lost you. I no longer had you! So, why couldn't I just live the way I used to live before you? But I could not! It was no longer possible.

"The Light part of me, the Angel you awakened, was gaining strength and power while I was trying to resurrect the Dark One—the Shadow— I was accustomed to him for so many years. But I could not. *Suddenly, the Dark became lifeless, cold, and terrifying.*

"Months passed, one after another. Everything blurred into a series of days, which seemed exactly the same.

"Susan, my assistant, was always there with me and for me. I saw, in her eyes, she understood perfectly well what I was going through and who was the reason for it. After all, the whole story was happening in front of her eyes! But she did not dare to speak with me about you, knowing and sensing that subject was too touchy for me. That made me feel a bit easier. I tried to dive into my work that had always been my refuge. But that wasn't helping either. Nothing helped. My once-beloved work, beloved friends and hobbies, all lost the meaning, joy, and excitement they used to have. Only reading books and rereading what you had written, somehow brought me some consolation and peace.

"I asked myself, *Among the hundreds of masks I wear, where is the real me?* And I couldn›t answer. It suddenly became so clear that I could be *real* only with you—sometimes not even with myself—*only with you.* I realized how much I needed you, like the air I breathe. But you were gone. How was I supposed to breathe? How was I supposed to live?

"At some point, I began to read everything I could find about Twin Flames! At first, I thought, this ridiculous tale, this unbelievable legend, could not possibly be true! But the more I researched the topic, the more everything was falling into place and, like connecting pieces of a puzzle, the whole picture *soon revealed itself!* A few months later, what had seemed crazy to me at the beginning, knowledge about One Soul divided into two bodies, *finally gave me all the answers I was searching for.*

"It became clear to me, why from the very first line of your letter, which Susan showed me, something seemed to awaken in me. Something that had been sleeping for a very long time! It was my Soul that woke up when it recognized you! *I realized that you were half of me! Half of myself!*

"It was a very unexpected realization, even ridiculous. I couldn't share it with anyone. They would laugh at me and this incredibly fantastic story— such a beautiful fairy tale with a very sad ending.

"You described us perfectly in the story of the Witch and the King. You were always that Witch—Sorceress from another world, a different kingdom. And we were separated by the magical waterfall of a Forbidden Forest. But the main thing separating us was the heavy crown of one King. That King, who was *enough of a fool* to lose *the woman who was his very Soul!*

"When a woman walks into a life of a man, brings him Light, and makes him truly happy, not every man is ready to accept her and this sacred Love. Such Love requires breaking through all those habitual boundaries and obligations, the fear of being judged, criticized, disapproved, or even laughed at. We are slaves to our formalities. *Each genie has his own lamp.* A genie has powers, but his powers make him a slave! I, too, was a slave, thinking that I could control the empire, and therefore was omnipotent. But I was a *King-Slave.* Strange, isn't it?

At some point, I developed a deep love for this one song. I do not sing as well as you, so, so not laugh. And he sang:

If we'd go again
All the way from the start
I would try to change,
Things that killed our Love
Your pride has built a wall, so strong
That I can't get through
Is there really no chance
To start once again

531

I'm still loving you.[39]

"'Scorpions'!!! Farhan! I am Speechless! I did not know YOU CAN SING! «Still Loving You" has been one of my favorite songs since I don't even remember when! They first released it, I think, over 30 years ago! Did you know the name of that album? *"Love at First Sting!"*

"Really?" He said with his boyish smile. "No. Did not know that! Sounds very symbolic!"

"I know, right? And you! Farhan, you sing beautifully! What a voice! I am astounded! You are full of surprises, Sir!"

"I also can play the guitar, but not very well yet. When you wrote to me that you melt when you see a man playing the guitar, *I bought myself one.*"

"I bet that guitar costs a million dollars? "I said smiling, feeling my heart melting with love to him.

"No, just a couple thousand."

He pulled me tightly to himself, embracing me in his strong, loving arms.

For some time, we were silent. I didn't say a word. I needed time to understand and accept everything he'd said. I was deeply shaken to learn that this path wasn't smooth and easy for him either. For some reason, I naively believed that only I was having a hard time. But I was wrong. *He had his own fight.*

Then, while gently caressing my hair, he said, "Why did it take me so long to see, to understand, to realize who and what you are for me? I don't know. I can't say for sure. The realization has finally come over me like a storm. And with it came my punishment, having to live without you, away from you. Away from the One who is half of myself. One with me. My Soul."

---

39 "Still Loving You." Track #9 on Love at First Sting, Dierks Studios, 1984. Scorpions. Music composed by Rudolf Schenker, lyrics by Klaus Meine.

Silence again. I lifted my head from his chest and looked into his eyes, instantly drowning in them like in Space—in Eternity. How long have we both been in this Universe? How many lives have we lived? How many hardships have passed; how many are still ahead of us? Who are we? He and I in this Eternity? How strong is our Love? Why do we prepare so many tests for ourselves in every life, and try to pass them? There was so much I wanted to tell him, so much that I couldn't find the words. So, I only said that eternal and ancient phrase that I had already told him thousands of times in thousands of lives, including this one.

"*I love you.*"

A smile touched his lips, which was both happy and sad.

"I love you more—much more, Lala! I am breathing you!"

"No! I..."

"Shhhhh..." he said, gently putting the finger on my mouth.

"Let me speak. We will argue later who loves whom more."

"I want you to know!" he said, hugging me so tightly as if afraid that I would break free and run away.

"You should know! I have never pretended to love you. Never! I *THOUGHT* I was pretending, but in fact, I was deceiving myself. *I LOVED you*! I have loved you from the very first line of your first letter, and I loved you more and more with every next word you wrote. To be exact, I was *REMEMBERING* my Love for you. I guess *I needed time to remember!* And then to believe you. After all, this is not the first or even hundredth and first life we have loved each other. But I wasn't aware of it. I did not understand it, didn't realize.

"Maybe because of my crazy life and so many years of 'ruling the kingdom.' Maybe among the dozens of masks that I have worn, I lost my true self. Or maybe, playing Love on the screen hundreds of times, I have never truly known what real Love was, and therefore *I could not immediately recognize it.*

"But when you did recognize it, why didn't you come? Why didn't you call? Farhan! Why did you continue to torment yourself and me?"

He sighed heavily. "For me, coming to you would mean to lose and losing meant humiliation. It would mean I would have to apologize. I would have to admit the fact that I was wrong. And the King cannot be wrong! The King cannot be weak! Plus, I was sure, sooner or later, you would come back anyway. When I knew you would not, I decided that I had lost you forever. And I almost put up with it. But I was reading everything you wrote and watched everything you posted. *I wanted to remember. I wanted to understand.* I continued to feel you and talk with you in my thoughts. My failed marriage, the fact that Cynthia was tired of playing the game of "Happily married couple "and announced our divorce to the press, her parents taking control over "My empire," the yellow press discussing me at every turn. *None of that really touched me much.* For some time now, everything that was occurring in my life seemed 'not real' to me. As if it was a performance on the stage or a scene from a movie.

"People around me seemed to be playing their roles, events where I participated, looked more like movie sets. Smiles, words, compliments, flirtations. All seemed fake, false. A pretense! I was suffocating among all this. The atmosphere I had spent dozens of years in and used to enjoy, seemed poisoning. Me, who used to be the King of pretense, *now hated it with all my breath.* I realized how little I had that was real. The real ones for me were only my children, my father, sister, and my faithful, wonderful Susan, and the fire of my Soul—You!

"I think Susan, to defeat my stubbornness, decided to unite me with you in such a romantic way! I just wonder if someone helped her, or she thought of it all by herself. How did she manage to lure you here? What did she tell you? You must have connected somehow. Otherwise, how could she convince you to come? Did you meet her?"

"Just once. In," I was silent for a moment. But I didn't want to lie to him or hide anything from him, "in San Francisco."

His body tensed.

"What did she tell you?"

"She, she was very kind to me and very supportive. She said that she believed we really were Twin Flames, knew each other in thousands of lives and our Love was true and eternal. But our path was fraught with challenges, and I had to be strong because we still had to go through lots of tests. When I was leaving, she hugged me. To be completely honest with you, your dear Susan turned out to be pretty much *my savior that night*. Her words and her compassion prevented me from breaking down completely. They gave me the strength to get up and move on. She's wonderful, Farhan! And she is very loyal to you and loves you very, very much!"

No, I would not retell him the conversation we had that night. It was not necessary, and I simply did not want to. I could read shock mixed with admiration on his face.

"Ah, Susan!" He said, finally, shaking his head. "She never said anything to me! Of course, I knew that you had touched her heart deeply, like everyone else who knew about you! But I could not even imagine it was that serious! So, she met you that night after the show? When I ran from you, like a rabbit from a wolf? Oh! My dear Susan! *How incredible is this woman!* How truly blessed I am to have her. I owe her so much. If it was not for her, we might not even... I do not want to even think of it now! But tell me, how did she get you to come here?"

"She said there would be a girls-only party, like a coven of witches," I answered with a laugh. "The famous Isabella Sullivan was to come here as well! I have read all her books and admire her endlessly! Susan said they were friends and Isabella wanted to meet me! Can you imagine? *Meet me!* Of course, I could not say no to that! Also, I've never seen the mountains! But when I arrived, she called and said that things got a bit complicated and she wouldn't arrive until tomorrow morning! Oh, Farhan! She planned it all!"

"Of course, she did!" He said, laughing. "She told me that the cabin would be empty, but Stephen, her assistant, had prepared everything for my arrival. When Stephen brought me here and I saw the light burning in the house, it did not surprise me at all. He gave me the keys, wished me a pleasant stay, and left immediately. I just could not understand why; all the way from the airport, I felt as if I was locked in a huge oven preparing to be served at the Christmas table instead of a turkey! I saw your face, I could sense you, and I heard your voice. I thought I was simply losing my mind!

Now I understand why I felt like that! *Because you were very close and with every minute you got closer and closer!* Then I came in and!

"Heavens! Can it even be described in words? So many times, *I have imagined you with me*, in my arms. So many times, I imagined that I could raise my hand and *touch you!* But I was well aware that I didn't have the guts to make my dreams a reality!

"And suddenly, you were right there, standing in front of me, looking at me with those impossible eyes of yours! For a split second, I even thought I had lost my mind entirely and was hallucinating! And then, Lala, it was exactly like you said.

"I looked at you as if I had come out of a dark cave into the bright sunlight. You were standing only a few steps away from me, and no power could make me go back into the cave. Nothing could make me do that! You were shining with some unearthly light, or so it seemed! I am not sure now. At first, this light was in you and seemed to be yours only. But a moment later, it was in me and became mine as well. It was as if a part of me could observe what was happening to me from the side.

"Rays of light were coming from you, as if from the sun but they also were coming from me. And when they touched, *our rays connected and intertwined.* Also, just don't laugh, I thought, I could hear some music. But I don't even know if we could call it music because these sounds do not exist on Earth. When I first touched you, looking into your eyes, the shadow, which had my same shape, *suddenly stepped out of me and disappeared in the radiance surrounding us.* I heard the words. I mean, they seemed to appear by themselves, not even in my head, but in my Soul, my very Essence.

"'*For what has been created as one shall be united as one!*'"

I sat up, looking at him, astonished. *"You heard those words?"*

"It was not like I heard them, but I don't know, Lala. They seemed to appear *inside me* out of nowhere. I don't know how to describe it. Why?" he fell silent for a moment, looking into my eyes.

"Did you hear them too?"

"Yes! Yes, I did! And it was exactly as you described it! I, Oh, Farhan!" My made-of-steel and at the same time gentle Soul could not bear so many overwhelming emotions and so much happiness. I was not used to it. I just burst into tears.

"My Love! What? What is it?"

"I... I... These are just, just tears of, of ha-a-pp-i-ness," I replied, stuttering, crying, and laughing, while he hugged me and stroke my head like a little girl. "I am just, so, so ha-a-a-p—p-y-y!"

"Okay. All right! You can cry with happiness. I allow you that. But only cry happy tears, okay?"

"Yeah," I muttered, burying my face in his chest. "But what will happen next, my Love?" I asked, raising my wet and happy eyes to him. "What are we going to do?"

Next!" he answered, throwing back a lock of hair from my forehead, "two things will happen! First, I will love you here in this house! Until I die, either from pleasure, or from exhaustion, or happiness, or from all of that combined! And then! Well, then together we are going to change this world! We will try to make it kinder, wiser, brighter, fairer and more beautiful, as you have always wanted it! We will inspire people to believe in Love and themselves, follow their hearts, listen to their souls. We will build schools and feed the hungry. We will fight against poverty and the suppression of women. But first, you will become my wife."

"*Wife?*" I felt my heart sink. Yes. I wanted to be with him, but a wife? I didn't want to be his wife. A life under a microscope, viewed by the whole world, did not appeal to me. Instead, it frightened me to death. Even the mere idea of it frightened me. I have lived my whole life as an ordinary woman. I had my own little world. My kids, my mother, our little house, my walks along the ocean, stars in the night sky, my solitude, and my Love for him—*the eternal and never fading Love to him, the fire of my Soul*— that was my life for many years. I've never even dreamed of hearing these words from him. I never even *thought of it*. It was an absolutely absurd idea. But now, once he said them aloud, I just got scared. I wanted to be with him. Yes, of course! I wanted to be his Sun and Moon, his inspiration and quiet joy, peace and softly streaming light. But *a wife?* No. I didn't want to be that. I did not want to get married.

Or maybe, and most likely, I just never considered this option because of its complete absurdity. And now, when it suddenly became my reality, I got scared. I tried to turn it all into a joke.

"Your wife? Why?" I said with a cheerful, as it seemed to me, smile, "Farhan, you do not have to...."

"What?" he frowned, interrupting me. He turned my face to his and intently looked into my eyes. *"You do not want to be my wife?"*

He looked shocked! Surprised, then almost as sad, as if he was a three-year-old boy like someone took his favorite toy truck away from him. When I thought of it, I laughed. My heart was overflowing with Love and tenderness to him.

"Farhan. I..."

"What's so funny, Lala?" His voice was sad, surprised, and even a bit angry.

"Um, Nothing. Forgive me, my Love! But I, may I *not be your wife?* We do not really need this, do we?"

He was confused and could not believe and understand how that was even possible. Why didn't I want to be his wife?

"Lala!" he said. "You love me, don't you? We are two halves of one. We are *Twin Flames.* One Soul, are not we? Or am I losing my mind and all this is just my imagination? *Do you love me, Lala?"*

"I do, Farhan. I love you more than life."

"Then explain to me, please, *why don't you want to be my wife?"*

"You see, I, I don't believe in the power of earthly marriage. I stopped believing in that a long time ago. All these papers and official ceremonies scare me. It's like some kind of promissory note that doesn't guarantee happiness. Instead, it forces people to obey laws established long before they were born. They do not protect you from hurt, betrayal, or loneliness. They honestly protect from nothing and guarantee nothing. From what I saw, within years, it becomes something like *a cage* two people live in, without the chance or courage ever to get out. They live like this for years and often for a whole life. Some hate each other and some live like neighbors or strangers. I do not want that! I was married, and you have been married as well. Why do we need all this? I'm already with you and you are with me. We are together. Nothing else matters, Farhan."

He looked at me, perplexed, not entirely understanding my reasoning. Suddenly, his face changed, and a smile shone on it, while eyes were sparkling cunningly. It was the smile of a teenager who had just received his first kiss from the most beautiful girl in the classroom.

"Lala!" He said, very matter of factly. "I believe that sex should only be between people who are officially married."

Now it was my turn to be shocked, and I could barely help laughing aloud at hearing this absolute nonsense and a blatant lie.

"Oh really? And allow me to ask you, my King, *exactly when* did your Majesty start to follow such a strict rule of morality?" I asked, hardly hiding the sarcasm behind a smile.

"Just now, Lala!" he answered without even flinching. "The strength of your Love made me a new man—a perfect man, an ideal man, *almost an Angel*! And this man decided from now on to do only the right things or at least try to!

"Therefore, my Love," he continued, running his fingertips along my cheek and lips, gently, barely touching my skin, "I'm sorry but unless you are my wife, I cannot make Love to you!"

"Oh, I see!" I replied, trying to speak calmly, although all I wanted was to close my eyes and lose my head, enjoying him caressing me. Using my iron willpower, I kept talking, trying not to pay attention to my body's response to his touch.

"A few minutes ago, my King, you made a highly moral decision to never make Love to a woman without being officially married to her. Is that correct? Then stop touching me, cover yourself with a blanket, turn to the wall and sleep tightly, *like a good boy!*"

"No, I cannot do that!"

"Why not?"

"I should try to use all the means available to convince you to accept my proposition! I intend to use my power and your body's reaction to my touch to my advantage. I will do this until you say that you will be my wife!"

"What exorbitant arrogance! Simply unthinkable!" I answered, shaking my head and trying to restrain laughter and not respond to his touch, tenderness and closeness. *Gods! How could one not love him and not want to shout to him a hundred times: 'Yes! Yes! Yes, I will be your wife! I will be your sister, brother, Guardian Angel, anything, I do not care what, as long as I am with you, as long as you love me!'*

But even the word *"wife"* frightened me, let alone the marriage with a man who is known to the whole wide world, a man whose personal life has always been and always will be a target for eyes and cameras. No. That was too much for me. Such a role is not for me. I am not cut out for that.

Marriage—such an unstable earthly word. Such a temporary and short-term earthly union. Why do I need this word? It will not change how I feel about him. But the marriage bond can for sure become the chain that might begin to weigh us down with time. The chain which one or both of us, free-spirited and freedom-loving Twins, will someday want to break free of. No. *I do not want to risk that!*

Or maybe I am scared of another betrayal? Of lies? Of pain? Do I really believe him? Could I answer positively to this question? No, I could not. *I wanted to believe him*, but I did not. The memory of the night in San Francisco was still too fresh! That agony, hurt, and numbness. *I WANTED* to believe, but... Ah, there is always this notorious *"But!"*

I needed to explain to him and make him understand why I didn't want to get married, without hurting him. I don't want to be his wife, not because of *HIM*, but because of *ME*. Added to all my fears and doubts, I was more than sure that I was not ready to be the wife of the great Farhan Ali! A mega movie star! I am no good for such a role! I am too open, too straightforward, *I hate a pretense*, and that world of his is full of pretense! It's insane even to imagine me in that role! His ex-wife Cynthia played that role for years, but even she at some point got sick of it. I would not last for even a week! All those polite fake smiles, the right fake words you must say, the masks you have to wear, and God forbid you to say or do something against *"the rules!"* Oh, no! That world is not for me! Even if I agreed, this all would fall apart in a month.

"Farhan, I...."

But he did not let me finish. He took my face in his hands and began to kiss me. These kisses were completely different than before. There was no daring desire in them nor withering passion. He was kissing me as if I was woven from dandelion feathers. I could never have imagined he could be so gentle—so painfully and beautifully gentle. He kissed my lips, eyes, eyelashes, hair, cheeks, again returning to my lips. He seemed to be begging me to be with him. Not with words, but with his lips only.

"Say yes," his lips whispered.

"Mmmmmm..."

"That is a wrong answer, Lala." He paused. "Look at me."

I obeyed. Looking into his eyes, I felt dizzy as if I had just looked into the depths of an enormous abyss and barely managed to jump away from the edge. He robbed me of my strength and desire to resist. *I did not want to resist* or fight. I was so tired of fighting and resisting. I just wanted to stay there in his arms and think of nothing, decide nothing. Just be with him. Just be.

Do I also have the same impact on him as we are two parts of the same Soul, or do I have this desire to succumb to him because he is used to commanding and holding the reins?

"Say yes," he repeated.

"Farhan! *I CAN NOT!*" I almost whispered. My voice still sounded like a plea for help, but I had already come to my senses and felt more confident. I must learn to communicate with the King as an equal. Otherwise, it will not work! I would just turn into his slave. *That was the last thing I wanted.* I had to explain to him!

My words made him freeze for a moment, the pain of a rejected little boy flashing in his eyes. He got up, wrapped himself in a sheet, went to the fireplace and sat in the rocking chair in front of it. Silently, he began to watch the barely smoldering logs. Suddenly, with my inner vision, I see him as a child! Maybe only five or six. His mother brought him somewhere. It looks like the house of a family relative, maybe an aunt or someone like

541

that. She leaves him there and goes away! He says nothing. He just watches her leaving. *Pain! Pain is in his heart and his eyes!* At that moment, he can't understand it was a necessity; he is sure his mother has gone because something must be *wrong with him.* Maybe mama doesn't want him or love him because he is not *good enough!* He feels *he deserves no love.* The pictures change to another, then another. He stayed in that family for many months. His mother did not mean to cause him trauma, of course. The family had problems and she thought it would be better this way. But unfortunately, it did cause trauma.

The wound cut deeply into his heart. That is why all his life he tried to be the best of the best! To *deserve the Love of millions and the Love of his mother!* He had to prove to her and the world, *he was indeed good enough and he deserved to be loved. Oh, Maa! Maa, why have you never told me that? Why do I see it only now? And I, I just have done the same thing to him! He did not see my reasons. What he saw, "I do not want to be your wife. I do not want you! You are not good enough. You do not deserve my Love!"*

I feel his pain like I've taken a blow to the chest from an invisible enemy. My breathing seizes up at its powerful intensity. I'm reflecting his pain, mirroring it. My guilt is getting mixed with it as I try to gather my thoughts and find the right words. But he did not let me do it.

"Come here!" he said softly, without turning his head.

I obeyed. I got up, put a soft woolen blanket around me, and silently walked up to him. He made me sit on his lap like a little child.

My head was lying on his shoulder, my lips touching his neck, his hands holding me in a ring of embrace. I inhaled the scent of his skin and I wished I could sit there forever.

"Lala," he began quietly, "what have you told me a thousand times about the Twin Flames? *Why are we coming to this Earth?*"

"To, to help people *remember who they are,* to light a fire in their hearts. We are like burning candles that help light thousands and thousands of other candles. Those, in their turn, will light others. This way, there is more and more Light on Earth and less and less darkness. People begin to shine. They change themselves, start to believe in their strengths and their ancient

542

Light, which is the spark of the original Source of Creation. They find or remember their true calling. They heal themselves and the others. Inspire. Create. Life and the world around such people, begin to change for the better. For this mainly, I believe.

"This means we are here to change the world. At least try to. Make it kinder, brighter, to force the darkness to recede, right?"

"Right. I know it might sound pompous, but that is how it is."

"Yes, I understand. And I know what we must do about that! But for this all to be possible, there is something you must understand as well."

He fell silent for a few seconds and then continued. "Do you remember how you used to start many of your letters to me? 'Go and tell them, Ram! Tell them, my Love! They will listen to you!' Do you remember?"

I nodded silently.

"You see, my Love, I don't want to do this alone anymore! *I want us to do this together!*

"Your words can touch the heartstrings of people in the same way as mine! You once wrote to me: 'If you allowed me, if it were possible, I would stand by your side shoulder to shoulder against the whole world, or IN FRONT OF the whole world! For we are ONE!' Did you say that?"

"Yes, but..."

"Do you want to be with me, Lala? Will you be with me? Or are you going to return to your little familiar world in a few days and I will have to return to mine? If so, tell me now!"

I sighed heavily, closing my eyes.

"Farhan, to be with you means to breathe. I have lived my whole life without breathing! Of course, I want to be with you and I will be, but only..."

"But only not as my wife, right?" He looked wounded and angry. I knew he saw no logic in my statements. "You want to remain just my lover while I offer you everything—my name, my hand, my Soul, my life and everything I have."

"Farhan ... It is just I am not..."

"This way, it won't work, Lala!" he interrupted me. "*It will not work!* You CAN tell people about the fire burning in their Souls, about their inner

Power, which they have forgotten and should finally remember. You can tell them about our Mother Earth and how we slowly kill her, about abandoned children... Yes. You can tell this all to them even without being my wife. *You CAN* speak about it. In America or Europe, perhaps many will even hear you, and your words will touch their hearts ...

"But in the Middle East and Asian countries, people will not listen to Lala, the lover of Farhan Ali! Do you understand? Even if they believe we truly love each other, still, you would be just my lover in their eyes! *NOT, A WIFE!* Some of those societies are somewhat archaic, Lala! Family values and ancient traditions are more powerful and important than even written laws.

"If you are my lover and not a lawful wife, not only will they not listen to you, they will react to you with hostility! Unfortunately, the way some societies treat women is far from decent, and it is especially those societies who *most need to hear your words* burning with the fire of your Soul! They especially need your Light! *Our Light!* They do need our help, Lala! But to help them hear you and listen to you, my dear, you must be my wife! *A WIFE,* do you understand? Only then, together, would we be able to start doing what we have come to do as Twin Flames. That is why we have gone through so much, survived, and experienced so many things! *We must do it together!*

I was silent. He was right. Every word of his was right but... Yes. That "But" again.

"Now... Let's not talk of our mission and everything about it. Let's talk about you and me—just us.

"Tell me!" He continued, lifting my chin and peering deep into my eyes. "*Why are you afraid?* Are you afraid of me hurting you again? Are you afraid of my fans, journalists, a huge crowd, or of me lying to you? Or maybe you trust my Love so little that you are afraid I would betray you with another woman, or not even one of them? Hmm? Tell me. *What are you afraid of, Lala?*"

I closed my eyes. Frankly, I was afraid of *all of the above* and, possibly, of what he hadn't even mentioned. I was afraid of my little world getting lost in his huge world. I was afraid of how his adult children would react to me. I have long loved them with all my heart, but would they accept me? Will they respect their father's decision to connect his life with a woman who is a stranger to them? Or maybe they will hide their grudge against him, not being able to understand and accept his choice? I would rather die than stand between him and his children. I knew, for him as well as for me; his children were the center of his universe! I did not doubt that my children would accept him, as the whole story happened in front of their eyes. I never hide anything from them but his kids. Will I earn, if not their Love, then at least their friendship? That one I did not know, and it scared me.

And what about his circle? All that "high society," all those "rich and powerful." What did I know about them and the rules by which they lived? Not much. But what I did know about them, was more terrifying for me than a deserted cemetery in the middle of the night on Friday the 13th.

Oh yes, many things scared me! That fear has put its chains around me like in my distant childhood. I had to somehow explain it to him. But how?

"Farhan, My Love, my life, my Soul!"

"Be my wife, Lala!" He said softly, almost whispering, preventing me from speaking. "I'm far from being an Angel and you are well aware of that. Life with me may not be, as you once wrote, 'a walk in a park early morning in May,' but it will be a real *LIFE*. Not an illusion! Not a pretense! Life! I need you, Lala! *I need you, you alone.* Do you hear me? No other woman has existed for me for a long time already. Hear me! Believe me, my Love! I only need you! And you need me! And this crazy, terrible and beautiful world *needs both of us. They need us to be together, Lala! Together!*"

"Farhan! Your children, your son and your daughter. I don't know if they ever can…"

"Lala, I think that our children, yours and mine, also came to this world for a reason, and it was not by chance that they chose us as their parents. They will understand. They will. *Believe me.*"

Oh! How I wanted to believe him!

I laid my head on his shoulder, and I closed my eyes again. The logs crackled as snow fell outside the window. Farhan stroked my hair as if I were a little girl and I just wanted time to stop so that we could stay in this snowy paradise forever—in this small cozy home in the middle of the mountains. Only the two of us. And nobody else. But we had people out there, away from this house, who needed us and loved us. We had, as he said, "*this crazy, terrible and beautiful world, which needs both of us.*" So, even if it was possible, I could not and would not want to imprison him in this tiny world, where only he and I exist. I have to let him be free. And myself as well. *Love is Freedom!* Love is a bird — she needs to spread her wings and fly up high in the sky. But he doesn't want to fly alone anymore. He wants me to fly next to him—wing to wing. Tell him to fly alone? Go back to my little world? But then, why have I been walking this extremely long and exhausting path since my very childhood, just to reject his huge world because it frightens me? Or was his world now also mine?

After all, he was absolutely right. We will be together. Whatever happens. Together. So if certain agreements and conditions are necessary for us to be together in this life, then let them be. Besides, I had promised him to stand by his side, *shoulder to shoulder*. And he remembered my words. How can I now refuse my own words? Together we should try to change this world for the better, even if just a little bit. *Every little bit counts.* We will be living, inspiring, creating, and most importantly, loving. We will be shining our inner Light, and with it, we will try to warm up the tired Souls and help them find and shine their own Light. That was precisely my dream—*the dream of my entire life*. I did not believe it would ever come true, but now he is asking me to do it together with him.

So, am I really that scared of the future? Am I scared of its uncertainty and unpredictability? That simply looks like *cowardice*. It seems like I am trying to find excuses for myself. No, I don't have the right to hesitate. *I do not have the right to have fears and doubts.* Do not have the right to be weak or, even worse, to be a coward. No! I don't!

"Do you need some time to think it over?" He asked quietly.

"No," I answered firmly, "I don't need time to think it over. Forgive me, my Soul! Forgive me of my doubts and fears. You are absolutely right. I am just a coward! I told you what I dreamed of, I told you what I wanted and now when you tell me we can finally do it together, I want to run and hide. No, my Love. I will not run…"

"*I will be your wife, Farhan.*"

He took my face in his palms as if shielding me from stupid fears and doubts. Like in a mirror, I looked into his dark eyes, trying to find answers to all my questions about the future. But in his eyes, I saw myself. I saw dazzling flashes from the burning logs and a myriad of stars of faraway worlds.

"*I love you,*" said the stars. And new galaxies were born.

"*I love you,*" said the fire. And became alive in millions of hearts!

"*I love you,*" said my Ram, hugging me tightly as if afraid that I would disappear.

We are finally one. We are protected from the whole world by the Power of Keepers of the Light and our Eternal Love. Free at last from the Power and influence of shadow and darkness. One Soul, divided in two, once again has come to Earth to become what it always had been—*One Whole*. Become one, after going through a million tests and trials, pains and disappointments, ups and downs. Finally, become One.

"*For what has been created as one—the moment darkness recedes, and shadows dissolve—shall be united as one again!*"

Will our path be easy? Probably not. But if my beloved grows weak, I will give him my strength, my Light, my fire. And if I weaken, he will bring me back to life, even from the ashes, with his Love. How can anything break us? We are created from the Origin of it all—The Source. The Eternal Fire. The Flame.

We

    are

       Twin Flames.

Chapter 56

The Mist House on the Lost Planet

Haan read the last pages of the story.

Firebird rearranged the glass balls on the shelves in a cabinet made of old dark wood, admiring the small worlds enclosed inside them. Sometimes she would warm a glass ball in her palms and watch tiny suns and moons shine there, behind the clear glass. Trees were swaying, clouds were running through the sky and flowers were blooming.

Helena and Joanna looked at her anxiously and a little expectantly.

"For what has been created as one—the moment darkness recedes, and shadows dissolve—shall be united as one again!"

Will our path be easy? Probably not. But if my beloved grows weak, I will give him my strength, my Light, my fire. And if I weaken, he will bring me back to life, even from the ashes, with his Love. How can anything break us? We are created from the Origin of it all—The Source. The Eternal Fire. The Flame.

We are Twin Flames."

Haan put down the last page and also looked intensely at Firebird.

"What! What is happening?" She smiled and suddenly began to cry. «Helena? Joanna? What is wrong with me? I, I don't understand... What is going on? What has suddenly gotten to me? Why does it feel so bitter and painful if everything ended so beautifully? Why am I happy and unhappy at the same time?"

Helena walked up to Firebird, hugged her and started to stroke her head as if she was a little girl.

"My dear girl, you, you remember now, do you?"

Firebird lifted her head from Helena's shoulder. She looked around at everybody. Her face instantly matured, shadows suddenly appeared under her eyes, her cheekbones sharpened, her lips seemed more clearly defined.

"Remember? Yes. Yes, I do. I remember. Lala, her story is almost exactly like my own. But still not mine. I had it all almost the same. My Love, my Twin. But…"

Tears and pain appeared in her eyes.

"He and I, we have not… I've never been in that home in the mountains. My life was very similar to the one described in the book, but it was not mine even though everything in that story was so painfully familiar to me—so painfully familiar till the last words. But this was not my life."

Joanna approached Helena.

"Firebird, dear, you are absolutely right. It is indeed not your life. Your Twin, He did not come. He did not believe you and did not want to change anything in his life. When you understood that, you swore to forget him. You married a wonderful man and moved to another country across the world. You forbade yourself to think about him and became a faithful wife and a mother. Till the end of that life, you two lived far away from each other. You considered the past to be too painful to remember. You did not want to remember him, so you swore to forget him. And you did.

«Your Observers and Keepers, even the Guardians, wanted to help you both. They were there for you. You two were extremely important and powerful! Key Twins! They tried so hard to unite you. They directed you both, encouraged you both, gave you two plenty of visions and signs, but despite everything, they failed. Your Twin, just like Farhan, in that life was a very powerful man. He did not want to risk what he had in the matrix for some «crazy love story" which was too good to be true. He rejected and deserted you! The Dark became dominant on your planet. It only took a couple of hundred years, and your land became forsaken. Another Lost Planet. Just like this one we are on right now.

"All that is left is the small glass globe as a symbol of loneliness. A model of the world without Love and without people. The only ones who can be there in those deserted worlds are the Observers."

Helena smiled affectionately.

"Joanna and I begged the Elders to allow us to give you two another chance because, in the future, you would make great Keepers, and after that, Guides and Guardians.

"Twin Flames, those who failed to unite even after a thousand incarnations, could easily understand other Twins in the future and help them avoid their own mistakes."

Firebird looked at Joanna in surprise.

"Did you and Helena convince the Elders to give us another chance? Who are you, women? Are you almighty?"

She burst out laughing.

"No, not at all! We are just like you. We are the Twin Flames. And just like you, we could not unite with our halves for a thousand and one reasons with a million lame excuses. One was running away. The other one was chasing. One was afraid; the other one did not believe. You know how that is. We didn't manage to get out of that circle.

"This, unfortunately, is tragic because it was us, the Twin Flames, the most powerful and brightest souls, who were to become the light and the guidance for other people. We were responsible not only for our own destinies but also for the destiny of the whole planet we lived on. Our Keepers helped us too. They helped us understand who we were and remember our lives and tasks. But still, we failed to unite. So later, after much long training, we ourselves have become the Observers and Keepers.

"And now we have prepared, I think, excellent successors, who will continue our work." She looked at Firebird, and for some reason, at Haan, and nodded slightly.

"We should have left you and moved to the level of the Guardians a long time ago, but due to some unauthorized prompts and additional assistance to our supervisors, we had to stay in this world for yet another life. But we are not sorry, are we!"

Joanna went to the little table, suspended in the air. She collected her paints and brushes and packed them into a wooden suitcase, where she kept her finished paintings. Looking around sadly, she sighed. When she waved her hand, the suitcase soared up high with a splash of small cold sparks and melted in the air.

"We don't have any regrets," she repeated firmly. "A long time ago, for thousands of lives, we were humans, as well. We all went through this. We were also helped by some kind and compassionate Keepers-Observers, back in our time."

She thought for a moment.

"So, my dear Firebird, we were not just reading and discussing the book of Lala. We were waiting for you to remember your own story, to relive that life again, so similar to yours, to overcome this pain, which made you forget him and the life in when he refused you. We wanted you to learn to rise after every fall, believe in your strength and finally, both of you to understand how to live, love and treasure each other.

"We hope that now, the two of you can begin your service; if you want, of course. Your experiences, your lives and your feelings would be invaluable to all the Twins who are out there. They need your help. And, therefore, to the planets that are still alive, breathing and vibrating with people searching for their shine and truth."

"They all need the energy of Love. True Love. Eternal Love. They need the Love of Twin Flames. And you already know how to help them. Now the salvation of those planets will depend on you and those you will be able to help and lead to union."

Helena walked over to the huge gold-rimmed mirror hanging on the wall next to the door. She looked intensely at her reflection.

Her expression remained unalterably kind and caring, while the features of her face started to change constantly in the mirror. There were women and men, again women, children, old and young, with all possible eye colors—blue, brown, green, yellow, hazel—all the people she had ever been were flowing through the mirror.

Finally, her reflection became more blurred, indefinite, and disappeared. But, for the three in the room looking at her, she remained the same—a woman with white hair.

"Joanna, we have to go."

Joanna walked over to Helena and took her hand. They looked at each other, and new images started flashing in the silver glass—beautiful, strong, weak, belligerent, peaceful, angry, confused, timid, confident—curling up, spinning, creating a tunnel that went deep into the mirror.

"Yes, Firebird. We have to go. You already know a lot and can do a lot. We have been teaching you. The most important thing is this: you must watch, observe, but you must not interfere," *she smiled with the corners of her lips,* "except in the most extraordinary cases, of course."

"You know what kind of risk Twin Flames take when they both incarnate! When only one incarnates, the other is leading, guarding and guiding. When both incarnate, they need all the help you can possibly give them. Help them meet each other. Lead them! Help them see the signs and be strong. Teach them not to give up, not to succumb to the shadow and the influence of the Dark, those constantly attacking them through fear, doubt, greed, jealousy, and so on. Help them keep on going and shine brightly, avoiding the mistakes you made, while being there, help them unite and realize their mission. Teach them to cherish their Love—nothing in the Universe is more powerful. Believe in them.

"Please keep us informed. Do everything possible to prevent the blooming and breathing planets from turning into glass-ball-planets. It only can happen if people succumb to the Dark and fail to learn to love and cherish each other. Teach people to protect Love and bring light and happiness to themselves, the people around them and to the world."

"Will you be gone forever? Will I ever see you again?" *Firebird's eyes filled with tears again.*

Helena and Joanna looked at each other.

"Of course not. Firebird! What are you talking about? Do you really think that we would leave you forever?" *Helena shook her head.* "No, sweetheart! Of course not! You and your Twin could not save your planet because your fears and doubts, ego and ambitions contributed to the destruction of humanity by the Dark Side. Now, to make things right, you must save other planets, which still have a chance to stand through the Dark and ascend to a new level. Twin Flames are there to help them, and you, while being here, will help these Twin Flames. They need you! Both of you!"

552

"Our World is a Crystal. It shimmers with its multifaceted sides, with countless shining faces. Each one of them has its own world. Altogether, it creates many worlds, many love stories, and many Twin Flames.

"You are to stay in the Mist House until the Elders consider that your karma has been fulfilled and lessons are fully learned. After that, you will be given the choice of either to rise to the level of the Guardians or the freedom to choose when, where and how you will incarnate as humans in your next lives. The goals, the lands, the circumstances, all that you will be able to choose and decide for yourself.

«Tomorrow, you are getting a new planet, which is on the verge of destruction and very close to being overcome by the Dark Side. Your task is to look for the Twin Flames. Help them to fill their world with Love. Love is the only protection from the Dark. Love. Nothing else but Love. Only Love.

"Our Mist House is completely at your service. You are allowed to appear in the worlds of the Twin Flames you are watching over as different people—people who can give them advice, support, inspiration, motivation, and strength to keep on going. You will know when and how that will be necessary." The woman with white hair smiled and said, "That always was my favorite thing to do! Goodbye for now, Firebird. We will see each other again. Remember. Nothing ever ends, only continues."

The mirror suddenly flashed white, both figures disappeared, breaking into swaying color spots—like the reflection in water from a thrown pebble—drawn into a spinning vortex right in the center of the glass.

Firebird looked in the mirror. She only saw her own reflection and—and the sad, lonely figure at the doorway.

"Haan…" she almost whispered. "You…"

She covered her face with her hands and sat on the chair, trying to calm her heart, which wanted to break free from her chest and fly away.

"I REMEMBER you now! I remember… You have been here, and I, I did not remember you all this time. Forces of Light, are we together again? How can this even be? You—in that life—You had renounced me! I fought. I fought so hard! I knew if I failed, we would both fail. We would lose our planet to the Dark. But you did not believe me. You did not want to see. You did not want to listen. Why? Why haven't you…"

"Firebird, it is useless now," he answered quietly. "Why haven't I, why didn't I... There is no point."

He closed his eyes for a moment and continued. He wanted her to listen; he hoped she would listen. He hoped she would understand and... Forgive him. Even if it took a thousand years. He was ready to wait that long, just to see her forgive him.

"While watching and reading this story of Ram and Lala, I again relived all the horrors, fears, doubts, disbelief of that life. And the worst of all was immense, unbearable grief from the loss—the loss of you. You swore to forget me, and you did. It made my torture almost unlivable.

"Oh, if only I could turn back time, Firebird!
　　　If only
　　　　　I could.
　　　　　　　If only...

To get back into that life of ours, to change it all, to live it all differently. But...

«I don't know if you will ever be able to forgive me," Haan turned to the girl and looked her straight in the eyes. His unbelievable dark eyes—lakes—were burning with hope and... Love. Eternal and immortal Love. Love as endless as the Universe.

Firebird got up. She came up to him without tearing her eyes away from his. He did not dare touch her. He stood, waiting for any sign from her, showing him that he had not lost her completely. There was still hope in him. She raised her hand and gently touched his cheek.

"Just leave it for now, okay? Let's not talk about it. Perhaps some other time, we will return to this conversation, but not now. We have a job to do."

He smiled. He told himself that even if it took an eternity, he would win her trust, her heart and her love back again. After all. They are Twin Flames.

"You really do remember me now, Firebird? Heavens! I thought I would lose it when I saw you here, every moment. But you did not remember me. I was so terrified I would reveal myself and my feelings.

The Observers said it was forbidden. I hurt you too much, and you had the right to forget me. I had to wait till you remembered me yourself.

"Yes. I remember you! I remember everything. Reading Lala's book, I also relived the last life of ours. I did not immediately understand why it hurt me so bad to hear their story."

She suddenly laughed and spun around the room.

«Oh, how glad am I that Lala and Ram are together. I hope we have somehow helped them. They are strong. Wonderful. Kind. They love each other so much! May they be happy—very happy—and teach others to be happy as well. Their power has grown immensely since they are united now. I know, together, they will do amazing and great things for their world."

He came up to her and dared to take her both hands in his. She did not push him away and his heart sang with joy.

"Firebird. I...."

"Haan," she said. "Let's open the window."

They came to the window and opened the huge white frames. Outside, green hills spread out, and the dazzling clear sky turned indigo blue. The bright, scarlet red sun, rising from the silver ocean, splashed heat and light onto the water and the land.

"This world is beautiful and perfect, Haan!" She said. "And we have all of the eternity for us! Isn't that wonderful? All of Eternity! Let's not repeat our mistakes! Can we do that? Or at least, try?"

"Maybe we can still make things right, my Love? Do you believe it is possible?"

"Anything is possible, Haan. Everything is possible, if Love is still alive!"

"Is Love... Still alive, Firebird?" *fear and hope sounded in his deep, beautiful voice. She turned to him, looking into his eyes, drowning in them. He drowned in hers. She raised her hand and gently traced his face with her fingertips.*

"How can it not be alive?" *she whispered,* "if it is eternal? In a couple of hundred years, when we live as humans again, please remind me of that. If something happens, and I forget, find a way to help me remember. Help me remember, Haan. Help me remember! And I will do the same for you. Do you promise?"

"I promise," *he said.* "My Love, I promise you, I will!"

Chapter 57

From the Author

Your eternal, immortal Soul, even before your birth, creates a map of your future life. She chooses the paths you must walk. She chooses the trials you must endure. Your road will never be easy, but your Soul KNOWS what she wants and she guides you. Love goes hand in hand with her. Your Soul is Love.

Love is Power and Creative Force. Everything in the multiverse is created by it—everything but the dark. There is no darkness in Light! Love is the Light, and nothing is more powerful than Love. Nothing ever will be. Follow the path your Soul—your Love—has chosen for you. And no matter how hard it might be at times, no matter what tests and challenges await you, do not give up! The Soul knows the right path ALWAYS. Follow it!

Love is the Eternal Truth, the Eternal Law, which conquers dark, evil, and death. Love is invincible, undying, and everlasting.

Love and be Loved. Shine your Light brightly and help others shine. May the Power of True Light—the Power of True Love—guide you and protect you every step of the way.

Thank you for reading my story.
Sincerely yours,

Lala Agni (*Firebird*)

Notes

Notes

Made in United States
North Haven, CT
26 September 2023

42019995R00311